A Candle for d'Artagnan

an historical horror novel
third in the Atta Olivia Clemens series

Chelsea Quinn Yarbro

TOR
HORROR

A TOM DOHERTY ASSOCIATES BOOK
NEW YORK

A CANDLE FOR D'ARTAGNAN

A TOR BOOK
Published by Tom Doherty Associates, Inc.
49 West 24 Street
New York, NY 10010

First edition: October 1989
0 9 8 7 6 5 4 3 2 1

For
Virginia

AUTHOR'S NOTES

Any mention of the Musketeers, let alone the name d'Artagnan, immediately evokes Alexandre Dumas' wonderful novels in all their swashbuckling glory; certainly my interest in the France of Louis XIII and the early years of Louis XIV was partly kindled by his Musketeer stories. However, marvelous as those books are, historical accuracy is not their strong point. For one thing, almost all the action takes place when the historical d'Artagnan was, in actuality, a child—at the time of the murder of the Duke of Buckingham, d'Artagnan was not yet ten years old. While there might be some confusion over the fact that there were *two* Charles d'Artagnans in the Musketeers, the first one died in 1633, long before the d'Artagnan known to Dumas had left his home in Gascony; at least part of the many questions about this man is due to the earlier Charles. Some of it is the fault of d'Artagnan's own "official" biography, which never let the facts stand in the way of a good story. It has been the task of historians to document or dismiss the various claims made in the "official" biography. While I sympathize with the official biographer—and being a novelist I have a hearty appreciation of a good story—I nevertheless prefer truth with all its knobs on whenever it is possible to get it.

For that reason, among others, in this book, I have made every effort to stay within the bounds of documented fact. When direct material was not available, I used the best secondary sources I could find in order to keep the events as authentic as possible. Where no reliable sources are available, I have made the best and most reasonable guess I can, which is part of a novelist's job when working with history. I am especially indebted to *D'Artagnan, the Ultimate Musketeer* by Geoffrey F. Hall and Joan Sanders, Houghton Mifflin, 1964 for filling in more gaps and answering more questions than any other single source consulted in the preparation of this novel.

Since it was usual to destroy private communication and covert diplomatic documents, there are many curious holes in authentic information regarding d'Artagnan's career; verification of certain key events in his life is all but impossible.

Because of the familiarity of Dumas' work, and the assumptions that go with it, I have elected to use the Gascon spellings of the characters most readers know better by the Parisian versions of their names. Hence, you will look in vain for Athos, Porthos, and Aramis, and will find instead the short-lived Arnaud de Sillegue d'Athos, d'Artagnan's good friend Isaac de Portau (who I have taken the liberty of numbering among the Musketeers three years before he actually joined the regiment), and their comrade-at-arms Henri d'Aramitz. However, I have made one exception to Dumas' literary tradition: I have retained the d in d'Artagnan, though he would be more properly addressed as Artagnan except when adding Monsieur to his name. Strictly speaking, d'Artagnan was not his proper name, but his mother's maiden name which d'Artagnan assumed when he joined the Musketeers, since it was more distinguished than his own. The Bearnais leader of the Musketeers, in Dumas called Treville, I have kept in the original version of his name—Jean-Arnaud du Peyrer de Troisvilles.

The treacherous years of the end of Louis XIII's reign and the long regency for the young Louis XIV under the care of his mother, Anne of Austria, and Cardinal Mazarin, Richelieu's handpicked successor, are difficult to sort out; the political situation in France was precarious and much of the concessions, trades, negotiations, agreements and the like was carried out in secret, as much from necessity as from any perverse love of the covert. As I have noted, oftentimes no records were kept, or were deliberately destroyed when negotiations were concluded.

There is also the matter of historical tradition as regards the actual persons of this story—legend far more than facts have come to color the general understanding of the motivations and personalities of these illustrious persons, which has made sorting out truth from misconception a particularly knotty problem, and one which often only adds to the confusion.

Because of that, and because rumor was always rife at the various royal courts, it is not uncommon to find more than one version of an event, often several accounts—all secondhand—exist, all very much at odds. Where there are conflicting accounts of events or their precursors, I have chosen the version that best serves this story.

And while this story concerns actual people who lived in the seventeenth century, they, the places and the events that surround them, are used fictitiously and there is no intention whatsoever to depict actual persons, places, and/or events.

Brest

Le Havre

Oust

Rouen
Amiens

Brest-Nantes Canal

Chartres
PARIS

Reims

Atlantic
Ocean

Angers

Meaux

Nantes
Tours
Blois

Loire

Orleans

Troyes

Poitiers

Nevers

Dijon

Charente

Bordeaux

Garonne

Lyons

FRANCE
ITALY AND
SPAIN
1644

Gascony

Rhône

Bearn
Toulouse

Avignon

Torino

Milano

VENETIAN
REPUBLIC

Durance

Genova

Po

SPAIN

Perpignan

Venezia

Marseilles

*Ligurian
Sea*

Pisa

Adriatic
Sea

Barcelona

Toulon

Arno
Firenze

Mediterranean Sea

Corsica
SPAIN

TUSCANY

Trasinero

PAPAL
STATES

100 mi.

Roma

KINGDOM
OF NAPLES

Tivere

Sardinia
SPAIN

*Tyrrhenian
Sea*

Napoli

PART I
Giulio Mazarini

Text of a private note from Nichola, Cardinal Bagni to Atta Olivia Clemens, delivered by personal courier.

To the gracious and most respected widow, Atta Olivia Clemens at her villa Senza Pari;

Word came from Parigi today, and some of it is encouraging. The great Richelieu continues his interest in Mazarini, and has said that he wishes to have him return to Francia as soon as it can be arranged. While it is true that this has been said before, our recent developments give us all reason to believe that the day is not far off when Mazarini will once again leave Roma.

We are proceeding on the assumption that Mazarini will, indeed, take up his work in Francia again, and before very long. Apparently one of the stumbling blocks is the matter of citizenship and for that reason we are advising Mazarini to accept the offer of naturalization. We have waved the matter of ordination; an Abbe in Francia is well enough for his work, and not so suspect. He has not quite resisted becoming a subject of Louis, but his family has many doubts. The Colonnas are being especially difficult, for they are the most noble of his relatives and they are offended that he would consider leaving Roma at all, let alone surrendering his nationality. They have their own arrangements, of course, and do not want to have their position questioned.

Why, you wonder, do I write of this to you? We know you are friendly with members of the Colonna family, and we are convinced that if you are willing to support Mazarini's requests, it must bear some weight with them. You are regarded as disinterested in the matter, and even so suspicious a household as the Colonnas must give some attention to you. Also, if you are willing to travel with Mazarini and his suite to Francia, it might persuade them that *they will not be without influence still. I am certain I can rely on your discretion in your dealings; the interest of the Holy See is concomitant with the interest of Roma.*

It appears that I must pile one request on the shoulders of the rest, and for that I offer only the expression of our gratitude and the assurance that your service will not go unnoticed: we would be most appreciative if you would consider this offer and undertake such a move. With you to accompany Mazarini, we are confident that his mother's family will rally the necessary approval; the Tuscan branch of the Colonnas is respected and powerful and they can make the rest listen. Since any mention of Mazarini's future coming from the Holy See must be viewed with skepticism and scrutiny, we are all especially obliged to those who are willing to give us aid at this difficult time. I cannot promise any direct recompense, but there are many clandestine favors that might well come your way from your assistance; I will be pleased to discuss them with you.

Certainly it is not my intent to offer you any insult, but I wish you to know that should you decide to journey with Mazarini and his household, or better yet, precede him, we would be more than willing to defray the costs to you, and to see that your villa is maintained in the style you would like for the time you are gone. Do not disdain this offer, for we can send soldiers from the Papal Guard to keep your villa and its grounds protected if there are any unpleasantries while you are away. You have only to issue the instructions for us to see that they are carried out.

I await your answer and I pray that you will perceive the advantage of having Mazarini once again in Parigi with Richelieu. It is said that you are a most intelligent and sensible woman, and that God has given you wisdom of a sort. I implore you to use it now, for the benefit of Roma and all the people of Francia. If you refuse, we will have little chance to influence the successor to Richelieu. If you accept, then the peace of our countries is assured, for which we must all thank God.

With my gratitude and my prayers, and with the certainty that you will help us in this difficult time.

Nichola, Cardinal Bagni
By God's Grace and Mercy

From Roma on the 17th day of November, 1637.
Nota bene: destroy this.

· 1 ·

From Advent to Epiphany there was a continuous parade of musicians and acrobats at Senza Pari; the entertainment, always an essential part of the season, was reputed to be superior at the home of Bondama Atta Olivia Clemens, more than the equal of any titled nobleman in Roma. No part of the festivities was neglected—food, dancing, music, amusements, all were lavishly available.

"Not that Sanct' Germain approves," said Olivia to her major domo as the two of them met in her library at the deepest hour of night. "He warned me that I bring too much attention to myself."

"You have said that he often lives splendidly," said Niklos, who had removed his shoes and was rubbing at his feet. "Who would have thought I could still get blisters." They were speaking a language they had evolved between them—part Imperial Latin, part Italian, part Frankish—in the long years they had spent together.

"It's my penchant for remaining in the same place and living conspicuously," said Olivia as she removed the elaborate pearl drops from her ears. "It's one way to have some protection. A woman alone invites attention; I prefer to command it."

"We've lived other places," said Niklos absèntly. "I wish we still had those Turkish chairs."

"There are many things I wish I had; many, many things," said Olivia, and for an instant her hazel eyes were spectral.

In all the time he had known her, Niklos had never learned to see these flashes of despair without sensing an echoing desolation in himself. Very deliberately he changed the subject, saying lightly, "What is the matter with that damned Genovese with the squint? He has run into me six times in the last two days. Every time I look up, there he is, squinting."

"He has a weakness for handsome men, or so I've been told,"

said Olivia. She dropped onto an upholstered bench and sighed. "I agree about the Turkish chairs. How many more days of this, Niklos?"

"Seventeen," said Niklos, straightening up and flexing his toes. "That's better."

"Why not wear softer shoes?" she asked, not completely paying attention. She fiddled with the short tendrils of fawn-colored hair that framed her face. "Whoever decided that showing all the forehead was immodest?" she asked of the air.

"Wrists, too," said Niklos with a slight laugh.

"Oh, yes," said Olivia, making no excuse for her sarcasm. "The view of an uncuffed wrist is enough to undo us all." She looked away abruptly, and when she turned back, she spoke more evenly. "Pay me no mind, Niklos. I am . . . oh, I don't know what I am."

"Bored?" suggested Niklos gently. He started to draw on his uncomfortable shoes, making sure the modest rosettes were fixed properly.

She considered her answer. "Perhaps I am. I'm restless for no reason, to no purpose. Perhaps there is nothing more extreme the matter than that I feel it's all so tedious."

As he got to his feet, Niklos said, "There is Bagni's suggestion."

"To go with Giulio Mazarini to Parigi?" She shrugged. "I haven't been there in . . ."

"Centuries," Niklos supplied bluntly when her voice trailed off. "If you want a change, why not Parigi?"

She made a complicated gesture. "It's too difficult and it's too easy, all at once." Her expression softened to rueful amusement. "It doesn't make any sense. I can't ask you to understand it, because it isn't sensible." As she put her hands into her lap, she toyed with the antique cabochon emerald in her largest ring. "What would be the point of leaving?"

"What would be the point of staying? You said yourself, in the summer, that it is approaching the time for you to have another disappearance. We have been here sixteen years straight." He paced down the room, his steps muffled by a splendid carpet brought from Persia three hundred years before.

"Yes, yes." She put her hand to her brow. "There are many people in Parigi who have seen me here; Giulio Mazarini is one of them. What is the point of picking up and leaving if there are those who know me? It would not be a successful disappearance." She clapped her hands together. "There's the New World, but the thought of crossing the ocean is . . . out of the question."

"It could be arranged," said Niklos gently. "You do not need to suffer."

"Certainly," she responded with alacrity. "I can stay off the water. After that nightmare in Portugal, I never want to sail beyond sight of land again." She touched her forehead. "I should return to my guests." But she made no move to leave.

"They will not notice that you do not eat if you wait until they are done," said Niklos, rising and adjusting his peplums so that they fell evenly from his high-waisted English-style doublet. Although the cloth was satin, it was plainly cut, and only the lace at the hem of the peplums suggested luxury, as was fitting in a major domo.

"Of course," said Olivia, sighing. "I wish we had a good Roman holocaust to heat this place, instead of these smoky hearths. We'd be warmer."

"We could have a holocaust and Roman floors," Niklos reminded her as he had many times before, "but it would give rise to comment."

"And we do not want comment, oh, Dio mi salva, no," said Olivia in exaggerated horror. She extended her foot from beneath the hem of her wide, brocaded skirt. "Next time I won't wear these chopines," she said, speaking of the Venetian shoes she had on. "They're miserable for dancing."

"You could change them now," Niklos suggested.

"It would account for my absence," she said, nodding in a remote way. She rubbed at her side where her corset was tightest. "They say the French are shortening the stomacher and are wearing less restrictive corsets."

"The Pope does not approve," said Niklos with a slight smile.

"The Pope is not *supposed* to approve," snapped Olivia. She shook her head once. "Pay no attention. I am in the mood to argue with someone—about anything."

Niklos chuckled softly. "Olivia, would I were a worthy sparring partner for you."

"You come closer than any other," said Olivia with asperity, but knowing that Niklos would not respond to any goad.

"Save one," said Niklos.

"Save one," she agreed. She lowered her eyes and pressed her knuckles together. "I suppose I must face them again."

"Is it so much an ordeal?" Niklos asked, and knew the answer from all his years with her. "They are not—"

One of the servants scratched at the door. "Bondama."

Olivia lifted her head, making a warning gesture for silence to Niklos. "What is it, Giorgio?"

"There is a messenger. He has just arrived."

Niklos shot her a quick glance. "Shall I leave?" he whispered.

"Why? You're major domo here." She went to the door, her face set in a smile that touched only her mouth. "Enter, Giorgio," she said to the young page, indicating where he was to stand. "Tell me who this messenger is and why he has come now."

"He is a personal courier from Alessandro, Cardinal Bichi. He has a letter for you." Giorgio ducked his head, turning suddenly bashful. At eleven, he was still awkward in his duties.

"Show him into the salon by the inner garden," she said when she had given the question a moment of thought. "See that he has wine and something to eat." She held out a silver coin. "For your good service, Giorgio."

The boy took the coin, bowed gracelessly once, and left.

"Alessandro, Cardinal Bichi," said Niklos, one dark brow raised. "Very interesting."

"That it is. First Bagni and now Bichi. How curious." She made sure the door was closed. "Niklos, for my sake, I want you to listen to what the courier tells me."

"That may be nothing," said Niklos without much feeling. "For that matter, he may know nothing."

"True enough," said Olivia, now doing her best to shake off the oppression of spirit that had taken hold of her. "I wonder if we'll hear from Barberini next—that would cover the French faction at the Vatican, wouldn't it? Bagni's note was covert. I will wager three gold angels that this messenger is unofficial as well."

Niklos shrugged. "And what is the official excuse for his being here?"

"Doubtless he is bringing greetings of the season for the holidays. I am wealthy enough that it isn't strange." The fatigue was back in her face once more. "It's foolish of me, to miss so much."

"And you do not mean all that has vanished, do you," said Niklos gently, very softly.

"No," whispered Olivia. Then she took hold of herself again. "Well, I had better see to this messenger before he decides that I am avoiding him."

"Wise enough," said Niklos. "I will need a little time to conceal myself." He indicated the room, nodding toward the small inner door that led to Olivia's private apartments. "Are you going to change shoes?"

She looked down at the tips of her toes emerging from beneath her skirt. "Probably not. Though I wish these were not so treacherous to balance on."

"You always say that about your shoes." He made a gesture of mock helplessness. "Except when you say that they are less than slippers and are good for nothing."

Finally Olivia laughed, and though the sound was tinged with a kind of grief, it was better than the wildness that had been in her voice earlier that evening. "You're right, and I am clearly being impossible."

"Not impossible," Niklos corrected gently. "Just unhappy."

She could not answer at once. "You know me too well, old friend." With that she gave a tug to her skirt so that it would hang properly, and started resolutely toward the door.

"What are you going to tell him?" Niklos asked.

"I don't know what he has to say to me." She opened the door and looked out into the hallway. "By the way, we will need new lanthorns at the door by tomorrow."

"I will attend to it myself," said Niklos, and watched her close the door. He tapped his fingers together, trying to assess her mood, feeling greater concern for her than he had been willing to reveal to her. Now, there was a strong line between his black brows and his ruddy-brown eyes were deep and troubled. He gave a short, hard sigh and crossed the room, cursing his shoes as he went.

By the time he slipped into the concealed room beside the salon, Niklos had resigned himself to his distress. He adjusted the old-fashioned oil lamp that hung in the little chamber and slid back the panel behind the largest painting in the salon. Now he could observe most of the chamber without being seen.

The Cardinal's personal courier was a young man, dressed in elaborately Spanish style—the preferred mode at the Papal Court—that was the worse for being rained on.

"You wished to see me?" Olivia said as she entered the salon unannounced. Her expression was carefully neutral and her words, though polite enough, did not encourage elaborate courtesy.

"Bondama Clemens?" said the courier, starting to bow and then hesitating.

"Yes." She indicated one of the two upholstered benches that faced the windows, dark and rain-spangled now. "Please. Be comfortable."

This time he did bow properly. "How good of you to receive me while you are entertaining guests."

"All the more reason to come to the point," said Olivia with asperity. "You have something to say, pray do so."

The courier sat down and shook out his bedraggled, shoulder-length curls. "I have been asked to arrange a meeting, if you are willing."

"That depends on who the other parties are," said Olivia with a slight, firm smile.

"Cardinal Bichi is eager for you to meet with Giulio Mazarini." He did not look at her. "They have certain things they would like to discuss with you."

"The same sort of thing that Cardinal Bagni might have mentioned to me?" Olivia suggested. "Or are you not at liberty to say."

"Well," the courier responded warily, "I have no knowledge of what the Cardinal might have said to you—"

Olivia shook her head in exasperation. "You have a very good idea, though you might not know the precise words. It has to do with Mazarini's going to France. I assume this is more of the same."

"It is . . . related," said the courier. He laid his hand on the hilt of his sword. "There are many who oppose this cause, and there are risks. You are a widow, and the Cardinals would understand if you were not willing to—"

"As a widow," Olivia interrupted, "I am especially useful to the Cardinals, and I would appreciate it if none of us denied that. I have no family to hold me here, and no family to demand difficult explanations from any Eminence who might be involved."

This time the courier made no attempt to answer. "I would like to tell my master that you will agree to a meeting."

Olivia held up her hand. "Why—other than my widowhood—am I so sought-after?" Before the courier could answer, she provided the reason herself. "It is my stud farm near Tours, isn't it? I have an excuse to be there, and there need be no explanation for my inclusion in Mazarini's suite."

"It . . . it is a factor." The courier was staring at her now, partly in fascination, partly in repulsion. "The Cardinals might not . . . feel the same . . ." His gesture was intended to be an answer, but it was not successful.

"I suppose I have no reason to be surprised." She went to the window and stared out past the glistening raindrops to the darkness. "And if not now, then they will try another time, won't they? Your master can be most insistent."

"Madama?" the courier asked, pretending not to understand.

"I know the Cardinals of old." She looked toward the vast allegorical canvas showing Susannah and the Elders, ironically amused to know that her gaze met Niklos'. "Once they are determined on a course, it is an accomplished thing."

"They are the lieutenants of the Pope," said the courier dutifully.

"When it suits their purposes." Olivia shook her head once, making up her mind. "All right. Tell your Cardinal Bichi that I will meet with him and with Mazarini—though he and I have encountered each other once or twice before—and any of the rest of them."

The courier regarded her directly. "You would journey to Francia if it were necessary?"

This time Olivia took a little time to answer, and regarded the painting of Susannah fixedly as she did. "Certainly. If it is necessary." Her smile was the more enchanting for its sadness.

* * *

Text of a letter from Giulio Mazarini to Cardinal Richelieu, written in Latin and carried by Richelieu's personal courier.

To the man who is most surely the hero of France and the model of all men of principle and purpose, at Paris; under seal and under the rose.

Rest assured that I have continued with the plans we have agreed upon, and that although there has not been as rapid an accommodation made as either of us would like to have, I remain confident and tranquil in the sureness that God could not have brought me to you only to have me fail in our great purpose.

The Cardinals who join in our cause have continued with their aid and assistance, both openly and privately; I am confident that there will be a satisfactory resolution to our venture in the very near future. So certain am I of this happy outcome that I have already begun to arrange for my companions in anticipation of my coming again to France. As you recommend, I have selected my suite from among Romans who have some interest in either my family or in France. My nieces are full of schemes; in their delight they indulge in every joyous whimsey in their plans for their arrival in Paris.

I have offered prayers for your returning health every morning and evening. I am convinced that God will not require you to abandon your goal with it so nearly accomplished, and you will be restored once more to your full strength. Without doubt you will be spared—and with God's Grace you will once again flourish as you have before. Be staunch and cheerful, for France has become great while you guided her in the Name of God and the King; such greatness cannot be swept away by a single misfortune.

Extend my greetings and my prayers to His Gracious Majesty, to Her Majesty the Queen, and beg that I may be permitted to assist them again in years to come.

How much wisdom you have given me, my master and my friend! And how much more I have to learn of you to have the smallest part of your knowledge. I thank God for His Goodness in allowing me to serve you. You are the peace of Europe and the center of the greatest Kingdom on earth, for which God be praised again and again.

With my prayer, my endless gratitude, and the hope that God will shower limitless blessings on you for your excellence,

Giulio Mazarini, Abbe

On the 19th day of February, 1638.
Caveat: to be destroyed.

· **2** ·

Outside the walls of Roma, most of the roads were mired and rutted; Olivia's carriage lurched and lumbered through them, her driver cursing the horses and the mud as they went.

"Where are the good Roman roads?" Olivia asked, addressing her personal maid. She hung onto the passenger strap as the coach swayed dangerously, then righted itself and continued on into another deep trough.

"I do not know," whispered the maid, who held her scent-soaked handkerchief to her face, as if the perfume would prevent the dizziness she felt.

Olivia peered toward the window. "How much longer?" She did not expect an answer and got none. "If I've been called out on a fool's errand, they will regret it."

"Of course, Madama," said the maid, her face taking on a greenish tinge. She blotted the cold sweat from her brow and crossed herself.

At that Olivia relented. "I don't mean to trouble you, Avisa. You have nothing to do with the state of the roads." She bounced against the back cushions as the carriage shifted to the side; from the box the coachman's curses grew louder. Olivia saw her maid blush at the string of obscenities he uttered.

Avisa avoided Olivia's steady gaze. "It is not fit for us to hear such words."

"Words cannot hurt you, Avisa," Olivia said gently and ironically. "Fear the things that can, not words."

"God is offended by such words," Avisa insisted, resisting the urge to clap her hands over her ears, but only because it meant giving up her secure hold on the passenger strap.

"Then let God rebuke the coachman, if He's of a mind to," Olivia said, adding with a sigh, "It would be easier to unhitch the horses and ride."

"We are unescorted," Avisa said, shocked at the notion.

"Lamentably we are," came Olivia's response at once. "And you would probably not want me to ride straddle, either."

"No gentlewoman rides in that manner," Avisa said firmly, her indignation lessening the nausea she felt.

"This gentlewoman does," Olivia reminded her. "But not to visit His Holiness," she went on resignedly. "When do we reach the Via Flaminia? It can't be that far."

Avisa did not approve of her mistress calling the roads and towns by their ancient and un-Christian names, but she held her tongue, saying instead, "It's leagues and leagues."

"Yes, that is painfully clear." Olivia tapped on the ceiling of the carriage with her long-handled cane. "Uberto, try not to tip us over, if you please."

Once again there was a long and colorful string of blasphemies from the coachman's box, which ended abruptly with a sheepish apology. "Your pardon, Bondama Clemens; it is the road and the Devil that angers me."

"As well they might," said Olivia, as much to herself as to Uberto. "I don't suppose there is another road we could use?"

"There is one, but it is just as bad," answered Uberto after a slight hesitation. "Possibly worse—it goes by a pig farmers' village."

"Spare us the pigs," said Olivia with a rueful shake of her head. She wanted to say something encouraging, but was not able to find honest expression beyond remarking to Avisa, "Once we reach the Via Flaminia, it will be easier. The old roads are never this muddy, and there are a few milestones, too." She remembered how diligently the roadbuilders had set up their markers at every thousand standard paces; the markers that remained always stirred her recollection. "The Romans built their roads to last."

"The old roads are the best," Avisa agreed, her handkerchief to her mouth once more. "Why does the Pope have to summon you at such a time?" she wondered aloud, then crossed herself. "It is always an honor to be summoned to the Pope, and doubtless His Holiness has excellent—"

"I think it's a nuisance, too," said Olivia, to help Avisa from becoming more embroiled in her denial. "But it is the Abbe, you see."

"Why is he so important? Why does the French Cardinal want him? Hasn't he Cardinals enough in France?" Avisa turned her bewildered eyes on Olivia.

"Oh, there are French Cardinals, and they are from noble families, most of them, and France is a kingdom at war and internally divided." She sighed. "They do not want France to be another Germany, with Catholics and Protestants killing each other year on year on year." She tapped the arm of the coach. "So they are looking for a man with dependable loyalties, who will not be suborned as some of the others have been."

When they had gone a little farther the left rear wheel bogged down a second time. Olivia thought of Niklos, riding on ahead of them to Pope Urbano's retreat to set up her apartments there. She wished now she had ridden with him; in another time she would have. In another time: such little words, she thought, and inno-cent-sounding. Who would believe what they meant to her?

Quickly she reminded herself that in those long-vanished days she would have required an armed guard as well, and would not have been assured of her welcome or comfort once she arrived, not after the Empire failed.

At last the carriage came free of the mud. Uberto blessed and cursed the vehicle and his team of four blood-bays indiscriminately, then scrambled back onto the coachman's box, bellowing over his shoulder to the two footmen hurrying to take their places once again on the rear of the coach. "We are moving, Madama!" he announced loudly.

Olivia restrained the urge to give a sharp answer, and said only, "Thank God."

"And the horses and the footmen; they got us out. If God wants to give us real help, He'll get rid of the mud." Uberto whistled and the team moved a little faster. "Never fear, Madama. We will arrive safely."

"You reassure me," said Olivia drily, looking at Avisa whose pallor was more marked than before. She leaned forward and touched her maid's hand. "Do you need anything of me?"

Avisa shook her head several times. "I need to stop moving. It disturbs me to move so much." She put one hand over her mouth. "I am ashamed."

"You have no reason to be," said Olivia. "Carriages do not upset me, but put me on any boat, and I suffer as you do now." She sighed once. "If it helps you, consider that."

Uberto shouted something; the coach stopped, shuddering as the horses tried to drag it free of a deep rut.

"Not again," muttered Avisa.

"I have an idea," Olivia declared, her patience all but exhausted. "There is a footpath beside the road here. Let us get out and walk awhile. It isn't raining enough to matter, and with the coach lighter, it will be out of the mud faster."

"Our clothes . . ." Avisa said uncertainly.

"They can be brushed later, or discarded, if that is necessary. But you would be the better for fresh air and I would be more pleased if I did not have to sit in this cramped box." She reached for the doorlatch.

"But if our clothes are ruined, and we must attend upon the Papal court . . ." Avisa stopped, her hands trembling in her lap. "Madama, we must not."

"The Pope will not be concerned about our clothes, Avisa. We have our reception garments in the trunks, in any case. Come. Put your zoccoli on." She indicated the wooden shoes tucked under the seat. "And lift your skirts when we get out. It doesn't matter if Uberto sees your sottane—for he has undoubtedly seen such before."

Avisa looked even more shocked. "Tell him and the others to look away," she insisted as she untied her soft kid shoes and pulled on the clumsy, utilitarian zoccoli.

"Of course, if you wish," said Olivia, changing her shoes as well. "But do not fear that Uberto will pay much attention to us. He has his team to consider." She listened to the sounds the horses made, frowning as she realized how fretful the team was. "Be quick."

"I am ready, Madama," said Avisa as he pulled her cloak around her shoulders and raised the soft hood. "Take your muff."

"I don't need a muff," said Olivia as she fastened her long, fur-trimmed chatelaine over her clothes. "Take mine if your hands are cold," she added as she saw Avisa shiver.

"It isn't fitting that I should," the maid protested halfheartedly. "But I am cold."

"Then take it," said Olivia, pulling her muff from under the seat and shoving it at Avisa. She rapped on the carriage wall again, this time sharply. "Uberto! Avisa and I are getting out while you free the carriage."

"But—" the coachman began to protest.

"We will walk along the path with one of the footmen; you may choose which." She opened the carriage door. "Will one of you lend us a hand?"

Uberto hesitated an instant longer, then shouted, "Guido! Tend to our Bondama!"

The slighter of the two footmen scrambled off the back of the coach, clutching his heavy woolen cape around him. His face was set with cold. As he brought down the passenger steps, he gave a little bow to Olivia, holding out his arm to her, too scared to speak.

Olivia placed her tall cane at the edge of the mud and used it for balance. "Lend Avisa your arm, Guido," she said as she stepped over to the pathway. As she waited for her maid, she squinted up at the lowering clouds. "Well, what do you think? Will there be more rain today, or is it over?"

Uberto was unbuckling the Hungarian reins so that he could guide each horse independently. He looked away from his task long enough to measure the sky once. "Nothing more today, I think. There are fewer clouds to the south and west."

The off-wheeler tried to rear and this set the other three horses plunging in harness; Uberto struggled to restrain the team as Avisa tripped in her hurry to get away from the coach.

"Here." Olivia held out her hand to her maid and kept her from falling into the mud. Guido watched in bemused surprise as mistress helped servant to her feet.

"Many thanks, Madama," Avisa said breathlessly. She looked back at the coach, shaking her head.

"Let them tend to their work," said Olivia, a bit wistfully; she wanted to help Uberto but knew her coachman would be dreadfully chagrined if she came to his assistance.

"Those horses are so wild," whispered Avisa as she moved away from the coach. Her wooden zoccoli left deep prints in the soft earth of the footpath.

"They're frightened," said Olivia, following Avisa, thinking of the many, many times she had come down this road, for it joined with another that led to the Villa Dacia, sometimes called the Villa Vecchia, but had once been known as Villa Ragoczy.

"That Spanish lord has planted more vineyards," Avisa observed as she quickened her pace.

"Yes," said Olivia, looking toward the new vines on the rolling hills. "He will have a bountiful harvest in a few years, if there is no blight or drought or war."

"He wishes to curry favor with the Church, by giving them his wine for Sacraments." Avisa sounded very disapproving, but her expression changed as Olivia spoke.

"I do the same thing myself," she reminded her servant. "But perhaps not quite for the same reason. The Spanish lord has men fighting in the Low Countries, against the Protestants, and he wishes to keep Papal favor, in case the war goes against his forces, for the Crown will not support him then, and he will have to come to the Church for allies."

"That is another matter entirely. You are not like that Spanish lord."

"No, I am not," said Olivia. "But many are, and some are caught up in that war. Which is why the Cardinals want to establish Mazarini's embassy before he arrives, so that he will have a modicum of protection if the war extends to France. It hasn't so far, but that is because Richelieu has kept the Protestants on the run, and why he wants an Italian Catholic to succeed him." She looked ahead. "Ah, see, there is the old road. Not far now." Her steps were careful, for though the path was not as muddy as the road, the footing was precarious. "Uberto will meet us at the cross-road. What do you say, Guido?" she called back to the footman behind them.

"I say it is not appropriate for a landed lady to stand at the side of the road like a peasant." He tried to keep the contempt out of his voice but could not disguise it entirely.

"Ah," said Olivia with a faint smile.

Avisa took Olivia's part, speaking emphatically. "How dare you speak to the Bondama that way?"

"If she has no concern for her station, it is for us to have it for her," said Guido stiffly, casting a quick, uneasy glance at Olivia as he spoke. "I do not mean to give offence; a lady of rank sent to attend the Pope must be careful in everything she does if she is not to bring scandal on herself and her family."

"I take no offence," said Olivia.

Two large carriages drawn by teams of six horses came down the Via Flaminia; both vehicles had arms blazoned on their doors and their drivers and footmen wore Colonna livery.

"Bound for Assisi as well," said Guido as the carriages lumbered by. "And if they notice you, Madama, it will not be to your credit when we arrive."

"You saw the livery?" Olivia asked, ignoring the criticism. "Colonna is Mazarini's family. They are supporting his efforts with the Pope. It is a dance and a chess game together, this meeting. They would be pleased to have one of their . . . blood be Richelieu's deputy. Doubtless we will have to listen to them at Assisi."

"They have estates to the east," said Guido.

"They have land everywhere," said Olivia. "And you are right. There are other reasons to be on this road, and other places to go other than the Pope's retreat, but still—" She looked down at the mud spattered on her woolen skirts. "This will have to be cleaned as soon as we reach the inn."

"Of course," said Avisa, a hint of offence in her voice.

From the other direction came a man leading a mangy donkey laden with baskets of cut wood and singing scraps of the plaintive folk song "Non lo sai" as he trudged along, cracking on the higher notes and humming where he forgot the words.

Guido narrowed his eyes. "There are many cutthroats who pretend to be harmless wanderers."

"And there are many harmless wanderers," said Olivia, thinking back to the times she might have described herself that way. "You have your pistol, and I have . . ." She tapped her leg, reminding the footman that she had a knife strapped below her knee.

"That would not stop a cutthroat," said Guido with gloomy satisfaction. "They would shoot you and then rob you."

"Perhaps," said Olivia, recalling times such plots had not worked.

Avisa's features were harsh with disapproval. "How can you take such risks so lightly?" she demanded, forgetting to show proper respect.

"I?" Olivia asked in sad amusement. "It is my age, I suppose. I am inured to risks." She looked back and saw that Uberto had brought the coach much nearer. "Ah. Lightening the load has helped, I see."

Guido waved exuberantly, as if they might not otherwise be noticed. "In buon punto!" he called out.

"It does not seem so to me," Uberto grumbled as he brought the coach onto the Via Flaminia. "Were I come in good time, you would not have had to walk." He indicated the state of the team. "We will be brushing mud out of their coats for three days."

Guido was not troubled since it was not his task. "We can resume the journey properly," he told the two women. "Our travels will be easier now."

Uberto laughed nastily as Olivia and Avisa got into the carriage and Guido climbed up behind, next to the older footman. When he set the team in motion, Uberto yelled out praises to San Antonio on behalf of the horses.

"When do you plan to stop for the night, Madama?" Avisa asked as she pulled off her zoccoli, wrinkling her nose in distaste at the mud caking them.

"It has been arranged," said Olivia, who had left such plans to Niklos. "Uberto knows where we are to go, and it is a place others of the Papal Court have gone, so you need not fret about my reputation." She stared out the small window, her attention suddenly very far away.

"Madama?"

Olivia did not respond at once, and when she did, she spoke as if to someone else. "You'd think I'd had enough of Popes, wouldn't you? Urbano VIII is just one in a long, long parade—a thought more capable than some, I suppose, and not as bloodthirsty. He's craftier than some, though. He probably has to be, given the German war and the Spanish."

Avisa crossed herself. "The Throne of San Pietro is a glorious honor and the triumph of faith."

"Not always," said Olivia after a brief hesitation. "Worldly policy and God do not always accommodate one another very well. We are going to Assisi for worldly reasons, Avisa, not for the Glory of God. The Catholic Church is at war and we are being calling into the lines." She bent to fasten the laces on her heeled kid shoes. "In a way, the zoccoli are more comfortable. Certainly they're more sensible."

"Madama!" Avisa protested, uncertain whether she should laugh or be shocked.

At that Olivia relented. "Pay me no mind, Avisa. Travel always turns my thoughts to peculiar matters." She stretched out her legs, letting the toes of her shoes poke out from her skirts. "When I was . . . oh, half my age . . . I would have got astride one of the horses, thought nothing of it, and would have ridden with Niklos and one man-at-arms for escort. Now I must sit in this thing."

"A hoydenish trick, not suitable for a respectable widow," said Avisa with determination. "You would certainly not do so now."

"I suppose not," said Olivia wistfully.

"The Pope must have correct conduct when you answer his summons," said Avisa. "No matter what you say, he defends all that is right and moral, and those who serve him must do so, too." Avisa smiled suddenly and the sternness faded from her face. "I have never before been to the Papal Court. My sister will be amazed when I tell her of it." Her face showed an innocent smugness at anticipation of her sister's envy.

Olivia shook her head. "When we leave you must let me know what you thought of it." She gestured mock dismay. "Perhaps then I will know which of the Cardinals are supporting the Germans. Bichi will not tell me."

"Why are you convinced that it was not the Pope himself who called you to his retreat court? Surely you are of a rank and position to merit such an offer—"

"Oh, Avisa," said Olivia with deep weariness, "Popes do not ask widows to so public an occasion as a retreat, and you know why since you are so worried about conduct. His Holiness has been persuaded to invite me, and I am determined to learn the reason."

"But surely you are of a rank and position that could gain you such an offer—" Avisa persisted.

"I am a Roman widow, which presents a difficulty. But," she continued briskly, "I have lands and money, and most are unencumbered but for the trustees the Church demands, and that elevates my worth." She tapped her toes, the only indication of her irritation. "But the Cardinals want more than lands and money just now—they want discretion and assistance and observance and who knows what else?—and so they are prepared to overlook my widowhood, or turn it to their advantage." Her mouth smiled but her eyes were grim. "Who knows what else?" she repeated softly to herself.

"Surely you don't assume that there is anything . . . improper in their proposals, do you, Madama?" It was a hard question to ask; Avisa knew the rumors as well as any Roman servant did, and she could not entirely forget all she had heard whispered of secret agreements and concealed influence being the stock in trade of those nearest the Pope. "Why would the Cardinals need one such as you?"

"For my appropriateness, I've been told. For my invisibility, perhaps?" Olivia suggested with a lightness she did not feel. "I am not part of the Church, I am not part of any powerful family. I am not known to harbor Protestant sympathies. I have no allegiances that could be awkward. Giulio Mazarini has been a guest at my house, without scandal. Therefore I might provide a cloak of respectability for Mazarini which would allow him to do those things he must and still appear without reproach. And he will have much to do with the French pulling at him from one side and the Church from the other. Providing, of course, that the French are willing to have me in their country, and that will depend on Richelieu." How absurd the notion was, Olivia told herself, that she, of all Romans, should be chosen to appear staid and ultimately proper. "We may guess ourselves foolish from here to Assisi and be not a mote the wiser."

"What is there to guess?" Avisa said, trying to find solace in her piety, for there were doubts in her now that had not arisen before, and which she did not like.

"I wish I knew." She frowned, her hazel eyes thoughtful. "I trust I will learn more shortly."

Avisa folded her hands once more, and looked down at her fingers as if they were entirely new to her. "You make it seem that the Church is as venal as any earthly King may be. It is distressing to think that the Cardinals spend their time trading influence and discrediting rivals. They are the Princes of the Church. They are not supposed to deal with Kings for earthly gain and for advancement. Shouldn't they be above that, Madama?"

Olivia said nothing in answer to Avisa's question. "I wish Uberto wouldn't trot the horses. They're tired enough as it is and what little time it saves us now it might well lose us tomorrow."

"Perhaps he wishes to arrive where we are expected before sundown. It isn't safe to be—"

"Abroad after that," Olivia finished for her. "Yes, I know. It is still foolish to press the team." As if in reaction to her admonition, the vehicle slowed as the horses were pulled back to a walk.

"They know your mind," said Avisa, trying to make a joke of this observation.

"I would like to think so," said Olivia quietly. Her hazel eyes darkened for an instant, and then she chuckled. "Do you mean Uberto or my horses?"

"You, Madama." Avisa was puzzled when Olivia grinned. "What have I said?"

"Nothing, nothing," said Olivia, amusement making her eyes dance. "I misunderstood." She looked away out the window and remained silent until Uberto swung the carriage off the road and drew up in a flagged innyard.

Shouts and the first-lit evening lanthorns and torches greeted the arrival of Olivia's coach. The innkeeper himself opened the passenger door and placed the steps for Olivia's descent, bowing deeply as she did.

"I pray God gave you a swift and safe journey here, Bondama Clemens," he said, addressing her shoes.

"My coachman certainly did his best to make it so," Olivia said lightly. "If God will do something about the mud, all will be well."

The innkeeper was slightly taken aback by her words, but recovered himself quickly and laughed. "The reputation you enjoy for your wit is surely much deserved," he said, indicating the door to one of the two private parlors of his inn. "Your major domo has ordered that this room be set aside for your use. He has also provided bedding for you and seen your quarters prepared."

"Excellent," said Olivia, pausing to be sure that Avisa had got out of the coach safely. "You have prepared everything for me, I trust?"

"Of course, Madama." The innkeeper snapped his fingers imperiously. "It was done hours ago."

Olivia nodded her acceptance. "I am grateful to you for your labors. Now, there are a few things I require of you: my servants will want their evening meal as soon as possible. I hope you will attend to them."

Again the innkeeper bowed. "And you, Madama? What am I to have the honor to do for you?"

"Provide me a half-barrel of hot water and some drying sheets," she said crisply. "I am smirched with mud and cannot retire until I have washed the worst of it away." She held out a golden angel. "For your good service."

The innkeeper took the coin and bowed again, this time with real satisfaction, for the donation was lavish. "To do other than my best for you, Bondama Clemens, would disgrace my family for three generations."

Olivia smiled briefly. "Would it?" Without waiting for the inn-keeper's effusions, she passed through the door into the private parlor, Avisa trailing after her and muttering like a hen on a clutch of eggs.

*   *   *

Text of a note from Alessandro, Cardinal Bichi to Giulio Mazarini, written in code on crossed lines.

To my dear colleague and great hope, blessings and favor from Heaven accompany these words.

I have called upon the widow at Senza Pari again, and have discussed the plans we have all striven to bring to fruition. She has heard me out most courteously and has said that if approval is given to bring you into service of the French Crown, she will con-sider joining your suite at Parigi and there will act in your service. What that service may be is not specified.

She has agreed to allow her stud farm at Tours to be used as a remount station for your messengers if their tasks take them in that direction. She has also said that she will place twenty of her horses at your disposal for the time she lives in Parigi. We have assured her that a minor misunderstanding she has had with Milano will be swiftly resolved, for which she has owned herself properly grateful.

The fortnight she attended His Holiness at Assisi, I had several opportunities to converse with her and have found her to be, as we have heard before now, a woman of superior sense. She is not as devout as might be wished, but in this instance I must believe that her pragmatism might serve us better than too intense a devotion would.

She has indicated to me that she is not interested in marrying again, that her husband left her with a distaste of marriage, and so we need not fear overmuch that she will spend her time in Francia searching for a sufficiently wealthy and noble partner. It may be that we will wish to arrange such a union for her in the future, for she has indicated that she is not adverse to men and has taken lovers before, but at present there is no reason why this would be advisable until you are established at Louis' court. Certainly it would be worthwhile for you to talk with her on this matter, but I think you will discover, as I have, that we have no grounds for anxiety on that issue. Keep in mind that she is a woman without family, and therefore she will be the more at your service than if she had other interests to serve.

With my prayers and my hope that we will succeed in this venture, I am in all ways your friend,

Alessandro, Cardinal Bichi
On the 2nd day of May, 1638, traveling north.
Destroy the code key.

· **3** ·

Though his study was hot, the west-facing windows bringing in the enormous afternoon sun, Antonio, Cardinal Barberini felt cold. It was not the tally of years that chilled him as much as the risky enterprise he and his fellow French-supporting Cardinals had undertaken. He stared at the letter he had just received, knowing that now none of them could turn back.

A knock at the door did not cause Barberini to turn; without taking his eyes from the sheet he held, he said, "Enter," in a distracted tone.

"Eminenza," said the simply habited Abbe as he knelt and waited for the Cardinal to proffer his ring to be kissed.

With a little shake to his head Barberini did this, motioning his visitor to rise as soon as the obedience was performed. "Well, we are assured of Louis' support," said the Cardinal without preamble. "I have just had word."

If this information evoked any emotion in the Abbe, nothing of it was revealed by his handsome features. "To what degree?"

"He will request that you become a citizen of Francia, that you be accepted into the diplomatic service of that country, and that you be made a Cardinal, as befits your station." Barberini placed the letter on his writing table and folded his hands.

"And ordination? Must I be a priest?" The Abbe touched his pectoral crucifix. "I have not that vocation."

Barberini sighed. "Giulio, what a stickler you can be." He closed his eyes. "Thus far, neither His Majesty nor His Holiness have insisted that you be a priest; it is enough that you are an Abbe. This is the least of our concerns."

Giulio smiled, his expressive brown eyes filling with warmth. "Not for me, Eminenza. Forgive me for speaking of this again, but it is no minor thing with me."

"Your 'tranquility of soul'—yes, I know," said Barberini as tolerantly as possible. "That was more than a decade ago. Surely . . ." He did not finish. "There is no reason for us to discuss this. There is no reason at all."

"As you wish, Eminenza." Though the words were dutiful, his manner was firm.

"More of your insolence, I suppose," Barberini said, his rebuke marred by a chuckle. "It speaks well of you. A diplomat needs insolence to carry out his tasks." He indicated the upholstered bench on the other side of his writing table. "Sit down. There are many things we must decide."

Giulio Mazarini sat down at once. "What is needed of me?"

"There are a few matters"—he indicated the letter without touching it—"suggested here that demand our attention before we respond. And we must respond quickly, before the official statements are issued."

"Certainly," said Giulio, his face once again without expression beyond polite interest.

"There is the matter of Richelieu and the Protestants." Barberini fully expected an outburst; he regarded Giulio narrowly.

"Our disagreements are known to you," he said carefully, hesitating just long enough to hold back any hasty words. "When I came back to Roma, we discussed the matter then."

"So we did," said Barberini. "But that was seventeen, eighteen months ago. There have been changes." He placed the tips of his fingers together and regarded Giulio over them.

"My purpose as extraordinary nuncio in Parigi was to establish peace between Francia and Espagna. How the great Richelieu dealt with the rest was not in my purview." He was sitting a little straighter, but nothing in the tone of his voice revealed his emotions.

Barberini shook his head. "Giulio, caro Giulio, this is not a diplomatic assembly. We are two friends, and what we say will not go beyond this door." He offered a kindly smile. "Tell me, Giulio, how you would assess the troubles Richelieu has had with the Protestants and—"

"I would not presume to assess, not after so long a time and at such distance," said Giulio more sharply.

"Your defense of Richelieu is admirable. I pray that if ever I require your defense you will do as well by me as you have by him." He coughed delicately. "But about the Protestants?"

"There are many Protestants in Francia. There are several factors to consider." He shifted on the bench. "Eminenza, I beg your forgiveness, but I do not believe that I can comment on what has happened in Parigi since I returned to Roma. It is not only that I do not wish to speak ill of my great mentor, but that I am not abreast of events there."

Barberini lifted one tufted brow, his childlike face suddenly very ironic. "What? In all this time you have received no word at all from Parigi?"

Giulio had the good sense to be silent. He met Barberini's gaze evenly, his attitude unchanged. "Perhaps we should speak at a more convenient time," he said at last.

"There is no convenient time to speak of these matters," snapped Barberini, relenting. "Very well. I accept your silence. I will not demand to know what has been sent to you under the rose. I have had my own observers there and I suppose I must be guided by what they tell me." He waited, leaving this opening for Giulio. "But if there is something . . . ?"

"No; nothing. Yours is a wise decision, Eminenza," said Giulio. He looked down at his long, shapely hands. "In the matter of citizenship?"

"You must accept those terms. You cannot act for Louis if you are not one of his countrymen." Barberini opened his hands, then laid the fingertips together once more. "Citizenship is for the sake of the world, not the sake of the soul. You are part of the Church, which is more than any nation. If to serve God and His Church we must make concessions in the world, it is a small enough price to pay."

"I do not object to the terms." Giulio looked up at the ceiling. "If Francia is to be my work, then"—he changed from Italian to French—"then I will be French. It is no disgrace to be French, Eminence."

Barberini's French was not as good as Giulio's, but serviceable enough. "It is no disgrace to be Christian anywhere in the world, so long as you are not Protestant."

Giulio crossed himself. "God will protect me."

"As He will all of us, we pray forever." This was an automatic sentiment, expressed with slight impatience. "Have you considered your suite?"

"I have," said Giulio, still speaking French. "I have relatives, of course, to be with me in time to come. Richelieu advises me to make most of my household with French servants, so that I will not seem as much a foreigner." He rose and went to the window. "For the most part I agree, though I have insisted that my cooks come from Roma."

"What does Richelieu say to that?" Barberini asked, amused.

"He concurs." Giulio took a deep breath. "For two reasons: he has advised me that there could be attempts on my life, and that poison would be the most expected means of harming me. His second reason," he went on with a most charming smile, "is that he knows Italian cooks are superior to French ones."

Barberini laughed once, and Giulio joined with him. "You're right. And so is His Eminence." He grew serious as he regarded the letter again. "What about the rest of your suite?"

"I have decided that I will employ French officers as my private couriers. This way it cannot be said that I have used my station to compromise Louis, since his own men would not act against their oaths to him." Giulio had become serious with mercurial swiftness. "I do not want to give any occasion for doubts to arise. I want the French to know that I am one of them."

"And your name?" said Barberini. "What have you decided about that? Giulio Mazarini is an Italian no matter what nation he serves."

"Yes," said Giulio with resignation. "I cannot dispute that. It is Richelieu's recommendation that I adapt my name, so that I will be French, but also so it will not appear that I am trying to hide my origins."

"Richelieu often has excellent sense," said Barberini. "So, what is it to be?"

"Jules Mazarin," said Giulio thoughtfully, tasting the name to see how it felt in his mouth.

"Mazarin could be Venetian," approved Barberini. "You will not find opposite to such a name here."

"Nor in France, I hope," said Giulio. "I've practiced writing it; the most difficult thing is to leave off the last *i*." He gestured self-effacingly. "Tell me, will Bichi and Bagni support me?"

"Of course. You need not ask," said Barberini. "Since your successful negotiation of the Treaty of Cherasco they have had faith in you, and they see that your affiliation with the French is for the benefit of the Church and the nation." He had drawn himself up and spoke as if addressing a large number of people instead of this single Abbe.

Giulio turned his back on the window. "I do not ask for pride, Eminence. That would show more clearly than any other sin that I am not suited to fill this post. I ask because once I leave for France, I will have to rely on your aid without being able to solicit it."

Barberini gave Giulio a measuring look. "We have striven for years to bring this about. You have no reason to suppose that we would desert you now."

"No reason," repeated Giulio, his eyes fixed on a point some distance beyond the opposite wall. "You will have messengers from those who will not wish me to continue in my work. You will hear things of me, and some of them will be lies."

"Certainly; that is the way of the world." Barberini waited until he had Giulio's full attention. "That is why you must choose your suite carefully, and why your messengers must be wholly reliable and devoted to you. Any other course is folly."

"Yes," said Giulio. He glanced once at the letter on the writing table, then looked deliberately away. "I have made several inquiries already. I will arrange for personal couriers after I have myself established."

"You and your suite?" Barberini suggested.

"You mean in case I should need to have it appear that I am not making use of couriers?" Giulio said, and just for a moment his attractive features hardened to show his tremendous will beneath his pleasant manner.

"Among other things," said Barberini, being deliberately obscure.

"I have not yet discussed the matter with those who have consented to come with me," said Giulio, choosing his words with great care. "That is not to say that they have not broached the matter to me; Bondama Clemens was most forthcoming."

"And the others?" Barberini inquired at his blandest.

"It will take time for me to be certain, but I believe that most of those accompanying me are astute enough to understand what our game is." He paused, one hand resting on the crucifix he wore. "Is it fitting, I wonder, for a churchman to expect others to compromise themselves for the sake of the Church? I believe that what we do we do for the benefit of all the souls in Europe, in Christendom, but for that benefit, I require those most closely allied with me to accept hazards that are more truly mine than theirs. What will God make of that when He judges my soul, do you think?"

"That you were obedient to the Will of God and the Pope," said Barberini at once. "You have work to do in the world, Abbe, and there is no reason for you to think that your work is less in the Way of God than the prayers of a cloistered nun. As long as we are on the earth, we must—"

Giulio held up his hand. "Yes, I have said those things to myself, and most of the time I persuade myself. But what of the others? Do they believe I am entitled to . . . ?"

"Why would they agree to form your suite if they did not?" Barberini demanded, his small eyes narrowing. "Who doubts your right?"

"No one. Save myself." Giulio crossed the study in four long strides.

"This from the man who rode between two attacking armies

shouting 'Peace!'?" Barberini nodded once. "It is no wonder that Richelieu and Louis want your services. If you were willing to do so much then, you are entitled to like service from those who have accepted your protection." He held up the letter. "You are not unopposed. Those who go with you know that, and they are aware that your protection is their protection."

Giulio crossed himself. "May there be no blood on my hands at the end of my life. God give me His aid."

"He has done so already, by bringing you to Richelieu's attention, and by giving you courage. Give thanks in your prayers that God made His Gifts known to you early." Barberini picked up a small silver bell and rang it. "My page will bring us refreshments."

"Thank you," said Giulio, who did not want any.

"Bichi will be joining us directly. He has some information to pass along to you." He read through the letter once more, shaking his head. "You must send a courier to Richelieu soon. I do not like what we have heard about his health. He is vulnerable if his health fails."

"He is vulnerable in any case," said Giulio grimly.

"But doubly so . . ." Barberini stopped as there was a discreet knock on the door. "Who is it?"

"Lionello," said the page in a high, nasal voice.

"Bolognese," said Barberini softly. "Don't comment on his accent, will you?"

"Naturally not," said Giulio. "Have him enter." He resumed his seat on the bench, resigning himself to boredom and worry.

"Come in," called out Antonio, Cardinal Barberini, reverting to Italian. "And bring our refreshment."

Lionello was no older than nine, taller than most for his age, but gawky, all arms and legs. He held the tray he carried as if he expected it to explode. It was not possible to bow, but he lowered his head, first to his master and then to Giulio. "I tried to find some berries, but they are not ripe yet, master."

"That's all right," said Barberini, directing Lionello to put the tray down on the corner of his writing table.

As he obeyed, Lionello looked toward Giulio. "They say you are going to Francia to serve the King."

"Yes, I have heard that, as well," said Giulio, doing his best to appear unconcerned.

"Such matters are not for pages to discuss; certainly there is no reason for you to talk of it." Barberini's words were sharp, and he directed them at Lionello in his most impressive tone. "If I learn that you have been listening to gossip, or spreading it yourself, then I will see that you are sent home to Bologna at once, and there entered in monastic service—preferably with a silent Order."

Lionello's hands shook as he stepped back. "I have said nothing. I repeat only what I hear, my master." He kept his eyes lowered as he said this.

"A little less defiance, if you will," said Barberini, reaching out and forcing the boy to look up. "It is in your eyes, carino, and God knows it as surely as He knows the limits of the oceans."

Giulio signaled to Barberini, then said in his mildest way, "Don't be too harsh with him, Eminenza. He knows that the others gossip and bear tales, and it is not surprising that he wishes to be like the rest, with his own tale to tell."

"No servant of mine is permitted to gossip," insisted Barberini. "If you do, boy, you will rue the day, you have my promise of it."

Lionello cowered back. "I never speak, Eminenza. Never."

"For your own sake I hope you are right," said Barberini with a significant nod to Mazarini. "The Abbe here will not hesitate to say that you overheard us speaking and therefore are to blame for the spreading of secrets, and distorting them as well." He indicated the door. "I will want you to return shortly, so do not dawdle in the kitchen."

"Of course not," muttered Lionello, bowing his way from the august presence of Antonio, Cardinal Barberini. He closed the door and walked away heavily, so that the sound of his retreating steps would be clearly audible to the Cardinal and his guest.

"Was it necessary to terrify him?" Giulio asked sympathetically.

"You know the answer to that; think of how many times plans have been compromised by the gossip servants repeat, or by information taken by subtlety or bribe. Why do you, of all men, ask me this?" He folded his arms and managed to look like an overgrown child. "You are intending to deal with the French, Giulio. Your servants will be the single biggest danger around you." He looked toward the tray. "Bless the Name of God and have some of this food, will you?"

Giulio crossed himself and lowered his eyes. "I thank you for your generosity and God for His Goodness."

Barberini shrugged. "How the work of God is to be done on scraps and a few sips of wine, I do not know, and do not"—he lifted an admonitory finger—"preach the Loaves and Fishes to me,

Abbe. I know that God's Word is enough to feed the soul of all men." He looked over at the tray. "Cheese and apples. It could be worse. And the wine isn't too bad."

"Italian?" asked Giulio as he reached for the bottle to pour some for himself and host.

"Umbrian, a bit strong." He held out his hand for one of the two large cups. "Apples, and wrinkled at that."

"Last autumn's apples," said Giulio, making conversation as he cut one of the two apples in half with the small knife provided. "His Holiness has given me permission to wear the pluvial while officiating in France, no matter what rank I have achieved."

"Sensible, given the post you are to fill eventually." He bit into the apple. "Too dry."

"Old apples are dry," Giulio said, eating as if this were the sweetest and ripest fruit plucked fresh from the tree. "The wine will end your thirst."

"Oh, stop it, Abbe," said Barberini with a combination of amusement and irritation. "You are not on diplomatic duty here, and if the apples are not to your liking, you may tell me so without hesitation."

"I would never give so much an offence," said Mazarini, in such a tone that it was impossible to be certain whether or not he was serious. He chewed in silence, then addressed Cardinal Barberini once more, this time with greater formality. "When I return to France, I will want to keep you and our friends informed of what I do, but that will require French couriers. Therefore I may require that we select meeting places away from Roma where a messenger would attract less suspicion than he might here."

"It will be decided," Barberini gave his word. "Before you depart all such sites will be established. We will also try to have messengers waiting for your dispatches at all times, but that is less certain." He yawned suddenly. "I don't know how it is, but just as most of the world is recovering from mid-day slumber, I am in need of it."

"Is it the heat of the day?" ventured Giulio politely.

"I don't think so," said the Cardinal as he took a generous sip of the wine. "If it were, the heat is greater earlier, and that should give me more fatigue."

"Then it is the Will of God," said Giulio gently.

"Or a failure of the flesh," said Barberini, his eyes growing hooded with a light in their depths that revealed little more than unacknowledged passion.

"Who is to say that is also not the Will of God?" said Giulio, wholly unperturbed.

The burning faded from Barberini's eyes as he refilled his cup. "Abbe, you are a formidable diplomat. I can find it in my heart to pity the French." He waved his hand as if shooing away a mosquito. "Take no offence, Giulio. Doubtless your skills are also the Will of God."

* * *

Text of a letter from the major domo Niklos Aulirious to a warehouseman in Paris; written in French.

To that most excellent merchant and dealer in household goods, the warmest respects of Niklos Aulirios, and a number of requests which I trust you will be able to grant.

First, this is to inform you that my mistress, Bondama Atta Olivia Clemens, widow of Roma, has been given the signal honor of forming one of the suite of the Abbe Giulio Mazarini to accompany him to your illustrious city upon the occasion of his return there when he enters the diplomatic service of Louis XIII.

To that end, we have secured a house for Bondama Clemens just outside of Paris, near Chatillon, not far from the road leading to Chartres and Tours, where my mistress owns a stud farm. The house is seventy years old and necessary repairs are being made in anticipation of Bondama Clemens' arrival there. I am informed that the renovations will be complete in three months, and that work has already commenced on what is needed. Since most of the house is empty, and what few furnishings there are do not suit my mistress, this letter will bring a purse to be used in the purchase of appropriate furnishings. My mistress, being Roman, tends to prefer Roman designs and textiles, but the current fashion in Roma, being Spanish, is not especially to her liking.

Let me recommend elegance in all things, for such is Bondama Clemens' taste. Elegance and usefulness are her constant guides in all that surrounds her. If there is a choice of two chairs, select the one that is the more elegant and the more sturdy. Bondama Clemens has little patience with flimsy chairs. In the matter of draperies and other window coverings, again I feel I must emphasize elegance. Where a design is more simple but more elegant Bondama would doubtless prefer it over those more flamboyant but less elegant. She has a decided preference for damask silks but is not fond of embroidery.

We understand in Roma that there are many styles of lace just now, and for that reason my mistress has requested that I advise you she prefers lace on her clothes, not on her draperies, or linen or upholstery. I hope you will keep this in mind when you select those items for her house. When she is pleased, she is very generous; when she is disappointed, then she keeps her purse closed. Those who have pleased her have not regretted it.

My mistress is dispatching me to Paris before September, and I will do myself the honor of waiting upon you then to review all that has been done to the house and to be certain that all will be to my mistress' taste upon her arrival.

You have been most highly recommended to me from many who have lived in Paris during the last ten years. For that reason, I am prepared to rely on you for this work. With these few guidelines I am certain that you can provide Bondama Clemens with all she requires of you. Tell your assistants to keep her preferences in mind, and they will benefit accordingly.

My mistress is expected to provide entertainment for those of the court who wish to speak with the Abbe in surroundings less restrictive than the court, but that does not mean that comfort and luxury are to be forgotten along with the rest of it. Bear in mind that those who are used to the caress of fine fabrics and the look of gold service will not be amused by appointments intended for a farmhouse.

The chateau, called Eblouir, will be available to you upon the presentation of this letter and the enclosed endorsement. I will give myself the pleasure of inspecting your progress upon my arrival in Paris, and at that time we will bring our accounts fully up to date. The endorsement includes the limits of your permitted expenses, and unless there is some reason you believe that there is a compelling reason to exceed your permitted spendings, I will assume that you will observe the boundaries you have accepted.

Your recommendation of a coachmaker would be very much appreciated, the appreciation taking useful form should your recommendation prove worthy.

Until I call upon you myself on my mistress' behalf, may God send you good health and good fortune.

Niklos Aulirios
major domo to Bondama Atta Olivia Clemens
On the 19th day of June, 1638, in Roma.
By the courier of the Abbe Giulio Mazarini.

· 4 ·

Crates were stacked in the central parlor of Senza Pari, the largest of them containing trunks filled with Roman earth. Though it was late in the day, the room was still uncomfortably hot and the men sweated as they struggled to finish their tasks before the evening meal.

"I wish there were a tepidarium out by the stables," Olivia said to Avisa as she stood in the door watching.

"A tepidarium?" repeated Avisa. "A thing of pagan Roma?" She was not as horrified by such a notion as she had been a year ago. "What is a tepidarium?"

"A bath, a very big bath, filled with cool water, where we would be able to swim. How pleasant that would be, swimming as the day wanes."

"Infamia," said Avisa with satisfaction. "What woman would want to do something so . . . debauched."

"I would, for one," said Olivia with a short sigh. "I wish Niklos were still here. But then," she went on with a quirky smile and a gesture of resignation, "I sent him to Parigi because I need him there."

"The perils of travel, Madama," said Avisa seriously. "For one of your station, and with your obligations, arrangements must be made." She indicated all the chests. "You are being most reasonable, most prudent, leaving so much here."

Olivia turned away from the parlor and started down the hall. "But then, I will come back here. I always come back to Roma; it is my native earth." She entered the dining hall and shook her head as she studied the framed paintings hanging there. "I will miss them; they are much too cumbersome to take with me."

"Out of their frames and rolled . . ." Avisa began, then stopped.

"I might as well take my carpets, too," said Olivia, pausing to look at a Caravaggio she had commissioned from the artist. "And while I'm at it, my chests and my tables and my chairs. No, no"— she shook her head—"I don't want to be tempted. They remain here, awaiting my return, for surely I shall return. In a way," she continued after a brief hesitation as she gave the room another quick, keen glance, "they are my bond, my surety that I will be back."

Avisa coughed delicately. "If that is your wish, Madama."

"That I return?" she inquired. "Why should I not?"

This time Avisa smiled, the same sort of smile a nursemaid might give to an adored child. "Who knows, but that you might find a husband to your liking in Parigi and decide to remain there." Her brows rose to accent the suggestion.

Olivia shook her head slowly. "Thank you for your good intentions, but I have had my fill of marriage."

"That is because you have not met one who can replace your husband in your memory," said Avisa piously.

"Thank God fasting for that," Olivia responded, her hazel eyes darkening at the memory of Justus. It was the one thing she disliked about Roma—the city constantly reminded her of him. Most of the time the recollections were fleeting and fragmented, but from time to time his image came back to her and she discovered she could still loathe him.

"Madama!" Avisa said, scandalized, as she always was at Olivia's disparaging remarks about her husband.

Generally this did not irritate Olivia, but now she spoke sharply. "You know my husband was debauched."

"So you have said, Madama," said Avisa, affronted.

In spite of herself Olivia laughed. "Oh, don't pucker so. I am not saying any of this to goad you, though you may think I am. It is my distress at leaving home that speaks, nothing more."

Avisa dropped the suggestion of a curtsy. "Madama."

"Don't take offence," said Olivia as she started toward the door. "None was intended." She paused, looking back at the paintings she would leave behind. "What a sad thing, to leave so much beauty."

This time Avisa did not say anything; her back stiff with disapproval she followed Olivia out of the salon and toward the side of the building toward the door that led to the stables.

Uberto emerged from the carriage-house as soon as Olivia entered the stableyard. He gave a nod in place of a bow and jerked his thumb in the direction of the smithy. "All new shoes on the horses, Madama. Every one of the teams will be inspected and tended to."

"You have given them the meal I provided?" Olivia asked, looking around at the bustle of activity.

"For the worm; yes. But, Madama, there is no cure for the worm. It works its way with horses." He shrugged emphatically.

"Do my horses die of the worm?" Olivia challenged.

"Not often," Uberto allowed, pointing to the long row of stalls. "There are two mares in foal, of that we are certain: the Neopolitan and the Hungarian mare."

"Those are the ones crossed with the Spanish horses from Andalusia?" Olivia asked, paying no attention to Avisa as she hung back at the entrance to the stableyard.

"Yes. The third mare did not settle." He spat. "It was the doing of curses."

"It was no such thing," said Olivia. "I have been at breeding horses for a long time, Uberto. There are mares who do not settle easily, and that French mare is one such. When she comes into season again, have Fulmine mount her, and be certain that she is turned out for exercise every day."

Uberto shook his head. "If she will not settle in her stall, giving her exercise will insure that—"

"She is the sort of mare who craves running. If she is deprived of that, she becomes troubled and ill. Do as I require, Uberto." Olivia cocked her head toward the carriage-house. "Are the coaches in good repair?"

"Yes, Madama," said Uberto with a sigh. "I have ordered all the axles tested, as you require, and there are extra wheels being made for the five coaches that will carry you into Francia."

"Very good," said Olivia, adding with a trace of mischief, "I know you think me quite mad, Uberto. But I have learned to make certain . . . preparations before I travel. Too often I have discovered, too late, that my plans were inadequate." She motioned him to follow her toward the paddocks. "I trust you will keep me informed of the breeding here while I am gone? I want to know about every foal."

"Are you planning to be homesick?" Uberto suggested with a wink.

"I'm always homesick away from Roma," Olivia said seriously, her hazel eyes as distant as if she were already in Parigi. "That is to be expected." She pointed toward one of the paddocks, her manner pragmatic and full of purpose once more. "What is being done about that gelding? Is his hock improving?"

"A little," said Uberto cautiously.

"How little? That bodes ill," Olivia challenged, her eyes narrowing. "Has he been able to move well, or is he still lame?"

"He's been pretty lame," Uberto admitted. "He hasn't been exercised. The sore is still open." This last he said guiltily with his face averted.

"Have the grooms used the poultice I gave them? I gave them an ample amount of it the day after Furbo was injured. If they have done their work, he ought to be improved by now." She waited for his answer, weighing his reaction.

"They have their orders," said Uberto, still not looking directly at her.

"My, my, what a very slippery answer." She tapped Uberto on the shoulder with her folded fan. "Meaning that they have not used the poultice as I instructed them, have they?" She paused briefly. "And as a result of their obstinacy Furbo is probably ruined. How much proud flesh is there around the wound now?"

"Not much. Nothing so severe," Uberto said, but his protest was little more than form. "He can improve." He looked around as if searching for allies, but none appeared.

"Oh?" Olivia asked, a bit too sweetly. "Explain to me how it could not be so severe. Tell me how a gelding is going to be good for anything if he is still lame and the sore is open on his leg?" She had one hand over her hip; the lavish support of her padded sottane and Spanish farthingale made her skirts billow out from her waist. "Well? What do you propose? He is an excellent horse, Uberto, but if we cannot use him . . ."

"He will improve," insisted Uberto. "The poultice takes time. I will attend to it myself. I will set myself a task—that Furbo improves." His face was ruddy now and he swallowed hard once. "He's hauled me out of trouble more than once, and I'll see to it that he gets better." He touched the medal that was around his neck on a ribbon. "By San Antonio."

Olivia inclined her head. "I wish you success. It strikes me that you will need some aid if you're going to manage it. Assign one of the grooms to tend him as well. All this for a gelding," she said, shaking her head once as if amused at her own temerity.

"Furbo is a good fellow," Uberto said with feeling.

"I agree," Olivia answered. "It's a pity that his mouth is so bad—I'd have used him as a stud if his mouth had been good." She gave a slight, quick gesture of resignation. "Oh, don't remind me that we do not breed unworthy horses here: that is my own rule and I have rarely broken it." She was walking ahead of Uberto now, and Avisa lagged far behind. "The six-week-old foal."

"She is doing very well. She's thriving," Uberto said with more enthusiasm than usual as if to compensate for his earlier lapses. "She is exercised twice a day with her mother."

"She is not being restricted, is she?" Olivia asked sharply. "I do not want any of these new foals brought to heel too young. Remember what happened to the legs of last year's foals? I want no more of that." She opened her fan and used it once as emphasis. "And while I am gone, I expect a full and correct report regularly. Niklos Aulirious will return from time to time and he will inform me if there is any trouble here."

"Madama, I do not write except to sign my name," Uberto protested.

"There will be those here who do. You are to see that they have your reports once a month. The Abbe has guaranteed me monthly contact with Senza Pari, and access to his personal couriers in emergencies." She had entered the barn where all the grain and salt was stored. "Before I go, I want a complete accounting of what you have on hand so that orders may be placed for those feeds you must purchase."

"Of course, Madama," said Uberto, sounding a little desperate now. "But am I not coming with you to Francia?"

"Yes, and you are then coming back. You are of more worth to me here than you would be in Parigi. I have coachmen in Francia already; you have been with these horses for almost ten years and you know them well." She folded her arms as much as her enormous stiff sleeves would allow. "I would prefer to entrust the breeding to you than to someone unknown."

"You honor me, Madama," said Uberto, a touch of suspicion in his manner, as if he doubted her intentions.

"No, I don't," Olivia responded. "I am requiring a great deal of work from you, which is something very different. There is a great deal of responsibility to this task, and I am asking you to shoulder it while I am away. You will have more to do than you think now. And I expect you to do the work I assign to you." She let him think over what she had told him.

"Of course," he said, still not wholly convinced.

"You think now that while I am gone," Olivia went on, her tone easier, as if they were speaking of nothing more than the prospects of a hot evening, "you will be the one to be master, but that is not correct; you will be my lieutenant, not my general." She read his startled expression correctly. "That is why I want regular reports. You may dictate them to Vittorio or Andrea, as you choose, but I want those reports. Give them to the Abbe's courier every month, or I will dispatch Niklos at once and you will have to answer to him."

Uberto's expression which had been lighter had now soured. "I am your servant, Madama."

"Yes," said Olivia cordially. "Little as you may like it, you are. You are also the most reliable of the lot, and I am depending on that." She looked around. "Where are the tally sheets on sheep and cattle?"

"Nino has them," Uberto growled. "He is in the storage shed. Surely you don't need to talk to Nino, do you?" There was a whine in his voice now, and he hated the sound of it.

"Is he drunk again?" Olivia asked without distress. "Your brother-in-law is carrying your family obligation much too far, don't you think?" She was walking toward the storage shed with a determined stride, her heavy skirts puffing around her toes like damask dust clouds.

"He . . . he does drink too much," Uberto had to admit as he hastened after Olivia. "He is not a happy man and his distress rankles him." It was a very poor explanation but it was the only one he could offer.

"Does he say the same thing to your sister, I wonder? Or does he bluster and tell her of what he is capable of doing but has been thwarted by others because they sense his superiority?" Olivia had lived too long not to recognize the chronic discontent in Nino that sufficed to excuse all his excesses through resentment. "Other men have made the same claim; almost all of them are forgotten, and those that are remembered are not loved."

"Dio," whispered Uberto, unable to disagree with his mistress, yet unwilling to invent another excuse for Nino.

Olivia swung open the door to the storage shed, using her fan as the dusty air swept out of the darkness. "Gracious, what do we keep in here these days?" she asked, wishing she could sneeze to clear her head.

From some distance behind her, Avisa called out, "Madama, it isn't fitting for—"

"Oh, Numi!" Olivia cut her off in exasperation. "I really don't have to have my maid as chaperone in my own buildings. Stay where you are, Avisa. If I need you, I will scream."

"It might not be possible," Avisa warned darkly as she made her way to the shade of a tall old fig tree; its fruit was just starting to ripen, and Avisa occupied herself looking for those first few delicious morsels.

There were barrels and sacks and bins along one wall, carded wool in loose-knotted hanks and rolled hides on the other. The doors at the far end of the shed were closed. The atmosphere was stifling and so full of smells that the air seemed the consistency of minestra alla cacciatore.

As she picked her way over the uneven and unswept floor, Olivia said to Uberto, "Where do we look for him and his tallies, pray?"

"I don't know," Uberto admitted unhappily. "Sometimes he goes behind the bins, back where the wine barrels are."

"Naturally," said Olivia, her face becoming set. "And does he broach any of them, do you think?"

"He has been told he must not," said Uberto with great care. "I have told him myself."

"I see," said Olivia as she pushed her way between a large bin half-filled with crushed oats and a barrel of bacala. Her nose wrinkled as the odor of the salted cod enveloped her. "Why don't we keep that in the kitchen cellars? I'm surprised all the feed doesn't reek of fish."

"I will attend to it, Madama," muttered Uberto as he followed her down the narrow access toward the tremendous barrels standing twice the height of a man where the wine was made. "He might be on the other side, by the small barrels."

"Thank you," said Olivia as she made her way around the end of the line of huge barrels.

Desperately Uberto added a warning. "He has an uncertain temper, Madama."

"So have I," Olivia countered, and in the warm, wine-scented gloom she began to look for Nino, finding him almost at once reclining against two of the smallest barrels, his head cradled on his arms, snoring gently.

Behind her, Uberto whispered, "Gran Madre Maria," and crossed himself.

"Ah." Olivia went to where Nino slept. "He smells more than the wine does." She reached down, her hand wrapping around the back of his grimy smock. "All *right*," she said loudly, tugging suddenly upward, dragging Nino to his feet and waking him all at the same time.

Uberto blinked, astonished at what he had seen. He stood in silence, regarding Olivia with an emotion between awe and distress. "Nino," he said as his brother-in-law blinked at him. "What happened." It was a foolish thing to say; he knew what happened.

Nino tried to take a step or two away and found that he could not. He stared at Olivia, his thoughts disordered. He shoved his hand through his hair and then over his stubbly chin. "This morning. Early. There was much to do. I . . . I wanted to rest . . ." He gestured toward the small barrels as if it were the most natural thing in the world for a man to nap on them.

"You stink of wine," Olivia informed him.

"Well, look where I am," Nino said, doing his best to smile.

"I did not say you smell of wine," Olivia corrected him with severity. "I said you stink of it. It is in your sweat." She released him and moved away from him. "You are here because Uberto vouches for you, and you abuse his trust. And you abuse mine." She cocked her head to the side. "Well?"

Nino smiled; it was a practiced smile, as guileless as a child with pockets full of sweetmeats. "All of us has a lapse from time to time, Madama. Who of us has not occasionally forgot himself and had a bit too much of wine? Eh?"

Uberto had tried desperately to signal Nino, to stop him on this disastrous course. His attempts were in vain, and so he tried to intervene. "The priest will pray for you, Nino, and I will pray and Angela will pray."

The smile disappeared. "Pray. That's all you're good for, the lot of you. All for this damned widow who hasn't the decency to re-marry or to turn over her estate to her relatives." He spat. "You know what kind of women do that, brother-in-law, and though they work other streets, they are the same meat."

Olivia's brows rose. "So you think I am a harlot," she said blandly. "Then you should be pleased to be gone from my service. Present my tallies to me, take your things and leave before sunset."

Uberto stood transfixed. In a voice that seemed to come from a great distance, he said, "Madama. He is my sister's husband."

"That is unfortunate for her." Olivia looked at Nino. "You are not to be on any of my land again. Is that understood? If you are, I will have you in front of a judge."

Nino laughed once but this time it was nothing more than bra-vado; his eyes were shiny with fear. "What judge would hear the likes of you?"

Olivia answered him sweetly. "Would you care to make a test of it and find out?"

"Iddio aiuto." Uberto clasped his hands together as if keeping them closed would somehow stop Nino's catastrophic words. "No, Nino. Be silent."

Without warning Nino rounded on him. "Why? Are you afraid I will ruin your place here with this woman? Do you fear her wrath?" He was angry now, his countenance darkening with each accusation. "You speak against me to my wife. You give me no privilege here. You could have made all of us rich, but you will not do it! You have decided to have it all for yourself, and your sister and I can starve! That's what you want, isn't it?"

Uberto was staggered. "Nino, it's nothing like—"

But Nino was too caught up in his own delirium of wrath to listen or to stop. "You plan to have it all for yourself. You won't share your treasure, will you? You're not going to—"

"Both of you be silent," said Olivia, her voice not much above her usual conversational level, but of so certain a purpose that both men turned and stared at her. "You, Nino, will leave before sundown as I have ordered. Your wife need accompany you only if she wishes to. If she would prefer to remain here, she would be—"

"So you can make another whore of her!" Nino bellowed, and swung his locked fists toward her.

Before Uberto could move, Olivia ducked under the two-armed swing and kicked Nino lightly on the back of his knee. With a loud cry, Nino toppled. Olivia moved out of range.

"To continue. Your wife can remain here if she wishes, in the company of her brother. She will continue to be paid for her work dying yarn, if that is what she wishes to do. You will not be allowed to take money from her, but if she decides to provide for you, that is her affair. If there is any attempt on your part to coerce her into aiding you, I will have you before a judge." This last, she realized, was a bluff. Not since her youth, more than fifteen hundred years before, had women been entitled to hold and administer their own money; in this world a woman's wealth was the property of her husband as much as the woman herself was. "Uberto will keep me informed of this."

Uberto thought of his monthly dispatches and sighed. "Madama, it is not fitting that man and wife should separate."

"It isn't fitting that man and wife should live with one filling the other with dread, but it happens." Olivia's words were hard and flat; Uberto sensed he would be wise not to question the reason for it.

"We were wed by a priest, joined together," Nino declared. suddenly trying to scrape some dignity into his demeanor. He was sitting on the floor rubbing at his ankle. "You are trying to sever what God has joined."

"Nothing of the sort," Olivia said. "I am trying to spare your wife more pain than you've already given her. I am doing my best to see that only one of you has to starve." She turned and started toward the passage between the barrels.

"You are a dangerous woman. You are worse than those who are poxy." He made the sign against the Evil Eye before he got laboriously to his feet, taking care not to put too much weight on his ankle.

"Nino, for all the Saints, think what you are saying," Uberto urged him, his voice low, as if Nino's accusations would be less real if they all spoke more softly.

"I do think," said Nino, nodding furiously. He was shaking now, but whether from wine or fright it was impossible to tell. "I think that a clever witch has been working on you and has done something to poison your mind against your family, that's what I think." He pointed toward Olivia again. "You are a vile creature and you will be destroyed."

Olivia had heard such threats many times in her long, long life. "And you intend to destroy me?" she asked sardonically.

"By God's Right Hand, I will," swore Nino. He moved

abruptly, shoving her out of the way and lurching toward the door of the storage shed.

"My, my, my," said Olivia softly, sarcastically, when Nino had gone.

"Madama," Uberto began, his features sagging with dismay, "I pray you, do not regard it. What am I to say? He is my brother-in-law, but what he has said . . . Madama, how can I apologize?"

There was a brittle edge to her lightness now. "You have nothing to apologize for, Uberto. You did not speak words against me, you did not make threats, Nino did. For what consolation it may be, I think your loyalty to him is misplaced but admirable." She took a short, deep breath. "Come. I think the odor will overwhelm me if we remain here longer." With a quick turn that revealed more of her anger than her words did, Olivia continued along the narrow passage toward the door.

Uberto hurried after her, saying, "Ah, Madama, the smell of wine is sweet, almost as sweet as wine itself," in an attempt to mollify her.

Olivia turned as she reached the door, her hazel eyes meeting Uberto's as penetrating as steel. "I do not drink wine."

* * *

Text of a letter from Abbe Giulio Mazarini to Abbe Luc-Simeon Gottard at the monastery of Sacres Innocentes, Tours, written in Latin and French.

To the most reverend leader of monks and wise advisor of the soul, Abbe Gottard, this brings the blessings and continuing good opinion of Abbe Mazarini, with the most respectful request that the good Abbe Gottard will pray for him and his endeavor.

Your King has requested my elevation officially now and I am told it is only a matter of time before I will be once again in Paris where I may begin to serve the country and people who are to be mine by adoption; and as in the case of an adopted family, you have my vow that France will receive my greatest attention and continuing care. There need be no fear that France and her people will suffer the fate of certain step-children, and be allowed to languish. I take up the cup from the most august and perspicacious hands: the honor that Richelieu does me is so great that I know I will never be wholly deserving of it, no matter how earnestly and faithfully I strive to fulfill his mandate, or what success in that effort I attain.

The first members of my suite will arrive in Paris before the end of the year and will be established there by the time of my own arrival, or so I hope. It is in respect to one of these that I write to you now, and request you will give my words your thoughtful and prayerful consideration.

There is a Roman widow, a woman of rank and fortune, who is soon to occupy a small chateau a short distance from Paris. She is not of the first youth, as sensible a woman as God has made and not sent into His Church, and discreet. She is also learned, but not so given to learning that she has forgot the world.

It is my understanding that she owns a stud farm near Tours and she has assured me that my couriers have access to her horses for their use and for remounts if ever the need arises. That is generosity that has more of charity in it than many of those who throw a few coins and trinkets to beggars and think that they are piling up bounty in Heaven for so minor an act. It is my hope that you might be willing to extend the hospitality of Sacres Innocentes to those couriers, if such becomes necessary, and to keep their presence unknown if the couriers so require. I am aware that you do not wish to be embroiled in politics. Those living as monks are often reluctant to be wooed into the world in such a way, and their devout attentions are cherished by all those who long for salvation. However, salvation is found on many strange paths, and for these couriers, a haven can be as much salvation as the Sacraments.

It is not necessary that you answer me now, or that you come to a decision at once. There is some time before I leave Roma, and so long as I have your answer by that time, it is sufficient for me. Forgive me, Abbe, for the requests I make of you, but it is the nature of the world that compels me, for I cannot compromise my oaths to your King Louis, as I cannot abjure my vows to God and His Church.

Should you decide to permit my couriers to come to your monastery, I will so inform the overseer of Bondama Clemens' stud farm and will provide him with proper letters of identification and necessary passwords. He will then contact you and whatever arrangements you deem appropriate may be set at that time. I have it from Bondama Clemens that the overseer has been her trusted agent for many years and has been faithful and honest in the discharge of his duties. Would that all servants acquitted themselves so well!

I will pray for your wisdom and compassion, I will place my confidence in you, I will ask Heaven to guide you in all your works, and I will accept your decision, whatever it may be, with a grateful heart and a tranquil soul.

May God raise you up, may He bring the world to the foot of His Throne, may He bless His servants and forgive us where we fail. May He restore the health of Cardinal Richelieu and spare the Kingdom of France from the scourge of war. Until I may pray with you myself, I place my trust in your wisdom and the Love of God which unites us all.

Giulio Mazarini, Abbe

On the 27th day of August, 1638, in Roma.
Keep covertly or destroy.

· 5 ·

By the end of September the harvest was well under way; the bounty of field and orchard and vineyard were given up to the farmers who fussed and sweated and swore with the task of reaping the largesse of the earth.

"I hate traveling now," said Olivia as she stared out the window of the coach. "I'd rather be back supervising the harvest. It's where I belong."

"Uberto will attend to it," Avisa said, her lavender sachet held close to her mouth.

"They say we will reach Firenze tomorrow," Olivia said a few minutes later.

"We make good speed," said Avisa, as if reciting from rote, for she had never traveled so far and thought the hours in the swaying coach were more torture than she could endure for the number of days Olivia had said the journey would take.

Olivia chuckled. "Be glad you are here, at the head of the line, not back with the other servants and the baggage on the big wagons, where you would breathe nothing but dust." She closed her eyes a moment, sensing that brief vertigo that claimed her at odd instants when she was away from Roma, a sense that she was drifting and rudderless, without any link to her self. It made little difference that the soles of her shoes and the floor of her coach were lined with her native earth; such necessary precautions were anodyne, but they could not replace the reality of Roma, and the sustenance provided by the place of her birth.

"Madama?" Avisa said uncertainly.

Olivia opened her eyes and did her best to offer a reassuring smile. "You are not the only one to be uncomfortable while traveling," said Olivia, indicating her brow as if she had a headache. "At least we are not attempting to reach Parigi in winter; then it would take us forever."

"It is not the height of summer, either," Avisa said with a wise nod. "A coach is an oven on wheels and we the loaves it bakes at the height of summer."

"Yes," Olivia agreed distantly. She frowned, then managed a good-humored shrug. "Firenze. It makes me remember I have a very old friend who used to live in Firenze."

"A very old friend?" Avisa repeated.

"I have known him most of my life," she said truthfully.

Avisa smiled with satisfaction and put one hand to the large ornate silver crucifix she wore around her neck. "That is an old friend; those we know in childhood are—"

"He is . . . much older than I am," said Olivia.

"A friend of your parents, then?" Avisa said, once again puzzled.

"A blood relative," said Olivia in a manner she decided Sanct' Germain himself could not improve upon.

Avisa gave an approving cry and clapped her hands together for emphasis. "How fortunate you are in your relations. Few women can speak so well of their families."

There was nothing Olivia could think to say. She closed her eyes again, and was immediately struck with memories of her mother, living alone in their old house, her treasures and her slaves stripped from her in spite of the protections of the law, all for the greed of the man Olivia had been given to in marriage. Even now the recollection was corrosive. She straightened up and opened her eyes. "Well, at least we have passage documents from His Holiness. That will simplify matters for us."

"It is a great honor he has bestowed on us," Avisa said as she crossed herself decisively.

"It is not precisely a gift; I am expected to accommodate the Abbe upon occasion," Olivia said without rancor.

"Madama!" Avisa said, scandalized.

"Not that manner of accommodation, and well you know it," Olivia rejoined. "One of the reasons we are to arrive ahead of Mazarini is because he does not want to give the least hint that we might have such an arrangement. Whatever the Abbe's tastes may be—or if he has any at all—they do not include me except in matters of entertainment."

"A strange reason to have you with him. I have said from the first that there is more to his request than apparent." Avisa folded her arms and did her best to look aloof, but her eyes were bright with curiosity.

"Occasionally the Abbe will require aid from someone who is not under suspicion," Olivia said carefully, knowing that it would be very unwise to reveal the whole of her agreement with Mazarini to her servant. "Undisputed ground, if you like; a place where courtesy may be relaxed."

"And there are your horses," said Avisa with great knowledge. "He has a use for your horses."

"He would have that use no matter where I lived," said Olivia in her most pragmatic manner. "I would be worse than a fool if I were not willing to provide such a trifle for the Abbe and his couriers." She turned toward the window again, watching men in the distant field bent over to harvest vegetables. How pleasant they looked, graceful as dancers, and how grueling the work was for the men doing it.

Avisa tried not to look out the window. It was apparent that she did not enjoy watching the world go by. She clutched her sachet more tightly and struggled to find a more comfortable position to sit. "I fear my foot has gone to sleep," she said a short while later.

"If you stand on it, it will be better," Olivia said distantly.

"Stand on it?" Avisa protested. "It will be full of pins then. Besides, how can I stand in a moving carriage?"

"If you bend at the waist you will manage it." Olivia leaned forward to indicate what she meant. "It will feel like pins no matter when or where you stand on it."

Avisa shook her head, her frown deepening. "I'd be sick, Madama, if I did that."

"Then by all means stay sitting," Olivia said at once. She turned to the place on the seat beside her where a leather case rested. "I have some willow bark tea—it's cold, of course—and that might help you."

"Madama, it isn't proper for me to take your stores," said Avisa, her manner that of a guilty child.

"Come to that, it isn't proper for you to be sick in my carriage, either," said Olivia with asperity. "Have the tea and be done with it." She took a sealed jar from the case and held it out to Avisa.

"Madama . . ." she faltered, wanting the willow bark tea and at the same time knowing it was improper to accept it.

"Magna Mater, what is the problem? Drink the tea and you will be better. Where is the difficulty with that? I have no use for the tea myself, and this evening I will prepare more of it for tomorrow." Her exasperation made her speak crisply but there was a softening in her face. "I know what it is to feel ill, Avisa. There is no reason for you to suffer on my account."

Avisa nodded and against her better judgment accepted the jar. "The seal?"

"Use your knife to pry it off," Olivia recommended. She watched as Avisa struggled with the jar. "Don't drink it too quickly; it works better if you take many small sips instead of a few large ones."

"Why is that, Madama?" Avisa asked as she pried the seal off and lifted the jar to her lips.

"It is the nature of the willow bark. Some herbs are better taken quickly, some are better taken slowly. Willow bark is one of the slow ones, along with pansy. Ginger teas are better taken quickly." She frowned as the coach slowed. "We are walking again."

Avisa, trying to drink the tea in many small sips, could only nod for a comment.

"I know we cannot trot forever, especially the rear wagons with such heavy loads, but when we walk, I believe we will never arrive." Her eyes clouded as she thought of the many times she had left Roma and how she had gone. The last time she had lived away she had gone to London, curious to see the country governed by a woman. For nineteen years she had remained there, after the death of Elizabeth and into the curious reign of James. She had kept a horse farm a day's ride from London, living quietly there, keeping away from the court. She had had two lovers during that time, one she still remembered with great fondness, the other with grief. It had been pleasant, but it was not Roma and in time the pull of her native earth was all but unbearable.

"Madama? What is it?" Avisa was holding out the empty jar. "I have finished, Madama."

Olivia shook herself. "Thank you, Avisa," she said as she took the jar and put it back in the leather case. "My mind was elsewhere."

"Do not worry about Senza Pari," said Avisa, mistaking Olivia's meaning. "Uberto will do his duty as soon as he returns and Gaetano is a capable steward."

"Yes, I know," said Olivia. "That was not what troubled me."

"And you must not be afraid of Nino. Men like that only make threats. He will do nothing more than bluster," Avisa said with great confidence. "Nino is a sot. Sots are only interested in wine; their vengeance is lost with the next full cup."

"I hope you are right," Olivia said.

"Of course I am right," Avisa insisted. "Men of that stamp make threats and promises with equal ease, but all that moves them is wine." She wagged her finger at Olivia. "You are not to be concerned about the likes of him, not with the Abbe Mazarini needing your aid. It is not fitting for you to be distracted from his requests by the likes of Nino."

Olivia nodded. "As you say, it is foolish to worry. I am going into Francia. He is . . . wherever he has gone." The admission that she did not know Nino's whereabouts was more bothersome to Olivia than she wanted to admit; there was something about Nino that worried her more than appeared necessary.

"Which is not Francia," Avisa declared, as if that had been a possibility. "It is too far for a man like that to go when there is wine aplenty to be had here or in Roma. He will forget what he has said by the next full moon." Her scorn was so complete that Olivia decided there was no point in challenging her conviction.

"Firenze to Pisa to Genova to Torino to Chambery to Lyon. Then Paris," Olivia said the last in French dreamily, reciting the rest of their route in an emotionless tone. "They tell me it will be at least thirty days before we reach our destination."

Avisa sighed and her face blanched. "Thirty days in a coach. I wish we could be there in half the time. I do not like the motion; it upsets me."

"Would you prefer to walk?" Olivia suggested with a slight smile. She had covered far greater distances on foot herself but had never come to enjoy it.

"It is a long way, Madama." She was looking down at the sachet in her hand again, afraid of the answer her question might receive. "Would you prefer I ride with the other servants part of the way?"

"I may," said Olivia and, seeing the shock in Avisa's face, went on soothingly, "but only if either of us becomes ill." She stared down at the floor, as if seeing through the boards to the lining of earth. "Or if I am too tired and need to rest."

"You never rest. You do not sleep at night." Avisa brought her head up sharply. "I know; I have seen you go to your library after midnight."

This alarmed Olivia; having her servants aware of her long solitary hours meant that she would have to be even more circumspect than she already was. She made a dismissing gesture as she strove to keep her composure. "Well, many another has trouble sleeping. If I cannot sleep, I might as well improve my mind with reading as lie in bed and fret." It was in the deepest part of the night that she visited various men as a dream. It was the only contact she had permitted herself for several decades.

"If you believe that is wise," said Avisa. "I was warned that too much reading leads to brain fever."

"Brain fever," Olivia repeated, thinking of all the other caveats against reading and learning she had heard over the centuries. "Yet, as you see, I have not taken brain fever."

"Not yet, no," Avisa agreed darkly.

"Why would reading bring on such a malady?" Olivia could not resist asking, repelled and amused at once.

"It excites the brain," said Avisa somberly. "It is more dangerous in females than in males."

"Because we are less capable of learning?" Olivia suggested sarcastically, but was not surprised when Avisa gave her a serious answer.

"Yes, in large part. I beg you, Madama, do not read overmuch. If you impair your health, you will not be able to assist the Abbe."

"Of course," said Olivia, realizing—as she had suspected from the first—that Avisa would place Mazarini's importance above her own. In spite of her understanding, Olivia was annoyed to discover her own servant more devoted to Mazarini than to her, and it took considerable will to keep from falling into an argument with Avisa.

"The honor the Abbe has shown you—" Avisa began.

"Yes, yes, I am aware of it," Olivia interrupted. "And I know what is expected of me. That was made clear enough, and I have agreed to the requirements. Never fear, I will not shame Giulio Mazarini, even when he is Jules Mazarin." She leaned back against the squabs and tried to keep her temper under control. She had little to say after that until they stopped for the night at the Fiori d'Oro, and then she confined herself to a few requests and instructions before retiring to the best room in the hostelry.

In Firenze Olivia took half a day to wander amid the treasures of the Medicis, remembering the heartbreaking letters she had had from Sanct' Germain when he lived here, almost a hundred fifty years ago. The statuary and paintings took her breath away; the Battistero doors awed her; the Laurentian library astonished her. At another time she might have been content to remain there for a while, but she was not at liberty to be idle, and secretly she feared that her melancholy might become greater if she permitted herself to think of the wonderful things that were lost in the Bonfires of Vanities when Savonarola had ruled the city. Reluctantly she got back into her coach and the train and outriders went on to Pisa and the Universita where students gathered to discuss law and astronomy in the shadow of the famous leaning tower.

Turning north up the coast, the five carriages were slowed by brisk winds off the sea. A number of squalls, early for that time of year, disrupted traffic on the coast roads and endangered shipping from Sicilia to the south coast of Francia.

"I am sorry, Madama," said Uberto as they pulled into an inn-yard at mid-afternoon. "They say the road ahead has been washed out, and we will have to wait here until it is safe."

"When will that be?" Olivia asked, trying to be civil.

"They say day after tomorrow. I beg you, Madama, take rooms here and wait for the repairs to be made. It would mean a far greater delay if we were to be caught in a slide. We could lose one of the carriages or wagons. We might have injuries. The horses might be hurt. Or the outriders could be lost." His smile was nervous and ingratiating.

"Yes," said Olivia quietly. "Yes, I do understand your concern. Very well. Speak to the landlord. I will want my own parlor. I will pay for however many of this train he can house. Since the horses worry you, you might as well make sure the teams get good feed while they're resting, as well." She dropped to the ground without recourse to the steps. "At least I am not moving anymore. That is something favorable."

"Madama," said Uberto, "I am very sorry we must wait here. I trust it will not disrupt the Abbe's plans."

"It is disrupting *my* plans," Olivia said abruptly, then relented. "Pay no heed to me, Uberto. My legs ache and my head is splitting. I don't blame you for the weather and the roads."

He bowed, removing his battered hat as he did. "You are gracious, Madama."

Olivia did her best to laugh but was not wholly successful. She noticed that the innkeeper was asking a higher price of those going north, confident that it would be met. That sort of minor venality irritated her, and at another time she would have been tempted to argue with him, but not now. With a sigh she laid out the gold coins that would purchase bed and board for herself, her servants, coachmen and outriders, and stalls and feed for her horses.

The landlord cast a furtive eye over his elegant guest. "What's a fine lady doing traveling without husband?" he asked as he took a ring of keys from the wall.

"That is an impertinent question," said Olivia.

Shrugging, the landlord gave a single snort of laughter. "There's many a fancy woman who sets herself up as quality. It's the lack of husband that gives them away." His expression had altered and now his sagging features were lascivious.

"My husband is dead. I am a widow." She gave him a direct, unflinching stare. "I am traveling at the behest of His Holiness and have documents to prove it."

The landlord was torn between doubt and dread. "What has His Holiness to do with pretty young widows, then?"

Olivia took the ring of keys. "His Holiness has requested that I lend my assistance to the Abbe Mazarini in Francia. Now you have enough for a month of gossip. If you detain me one moment longer or make any more insolent remarks, I will send word to the Abbe. Which room is mine?"

"Ah . . ." the landlord faltered. "My serving wench will lead you up, and your lady's maid." He did not quite bow, but he lowered his head a bit and was no longer willing to meet her bright hazel eyes.

For the next three days Olivia remained at the inn, spending most of the time indoors with Avisa for company. At the end of the second day, Olivia would have preferred being in her coach on a bumpy road to the continuing irritation of delay.

"The word is good," Uberto said on the morning of the fourth day. "There was no rain for all of last night, and this morning they have sent word that the road will be open by mid-day."

"Then we had better be ready to travel shortly, or there will be a line of wagons and carriages and donkeys going all the way to Livorno," said Olivia as she shook out her skirts. The fabric, still creased from being folded in a trunk, refused to hang properly.

"We're not so pressed for time," Uberto said, beaming at Avisa. "There is no reason to hurry."

Olivia sighed impatiently. "Indulge me, Uberto. Have the wagons and coaches loaded and the horses put to. If we have to wait to use the road, so be it, but I would rather that than fall to the end of the line. And there will be a line."

Uberto looked flustered. "Madama, there is no need—"

"If I say there is a need, then there is one," she reminded him politely. "I ask you to be ready to depart within an hour. Will you do this for me?"

This time Uberto bowed. "Si, Madama. Volentieri."

"I doubt it," Olivia said, almost smiling. "I think you suppose I am being demanding and fussy. Perhaps you are right and if you are, you will have every opportunity to remind me of it when we reach the place where the road has been repaired. But Uberto, consider this: if the repairs are not strong enough, the more carriages that go over it, the greater the chance of another slide." She did not give the warning lightly; two hundred years ago she had been caught in just such an accident on Corsica.

"An unnecessary precaution, Madama," said Uberto, his tone becoming indulgent. "But we will do as you ask, since you are so worried."

At another time Olivia might have argued with him, but not now, while she longed to enlist his help and speed. She knew it was useless to remind him that she employed him, for Uberto was still puzzled by this. "The sooner you begin the task, the sooner it is done."

"Certainly, Madama." He was able to wink at Avisa before he left the parlor.

"Well!" Avisa burst out as soon as the door was closed. "He has no right to address you in that way! How could you let him do it?"

"Because I would rather have the wagons and coaches made ready than sit here and wrangle," said Olivia, a warning to Avisa in her words. "I meant it when I said I wanted to be away from here within the hour. I will be satisfied if we are gone in less than two, but I won't tell Uberto that, or we might not be on the road until tomorrow."

Avisa's expression changed. "That was very clever," she said in a different tone, one that was filled with discovery and surprise, as if she had stumbled upon an unexpected truth. "You are a clever woman, Madama."

"You get that way," said Olivia, her words light and faintly bitter, "when you've lived as long as I have."

*　　*　　*

Text of a letter from Niklos Aulirios to Gaetano Fosso, acting major domo of Senza Pari.

To my most excellent deputy, I, Niklos Aulirios, send greetings and news.

A messenger of Cardinal Richelieu informed His Eminence that he met our mistress in the town of Chambery on his return from Milano. He, being mounted and remounted on couriers' horses, has made far faster time than Bondama Clemens and her train have. The messenger informed His Eminence that all was well with our mistress, though one of the wagons carrying goods had needed a new wheel, which in turn required them to wait in Chambery for

*two days. From what I know of our mistress, she must not have
been pleased.*

*One of the coachmen driving the wagons has suffered a broken
arm, the result of trying to fix the wheel himself. Olivia has
tended to the injury—she is very capable in such matters—and
the man was said to be improving. He will remain at Chambery
and will return to Senza Pari with Uberto when he comes back
from Parigi.*

*While it is true that Olivia is now six days behind her proposed
schedule, there is no reason to fear that she has been inconvenienced
by the slower travel. Often in the past delays have boded ill for her,
and it is not unusual for her now to believe that if she is made to
wait it is because her situation is becoming more dangerous. I mention that so you will understand why she puts such store by prompt
reports, and why she will be more apt to aid you if you send your
reports as she has requested.*

*The house here is almost ready to receive her. We lack carpets and
some draperies, but those are to be delivered within the week, and it
is not likely that Olivia will be here before that time. I have commissioned one of the court artists to complete a set of murals in the
two main salons, and three of these are under way, though there are
another seven to go. I doubt they will be finished by the time Olivia
gets here, but it is not crucial, for she may occupy the house and
even entertain while the murals are being done.*

*We will need four matched carriage horses by late spring. Uberto
has already been informed of this, but I believe it is necessary for
you to be prepared before Uberto returns. I would recommend that
the Neopolitans be considered. They are heavy enough for light carriage work, especially a team of four. In this case, the showier they
are, the better. Olivia has said that she does not want to use horses
from her Tours stud farm because those horses are reserved for the
use of Abbe Mazarini. So it must be from Senza Pari, and the
Neopolitans are the showiest of the lot.*

*I would also want to arrange for two large barrels of wine to be
delivered at that time. Do not use the Neopolitans to pull that
load, use mules or the liver-chestnuts for that. Having her own
vineyard will do much to enhance Bondama Clemens' prestige in
the eyes of the nobles here, and will provide another reason for her
to maintain regular contact with you at Senza Pari.*

*The signs here are for an early winter this year, and for that
reason, I recommend you dispatch your messenger a few days earlier*

than planned. If the passes are closed, he is authorized to go around by the coast and come up through Avignon. Be certain that he travels with extra money to pay for delays on the road, and that he carries the Abbe's writ so that he will not be detained on his way.

With thanks on behalf of Bondama Clemens, whom we both serve, I pray God will bless and watch over you now and for years to come.

> *Niklos Aulirios*
> *bondsman and major domo to Bondama*
> *Atta Olivia Clemens*
> *at Eblouir, near Chatillon*

On the 4th day of October, 1638
Retain for estate records.

· 6 ·

Padre Riccono leaned back in his chair and took another sip of wine. "Patience, Giulio; you must have patience."

Mazarini glared at the Pope's cousin and held back the retort he had been about to make. "I pray for it daily," he said, more brusquely than was polite. "King Louis has requested that I be made a Cardinal, and apparently this is possible; I am supposed to be welcome again in Francia, and that is good news, most certainly. I am thankful that His Holiness has received the petition from Louis, and I am confident at the outcome. But here I am in Roma and I am no nearer to leaving than I was at the start of summer." He paced the length of the library and came back to Padre Riccono. "So what am I to do?"

"Wait," the Padre said with a benefic smile that was colored by an unexpected ferocity which often lay concealed in his good-natured pose of ineffectiveness. "You must wait, Giulio. Pray if it passes the time well. It will not be much longer."

"How many times have I heard that?" said Mazarini, but he

selected one of the other three chairs and flung himself into it with an exaggerated sigh. "Very well. Since I must wait, I will wait. I have prayed already and I do not wish it to appear that I am ungrateful to God. But do not advise me to take no active part, for that—forgive me, Padre mio—I cannot and will not do." He had very expressive hands, large, long, and lean. He placed two fingers at the center of his brow as if to pinpoint a headache. "You do not know what you ask of me. Waiting can be worse than outright defeat."

"I have some notion of it," said Padre Riccono, cordially but drily. "But if you wish to explain it to me, pray do so." His smile this time had lost its hidden wrath and instead was self-mocking. He had been one of the many Vatican secretaries for many years and was as skilled a strategist as any successful corsair. "In the meantime, have some of this excellent wine. It is a gift from that protegée of yours."

"I was not aware I had a protegée," said Mazarini in his most depressing manner, though he poured himself a glass as he spoke.

"Your protegée. The widow who is already establishing herself in Francia," said Padre Riccono in the slow and deliberate way some persons talked to the deaf.

"She is not my protegée. She is part of my suite." He tasted the wine. "A good vintage."

"Yes. Her steward had it delivered a few weeks ago. There are four barrels of it, and I for one will be sorry when it is gone." He finished his glass and looked sharply at Mazarini. "How do you mean, she is part of your suite, but she is not your protegee?"

"You know exactly what I mean, Padre," said Mazarini, his tone growing sharper in spite of himself. "She is not part of my family, she is not my mistress, she is merely a Roman woman who has agreed to assist me with my dealings in Francia and to provide me a few needed favors from time to time. Clearly she is not under my protection."

"Clearly." He lifted his glass in what might have been a toast. "I heard she is a handsome woman," said Padre Riccono, a speculative light in his eye.

"She is. Many another has said so." It was becoming obvious that he did not want to answer more questions about Bondama Clemens.

"I have never seen her. Tell me about her," said Padre Riccono in a flat voice.

Mazarini sighed and capitulated. "Mind you, I do not know her very well, and I am not completely familiar with her background."

"Understood," said Padre Riccono.

"I would guess her to be perhaps thirty from her face, but she must be more than that; her manner and her fortune suggest that she is older." His eyes grew distant as he went on. "She has a title to her estate that can be traced back as far as the Crusades, so there is no question to her place in society. According to the records one or another of her blood relatives—that is her phrase—has lived there since that time. She has provided patronage to artists and musicians from time to time but not in an unseemly way."

"These patronages, is that all they were?" Padre Riccono asked, suspicion making his genial features sharp.

"You mean was she rewarding lovers? I don't know. I have met men who had dreamed about her, but in the matter of lovers, Bondama Clemens is most discreet." He set his wineglass aside. "It was good of her to send this."

"Or clever," said Padre Riccono. "Are you certain that she is committed to your work?"

"No," said Mazarini. "But I am sure that she is not committed to anyone else's work." He coughed delicately. "She has said she dislikes politics and I believe her."

"And you sent her to Francia?" marveled the Padre.

"Of course. If I sent someone from my family, or someone who was known for what he has done in the world of politics, there would be endless difficulties, for everyone in Parigi would be instantly suspicious. It would be an unfortunate beginning, one that could lead to unpleasant repercussions later. But under the circumstances, how can there be offence given or taken since the woman who is in Francia is known for her dislike and distrust of politics?"

"Someone will find a way to be offended," said Padre Riccono, taking a gloomy satisfaction in his prediction.

"But fewer than might be," said Mazarini with determination.

"I will allow that," said Padre Riccono when he had thought this over. "Still. You will want to take care as we approach the time for your departure to Francia. Remember that though you become a citizen of Francia, you will still be an Italian in the eyes of many, and they will scrutinize all you do. It will be crucial that those in your company deport themselves properly so as not to give more grounds for suspicion."

"I have considered this, Padre, and I thank you for instructing me." Mazarini's large brown eyes were growing harder. "Is there anything else I might have overlooked that you wish to point out to me?"

"Ah, you've taken offence," said Padre Riccono. "You may do that here with impunity, but once you enter the service of Louis, you will not have such luxury again. Learn to school yourself, Abbe, so that those who are your enemies cannot use your anger against you."

It was useless to argue, and Mazarini knew it; he sat in silence for some little time before speaking again. "You have given me much to think about, mio Padre. I am grateful for the interest you have in the work I am to do."

"Of course, of course," said Padre Riccono with a wicked chuckle. "And in time you will come to understand why I have done this. You will."

"Will I? I pray that God will send me such wisdom." He rose slowly. "I am supposed to meet with Cardinal Bichi. There is a prelate here from Parigi he wishes me to meet; a scholar of some repute there, I'm told."

"I have heard of this man," said Padre Riccono. "Let me remind you of my advice again before you speak with this scholar from Parigi." He had his rosary in his hands but appeared only to be playing with the large ivory beads. It had been a gift to him from His Holiness and the Padre often found reasons to display it.

"My thanks to you and to God," said Mazarini without as much humor as he wanted to show. It was difficult to maintain a diplomatic wit when he was dealing with those so ruthless as Padre Riccono. Who was he speaking for? Mazarini wondered. Was the Padre reminding him of the power of the Pope, or was he trying to use his influence on behalf of others, such as those Cardinals who supported the Spanish instead of the French? He offered Riccono a more formal bow than courtesy required, then swept from the room, doing his best to ignore the soft, amused laughter that followed him out of the library.

For a quarter of an hour, Mazarini walked through the chapels and hallways of the Vatican, deliberately seeking out the things of beauty that served to quiet his soul, to restore the tranquility he found all too infrequently now. He did not want to give offence by arriving late to speak with Cardinal Bichi, but he knew that if he attempted to speak with this new man from Parigi, he must not appear inattentive or ungracious. Only when he was certain that his skills would not fail him did he start toward Cardinal Bichi's apartments.

"I ask your indulgence for my tardiness," Mazarini said as he came into the reception chamber and knelt to kiss the Cardinal's ring.

"It was most unlike you, my son," said Bichi in what Mazarini thought of as the Cardinal's official voice. Lazily he motioned to Mazarini to rise. "Abbe Mazarin, let me make you known to Pere Pascal Chape," he said in French.

A lean, middle-aged man in the black habit of the Canons Regular of Saint Augustine came forward, blessing Mazarini as he did. "I am honored that you will receive me, Abbe."

Mazarini returned the blessing. "It is you who honor me, for I am coming to your country as . . . as one who is an orphan and who dedicates himself to the welfare of the family who has taken him in." He listened to himself with a little amazement; he had not known how naturally he could spin out compliments and pleasantries until now.

"No Christian is an orphan, mon Abbe," Pere Chape corrected him with sternness.

"Possibly not, but in the world, we see every day that men are—" Mazarini began only to have Cardinal Bichi interrupt him.

"This dispute would agreeably fill an hour, but, mon Pere, our time is short and there are other matters we must discuss. You may practice your statecraft at another time; now we must attend to the business that has been laid before us." He indicated two letters on his writing table, both with broken seals. "Pere Chape brought these to me, and I wish you to read them. They are reports on the state of Cardinal Richelieu's health and the current progress of the war." He tapped the edge of the letters impatiently. "We must have you in France, and soon. Those who would rather keep you here must be stopped."

Mazarini crossed himself, his face noticeably paler than it had been a moment before. "Is Richelieu ill? Again?"

"It is more a question that he continues ill, for he has never made a proper recovery, though there are times when he is improved for a while," said Pere Chape. "His physicians, of course, are silent, and they will not reveal how the Cardinal fares. His servants are as circumspect, refusing all questions about their master. Richelieu himself has not discussed the matter with anyone, except—perhaps—His Majesty. Whatever is wrong with him remains speculation, nothing more, which is what Richelieu desires. Still, he is not as strong as he was and he has admitted that he cannot continue to work as he used to. He says little about pain, but the lines in his face give him away."

"Oh, dear God," whispered Mazarini, and the words were filled with sadness. He looked toward Cardinal Bichi, then toward the crucifix on the wall. "Richelieu."

"He needs you, Abbe," said Pere Chape as candidly as he could. "He has need of an ally he can trust, who can take up the reins when he can no longer hold them."

It was not Mazarini who responded to Pere Chape's remarks. "You sound as if you fear the day is near," said Cardinal Bichi, his eyes narrowing as he looked from Pere Chape to the letters in front of him once more. "You speak as if we ought to be preparing black crepe for the altars and canticles for the dead."

"I fear that time is not far off," said Pere Chape. "I wish I could tell you otherwise, that I could offer some hope that the Cardinal will recover, but there is no reason to think that God will continue to spare him. Nor would you want Him to do that, if you could see how the Cardinal suffers."

Mazarini turned away abruptly. "The man is the light of Europe, all of Europe. He is the spirit of reason in faith and of diplomacy. He is the greatest minister France has ever had. It is impossible that he cannot finish his own great work." He folded his hands and raised them as he began to pray silently.

Pere Chape studied Mazarini, then regarded Cardinal Bichi with a questioning lift to the brows. "Well?"

"Oh, believe what you see, Pere," said Cardinal Bichi. "He"— he nodded toward Mazarini—"will not give you false coin. His admiration of Richelieu is entirely genuine, do not doubt it. Little as it may seem possible, his faith is genuine. He is not one of your political religious—he is a religious who is also political."

"Sophistry," said Pere Chape.

Cardinal Bichi was about to protest when Mazarini turned around. "No," he declared. "No. Let me explain it to you." It was apparent from the fire in his large, dark eyes that he was offended. "You expect me to be some self-serving creature, a tool of the Colonna family, perhaps. I am an Abbe and I serve God in the world as ably as I can. I have dedicated myself to the cause of ending the strife in Europe, and to the goals of Cardinal Richelieu in particular, for I truly believe that unless his vision is fulfilled, our countries will be lost to war again before the next generation is old enough to bear arms." He was speaking quickly, with abiding feeling. He trembled with the force of his emotion. "You expect me to become the pawn of France, a servant of the Pope, and a lackey of King Louis. Well, mon Pere, you are mistaken. I have dedicated myself already and I will not be swayed. I will bring France under the single rule of the Crown or I will retire to a monastery." He turned to Cardinal Bichi. "Why have you wanted to subject me to this, when you know the goals for which I strive? What has made you bring this man to me?"

"You will have to answer such inquiries many times," said Cardinal Bichi at his most imperturbable. "There are those who doubt you and there will be many more. You might as well accustom yourself to such skepticism."

"It is offensive to me," said Abbe Mazarini, looking from Cardinal Bichi to Pere Chape. "I accept your explanation, that you have done this without intention to give offence, but still I am offended." He nodded in the direction of the door. "Is there anything else for us to talk about?"

"A few things," said Pere Chape in a more conciliating tone. "Nothing so urgent as Richelieu's health, but still of some interest. We have had word that the first of your suite is about to arrive at Paris. She may well have done so by now, which is all the more reason for us to review what you know of her." He indicated one of the chairs. "They say she is a widow."

"Yes," said Mazarini, trying not to be short-tempered. "She has position, wealth, and an excellent reputation." He stared at Cardinal Bichi. "You know her; you tell the Pere about her. I do not want to be questioned about my motives again."

Cardinal Bichi nodded. "Yes. A woman of property and of propriety. She has an estate north and a trifle east of Roma. She is said to be capable manager and a just mistress."

"High praise," Pere Chape said so dubiously that in spite of himself Mazarini laughed.

"You need not think that this is a fabrication," he said. "Bondama Clemens is not one of those women who is the handmaiden of power. Never have I heard of any instance when she was a willing pawn, or served as the tool of others."

"Yet you have asked her to do such things for you," Pere Chape pointed out.

"Reluctantly, and because I knew that it was foreign to her nature. She is not a woman to become the plaything of those in power, or to choose it for herself. In fact, for one as well placed as she is, she is much inclined to avoid it. If I had left her to her estate, she would have been just as pleased." He looked directly at Pere Chape. "I would consider it a personal affront if I learned that there had been rumors spread about her in Paris. She is to suffer no calumny because of me."

"If there are rumors, they are none of mine," said Pere Chape stiffly, after one fulminating glance at Cardinal Bichi. "I fear you have mistaken me. I have no excuse to offer for my conduct or my suspicions, and I will offer up my fault in prayer. But there are . . . many things, many things that have convinced me that this woman might be . . . persuadable. Our own Queen, who has had much travail in the past, certainly, has often made . . . inappropriate friendships that have led to gossip and other speculation. And Louis has also . . . certain inappropriate friendships." He grew noticeably more uncomfortable as he spoke.

"When you express yourself in this way," said Cardinal Bichi, sounding far more bored than he was, "I am puzzled as to your meaning. What is inappropriate about the friendships?"

Pere Chape pursed his lips before he answered. "Well, the Queen, several years ago, was unwise in her dealings with the English Duke of Buckingham. Sadly, the Englishman was not very discreet in his attention to the Queen, and this caused His Majesty embarrassment and annoyance. Not even the English King could curtain the Duke's extravagances, or his public demonstrations of his feelings for the Queen. Some say his servant killed him because of the relationship." Pere Chape hesitated before continuing. "His Majesty often . . . prefers the company of gifted youngsters rather than his Queen."

"Gifted youngsters?" Cardinal Bichi said, his brows rising. "Young men of rank, you mean? Then those rumors are not malice?"

"Regrettably they are not," said Pere Chape. "The young men who gain his . . . favor obtain power and influence as well, for as long as the King's fancy lights upon them. It would be one thing if he confined himself to pages or . . ." He closed his eyes. "We have prayed for a change of heart."

Cardinal Bichi turned his razor gaze on Mazarini. "Giulio," he said dulcetly. "How is it that for all the time you were in France, you made no mention of this?"

Mazarini was prepared for the question and answered it very directly. "I saw nothing of it for myself, Eminence, not personally. There were rumors, of course, but you have warned me against rumors. There was no advantage for any of us in promoting tales to the discredit of the King if there were, in fact, no basis for them. Since gossip was all I knew, I remained silent. To be frank," he went on, looking at Pere Chape, "I am sorry to hear my worst apprehensions confirmed, for it could mean that Louis' heir will be questioned and his legitimacy doubted."

Pere Chape nodded once in agreement. "And with good reason, I fear. They were married so very long before their first son was born, and the King did not conduct himself well at the lying-in, I am ashamed to say. It is acknowledged that Louis avoided Anne for more than fourteen years."

"And the King of Spain did nothing? Under the circumstances, he would be excused taking action on behalf of his own daughter," said Cardinal Bichi. "Why would he refuse?"

"There has been trouble enough between France and Spain," said Pere Chape.

"Of course," said Mazarini. "Of course. We must strive to maintain the peace between France and Spain: this revelation would end all that we have worked to maintain." He rocked back on his heels. "Still," he said in a soft, speculative voice, "I am surprised that Richelieu did not confide in me."

"He is dedicated to the protection of the Queen and her children," said Pere Chape.

Mazarini nodded. "And he would not speak against his King until he was certain I was pledged to France. He has always been wise." He hesitated, looking away from Cardinal Bichi and Pere Chape toward the windows. "But I wish he had trusted me."

From what seemed like a great distance, Pere Chape said, "He has more than himself to consider—he has his duty to the Crown, and to the Queen."

"Yes, the Queen," Mazarini said gently, his expression softening. "Poor Anne."

＊　　＊　　＊

Text of a letter from Jean-Arnaud du Peyrer de Troisvilles to Paul de Batz-Castelmore.

Monsieur de Batz-Castelmore,

Your family is well known to me, as are many of the Gascon families who have sent their sons to defend the King's Honor. If it were possible I would be delighted to welcome your brother Charles into our ranks at once, but at this time we are full. Should there be a vacancy in the Musqueteers, then it will be my pleasure to receive your brother's application once more.

The Guard may be a less illustrious company, but be assured that the skills gained there, and the promotions, are most useful and will serve him in good stead when he again attempts to secure a position with my men. Pray inform your brother on my behalf that his application to this company will always be welcome to me, and that I will review his career from time to time if he will but keep me informed. It is nothing to me that he is not adept with letters; I am more concerned with his skill at arms than his gift for persiflage.

I thank you for your kind words in regard to the Italian Abbe. I will resist his rise to power with all the strength I possess, and with the determination of my men, if that is necessary. No man fighting for France can wish to see the reins of state held by a foreigner. They say that he is giving up his country to become a Frenchman, but we all know how deeply bred in the blood and bone the country of nativity is, and this must be true of Mazarini as it is for any Frenchman, or Gascon, for that matter.

Not only does Richelieu continue to ail, but His Majesty has not enjoyed good health for some little time now. He has been in the care of his physicians, but they do not appear to be in agreement in regard to the best treatment for his ills. Again we are made to recall that all, from the most mighty to the lowliest, are in the Hands of God, and our days on earth are at His pleasure, not our own. Those who are faithful subjects of Louis XIII will address Heaven on his behalf, for surely that is where the hopes of all of us lie.

Let me hear from you again, and ask your brother to present himself to me at his convenience. We of the King's Musqueteers are *ever searching for men of courage, and from what you have told me, your brother Charles is one such. I will be pleased to see him at any time he presents himself.*

With my regards and prayers to you and your family, and the distinguished family of your noble mother,

Jean-Arnaud du Peyrer de Troisvilles
The King's Musqueteers

At Advent, 1638, in Paris.

A bona fide copy has been entered in the records of the King's Musqueteers.

· 7 ·

On Twelfth Night, Olivia gave her first grande fete at Eblouir, officially marking her entry into French society. The planning took well over a week, and by the time the guests were expected, four cooks had been busy in the kitchen for the better part of two days and a dozen lackeys scurried throughout the chateau putting the last touches on Niklos' and their mistress' instructions for the occasion.

"It must be very grand, as splendid as we can make it and not offend Richelieu. And all can only be very, very Italian," she reminded Niklos as he showed her the decorations in the largest salon. "At least the cooks and the musicians are Roman, that's something."

"So is the wine," Niklos reminded her with a wink. "From your own estate."

"Excellent," said Olivia without much enthusiasm. "Predictable, too, but what's to be done."

Niklos lifted his brows and looked at her. "How is this, Olivia? Still downcast? What's wrong?"

"Oh, nothing, I suppose. Nothing at all. The same complaints; pay them no mind." She lifted one shoulder, trying to make light of her distress. "You have heard it all before: I feel old. My home is a long way off; I am in a strange place, far from my native earth, and my friends here are few and untested." She shrugged, indicating the splendor of the room and the lavish decorations. "Still, this may persuade a few more to recognize me—what do you think?"

"I think you are worried," said Niklos honestly, his ruddy-brown eyes meeting her hazel ones directly. "Now, don't stiffen up that way. I do think you are worried. And I think you are lonely."

Olivia made an impatient gesture as she turned away from him. "I wish you would not start that again," she said, her voice unsteady, for although she had no tears to shed, some words caught in her throat when she uttered them. "I am not . . . truly lonely."

"But you are," said Niklos, more firmly and more sympathetically than before. "What else would you call it? Don't answer me yet, Olivia; I'm not finished." He waited to see if she would permit him to continue, and when she gestured her permission, he nodded. "You are not the only one worried. I am worried for you. I see the expression in your eyes and I wish for the power to end the pain I read there." He saw her start to turn away but he would not stop now. "I listen to you speak. Give me a little credit after all these years, these centuries. You are a spectre at a feast, Olivia. You hunger for the food you need but you will not eat."

Olivia had put one hand to her eyes. "I wish we had discussed this another time," she said softly. "There is no time. It is too difficult with over a hundred people arriving here this afternoon." She looked at him, aware that he would not be put off with facile answers. "All right. I will see if there is anyone who might not object to a vampire for a lover, who would not betray me—and you—to the King's men, or the Cardinal's men, or the Pope's men. And if there is such a man and he wants me as well, then perhaps I will be more than a dream to him. Will that content you?"

"It is not my content that concerns me," said Niklos. "But yes, it is sufficient. I have never known you to abjure your word."

Her eyes darkened and though she did not frown, her face seemed shadowed. "It has happened. But that was long ago."

"It must be, if it was before we met," said Niklos, making a point of regaining his good humor.

"It wasn't," she said abruptly. "Come. I ought to have Avisa do something about my hair. There are times it is the very devil not to be able to tend myself in the mirror."

"That's not amusing," said Niklos, a line appearing between his brows. "Not even as a joke."

Olivia turned to him with an apologetic smile. "Forgive me. I did not mean . . ." She hesitated. "Or perhaps I did. I've been called devilish for so long that I must be getting used to it." Pausing to take a last look around the room, she said, "I want the napery edged in gold for the buffet."

"Of course," said Niklos, following her and signaling for a lackey to close the door behind them as they started down the wide gallery that connected the grand salon with the spacious library. "I have ordered evergreen boughs in the library, and sprays of evergreens over the coaching entry."

"I thought we were supposed to be Italian: all that evergreen sounds more English." She had regained some of her buoyancy but Niklos knew what an effort it cost her. "I wish the Abbe were here. It would be much easier to manage if his arrival could be approved at once." She stopped to pick up a comfit dish, examining the sweetmeats and candied fruit presented on it. "I suppose it doesn't matter where we are, or who the guests are. We have been strangers for so long that it is all the same."

"Is that the excuse you give yourself?" he asked bluntly, and before she could continue, he went on, "How long has it been since you trusted yourself to take a lover? Twenty years?"

"Stop it, Niklos," words sharp, coming in Italian instead of French. "We have been over this ground until it is sterile and repeating ourselves will change nothing. Whether I take a lover or not it is no concern of yours. I have promised Mazarini that I would conduct myself with dignity, and you know that dignity is another word for celibacy for widows." She walked slowly away from him, then looked back, her features as immobile as those of a statue. "Who would be safe here, even if I wished to have a lover? Assuming that there might be a man who would not be distressed by my nature, it would be dangerous to know me. We are in France, part of the Abbe's embassy and there is no one we can count a disinterested friend. I would be more of a fool than I am to look for . . . something more than sweet dreams."

"Mi sono detto," Niklos began in Italian, finishing in heavily accented English, "'The lady doth protest too much.' That is the quote, isn't it?"

Olivia glared at him. "It comes from Shakespeare."

"I remember," said Niklos. "He was right." He leaned back

against a tall, antique chest decorated in red lacquer as he folded his arms and crossed one foot over the over. "I say it again, and nothing you tell me will change my mind: you are lonely, and it makes you . . ."

"Makes me what?" Olivia challenged.

"It makes you less than you are; it limits you. And that breaks my heart, Olivia." His smile was lopsided. "Don't tell me that ghouls cannot have broken hearts."

This time Olivia did not argue with him. "Very well, I am lonely. I have been lonely for more than a thousand years if you were to count the sum of them," she conceded, her eyes growing weary. "But that does not alter any of my objections. We are part of Mazarini's suite, answerable to the Abbe and therefore under scrutiny. We are at risk here. No words, no longings, can change that."

Niklos gave a short sigh. "Won't you at least consider taking a lover—not a man you visit as a dream, but a lover, one who knows you are with him, who welcomes you?"

"Stop, please, Niklos," said Olivia, one hand raised. "Please."

"So you will deny it?" he asked, compassion in his handsome face. "You have denied yourself much too long, Olivia."

She did not answer at once. "Sanct' Germain is far older than I am, and he has learned to bear it." Her smile was quick and rueful. "Perhaps he's right, and too long denial turns to a loss of . . . savor."

"Don't mock yourself," Niklos warned her. He raised his head. "Coaches."

"In buon punto," said Olivia, straightening the heavy gathers of her taffeta skirt; she put a hand to her hair. "I must find Avisa. See to the formalities at the coaching door and direct the servants to their quarters." She had already started away from him.

"I do know my duties," Niklos reminded her as he watched her rush toward her own apartments in the chateau. He noticed that the young lackey who had secured the salon door was showing great interest in Olivia, which troubled him. There were always spies in a household like this one, and as the first of Abbe Mazarini's suite to be established in France, Olivia was more vulnerable to spies than others might be.

Some of the same unhappy thoughts plagued Olivia as she hurried into her dressing room. She reached for the bell that would summon Avisa, ringing it with more determination than usual. "Avisa! My hair!"

A few moments later, Avisa came into the dressing room carrying a small lamp and a number of crimping irons. "You should not have waited until the last to have this done."

"But if you had done it earlier, it would all be nothing more' than wisps," said Olivia reasonably as she settled herself in the chair and gave herself over to Avisa's ministrations.

"Your guests are starting to arrive—" she began.

"My guests' servants are starting to arrive," Olivia corrected her. "The guests will be behind them by less than an hour." She blinked as Avisa brought the hot iron near her cheek. No matter how many times Avisa performed this simple task, Olivia winced as she felt the hot metal near her skin. Fire was deadly to her as few things in the world were, and no matter how minor the burn, it carried with it a reminder of her own provisional mortality.

"I did not touch you, Madama. I am not a clumsy girl. I have done this before, many times, to your satisfaction," said Avisa with more certainty than she felt. She held the crimping iron in a thick rag mitten, smelling Olivia's hair.

"No, you did not touch me. I know it," Olivia said a bit faintly. "You do your work well." She did her best to sit more comfortably and let Avisa get on with her chore, but again as the next hot iron came near her skin, she had to resist the impulse to cringe.

"I will take great care," said Avisa, looking critically at the results of her first effort as she tended to her second. "Your hair is very silken, Madama, very lovely. It is so pretty that who can blame you for wearing it uncovered, widow or no."

"Such is the nature in my House," she said, aware that all but she herself had died out fifteen hundred years ago. "My brother Drusus had beautiful hair, a little curly and shiny like a metal cap, not light brown like mine." It reassured her in a strange way to discuss the past while Avisa wielded the crimping irons. "He was a very pretty boy, very straight and soldierly."

"Was, Madama?" asked Avisa, who could not disguise her curiosity about Olivia's history, and was always eager to glean more information about her past. The few tidbits she had were intriguing beyond anything she could imagine for herself. "You have not told me about this brother."

"He died young," said Olivia, unwilling to recount her own husband's deliberate betrayal of her brother and father. "But he was the best-looking of us all." She leaned back and locked her hands together. She wished she could use a mirror to mark Avisa's progress.

"You miss him?" Avisa asked, not giving her answer as much attention as she would have liked. She was speculating already as to the cause of death for the beautiful brother.

"Not anymore," said Olivia, then amended this denial, "or not very often; that was a long time ago." Then she deliberately changed the subject. "Do I need color on my cheeks or will I do for Twelfth Night?"

Avisa stopped her task and looked down at Olivia's face. "You are fair, Madama. I think it would be wise to remain fair. The Frenchwomen may paint their cheeks and redden their mouths, but you do not need to augment your beauty."

Olivia laughed, her spirits lifting a little at this flattery. "How very diplomatic you are. Mazarini should have made his bargain with you." She would have nodded but Avisa was once again setting another hot iron in her hair. "I will follow your advice and appear just as I am. I will add the diamond clip to the pearls around my neck, but that will suffice."

"You are too modest, Madama," said Avisa, this time so bluntly that Olivia knew she meant it. "You are the most elegant woman and no one will rival you tonight. The jewels on your stomacher are sufficient to make all the others devour their own entrails from envy. That you are beautiful enough to dare to appear without macquilage—"

Olivia cut her short. "Come, Avisa, there is no reason to toady to me. Doubtless I will have my fill of that in the next few hours. Speak directly, I pray you."

"I do speak directly," said Avisa, with a trace of pride. "It is not often that a maid is given the chance to dress and do for a beautiful woman. Then, most beautiful women are spiteful and you are kind." This last caused both of them some embarrassment, and it took a few moments before Avisa was prepared to go on. "Bondama Caldopiove was good to me, but she was plain as a sack of flour. She understood that I could not do more than God had willed, and she bore this patiently. She was blessed with a most wonderful voice; I suppose that made up for her face."

"Mauro Caldopiove certainly thought so," said Olivia. "She was fortunate in her husband."

"And well she knew. It is five years since she died and he still has not remarried, he, with his title and his money." Avisa sighed. "He doted on her."

"No," Olivia corrected her seriously, "he loved her. There is a difference."

Avisa set one more crimping iron, then stood back, examining the results. She reached for a brush and tweaked the crimps with it. "There, Madama," she said. "Your hair is ready."

* * *

Text of a letter from Gaetano Fosso to Niklos Aulirious.

To the major domo of the distinguished Bondama Clemens, now in Francia at the behest of Abbe Mazarini, the requested reports on the estate Senza Pari are tendered with all duty and respect.

The early planting has gone well, and aside from some minor amounts of spring rot in the planting, all the land should come to harvest. The spring rot has been contained and the land washed in vinegar; it will lie fallow this year and be planted again next spring, when, with the aid and good Will of God, the new plantings will flourish.

Of the four horses you sent authorization to sell, three have been taken for the sums you set. The sole exception is the gelding Furbo, who is ailing again. The farrier has looked at him and prepared hot mashes for him, but I fear he is not going to be marketable for some months. What would you wish me to do about this horse? If he cannot be made well again, it is a waste of money to keep him. I will continue to follow the advice of the farrier and Uberto until other orders are received from you and Bondama Clemens.

Uberto has asked that I inform you that he has lost track of his brother-in-law Nino, but has given orders to his family to notify him if the fellow presents himself again. It is Uberto's belief that the man has found someone else willing to keep him drowned in wine, and that we will not be bothered with him again. Uberto's report on the horses is included with this report and you will see that the mares in foal are doing well. Two more of the Hungarian mares have been bred, as Bondama Clemens requested, and the farrier informs me that they have settled and will deliver in ten months or so. Uberto will continue to report on their progress.

There has been a request from Paolo Germoglio da Luccio to purchase part of the ridge where his land and Senza Pari meet. His letter is also enclosed, and I am to tell you on his behalf that he believes that with Bondama Clemens and you gone from this estate that it cannot prosper as before and therefore it is his wish to do all that he might to keep the estate from falling into ruin, which he fears it will.

Word has come from Cardinal Bichi that it may be a few more months before Abbe Mazarini comes again to Francia. There are those who object to a mere Abbe being elevated to Cardinal without being ordained as a priest. His Holiness has promised to reach his decision soon, and has been willing to have these messages carried by his own courier, who is also bringing dispatches to King Louis.

There was fever in Roma this winter, and many were ill. As Bondama Clemens instructed me, I extended the aid of Senza Pari to those in need; food and blankets were distributed to the poor and four of the household lackeys were sent to the local monastery to assist the monks while half their numbers were taken with fever.

We have purchased the sheep you informed us we must have. All but four have arrived, and the rest will be here in the next week. All appear to be uninfected, and it is the opinion of the farrier that they will give good wool. Such long-haired sheep they are! Some of the landholders nearby have come to see them. They all agree that if their wool is of good quality that Bondama Clemens will have much to be pleased with when the first shearing comes. Of course, there are those who say that such sheep are an expensive and foolish waste of money, for they will not thrive in the Roman summer. Bondama Clemens has said that they come from a country where the summers are as hot as they are here, but most of her neighbors do not believe that. I will keep you informed about the progress of these sheep.

Three dozen pigs were taken to market and brought a very good price. The large black sow went for the greatest amount; you will observe this in the accounting I have included with this report. Of the sows remaining here, five are piggy and should deliver by April.

The Christmas benefices were gladly received by the servants here, and the allowance for two new suits of clothing for the household staff is most welcome, though it might not be prudent to give both a generous benefice and an allowance for two suits of clothes when one would suffice, under the circumstances. While Bondama Clemens is known for her generosity, she need not be so lavish with lackeys and cooks. In most households a single new suit of clothing is considered sufficient when there has been a benefice given. I intend no criticism, but as your deputy while you accompany her, I feel it wise to make this observation. If I give offence, I ask pardon of you and Bondama Clemens, for I do not wish to offend either you or her.

Permit me to recommend you review not only Uberto's report, but his remarks on the conditions of our coaches, carriages, and wagons, for there are three requiring repair before they can be used safely. Two of the vehicles that Uberto returned here to Roma after they carried our mistress into Francia are much the worse for their long journey and are in poor condition. I realize that funds are available to replace such vehicles, but I do not think it wise to purchase new when the old might be repaired adequately. Uberto has agreed to do nothing until word is brought from you, but he has said that one of the wagons is past saving, and it is his belief that it would be wiser to replace that wagon. I await your orders on this and all other matters.

With the prayers of this household and all our families for the protection of Heaven and betterment in the world for you and our esteemed Bondama, I extend my most sincere salutation and solicit your prayers on our behalf as well.

> Gaetano Fosso
> acting major domo of Senza Pari
> by my own hand, with appended
> documents, previously described

On the 18th day of February, 1639.
Two bona fide copies retained at Senza Pari.

· 8 ·

Richelieu's face was drawn and his large eyes appeared to have sunk into his head. He put one hand to his brow, almost concealing his frown as his lackeys aided him out of his sedan chair and supported him up the four shallow steps to the enormous doors of the hotel d'Arruretordu.

The lackeys who opened the door both knelt to kiss his proffered ring, then escorted him to the private salon where this meeting has been arranged. Their host was conspicuously absent. "Eminence," said the senior lackey, and bowed Richelieu into a room of pleasing proportions with tall windows overlooking a tiny, elegant garden.

Pere Chape was already on his feet; he knelt to kiss the Cardinal's ring, then stood aside for Atta Olivia Clemens to make the same obeisance.

"I have a little more than an hour," said Richelieu. "Then there are others who have a claim on my attention."

Pere Chape accepted this at once. "We are grateful for any time you are willing to spare us." He stood at a respectful distance while Richelieu went to the largest of the upholstered chairs. "Were it not that there has been so long a delay and so many rumors, we would not have trespassed on your good nature this far."

Richelieu glanced at Olivia. "Is that your opinion as well, Madame?"

"Essentially," Olivia answered with a steady look.

"That implies that, in fact, you disagree." He made a sign to Pere Chape, who was about to intervene. "Pray, tell me why you disapprove, as I assume you do."

"It is not for me to approve or disapprove. I came here at the request of Giulio Mazarini to be of assistance to him upon his return to France. However, that day seems as far off now as it did when I left Roma. Occasionally I wonder why I am here and what is expected of me."

Pere Chape had raised a warning finger, but was prevented from speaking by Richelieu. "I share your disappointment, Madame, and I am as confused by it as Mazarin is. You must call him Mazarin here, for in France he is French."

"As you wish," said Olivia, curious about Richelieu and willing to let him steer the conversation as he liked. "Mazarin he shall be."

Richelieu nodded once. "You have received messages from Mazarin?" Although this question was directed at Olivia, Pere Chape took it upon himself to answer.

"I have, Eminence," said Pere Chape eagerly. "I have word from him faithfully every month."

The expression in Richelieu's sunken eyes was not pleasant. "I inquired of Madame Clemens, mon Pere. I will speak with you directly." He turned back to Olivia; when he spoke again, it was in Latin. "I have been told you are a woman of some education, and that you have an understanding of the Church's tongue."

Olivia responded, "I speak Latin, if that is your meaning. Also Italian, French, a little Spanish, some English." She knew more languages than that, but was aware it was risky to admit it, or that some of the languages she knew had now all but disappeared from the world.

"Most impressive. How do you come to know it?" He had rested his elbows on the chair's arms and now placed the tips of his fingers together.

"I learned from my father and mother," said Olivia with complete honesty.

"A scholar's family, then," said Richelieu. "And it would account for your curious accent. Whoever told you to pronounce the letter *C* in that fashion was most capricious."

It was an effort for Olivia not to return a sharp retort, since her Latin was that of the upper-class Romans of the first Christian century. She coughed once. "It was the way I learned to speak, Eminence."

"Scholars," said Richelieu, dismissing all of them in a single word, though with an indulgent expression, as if he and Olivia shared a private joke. "Yet it is odd that you were taught. Did you have no brothers?"

"I did," said Olivia. "All of us spoke Latin."

"And French and Italian and some Spanish as well as English?" Richelieu asked archly, plainly enjoying himself.

"No," Olivia said after a brief hesitation. "Not . . . all of us had . . . the opportunity." She wished now she could change the subject, but did not want to alert the Cardinal to her distress. "I outlived my brothers and sisters," she said.

"Ah," said Richelieu, crossing himself. "My condolences." He sighed. "No wonder your father lavished such attention upon you. And how fortunate you proved an apt student." He fell silent, his eyes never leaving her face. "I understand you are a widow without children, or so Mazarin informs me."

"That is correct," said Olivia, wondering where Richelieu was leading their conversation now; she made no effort to change her Latin accent as she went on. "I have supposed that is one of the reasons the Abbe asked me to be part of his suite; I have few obligations to keep me in Roma." The one that held her was so strong that the demands of family—if she had any surviving—were inconsequential in comparison. The tie of her native earth was as all-encompassing as the bonds of blood.

"He is a most astute man," said Richelieu, then looked to Pere Chape and spoke once more in French. "You report to him, do you not?"

"Of course," said Pere Chape, taken aback at the question.

"And the reports you render, are they candid? Or are you a politician at heart, ever currying favor and seeking to improve your place in your patron's esteem?" His tented fingers pressed together and his fingers closed over his hands. "Well?"

"I am faithful to the task that has been set me," said Pere Chape after a tiny hesitation. He stood a bit straighter and did his best to appear indignant. "I have no purpose in my reports but to inform the Abbe of what has transpired in my parish, that is, as much as I may do without violating my vows."

"Commendable," said Richelieu drily. He regarded Pere Chape a little longer. "Do you report to others? Is your intelligence intended for the Abbe alone, or are there others you include in your work?"

"Cardinal Bagni, for one, has asked for reports," said Pere Chape, high color in his cheeks like fever spots.

"And the others," Richelieu inquired, as polite as he was icy. "Will you tell me, or am I going to be made to guess?"

Pere Chape coughed. "The secretaries of His Holiness."

Richelieu took a long breath. "His secretaries?" He tightened his locked hands. "For the benefit of the Church?"

"I am an ordained priest," said Pere Chape.

"You are also a Frenchman," Richelieu reminded him sharply. He leaned back, regarding the priest as if he were a perplexing stranger. "All right; you have your duty and you must perform it as you see fit; I will not dispute that. I have my duty, as well, and I will not tolerate your interference in it." He opened his hands and indicated the way to the door. "I wish to be private with Madame Clemens. You may leave us."

"Eminence—" Pere Chape began.

"I have said you may leave us: need I repeat?" He waited, hardly moving, until Pere Chape bowed and went to the door. "I will have you sent for when you are wanted."

"Of course, Eminence," said Pere Chape in a tone that was barely civil. He slammed the door behind him as he left the room to Olivia and Richelieu.

"So," the Cardinal said when he was satisfied that Pere Chape was truly gone. "To repeat to you what I have already told Pere Chape, you may be as candid as you wish, Madame. I welcome your candor, and I trust—I pray—it is more genuine than I suspect his may be."

"About what am I to be candid?" Olivia countered, her attitude respectful to conceal her alarm.

"Why, whatever you like," said Richelieu. "But I trust that you will speak to the matter at hand—this delay that keeps Mazarin in Rome is not convenient." He very nearly added more, but then held his silence.

"For any of us," Olivia said with asperity, hoping she was not interrupting him, for it was clear that the Cardinal disapproved of such behavior. "I anticipated that Mazarin would have received permission to leave Rome before now. When I left, it was understood that the Abbe would not be long in coming, and that he would be wearing a red hat as well."

"That was my understanding also," said Richelieu thoughtfully. "And I wonder why it is that the Pope should be so slow to act." He lowered his hands into his lap and looked down at them, becoming remotely studious. "I fear he is awaiting news of my death, so that he might use that event to his advantage."

"Surely, Eminence, you cannot believe that His Holiness is so"—she hunted for just the right word—"unscrupulous."

Richelieu gave a single, humorless laugh. "I have few illusions about His Holiness—no man in my position can afford illusions—and although I am the sincere and devout son of the Church, I realize that no Pope in this age may act with complete impunity when involved in matters of state. So I cannot help but doubt his intentions when he so resolutely refuses to grant my requests." He met Olivia's eyes directly. "You see, I, too, can be candid."

"So it appears, Eminence," said Olivia, startled in spite of herself. "It puzzles me, however, that you are so forthcoming with a stranger, and a foreign woman at that."

"You are most astute, Madame," said Richelieu, and once again spoke in Latin. "I have my obligations to France as I have obligations to the Church and to God. To that end, it is my sworn purpose to protect this country from all depredation. I cannot in conscience leave it to the caprice of the Pope, nor the . . . disposal of the King."

Olivia made little effort to hide her ironic amusement, yet she also made every effort not to appear to be mocking him. "Eminence, it would seem that it is the right of the Pope and the right of the King to do as they see fit, for it is within their Right to act, whether it suits you or not."

"Perhaps," said Richelieu, an odd twist at the corners of his mouth that might have been a bitter smile. "It is my task to turn the kingdom over to Louis' heir intact and prosperous, no matter what King and Pope may say. Any other legacy would be my disgrace."

"And you fear you will not be able to do this?" Olivia asked directly, her gaze meeting his.

"Yes," said Richelieu with equal bluntness. "If I die before Mazarin is established here, the Queen will not be able by herself to protect the heir, of that I am sadly certain. Anne of Austria is Spanish, and Spain and France . . . well, she is mistrusted, and much of it because of the King's . . . aversion as much as her foreignness." He shook his head. "I have given my life, and gladly, to the cause of my faith and my country; to be so close to securing France against her enemies, inside and outside the country, and to be at risk of losing all because the Pope does not wish to offend any of those who support him is maddening."

"Yes," said Olivia, for the first time feeling genuine sympathy for this reserved and formidable man.

"Right now, only I stand between the heir and chaos, and I will not be able to protect him much longer. Without Mazarin, it will all be for nothing." He rose abruptly and began to pace the room, the hem of his habit whispering against the floor as he moved. "The King is a man of unsteady temperament and dangerous affections. He has made certain promises that I am not convinced are reliable." He rounded on her. "You are not to repeat that to anyone, not even to Mazarin in your confidential reports; if you do, I will learn of it, you may be sure, and I will have you cast out of France."

This threat was all the more believable because it was delivered in a low, steady voice; Olivia was indignant. "You have no reason to entertain such a poor opinion of me, Eminence," she said, matching his coolness with her own. "If you think I will betray your confidence, then it were best that you extend none to me. If you want me to leave France, you have only to say so, and I'll arrange to return to my home at once."

Richelieu shook his head. "Good Madame, I only wish to give you a warning, not to accuse you. Coming as you do from so far away, you might not quite understand the gravity of what transpires here. You have been described as a woman of excellent judgment, and certainly it is plain that your wits are quick, but that does not also guarantee that your tongue is as discreet as it must be while you are here."

Olivia watched him pace. "Mazarini made that clear to me in Roma," she said in Italian, then reverted to Latin. "I may be a woman, but I am not foolish. I have seen too much of the ways of the world—the ways of men, if you will—to put myself in a more compromising position than that which I occupy already. I know something of the past, and the place of women in it, and I have read what de Pisan wrote; her words are more eloquent than mine, but I would defend the City of Ladies as staunchly as she did, given the opportunity."

"You are eloquent enough," said Richelieu, stopping his restless walking long enough to regard her with greater curiosity. "Tell me, Madame, does your militance extend itself to Queen Anne? Or are you one who propounds a notion for no purpose other than your own gain?"

Olivia bit back the sharp retort she longed to give; Richelieu was too formidable an opponent to be shaken by unkind words. "I am a Roman," she said. "And well I know that the place of women has"—she nearly said *sunk* but caught herself in time—"changed since the time the Caesars ruled." It was tempting to catalogue them, but she knew it would serve no purpose but to fuel her indignation. "Peasant or Queen, women are forever disadvantaged, and for that reason, if no other, there is ample reason for me to lend what aid I can when another woman requests my assistance."

"A most . . . unusual attitude," said Richelieu, starting to pace again. "Most women, no matter what fondness they profess for other women, would scar the cheeks of every other woman they know. And those that would not are either out of the world in cloisters or are as unnatural in their affections as the King is in his." He narrowed his eyes and directed a piercing look at her. "Are you very clever, or are you genuine, I wonder."

Olivia did not flinch at Richelieu's scrutiny or accusations. "You will have to discover that for yourself, Eminence, since I suppose you will doubt any answer I give you."

"There is some truth to that," he said, less pugnacious now that Olivia had spoken so coolly. "And you may be assured that I will watch you, that I will have reports of you regularly."

"So I supposed; as Mazarini will, and undoubtedly his supporters will, as well as the Pope." She indicated the chair Richelieu had left. "Eminence, you look tired. Pray sit and rest, and let us discuss what you require of me on the Queen's behalf."

Richelieu stopped in front of the hearth and leaned his shoulder against the marble mantelpiece. His face was pale and the smudges under his sunken eyes appeared muddy now. "I am a little tired," he admitted. "And I have little time left for my stay. There is so much left to arrange."

"For the Queen and the heir?" asked Olivia, who had caught something in Richelieu's expression that surprised her; for the briefest of moments there had been a softening in his face and a light had come into his eyes that had nothing to do with his health. She wondered if some of the most outrageous of rumors she had heard whispered in the last six months might have a kernel of truth in them. "Eminence?"

"For the Queen and heir," said Richelieu softly. "I cannot leave the world knowing they are in danger. Mazarin—you must call him Mazarin, I remind you—will have to be very careful and do all that he may to guard them." The light was in his eyes again, in spite of his pain and his icy discipline. "The Queen . . . does not give her trust easily, and too often it has been betrayed. That is why I want your assurance, as I have had from Mazarin, that you will put the preservation of the heir first, along with the safety of his mother. All that I have worked for in France is nothing if I cannot do this for them."

"Your . . . legacy," said Olivia, choosing the word Richelieu himself had used.

"Yes," said Richelieu. "When I went with the Queen Mother into exile, I saw what could become of France if the Crown was compromised and endangered. I vowed that it would not happen again were I able to prevent it."

"And you are certain you can prevent it, Eminence?" Olivia asked, this time with kindness.

"With God's aid, yes." He crossed himself, then went on with more asperity, "However, it appears that God is not as urgent a problem as the Pope. I must have Mazarin with me, and soon. He has been granted French citizenship, and the Church has agreed. Why must the Spaniards continue to delay?" He slammed the flat of his hand against the marble. "They wish to thwart me, to wait until I am in my grave, and then they will descend on France to pick her bones. They will say that Anne of Austria is a Spaniard, and for that reason they must seize the throne and remove the heir. I know this is what they want. The Pope must know it, too."

"The Pope has many Cardinals, and each Cardinal has demands," said Olivia, repeating what she had been told many times over the centuries.

"The justification of cowardly men!" scoffed Richelieu, and Olivia nodded in agreement. "They are afraid to disturb the little peace that has been cobbled together. But if the peace is so fragile that a single Abbe can end it, then it is no peace at all, merely a calm between battles."

"In fact," Olivia went on for him, beginning to like the man in spite of himself, "the battles continue, but they are fought by ones and twos in the dark."

Richelieu laughed once. "And what does a widow know of battles?"

"More than you suppose," said Olivia, her thoughts going back to the Legions, to the armies of Byzantium and the Ostrogoths, to the Persians riding against Greeks, to the raiding Islamites in Spain, the marauding bandits in Corsica, to mounted Crusaders collapsing in the inexorable sun, to Ottoman troops on the Dalmatian coast, to Swiss mercenaries in Germany clashing with Protestant Dutch.

"Your husband, then, died in battle?" Richelieu asked, seeing something in her face that he could not fathom.

"No," Olivia said. "He did not die in battle."

It was apparent that Richelieu wanted to learn more, but would not allow himself to be distracted. "Well, whatever your reason for distrusting battles, I pray it will sustain you while you are here, and will give you the faith to continue to aid the Queen and the heir." He came back to the upholstered chair and sat down, moving stiffly.

"Eminence, is there something you require?" Olivia asked, realizing that the Cardinal was in pain.

"No, nothing," he said. "God remember you for your kindness." He closed his eyes, the double lines between his brows deepening. "It will pass."

"I will send for—" Olivia began.

"You will send for no one," said Richelieu sharply, looking directly at her. "Jesu, there are whispers enough about me; I do not need to have everyone know that I am not as strong as I was. It is one thing to have it suspected that I am growing more ill; I will not help my enemies by confirming their suspicions."

"As you wish, Eminence," said Olivia, her voice dropping.

"I do not want you mentioning this to Mazarin. What he needs to know he will learn from my couriers and under my seal." He let out his breath slowly, not quite evenly. "So. The matter of the Queen and heir: I wish you to devote yourself to their interests and the interests of Mazarin, for that is the salvation of France."

It took Olivia a moment to decide to ask, "Eminence, you are devoted to the Queen and her boy; why is that?"

"She is Queen and he will be King," said Richelieu, a bit startled at so obvious a question. "They are the hope of France."

"Pardon me if I intrude, but it seems that there is something more. May I know what it is?" She did not look directly at him, but she observed him with keen attention.

This time Richelieu hesitated. "I am dedicated to the preservation of France, and her Royal House," he said, then added, "and I esteem and revere Queen Anne; I pity her for what she has been made to endure because of her marriage. That God has given her a child after so long and . . . unrewarding wedded years is a sign of the greatest favor." He looked away from Olivia.

"I have heard that for many years you were at odds." She half expected the Cardinal to become angry and depart.

"Yes," he said slowly. "Yes, there was a time that every time we met we argued, but that was before she . . . she came to trust me." His face was less severe and remote now, and there was a warmth in his voice that Olivia had not heard before and had not thought he possessed. "She had made some . . . unworthy connections, and the King was distressed to learn of it. Her association with the Duke of Buckingham had been bad enough, but it did not touch France directly. The other was more serious, and Louis wanted more than ever to be rid of his unwelcome wife. He wanted to accuse her of . . . oh, terrible crimes. I did what I could to prevent this."

"For Anne," said Olivia.

Some of the reserve came back into his manner. "For France, and to prevent a worsening of our dealings with Spain. Her brother would not have tolerated abuses beyond what she had suffered already." He looked at Olivia. "I hope you are as discreet as Mazarin said you are."

"Certainly that is my intention, Eminence," said Olivia, her brows lifted slightly.

"It would be most unwise of you to discuss any of what I have said." His manner was polished now, and cold.

"Why should I, Eminence?" she asked, uncertain how to proceed with Richelieu now that he had retreated from her so completely.

"Any reason you might have worries me," said Richelieu, not answering her directly. He gripped the arms of his chair tightly. "Give me your word. And then call that fool Chape. It is time I was leaving."

Olivia sensed the tremendous fatigue that engulfed Richelieu, and the disease that wrought it. "You have my word that I will keep your confidences, Eminence, no matter what they are." She started toward the door, then paused, watching Richelieu struggle to rise. "Shall I call Pere Chape?"

"Your word," Richelieu mused as he got to his feet. "Well, I will have to accept it, for the Queen's and the heir's sake as well as my own." He signaled her to open the door, then held out his ring to be kissed.

* * *

*Text of a letter from Alessandro, Cardinal Bichi to Atta Olivia
Clemens.*

To the esteemed and well-respected widow, the distinguished lady
Atta Olivia Clemens currently abiding in Francia, the blessings
and greetings from my hand and soul to yours.

I cannot express sufficiently the chagrin I feel at the inconvenience of your current situation, being in Francia with Mazarini
continuing here in Roma. To be the first of his suite to arrive there
and then be forced to endure these endless delays in the arrival of
Mazarini is an ordeal that I would not wish placed on any shoulders, let alone those of a worthy and proper widow. You have been
deserving of better treatment than we have been able to accord you
thus far, and you have my assurances that as soon as Mazarini
arrives in Parigi, all will change. The Abbe has undoubtedly said
much the same thing to you in his dispatches, and means them as
sincerely as I do.

We have reason now to hope that by the end of this year it will be
possible for Mazarini to be in Francia to take up the duties Cardinal Richelieu wishes to share with him. The burdens of statecraft
are heavy indeed, the more so for the leagues between Parigi and
Roma, and our reliance on your presence has gone beyond what
any of us anticipated; so will you be commensurately rewarded by
Mazarini for your aid and duty in these difficult times.

We have reason to believe that some of the reports we have been
sent have not been as accurate as we wish them to be, and we must
impose on you once more in this regard. There are those who from
time to time inform us of various activities in Francia, as you do,
and of late the reports supplied by certain of our associates have
contained material which has proven to be inaccurate, which distresses us more and more, for we are required to act on faulty information, which serves only to strengthen the position of our enemies
and the enemies of Francia. Therefore, we seek to ask for more reports from you, on the subjects we will indicate, and implore both
haste and silence on your part until we are confident that those who
provide us with this material are honestly mistaken in what they

have said, or have been erroneously informed themselves. That will then enable us to make necessary decisions in a responsible manner in regard to those who have obtained the information.

It is awkward to have to continue this way, but for a short while longer we must. If Mazarini could leave for Parigi at once, then your service in this unpleasant matter would not be required. For that I ask your understanding and pardon, and assure you that you will not have to perform this service for very long.

The first matter we wish you would explore more in depth is the true position of the various military leaders, since our reports are so varied and confusing as to be worse than useless. I know that such men are often distasteful to women of your station, and that to single out any of these men could be compromising to you, so this is not being asked. Instead, we urge you to attend those functions where these men are present, and to learn what you can of them. It is often the case that such men believe women to be more foolish than God made them, and will say things to them they would not vouchsafe to another man; if you are willing to undertake these inquiries, I am eager to hear all you may learn. The information you gain will be of importance to us, no matter how little it is, for it will enable us to know which of our other reports to believe.

We are grateful for all your work on our behalf, and to show this gratitude, we have licensed your stud farm at Senza Pari to service to the Papal Court, at the maximum fees. This honor will bring distinction to your horses and gold to your coffers, and in some small part it will acknowledge your assistance to our work in Francia.

May Our Lord and His Virgin Mother watch over you, keep you in the way of virtue and faith, and may you find earthly joys as well as those in Heaven. Be sure of our gratitude as you are sure of the rising of the sun.

Alessandro, Cardinal Bichi
By God's Grace

From Roma on the 11th day of April, 1639.
Destroy after reading.

PART II
Charles de Batz-Castelmore

Text of a letter from Giulio Mazarini to Atta Olivia Clemens, written in Italian.

To my dear friend and staunch ally, Abbe Mazarini sends his most respectful and heartfelt greetings, and expresses his thanks for all that Atta Olivia Clemens has done in his cause for far too long.

I am relieved to tell you that at last the barriers to my return to Francia are being broken, and all that has stood in the way is ending. I have had word—though it is clandestine and I cannot allow you to acknowledge what I tell you—from the Queen telling me that those in Francia who oppose my coming have been brought to heel and are not resisting my arrival. Your information on the military men was most hopeful in this regard, the more so for being odious to you. I pray most fervently that you will never again be asked to perform such a task for any reason whatsoever. That you have done this for more than six months is more praiseworthy than I can say, and I beg you to accept my obligation to you as token of all you have done for me and for Francia, little as anyone there may appreciate that.

I have been assured that I will be summoned to Parigi before the end of the year, and I am putting my household in readiness to travel at the end of this month. Once word has come, I do not wish to contribute to the delays through my lack of preparedness. My goods are much the same as yours, and we anticipate five to six weeks on the road, providing the weather is not severe. Due to the lateness of the season, we may have to add another week to the travel, coming along the coast into Francia and then proceeding to Aix-en-Provence, and from there to Avignon, coming north along the Rhone to Lyon. If the weather is mild, we will come through the mountains. Word will be sent from along the road by courier, so you will know well in advance of my arrival.

I cannot tell you how I long to see Parigi again. I recall the first sight I had of it, that splendid city, the old walls as grand and imposing as any I have seen. It was a windy day, and all the windmills were turning, their sails making them appear to be a fantastic landlocked navy come to besiege this treasure of a city. That you have chosen to live outside the gates means that you are one with those windmills. I have heard such wonderful things of Eblouir, that it is the jewel of Chatillon, and that to be asked there is an honor. You must tell me when I visit you there if you love the countryside as much as I do, and the vision of Parigi east of you.

Your note to me with the last courier's pouch was most distressing, for if your observations are correct, the great Richelieu will not live as long as we all have hoped. Perhaps it was a more difficult day for him than others, and you did not see him at advantage. Perhaps, too, as you suggest, he has been skilled at hiding the seriousness of his condition, and that few courtiers are aware of how ill he has actually become. I confess I hope that he is in better health than you fear, but I know I must not assume otherwise, and I am truly saddened at this information. There has never been a greater man in Europe, and to lose him at the point of fruition of his plans is gall to me. I pray that I will be given the perspicacity and strength and wisdom to continue his great work, for he is entrusting it to me, and I am obligated to persevere in his tasks for him.

Until I have the felicity to speak to you face to face, I send you my warmest greetings and pray that God will continue to protect and favor you for all you are doing on my behalf.

Giulio Mazarini, Abbe

From Roma on the 21st day of September, 1639.
Place under lock and seal or destroy.

· **1** ·

Peyrer de Troisvilles leaned back in his chair and rubbed his eyes, wondering as he did if he needed spectacles, like one of the old priests he knew. Four letters, all petitions to join the King's

Musqueteers, lay in a disorganized pile on his writing table. All would have to be answered, and he was more reluctant than usual to answer them. "What am I to say to them?" he muttered to the walls. "That damned Italian Abbe is coming, and who knows what work he will make of the Musqueteers." He sighed, the thought of disbanding the Musqueteers hurting him like an old, ill-healed wound.

There was a discreet knock at the door; when de Troisvilles did not answer at once, it was repeated.

"Come in, come in," de Troisvilles said brusquely, gathering the letters together and forcing himself to attend to business.

Isaac de Portau favored de Troisvilles with a short, respectful bow. Both were Bearnais, and both spoke that dialect more comfortably than they did the French of Paris. "God give you good day," said de Portau, coming to stand on the other side of de Troisvilles' writing table.

"Is anything the matter?" de Troisvilles asked, staring up at de Portau. "Why did you interrupt me?"

"I have heard that the King will summon the Italian here officially in the next month." He cleared his throat. "I heard it from one of the lackeys in the Royal Household, a fellow who has been reliable in the past."

"I have heard much the same thing," said de Troisvilles heavily. "It would have to happen eventually, I suppose. But if only it could have been longer; with Richelieu in such poor health, he cannot hang on much longer." He leaned back in his chair. "It is a sin to pray for the death of another, and a Cardinal at that, but every night I beg God to gather Richelieu to His bosom before this Abbe can be summoned."

"God forgives such requests," said de Portau in an offhanded way. "Especially in matters of state."

"So I hope," said de Troisvilles in a soft, weary tone. "I tried to stop his coming. I dread what may happen to us at his hands. No matter what the King declares, the man is a foreigner, and cannot be trusted. He is related to the Colonnas! How can we permit such a creature to hold the reins of France?"

De Portau's merry little eyes glittered. "How can we permit the French to hold the reins of France?"

"The French," said de Troisvilles, making the word a curse. "When I was a child we did not allow Frenchmen to enter the house. We gave them no hospitality, for they were not Bearnais, and could not be trusted. And now, look at us: here we are in

Paris, speaking their language to them because they disdain ours."
He glanced toward the window. "Close the shutter for me, will
you? It looks as if we're going to have more rain."

"A wet winter," said de Portau as he drew the shutters in and
locked them. "My sister sent me a letter last week and said that all
the signs are for a wet winter. Her husband's brother is a monk and
writes for her."

"What Order of monk?" asked de Troisvilles sharply.

"Benedictine," said de Portau. "A Gascon; my sister would not
have married other than a Bearnais or Gascon. She said also that
there have been Spanish scouts in the mountains."

De Troisvilles made a gesture of helplessness. "And we are to do
nothing. My last petition to His Majesty, asking for an increase in
our numbers, was denied. You know at whose door that refusal
may be laid."

"Richelieu," said de Portau roundly as he busied himself lighting the candles, for with the shutters closed the room was dark. "I
saw some of his Guards on the street this morning. I did not return
their salute."

"Not that they are troubled by such conduct," said de
Troisvilles. "They know that thanks to their Cardinal, our hands
are tied and we are useless."

De Portau for once had no easy answer. "Is there a way to increase our numbers without the permission of the King?"

"How?" asked de Troisvilles. "Oh, there are men who would be
pleased to serve with us." He indicated the letters on his desk with
a fatalistic smile. "Yet I must refuse them. His Majesty has given
us no funds for more men and weapons, and he is not likely to. To
bring in new men now would make it appear that we are cutting
ourselves off from the Crown, and that could mean prison or
worse for all of us."

"Surely the King would not go so far," said de Portau.

"It is not the King who must concern us, it is Richelieu. Always
Richelieu."

"And that Italian," added de Portau. He pulled up a wooden
bench and sat down. "Is there anything that can be done about the
Italian?"

"Not any longer, I fear. He will be back in France within six
months; I'd wager my eyes on it." De Troisvilles glared at the nearest candles. "I have tried everything I know."

"What of the Queen? Would she aid you?" De Portau leaned

forward as he offered this suggestion, as if that would increase its possibility.

"If the King and the Queen were less at odds, I suppose it might. But she will not set herself directly against him, not with the fate of the heir so precarious, and her future as well." Now de Troisvilles looked haggard. "And who is to blame her, given the circumstances? There are rumors already, and if she defies the King, even the most outrageous of the rumors will be believed." He rubbed the bridge of his prominent nose. "A few are believed already."

De Portau had to screw up his courage to ask, "You, what do you think? Is the child Louis' get, or did the Queen come to her senses at last and make other arrangements?"

"I would not fault her if she did," said de Troisvilles. "After so many barren years, and the King a stranger to her bed, she would not be the first woman to allow herself to be persuaded by the promise of a child and an ally." He coughed. "I haven't answered your question, have I? It is because I cannot. I am of two minds; I do not know what to think. I am grateful there is an heir, for France needs one desperately, yet I would rather not endorse a child who had not the Right."

"But how could you learn? How would you know? Isn't there some way to be certain? The doubt alone is—" De Portau suddenly fell silent, his hand raised in warning.

"Is someone there?" de Troisvilles called out sharply. He, too, had heard quiet steps in the hall.

"They had the surgeon in earlier," said de Portau quietly. "It could be the surgeon."

"It could be anyone, and whatever we have said could bring us to a traitor's end at the block."

"Surely nothing so severe," said de Portau.

"The King cannot afford to have questions asked, not after the Buckingham affair. His position is much too vulnerable." He cleared his throat. "Do you hear anyone now?"

De Portau gave a signal for de Troisvilles to continue speaking; he rose and went silently to the door, indicating all the while to de Troisvilles that he should go on talking.

De Troisvilles nodded his understanding. "All of France has questions about this birth, and who is to say they are without reason? Whether the King has his favorites or not, he is known not to admire women, and when his Queen has been so ill-used and has waited so many years to have children, there must be those who will be suspicious. It is not for us to determine if the Queen has erred, but to uphold the King."

Without warning de Portau flung open the door and sprang into the hall, one hand on the hilt of his dagger.

A lackey cowered back as de Portau caught him by the sleeve, his manner so cringing and servile that de Portau wanted more than ever to have an excuse to pressure the man. "Well, see what I have here," he said with false affability.

"Cados," said de Troisvilles, more shocked than he wanted to admit. "How it is you are listening to what we have been saying?" He made a gesture to de Portau.

"Let's not stand here in the hall," said de Portau, taking a strong grip on Cados' arm and forcing him to enter de Troisvilles' room. "We can be more private this way, fellow."

Cados was horridly pale and he looked from de Troisvilles to de Portau as if he had been trapped between wild animals. "I . . . there is no reason for this, Monsieur de Troisvilles. You are mistaken. I was not listening to you, or nothing deliberate. I merely heard you mention the heir, and I am as curious as the next man . . ." He tried to go on, but he could find no words.

"Idle curiosity, nothing more?" said de Portau, pretending solicitousness.

"Yes, yes, idle curiosity. The same as any man." He took a step toward de Troisvilles, but was stopped when the leader of the King's Musqueteers raised his hand. "It was nothing, I swear it. It was nothing."

"Nothing," said de Troisvilles in a contemplative way. "How strange. From the way you have been behaving, I would suspect you anticipated worse at my hands than a few questions. It is odd how deceptive appearances are."

"But, Monsieur de Troisvilles," protested Cados, "there is no reason for you to think the worst of me. I have given you no reason to do it, have I?" He looked once toward de Portau, as if he expected to be physically restrained, then hurried on. "You are too hasty, Monsieur. You are assuming—"

"I am assuming nothing. I have discovered you listening at my door, and I am waiting now to find out why you have done this." De Troisvilles moved his chair back from his writing table and folded his arms. "The only opinion I have formed is that you have conducted yourself unwisely."

"You are wrong," said Cados, not as polite as he had been a moment ago. "I have done nothing unwise. I have done the bidding of the King."

"The King," said de Troisvilles with the look of courteous disbelief, though inwardly he grew cold—what if Louis had asked Cados to watch him? The idea was absurd, of course, but it was so ridiculous that it might be true.

"His deputy came to me," Cados explained. "He had the Royal Seal and he told me that I was needed to do the work of the King. I am a true Frenchman, more of a Frenchman than Bearnais and Gascons." The last was said haughtily.

"More of a Frenchman," said de Portau. "I would not be so pleased as you are."

De Troisvilles agreed with de Portau. "Listen well, Cados, for de Portau is right: in this room, one does not boast of being a Frenchman."

Cados started to speak, then thought better of it. He refused to look at de Troisvilles, directing his gaze to the closed shutters as if he could see beyond them with ease. His expression had become scornful.

"You are churlish, my good man," said de Portau, clapping one hand on Cados' shoulder with more force than was necessary. "Here is Monsieur de Troisvilles who has given you honorable work and a respectable wage, who has given you his confidence, his trust, and you have rewarded that with treachery." He fixed his fingers more tightly, ignoring the way Cados winced at this treatment. "You have not done honorably, Monsieur, and have much to answer for; Monsieur de Troisvilles wishes to hear what you have to say in your own defense."

"I was acting at the behest of the King," said Cados, more loudly than before, looking at de Portau's profile as if that would make him move his hand.

"As are we, as the King's Musqueteers," said de Troisvilles with extreme patience. He inclined his head to de Portau. "Every man here is the King's man. Yet you behave as if we bow to different masters."

"The King has need of those to aid him," said Cados, his face heating. "He must discover who among his subjects is worthy of his trust and favor."

"Trust and favor," repeated de Troisvilles, musing. "So. You believe that we of the King's Musqueteers have failed His Majesty: it appears that we are at an impasse."

"I have done what the King wished," said Cados emphatically. "What you say is true, yes. You say you are King's men, all sworn and loyal to the Crown, but the King has his reasons to doubt that. He desires to know if you are his defenders and champions or if you are working with his enemies to bring ruin upon him."

"We seek to do the King no harm," said de Portau. "Our actions show that clearly. We have been first in battle for his honor and our own, all the world knows it. But it may be that the King has listened to poor counsel and wishes bad cess upon us." He looked at de Troisvilles for confirmation.

"If not the King," said de Troisvilles sourly, "the Cardinal. This fool was not suborned by the King, but by Richelieu. We are all suspect and the Musqueteers are brought into bad circumstances because of my opposition to that Italian." He faced the wall on his left where his books and maps were stored. "It was the Cardinal's man, not the King's, who approached you, wasn't it?"

Cados straightened himself. "I was told he was from the King," he insisted, but there was an unsteadiness in this objection that made it ring false.

"Whose livery did he wear?" de Troisvilles asked, suddenly feeling old and tired. How had he got enmeshed in politics after so many years of keeping away from it? What had he overlooked, who had he offended, that his men were made to pay for his blunder? Why had he allowed himself to be drawn into the debate over the Italian? It was an effort to listen to Cados with all the questions and accusations ringing in his thoughts.

"The King's livery," said Cados, glowering at de Troisvilles as if he would not tolerate more contradiction. "He had the badge on his sleeve and the colors—"

De Troisvilles arrested the flow of words with a wave of his hand. "No doubt, no doubt. How many of the Cardinal's supporters are in the Royal Household?"

"It was the King's—"

"—man, yes, certainly it was," de Troisvilles finished for him, his voice quiet. He continued to look at his books and maps. "How did this man come to choose you, did he tell you?"

"He knew I was part of your establishment," said Cados, beginning to feel more important. "It wasn't my livery alone that informed him; he said that he had observed this place and had learned to recognize many of your servants. I was selected because I am a Parisian, not some arrogant bully from the provinces." This last was intended as an insult and both de Troisvilles and de Portau took it as such.

"I had no notion," said de Troisvilles as deliberately as he could, "that being employed here was so bitter for you. We have asked you to assume an intolerable burden, I see that now. Well, I have no wish to continue your distress now I have learned of it. Since you find . . . arrogant bullies from the provinces so unbearable, you are relieved of that oppression at once. You may present yourself in my office the first thing in the morning and your wages to that day and hour will be paid in full." He did not permit himself the luxury of smiling.

"Paid in full?" Cados repeated in a numb, tense way, his eyes growing wide. "How do you mean?"

"I mean you will be paid and released. We have no desire to cheat you of your wages, and so you must permit us the night to gather together the necessary records. A purse and accounting will be ready by the end of Mass tomorrow." He looked at de Portau. "Will you provide him the appropriate escort?"

"When?" asked de Portau. "Tomorrow?"

"Yes."

Cados looked wildly from one man to the other. "Wait!" he cried out. "I have a wife and children. They do not deserve this of you. You cannot do this to—"

"Perhaps you might have done better to have thought of that before you acted on behalf of the Cardinal. Or the King, if that's what you desire to have us believe." De Troisvilles got to his feet and approached Cados deliberately. "You have not considered your position. I could find it in my heart to pity you, but not when it is my men you have harmed."

"I have not harmed them," said Cados, but by now he lacked conviction. "Nothing I have done would harm them. They need only fear if they are in error."

"By whose terms do we decide error?" de Troisvilles asked, wanting to end the game. "Oh, get out, Cados. Go and toady to the Cardinal or anyone you like, but leave us alone." He indicated the door and let de Portau shove the lackey through it. As de Portau closed the door, Cados' threats began.

"What do you think?" de Portau inquired, his head cocked to the side.

"He'll leave soon enough," said de Troisvilles, pinching the bridge of his nose as much out of habit as headache. "What is the matter with me that I could not see what was happening?"

"You mean with Cados?" de Portau said, jerking his thumb in the direction of the door. "What man has time to question all the lackeys for the regiment? It's ridiculous." He dragged his chair near de Troisvilles' writing table. "Why should you be suspicious of a troll like Cados?"

De Troisvilles would not be coaxed out of his grim thoughts. "Ever since Richelieu first proposed bringing the Italian Abbe to France, I ought to have been on the alert. I have been in more obvious matters. I know that the reason we cannot increase our numbers is more the Cardinal's decision than His Majesty's. Yet I overlooked something so simple as household spies."

"But we all use lackeys for information," said de Portau reasonably. "And some of the time, they have useful information for us. Other times, we waste our gold, but"—he shrugged philosophically—"what can you expect from lackeys, in the end? They are nothing."

De Troisvilles looked away from his companion. "I made an error, a foolish, stupid, tactical oversight, and it may be the end of all of us." He stared down at the letters piled before him as if he had never seen them before. "Look at these! What do I tell them? Do I warn them that if they want to join the Musqueteers it may mean making an enemy of Richelieu because I—*I*—do not like Mazarini?"

"Most of us are not admirers of Richelieu," said de Portau with exaggerated nonchalance. "And a few think it would be no bad thing if the King preferred a Frenchman to fill his post."

"The King does not consult with us on such matters," said de Troisvilles distantly.

"Perhaps he should, since he listens to your advice on other issues," said de Portau. He scratched his jaw, where the neat beard gave way to day-old stubble. "A man given the task of defending the kingdom should be heard. The Musqueteers are known as the best fighting men on foot. That should count for something with Louis."

"But does it?" said de Troisvilles, listening as the first drops of rain splattered on the closed shutters. "Just in time."

De Portau would not be distracted from his theme so easily. "It would be very sensible, very wise, for the King to listen to what you have to say about protecting the kingdom, including from foreign Abbes and churchmen. He has taken your advice about armies and such—then why not about his . . . deputies? If you told His Majesty that an army officer, though he was of high rank and in mounted troops, was not reliable or was not trusted by his men, the King would listen to you and consider what you say. If a soldier fled under fire and you said to the King that the soldier was right to do this, Louis would accept your judgment. So there is no reason he will not—"

"He has not thus far, not where Mazarini is concerned," said de Troisvilles in a tone that closed the matter.

De Portau coughed. "Well, I wanted to think of some advantage in all this."

"I know," said de Troisvilles heavily. "I thank you for that, Isaac." He got up and went to take down one of the rolled maps.

De Portau reached across the writing table and picked up the letter that lay on top of the stack of four, squinting at it as he read with difficulty. "Isn't very good at letters, is he?" he said as he put the letter back on the pile.

"Who?" said de Troisvilles, then answered his own question. "Oh, you mean de Batz-Castelmore?"

"Yes; Charles de Batz-Castelmore," said de Portau. "Sounds like a Gascon."

"He is," said de Troisvilles, coming back to the writing table with a map half-unrolled between his hands.

De Portau moved the letters out of the way. "What's he like, do you know?"

De Troisvilles was more engrossed in the map than in his conversation with de Portau. It took a little time for him to answer. "Batz-Castelmore? A typical Gascon: tell him it's for honor and he'll eat a Turk for breakfast."

"Oh, then you've met him?" de Portau asked with a trace of surprise.

"Yes," said de Troisvilles as he traced one of the tributaries of the Marne with his finger. "He came here a few months ago. We had no place for him, but I promised I would enter his name on the lists. I believe he joined the Guard; I told him it was a good place to start. I heard that he went there, though he was most insistent about being a Musqueteer."

De Portau clapped his wide, square hand to his chest. "I started there. As you say, it makes a good beginning."

"For most of the regiments in France," said de Troisvilles, his finger stopped at Ecury-sur-Coole. "What is the ground like here?" He tapped the map twice.

"I've never been there," said de Portau after craning his neck to look at what de Troisvilles was indicating. "You might ask one of the older men; some of them probably remember."

"Of course," said de Troisvilles absently, going on as if to himself, "I'd like to be on campaign now. In war I know what I'm doing. I'd like to be doing something more than waiting for the King to tell us we have to protect that damned Italian." He signaled to de Portau. "Have someone bring us wine; I'm dry as a bucket of dust."

De Portau complied with alacrity, hauling the door open and bawling his orders to the confusion on the floor below. As he slammed back into the room, he said, "Cados is gone."

"Just as well," said de Troisvilles, trying to make himself believe it. "That's one less thing to worry about."

* * *

Text of a letter from Atta Olivia Clemens to Ragoczy Sanct' Germain Franciscus, written in Latin.

To my dear, dear, dear Sanct' Germain, my greetings from Gaul, and my hope that this finds you more contented than I.

I have followed Rogerian's instructions and handed this to that Spanish Franciscan whose name you gave me. The man is much aged—in only ten years—and his face has that pinched, dried look that does not bode well for him, and in future it may require other means for me to reach you. Still, Frey Alejo tells me that all is in readiness; he has said he will arrange this to be sent where you are, although why you should have traveled such a very long way, and over water at that, I am at a loss to comprehend.

Of course there have been postponements and delays and heaven knows what else, and Abbe Mazarini has still not left Roma to come here. I don't know why this astonishes me, but it does, and I am indignant to no purpose, since my indignation means nothing to any of the worthies who are jockeying for favor or power through Mazarini, Richelieu, and the King of France.

I have met Richelieu twice more, and I am certain that he is not going to live much longer. No, this is not despair that comes upon our kind from time to time, seeing nothing but brutality and brevity everywhere: Richelieu does not thrive. He masks his suffering well, but it is difficult to keep such secrets from those of our blood. I persist in my assumption that he has been protecting Queen Anne for many years, for no reason but his own love of her. Whether she loves him, or is indifferent to him, as I have heard, or whether she is aware of his protection, I do not know. I have met her only once, and that for nothing more than to touch her hand, curtsy, and say that the gathering was brilliant. I tend to discount the rumor that her son Louis was fathered by Richelieu—though the company of saints will testify that Richelieu is more of a father to the boy than Louis has been—though it is not impossible. But I cannot forget that Anne of Austria is a Spanish Hapsburg and she might not accept a priest as a lover because of his vows, which may be short-sighted where Richelieu is concerned.

Sanct' Germain, why did you have to choose this time to go to the New World? It is less than a year since you set foot on that cursed ship, and already I miss you as if you were gone for a century in the heart of Africa. When you are not where I can reach you, I am uneasy. And it is not the same that Niklos is here and fusses over me; it is not the same at all.

I thank you for your advice—the same I have given you on more than one occasion—but I find myself unable to act upon it. Certainly I have visited men in their dreams when the need was upon me, and left them unharmed but for what little I had of them. You are right, of course, and it is poor nourishment, without love, but better than starving. I find I am not as willing as I was once to risk being despised. Once, perhaps, it was not as important to me, but now I dread that sickness of the soul that shows in their eyes when they know what I am and what I have done. That, I suspect, makes me a coward, and if I am, so be it. I have made a kind of truce with life. True, I miss the passion, but I am spared the odium. If this is a sign I am growing old, who (but you) has a better right to age? You ask would I take a lover if there were a man who wanted me and was capable of accepting what I am? Yes, yes, I would, so long as he gave himself as well as his blood; if not, then I prefer the honesty of loneliness to the deceit of closeness where nothing more than skin touches.

There, now I am starting to despair, which is useless and foolish. Tomorrow the court is supposed to go to Fontainebleau because the King has a taste for mushrooms or some such nonsense. I have been invited to attend, and since it is what the Cardinals want of me, I suppose I must go, though it has been raining most of the week and the roads are hip-deep in mud. Why it is necessary to order two or three dozen coaches to take to the road at such a time completely baffles me, but I suppose that is what makes royal caprice what it is.

Come back soon, my best and dearest friend. Europe seems awfully empty with you gone from it. Nevertheless it does not matter where you go—be sure that this brings you my love no matter how many years go by, no matter how far away you are. Send for me and I will come, Cardinals and Kings and Abbes be damned: their hold is nothing compared to the bond that links us and has linked us for more than fifteen hundred years.

There; I promise, no more morbidity. It is useless, as I have told you before. I will not languish nor despair, at least not for long.

Niklos informs me that it is time to go. I have come to my senses and sent word to the stables that we are to follow the court. My maid is in a terrible humor because of the haste I require of her, and if it were not that she will be near the Crown, she might sulk and refuse to accompany me. She, you understand, is overjoyed at the thought of seeing all the grand ladies and gentlemen. Sadly, I do not share her enthusiasm; I will prepare to be agog at mushrooms and talk inanities from dawn till midnight. And I will miss you, your smile and your voice. You would think after all this time apart that I would stop missing you. But I haven't.

Olivia

At Eblouir, near Chatillon.
On the 2nd of November, 1639.

· 2 ·

One lackey went to wake Niklos, who bundled into a long dressing robe and issued a few sharp orders as he searched for his shoes;
the other went to Avisa's chamber to instruct her to summon her
mistress.

"Good Lord God," whispered Avisa, crossing herself and searching for her engulfing night wrap. Her hair, covered with a modest
cap, poked out around her face giving her the look of a poorly
made doll. "What has happened?"

The lackey had no answer, but said, "There is a courier from
Mazarini. He has—"

"San Michele proteggimi," she said, speaking a trifle more
loudly. "The Abbe's courier at this hour! From Mazarini himself!"

"Yes," the lackey declared, hoping that this impressive news
would spur Avisa to action. "Bring your mistress at once. The courier is waiting and he has been riding since sunset. He is tired and
hungry and cannot rest until Bondama Clemens has the letter he
brings to her."

This information at last goaded Avisa into activity and she
plunged through the short connecting corridor into Olivia's private
room, calling to her mistress to rise. "I'm sorry," she added as she
approached the bed, "cara madama, to call you so early, but—"

It was then she noticed that Olivia's bed was empty and, aside
from the impressions in the pillows, showed no sign of being slept
in; not even the embroidered satin spread had been pulled back.

"Dear God," said Avisa, clapping her hand over her mouth and
trying not to scream. "Bondama!" She stepped back, then stared at
the bed once more, as if she might have been mistaken the first
time. She rocked back on her heels, her thoughts dithering, as she
heard the lackey knock more forcefully on the door to her room.
"Dear. Dear dear dear," she said, biting her knuckles. "Oh, Bon-

dama, dov'e?" She turned suddenly, as if she might catch Olivia unaware and lurking in the corner. Then she almost ran from the room, back to open the door for the lackey.

"How long will your mistress need to prepare?" the lackey asked, showing a careful blend of authority and subservience.

Avisa gathered her hands together under her chin. "She is gone!" she announced as dramatically as she could.

The lackey looked at her as if she were suddenly mad. "Did you tell her who was waiting for her, woman?"

"She is not here to tell. I can't find her!" Avisa said, more loudly and slowly, as if the lackey were hard of hearing.

"What do you mean, can't find her?" the lackey demanded contemptuously, hands now on his hips. "The courier is waiting. Get her up."

"She is not in her room," Avisa said, and burst into tears.

"Lord spare me a woman's weeping," said the lackey, blustering as he retreated. He did not turn as Avisa called after him.

"We must find her! We must find her!"

The lackey returned to the salon where the courier had been taken to wait for wine and a meal, found Niklos Aulirios already there, and was uncertain of protocol. Then he bowed to the courier and nodded to Niklos, making a careful distinction between the two men. "Apparently Bondame Clemens is not in her quarters and I regret to inform you that she has not yet been located," he said smoothly to Niklos, doing his best to make this news sound both unremarkable and intriguing at once.

"What?" Niklos said, more amused than alarmed.

"Her maid told me she was not in her room." The lackey opened his hands as if to absolve himself from anything Avisa might say.

"That's impossible," said Niklos, turning to the courier who by now was sprawled on one of the divans near the curtained window. "Will you permit me a few minutes to find my mistress? As you know, we have no guests here at present, and there are no entertainments after supper. However, Bondame Clemens occasionally suffers from sleeplessness"—he did not add that Olivia rarely needed more than two hours' rest in a day—"and if this is one such night . . ."

The courier lowered his eyes to the dispatch case strapped to his sash. "I must present this to her myself; if you know where she is, bring her, in Mazarin's name."

"Certainly," said Niklos, signaling to the lackey. "Go to the kitchen and see why wine has not been brought, and as soon as it is presentable, bring it. I do not want this house thrown into an uproar simply because Bondame Clemens has nights she cannot sleep." Where was she, Niklos asked himself, and how could he account for her absence if she were not in the house at all? He made himself deal with immediate problems, not anticipation and worry. "Come, man; you see the courier needs refreshment. Hurry."

The lackey longed for one of those households where the staff had free access to all the secrets under the roof, but this was not one such. Even idle speculation was frowned upon by Niklos, and the lackey had learned that the Greek major domo had unpleasant ways to deal with servants who forgot. Much as he would have preferred otherwise, he bowed slightly. "Certainly, Aulirios." Using Niklos' last name was a compromise the staff had reached in assessing the man.

"Now," Niklos insisted pleasantly, indicating the door. As soon as the lackey was gone, Niklos bowed to the courier once more. "I fear I must excuse myself a short while. As soon as I locate my mistress, I will present her to you."

"I am grateful," said the courier, making a gesture of dismissal.

Niklos knew it was folly to appear harassed or anxious, so he made himself walk at his usual pace. His first destination was the library, which he found empty. He stared into the dark, cavernous room, his thoughts momentarily blank. Then he went to his quarters to get his fur-lined cloak. As he opened the larger of two armoires, he rang for a lackey.

He was drawing on his boots when the lackey—a sleepy youth from Chatillon—entered his room. "I need a lanthorn and someone to accompany me," he said as he rose and pulled on his cloak. "I want no word of this to reach the courier."

The lackey bowed. "One of the other lackeys, perhaps?"

"You," said Niklos. "Get your cloak, bring the lanthorn and meet me at the stableyard door. As soon as possible."

The lackey blinked and gave a nod that was almost a bow. "Certainly, Aulirios."

"Thank you. Hurry," said Niklos, all but shoving the young man out the door. He glanced quickly around the room, and on impulse decided to carry a dagger with him. He tucked it into his sash at the waist. Satisfied, he left his quarters.

The young lackey was waiting at the stableyard door, not far from the pantry. He had wrapped himself in a threadbare cloak and carried a hooded lanthorn. He was not completely awake yet, but he appeared more alert than he had been before. "I am ready," he said in a tone that was not as convinced as his words.

"Good," said Niklos, indicating the young man should go ahead of him. "Have a look around."

The lackey did as he was told, reporting, "The stableyard is empty." He wanted to ask what else it would be at that hour, but could not summon the courage to speak.

"Fine," said Niklos, coming to his side and taking care to close the door.

"Where are we going?" asked the lackey, looking around in his apprehension. He had heard a few tales of the strange comings and goings at Eblouir and hoped he was not to be included in them, whatever they were.

"To the stables, of course," said Niklos as if it were a foolish question. As they walked through the blowing night, their steps revealed by a feeble circle of amber light from the lanthorn, he added, "What's your name?"

"Meres," said the lackey.

"You came here in August, didn't you? along with the two kitchen maids and a seamstress?" Niklos entered the shadow of the roof of the first rank of stalls; the greater darkness was less offset by the lanthorn, and the stable seemed to loom around them.

"Yes," said Meres, whispering.

Niklos chuckled. "There's no need to do that. Better to speak up, so we will not be treated as intruders."

Meres nodded, but could not bring himself to speak more loudly when he first tried. "Why would anyone . . . anyone suspect intruders?"

"You do not expect intruders," said Niklos patiently, a hint of a chuckle in his voice. "They arrive without invitation. And are not met with welcome."

"Yes," said Meres, repeating the word with more force. "But who would meet them here?"

"Oh, grooms, stablemen, farriers, horsemen," said Niklos carelessly. "And horses, certainly." He swung back the massive door that led to the corridor of stalls, whistling loudly as he did. He waited; there was an answering whistle. "I knew it," said Niklos to himself. "I knew it."

"What?" Meres asked, more confused than frightened now.

Niklos drew Meres through the door and secured it from the inside. "Which stall?" he called out, not loudly but sufficient to be heard.

"The seventh, left side," answered Olivia. "With the black yearling." Her voice was loud enough to be heard but steady and soft. "I finally got his foot into a bucket. Don't startle him. I'll have to do it all over again."

Niklos and Meres followed the sound of her voice to the stall she indicated. Lifting the lanthorn, they saw her seated on the straw bedding of the stall, dressed in men's clothes, her attention on the black yearling that stood fretfully with his right rear leg in a bucket. A strong odor of crushed herbs and camphor hung on the air.

"Don't bring the light any higher," Olivia said in the same calm way. "He's nervous enough without that. And he's restless, poor fellow. Try not to bother him, if you can." Very slowly and gracefully she got to her feet, patting the sleek black shoulder as she stood. "Good boy," she said to the horse. "Keep that leg soaking a little more." Then she looked curiously at Niklos. "Why have you come looking for me? It's late for anyone to be up. It must be after midnight."

"It is," said Niklos, smiling at her in a way that might have seemed indulgent in another. "However, one of the Abbe's couriers is waiting for you with an urgent dispatch. He's in the east salon with food and wine. The poor man looks worn to the bone. Whatever his errand, it must be important. I've tried not to rouse too much of the household." He indicated Meres with a nod. "Meres here has been very helpful."

The lackey blushed. "I have done . . . very little."

"And thank God for that," Niklos said softly and with feeling. "There are those on the staff who would have clarions and bells going by now. A courier's presence is generally supposed to be . . . clandestine. The Abbe has had such uneven fortunes this last year, it's no wonder he is being so cautious."

Olivia let herself out of the stall and secured the door behind her. "Well, I have to tend to Sabato here, but I suppose he can be left for a little while. I dislike leaving him unguarded; he's apt to kick the bucket over and make things worse. But the courier—" She shook her head.

"He must be seen at once, before more attention is drawn to

him." Niklos had that tone in his voice again, a warning that was more than it seemed to be.

"Yes, yes," said Olivia impatiently. "And you?" she added abruptly, turning to Meres. "What will you do?"

"Meres will do as you instruct him," said Niklos in that same quiet, pointed way. "You may rely on him."

Olivia regarded the young lackey, her expression all but unreadable. "It seems you are a very discreet fellow," she said to Meres. "Very well; I am grateful, and you will have proof of it," she promised, then gave her full attention to Niklos. "Tell me about the courier. What is he here for? Why has he come?"

"I don't know," said Niklos. "I am fairly sure he does not know why himself. He has a letter that is for your eyes only and he cannot retire until you have read it in his presence. It is twice sealed: very impressive. I hope none of the servants saw it when he showed it to me. Whatever is going on, it is most important and you may be sure it is secret. You chose the worst possible night to be out of the house." It may have been a trick of the lanthorn's unsteady light, but his features sharpened, shifted briefly, becoming menacing, then returning to the handsomeness that was familiar.

"I was not able to sleep, Niklos," said Olivia, her tone keener. "And this colt Sabato has a swollen leg—hock to pastern. So long as I could not sleep, I thought it might be best to get up and take care of him."

"So it seems, Olivia," said Niklos, taking a liberty that few French servants would dare to show to their masters.

Belatedly, Meres interrupted. "Do you mean you have been sitting out here in this stall, in the dark, with that colt? For hours? Alone?"

Olivia looked at him, a kind of amusement in her hazel eyes. "Yes. Is there some reason I should not?"

"But a dark stable, alone . . ." he protested.

"What is there to fear?" asked Olivia as she opened the stall door once more and spoke softly to Sabato. "I'm coming back, colt. Don't get bothered."

Meres came to the door of the stall. "What if the horse should injure you?"

"Him? Injure me?" Olivia said with disbelief. "I've been around horses for most of my life. Ask Niklos. He made a horsewoman out of me, when we were both much younger." As she spoke she bent and eased Sabato's leg out of the bucket. "You need another hour of that, but perhaps tomorrow night." As she straightened she picked up the bucket.

At once Meres moved to take the burden from her. "Madame," he objected. "No, you must not."

Olivia motioned him away. "Be careful. You'll frighten the colt." She gave the black a pat on the rump and he stepped aside, his movements quick and fidgity. As she left the stall, Olivia once again closed and braced the door. "The colt doesn't know you, Meres, and he is in a bad humor. Don't try to get near him now."

"But you must not carry buckets, Madame," said Meres with conviction. He had not learned all his responsibilities yet, but he was quite certain that the mistress of the household ought not to be permitted to carry buckets in a stable. He was, now he thought of it, not at all sure she ought to be in the stable, let alone tending horses. That she was wearing men's clothes was so shocking that he was not able to think about it at all.

"Don't be silly, Meres," said Olivia with her most winning smile. "I have been tending horses since before you were in swaddling bands." As she spoke she relinquished the bucket to Niklos, who had reached out for it. "Come. Back to the house. I need to think of a plausible excuse to account for my absence," she said in a more practical way. "Whatever I tell him, he is bound to report to the Abbe."

"Tell him the truth," suggested Niklos. "Mazarini knows that you care for your horses. Don't bother about the courier. His opinion means nothing." As they reached the enormous doors, Niklos paused to empty out the bucket. "It were better to see him now than require him to wait longer."

Olivia nodded, her face turned away from the lanthorn. She did not speak at once. "I suppose I must."

"It is nothing so dreadful," said Niklos. "The chances are that after so long a ride, he will not notice that you are dressed like a boy." He looked over at Meres as he put the bucket down. "What do you think?"

"It is sensible," said Meres, trying to puzzle out what these two required of him. He offered them the safest answer he could think of, though it sounded woefully inadequate to him, and hoped it would be enough.

"How diplomatic you are," said Olivia, laughter tingeing the words. "Very well, take me as I am, and we'll tell the poor man the truth." She reached back and untied the ribband that had secured her fawn-brown hair at the back of her neck. As she shook her head, it spread over her shoulders; the shorter tendrils that framed her face were not crimped, but hung loosely, like a child's crop. She did not look her age.

Niklos led the way across the stableyard. "Meres, before you retire for the evening, stop by my quarters." He opened the door and stood aside for Olivia to enter.

"As you wish, Aulirios," said Meres, more baffled than before.

There were a few night candles burning in the kitchen, and Olivia paused in the light of one, ignoring the stare of the scullery maid who had risen from her bed near the hearth when she heard voices. "Look at my hands," she said, holding them out, showing them water-wrinkled. She sniffed at them. "It is hardly perfume, is it?" She turned to Niklos. "Take me to the east salon, and then have someone fill my bath for me."

"Certainly," said Niklos, apparently unaware of the shock he saw in Meres' face. "Follow me." As he started down the hall, he said to Olivia over his shoulder. "You really look disreputable, Olivia. You do."

Instead of upbraiding her major domo—as Meres fully expected she would—Olivia laughed. "Well, you know what Roman widows are."

Meres watched them; he had no idea of what he ought to do next. He heard Olivia call his name. "Come, Meres. I need your help to lend me a little respectability." From the tone of her voice she was still amused. "Come," she repeated.

The courier was finishing off the last of a roast chicken and a plate of cabbage cooked in milk. He rose as Niklos entered the salon to announced "Bondame Atta Olivia Clemens," then stared as the woman herself strolled up to him.

In the hall, three lackeys gathered to watch until Niklos closed the door on them; of their numbers, only Meres would be privy to what happened in the east salon.

"Madame?" said the courier, reaching to take her hand, and then hesitating as he looked at her. He recovered himself and compromised with a bow. "Bondame Clemens?"

"Yes," said Olivia. "I ask your pardon for coming to you in this way, but one of my horses is not well, and I have been attending to him. I . . . lost track of the hour." She motioned to the divan. "Be seated, I pray you. Under the circumstances, there is no reason to stand on ceremony."

The courier murmured his thanks and resumed his seat. "Your servants have been—"

"Kindly and efficient, I trust," said Olivia. "It is no less than what I expect of them." She started to move a chair nearer the divan, but Meres intercepted her and carried the chair for her. "My lackey is an excellent example," she said, a bit drily. As she sat down, she indicated the leather dispatch case the courier carried over his arm. "You have something for me, I understand."

The courier nodded. "Yes. A letter. It is double-sealed and I must have your signature across the broken seals. I am charged to give it to you and to watch you read it. If there is a response, I am asked to take it to Cardinal Richelieu on Mazarin's behalf." He had assumed a more formal manner as he spoke, as if the words themselves imparted dignity and importance to the occasion.

"Ah," said Olivia, motioning to Niklos. "I require a pen and my inkstand, it appears. Bring them here, will you? And while you are away, be sure that a bedchamber is ready for our guest." She looked toward the courier. "It is proper to rest, isn't it?"

"I have to reach Richelieu before mid-day," he said, but went on, "I am grateful, Madame, for what you offer. I will accept the bed gladly, and bless your name tomorrow when I ride to Paris." He let the wide leather strap of the dispatch case slide down his arm.

"I will fetch your writing tools," said Niklos, bowing. He signaled to Meres as he opened the door. "Stand here. No one is to enter but myself. And when it is finished, you will forget what you have seen."

Meres swallowed once. "I will forget."

Niklos gave him a slap on the shoulder. "Good fellow," he said before he let himself out of the salon.

"How is the Abbe?" Olivia asked the courier.

"He is . . . fretful," said the courier, choosing the word with care. "There have been so many delays, and there is the question of ordination . . ." He reached out and took a sip of wine from the tankard.

"Which he still refuses?" Olivia asked, although she knew the answer.

"He declares he does not have the vocation, and will not profane ordination if it is lacking," said the courier, coolly repeating what he had heard so many times. "There are Cardinals who do not wish a . . . mere Abbe in their company."

"That is the excuse they give, I am sure," said Olivia, looking speculatively at the courier. "How long have you been in Mazarini's service?"

"He accepted me five months ago," said the courier. "I was recommended to him by my mother's second cousin once removed, Armand Jean du Plessis, Cardinal Richelieu." The Cardinal was his most exalted relative and it always gave him a moment of pride to reveal this connection.

"A most capable man. I have had the pleasure to meet him on two occasions," said Olivia, with the appearance of more interest than she felt. Titles and relatives had long ago lost the power to impress her.

"Yes," said the courier. "He honored me with the introduction to Mazarin." He opened his dispatch case. "The letter is—"

"Double-sealed," Olivia finished for him. "Yes, you have said so." In spite of herself, she was becoming curious about the contents of the letter. Perhaps, she thought, it would recall her to Roma. It would be unwise to return so soon, but it was tempting; she missed her home, her language, her annealing native earth.

"Madame?" said the courier, seeing something of her thoughts reflected in her face. "Is something the matter?"

Olivia gave herself a mental shake. "No, nothing. The hour, I suppose." She looked up as Niklos came back into the salon, carrying the small case that contained her writing tools.

"There are two trimmed pens," said Niklos as he brought this to her. "I refilled the sand."

"Many thanks," said Olivia, putting the little case on the table and opening it. "Very well, then, courier: let me see what you bring me from Mazarini."

The courier rose and bowed as he handed her the letter, looking a little surprised that she did not do the same. Olivia took the letter in her hands and kissed the first of the two seals, looking with curiosity at the Colonna arms pressed into the wax. She lifted the ends of the enclosing ribband and pulled the seal from the letter. Then she leaned forward, dipped one of the pens in the standish, and scrawled her name across the place where the seal had been. Out of this first envelope, she drew a second, once again kissed the seal before she pulled it off and signed her name. As she spread out the sheet, she crossed herself, and the courier nodded with approval as he drank his wine and watched her read.

Olivia's face was emotionless as she read; it was only after she had perused the document twice that she smiled. "I am pleased to receive the news you have brought me," she said carefully, knowing that she was not permitted to reveal the contents of what she had read. "I will do as the Abbe requests and I am in readiness to fulfill his commands at any time." It was a safe enough formula, and she looked directly at the courier. "Tell Mazarini and Richelieu that I will burn candles."

The courier touched his right hand to his chest. "On my honor," he declared.

"My thanks to you, once more," said Olivia as she rose. "I am told to destroy this after reading." She walked to the hearth and looked down into the low-burning fire there. "You may observe me do as I have been asked." With that, she dropped the vellum sheet into the flames, then stood watching until the sheet was nothing more than a curl of ash. When she turned, she bowed to the courier. "I thank you again," she said, then motioned to Meres. "As soon as the courier is ready, pray escort him to the blue bedchamber on the second floor, the one that faces south."

Meres bowed. "As you command, Madame."

Olivia favored him with a faintly mocking roguish grin before turning to Niklos. "Attend me."

The courier gave a single diplomatic cough. "There is no other answer you wish me to carry?"

"Only what I have told you," said Olivia. "It is often wisest to have care in answers, don't you agree? There was nothing in the letter that required more than I have told you." She offered him a farewell gesture that was more of a salute than a wave. "God give you good sleep, courier," she said as she left the room with Niklos.

"All right," whispered Niklos in Byzantine Greek as they went down the hall. "What was in the letter?"

"Our employer will soon be coming back to France; it's finally been arranged. He will leave Roma before the end of the year. The official documents are being drawn up now, and no one has stopped them. There will be a formal notice within the month," said Olivia in the same language. "And why must we speak this awful stuff? It reminds me of Justinian."

Niklos shook his head. "No; and not Belisarius. It reminds you of Drosos."

Olivia did not answer at once. "Yes," she admitted as they started up the stairs to her apartments. "It does. Poor Drosos," she said softly. "No one should have to endure what he did." Her mouth was a thin, hard line, and then she managed a bit of a smile. "But you're right. It is the safest language. Who in this household can speak it but us?"

"Exactly," said Niklos, pointing down the hall. "The bath will be ready in a short while. You might as well get undressed and into your night rail."

"No." Olivia made a face. "I don't want fine muslin and lace to smell of horse linament," she said, stopping at the door to her apartments. When she spoke again, it was not in the old tongue of Constantinople, but in French. "Is Avisa still awake?"

"She was a quarter hour ago," said Niklos. "She said she wanted to take a composer and go to sleep."

"I'll look in on her, in case," said Olivia, and resumed her Byzantine Greek. "Niklos, how much longer do you think Richelieu can hang on?"

"You know that better than I," Niklos said in French, evasively. "He is failing steadily, we know that, but with a will like his . . ." He lifted one of his hands, palm up and open to show that no one could judge Richelieu's will.

"In Greek, Niklos. We may be watched," she cautioned him. "About Richelieu: Mazarini must be aware." She looked over her shoulder, her brows drawn down in concentration.

"You've mentioned Richelieu's health in your reports, haven't you?" Niklos said, wondering why Olivia was distressed.

"Yes, but . . ." She made herself stop. "There is nothing I can do, is there? I am not the only one who reports to the Abbe. Mazarini will have to see for himself. Now that he is finally going to be Mazarin." She sighed, her tension fading. She returned to French. "It was fortunate, I suppose, that all I was doing was tending to a horse tonight. If I had been . . . elsewhere . . ."

"But you weren't," said Niklos, continuing to use Greek. "And if you were, no one would know it, in any case. You still visit your men in dreams, don't you?"

"Yes," she said with defiance. "And I will continue to."

Niklos looked at her with mild annoyance. "You will not have a lover? When you know how much you—"

"Only if a lover will have me," said Olivia, sadness replacing defiance.

For a brief moment the two looked at each other, a stillness between them. Then Niklos sighed. "Go take your bath," he said in French as he turned back toward the stairs.

* * *

*Text of a letter from Jules Mazarin to his fourteen-year-old sec-
ond cousin, Gennaro Colonna, written in French.*

May God bless and keep you, Gennaro, and give you a love of
learning as well as a quick tongue, for your last letter shows me
that you are not as attentive as a youth of your station must be if
he is to fulfill his position in life. In the hope of rekindling that
devotion which gave you such promise, I greet you in the name of
our family and in the name of the good people of France, who are
our most worthy friends.

It is now a little more than a year—a year and five days, to be
precise—since I returned to Paris. It has been an eventful year,
although that is of no concern to us now, other than the demands it
makes on my time and skills at the pleasure of the great Richelieu.
It is a great honor to be able to serve so great a master and to act on
behalf of the good people of France.

I am pleased to tell you that the winter has not been dreadful,
though, naturally, it is more severe than what you are used to. The
new canal linking the Loire to the Seine has proved most valuable
and those who scoffed at its worth have seen this winter how useful
such a waterway is. The previous objections are now silenced.

The problems with Catalonia continue, and I fear they are not
going to be ended easily or swiftly, though we are praying this
might be so. Portugal has elected Joao da Braganza to be King and
has declared that they are no longer under the rule of Spain. I fear
that the Queen and I are in disagreement on this issue, and I have
been reluctant to discuss it with her, for it sends her into such
displeasure. Were it not for the revolt of Catalonia, it would be
impossible for Portugal to defy Spanish rule in this way, and as
France supports Catalonia, Her Majesty is in great distress.

Yes, we understand that what you have heard about money in
England is true: its value has been decreased and is now worth less
than a half of what it was before. This is causing great hardship,
because so many find that they cannot afford food and shelter.
There are rumors that many merchants have reduced their invento-
ries because no one is able to purchase what they have.

It is not prudent for me to tell you anything about Richelieu's health, for that could easily be misunderstood by others to the disadvantage of His Eminence and his work. I would not be worthy of the trust he has placed in me if I said anything to you. As to the health of the King, His Majesty continues to suffer from poor digestion and other minor complaints. He has recently lost flesh and has been prey to every little malady, which troubles his physicians. This is known in the world, and prayers are offered everywhere for his speedy return to health, which God grant for the betterment of France.

The Heir is an active child, one who is cossetted and guarded with care. Whether this will prove to be a wise thing when he is older is uncertain, but I have given my word to His Majesty, Her Majesty, Richelieu, and God that I will be at pains to be sure that nothing harms the boy. His mother is devoted to her boy and shows him great affection. Because of the child, she, who for so long has lived in obscurity and neglect, has now some position in the court for the sake of the Heir, and she uses it well, for she has few illusions. The years she spent in virtual exile in her own apartments taught her not to trust the favor of the court, nor to rely on the promises of courtiers.

While I was visiting Her Majesty two days after Christmas, I happened to hear one of the ladies-in-waiting telling a tale to the little boy, who surely did not understand it. But I thought it an interesting tale, similar to ones I have heard in my youth. It has, I believe, a lesson apropos to you, and so I will relate it to you.

There was a poor man blessed in nothing but the number of children he and his wife brought into the world. He worked day and night to provide for them and to try to find a place for them, and protection of those who could provide more than they for their children. Imagine then his despair when his wife presented him with a thirteenth child. Not only was the boy another mouth to feed and provide for, but he was a thirteenth child, which was considered most unlucky. The poor man could find no one to be godmother or godfather to this last child; all the goodwill of their friends was exhausted, and none wanted to sponsor so ill-placed an infant. Then, when the poor man was walking from his fields to his home, a great black carriage came along the road and stopped by the poor man. The door opened and a woman dressed in a black cloak stepped out.

She explained to the poor man that she was Death and that she

would serve as the godmother to the thirteenth child, who was chris-
tened with the name Want, for his family was poor, and he had
been in want of a sponsor until Death offered her services. Death
promised to protect her godson and help him to prosper and advance
in the world, and to that end, she took Want into her household
when he was twelve.

Want was a respectful and attentive boy, and proved himself of
use to his godmother. She, in turn, provided Want with a secret he
could use in the world, as she had told his parents she would. She
said to him: "When you are called upon to treat those who are
injured or ill, if you see me standing at the foot of the bed, you will
know that person will recover. If you see me standing at the head of
the bed, you know the person will presently die. Use this secret to
make your fortune."

Soon the fame of Want spread, for everywhere it was known that
he could cure all those he agreed to treat. He prospered even as his
godmother promised, and he was soon so famous that when the
King's daughter grew ill, the King sent his own carriage for Want,
to bring him to the palace to treat his daughter. Want was over-
joyed at this opportunity and thought himself the most fortunate of
men, until he arrived at the palace and discovered that his god-
mother was standing at the head of the Princess' bed, and the beau-
tiful girl was marked to die. He knew it was useless to plead with
Death, for she heeds no prayers. Want had only his wits to guide
him.

The answer came to him in a flash. He told the King to bring
four men-at-arms to turn the Princess' bed around, so that the head
was now where the foot had been, and Death was at the Princess'
feet.

The Princess recovered at once and professed herself grateful to
Want and thankful to God for sparing her. But Death was not
pleased, and would not stay to speak with her godson.

The King promised to ennoble Want and to make him his son-in-
law, which filled the Princess with such happiness that she sang all
day long and prayed half the night. The wedding was celebrated
with pomp and grandeur, and Want decided that he was the most
favored of all men.

It was at the height of the festivities after the wedding that
Want's godmother suddenly appeared, arriving in her black car-
riage. She was dressed in her black cloak, and those who looked
upon her were fascinated and afraid. She treated her godson with

respect and did him honor, and then declared that she needed to have a last word with him, to present him with his wedding gift, and bade Want to follow her. Until that moment, Want had never feared his godmother, but now his entrails turned cold and his knees shook as he followed his protectress into a deep cavern in the earth where she had heaped up the treasures of her long life. "Here," she said. "You may take what you may. But for everything you take, one of the candles lighting the cavern will be extinguished."

Want felt relief, thinking that his godmother was not distressed with him as he had feared she might be. He began at once to gather up gold and jewels and coffers filled with coins and all the while the candles, one after another, flickered and went out. "There is only one candle remaining," Death told her godson when his arms were fully laden.

"Then I will take that crystal chalice," said Want, and reached for the glorious cup.

In that instant, the cavern was completely dark; everything vanished, and Want heard Death say to him: "I am not tricked, godson, not by you or any man. For the candles are the years of your life, and once they are gone, this cavern becomes your grave." Then there was a great darkness as Want met his fate.

My cousin, when you long to be profligate again, remember Want and his cavern of candles, and do not waste your time in accumulating vain treasure, but seek to improve the state of your mind and your soul. Surely these are of greater importance and are more enduring than the amusements you have sought so heedlessly. If you fritter away your time, there will be nothing for you at the end of your life, and it will come all the sooner for your venality. You have been the hope, the flower of your family, and you now forsake them as easily as a man turns a cur from his door, which is to the shame of all. Return to the ways of piety and virtue and the treasures of Heaven will be yours.

Throughout Lent I will say special prayers for you, and I will beseech Our Lord and the Virgin to bring you once again to Grace. It is the hope of your mother that you might one day enter my service, but that will not be possible if you continue as you have been behaving these last two years. Think of what I have told you and repent. There is great harmony to be achieved by those who free themselves of sin and place their hearts humbly into the Hands of God.

Let me hear from you before Easter, and let what I hear be more promising than what I have been told of late.

Jules Mazarin, Abbe
By the Grace and Mercy of God
In Paris on the 10th day of January, 1641.
Keep this with your journals.

· 3 ·

April was unseasonably warm; the sails of the windmills hung listlessly in the sultry air as Olivia entered her coach and prepared to be driven into Paris. She carried a fan and used it occasionally, though there was no sign of sweat on her lip or her brow. As they neared the walls of Paris, the coachman reined his team into a walk, for the roadway was crowded.

At the gate, Olivia's coachman presented her invitation to visit Richelieu to the Guards and the carriage was let through at once. Entering the city, their progress was slow, for the narrow streets were crowded with every kind of vehicle and with vendors, some with carts or donkeys, some on foot, all crying their wares. The din was constant and incomprehensible.

It might be faster, Olivia thought, if I simply got out and walked the rest of the way. She chuckled, thinking of the times she had done just that. How distant those times seemed to her now. Her mind drifted back through the centuries as she did her best to forget the noise, the smell, and the heat. There had been heat in Tyre and Alexandria, but it was different from this, less sodden, sharpened by desert winds. There had been heat in Gran after the Mongols came. Jajee was hot, a little more than a hundred years ago, when the Ottomites had come—no wonder she had gone north to London after a brief return to Roma. She was recalling that hideous sea voyage with some rueful amusement when the carriage stopped suddenly.

"Bueve," Olivia called out to her coachman. "What's the matter?"

"There's something up ahead. Men are fighting. I can see them, but I don't know who—" The coachman sounded hesitant, which was unlike him.

"Then go around them," said Olivia, starting to lean out one of the windows. In the next instant she ducked back inside as a rock thudded against the door panel. The sides of the coach rattled as more rocks struck it and she heard Bueve utter a sharp oath as one of the stones struck him. "What on earth!" she said, anger replacing confusion. "What is going on? Why are we under attack?" She rapped hard on the ceiling of the coach. "Bueve! How badly are you hurt?"

"I'll have a lump and a bruise," he said, his voice weaker than usual. "The off-side wheeler's taken blows to his legs from the rocks. I don't know how—"

Another rock struck and this time Bueve howled.

"Bueve!" Olivia shouted, and when he gave her no answer, she moved with determination. Despite the angry shouts and the continuing rain of pebbles and rocks as well as other, less appetising, things, Olivia shoved open the coach door and set her foot on the steps to the coachman's box. She could hear the team whinnying and one of the horses was kicking steadily at the body of the coach. Ignoring the shouts and missiles around her, Olivia pulled herself into the box and took the reins from Bueve's nerveless fingers. She gave him a perfunctory examination, determining that he was only unconscious, though his color was not good. She then gathered up the reins and reached for the long coaching whip, swinging it expertly over her team's heads to bring them back under control.

When half a brick struck her shoulder, she turned abruptly and flicked the whip over the heads of the mob, then gave her attention once again to her horses.

The fighting up ahead grew worse, and at last she could see that some of the combatants were in the mantle of the Cardinal's Guards. The rest appeared to be poorly dressed citizens, a few of them with narrow green sashes tied around their waists. The Guards had been backed up against the side of an old church where they could not easily defend themselves, which leant fury to the people attacking them.

Suddenly there was a change in the crowd: a troop of King's Guards emerged from one of the nearby alleys, all with swords at the ready. The crowd, seeing them, faltered, and a few tried to push through their numbers to get away. Four men in blood-spattered clothes tried to climb into Olivia's coach.

Olivia had just slid Bueve onto the floor of the coachman's box and was not yet in position to ward off these rioters. She pulled herself upright and tightened her hold on the whip. "Back!" Olivia shouted, and used her whip to fend them off. She drew in the reins as closely as she could, but even her enormous strength was put to the test by her four terrified horses.

A woman with big arms and her hair tied up in a makeshift turban tried to grab the harness of the on-side leader, and Olivia struck out at her as well, flicking the lash off the woman's back. She was so occupied keeping her horses under minimal control and preventing her coach from being taken or turned over that she was not aware of the alteration in the battle before her, though she could feel in the movement of her horses the shifting eddies of the force of the crowd, like a turn of tide and current.

She had just stopped one scar-faced cheese vendor from climbing up onto the box by delivering him a sharp kick with her square-heeled shoe when she felt the coach list back and to the right, and realized that two men had climbed to the roof from behind. It was impossible to release the reins, for then the horses would bolt and the carriage would very probably be wrecked. Tearing the shoulders of her puffed brocaded sleeves, Olivia swung around as far as the confines of the box permitted, her arm drawing the whip back, sensing already that she was a heartbeat too late.

Before she could strike, one of the men seized her arm and wrenched the whip out of her hand as the other lunged toward her, a dagger held low, aimed at her pearl-embroidered plastron. His grin was predatory, showing broken front teeth, and he began to curse her as he moved forward, signaling the other man to work around behind her. His eyes, red-rimmed, were full of hate and greedy lust.

"No," said Olivia as she struck out with the heel of her hand in a sharp, upward blow that caught the man with the knife under his jaw and snapped his head back. The man swore and clung precariously to the roof of the carriage, but did not fall.

His accomplice, taking advantage of this, threw himself forward, trying to confine Olivia's arms as he grasped her around her waist. Holding her was more difficult than he thought it would be, and it required all his concentration and strength to hang onto her, muttering obscenities as he did.

Below in the street the crowd was milling, trying now to disperse. The King's Guard and the Cardinal's Guard, ordinarily the most bitter rivals, joined their ranks to move the rioters from the street. The rioters now were shouting more and fighting less as they looked for ways to escape.

The first man had recovered enough from Olivia's blow to be enraged. He shook his head once as if clearing water from his eyes, then started toward her, making tentative, threatening strikes with his knife. He growled as he neared her, raising the knife so that it now moved only a handbreadth from her face.

Olivia tried to block this with her elbow, but between her hampering clothing and the man wrestling with her, she was not able to swing her arm far enough, and all that she accomplished was another long rent in her brocade sleeve. "You are scum, vermin," she hissed at the two through her teeth, though she realized it was folly to provoke them more.

The carriage rocked as three fighting men lumbered into it, and the horses almost broke from Olivia's failing hold on the reins. The men atop the coach struggled to keep their purchase as the vehicle teetered, then righted itself. One of the horses squealed as a wild thrust from a long dagger wielded by a limping onion-seller bit into his shoulder, and Olivia strove to gain enough control of the reins to hold the injured animal in check.

The man with the knife made a sudden swipe, and a thin line of blood appeared on Olivia's forehead. "Look, she bleeds like a common trollop." His laughter was more angry than his grumbled blasphemies had been.

Olivia spat at him, then tried again to break free of the hold of the second man.

"She's a handful," gasped the second man as Olivia almost succeeded in getting her foot free of her skirts to kick out again. "Be careful!"

Again the first man laughed, a sound like steel scraping on stone. "That's good, that's good. Don't want her to be too easy. Don't want her laughing at us. No fun in that." His knife swung toward Olivia, but this time she was ready for it, and avoided its blade. The man cursed vilely and thrust out for her throat.

Then his arm faltered, the dagger dropped from his hand and he made an odd coughing sound before falling slowly off the roof of the coach.

"Release her," said a young man with a Gascon accent who appeared over the edge of the roof. He was wearing the mantle of the King's Guard, his red-bladed sword aimed directly at the belly of the man who clung to Olivia. "Now. Unless you want to join your companion."

The man drew back, half-raising his hands to show that he had let go of Olivia. "No, no, Monsieur—"

The Guardsman was on the roof of the coach now, and he reached out to Olivia. "Move nearer to me, Madame," he said, and as soon as she complied, he struck out with the hilt of his sword, hitting the man on the shoulder and sending him sprawling backward into the dwindling crowd.

Olivia turned to her rescuer to thank him, but the words caught in her throat as she saw the shocked expression on his face. In the next instant, she felt blood from the cut spread into her eye, and she brought her hand up.

"No, Madame," said the Guardsman, wiping his sword and sheathing it before taking her arm. "Do not touch it. We do not know how severe it is," he said, the horror gone from his large brown eyes.

"It isn't severe," said Olivia, her tone more uneven than she thought it would be. She wanted to smile to reassure him she was not seriously hurt, but her mouth began to tremble and she could not do it.

"You do not want it to leave a scar," said the Guardsman, coming to the edge of the coachman's box.

"It won't," said Olivia with complete certainty. Not since she clawed her way out of her tomb to Sanct' Germain had her skin taken any blemish, and this cut she knew would be no exception. "Truly," she added, her manner softening to him as her fright and indignation began to fade.

The Guardsman got into the coachman's box beside her. "You are very brave, Madame. A paragon. But let me tend to that cut. And your team, if you will hand me the reins." His smile was impulsive and generous, very like the one she had intended to show him; he held out his gloved hand. "I will get us off this street and then I will examine your forehead. Will that satisfy you?"

To her inward surprise, Olivia nodded her acceptance without objection. "That might be best. One of the team has been cut; I need to see to that. And to my coachman."

"Ah!" said the Guardsman as he looked down into the bottom of the coachman's box and saw Bueve crumpled there. "I feared he fled and left you to your own devices—which were impressive, but still . . ."

Olivia did not respond. She started to bend over to Bueve, but as she did, her vision wobbled as she became dizzy and had to lift her head again. "I . . . I will need your assistance to pull him upright," she said, embarrassed by her request.

"Of course, as soon as we are off the street and I have seen to your cut," said the Guardsman as he gathered the reins in his hand and began to coax the team into moving once more. "A pity you haven't another whip."

"Yes," she said, watching him handle her team with critical eyes. "Take care. Nerone, the off-side wheeler, is nervous of loud noises."

"I will keep that in mind," said the Guardsman, his face alive with curiosity. "How does it come you know the temperament of this team?"

"I bred them," said Olivia bluntly. "I know my horses." She felt the first bite of a headache—a rare occurrence for her—and she winced as the coach began to move again.

The Guardsman stood up in the box and shouted down to a few of the Guardsmen nearby who had finished with the rioters. "Arnaud! Ehi! Arnaud!" He struggled with the team as one of the Guardsmen on the street finally approached the carriage. "Be a good fellow and tell des Essarts that I am escorting this Bondame to her destination."

Arnaud cocked his head, his shoulder-length curls in bloody disorder. "How long will you be?"

"That depends on where she is bound, I suppose," answered the Guardsman, inclining his head toward Olivia. "Where are you expected, Madame?"

"His Eminence Richelieu has invited me to visit him," said Olivia with all the propriety she could muster. She wished that she were not sitting in the box of her coach with blood on her face and her clothes torn.

"The Cardinal," Arnaud said, impressed and wary at once, for the King's Guard did not often support Richelieu unless ordered to do so by the King. He looked at his comrade with a speculative gleam in his eyes. "And will you make a report to His Eminence, Charles?"

"I leave that to his Guard," said Charles a bit stiffly. "Let us get under way. And assure des Essarts that I will not forget myself."

Apparently both Guardsmen found this funny, for they laughed and exchanged casual salutes as Charles continued to maneuver the team into a gentle turn at a very slow walk. "I do not want them to go any faster, Madame," he explained to Olivia.

"I would do the same myself, Monsieur." She cleared her throat, going on, "I fear all your name I know is Charles."

"Charles de Batz-Castelmore," he said, introducing himself with nothing more than a touch to the brim of his plumed hat. "I will offer my bow later."

"You are a Gascon," said Olivia, hating the way her head rang as she spoke. Few things caused her hurt and nothing gave her lasting injury except what brought the true death as well; but those few pains she did suffer were acute, as if to compensate for her great durability.

"Yes, and proud to be one. Better a poor Gascon than a rich Parisian." He hesitated. "I mean no offence, Madame."

"You give none; I am a Roman." Olivia paused, realizing that it was not proper for her to provide him with her name without another person to introduce them. How many foolish restrictions had been put on people over the centuries! she thought, and said, "I am Atta Olivia Clemens, a member of—"

"The Italian's suite, I'll be bound," said Charles with ill-concealed irritation. He did not look at her, being occupied with getting the wounded horse to keep moving—without a whip this took great skill with the reins.

"I am sorry if that distresses you." Olivia had to cling to the side of the coachman's box to keep from swaying as the vehicle began to move down the cobbled streets. Magna Mater! this was almost as bad as being at sea. What had that cut to her head done? It had been decades since she felt so faint.

Charles brought the team to a halt and turned to her. "You are in pain, Madame."

"Not . . . badly," said Olivia, drawing breath more quickly. "It will pass."

With a swift move, Charles set the brake and wrapped the reins around its handle. Then, as he pulled off his gloves, he turned Olivia's face toward him. "You *are* in pain, Madame," he repeated, this time with concern, and he brushed the crimped hair off her forehead. "It is still bleeding a little."

Olivia nodded twice, like an automaton. What a beautiful young man he is, she thought, and mocked herself for thinking it.

Still, she liked his face, especially the up-tilted flying brows over clear brown eyes. His hair, a rusty chestnut color, was not as curly as fashion demanded, fell in waves to his shoulder. He had a small, neat beard and moustache; Olivia thought these looked a bit silly on a man so young, but held back her comments. "It will be all right," she said.

"I have a cloth," Charles announced, and reached into the wallet that hung from his sash. "Here." He held it out to her, then kept it and dabbed gently at the wound himself. "You must tell me if I hurt you."

"No," she said, trying not to stare at him, silently upbraiding herself. How old is he? she demanded inwardly. At most, twenty. It is your coach and fine clothes that make him courteous and helpful. He seeks a reward, being a poor Gascon in the King's Guard. He is not interested in a woman your age, even one your apparent age. She realized she had put her hand over his as he finished brushing her face with his cloth.

"It is as much as I can do now, Madame," he said, his eyes directly on hers. "I will pray to the Virgin to thank her for this." He brought her hand to his lips.

Olivia tried to make light of this gallantry and found she could only stammer. "I . . . a-as well."

A grin broke out on Charles' open features. "Madame," he said briskly. "Let me take you to the Louvre at once. I will wait there to see that your coachman receives proper attention from the physicians, and then I will myself escort you to your home, for you will need protection." He was clearly pleased with himself.

"You have duties as a King's Guard," said Olivia, recovering herself somewhat at last.

"And none more pressing than guarding honest folk in service to the King and his court," said Charles promptly with wicked amusement in his eyes. "You are part of an embassy. It is shocking that you should have been treated so . . . so barbarically here in Paris. I am obliged to see that no further incidents befall you." He reached for the reins and loosed them, then he released the brake. "While you confer with Richelieu—and I warrant he has not had many visitors like you—I will send word to des Essarts to tell him of my plan." He nodded with satisfaction as he got the horses moving again.

"And if he does not give permission?" Olivia inquired, her feelings so confused that she wondered if she should ask Richelieu to arrange other transport for her.

"He will," said Charles happily. "It will mean showing up the Cardinal's Guard, for they were there and they did nothing to assist you. Des Essarts will give me three days' leave to escort you if I ask for it." His eyes suddenly narrowed. "Unless you refuse to have me."

There it was, thought Olivia with a tiny sigh. He has only aided me, and if I do not let him continue to aid me, I will give him a slight for his kindness. She looked down at her hands and was surprised to see bruises on her knuckles and two broken nails. "If your Captain will allow it, then it would be churlish of me to say no."

Charles laughed aloud. "This is the Bondame Roman, not the lady I saw fighting ruffians."

Bueve moaned and half opened his eyes. Peering through purple, swollen lids, he blinked at the team and then at the Guardsman handling the reins. He made a garbled sound and grabbed out for the reins.

Before Charles could do anything, Olivia restrained her coachman, holding his arms down and forcing him back in the hard wooden seat. "Bueve, no. Leave him alone."

The coachman tried to speak, then spat out three teeth and a mouthful of blood. Where he was not bruised he was the color of new cheese, and there was a film of cold sweat on his face. He put a shaking hand to his mouth and muttered something.

"Do not worry, Bueve," said Olivia with more purpose than she truly felt. "The Cardinal will see that your wounds are tended, and those responsible will—"

"I will attend to them," said Charles, holding the team to a walk. "It will not be difficult to learn who started the fray, and then all I need do is find them alone long enough to teach them manners with an arm's length of steel."

Olivia knew it was proper for her to object to this plan, for a member of a King's regiment was under oath not to pursue private battles; her own inclinations were as fierce as those of the young Guardsman beside her, but she compromised with what was expected of her and said, "I have known those in Roma to settle disputes in that way."

Charles nodded once with great determination. "There is something to admire in Romans after all. Other than their women, of course." He grinned, then gave his attention to the reins as they crossed the Seine and neared another open square. "The Place des

Enfantes," said Charles. "They don't bring children here now, but I was told they did once, a long time ago."

"Oh?" She put an arm around Bueve, who was swaying with every motion of the coach.

"When Paris was under siege, before the Crusades, or so they say." Charles shrugged to show that he did not necessarily believe this. "One of the other Guardsmen says they were Germans, but des Essarts says they were Danes."

"So many years," she said, thinking yes, long ago when Viking ships came up the Seine to bring raiders. Then there had been a squat, walled monastery whose monks—had they been Ambroisians?—had sheltered children while their parents battled the Norsemen in their long ships. She had witnessed two such battles, and had, in fact, been badly wounded in the first. It had taken her months to recover and a few of the monks were afraid when she did, for she had no scars when she was healed. As she looked around the Place des Enfantes, she saw almost nothing she recognized now but a small portion of the wall that had once enclosed the monks' vegetable garden.

"And a foe we need not fear again. No German army shall set foot in Paris again." He guided the coach into the next street.

"Watch the off-side wheeler," Olivia warned, for the gelding was starting to toss his head. "He'll get behind the bit if he keeps that up."

Charles jobbed the rein expertly. "Now he will not." He turned to Olivia for an instant. "You are knowledgeable with horses, Madame, that is plain."

"I raise them," said Olivia, not quite smiling. She looked down the narrow street and saw with disappointment that they were nearing the Louvre. When the Vikings had attacked, it had been nothing more than a small keep with enormous kennels around it, the dogs bred for hunting and for battle. Philippe Auguste had changed all that, and Charles V had expanded and improved the chateau until it was a self-contained city. Olivia had never liked the place.

Charles brought the coach to a halt at one of the side entrances and identified himself to the officer of the Household Guard on duty. "I bring Bondame Clemens to her meeting with His Eminence Richelieu, and request that a physician be brought at once." He climbed out of the coachman's box and waited while an official groom came to lead the team away. "They have been ill-treated by rioters," he said.

The Household Guardsman saluted and made a gesture of dismissal. "Thanks for your good service," he said to Charles.

But Charles did not leave. He held up his hand to assist Olivia down from the coach, saying to the Household Guardsman and to Olivia at once, "Your pardon, sir; I am charged with the protection of Bondame Clemens until she is once again safe within her own walls."

As Olivia descended the side of the carriage, she marveled at Charles' audacity, and was not terribly surprised when he met her eyes and winked.

*　　*　　*

Text of a letter from Jean-Arnaud du Peyrer de Troisvilles to Henri Coiffier de Ruze.

Monsieur le Marquise,

For a man of great position, you are not acting wisely. Since you have solicited my comments, you may have them only as courtesy to your position at court and your rank.

First, yes, I am, as I have always been, still opposed to the policies of Richelieu. My sentiments are not unknown to His Majesty, nor, I expect, to the Cardinal. I am known to have spoken against the Italian Abbe; I do not deny that he is a capable man of a sort, and his bravery is a matter of record, but I am not convinced that he acts in the best interests of France as I understand them. I am sworn to uphold the King unto death, and I pray God I will have the opportunity to demonstrate my loyalty on the field of battle.

But as regards your suggestion that assassination is the solution to our difficulties with the Cardinal, this does not convince me. Such deaths may appear expedient, but they are not acts of patriots but of those determined to destroy government. If the outrages you have described are as many and as flagrant as you have said, then bring this to His Majesty. If the King orders me to arrest anyone, I will do it for honor, and for my oath as his officer. The King's Musqueteers are not brigands to be hired or bribed, and it demeans every one of them to have your request brought to me in so clandestine a fashion. If it is not the King's will that I do such a thing, then it would dishonor me, my family, and my regiment for as long as the Kingdom of France endures.

You hint of illustrious supporters and many offers for fighting men and supplies in order to bring about the change you seek, but nowhere do you say who these men are, or what they expect to achieve in joining with you, and this causes me great concern, for if you have set yourself above the King in your actions, then you are no different from Richelieu himself, and you are as much a part of what I am sworn to end in France as is Richelieu and his Italian Abbe.

I will continue to oppose Richelieu, but only as the King permits. To act on your suggestion without the specific orders of the King is repellent to me. Until you can present such orders, I cannot participate in your venture, whether or not I agree with the ends you claim to endorse.

If you are planning to bring down Richelieu without the support and knowledge of the King, then realize that Louis may well regard what you do as treason, not assistance. You may be assured that I will not betray you: you were given my word when you first approached me and I will stand by it. That you question it at all is an offence that in another fighting man would demand that we meet on the field of honor. You, being a man of rank and under the protection of my master and his vicious dog, are untouchable by such a man as I, and I would be more than imprudent to risk so great a transgression for the satisfaction of meeting you. You may continue to rely on my silence and upon my oath taken to protect His Majesty for both spring from the same well and both are sacred to me.

Jean-Arnaud du Peyrer de Troisvilles
The King's Musqueteers

On the 18th day of July, 1641.

A notarized complete copy of this letter has been retained in the records of the King's Musqueteers.

· 4 ·

His expostulation was pithy and expert, in the lowest gutter Italian, and for those few moments, Jules Mazarin was once again Giulio Mazarini. Then he brought himself under control and returned to French. "I was promised! I was assured that they would make me a Cardinal whether I was in Rome or not, whether I was ordained a priest or not. I was not the only one: Richelieu was told it would happen!"

Olivia had stopped making notes on the report Niklos had prepared for her on the small harvest at Eblouir as well as the most recent letter from her stud farm at Tours. She had taken to spending part of her afternoons here in the library, and it was here that she received her unexpected visitor. "What is necessary, Eminence?"

"If I am to succeed Richelieu, I need that hat! Without such rank, I will not be able to step into the shoes Richelieu is readying for me; I will not be in a position to do the work the King will expect of me." He paced in front of the six tall windows, looking out once toward the walls of Paris. "Or that may be the purpose in this delay, to ensure I will not be able to perform the task for which I was summoned to France, for which I gave up my citizenship to become a Frenchman. Perhaps there are those working through the Papal Court who are striving to block me in my advances so that France will be unprotected when Richelieu is . . . no longer at court."

"And that is likely to be sooner than later, isn't it?" Olivia asked gently, going on when Mazarin turned to her in shock, "Someone must say these things, so that you may be prepared. It isn't pragmatically sensible to leave the questions all unanswered because you fear to be impolite or . . . oh, any number of things." She took a cleaning rag and rubbed the nib of her pen dry, then set it aside. "You have said yourself that you do not know how much longer Richelieu can last."

"That is true," said Mazarin, the color fading from him. "I did not intend to speak so . . . brusquely."

"You—brusque?" Olivia said with a warming in her hazel eyes. "Giulio, you haven't it in you to be brusque." She moved her chair back from her writing table and came toward him. "Tell me; who should I contact and what should I say?"

Mazarin faltered. "I don't know. I was certain that it was all settled. Buon Dio, Richelieu was sent word two months ago that the last barrier had been surmounted. He sent an official letter acknowledging the news." He clasped his hands on the pectoral crucifix that hung on his habit.

"Well, you know what the Pope is like, and you have been at the Papal Court," Olivia said in her most reasonable way. "If this is more of what we have seen before, it is only a last effort to bargain."

"Bargain," Mazarin repeated darkly. "That the Church should be reduced to a marketplace."

"Or a tribunal," Olivia added for him. "But that is the nature of the Church, or it has been for as long as I can remember." She put her hand on his sleeve. "Let me send a few letters for you, clandestine, of course. Perhaps I can find the place where the opposition is weakest. A nudge there will bring the whole thing down. It's just like blowing up a castle."

Mazarin grinned at her analogy. "You have no respect, Madame."

"No, not respect," she said, her eyes growing oddly serious. "I have respect in plenty. But I do not have awe. Not a jot. Not for any of the absurdities we turn to monuments." It was not entirely true, but she wished it were.

"You must be a trial to your confessor," said Mazarin, letting himself chuckle once. "What does he recommend for your obduracy?"

"Nothing. I don't mention it," said Olivia, her shrug slow and unconcerned; already she was thinking of the letters she would have to write and how best to have them carried without attention. This was one time it would not do to use Mazarin's couriers.

"What do you mention, then?" asked Mazarin. "There must be enough heresy in this library to keep half a dozen confessors busy with penances." He indicated one set of shelves with a number of enormous, ancient texts chained to the case itself. "It must have been difficult to obtain those."

"Yes, it was," said Olivia, finding it embarrassing to look at her greatest treasures.

"And they are all questionable—at least questionable." There was far more curiosity than blame in Mazarin's tone but his dark eyes had an underlying doubt that made Olivia answer him.

"Have you ever considered," she said distantly, "all the books that have been destroyed in the name of faith? Why is the first test of faith the destruction of learning?"

"Only the zealous believe that," said Mazarin at his very smoothest. "The Church has been . . . mistaken in the past, at times when the foundations of Christianity were being shaken by every enemy of God and man that walked the world. We have come to know that there are lessons we must learn, if we are to bring the world to Christ."

"Oh, yes; bring the world to Christ," said Olivia. "I have an old, old friend who is in the New World with Spaniards who claim to be doing precisely that. They are on a holy mission, or so it is claimed."

"They are," said Mazarin, puzzled at the strange direction their words had taken.

"Poor Christ, having to bear the burden of so many ventures and so many activities and so many terrible things down the years since He died. Do you think He would approve of what is done in His name, Abbe? Do you think He could have read those books, and if He could, that He would have cared what was written in them? Do you think He would have wanted them burned if He disagreed with them—He, who embraced lepers and pardoned whores? Might not He take the side of the book instead of the torch?" She recalled the first Christians she had known, before she had died, and how completely unlike the later Christians they were. "Do you think a man who built houses in Judea would understand why it was necessary for the Church to go into the world and bring all people under her wing, in His name?" She cocked her head and looked at him. "Well, Giulio?"

"You pose arguments even the greatest Doctors of the Church cannot answer in agreement. I am an Abbe, and a worldly man after my faith. How can I speak to you of these matters, but to advise you not to think of them at all, for they can endanger your belief and your place in Heaven." He looked from the books to

Olivia. "I wish I had not seen them. I do not want to know any-thing more about them."

"Why is that?" Olivia asked, taking care that there was no hint of accusation in her question.

Mazarin took a deep breath before he answered. "Do you ever pose such questions to your confessors?"

She smiled sweetly. "Certainly not. What could a confessor do but insist I burn the books and spend the night on my knees? I will not destroy those books, and there are better things to do in the night: I tell them of the dreams I have." That was not entirely accurate: she told of the dreams she brought to sleeping men, which was a different matter. "I lust in my dreams, Giulio."

"Because you are a widow," said Mazarin, comfortable now that they were once again in more comprehensible areas. "A husband could be found, if—"

"No," said Olivia sharply. "No husband. I have said before I do not want to marry again. Once was enough."

"It has been a long time," Mazarin ventured. "A suitable match would be very different now."

Olivia brought her heel down on the floor. "And when my hus-band had all my estates in his hands, what then? He could sell off all my stock—stock that I have been at pains to improve for years and years—or give it over to managers who would not handle the animals well. As a wife, there would be no recourse for me, would there? It would be my husband's to command as he saw fit, and be damned to what I might want." She looked critically at Mazarin. "Ask the Queen if you doubt me."

But Mazarin had already held up his hands in good-natured surrender. "Don't tax me further, Olivia, I beg you. You are too skilled for me."

She made herself smile at this. "From a diplomat, I gather this is some of your diplomacy." Before he could object, she said, "Promise you will not think of husbands for me again."

"And you will continue to confess your dreams?" asked Mazarin lightly.

"Certainly," said Olivia. "Unless I take a lover." She read shock in Mazarin's face, and went on in a different tone. "Oh, come. You are not surprised I would consider a lover, are you? You heard rumors in Rome, of course. I deny the most outrageous of them, but not every one. Look at me. I am not so sunk in years that I do not know the joys of the flesh, and if it can be done without hazards and with honor, I will taste them again." She wondered briefly if Niklos was listening, and what he thought. "I would be overjoyed to find a lover, my friend, if he were seeking me."

"What an odd turn of phrase." Mazarin lifted his hands once more. "I cry you mercy," he said, amusement making his eyes bright. "I will not dispute with you. If it suits you to take a lover, then do so with my blessing; I rely on you to be discreet for your own sake if not for mine. You are part of my embassy and there are certain—"

"I know," said Olivia, her voice less serious than her eyes. "I will not embarrass you. It would not serve my purpose, nor yours. And it may be that there will be no lover, and we have spoken in vain." She reached for a bell that stood on her writing table and gave it a single ring before setting it down again. "Come. The garden is very nice just now, and the doors open onto the terrace. There is rosemary in pots all along the walkways. We will have refreshments out in the air, where it will be more difficult for the servants to listen without being noticed."

"As you wish," said Mazarin. "But if you are so uncertain of your servants why should you employ them?"

"Magna Mater! if I dismissed every servant I ever caught at a keyhole, there would be only Niklos to take care of the house. And the reason he does not listen is that I tell him everything." She started to open the door, but saw distress in Mazarin's expression. "Servants are as curious as anyone, Giulio, and they can be excused for their interest in the household they serve. It is not done for spite or for gain, or not very often. I would as soon lessen the temptation for those who cannot resist their inquisitive natures." She looked up as she stepped onto the terrace, her eyes on the horizon where a few clouds gathered. "Do not be worried about Niklos, Abbe. Niklos knows all my secrets and has known them for . . . for more years than I like to remember, and he has never used them against me. If he will show such honor to me, what have you to fear?"

As Mazarin stepped through the door, he sighed. "You may be too trusting, Madame. But if you insist that the fellow is reliable, I will take your word, at least for now." He saw that a marble table had been placed on the terrace with two marble chairs brought up to it with bright cushions lying on their seats to make them comfortable. "Ah, a good Roman trick," said Mazarin, nodding to the cushions.

"Yes, a Roman trick," Olivia agreed, thinking back to her youth and the cushions she had carried to the Ludi Maximi at the Flavian Circus. "Pray, select one." She stood back so that her guest would not be influenced in his choice.

"This one," said Mazarin, choosing the chair that gave him a view of a small section of the distant walls of Paris, the terrace being on the north side of the chateau and affording limited sight of the city. "On days like this, with the windmills all turning, it is quite wonderful to see. They are like enormous butterflies, aren't they? I have always been taken with these windmills."

Olivia was not so captivated by the windmills, but said, "They are very distinctive." She indicated the fields that lay due north. "When the Seine followed the ancient course, where the old northeastern city walls stand now, have you thought what this place was like then?"

"It was not Paris," said Mazarin, dismissing it entirely. "It was not even a garrison for the Legions of the Caesars; it was nothing more than a collection of huts at the edge of a swamp." He slapped his hand down on the green-and-white mottled surface of the marble table. "You see, I know a little of its past. Paris is tidier about her past than Rome is."

"You have been studying," said Olivia with a little surprise. She would have gone on, but there was a sound and Meres appeared with a large tray in his hands. "You come in good time," she said, signaling her lackey to bring the tray forward. "What have you got for our distinguished guest?"

Meres put down the tray and bowed to Mazarin, then to Olivia. "Fresh bread, fresh fruit, honey just from the hive, butter less than a hour out of the churn, a brandied compote, aged wine, cream, mincemeat in crusts, and goat cheese." He bowed again and offered fresh-laundered linen napkins bigger than saddlepads.

As Mazarin took his, he watched Olivia refuse with resignation. "You still do not eat with your guests, fearing an impropriety," he said as he cut some of the cheese and gave his attention to the bread that was still warm to the touch.

"It would not be well-mannered of me to share a meal with you alone, and you know it," said Olivia, deliberately making light of this social stricture. "It is one thing to be a part of your suite, but another to be the object of gossip that would compromise you as well as me. There is already speculation that we might be more than we are to each other, and there is no reason to justify that assumption by our behavior. Which is another reason to eat here on the terrace." She reached for the wine and filled the single cup. "It is a very good vintage, or so I am told. I had it brought from Senza Pari."

Mazarin paused in the act of buttering a slap of bread. "You miss your estate, do you not?"

"It seems a part of me," said Olivia quietly. "I have lived there so long . . ." When she did not continue, Mazarin took a generous swig of wine to wash down the bread and cheese and said to her, "You were there more than twenty years, weren't you? No wonder it is so important to you."

"Yes, more than twenty years. And . . . it goes back in the records to the time of the Crusades." The first time she had seen it, after that arduous journey, it seemed to her to be the most beautiful estate in the world. Senza Pari had been smaller then and its walls stouter to keep out invaders, but she had loved it then and she loved it now. "The holdings were smaller when . . . my family first acquired it. But we prospered and the estate has grown."

Mazarin did not answer immediately. When he did, he put his food aside so that he could stare at her directly. "It was not my intention that you would have to be gone from it for a long time, but I fear it may take more time than we first assumed for my situation here to be made secure."

"I am entirely at your service, Abbe," she said with nothing more than a hint of a sigh. "If you look over toward the duck pond, you can see the geese I have recently purchased."

"Geese." Mazarin took another generous slice of bread. "You have an excellent cook. And I will not trespass further in the matter of your Roman estate." He sniffed at the compote, his nose wrinkling. "A very strong scent."

"Last year's fruit," said Olivia, as if that and not the brandy accounted for the smell. "The cook here likes to keep busy during harvest."

"A commendable virtue in a cook," said Mazarin. "I brought two of mine from Rome; one is doing very well, the other is so homesick that he cannot do a simple batter without weeping into it. I am at a loss to know what to do with him."

"Send him home," suggested Olivia, a little surprised that so obvious a solution would have eluded Mazarin.

"That is something of a problem," said Mazarin after chewing bread-and-cheese thoughtfully. "I brought him here at the request

of his family and he would be in disgrace if he were to be sent back
to Rome. Since I am not displeased with his cooking, only his
melancholy, I do not know what is best to do."

Olivia considered the problem, delighted to have something so
minor to occupy her thoughts for a change. "Why not arrange for
an advantageous post for him, with one of your Cardinal friends.
That way his return would hardly be disgraceful, since it would
move him nearer the Papal Court—"

Mazarin gestured to her to stop. He drank more wine, swallowed and said, "That is the problem. He cannot be sent to the
Papal Court. He would not . . . be completely welcome there."

"Oh?" Olivia's hazel eyes glinted with wicked humor. In the
distance she could hear the honking of geese and the whinny of
yearlings playing in the fenced field behind the stables. "Whose
bastard is he?"

It was with tact and difficulty that Mazarin answered. "His
mother was the—"

"His mother was? *Was?* What happened to her?" Olivia was
interested now, and made no attempt to hide this. "How did she
die? since she must be dead."

"She . . . took her own life, not long after the boy was born.
There was fear of scandal, you see. The family kept her confined,
as they had before the baby was born, but she obtained a vial of
poison and drank it. No one knows who gave her the poison. For
the sake of the household it was said she was mad, and she might
have been." Mazarin put down his cup and looked directly at
Olivia. "The boy is not only the nephew of a certain high-ranking
Cardinal at the Papal Court, which is embarrassment enough, he
is also his half-brother."

"Ah," said Olivia. "No wonder you brought him here. And you
have him with you so that everyone can forget this? You are a most
adept diplomat, Giulio, I have said so before, but it bears repeating." She leaned back in her hard stone chair, the cushion providing no support for her shoulders. "You have a difficult problem,
there is no doubt."

"And one I am at a loss to deal with," said Mazarin. "I've spoken to Richelieu, but he cannot act in this case. He does not want
the cook in his household, not with so much opposition to him
building up in Rome, and his position so precarious. If he were to
take in this cook, it would be regarded as a deliberate insult by the
Cardinal in question, and—"

It would have been easy to laugh, Olivia realized. Such exaggerated care to avoid affronting a man whose father had impregnated his sister. Olivia stifled her own heartfelt desire to suggest that the Cardinal's father was the one at fault and deserved the odium of the Papal Court, not its protection. But that, long and bitter experience had taught her, was not possible. She frowned at the nearest pot of rosemary. "What is it the cook misses most, do you know?"

"I have spoken with the boy once," said Mazarin. "He is cold all the time. He says that he can never learn French. He wants to be with people he can understand." He wiped his fingers before cutting more bread and smearing butter and honey over it. "This is excellent fare."

"Thank you," said Olivia, her manner a bit distracted. "He wishes to be among those who speak Italian." She tapped the marble with her finger. "Those who speak Italian." With that she lapsed into a silence that lasted a short while. "What of the south of France? What of the Genovese holdings? They are clients to Spain, but surely that is no difficulty for you. What of Nice? It is not Rome, but there are Italians. Surely someone there would be pleased to have this cook."

"Nice?" repeated Mazarin. "I had not considered Nice, or Genova, or the south." He finished his bread. "I know a fellow there; his uncle is in Orders in Rome. He might be the very man to take on this boy." He gave Olivia an appreciative smile. "You see, you are more apt at this game than you know. I should have come to you weeks ago."

Olivia shrugged. "Abbe, I am no able negotiator, and the endless games of diplomacy exhaust my patience." She started to rise, then sank back on the cushion. "As long as we are out here, is there anything else of a delicate nature you would like to discuss, or shall I signal Meres to take these things away?"

This time Mazarin made a deliberate display of helping himself to another bit of cheese and then filling his cup with the last of the wine. "There are one or two minor matters that it would probably be best to speak of now."

"One or two minor matters," said Olivia in a politely disbelieving tone. "Go on. I am curious to know what these matters are." She folded her hands like a schoolgirl and waited while Mazarin composed himself.

"First, I have a cousin. Not as awkward a relative as my cook is, but a . . . careless young man. He has had good instruction and was a satisfactory pupil in most studies; he is a pleasant-faced youth, not destined to inherit much but not wholly without substance . . ." He took a sip of his wine and gave Olivia a sidelong look.

"What is the problem with this paragon?" Olivia asked with deliberate irony.

"He is becoming debauched. I have had letters from his family and from others. He is a young man, not yet fifteen, and until May, he was affianced well. Now the bride's father has ended the betrothal because it is known that Gennaro spends most of his time in brothels. There may never be another opportunity to ally him so well, since it is feared he has taken the pox." He took another draught of the wine, this one longer than usual. "I have been asked to write to him, and I have done this, admonishing him to reform and to consider how little time he has upon the earth."

"And it was to no avail?" asked Olivia, already sure of the answer. What wayward youngster had ever listened to the cautions of others, especially one caught up in debauchery, she wondered.

"Sadly it was not," said Mazarin. "I had a letter from his brother that told of greater excesses." He put down the cup and sighed. "It is possible to get him a commission in a regiment, I suppose, but officers are often the worst example for boys like Gennaro. How am I to make such a suggestion when I suspect that he will only seek to emulate the most reprehensible of them?"

"What about a ship?" said Olivia, feeling a bit queasy at the thought. "It would be possible to—"

"Not where he is concerned," said Mazarin. "The more influential members of the Colonnas do not want to be hindered by this boy, and they seek only to put an end to his behavior. If he were young enough, they might want to enroll him as a castrato—that way whatever he did, there would be little to offend anyone." He did not smile, but there was a hard amusement around his brown eyes.

Olivia made a sign to Meres, and the lackey, interpreting it correctly, left the terrace to bring another pitcher of wine. "But his voice has changed, so there is no reason to clip him."

"No acceptable reason," said Mazarin. "There are many reasons I could offer that are sensible but they would not be regarded well." He drank the last of his wine and stared out across the fields. "I have given my word to my family that I will not abandon the boy as long as there is a trace of virtue left in him. Though I fear my exhortations are useless in persuading him, I will not cease them." He lifted his long, large hands in resignation. "I admit that I have used every means I can short of forcing the boy into Holy Orders. I have no other ideas of what I might do."

How many thousand of these wild youths had Olivia seen over the centuries—she could not count them. There were always a few raging boys, hardly more than children, bent on rebellion and destruction. "What of the New World?" she suggested, knowing that Sanct' Germain would disapprove.

"With the Spaniards?" Mazarin asked, looking up sharply as Meres approached across the terrace with a second pitcher of wine.

"Please serve the Abbe," said Olivia smoothly. "Well, why not? It is far enough away that no one in your family can object to sending him there. For those who are adventurous, there are fortunes to be made; God knows there is debauchery everywhere, but perhaps if he had to fend for himself . . . ?" She let the question hang between them, all but visible on the air.

Meres bowed to Olivia and Mazarin, then took up his place at the edge of the terrace.

"The New World . . ." began Mazarin as if to object, then let the words trail off. "It is a dangerous place."

"And he might do you all a favor and die while he is gone," said Olivia, laughing a little to show that she did not intend this as the purpose of sending the young man away. "Or he might become worse than he is and return like one of those Swiss mercenaries who murder children for amusement." She lifted her hand to her face. "Or he might make a man of himself."

"He might," said Mazarin as he tasted his cup of wine. "A different vintage, a lighter one."

"I hope you find it pleasing," said Olivia, her mind on other things. She did not speak again until Mazarin set his cup aside and motioned for her to go on. "To be candid, Abbe, I can't think of anything else to do with such a boy that would not offend some part of your family. I'm sorry." She hesitated. "What is the other matter? And why do you discuss any of these things with me?"

"For your prudence, Madame," said Mazarin, nodding in her direction as if bowing. "And there is no one else in my embassy who is as . . . disinterested as you are."

"I see," she said, and was about to say something more when Niklos came out onto the terrace and came toward her, his handsome face unreadable. "What is it?" she asked sharply, since Niklos rarely interrupted her when she was with Mazarin.

"There is someone here to see you," he said after a formal bow to the Abbe. "I explained that you were not at liberty, but he has set himself up in the yellow salon and has stated—quite cheerfully, by the way—that he intends to remain there until you receive him."

Mazarin permitted himself a crack of laughter before he poured himself a bit more of the wine.

Olivia was not as amused. "Who is this uninvited guest?"

"Someone you know," said Niklos, his ruddy-brown eyes bright with amusement.

"Who?" Olivia demanded, somewhere between indignation and chuckles.

"You must greet him, of course," said Mazarin. "Whoever he is." He leaned back in the stone chair, the cushion flaring out behind him like short cherub's wings.

"We have unfinished business, Abbe," said Olivia with a trace of formality.

"It will wait a while longer. Go attend to your guest. I will wait for you in the library." He motioned Olivia to be gone, the corners of his mouth turning up to match the gallant curl of his moustache.

Olivia rose and offered Mazarin a curtsy before falling in beside her major domo. "Well?" she demanded as she entered the house. "Are you going to tell me?"

Niklos relented. "He is a member of the King's Guard—a Gascon by the name of Charles de Batz-Castelmore."

* * *

Text of a letter from Gaetano Fosso, acting major domo at Senza Pari to Niklos Aulirios.

To the excellent major domo of the distinguished Roman gen-

tlewoman, Atta Olivia Clemens, currently residing in the Kingdom of France, this report on the state of Senza Pari is respectfully submitted.

Your remarks of the summer are very useful and have been taken to heart by those who have been informed of them. If it is the wish of our mistress that there be a distribution of second-grinding flour to the poor, then it will be continued whether she is here or not, and we will continue this charity until we are told to desist. We have also permitted the poor of this locality to harvest all windfall fruit, as Bondama Clemens has requested.

The price for swine has fallen, and therefore the profits on the current stock are very disappointing. We have taken steps to improve the price we receive through restricted breeding and superior feed, so that the flesh is more savory, but the results of these actions will not be apparent for some little time, and for the next month or two, I fear that we will not show the return usually gained from the slaughter of pigs. We can delay the slaughter, of course, but then the animals will have to be tended and fed, so that even when the market is better, the profit will be less. If you have any suggestions regarding the pigs, we will welcome them.

The grapes are another matter: our vineyards are bounteous in yield this year, and the amount of wine yielded should be higher than it was for the last three years. We have already filled eight more barrels than last year and there are a few more vines to be picked, especially the small grapes our mistress brought from Hungary more than twenty years ago. I have ordered more barrels for next year, but it is possible that we will not have similar good fortune again for some time.

Paolo Germoglio da Luccio has renewed his offer for the ridge land where his land joins this estate. It is more generous than his second offer, but he declares he will go no higher. He has asked that I include his letter to Bondama Clemens so that she can see for herself that he is willing to give her a reasonable sum for the area in question. He is determined to have the ridge and has said that he will not be stopped by the whim of a woman who has no notion of what use that land can be.

Uberto informs me that the new foals are doing well but for one filly with delicate hooves. The farrier has prepared several compounds, but the filly has had many cracks and injuries that do not bode well for the years ahead. Uberto has said he will take the filly for a year, and if she is not able to develop sound feet, he will tend to destroying her himself, since such a defect cannot be permitted in breeding stock.

Also, Uberto has been told by his sister that Nino has joined one of the regiments that passed through Roma not long ago. The regiment uses cannon and other such items of war, and apparently Nino is being taught to prepare cannon for firing and other similar things: grenada bombs and petards. He will not be able to ply his trade-in-arms if he continues to soak himself in wine all day, but that misfortune would not be overwhelming to anyone. The regiment has left Roma and is not supposed to return for some time. Nino gave a small sum of money to Uberto's sister with the promise of more, but Uberto does not believe there will be any. He has said that it is blessing enough to be rid of Nino and he will be thankful to God for that; other recompence is not needed, he has said.

The sheep we have crossbred, as per the instructions of Bondama Clemens, have done well and the wool they have produced is plentiful and of superior quality. Since you have given me permission, I have entered into agreement with two mills, one in Italia, one in Genova, to supply them with the first shearing of the sheep we now breed. I must remark here that the young lambs are not particularly strong and they do not tend to fare well in winter. I have been at pains to be certain that as many survive as can, but we are still losing one lamb in twenty, which is not entirely satisfactory to me. If there is some precaution known to you or the Bondama, I pray you will inform me of it at once so that more of these lambs will flourish and breed more of their breed. I have, incidentally, taken the meat from the weakest lambs who are killed earliest and given it to the Church for distribution to the poor, as the Bondama has requested, and I have letters of acknowledgement of these gifts from the local priest and from Cardinal Bichi himself.

Uberto has sent a request in another dispatch asking for permission to employ the Hungarian coachmaker he met not long ago while in the north of Italy. The man is capable, trained in Kocz, and known to be a gifted artisan. It is true that we have carriages that are in need of refurbishing as well as a few that must be replaced. Pray inform Bondama Clemens that I second the request that the coachmaker be hired and set to work at once so that we will have all our carriages in fine working order for any occasion that may arise. If there are any doubts as to the man's competence, he has letters to present attesting to his abilities.

We have been asked to increase our tithe this year, and with the good harvest, this is no imposition. But I believe that once a tithe is made larger it is difficult to make it smaller, and so I have asked that the tithe be reviewed, and that consideration be made that Bondama Clemens is already acting in the aid and interest of the Church and Abbe Mazarini. I will voluntarily give more from the estate if you authorize such a donation, but I fear the consequences of making such a gift a tithe.

In accordance with Bondama Clemens' instructions, we are preparing for a reception feast at Advent, and have arranged a countrymen's fair to be held on the estate, with tent shelters in case of bad weather. It has been announced in the district churches already and there is much excitement and anticipation. Many have offered prayers of gratitude on behalf of Bondama Clemens and all have said that it is sad she will not be here to join in the festivities. I am often asked how long Bondama Clemens will remain in Parigi, but I have no answer to give them. I pray that it will not be too long before we may welcome her return to Senza Pari.

It is my sad duty to inform you that six of the children of families working on Senza Pari have succumbed to fever since the end of summer. Also, the wife of Carlo da Termi has died giving birth to twins who did not long survive their mother. The aged father of Antonio Nuccio has died after taking a chill and a cough. The priests at San Andrea are warning that the Grey Cough is on the rise again and that we must guard against it, especially in children. The monks from Santissimo Redentore have said they will visit every family in the district once a week while the danger of the Grey Cough exists. I have followed Bondama Clemens' orders and put the medicaments of Senza Pari at the disposal of the district churches. We all hope that they will not be needed.

With my personal regards and good wishes and prayers for your safety and the day of your return, and with gratitude for the trust you have reposed in me, I send to you and to the esteemed Bondama Clemens my salutations for the Nativity.

> Gaetano Fosso
> acting major domo of Senza Pari
> by my own hand

On the 9th day of November, 1641.

Two bona fides copies are retained in the muniment room of Senza Pari.

· **5** ·

With visible effort Richelieu rose from his knees. He kept one hand on the small, gorgeous altar to steady himself as he strove against the pain. In spite of everything, he was smiling. "God has given me one last Christmas gift," he said softly, addressing the crucifix but heard by the three other people in his private chapel. "And I thank Him humbly and with a joyous heart."

Anne of Austria looked at her son as she heard Richelieu's words. "How is that, Eminence?" she said in a low voice. Now that their morning Mass was over, she was anxious to return to her apartments where she knew her boy would be protected.

"Rome has capitulated at last," said Richelieu, turning to face her. "They have delayed and delayed and thrown every barrier and difficulty in my path, but finally—" He moved away from the altar, pausing to turn back, genuflect painfully, and cross himself.

"Finally?" Anne prompted as she rose from her bench and knelt to the altar. As she crossed herself, she motioned to her son with her left hand, urging him to join her.

The third person knelt at the rear of the chapel, his habit making him inconspicuous next to the finery of the others. He crossed himself and whispered a prayer for patience, as he had every morning for five years. As he rose, he went toward Richelieu to offer the Cardinal his arm. "What is the news, Eminence?"

Richelieu regarded the Abbe with speculation. "It is as much your news as mine," said Richelieu at last. "Eminence." He favored Mazarin with a slight but distinct bow. "You will be elevated; it is assured."

Mazarin clasped his hands to his pectoral crucifix. "Truly?" he asked, feeling suddenly breathless.

"It is not a thing I would joke about," said Richelieu with severe humor. He looked toward Anne and her son. "Majesty, you will not be left unprotected and without support when I am gone. God has shown His will at last."

"Does the King know?" asked Anne, two deep lines appearing between her brows as happened so often when she spoke of her husband. "Have you spoken to him?"

"He requested the elevation just as I did," Richelieu reminded her.

"Because of you," said Anne grimly. "Had I asked it, he would have seen Mazarin banished to the most remote mission in the New World rather than have him set foot in France, and well you know it." She drew her boy close to her side, ignoring his fidgiting. "It was done because of you."

Mazarin moved closer to his mentor. "Her Majesty is correct, Eminence. I will give thanks to God, but well I know that you are the mover in this."

Richelieu shook his head. "At best I am God's most minor deputy. If it were not God's Will, then you would not be elevated no matter what I or the King or any temporal power in the entire world demanded." He motioned to Mazarin. "Take my blessing for your perseverance and good-heartedness."

"Eminence," said Mazarin as he knelt for Richelieu's blessing. "There is nothing I can say that will tell you what great emotions fill me."

"Reveal them to God in your prayers," Richelieu said, holding out his ring as he concluded his blessing. "Before the end of the year, the hat is yours." He looked again at Anne. "I want you, Majesty, to give us a little more of your time and to favor us with your thoughts, for there are many things we must understand between us, now that our hands are no longer tied."

Her long years at court had made Anne adept at interpreting these vague remarks, and she responded in the same manner, confident that Richelieu would know what she meant to convey. "I shall endeavor to avail myself of your good instruction, Eminence, and I am confident that I will profit from what you tell me." She glanced at Mazarin. "Abbe, it is time that you knew my son better. I would deem it a favor if you would place some of your time at his disposal."

Mazarin was quick to answer. "It is my honor and duty to be at your service, Majesty." His bow included both Anne and her boy and showed a nice blend of respect and authority. "I place myself entirely at your service but for the obligation I have to God through my vows."

Louis broke free of his mother's grasp and began to skip around the chapel, singing to himself and grinning. He paid no heed to his mother's warning call.

"Leave him be, Majesty," said Mazarin. "He has so little chance to show his spirits. This boy will rule France one day, and that will drain the gaiety from him, no doubt."

"As it has my husband?" suggested Anne uneasily.

"Perhaps," said Mazarin, knowing that Louis XIII's temperament was mirthless and it did not matter whether he was King of France or a swineherd or a luxurious Turk, he would be a man of extreme and morose moods. The boy was altogether different than his father, and it was easy to see why—even if Louis were not known to prefer the company of handsome young men to that of his Queen—there were rumors about the heir's parentage. "Let him have his enjoyments."

"But playing in the chapel—" Anne said, looking to Richelieu to aid her.

This time the Cardinal said, "Majesty, Jesus said that we must be as little children if we wish to enter His kingdom. God is not offended by a happy child." He watched Louis, smiling slightly. "Jules is right. Let him enjoy himself."

Louis squealed as he slipped on the slick inlaid flooring, skidded, slid, then fell. For a moment his face reddened and puckered; then, as his mother started toward him with a worried oath, abruptly he laughed.

"There, you see," said Mazarin, going to help the boy to his feet. He smoothed the blue velvet doublet with the long, lace-edged peplums, smiling at Louis as he did. "You are very good at running, mon Dauphin." He stumbled a little over the title, but covered it with gentle laughter. "It is good that you run well."

"I do," said the boy. He looked up at his mother. "She doesn't like me to run."

Immediately Anne's face changed. "I want you to be careful of yourself, Louis," she said, correcting him sweetly so that he could not become angry with her. "You are the hope of France. It would not do if you were to hurt yourself." In an undervoice she added to Richelieu, "Since le Duc de Soissons, I do not feel safe for him. I know that I am in disgrace, but since the revolt, I think we are surrounded by enemies."

"De Soissons paid the price of his treason, Majesty," Richelieu said, then gestured toward Louis, bending toward him as far as he could without pain. "You are a very remarkable little boy, Louis. So many have such high hopes for you."

"I am not a little boy," he said indignantly. "Babies are little. I'm not a baby." He lifted his head, his eyes bright with challenge. "I'm not a baby," he repeated forcefully.

"Of course," said Mazarin. "But mothers are like that. They always think we are little children. My own mother was forever fussing over me when I was young, trying to guard me and to keep me from harm." It was not the truth but it had the desired effect.

Louis heaved an enormous sigh and went slowly back to his mother's side. "You are a good mother, Mother."

She leaned down, though it was awkward to do so, and kissed the top of his head. "Thank you, mon Dauphin."

Richelieu favored the two with a rare, unguarded smile. "It does my heart good to see you this way, my boy," he said to Louis. "And you, Majesty," he added to Anne, warmth in his pain-dulled eyes. He gestured in the direction of the door. "Come; let us walk a little way together," he said, knowing that the servants would notice this and that word of it would pass to their masters. It would still some of the more unpleasant rumors circulating in the court, at least for a while. "Now that you are to be a Cardinal, Abbe, you may walk beside me."

"It is a great honor," said Mazarin with feeling, for he was aware of the shifting currents of the court and recognized what Richelieu planned by this. "Do you think," he went on, bending down to address Louis, "that I might have the privilege of holding your hand, Highness?"

"I can keep up without holding hands," Louis said grandly.

"I can see that," said Mazarin, wholly unflustered. "But it would be a generous thing for you to do, if you are willing. You are the Dauphin, the Heir of France, and therefore I would be fortunate to be permitted to hold your hand while we walk." He did not want the boy to realize that he was being held back, that he was being guarded, for the independent three-year-old would want to run off on his own, which could not be permitted.

"I will consider it," said Louis, making his thinking face. He pointed to Richelieu. "What do you say? You are the First Minister of France; would you let him do this?"

"I've already asked him, mon Dauphin," said Richelieu, his

face showing the depth of his devotion to the little boy. "But you must decide for yourself."

"Is he trustworthy?" Louis asked, using a word he did not quite understand but had heard often in the last few months.

"I believe so," said Richelieu. "I trust him."

"So." Louis folded his arms and glowered. "All right, Abbe, you may hold my hand while we walk, but only until I say you must stop."

Mazarin bowed. "I thank you, Highness." He held out his hand, doing his best not to engulf Louis' completely.

"There," said Louis, holding his arm up to show his mother and Richelieu that he had done it. "We can walk now."

They were a strange procession, the two churchmen flanked by the Queen and the Dauphin. They went slowly down the halls of the Louvre toward Anne's personal apartments. Servants bowed as they passed and occasionally courtiers moved gallantly out of the way for them.

"Le Duc de Soissons chose his hour badly, for himself," said Richelieu, including both Anne and Mazarin in his audience. "Had he been more alert, he would have realized that it takes more than one battle to win a campaign."

"And he died in that battle," said Anne with hard satisfaction. "There was no victory for him at all."

"No, there was not," said Richelieu, leaning a little more heavily on Mazarin's arm. "Still, it is a warning to us all to be alert to treachery. De Soissons was not the only discontented man at court, Majesty, and it is fitting that none of us deceive ourselves into believing otherwise."

"I have not been deceived that way since I came here as a bride, and that was more than twenty-five years ago." There was a look in her face then, of despair and outrage, but she hid it at once behind an assumed serenity. "I remember when you joined the King's Council. I had already been married ten years."

"I remember as well, Majesty," said Richelieu, enjoying his moment of nostalgia. "That was in April, and by the end of August La Vieuville was gone and I was First Minister." He looked over to see how the Dauphin was managing.

"I can manage for myself," said Louis with great pride. "Mazarin is not holding me up."

"Certainly not," said Mazarin, who was. "Le Dauphin is so strong he has no need of me."

Richelieu shook his head. "Ah, no. That is an error of youth, mon Dauphin, to think that your strength alone is sufficient for the Heir to France. You will need the strength of many to hold you up, for there are others who will try to bring you down. Courtiers are fickle, but friends are true."

Louis had been listening with mild curiosity, but at the last he shook his head. "My father's friends are courtiers." The last word brought a frown to his pretty face.

"So they are," said Richelieu in a tone so neutral that while Louis looked confused, Anne stifled an irritated laugh.

"Listen to the Cardinal," said Mazarin. "He loves you, mon Dauphin, and he gives you his wisdom."

"I know," said Louis, his attention taken by two women dressed at the height of style, their puffed, brocaded sleeves so full that the rosette confining them at the elbow was of heavy ribbon twice-sewn. Their shortened stomachers were edged in jewels and pearls, and since they had just come from Mass, each wore a crucifix suspended on the corsage. For head covering they had wired hoods on their capes. Louis laughed and pointed. "Bird cages!" he shouted in delight. "They are bird cages."

One of the women turned toward him indignantly, then realized who it was and dropped him a curtsy, simpering.

"You're very charming," said Louis, using the compliment he had often heard addressed to his mother.

"Thank you, mon Dauphin," said the woman, prepared to linger and take advantage of being in the presence of the Queen and the Dauphin.

Mazarin intervened. "Pardon, Madame," he said with courtesy, "but we do not wish to detain you."

The young woman stepped back at once, looking uncertain and affronted. "I did not mean—" she began.

"No one thought you did," Mazarin lied smoothly.

She gave a little curtsy and withdrew, her cheeks scarlet.

"Very neat," Richelieu approved. "I lack your patience."

"It comes from attending the Papal Court," said Mazarin. "There we do not mention that two of the Cardinals and a host of lesser prelates are blood relatives of the Pope—it is bad manners, you know. You learn not to speak of such things, to pretend they do not exist, all the while knowing what everyone else knows. The court here does not seem so complicated, or not in that way, for here one need not speak indirectly all the time. This is easier, but the other is excellent preparation for the diplomatic life." He inclined his head toward Anne. "If you would rather I assume a more oblique manner, Majesty, you have only to request it and I will comply at once."

Anne shook her head. "No. Continue as you consider best."

Mazarin was about to answer, but Louis demanded his attention. "I want to have a musquet. I want to learn to shoot."

"Not again," murmured his mother.

"I want to shoot my enemies!" Louis hooted loudly.

"Mon Dauphin," said Mazarin, undismayed by this sudden outburst of childish ferocity, "when you can hold the musquet properly and fire it without assistance, then we will ask Monsieur Peyrer de Troisvilles himself to instruct you."

"That man!" said Anne with feeling.

"He is the leader of the King's Musqueteers," Mazarin pointed out. "He is surely the correct teacher for the Dauphin, when the time comes. Or, if Monsieur Peyrer de Troisvilles is no longer their leader, whatever man holds that post must instruct the Dauphin."

They had reached the door to the Queen's apartments; several ladies-in-waiting were in the first salon, most of them occupied with sewing or reading. They all rose as Anne and her company came through the door, and all curtsied, first to the Queen, then to the Cardinal.

"And to me!" Louis crowed, and stood at chest-out attention while the ladies-in-waiting curtsied to him as well.

"Majesty, we will leave you here, in the hands of your good ladies." Richelieu stepped back and gave a general blessing. "Pray for the welfare of the King, the Queen, the Dauphin, and the Kingdom of France," he said, and turned to leave.

"Eminence," Anne said, stopping him. "I want to consult with you before tomorrow."

Richelieu nodded at once. "This evening. The Abbe will accompany me, to prepare him for his tasks to come." He did not bother to look at Mazarin, but once again moved away, relying on Mazarin to stay at his side.

"My coach is waiting to take us to my palace," said Richelieu. "It is all very well to have my own chapel and apartments in the Louvre, but the servants here are worse than a nest of serpents. I want to have my staff about me, and no unfriendly ears pressed to the keyhole." He kept his voice low now, and he motioned to Mazarin to do the same.

"I can understand very well, Eminence," said Mazarin at once, with an involuntary glance over his shoulder. "Is it the de Soissons affair again?"

"No. And nothing more of that until we depart." He sighed once, his eyes distant. "It is difficult to know when one is acting in their own interests if they appear to be acting in yours."

"Truly," said Mazarin, uncertain where Richelieu was leading. "I have seen it often in Rome."

"Oh, yes," said Richelieu, world-weary. "For all the intrigue we endure here, I have no doubt that the Church is far more extreme."

"It is accomplished in different ways. Here it is known that blood ties are of great meaning, but"—they were nearing the coaching gate of the west courtyard and there were more people in the wide corridor—"in the Church it is said that the Blood of Christ supercedes all other blood, and that the ties of family are behind—"

"That is the same everywhere!" snapped Richelieu, his patience growing thin.

"—but it is not so." He would have gone on to describe the ways in which Cardinal Barberini and the rest were related to Urbano VIII, but sensed that Richelieu was not in the mood to discuss what he already knew.

Four lackeys hurried up and knelt in front of Richelieu. As he extended his hand so that they could kiss his episcopal ring, he said, "I want my coach at once. There is a doucement for you if we do not wait more than a quarter of an hour."

The oldest lackey jumped to his feet and signaled the others to come with him. "At once, Eminence."

"I left word that the horses were not to be unharnessed," Richelieu mused. "I trust they obeyed my instructions." He gave Mazarin a critical look. "When you have your own palace, you must take care to staff it well. Make sure your servants know that it is you they must please. If they do not please you, you must dismiss them at once, or they will sow dissension among their fellows and you will be subject to intrigues and distress." He regarded the activity in the courtyard where a squad of King's Guards were drilling. Three officers of the Cardinal's Guard were watching them from the outer gateway. "You see, the lackeys have not informed my Guards that they are to be ready for escort duty at once. They do not have their horses ready, they are at leisure, which means that it will be at least a quarter of an hour before we depart. I will complain of these lackeys to the King, and perhaps something will be done."

"And if nothing is done?" Mazarin asked, curious to know how far Richelieu was prepared to pursue the matter.

"Then I will speak to my Guard, and they will attend to the matter." He squinted as one of the lackeys went running up to the three Cardinal's Guard officers, gesturing urgently. The Guards straightened their mantles and went toward the stable. "I will not say that the lackeys are redeemed," Richelieu remarked as he watched his officers, "but one of them has shown a little sense, and that is a valuable thing."

"Eminence," said Mazarin, knowing how quickly Richelieu tired, "shall I send for a chair, so that you may sit down until your coach is brought?"

Richelieu shook his head, and fell silent. Although he was clearly in some pain, he paced in the entrance, making an occasional observation to Mazarin until his coach was brought to him. "Come, Abbe," he said as the steps were lowered and one of his personal lackeys stationed himself to assist the Cardinal into the carriage.

Mazarin complied, settling back onto the squabs with relief. "Did they earn their doucement?"

"No, but I want to learn the name of the young lackey who alerted my Guards. I may have work for him one day." He dragged his traveling cushions around him to protect him from the discomfort of the short journey to his palace. "I must make an effort to find out his name."

"Would you like me to attend to that, Eminence?" Mazarin offered.

Richelieu did not answer at once. He listened to the sound of his Guard approaching on horseback, then felt the coach lurch as his two lackeys climbed onto the back. "I would deem it a favor, Jules."

"It is done," said Mazarin with pride. "By the end of the week, I will give you the name."

"Thank you," said Richelieu as the coach started to move. "We must talk. We must talk," he said in an undervoice. "There is something afoot, and it troubles me."

"Something afoot?" Mazarin repeated as the coach passed through the gate. "The de Soissons plot is not ended?"

Richelieu waved that aside. "It is not de Soissons. Or if it is, we can find no link." He steeled himself as the coach swung onto the uneven cobbles of the Paris streets. "But I can smell treason. It is in the air. Someone, someone very high, is attempting . . . I do not know. It may be open revolt, like de Soissons, it may be something more insidious. I do not know, and that is the worst part of it, that I do not know." His voice became harsher and his eyes— usually cool—grew hot.

Mazarin could think of nothing to say for a little while; at last he said, "Is there no one you might speak with?"

"Oh, I might speak with any number of people," said Richelieu sarcastically. "And that would serve no purpose but to warn my enemies and the enemies of France that they must be more cautious or strike at once. I am not willing to aid them so much. Well, you will be a Cardinal by Christmas, and that might make a difference to them."

"How?" asked Mazarin, sensing that Richelieu was gambling.

"They are not counting on support for me or for King Louis. They—whoever they are—have assumed that my position would be essentially unchanged; now that you are finally going to be elevated, matters are very different. Perhaps all those infuriating delays have worked to our benefit after all. It allowed them to assume: assumptions are dangerous." He stared out the window at the shop signs in the narrow street. "I remember when my niece married d'Enghien last February, I thought then that I sensed something in the wind, but I attributed it to the envy of those who had not been as fortunate as Clemence was in her husband. There were plenty to mutter that a de Maille-Breze did not deserve a Prince of the Blood, and I put it down to malice. Cinq-Mars made a few jokes about it, and some of the others as well."

"You warned me yourself, Eminence, that malice often hides itself in mirth. It was insulting for him to make light of your niece's marriage, no matter what he thought of it." Mazarin's indignation was as keen as if the insult had been personal, which to some degree it was, since he was a man with nieces of his own.

"Cinq-Mars is a favorite of the King's. What would be an insult in another is a good jest from him." Richelieu pointed out the window. "Le Chat Ivre. I've always liked that one." The sign showed a portly tabby cat sprawled back with a cup spilling wine in one paw.

"It is amusing," said Mazarin, aware that Richelieu had closed him off for the time being. "I like the one at the corner, with the dancing calf."

"Yes," said Richelieu, becoming more withdrawn. "There will be rain again before nightfall. That will make our return to the Louvre inconvenient, but . . ."

"But it is for the Queen and the Dauphin," Mazarin finished for him.

"Yes; for Anne and her son."

* * *

Text of a letter from Pere Chape to Padre Fabriano Riccono.

To that most pious and dedicated priest, Padre Riccono, his Brother in Christ and the Church sends words of report and of warning, and prays that God will protect this letter and the courier who bears it from danger and from harm.

Now that Mazarin has been made a Cardinal, Richelieu appears to have gained strength. Two months ago that would have seemed impossible, but to the astonishment of many here, the First Minister has rallied and is vigorously endorsing the work of his Italian lieutenant. Many have remarked that they did not know Richelieu was able to do this, for his health, as I have reported in the past, has been failing.

There are more and more rumors at court that the tide has turned against Richelieu and that there are powerful and discontented nobles who wish to bring Richelieu down before he can entrench Mazarin. There has always been opposition to Richelieu, of course, but with Mazarin now a Cardinal, some of the noblemen are afraid that Richelieu's influence will extend beyond the very jaws of death. Many fear that Mazarin, for all his new French citizenship, would be a foreigner in great power and that he would use it to the benefit of his family and to the detriment of France. Mazarin has repeatedly insisted that he has taken his adopted country to his heart, but against that are the stories one always hears of step-children who turn on those who have taken them in.

Among those most openly opposing Richelieu—and Mazarin even more—is Monsieur Peyrer de Troisvilles of the King's Musqueteers. He, along with Monsieur des Essarts of the King's Guard, has declared that he will do nothing to support or advance either Cardinal or the policies the Cardinals propose. The King is aware of this and thus far has not interfered in the dispute. I have noticed that Richelieu does not often permit himself to be dragged into open conflict with des Essarts or de Troisvilles, but it would be foolish to think that he is unmoved by the oppositions in his own court.

Mazarin has told me that Bondame Clemens continues to be most useful to him, and has said that her service to his embassy has been so great that he dare not permit her to return to Rome and that the Pope's concern about the reputation of Bondame Clemens is not truly warranted; what gossip has been spread concerning her has not brought either the Cardinal nor Bondame Clemens any real embarrassment, and unless that should occur and not be answerable, it is Mazarin's contention that the good Roman widow remain at her post at Chatillon. It seems that having a meeting place outside the gates of Paris is more advantageous than was first believed, for messengers may come there and depart from there and leave no record of their passage because they do not, in fact, have to pass through the Paris gates, where records would be made.

Related to that consideration, it is of some interest that Bondame Clemens' stud farm at Tours has been prospering. Her most recent accounting from there has shown a rise in profits which she accounts for because of her presence in France. She has yet to go to Tours, but plans to go there again as soon as the roads are clear. The Cardinal has told her that he approves of this venture so long as she is not gone long and takes proper escort so that she will not be in danger from the highwaymen who prey on travelers.

I plan to journey to Rome after Lent and the Pascal feasts, should the weather and movements of armies permit. I will beg an audience with His Holiness, your cousin, for purposes of imparting to him my private impressions and to answer any questions he might have that are of too delicate a nature to consign to paper, even paper of this sort which will be ashes minutes after you finish reading it.

Your kindness to my cousin means much to me, and on behalf of all the family I extend humble thanks. Those of us coming from families of little means do not often have the opportunity to progress in the world; that you are willing to extend yourself on their behalf puts me all the more in your debt than that which I already owe to you for the advancement you have bestowed on me in the missions you have required of me in the name of His Holiness and the Church. I have admonished my cousin to remember your kindness in all his prayers and pray also that he be deserving of the distinction you have shown him, as I pray to be deserving of your continuing favor.

In the Name of God and His Church, and with the unfaltering belief in their righteousness in this sinful world, I commend myself to you and beg you to review what I have said here with all the subtle wisdom you command. Be sure I will write again in sixty days or less, and that if there are any unexpected developments that might be significant to the Church, you will know of it as swiftly as a courier may bring you word.

Pere Pascal Chape, Augustinian
By the Grace of God

On the Feast of Saint Titus, the 6th day of February, 1642. Destroy after reading.

· 6 ·

The villa at Tours was not so grand as Eblouir; it was older, more sprawling, and less elegant, a practical pile of a building with heavy, barred shutters for all the windows and a massive brace to close the gates at night. The stables were extensive, with large paddocks; even these were enclosed by high stone fences and protected with braced gates.

"Does it disappoint you?" Olivia asked her companion as they rode up to the front gates. Her face was rosy from the chill wind and her smile was open and unguarded.

"It reminds me of home," said Charles de Batz-Castelmore, his

King's Guard mantle askew from their long ride. "In Gascony most of the nobility live like this." He reached out and tugged on the bell chain to summon one of the staff. The sound of the bell was as unmelodious as it was loud and both his and Olivia's horse shied at the brazen noise.

"I think perhaps I should replace that," said Olivia as she brought her horse under control.

"It will bring assistance," said Charles confidently. "No one wants to hear that sound twice." Then he grinned at her, his eyes glinting. "Before your staff comes, I want to tell you something: you surprise me, Madame."

"I?" said Olivia. "How do I surprise you?"

He shrugged. "We've been in the saddle for almost seven hours, eight if you count the meal I had at that dreadful inn—I don't blame you for not touching it, but soldiers can't afford to be overly nice about food—and you've held up like a seasoned trooper."

"I told you I was used to long rides," said Olivia, faintly amused by his remarks.

"Yes," said Charles, listening for the sounds of approach on the other side of the gate. "But I was afraid what you meant was that you had learned to go on long, pleasurable jaunts around Chatillon or Rome, and would not be able to keep up on the road."

"You do not know some of the roads I have ridden. This *was* nothing more than a jaunt around Chatillon when compared to— oh, many worse places." She ended lamely, her face clouding.

Charles saw the change in her face, and made a shrewd guess. "Were you displaced by war? Is that it?"

"Among other things," Olivia said in truthful evasion. "Ah. At last."

The brace made a scraping noise as it was drawn back, and the enormous iron hinges groaned as one side of the gate was opened and a squat man in a farmer's smock stood to block the way. "Well?" He looked from Charles to Olivia and spat.

"Show respect, you peasant!" Charles ordered sharply, but Olivia gestured him to silence.

"Forgive the Guardsman; he did not intend any offence." She looked at the man, reading implacability in his surly expression and defiant posture; she decided to ignore this and to behave as if he had accorded her a reasonable welcome. "Where is the major domo? I would like you to fetch him. Pray tell him that Bondame Clemens wishes to speak with him."

"I have work to do," said the fellow in the smock, not moving and unimpressed with her gracious manner.

"For this stud farm? Is this where you work?" Olivia asked with the same determined courtesy.

"Yes," he said, and spat again, just missing her horse's front hooves. "For what that may be to you."

"Then I recommend you bring the major domo at once." She favored him with a deliberate show of teeth that was not a smile. "If you do not, I will order part of your wages be withheld—for churlishness." Her horse was sidling, lifting his head, aware of others of its kind nearby. She wanted a little time to quiet the restive animal but contented herself with slapping him with her crop and ordering him to stand.

He gave a single hostile bark of laughter. "You have nothing to say on it. Now go away." He started to close the gate, but Charles anticipated him, moving his horse up to block him. "Move back," said the peasant, his stance more threatening than before, his arms braced for resistance.

"Never," said Charles merrily.

"Bring the major domo," Olivia repeated, this time in a tone that tolerated no opposition.

The peasant folded his arms and glowered. "I am not a fool, me, and I won't be ordered about by a fancy woman and a fop in a King's Guard mantle and a hat with feathers." This last was so condemning that Olivia had to keep from laughing.

"You'll be ordered about by this woman," said Charles, clearly enjoying himself. "You will do whatever this woman requires of you or you will regret it. She employs you." He grinned as he delivered this most unwelcome news.

The man in the smock snickered. "The woman who employs me is a Roman widow, or so I am told. She never comes here." He pointed at the jaunty plumed hat perched on Olivia's fawn-brown hair. "What widow looks like that."

"This one does," said Olivia very clearly, growing tired of the game. "How I conduct myself is not for you to judge, no matter who I am. Stand aside, fellow. I am weary of arguing with you." She tightened her hold on the reins and wished, as she had for most of the day's journey, that she could ride straddle and use the pressure of her legs to guide her horse.

"You cannot enter," said the peasant, but he moved back as her mouse-colored horse pressed through the narrow opening.

Charles was right behind her, his horse's shoulder pushing at her horse's rump. Once inside, he swung his mount around and leaned to move the brace back into position. "We have entered," he said to the intractable peasant, gesturing at the stone-flagged courtyard in front of the villa. "Where do we find the major domo, since he appears unwilling to find us." He looked back once at the peasant who stood with hands on his hips. "What makes that man so . . . so resentful?"

"Nothing that has happened to him here, I trust," said Olivia, and the tone of her voice promised that she would discover the truth of the matter.

"He's a peasant," said Charles as if that explained it.

"In my employ," Olivia appended, then went on in a lighter way, "It may be that Niklos was right," as she rode up to the wide, shallow steps at the front of the villa. "Perhaps I should have arrived with two coaches and my six outriders and all the rest of the panoply. That man might have been convinced." She kicked her feet free of the wide footrest and waited for Charles to dismount and help her down, though she was completely capable of managing on her own.

Charles was out of the saddle at once. "How do you women ride with all those skirts?" he marveled as he reached up.

"Sometimes I wonder," she said as he put her down.

Near the door three stag hounds lounged in the shadows; two raised their heads at the newcomers, one giving a tentative wag to his tail, the other merely watching. Apparently satisfied, they dropped their heads back on their long paws.

"Handsome brutes," Charles approved.

Olivia frowned. "Yes, I suppose they are," she said, recalling no mention of stag hounds in any of the reports she had received over the years. Dogs were part of farm life, she knew, but so large and specialized a breed as these surely deserved some mention. She walked up the steps, secretly glad to be out of the saddle.

Before she could touch the enormous lion-headed knocker, the door was opened by a plump woman in early middle-age, her hair concealed under a discreet widow's cap and her clothes covered by a long apron. "God give you a good day, travelers," she said, bobbing a curtsy, the deeper one to Charles in respect for the mantle of the King's Guard.

"And you," said Olivia, wondering who the devil this creature was.

"Come in, in the name of our mistress," said the middle-aged woman, and looked affronted when Charles laughed.

"Thank you," said Olivia with a warning glance at Charles.

"Our major domo is . . . is not available just now." She looked anxiously over her shoulder as if she expected him to appear and make her a liar. "But if you will wait in the salon, I will send word . . ." Her manner grew vague and she hitched her shoulders in an uncomfortable shrug. "It's . . . in there," she added, pointing toward a door in need of paint.

"Thank you," Olivia said a second time, and nodded Charles in that direction.

"I will ask someone to . . . to bring you refreshments," said the woman from the doorway. She was tugging on the largest of her apron pockets, for all the world like a naughty child caught with sweetmeats in her hands.

"Wine and cold meat," said Charles promptly, his flying brows lifting in amusement. "We've been riding since dawn."

The woman made a sound in her throat and hurried away.

"Well," said Olivia when they were left alone in the salon. It was a room of medium size, its ceilings lower than fashion decreed, the floor no longer even, its paneling lusterless from lack of care, part of the ceiling water-spotted. Two sagging chairs flanked the hearth with a plank table between them and an old-fashioned upholstered bench was placed against the wall, clearly intended for visitors. "I see I have been gone too long."

Charles dismissed her concern. "Better that the farm run well than the woodwork shine," he said, and sat on the sturdier of the two chairs. Dust rose around him, and he smacked at it with his hat. "I'll wager they haven't had a maid in here in a long time."

"Undoubtedly," said Olivia. She went toward the windows which were largely obscured by vines on the outside, flyspots and dust on the inside. One or two branches of the vines were so tenacious that they had forced in a few tendrils through the old caulking around the windows. As she took stock of the neglect, she became somber. "I have become lax."

"Your staff is lax," Charles corrected, watching her appreciatively, a brightness in his eyes that Olivia tried not to see. "That's another matter entirely."

"No," said Olivia, and her manner made it clear that she did not expect him to disagree with her. "This is my land and my holding, and I have not taken the care I should have. Look at this place. What on earth is the matter with the major domo?"

"If they ever find him, we might discover an answer," said Charles, going on at once, "Don't be troubled, Olivia. It rends my heart to see you troubled."

She closed her eyes to keep from looking at him, knowing that he would see her longing there, a longing that she denied. "Charles, please." Magna Mater, how she wanted him, so fiercely that her desire was an ache within her.

Charles occupied himself brushing off his sleeves. "You told me that you could not stop me thinking whatever I like. You said that yesterday, in the coach." He stopped what he was doing. "Is that why you wanted to ride today? so you would not be alone in the coach with me?"

"No," she said, but the word lacked certainty. "I wanted not to be . . . surrounded. It is worse than being a captive, sometimes, this requirement to have servants and staff and guards all around. It seems that all my life long I have been enclosed by servants and all the rest. Occasionally, just occasionally, I have to break free of it."

"That is dangerous," he said, his concern genuine. "For a woman like you to be off on her own—"

"Oh, I know the hazards," she said, cutting him off. "I've known them for longer than you can imagine." The most absurd thing of her ridiculous fascination for him, she thought, was that she wanted to tell him all about herself, to tell him about the risks she had taken, the places she had been, and when. She wanted to believe that his infatuation would lead him to accept her for what she was, though experience had taught her otherwise. It was foolish to hope that he would be different from the rest, that he would not flinch in repulsion and abhorrence when he learned of her nature and her need.

"What is it?" Charles asked, feeling her turmoil in her silence.

Whatever her answer might have been—and she had no notion of how she would answer him—it was lost as the door opened and a skinny youth came into the room with a tray. He put it on the plank table, bowed to Charles, and, as an afterthought, to Olivia, mumbled a few incoherent words, and bolted.

"Who has been training them?" Charles asked the air, doing his best to lessen the tension building between them. "He can't have got that bad without instruction." He leaned forward to inspect what was on the tray. "Slices of ham and beef," he said. "It smells fresh."

"Good," said Olivia, grateful for the reprieve. She dropped onto the upholstered bench and watched as Charles rolled up one of the slices of ham and began to eat.

All but one slice of beef were gone when the door was opened again, this time by a stocky, bald man bearing a branch of candles, for the day was waning and the salon was now deep in shadow. His face was flushed and his clothes were dusty. He bowed deeply to Olivia, who watched him with curiosity.

"You are not Octave," she said coolly.

"I am his brother, Perceval." He bowed once more. "I have seen your portrait, Madame; it hangs in the dining room. If you will permit me to tell you, it does not do you justice." His effusive welcome was marred by the nervous, darting movements of his eyes and the shine of sweat on the dome of his head. "Octave . . . sends you his greeting, of course . . . but regrets he cannot attend you now."

"That does not surprise me," said Olivia austerely. "By the look of the villa, he has not attended to much at all."

Perceval rubbed his hands together as if trying to get something sticky off them. "It is . . . a temporary difficulty, one that we—"

Olivia interrupted him. "Those vines over the window are not temporary. They have been neglected for years, by the look of them." She rose from the bench and came toward Perceval, and though she was almost a head shorter than he, he gave ground at her approach. "The walls here have not been waxed. The floor is chipped and sagging and there are slates missing. By the look of the villa, it is ready to fall into ruin."

"Hardly ruin," protested Perceval with bravado, but his heart was not in it. "Madame, you must understand that—"

"Yes," said Charles, stepping forward for the first time. "What must Madame understand?"

Perceval yelped at the sight of the mantle of the King's Guard. "Madame! Monsieur!" He backed toward the open door. "It is not my doing. I had no part in it. It was Octave who let it decay. None of it is my doing."

"You throw your brother to the wolves and let him take the brunt of your mistress' displeasure?" Charles demanded. "Such courage."

"Madame!" Perceval objected, his voice a yelp. "Please!"

Olivia relented. "Never mind, Charles; we'll get no answers to-day." She turned back toward the window. "Do you think some-one could lay a fire in the hearth or will the chimney go up in flames? And I want a bath. I trust that my bath is not totally de-stroyed?" She saw Perceval nod, his features sagging with relief. "Good. I want Monsieur de Batz-Castelmore given a decent sup-per, with some of the best wine, if there is any left." She watched Perceval blanch. "All gone, is it? Tomorrow you will explain how that came about, if you please. I want rooms prepared for me and my companion. The bedding is to be fresh. I want someone to wait upon Monsieur de Batz-Castelmore and someone to tend to me. And after morning Mass tomorrow, I want a complete expla-nation and accounting of what has happened here. Then I will conduct a full inspection of the property. Oh," she added. "My major domo, with two coaches and outriders, will arrive tomorrow by mid-afternoon. They are to have rooms ready and supper laid for them. Engage extra servants if you need them to complete the tasks. Is that understood?" She waited, her hazel eyes unflinching. "Is it?"

Perceval bowed deeply. "Yes. Certainly." He looked once at Charles. "I will . . . attend to it." He backed himself out of the room with alacrity.

Olivia stood in silence as Perceval's footsteps retreated down the corridor. "I suppose," she said when the salon was quiet, "that I had better go find out what has happened to the bath."

"Do you really intend to bathe?" Charles asked.

"Naturally," said Olivia. "Would you like to?"

Charles turned his palms up, to show that he had no opinion. "Best see if they can do it first, Olivia. Then . . . why not?" He came over to her and put his hands on her shoulders. "I'm sorry you've found this."

She tried to break free and did not succeed, though she was well aware that if she had wanted to get away from him, he could not have held her. "What have you to do with this? You have no part in what has happened here."

"I am sorry because you are vexed; your trust has been abused, that much is certain." He leaned forward suddenly and kissed her hard and long on the mouth. "I am not sorry about that, Olivia."

"No," she said, not knowing how she meant it.

He looked down into her face. "I adore you; I wish you believed that."

"I am no goddess," said Olivia, then caught her lower lip in her teeth.

"Olivia." He shook her twice, very gently.

"Charles," she whispered.

He released her. "Go. See about your bath. Take care how you walk, though. I don't trust the floors, they're so uneven."

She shrugged and started toward the door. "Thank you."

He looked startled. "Why?"

"Because you are with me. It would be more difficult if you were not with me." She was puzzled when he laughed.

"If I were not with you, you would be back in your coach and would arrive tomorrow with servants and your major domo and everyone in this villa would jump out of their skins," he said. "One Guardsman isn't much compared to all that."

"One Guardsman," she said, looking him directly in the eyes, "when that Guardsman is you, is sufficient."

He sighed extravagantly. "Would it were so," he said, and waved her out of the room.

Olivia's suite of rooms, including her bath, were at the south end of the L-shaped villa. Built over a thick foundation of her native Roman earth, the apartments were restorative to her in the way nothing else could be, and she was more eager for that comfort than she wanted to admit. The door that separated the south wing from the rest of the villa squalked in protest as Olivia opened it. The smell of the air beyond was musty; spiderwebs and dust covered the chairs and tables in her sitting room; the brocade hangings over the windows—once a rich forest green—were faded to a non-color, and in several places were torn with age. Her bedroom was much the same except that the mattress stuffing littered the bed where mice had got at it. Olivia took off her hat but continued to carry it, having no place she wanted to put it. Finally, with apprehension, she entered the large, Roman-style bath with its deep, sunken tub, which was dry. At least, she thought as she examined the tiles, nothing is cracked—it could be cleaned and filled safely.

Disheartened, Olivia wandered back to the main part of the villa, her face set in hard lines. She stopped the first servant she saw—a lackey bent with age—and asked that Perceval be sent to her at once. She repeated the message twice, loudly, when she realized that the man was quite deaf. Then she returned to the salon, and found Charles sipping a cup of warm wine.

"More difficulties?" he asked as he caught sight of her. The room glowed in the light from the candles and the newly kindled fire.

"There used to be a carpet in this room," said Olivia, speaking to herself more than to him. "It had a pattern of wildflowers on it. I wonder what happened to it?"

"Mice." Charles cocked his head to the side. "Decay. Theft." He lifted his cup to her.

Olivia dropped her hat on the upholstered bench. "I feel I should apologize to you; this cannot be what you expected."

"No," Charles agreed. "But I think it is more upsetting to you than to me. This is not my land, nor my house. And in Gascony we have poorer places than this, I promise you."

"Still." She sat down beside her hat. "I was told that all was well here. That displeases me." Her flesh tugged at her bones, her fatigue gathering in her with an intensity that was disturbing. It had been so long since she had permitted herself to be drawn to a man. Why, of all the males in France, did it have to be this rambunctious Gascon with the tilted eyebrows?

Charles put his wine aside and came to her, standing before her in anticipation. "Here," he said, taking both her hands in his and pulling her to her feet. "We may not have another time together." He wrapped his arms around her.

"My rooms are a disgrace," said Olivia, hearing her excuse for what it was. She leaned her head against his shoulder and did her best not to listen to his pulse racing, and all the while his light, nibbling kisses fell on her cheeks, her brow, her eyelids, her lips like rain on parched soil. Slowly she felt herself succumb to him, to his ardor.

"The servants might come," he said roughly some little time later. He was breathing unevenly and his face was flushed. "It would injure your reputation, and disgrace your husband's memory. Oh, God, Olivia!" He moved her away from him, holding her at arm's length.

It had been so long since she had let herself know desire that she was dizzy with it. "My husband's memory?" she repeated, choosing the first words that came to her. "How could we disgrace my husband's memory?"

He tossed his hat aside and ran his hands through his chestnut hair. "You . . . you revere his memory. To permit your servants to see you compromised would—"

"I detest my husband's memory," Olivia said quietly. "I despised him. And I don't care what the servants think of what I do. They have made it plain enough they have no regard for me." She indicated the room.

Charles stared at her. "Surely . . . the Cardinal . . ." He was almost master of himself again, and he stood straighter.

"Oh, they would rather I appear chaste. It serves their purposes, both Richelieu's and Mazarin's." She yearned for him, but could not bring herself to act. "It is the appearance that matters to them."

"But a poor Gascon, a Guardsman, how could they permit you to . . . to be my mistress"—this last was almost defiant—"when I have no fortune, no position."

"I have fortune enough for both of us, if that troubles you," said Olivia, grateful that they were speaking of such practical things.

"It does, come to that," said Charles, then looked up as Perceval bowed his way into the room, his face stretched into something that he intended as his most ingratiating smile but was more like a grimace of pain.

It was nearing midnight when the house had been put in enough order for Olivia to retire to her quarters, and for Charles to be provided a bed in the most acceptable guest chamber.

Olivia had at last bathed in an ornate tub of painted zinc, which brought her none of the relief that her Roman-earth-lined sunken tub would have, but at least the grime of the road was gone and the back of her neck no longer felt gritty. Little as she wanted to admit it, she missed Avisa, who would have scolded her and the servants, and tended to her clothes and the sheets on her bed. There were things Avisa could say to the servants that would gain their cooperation more quickly than anything Olivia herself could do; servants trusted other servants far more than their employers, no matter how reasonable or fair. Usually Olivia relied on Avisa to gain the confidence of her domestic servants, aiding Niklos and her in many ways. Tomorrow, she told herself. Tomorrow Avisa would arrive and Olivia could leave such matters in her capable hands.

She had not expected to sleep—being on her native earth once more did more to restore her than any rest could—but she lay down on the improvised bed that had replaced the disaster in her bedroom, a branch of candles lit and a copy of Tassoni's *La Secchia Rapita* to amuse her.

But the candles burned down and the heroic satire could not hold her attention as it had before; the humor was stale, she thought. Her mind was drawn inexorably back to Charles, now sleeping three rooms away. And in spite of all her hard lessons from the past, she wanted to go to him, to visit him in his dreams, to have at least the echo of his passion with the taste of his blood.

"You're taking too great a risk," she whispered, though her voice sounded like a shout in the darkness to her.

"It doesn't matter," she answered herself. It had been so many years since she had indulged in the sweetness of love, of touching, of joining, of *knowing*, that she felt the lack of it as she would miss her native earth were it not in the foundation of her room, the lining of her mattress, the soles of her shoes. She stared at the improvised canopy of her bed, her vision little hampered by the dark, and she did her best to put Charles from her mind. As she memorized the way that the ancient, sagging velvet hung, her mind continued to work. You are getting sentimental in your old age, she told herself forcefully. You are letting yourself get carried away, indulging yourself in foolish, vain hopes, imagining he will not mind when he learns the truth about you. Drosos was not the only one to call you a monster, nor Vasili, nor Rainaut, nor Mauricco. Do you remember how that Englishman felt, only a century ago? Have you forgot what he said to you, the threats he made? Do you remember that Spanish painter with eyes dark as charcoal? He told the Inquisition about you—if it were not for Niklos, you would never have left Spain alive, for the fire is as deadly to you as it is to any heretic, and the Inquisition was searching for her. She pulled on her sheets and wished she knew what time it was.

A little while later, still upbraiding herself in her thoughts, she rose from her bed, left her chamber and made her way through the dark, sleeping villa to the room where Charles lay. As she opened the door—so carefully, so quietly—she promised herself that she would only lull him into deep sleep, as Sanct' Germain taught her to do, gratify her hunger if not her longing, and be content with the frenzy of his dreams.

As she came to the side of the bed, she thought, Magna Mater, how young he was! She looked down at him, at his sleep-softened features, at the muslin chamisade with the lace-edged collar he wore to bed. Carefully she moved onto the bed, sitting beside him, nearly touching him, bending over him. Her hands trembled and she pressed them together to stop it. In a voice that was less than a whisper, she began to speak. "You are sleeping, Charles, my Charles, sleeping more peacefully, more sweetly, more comfortably than ever before. You welcome your sleep and take delight that it has come so pleasantly and so deeply. It is a joy to be asleep. Sleep fills your being, bringing wonderful rest, sweet rest that takes away all fear, all distress. Nothing painful or unpleasant reaches you now; there is only satisfaction and delight to your sleep. You are happy to sleep so full of peace and pleasure. You are sleeping deeply because it is so pleasant to sleep, to have joyous dreams that come with your wonderful sleep."

Charles sighed and stirred, a faint smile turning his lips up. His right arm slid out from under the covers and Olivia noticed that the cuffs were lace-edged, too, and wondered if his mother, his sister, or his promised bride had made the lace.

"It is so delightful to sleep that you do not want to do anything else. You take pleasure in your sleep and your wonderful dreams. You are so happy to sleep that you are content to sleep through the night until the morning bells ring for Mass. You are deep in your sleeping, and your dreams are filled with all the things you love. Your dreams are so beautiful that you do not want to waken, but you would rather sleep deeply, to enjoy them more fully. You can experience all the passion, all the delights of love in your dreams. Everything you have sought in love, have longed for, is within your grasp. Your dreams are as real to you as anything in life, more real; they reach into your soul and satisfy you, bring you love." She felt a tweaking envy that he would be gratified more completely than she, if he believed in his dream. She leaned nearer, her hands slipping beneath the covers. Delicately she worked the tie that held his chamisade closed at the neck. "You know your deepest desires, your most cherished joys, and they are accessible to you."

"Yes," whispered Charles, not in the murmur of sleep, but with full and immediate passion. His arms closed around her and he kissed her mouth, opening her lips with his.

Olivia froze, unable to move, barely able to think. Never in all the centuries since she left her tomb had anything like this happened to her; no man, even those who had pursued her, had used such tactics. Belatedly she tried to push away from him, and found that short of an actual fight and a strong rebuff, he would not release her.

He pulled back from her enough to look into her eyes. "I have prayed for this," he said softly, happily. "God heard me."

"Charles—" she began, not knowing what more she would say to him.

He put two fingers to her lips to silence her. "Don't speak."

"You were asleep," she said.

"I was in ambush," he corrected her with unconcealed satisfaction. "A good soldier knows how to lie still and wait for the game or enemy to come to him. Or his lover, for that matter." His eyes brimmed with mischief that could not hide his ardor. "You are mine, Olivia, and I will have you, though the Devil come and roar for you, you are mine."

Olivia's smile was sad with memories. "And if the Devil does roar, what then?" It was all well and good to have this impetuous young man infatuated with her: once he learned what she wanted of him, she was suddenly terrified that his desire would vanish and he would believe that she and the Devil were one in the same. "Charles—"

"What Gascon fears the Devil?" He kissed her again, more slowly and thoroughly, and he tugged at the closure of her night rail.

"You'll tear it," said Olivia when she could speak.

"Good." He pulled one last time, and the embroidered ties broke free of the fine white lawn. "I have wanted to do that since I saw you on your coach. I have wanted to see you naked."

Olivia flinched. "Why?" After all this time, could she have been mistaken, and come upon a man who wished her harm instead of fulfillment.

"Because you are so lovely," he said, his words a soft caress. "You were the most magnificent woman I have ever seen; I could not bear to think that anyone else might try to aid you."

Her laughter was not as knowing as she had intended it to be. "Oh, yes. With a cut face and a ruined dress, I must have been irresistible."

"Oh, yes," he echoed her, very seriously. "You were." He kicked at the covers suddenly, and pulled her closer to him. "Here. Come here."

She slipped out of his embrace—there was shock and pain in his face as she did—but only to remove her night rail. "I am not what you think me, Charles," she warned him, because it was unthinkable not to.

He stopped in the act of tugging himself out of his chamisade. "That's impossible. I think you are Olivia." Then he dragged the garment over his head and flung it across the room. He knelt on the bed, arms out to her.

With a quiet cry made up of surrender and victory, Olivia went into his arms, feeling his skin burning against hers, his hands trembling as his touch changed from awe to adoration. She abandoned herself to his kisses and the sweet plundering of his hands, his desire, and his occasional clumsiness. She had known men more practiced, more experienced with women, but only one other so honest in his passion, and so generous. Once she laughed as his moustache tickled her; he chuckled and grew more audacious, surprising even himself in the pleasures they exchanged with increasing fervor. At last he went into her in a tender frenzy that possessed them both so wholly, so completely, that when culmination overcame them, their rapture seemed miraculously endless.

And when they finally lay in each other's arms, joyously weary, Charles tangled his hands in Olivia's hair and held her so that her mouth was pressed to his neck still. "You have me now, you have me now, you have me now," he whispered to her, and, to her amazement, laughed in triumph.

* * *

Text of letter from Isaac de Portau to Jean-Arnaud du Peyrer de Troisvilles.

To the leader of the King's Musqueteers, greetings.
I have followed the instructions you have given me, and I must

report that your fears appear to be well-founded, for although I have not identified those active in the conspiracy to bring down Richelieu and his Italian sycophant, I am convinced now that such a conspiracy does, in fact, exist, and that those active in the plan must act quickly or be discovered, for ours is not the only service investigating the current state of affairs.

I suggest that His Majesty's brother, d'Orleans, might be approached. We know he is ambitious and that he has not achieved all that he has wanted in life, but he is not a traitor. He does not always get on with Monsieur le Grand, nor can it be said that Cinq-Mars is any better inclined to him. D'Orleans has the advantage of position, and though he has not always been the recipient of the King's good attention, he is his brother and a man of some character. The courtiers dare not ignore him or slight him, except those closest to His Majesty.

In regard to those who are close to Louis and in his good graces, there are those who have heard Cinq-Mars complain of the treatment the King has shown him of late. His Majesty has always demanded much of those he favors, and Cinq-Mars is no exception, though it is plain he wishes to be—why else is he called Monsieur le Grand? How many times has His Majesty upbraided his favorite in public, or slapped him for bringing displeasure to His Majesty? We have seen how His Majesty has vented the extremity of his temperament on the young man, and offered advancement in place of apology. Yet Cinq-Mars has power, of a kind, and as long as the King places his affection on that handsome young man, Cinq-Mars will look to higher things for himself, for he has grown more arrogant as the years have passed. You would think that he were Louis' heir.

You know more than I that the King is a man of mercurial mind, and that he often passes from the keenest enthusiasms to the deepest melancholy without apparent reason. When he is in good humor, he is willing to extend himself for those around him, but he will not tolerate any slights to his position, and increasingly it is thought that Cinq-Mars has trespassed in that way, which might account for the conduct Cinq-Mars displays.

Some of the discontented courtiers are inclined to blame Richelieu for their difficulties. I am no friend of the Cardinal's, but it is useless to blame him for everything, as some do. If Richelieu is to be brought down, let it be by honorable means, not treachery. You see, I do not think the King is the object of these rumors we have heard whispered for so long, but Richelieu and Mazarin. It is

*bad doings to plot against Princes of the Church. Those who at-
tempt to do away with the Cardinals will be excommunicated without doubt, and therefore they would not be tolerated at court.*

*I propose that you be at pains to protect yourself from whatever
the future brings in regard to Richelieu. If Henri Coiffier de Ruze
believes that his position as Monsieur le Grand will protect him
from the Cardinal or the King, he, or those who like him enjoy the
privilege of the King's favor, will discover their error before they are
much older. Whether it is Cinq-Mars himself or his associates who
are behind the rumors, I do not know, but it does not matter. De
Soissons rebelled, and he is dead, though he was a Prince of the
Blood. Le Grand Cinq-Mars has no Blood Royal to protect him; the
King's affections are not enough to save him from Louis' wrath, if
His Majesty is pressed, not with his caprice and his brooding, for it
is said that His Majesty sees enemies everywhere when that blackness is upon him. You yourself have remarked on this to me before;
from what I have learned, your assumptions are correct.*

*If you wish me to reveal what I have learned, pray tell me how
and to whom. I will carry my report and any message you wish to
whomever you designate, and I will keep the entire affair a matter
of secrecy. I will put myself at the disposal of anyone you require I
do. If you would rather I speak only to you, or that I speak of this to
no one, I will do so. I am your man, and the King's man unto
death.*

*Isaac de Portau
The King's Musqueteers
First Company*

*On the 20th of April, 1642.
Do not keep.*

· 7 ·

Richelieu's eyes were wet stones in his face. "Are you certain?"
he asked the frightened boy who stood on the other side of his
writing table. The windows of his study were open and the scent of
May drifted in on the slow breeze.

"I am, Eminence," said the page. "I have seen them meet several times now, and they . . . they speak in whispers."

"Which you are at pains to overhear?" Richelieu asked, expecting no answer and getting none. He moved back in his chair and studied his visitor. "Why did you decide to come to me?"

"I . . . I thought that . . . you would have to know." He stared at the standish, as if he could read his future in the ink. "It was . . . wrong of them to . . . to—"

"Plot," said Richelieu directly. "It was wrong of them to plot against me."

"But they were found out. They were. The King's brother has . . . learned of this. He has watched them . . . and he is working to trap them." The boy coughed once, then fiddled with his soft lace collar.

"Are you certain?" Richelieu demanded, his voice low and his eyes harder than ever.

"Yes," said the page. "You see . . . he caught me listening. A few days ago." This time instead of coughing he cleared his throat. "I don't know how he found me, but he did. He knew I was listening. He wanted to know if I had listened before. He made me tell him what I knew, and then made me swear that I would do nothing. He said that I was not to inform on anyone and that I should speak only to him. But I couldn't do that, could I?" This last was a plea as his blue eyes brimmed with tears.

"It would seem not," said Richelieu. "Tell me, how long ago did d'Orleans catch you? How long has he known about this?"

"It was . . . three weeks ago," the page said uncertainly.

"Three weeks ago?" repeated Richelieu. "No more?"

"A day or two, perhaps," said the page, his gaze now fixed on the squared toes of his shoes.

"So, it is at least a month since d'Orleans learned of the plot. Yet he has said nothing of it. Or if he has, it has not been to warn me, as you have done." He tapped his fingers on the shiny surface of his writing table. "Then what is his purpose?"

"He . . . is going to trap them," said the page unhappily.

"Is he." Richelieu sighed once and closed his eyes for an instant as the pain in his vitals flared. "Undoubtedly he will, in good time."

The page gave a sickened, relieved smile. He stood a little straighter, but his manner was far from confident. As he watched the Cardinal, he began to fidget again.

"It was wise of you to come to me," Richelieu said at last. "I will see that you are rewarded for all you have done." He moved his chair back a little farther. "You have spoken to no one other than the Duc d'Orleans about the plot, you say?"

"Only to you, and to him because he made me," said the page. He rubbed his hands on his long velvet peplums.

"I think perhaps it would be best if we continue in this way for a while. Do not let d'Orleans know that you have spoken to me; if you do, you will suffer for it, I promise you." Richelieu spoke almost gently, but his implacability was apparent in every aspect of his demeanor. "I will feign ignorance for a while longer, to see if we can avert scandal. After de Soissons, His Majesty does not want scandal." He studied the page again, as if looking for the one weakness he could use. "I wish you to report to me every morning, promptly after Mass. I will hear what you have to say. It does not matter if you have nothing to tell me; I would rather that than have you make up something, for that would confuse my purpose, and you would answer for it."

The page had been listening closely, his eyes large. It troubled him to admit that the Cardinal was an impressive man, one who commanded more than respect or obedience, but devotion. "Yes, Eminence," he said, not knowing what he was expected to do next. He wanted to leave the room, but he dared not make a move without Richelieu's permission.

"If I learn that you have attempted to gain advantage with others through revealing this information to them in any way, I will see to it that you are sent to the Choir. You are still young enough for them to make use of you." He let this sink in, then added for emphasis, "Betray me and you will sing soprano all the rest of your life."

The page was white as new linen. "I understand, Eminence."

"Tres bien," said Richelieu with a slight, flinty smile.

"Every morning after Mass." He bowed his head, trying to keep his teeth from chattering.

"And if anyone should wonder at the sudden piety you show, you may tell them that you have a relative and you are seeking my aid in securing him a post. Let it be known that you are pestering me, so that the court will be amused." He looked at the boy's face. "Complain of my hesitation and lack of concern."

"Eminence," said the page, perplexed. He concentrated on what Richelieu was telling him, knowing that the Cardinal would carry out his threat if he were to fail in the task set.

Richelieu glanced away toward the window. "What is your name, boy?" Such a pleasant day, he thought.

"Fontaine de Rochard," he answered at once, trying to make this sound more impressive than it was.

"I am not sure . . ." said Richelieu, letting the page know from his lack of knowledge of his family that Fontaine was not well-connected, if the boy did not realize that already. "From Auvergne, perhaps?" It was his one concession; it gave Fontaine some small part of his dignity.

"The estate is a small one, near Riom," said Fontaine. "There are four sons younger than I am, and our means are . . . modest." His father had taught him to use such language and now that he was at court, he was grateful for it.

"An excellent reason for you to pester me," said Richelieu with another hard smile. "Five sons. And a small estate, you say? How small?"

Fontaine took a little courage from this question. "There is a chateau, and lands attached. We grow oats and barley, we raise sheep and hogs and have a dairy, cows and goats."

"Cheese, then?" suggested Richelieu. "Much like the farmers in the region."

"Yes," said the page, flushing at this description. "My father is a younger son and we are a cadet branch of the family." It was not an easy admission to make, and he could not look at the Cardinal as he said this, but he managed to stand straight through it all.

This time Richelieu's expression was more sympathetic. "It would be well for you to be diligent, Fontaine, for a boy in your position has need of powerful friends if you are not to end up farming as your father does." He intended his statement to cut, and saw from the expression on Fontaine's face that he had succeeded.

Fontaine bit back the retort that sprung to his lips. He ducked his head. "Yes, Eminence."

"You can turn this difficult time to your advantage. You may decide that it is best to serve my interests as a means to serve your own." He looked directly at the boy, giving him time to think. "I reward those who are in my service. I will look out for your welfare if you discharge the tasks I set you."

"Eminence." Fontaine was squirming inwardly, but did little more than scuff at the carpet with his shoe. He was not pleased to be so completely in the Cardinal's hands, but was wise enough in the ways of the court to know that if he were to rise above his current place, he would do it only with the aid of a powerful patron—and few were more powerful than Richelieu.

"Well?" Richelieu asked when he was sure that the boy had considered his plight.

"I am . . ." He faltered and tried again. "I am honored to be chosen to assist you, Eminence. I will strive to be worthy of your confidence." This time his bow was formal and faultless.

"Very wise," said Richelieu. "Now, be about your duties and listen carefully to all that you hear. Make sure that what you tell me is accurate; do not attempt to change what you have heard and seen: above all, do not interpret what you have heard; I want only to know as precisely as possible what it is. If you are accurate your rewards will be greater than if you are not. I will await your report tomorrow morning." He held out his hand so that Fontaine could kneel and kiss his ring, then he lifted a little silver bell, ringing it once.

A lackey came through the door and bowed. "Eminence."

"This page is Fontaine de Rochard. He has four younger brothers. Is there any place for them in my service?" Richelieu watched the lackey without expression.

"I will inquire," said the lackey, bowing again.

"Good. Take the boy with you and find out what you can about his family." He made a gesture of dismissal, then took a document from a case and began to read it, not looking up when the door closed.

A short while later, however, he left his study and went slowly toward his private apartments, alone. He was tired to the core, but knew there was no rest for him this side of Heaven. His head throbbed and the constant acidic ache in his side seemed worse today than it had been for a while. He had drunk pearls dissolved in wine on the recommendation of his physician, but it seemed to give little benefit, and had destroyed three pearls as well. He thought of the women he remembered from his youth, who made potions and salves from herbs. If the pain continued to worsen, he would be driven to speak with one of those crones, and that made him shudder. It was in God's hands, he reminded himself. As a Prince of God's Church, his body was entrusted to His keeping.

Once in his bedroom, Richelieu allowed himself the luxury of resting on his chaise, extra cushions making him sigh with the only comfort he trusted. As he lay back, he weighed what Fontaine had said. It made an infuriating sense, and that worried him. He could readily believe that Cinq-Mars would mount an attack against the First Minister, confident that the King would deny him nothing once Richelieu was gone. The rest—that Cinq-Mars was conducting secret negotiations with another country—was less credible, but not impossible, given the audacity Cinq-Mars had shown of late. Richelieu closed his eyes, trying to decide how he would proceed. He did not want to challenge Cinq-Mars outright, for the King was currently despondent and could not be relied upon to act for the benefit of France. There would have to be another way, and Richelieu would have to be certain that he did not enter into the dispute directly unless it was absolutely necessary.

And there was Anne, he thought. She needed his protection more than she had before; if Cinq-Mars were plotting against him, he was also plotting against Anne, for as the Queen and Louis' wife, she was as much a stone in his path as Richelieu was.

Unless, said a part of his mind that seemed never to sleep, she is part of it, as well, and is trying to gain power not only over you, but over the King, to insure that her children would not be subjected to any more mistreatment or suspicions. If she thought that with Cinq-Mars as an ally she would at last be rid of the stigma of bearing sons not of the King's loins, then she might throw in her lot with him. He sighed, and the pain flared. Anne, Anne, Anne, he thought. You cannot be part of this. You cannot have taken such a foolish chance with your life and the lives of two sons. She had been unwise before, he reminded himself with stern rigor. There was that Englishman Buckingham, who had courted her so openly that it was the talk of Europe. Perhaps it was just as well that his manservant killed him for his idolatry of Anne. There were other instances Richelieu was aware of, a few of them concealed from the King, that revealed more of her unhappiness and desperation than her political acumen. If Anne has sided with Cinq-Mars, he thought, he did not know what he would do to extricate her before the plot was revealed. He frowned, his eyes closed. He had to consider how best to proceed.

Cinq-Mars had to be brought down, he decided as he drifted into an uneasy half-sleep. It was most crucial that the rule of Monsieur le Grande be ended. Gaston, Duc d'Orleans was the key.

Shortly before sunset Richelieu was awakened by one of his manservants, who bowed to the Cardinal and reminded him that he was to dine that night at the King's banquet. He brought a basin filled with warm water and a ewer of spirits of wine so that Richelieu could wash his hands.

Richelieu made himself stand and go about his toilette as if nothing unusual had happened that day. "I will need a fresh collar," he said, indicating the wilted lace of the one he was wearing. "Something more fitting for the occasion."

"As you say, Eminence," the manservant agreed, inclining his head.

When he had dried his hands, Richelieu daubed attar of roses at his wrists, sniffing the overpowering odor of roses with satisfaction. "I would like my writing set brought to me here," he said when his manservant had given him a new, wider collar of gorgeous Belgian lace with gold thread mixed with the white.

"At once, Eminence," said the manservant, and withdrew.

But when the paper, standish, quills, and sand had been brought to him, Richelieu sat for some little time, staring toward the branch of candles set on his table. His salutation to Anne of Austria was all he had written on the page. After a while, he put a corner of the paper into the flame of the nearest candle and held it until it was burning. Then he dropped it into a vase before leaving his private apartments.

The Louvre was shining with torchlight; a line of splendid carriages waited to discharge their titled occupants at the largest of the coaching doors. Richelieu used his time to gather his thoughts, wondering how he might find an excuse to speak with Gaston d'Orleans alone without half the guests taking note of it.

"Eminence," called out one of his escorts, for at night he traveled with six of his Guards to protect him.

"Yes?" He did not like the testy sound of his voice, for it often seemed that his men thought he was afraid when he spoke in that tone. "Are we there?"

"The Duc d'Orleans is in the carriage behind you and has asked to be allowed to go ahead." The Guardsman said this without expression, merely reporting the request of the man behind him who was of superior rank.

Richelieu smiled. "It is the pleasant duty of all subjects of France to defer to the Blood Royal," he said with habitual smoothness. "Pray inform le Duc that I will allow him to pass."

The Guardsman touched his hat and rode back to the carriage behind. When he returned, he reported, "D'Orleans sends his thanks, Eminence."

"Excellent," said Richelieu, confident now that he would have his opportunity to converse with Gaston d'Orleans without any undue comment. He allowed himself the first real hope he had felt since the page Fontaine had come to him. Even when his coach did not advance and Gaston d'Orleans' rattled past his—which Richelieu would ordinarily consider to be a terrible affront—his good humor did not desert him.

As courtesy demanded, Richelieu left his coach to find the Duc d'Orleans waiting for him, his retinue around him. As he held out his ring, he said, "It was a privilege to do this service for you, Duc."

Gaston d'Orleans, rising from his knee, looked Richelieu directly in the eye. "Precedent, Eminence."

"Certain; a Duc of the Blood Royal must always have claim of a Duc's relative such as I am. I, too, have an elder brother." He gave d'Orleans a wintery smile. "But then, I gave up the claims of precedent for Armand-Jean du Plessis de Richelieu when the Church became my estate and the Kingdom of France my ward." He bowed to d'Orleans, making much of the courtesy since it was not strictly required to show such deference to the King's younger brother. "Give me the pleasure of your company as far as the banqueting hall." It was a marvelous trap, thought Richelieu, for if d'Orleans were to refuse, the insult would be so overwhelming that it would bring too much attention to both of them. "It has been too long since we talked, has it not?" He indicated the wide corridor. "And if we linger here too much longer, we will cause as much of a line as the carriages do."

Gaston d'Orleans did his best to appear delighted with Richelieu's suggestion. "It is always a pleasure to walk in the company of so august a minister as yourself, Eminence." He gestured to three of the men accompanying them. "Go ahead. The Cardinal and I will follow."

Two of the three exchanged uncertain looks, but were sensible enough not to question Richelieu here where all the world might see. One of them bowed to Gaston. "It is our pleasure to follow you."

D'Orleans waved his agreement to the three. "I did not anticipate meeting you, Eminence," he said to Richelieu as a ploy to bring their conversation to an early conclusion.

"Nor had I," said Richelieu. "It is fortunate the way such things fall out, don't you agree?" He paused to bow to the Spanish Ambassador. "I have had it in my mind for several days that I should ask you to spare me a few minutes for conversation, but my duties are such that it did not seem possible. Then God was good and threw us together in this way."

"Yes," said d'Orleans, scowling.

"I believe it would be wise for us to discuss the Dauphin, who is your nephew and will one day rule France." He was being unusually blunt, but feared he would not have much more time to speak with d'Orleans.

"With the guidance and mercy of God," said d'Orleans with the same tone as he used for the responses in Mass.

"Truly, truly," said Richelieu, concealing his irritation. "But God relies on His children to use the sense He gave them. We must do what we can to protect the boy and to ensure his reign will be a long and prosperous one, unbeset with unrest and injustice."

"You believe that we have had such under the rule of my brother?" d'Orleans inquired haughtily.

Richelieu refused to respond to this blatant challenge. "I can only pray that God will show us His compassionate face, for there have been many unfortunate incidents during His Majesty's reign that will have to be answered before the Judgment Seat. As First Minister of France, I pray God may grant me His vision for wisdom so that our sins will not be multiplied." He turned the corner and saw that they were nearing the banqueting hall. "I have been concerned of late at the unrest that is present in the court, and the wrongs which have gone unredressed."

"If God will not hear you, whom will He hear?" D'Orleans laughed at his own witticism. "The Dauphin is a little boy. He has many years before there will be any burdens placed on him." He shrugged. "It is not for me to decide, in any case. My brother is King, not I, and his wife is the mother of the Dauphin." With that calculated insult, he bowed to Richelieu and entered the banqueting hall on his own.

Richelieu watched him go, his anger growing steadily, though no trace of his emotion appeared in his demeanor. He allowed Roger de Saint-Lary de Bellegarde to kiss his ring and gave his blessing to the Archbishop of Paris, Jean Francois de Gondi de Retz; his temper began to cool.

One of Louis' favorites came up to Richelieu; he was resplendent in blue-and-gold velvet, with a profusion of lace at his wrists. He wore a golden sash that gathered in a rosette above the lace-edged peplums and his sword was for nothing more episcopal than ceremony. With an elegant flourish, he knelt to kiss the ring before saying that the Cardinal was awaited.

"I shall come at once," said Richelieu, starting to fume again at this unsuitable escort. What was Louis thinking of, to send one of his creatures to fetch him as if he were nothing more than a servant or one of his housemen? He schooled his features to a calm he did not feel and made his way through the enormous hall toward the high table where the King and those of his nearest court ate.

He had almost reached the dais when he saw Mazarin signal to him from a place not far below. "Your pardon," he said to the courtier who accompanied him. "I must have a word with Cardinal Mazarin."

The courtier stopped, looking a bit bewildered in all his finery, for he was not used to having to acquiesce to anyone but Louis. "If . . ." He did not know how to go on.

Richelieu did not wait for any response from the courtier, for that might be interpreted as waiting for permission, which he would never do. He stepped to the side of the vast table and waited while Mazarin made his way to his side. "What is it? Half the room knows you are speaking with me."

"I am your . . . assistant. It is fitting that we speak in public," said Mazarin, displaying more Roman sensibilities than Parisian. "They all know we speak—they might as well see it happen."

"You may think otherwise when you hear the gossip; never mind." He looked at Mazarin with curiosity. "What is it?"

"Gossip, actually. There has been a fresh spate of curiosity as to the parentage of Philippe." The Dauphin's brother, two years younger than Louis, was a baby that most of the court tried to forget.

Richelieu grew tense. "For how long?" he asked.

"A week, perhaps two. There are those who are saying outrageous things . . ." He hesitated. "Amico mio, there are those who say that they are convinced that . . . that you are the father of the boys, that you have been the Queen's lover many years . . . for all the years her husband has not been." He folded his arms, his face revealing nothing of what he said. To those watching them— and there were many—they might have been speaking of nothing more than a question of courtesy.

"Ah. They are trotting that one out again, are they?" said

Richelieu, his voice all but purring. "The page was right, I see now." He gave Mazarin a single nod. "You did well to warn me, and I thank you for your concern. I will bear this in mind while we dine this evening."

Mazarin's long, handsome face did not alter, but there was a frown in his eyes. "I must speak to you. It is urgent."

"Yes, yes," said Richelieu. "Tonight, then, when this is over. Come to my palace and we will discuss this in more detail." He looked over his shoulder and saw that Louis was scowling at him. "After this interminable banquet."

"As you will, Eminence." Mazarin lowered his head. "I did not intend to alarm you unduly."

"You didn't," said Richelieu. "You have only confirmed my suspicions. I will speak to the Queen and—" He made an abrupt gesture. "Tonight."

"Tonight," agreed Mazarin, turning to make his way back to his place at the table.

Richelieu hurried to the dais, taking his place four seats from His Majesty's right hand. He murmured a brief apology, which the King did not hear, but accepted, and waited while a lackey pulled out his chair for him. Gradually the room grew silent, and attention was directed toward him. He stood, his hands placed together, and began to invoke blessings on the banquet, the food, the company, and the glorious reign of Louis XIII, all the while hoping to discover who among the company was plotting against him, who was so implacable an enemy that he or they were willing to bring down the kingdom to destroy him.

❧   ❧   ❧

Text of a letter from Cardinal Jules Mazarin to his second cousin, Gennaro Colonna, written in French.

May God, Who watches over all His flock, even those who are strayed, guide and keep you in these difficult days. I am not astonished to learn of the decision of your parents, for surely you have tried their patience and the patience of those who have known you for many years. I pray that you will consider your current difficulty and accept the suggestion I am going to make to you.

To have the sin of another on your head, especially so grievous a sin as suicide, is a fate that I would not wish on the most obstinate heretic, and yet you, who are my blood, have brought it on yourself. The dishonor touches us all, and I must support your father in his decision. No man wishes to disinherit and disown his children, especially his sons, yet in a case such as yours, you have brought such disgrace to the name that to allow you to remain within the family would besmirch the name more than is permissible among noble families.

Whatever convinced you that you could lie with Dona Levana, make her your mistress, or rather your whore, and not have any consequence to your act? This was not some common slut, or girl from a brothel, this was a woman of birth as good as your own, with a contract of marriage arranged for her from the time she was ten years old. That you could seduce her deliberately, compromise her so completely that not even the most penitent convent could receive her, is debauchery of a sort that I can hardly fathom, though I see sin around me in plenty every day. You have betrayed her, Gennaro, and you have betrayed the family.

This has been a summer of betrayal, it appears. Not two weeks ago the King's brother, Gaston d'Orleans revealed a terrible plot against Cardinal Richelieu. The King's favorite, Henri Coiffier de Ruze de Cinq-Mars, was revealed to have entered into secret treaties with the King of Spain, and to have planned the murder of Richelieu as well as others.

You may consider Cinq-Mars' plight, cousin, and be thankful that yours will not end on the execution block. You, like Cinq-Mars, have been favored with an active mind and a high station in life, but both of you have squandered your gifts in debauchery. You both have reason to be grateful to those above you and to your families, but you both have treated those who have aided you and your families with a contempt that is not shown a starving cur in the streets. You both have sinned with your bodies and have abused the flesh God has seen fit to clothe you in. Dona Levana della Robbia, in her despair at what you wrought upon her, has taken her life with her own hand, and the guilt for that lies on your soul as much as hers. Cinq-Mars has betrayed the affection of the King and has brought ruin upon himself for what he attempted to do. He has shown himself unworthy of the favor the King had lavished upon him, and he will pay the price of his treason with his life in this world and with his soul in the next.

Bearing all this in mind, I admonish you to pay close attention to what I have, for the sake of your father and of the family of the lady you have ruined, arranged for you. It is apparent that you cannot remain in Italy, or, indeed, in Europe. Therefore, with the assistance of friends both here in France and in Spain as well, I have entered your name into a company of men bound for the New World with the Spanish to the city of Tenotsticlan, which is the capital of a people who live for the shedding of blood and who are obstinate in their refusal to accept Our Lord as their savior. The fighting men will be needed when these savages attack those who have come in the name of God to offer them salvation.

I urge you to accept this opportunity at once and to go to Madrid for the purpose of joining the company of men in question. As you see, I have enclosed a letter of introduction to the company, and the assurance that you will be loyal to the leaders of the expedition. You will have some chance to improve yourself if you are willing to travel to the New World.

Should you believe that it would be acceptable to remain here, confident that in time your father will welcome you back as his prodigal son, or that the della Robbia family will in time come to forgive you for what you have caused to happen to Dona Levana, I offer you this tale in the hope you will take it as an example and learn from its precepts.

Many centuries ago there were two brothers, sons of a King, though each was from a different mother, who were the delight and hope of their father, and who were given every advantage that the sons of Kings may have. Each was taught the way of arms and of letters, so that they might better govern. Because each was the son of a Princess and of Royal Blood, it was agreed from the first that when the time came, the King should arrange a series of tests to determine which of his sons would be his heir.

One of the sons excelled at arms and was known for his skill as a soldier. In battle there was no one braver or more fierce; the very mention of his name brought dread to the enemies of the King when they heard it. The other son was of a more subtle nature, more given to learning and to study, and he excelled in the ways of the court and of religion. He learned to value the teachings of God and the treasures of the mind. Yet there was a secret between them: one brother was of a chaste temperament and the other was debauched.

But so close was their bond that neither revealed this dreadful secret. When the King came to hear of it, he refused to believe it until proof of such debauchery was procured. Then he summoned his two sons and addressed them: "It has come to my ear that one of you has taken it upon himself to bring disgrace to this House, to conduct himself in a way that no son should, let alone the son who will one day rule in my place. I demand that you reveal which of you has become debauched."

To the astonishment of the court and the King, both sons insisted that he was the one, and the only one, who was debauched. No argument or exhortation could change them from their assertions, and no action on the part of the King was able to wring from them the truth about their actions.

In desperation, the King took the advice of his aides and decided to put each of his sons to the test, subjecting both to the same tests, not only to determine who would rule, but to find out which of them was the debauched son and undeserving of advancement and favor.

The first test was given to both, and though it favored one over the other, it was decided that it would be fair, since the second test would favor the other. The first test was this: it was known that the forces of the enemy to the east had gathered on the border and were prepared for war. Each of the King's sons was sent to the place, and given the task of subduing the enemy and restoring order. The first son gathered his company of soldiers about him and rode with all due haste to the border, where he caused the nearest towns to be walled and reinforced their ranks with his soldiers. When he was satisfied with the preparations, he led his men on a daring midnight attack and caught the enemy napping in every sense. The force of the northernmost flank of enemy soldiers was defeated, and order was established in the region, with the King's son preventing all looting and similar excesses with the full might of the King's law.

The second son approached the matter in a different way, going with two scholars to the center of the realm of the enemy; and presenting themselves as nothing more than men in search of learning, they set out to confound the enemy with false reports and misleading documents, and with the discovery of the plans that had been laid. For every letter and dispatch they intercepted, another one was substituted, misleading and filled with lies. In this way, the order of the opposition was quickly destroyed, and the King's second son left the capital of the enemy without ever being discovered.

When the aides of the King assessed what the two brothers had done, they were constrained to believe that each had proved as capable as the other, and could not advise the King in regard to the favor of either youth.

So it was determined that a second test would be made, and that both would be asked to address the same problem. But this time it was agreed in the King's Council that there would be a temptation added to the task, so that the debauchery of one or the other could be established.

In the kingdom there was a monastery where the monks had devoted themselves to the care of those afflicted in their minds. Among those living in that place was one who was believed to have murdered many people in terrible ways. It was set to the King's sons to go there and discover who among the mad was the murderer and to bring him to justice. It was thought that among the mad the debauched son would make himself known to them.

The first son set out alone but for his squire, determined to challenge those who were mad and see which among them would answer his challenge. In this way he was convinced he would learn the identity of the murderer. He was admitted by the monks with all respect and deference, and taken to the infirmary where the mad were kept.

He delivered his challenge, but reckoned without the subtle ways of madness, for many answered his challenge, some as cunning as foxes, some angry as bears; he was forced to battle with many of them, and at the end of it came no nearer to finding the murderer. He ordered all those who had opposed him locked in chains, which the monks at once did. Again he issued his challenge, this time upon threat of torture, then he set about testing each of the madmen in turn. At the end of it he was no nearer an answer than before, and the monks were displeased at the conduct of the son, who was then decried as the debauched son for the torture and killing of the madmen.

With sorrow in his heart, the King bade his first son to leave his kingdom and to enter into the service of his mother's people, for he would not accept debauchery in his heir.

So the second son was made heir and his wedding to a great Princess was arranged and celebrated with feasting, joy, and pomp.

The first son did not make merry at his brother's wedding, but his disgrace was seen as the reason for it; in a short time he departed into the land of his mother.

Then did a great burden descend upon the King, for he discovered that the uses his second son made of his bride were those no man should speak of, and his treatment of those in his service was without honor. Now that his brother was not at court to keep him in check, the second son gave such liberty to his excesses that in time his father died for the shame of it, and his wife threw herself into the ocean.

Finally his brother could tolerate such abuse of House and blood no longer: he gathered an army about him and showed again the prowess that he had demonstrated from the first. He returned to his home as a welcomed conqueror, and brought his debauched brother to the judgment of the nobles, who demanded that his life be taken as if he were the greatest traitor, for that, in fact, was what he was. The first son, who had prevailed against deceit and calumny, was crowned and anointed, and the kingdom rejoiced in his reign.

I pray, Gennaro, you will study this tale and take its lesson to heart. You have been permitted far more license than you ought to have had, and you have come near to destroying yourself as well as those around you. Before more and severer punishments are brought upon you, before your House is required to demand such recompense of you that you will not be able to pay, seize the opportunity being offered you and journey to the New World. Your audacity, which has led you to such disastrous ways here, may well sustain you in the New World where many are driven to the point of madness by the world around them, and where excesses such as those you have practiced are enough to endanger your life.

With my prayers and most earnest entreaties that you accept this most compassionate arrangement and show yourself compliant to the will of your House, or accept their decision to cast you out forever, I place my trust in God to bring you to true understanding and repentance through the ordeals of your distant journeys.

Your cousin
Jules, Cardinal Mazarin
By God's Grace

On the 27th day of June, 1642.
By my own hand.

· 8 ·

He caught up with her in the stables, panting a little from his exertion. He was half-dressed and carried his sword at the ready. "What in the name of God's Spikes made you do that?"

Olivia swung around to look at him, the shine from the lanthorn turning one side of her face a glowing amber and throwing the other side into darkness; her eyes fixed on his with an intensity he had not seen in them before. "I've explained to you—"

"You've told me a fable." He flung his sword aside. "If you wish me to be gone so badly that you are reduced to making up stories, you need not: you need only tell me to leave and I will go."

Her face changed subtly, revealing sardonic amusement. "Will you?"

"No," he growled as he pushed the door to the empty stall open. "No, and well you know it." He reached out for her, pulling her near to him, pressing her face to his newly shaven chin. "No, I will not go."

"Though it is wisest?" she suggested, afraid of giving in to his desire.

"There is nothing wise in walking away from love," he said. "There's no honor in it, either." He had his arms around her waist. "You cannot make me leave you, Olivia. You've said that to me yourself."

She nodded once. "That's true." With an effort she moved back from him two paces. "Charles, you've got to listen to me. You must." She touched his shoulder, telling herself it was for emphasis, but knowing that what she sought was his affection and love that would be strong enough to survive the truth. "I know you don't believe me. I know you are convinced that what I've said is impossible. But please, please, listen to me; hear me out. Because if you won't, I will have to stay away from you. And I don't know whether I can. You . . . Charles." She wanted to find the words to explain, but all she could think of was that she must warn him, though she lost him for it. "We are too much at risk now; another night, another hour in each other's arms as lovers and—"

"And what?" he asked when she broke off. "You aren't going to repeat that nonsense about being almost immortal, are you?"

"It isn't nonsense. Ask Niklos if you don't believe me." She was tempted to lean against him, to accept what he so openly offered her, but she could not until she was satisfied he knew what the cost would be.

"Your major domo will say what you wish him to say. Ask him to say he comes from the moon, and he will." His voice was gruff but his hands were gentle as he drew her back into his embrace. "You are a widow, and older than I am."

"I am much older than you are, much older; I've told you that." She looked into his eyes. "I told you when I was born."

"You told me an intriguing story," said Charles, the wicked amusement back in his eyes. "You entertained me."

"Entertained!" She threw it at him. "I told you when I was born," she repeated, this time so somberly that he released his hold on her a little. "I have no reason to lie to you, Charles; perhaps every reason to say something more plausible. I was born in Rome, in the first century. My father was a Roman nobleman, my husband a Senator. That is the truth." She touched his face where his beard had been. "Why should I make up a story, an entertainment like this?"

"Because you do not want me to know . . . that you are no widow, perhaps? Or that your husband died unnaturally." He spoke the words as if they were bitter to taste. "Or that you have fled a convent, or a husband who is . . . like His Majesty, but alive, and you are not a widow." His fingers closed around her wrist. "I don't care. I don't care if you killed ten husbands, or lived in a brothel, or a madhouse, or your father was a highwayman, or you were sold to a Turk, or . . . or ran away from the Grand Sultan himself."

"But you do care that I was born in Rome when the Caesars ruled," she said sadly.

"No. No!" He leaned forward and with his free hand turned her face toward him. "No, Olivia. It doesn't matter to me at all: I don't care if you were born when Joshua brought down Jericho." He kissed her emphatically, insisting that she respond to him.

Olivia felt she was drowning in light; her skin was suddenly tender, as if she had lain in the sun for an hour without the protection of her native earth. It was wonderful and maddening to stand here with Charles, to be caught between the Scylla of her need and the Charybdis of his desire. It was exhilarating to be known for what she was, and at the same time she trembled. How reckless she was, telling him so much about herself, revealing things that she had kept secret for centuries. And there was her own passion, as well as his. She had guarded against it, schooling herself to more prudent gratification. Now, she reveled in the intensity of her esurience.

"You want me," Charles whispered to her. "You want me."

"Yes," she answered. "Oh yes."

"Then the rest is nothing. If you did not want me, the rest would not matter, either." This time his kiss was almost chaste, barely the brush of his lips over hers. "Listen to me, Olivia," he said, his voice low and rough with emotion. "If you were at the ends of the earth, you would still be mine and I would find you, I would have you as long as you love me."

There was irony in her smile, the same irony that she had seen in Sanct' Germain's all those centuries ago. "That is apt to be a very long time," she said. "Among those of our blood, the bond is not—cannot—be broken except by the true death."

He laughed, but the sound was quiet and tender. "All death is true, except before the Throne of God." The scent of hay was very strong in the stall.

"Not with us," she said, her hazel eyes as direct and unflinching as an honorable foe's.

"Death is not revokable, except by the Will of God," Charles said insistently, straightening a little as he spoke.

"It is for us," Olivia said, going on as if reciting, "I died while Vespasianus was Caesar. I was walled up in a tomb, and I died." She waited, meeting his eyes until she saw acquiescence there. "I died. But that was not the end for me, as it will not be the end for you if you continue as my lover."

"It is most convenient, your sort of death. I need not fear the cannonfire and the—" he began gallantly only to be interrupted.

"None of us are proof against injury, and we die as surely as anyone when our bodies are destroyed. If your neck, your spine, is broken, if you are crushed or burned, you will be as dead as any other man. But short of that, you will survive." She moved out of his arms. "I have been shot, I have taken sword-thrusts in my arms and legs and body. I have had brands pressed to my skin and my limbs wrenched from their sockets, and lived through it all, but not without pain, not without hurt, though there is no mark on me to show it."

He brought his hand to her lips, dismay in his clear brown eyes. "No, Olivia. Not now. Nothing more."

"Yes!" she burst out. "I must convince you, don't you understand? If I do not, I cannot stay with you, for your own sake as well as mine." She came back to him, taking his arms in her hands. "Charles, Charles, please. Please believe what I tell you, so that I can love you. Please."

He scrutinized her face, concern and care in his eyes. "Eh bien," he said; he looked down at her hands. "I'll listen to everything you tell me. I will try to believe what you say." He stood while she released him, then moved away from her, leaning against the empty manger.

Now that she had his attention, she hesitated. Without being aware of it, she began to pace, the old straw cracking under her feet. "How can I tell you? You don't understand. You're Catholic and I—"

"I am more your lover than I am a Catholic, and if that damns me, I am a fortunate man," he said lightly but with an underlying purpose that surprised her.

"But to you I am . . . demonic. How can I—"

He stopped her. "You were born in Rome during the reign of Vespasianus. Your husband was a Senator."

"Yes," she said, steadied by this. "He was debauched and he debauched me." She looked at him suddenly, her head up in defiance. "If you pity me, I will never—"

"I don't pity you," said Charles quietly. "But I would like to kill him."

"Why waste your anger. He died in the Flavian Circus long, long ago," she said, and her rigidity left her.

"I would still like to kill him," said Charles, watching her in the guttering light of the lanthorn. "I would wish him alive again so that I might kill him for you."

Olivia's smile was faint and tentative but within her she sensed the first stirrings of happiness that had eluded her for so long. "The Emperor himself condemned my husband."

"Then you were not without aid," he said darkly.

She pretended she did not hear the possessive note in his voice. "I had one ally, and without him I would have remained in that tomb. I would be less than dust now."

"Then I am grateful to him, but I am jealous as well." He cleared his throat. "So. In the Rome of Vespasianus you had a debauched husband and an ally. You were entombed alive. You were rescued from the tomb and—"

"The tomb where I died, where I was confined to die," Olivia said, trying not to look at him as she said this. "I want you to understand that I died."

"Yes. You have repeated it enough." Charles capitulated. "You died."

"And now I am blood of the blood of my ally, and those who love me knowingly . . . who accept what I am and the nature of my love . . ."

"There have been others," he muttered.

"Yes, many others," she said, doing her best to salve his pride. "No one has been like you. No one has pursued me as you have."

"How convenient, so that you will not confuse me with the rest," he snapped, and in the same breath relented. "No. No, they are in the past. They are ghosts. I do not want to be your first lover, but your last."

Her expression changed and her eyes were distant. "My last lover . . ." She trailed off, then recalled herself. "If you had continued to sleep you might have had my love without risk."

Charles' laugh was more angry than amused. "I would have nothing. I do not want a dream, I want a woman; I want you. I would be less than a man if I accepted so little when you are much, much more than a dream." He moved toward her.

"But we have reached a turning point," Olivia said carefully. "You may lie with me, knowing me and the nature of my love, at most six times. Until that time, there is little risk that you will be . . . tainted by me, that you will take anything more than pleasure from me. You may love me and there will be no lasting . . . harm. After that, you will have too much of me, and"—she looked around as the lanthorn sputtered out—"and you will be as I am when you die, unless your body is destroyed or your spine broken."

"We have reached that sixth time," said Charles, the amusement returning to his voice. "Only six times, and already you are part of me."

"Yes." She locked her hands together in front of her as if they could shield her from him.

"What would be needed to insure that you and I are bound for all eternity? You say that with the blood is a bond: how do I strengthen it?"

"Sleep with me again, and—" she started only to have him interrupt her.

"No, something more than that. I want no risk, I want certainty. If you are upset because of what I *may* become, then let us make it absolute. Then you may give yourself to me without reservation." In the dark his eyes found hers. "What will make it so, Olivia?"

Bemused, she answered, "If you were to taste my blood as I have tasted yours, then even if this were only the first time we lay together, it would be the same as if we had been lovers for years and years." She took a step nearer to him. "You can't want that."

"It would settle the matter, wouldn't it?" Charles said. "Neither of us would be troubled again." He reached out for her, fumbling in the gloom.

She took one of his hands in hers. "But there would be no going back; you would be as I am. And when you die you will be one of those who do not lie still. It is a . . . difficult way to . . . to live, Charles."

"It is a fortunate thing for a soldier to be able to rise again. What King would not pray for such men to defend him." He kissed her cheek.

Olivia shook her head. "Charles, don't make a jest of it. Long life, as those of my blood have it, is not always a blessing. There are those who are fearful of us, and in their fear they hunt us. There are those who despise us and our love. And there are preparations you will need to make, precautions that will be necessary, for we are not invulnerable."

"Tell me what I must do, and come to my bed. Then I will be as you are," he said, pulling her close to him. His breath was warm on her neck.

"There is no going back, once you take such a step," she said, amazed at how willing he was to accept her; she hoped he would never regret his decision. "If you think you might have reason, later, to abjure the bond, then do not make it. You do not pledge your word to me, but your blood."

"As you have already done to me," said Charles with certainty.

"Yes; but I know what I am doing, I know the consequences. I have lived long enough that I recognize the nature of the bond." She smiled painfully, looking at his young and handsome face. "You . . . you are how old?"

"I am twenty-one," said Charles with some heat.

"Twenty-one," she echoed, wondering if she dared continue to love him. Twenty-one, she repeated to herself in her mind. When she was twenty-one, Nero ruled Rome, she had just married Justus and suffered the miscarriage of her first—and only—child. How could anyone so very young comprehend what her life was, what would come of loving her?

He all but read her thoughts. "I am a man grown and I know my own mind," he said with some heat. "Do you doubt me?"

Though she did, Olivia said, "No."

"If I were a greybeard and so filled with wisdom that my head ached, I could make no other choice. You are what I want. I have never wanted a woman as I want you. I never will again." A wistfulness crept into his voice. "One day I will marry, because I must. I know my duty to my family. But no woman will be to me what you are, Olivia, and that would be true if all you had told me were fanciful stories." He wrapped his arms around her and stood that way, his jaw against her forehead, his lips on her shining fawn-brown hair.

"They are not—" she protested a short while later.

"Stories. I know that. Ssshh," he whispered.

She started to give him one last warning, but he silenced her with his mouth, his kiss turning urgent, demanding, and his hands, which had sheltered her a moment before, moved impetuously to the ribbons that closed her robe de chambre. He unfastened them, taking care not to rip them, all the while continuing to kiss her. He broke away from her long enough to drag his chamise over his head and throw it into the manger. Then he opened the front of her robe de chambre, so slowly and reverently that it was almost an act of worship.

"Charles," she said, so softly that the wind, the sounds of the horses in their stalls, were louder.

"Look at you," he said. "Look at how beautiful you are. Look what you do to me." He gestured to the bulge in his striped breeches. "I love what you do to me." His fingers touched her nipples, barely grazing the skin. "I tremble when I see you." As he came a step nearer, he smiled down at her. "Do you tremble at the sight of me?"

"Yes," she said, surprised that it was so.

"What will your Roman Cardinal think when he learns of this?" It was the only note of caution he sounded, and as he spoke his hands were beginning their sweet plundering of her body. He was more sure of himself than he had been a month ago.

"He will . . . be relieved, perhaps," said Olivia, hoping that her guess was right. It was not easy to keep her mind on Charles' question. "He is not an unreasonable man."

"Isn't he?" His hands cupped her breasts now, and before she could think of the words to answer him, he lowered his head, and her thoughts were forgotten.

Olivia gave herself over to the rapture of his touch and the frenzy of his kisses. She let him take possession of her without resistance, returning his passion with her hands and lips when she could, reveling in what he gave to her when she could not. It was almost impossible to remain standing, but Charles was not ready to fall into the hay.

"Does this please you?" he asked a short while later as he knelt before her, his hands between her thighs.

She nodded, her body quivering with the intensity of her desire. "Yes," she murmured, as if speaking would break the spell. She went on as if sounding words out that she did not know. "It would please me more"—there was mischief in her voice—"if we were lying down. I don't think I can stand up any longer."

He chuckled, wrapping his arms around her knees. "So be it," he said, toppling her.

The straw was warm, and August hung on the night air like the smell of a hot stove. Their clothes spread on the straw was bed enough for them, and by the time Charles kicked off his breeches, his body was ready for her. As he moved over her, he growled, "I want to be part of you. I want to be part of you." He was avid for her, moving into her as if he wished to fuse the two of them forever.

It was astonishing to Olivia to plumb such depths of mania as she did with Charles. She had rarely felt so close to madness, and never so joyously. It was as if all the yearning, all the ecstasy she had denied herself for those long, long years, were returned to her tenfold; what was more amazing was that Charles' need equaled her own. She rocked with him, joyous in their intimate dance.

"What must I do?" he panted, sweat standing out on his flesh. "Tell me."

"If you're determined," she said, finding it difficult to speak.

She was caught up in the marvel of his touch, his lips. Speech seemed hopelessly clumsy in comparison. "You do as I do."

"And when?" He pressed into her more deeply. "I can't last much longer."

"When I do," she said, unable to keep the doubt from her tone.

"What is this, Olivia?" he asked urgently. "Don't you want me—"

"I worry for you," she said. "Be certain."

He gave a breathless laugh. "I am." He wrapped his arms around her more closely. "I am. I am."

Olivia could no longer argue. As she felt him gather, she put her lips to his neck and gave herself over to the elation he offered, and that he claimed for himself.

"Bon Dieu, I have scarred you," Charles burst out when he had come to his senses. He stared at the rivulet of blood that ran from just below her collarbone to her side.

"No," said Olivia. She was happily languorous in the aftermath of their passion. The straw on which they lay seemed as luxurious as a featherbed. "That is no longer possible."

"Scars are always possible," said Charles, unconvinced.

"Among the living," Olivia reminded him. "Not for such as I am."

"And I will be," said Charles with satisfaction. He kissed the corner of her mouth and one hand strayed to the curve of her breast. "I will never, never have enough of you. There is not enough time before Judgment Day."

"And you may see most of those years," she said. She repositioned herself so she could rest her head on his shoulder.

He smiled lazily. "To live from now to Judgment Day. What wonders I will see."

Olivia sighed. "I hope you will not come to hate me for those years, and the things you will see."

"How could I hate you? especially now that blood will bind us." He touched his neck where her lips had been. "There is as much of me in you as there is you in me."

"I pray you never change your mind," she said, a frown starting.

"Why should I?" Charles asked. With one hand he began to play with her fawn-brown hair.

"Others have," she said, her mind far away.

"They were fools, to have you and to let you go," said Charles, his expression darkening.

"Eventually we must let each other go," said Olivia, staring up toward the ceiling. "When you come to my life, the bond remains, but the rest . . ."

"What?" Charles prompted when she did not go on.

Olivia did not answer him at once. "When you come to my life," she repeated, "what we have now is . . . no longer possible."

He turned, grabbed her upper arms. "What are you saying to me?"

There was dismay in her face. "Do you regret this already?"

"I regret nothing, nothing; but you have to explain," he said emphatically. "Olivia. Tell me what you are saying."

She looked away from him, then met his eyes with her own. "When you die, we will no longer be lovers, though we will share our bond and our . . . nature. That is what will make it impossible for us to continue, for we seek life, Charles." She waited, and when he said nothing, she went on. "I will always love you, Charles; nothing else matters."

"But we will not be lovers," he said, scowling. "A fine state of affairs." He all but flung her from him but could not bring himself to let go of her.

"Not as we are now," she confirmed, a desolation sweeping over her. In all her centuries there had been so few times of lucid happiness, and now this one, treasured and rare, seemed to be slipping away from her.

Charles lay back, still holding her close to him. "Then we must make the best use to the time we have," he said decisively. He went on in his practical way, "I assumed we would have decade upon decade to make love, but as it will only be until my death, we will have to devote more time to love. I can see that it will be essential if we are not to be cheated later, and come to resent our bond." He gave her a hearty, deliberate kiss.

"You are not . . ." She could not find the word for what she feared.

"Disappointed?" he suggested. "Certainly I am, but we must accommodate." He gave her a close look. "You're not cold, are you?" He rubbed his hand over her shoulder in a token gesture.

"No; those of my blood are rarely cold," she said, oddly touched at his solicitousness. "Are you cold?"

He clapped his free hand to his chest. "I am a Gascon. It is not conceivable that I would be cold on an August night."

Olivia's laughter was warm and soft. "And a soldier as well." She leaned over and took his hand, bringing it to her lips to kiss.

"Olivia," he said with shock. "You must not do this; it is for me to kiss your hand."

"How absurd," said Olivia, kissing his hand a second time, then adding more seriously. "I kiss your hand because of our bond, Charles, not for courtesy."

He thought this over, then smiled a little, his flying eyebrows lifting at the corners. "Then it must be all right," he told her before catching her in a second, breathless hug. "We still have hours before sunrise."

"Aren't you sleepy?" Olivia asked, grinning with him.

He gave a snort of contempt. "Sleep is for those with nothing better to do. You and I have much more important things to do other than sleep." His kiss was lingering and impatient all at once. "And what is more important than this?"

Olivia laughed for delight. "I can't imagine."

✻   ✻   ✻

Text of a letter from Pere Pascal Chape to an unidentified person.

To the most exalted of those who attempted to right the injustices perpetrated on France, and who God in His Mercy has spared from death and dishonor, I send my most sincere greetings and pray that I will be permitted to act again in your interests whenever and however you may decide to command me, for next to God there is no one to whom I owe more binding allegiance.

It is most unfortunate that Cinq-Mars was discovered when he was so close to our goal; the price he has paid will be demanded of all of us at God's Hand one day. I pray that Cinq-Mars was received in Heaven as the martyr he is, and that his cause—our cause, if I may be permitted the liberty—will not wither and die because of cowardice on the part of those who are near to you who have been horrified by how the not-to-be-sufficiently-damned Richelieu and that Italian poppinjay who is his lieutenant have moved against those in league with Cinq-Mars.

More than ever France cries out for a King who will serve her in honor and glory, who will leave not two puny sons behind him, but more children than any noble could wish for, all of them vital and devoted to the cause of their father and their country. What we have now is the puppet of his desires and those who find favor through his desires. This disgraces us before God as well as before the eyes of the world. That a Prince of the Church should support such a terrible regime is the greatest shame of all; Richelieu knows better than most that his position is untenable, both in terms of the country and any moral standard set forth by the Church.

I ask a favor of you, in that wonderful time that you rise to power and become the master of the kingdom, as you have every right and claim to be: that I be allowed to set out the punishments to be visited on Richelieu and that Roman Mazarini. I long to wield the sword of righteousness and to strike down those who have betrayed us all. Assure me that it will be my sentence that will fall on these two and I will never ask another boon of you, not for myself nor any part of my family nor any other man alive.

As far as I have been able to determine my role in our venture has not been discovered. I pray you will permit me to continue as I have been, sending you dispatches from time to time as they are needed and as I deem it is prudent to do so. I will employ a different courier each time and never one who is likely to serve me ill. Those I have used to date have been in Orders, and it seems to me that they are more apt to carry out my instructions without question than those who are not devoted to the religious life. I have also striven to choose those whose convictions march with our own and who are willing to risk disfavor in this life for the rewards granted to the virtuous in the next. I have pledged those who have served me to absolute silence, and my faith reposes in their vows.

I have been informed that you may come to court for the Nativity fete. If this is so, I ask that I be allowed to visit you, under such circumstances as would occasion no unwise remarks or speculation. I will count it a most profound honor if you are willing to admit me; if you have any reason to refuse, I will bow my head in acceptance, of course. You are the hope of all France and we who serve you have fixed our eyes on your star.

Permit me to make a recommendation at this point: it would be prudent to sever the courier links to Rome currently employed by the Italian Cardinal. I am certain he uses the house of his countrywoman, the Clemens widow, as a place of message exchanges. It is much easier to cut the chain there than in Paris or Rome; the route traveled by his couriers is changed from time to time, and so it is not as easy to interrupt the messengers once they have left Chatillon. I advise a constant watch on the widow's house for now, so that when the time comes to act, we will not have to guess at what we do. We must also suborn one or two of Mazarini's house servants—lackeys will do—so that we may know what is taking place there. As long as we have no means to decide which events are significant to our purposes, we increase our risks and by extension add to Mazarini's strength, which would be most unfortunate for all of us.

Your request that I question those of noble rank as to their current sentiments concerning Richelieu and Mazarini is perhaps a bit premature, for Cinq-Mars has been dead for less than two weeks and there are many who fear that suspicion may light on them. By the time you come to Paris, such sentiments will have given way to reason and the resentment all true Frenchmen feel will have returned many fold. At that time, I may be of greater use to you and to the cause of justice we all serve.

I pray night and morning for your health and your advancement, and I ask God to show His favor by bringing you to the Crown you deserve. Be certain that I have not faltered in my convictions and I never will.

With benedictions and devotion, I have the honor to sign myself to you,

> Pere Pascal Chape
> Canons Regular of St. Augustine

On the 22nd day of September, 1642, the day following the Feast of St. Matthew the Apostle.

Destroy this.

· 9 ·

At the monastery of Les Sacres Innocentes the roof of the smaller chapel was leaking. Most of the monks continued with their duties, but a few of them were busy trying to repair the broken slates before any more damage could be done.

"A fine way to keep the feast of Saint Martin," Frere Herriot grumbled as another of the slates got away from him and went clattering down the roof.

"I tell you," Frere Aubri agreed as he flapped his sodden habit at the others, "I would not mind the loan of his cloak about now."

It was a feeble joke, but the other four monks perched on the roof did their best to laugh.

"The Abbe wants this done before nightfall," warned Frere Gautier, who was the first to fall silent.

"If we're fortunate, and if God wills it, then we will be done by nightfall," said Frere Crepet, who was known not to be entirely right in his mind. "God will guide us."

Frere Herriot and Frere Servie nodded and crossed themselves; Frere Aubri scoffed. "God isn't going to wield this mallet for me, or shape new slates. If He'd slack off the rain, I'd be pleased."

Again the other monks laughed dutifully.

"A pity we don't have carpenters among our lay brothers," said Frere Herriot. "It would mean we could stay inside at prayers and not have to—" He held up his mallet to express his irritation.

"God save us," sighed Frere Servie. "Hold your tongue, or we'll have to confess blasphemy and who knows what else." He stared up into the rain. "We have one thing to be thankful for: it's not windy."

"A consideration," Frere Aubri said. "Or we could have frost or snow. The roof wouldn't be leaking, but . . ." He went back to work on the slates, muttering the "Dies Irae" with each blow, letting the prophesy of doom set the rhythm for him.

"But," said Frere Gautier, running his hand through his thinning hair, "if we had snow, the roof might collapse. We're better off with rain."

Frere Servie, who was closest to the edge of the roof, started to lean forward. "What?" he called down through the steady drumming of the rain.

"Be careful!" Frere Crepet warned him, moving a little nearer the older monk, though he was known to fear heights as he feared so many things.

But Frere Servie was pointing down to the road that ran beside the chapel. "Look. There's a man down there."

"There are always men down there," said Frere Aubri with a hint of disgust. "Men in the road!" he exclaimed in mock horror. "What is the world coming to?"

"But look," Frere Servie persisted. "He's waving to us."

"A humorous fellow," scoffed Frere Aubri.

"The poor man," whispered Frere Crepet, though the other monks could not find the reason for his distress.

Frere Gautier came nearer the edge and looked over. "You're right; he's waving."

"I wonder why," Frere Herriot said, but he did not leave off his work. "If he wants something of us, let him go around to the pilgrims' gate."

"He looks like a soldier," said Frere Gautier, who had been with the Compagne de Flandre just five years before.

"A deserter, more like," said Frere Aubri without enthusiasm. "Seeking the monastery to take him in."

"Well, you took *me* in," said Frere Gautier reasonably. "The Abbe will not turn away another, not if he wishes to join the Order." He held up his arms to get the man's attention, and when he was sure he had it, he gestured instructions for finding the pilgrims' gate. He repeated the process before he saw an answering signal of understanding from the man on the road.

"Abbe Gottard will be displeased," said Frere Aubri as they returned to their work.

"He would be more displeased if we turned anyone away from our doors when they are in need," said Frere Gautier in his most practical manner. "We are supposed to minister to those in need, aren't we?" He started to wring the water from his sleeve, then shrugged. "We can put a few more slates in place before we get down." As he swung his mallet expertly, he looked away over the roofs of the nearby town. "What must Tours have looked like when Saint Martin was Bishop here."

"A smaller place, the houses more like huts, and stouter walls." Frere Aubri gave a sweeping gesture with his arms. "And probably fewer farms, and most of them walled." He sneezed once, twice, and blessed himself. "Come on, Brothers. A little more work and we're done."

"Well enough," said Frere Herriot. "Labor and prayer are the same in the eyes of God." He repeated it as he tended to repeat all lessons, in a kind of singsong voice that made him sound like a sulky schoolboy. He brought his mallet down with such force that he chipped the slate he was putting in place.

"Restraint," suggested Frere Servie; he had been making more progress than the others, keeping at his task with rote steadiness. "The sooner we have our slates in place, the sooner it will be possible to get warm and dry again. And we need not fear the roof falling on us while we're at prayers."

"It could have happened to the nuns' chapel," said Frere Gautier wistfully. "All those good Sisters with their orphans' school."

"That's a worldly thought to hold," said Frere Servie. "Do not bring sin on yourself, Frere."

Frere Gautier took the rebuke without anger. "Oh, not sin: nostalgia." He grabbed a new slate and set it in place expertly. "God does not expect us to forget we are men."

"But He *does* expect us to make an effort to rise above it." Frere Servie shook his head as he kept on working. "I will pray for you, Frere Gautier."

"And I for you," said Frere Gautier at once. He winked, but only Frere Crepet chuckled.

It was nearly two hours later that the five monks, dried and in fresh habits, gave themselves to ministering to those who had come to the monastery for charity, offering their sympathy and prayers.

Frere Gautier made it a point to speak with the fellow he had seen below them. It was not correct for him to place the needs of this one man over anyone else's, but his curiosity was piqued and that he decided was sufficient. He approached the ragged fellow who was sitting on a bench eagerly sucking up the last of the simple pork-and-onion stew. "Stranger," he said as he would have said to anyone in the room, "be welcome in the Name of God and the Holy Innocents slaughtered in His stead."

"To you," the man said while continuing to eat.

"You were the man I saw on the road, aren't you?" He read suspicion in the other's features, and he shook his head. "I and four of the others were repairing the roof."

"Oh," said the stranger, less guarded. "Is there a chance I could get some more of this stew?" He spoke with an accent and although he managed the words well enough, his rhythms were from another tongue, something more musical.

"Are you starving?" asked Frere Gautier, studying the man's face: it was lean but not pinched and his eyes were not sunken.

"Not yet, but I'm very hungry, and stanco . . . tired," said the stranger. He held up the empty bowl. "Not much there to fill a man."

"Enough," said Frere Gautier with a new sternness in his attitude. "It is all we monks are given."

The stranger had the grace to cough. "But still, you are monks, living here, not walking down these infernal French roads."

"Where are you going?" He was all but certain now that this stranger had been a soldier—he had the manner—but the stiff leg that poked out from the bench would have made him a liability to a regiment, for it would slow him down.

He sighed. "I don't know. If things were otherwise"—he slapped the thigh of his stiff leg—"I might go home. My wife may have softened to me, for I've been gone some time. Her family opposed our match, and since we were poor, in the end it was easier for me to leave, to become a soldier, than to remain where we spent so much time arguing. So long as I was going to fight," he said with a faint smile, "I thought I would like to be paid for the risk and have a chance of a victory or two."

"Where is your home?" asked Frere Gautier; in his years as a soldier he had heard tales of many men who had followed the drum to end their poverty as much as for honor.

"In the Papal States," answered the stranger at once. "A little place not far from Rome. You won't have heard of it unless you'd been there." He leaned back against the wall. "I had hoped I would bring something home to my wife, to show that we would not always be scratching in the dirt like chickens."

"Many another has suffered the same fate," said Frere Gautier. "Where were you wounded?"

"You mean the leg? It was during La Marfee when the Duc de Soissons was killed, before de Bouillon surrendered. I was on the line of cannon when one of them . . . blew up." His chuckle grated, like the sound of a saw on a brick. "Not even enemy fire. There might have been some glory in that."

Frere Gautier knew that the stranger probably received no money for the wound, since it did not come from the enemy. He shook his head, saying with feeling, "That is unfortunate."

The stranger shrugged. "I am not the only man to suffer this." He looked keenly at Frere Gautier. "How long has it been since you rose to trumpets instead of bells?"

"Four years," said Frere Gautier. "So you see, I do know what can happen, even to the best of soldiers." He hunkered down so that their conversation could be more private. "What are your plans, then? Back to Italy?"

The stranger faltered. "I . . . truly, I don't know. I am not sure . . . My wife and I did not part on good terms. Her family took her in, and I know they have the money to care for her better than I can. I have a little land of my own, and I could work it, but with my leg, I might be less successful than before. I'm strong enough, but a lame man . . ." He shook his head. "Perhaps it would be best if I sold the farm and gave the money to my wife and never came home."

"She is still your wife," Frere Gautier pointed out, less willing to believe that any man would want to stay away from a spouse whose family was better off. "Under the circumstances, might not her family arrange for some help?"

The stranger gave a gesture of mixed impatience and resignation. "I can't be sure." He caught his lower lip between his teeth before continuing. "I admit that by the time I left, I was glad to be free of her. We had done nothing but shout or be silent as stones for months and months. I had not brought in a good crop and we had even less money than we had anticipated, which was very little, not more than two dozen scudi to last through the winter."

"Two dozen scudi—" began Frere Gautier skeptically.

"Silver scudi, not the gold ones they make in Milano." His disgust was very strong. "I was angry with her, and with her family who said that I was a wastrel and other unkind things. One of her brothers offered to help me, but it came to nothing, and Angela went back to them."

"But your leg . . . surely they will provide assistance." He hesitated. "And there will be sons."

"No," said the stranger, shaking his head slowly. "No children. I have been told by the physician of the local landowner that there is some defect, some lack in my wife that will not let her breed as she ought. Her family blames that on me as well as all the rest. They say that if she had not married a poor man, she would have children." He folded his arms and looked belligerent.

"It is the Will of God, perhaps," said Frere Gautier.

"It doesn't matter whose will it is," said the stranger with muted fury. "She's barren as a post."

Frere Gautier frowned, thinking. He was taking a great deal into his hands, but he said, "We have need of lay Brothers here, who take no lasting vows. You could work here awhile until you decide what you wish to do."

"What?" the stranger said, his wrath turning to astonishment. "What are you saying?"

"It is something to consider," Frere Gautier said a bit more cautiously. "If you think you would want to live in a monastery and eat simple food."

"Simple food!" The stranger gave a single bark of laughter. "What soldier isn't used to simple food? Half the time it's a duck stolen from some farmer and cooked on a spit." He leaned back. "It's a generous offer, but what use am I to you, if I am not any use as a farmer?"

"Oh, there are other things," said Frere Gautier. "We have a smithy and a wheelwright; if you could climb to the roof, you could repair the slates."

"The way you were doing?" the stranger asked. "I am not much use on a ladder, I'm afraid."

"We make cheese as well, and need cowherds and dairymen." Frere Gautier got to his feet. "I'll leave you now, but perhaps you will allow me to speak to the Abbe on your behalf?"

"I'll . . . think about it," the stranger said, his tone indicating he would. "What of those near here? Might not it be better if I found employment with someone else?"

"Well, there is a stud farm adjoining most of the northeast side of our land, and the work there is controlled by an evil fellow named Octave and his brother Perceval. They would not take in one they do not know. They are left to run the place alone and they abuse their master by stealing from him and giving the profits to themselves." Frere Gautier had the strange sensation that the stranger was too eager to know about this place.

"Who is the master?" he demanded.

"Actually, it is his widow who has inherited the place, and she is never there," said Frere Gautier. "Women—"

"Yes," said the stranger, his accent growing stronger. "I know how capricious widows can be. They have no business running stud farms, or anything else, for that matter." With a visible effort he calmed himself. "Perhaps I have come to the right place," he said, looking directly at Frere Gautier.

"We would not coddle you, if that is what you are hoping, but we will not despise you for the ill God has visited upon you," said Frere Gautier, starting away from the stranger only to be called back.

"What would the Abbe expect of me?" He rubbed his stiff leg without paying attention to it. "I am willing, but there is much I am not certain I can do."

"I'm sure that's understood," said Frere Gautier. "For six months there is no reason you must take any vow at all. At the end of that time, you may become a lay Brother, or, if you find you have a vocation, you may begin to join us as a Brother. It would have to be secondary, for your wife is still alive."

"As far as I know," the stranger appended. "I have not been able to send word to her very often, nor she to me. Neither of us can read or write, and I think she begrudged the price of a scribe." He coughed. "I had a letter sent to her just after I received this"—he slapped his leg again—"but since then I have not been able to afford . . ."

"We will remedy that," said Frere Gautier with a smile. "Tell me where to write, and to whom."

The stranger gave a smile that Frere Gautier suspected was forced. "It is best to write to her brother. He works at the biggest estate in the area. It's that or the parish church, San Andrea."

Frere Gautier regarded the stranger. "And what is your name, so I may tell the Abbe?"

The stranger smiled. "I am Nino," he said, providing himself a grand family name. "Nino Colonnello."

"A cadet branch of the family?" suggested Frere Gautier, not wanting to give offence to any relative of Cardinal Mazarin's, no matter how remote.

"Not quite that, but related, nonetheless." It was a lie that no one would bother to investigate, in case it would stir up scandal that was better forgotten. "There are documents, somewhere."

"It has happened before," said Frere Gautier, knowing how he could approach Abbe Gottard now. He gave Nino an encouraging gesture, one that had more soldier than monk in it. "I will have an answer for you by morning."

"Thank you," Nino said, doing his best to sound grateful and humble while he let himself imagine the revenge he would take, with Bondama Clemens almost in his hands.

*   *   *

Text of a letter from Charles de Batz-Castelmore to his older brother Paul; dictated to Niklos Aulirios.

My dear brother,

It is fortunate for both of us that you do not have to struggle through my horrible efforts at writing; for once I have found someone willing to take down what I say as I say it and will ask nothing of me but my signature, which I can manage well enough.

I have had another interview with M. de Troisvilles, and he has advised me that I will not be admitted to the Musqueteers this year, but perhaps there will be an opening next year. He has encouraged me to make an effort with the King's Guard, so that I will have a reputation to offer the Musqueteers when I am permitted to be among their numbers.

For he does not rule out all hope—in fact, he has been most encouraging—but rather is bound by the regulations that make it impossible for him to install more than a certain number of new men at any time. I am attempting to be sensible and to accept this state of affairs without chafing, but that is often more difficult than I want to admit.

I am following your suggestion and making what friends I can who may be of use to me later; in one case it is far more pleasure than ambition that drives me to seek out the company of this member of the new Cardinal's embassy. Lest you fear that I am coming to support the Italian, I wish to remind you that I am aware as any good Gascon of the danger he represents, just as I also know there is no one who is a stronger friend at court now that Richelieu is dead. If Mazarin is willing to aid me, then I would welcome it, and gladly, though he were the Devil himself.

As part of my attempt to improve my place in the world, I have consulted M. de Troisvilles as to the use of our mother's name, for her family is more noble than our father's. I do not hold our father and his family in any less esteem, but you yourself have said that I must make use of what connections I may since I lack fortune and exalted title to provide me with the opportunities I seek. If you do not object to this change, I will assume her name at once, and inform M. de Troisvilles of what I have done, for he will take that change into account when he evaluates the various candidates he has for the Musqueteers.

When you wrote two months ago you inquired into the health of the King; I am sorry to say that His Majesty has not improved. There are those who say that the shock of Richelieu's death—though why it should be a shock, I do not comprehend, for he had been ailing steadily for years—has worsened His Majesty's condition. His physicians continue to treat him, and have said that they expect an eventual recovery, but for now it is understood that Louis XIII requires rest and the medications and procedures recommended by his physicians. I was told that His Majesty has been made to sit with his feet in the warm blood of fresh-killed bulls to aid in the return of his strength. Perhaps if he drank the blood as well, it would help him more, for blood, I have been assured, has special powers to restore vitality.

It will not be possible for me to return to Gascony for several months. Not only does the weather prevent me—you know what the roads are like—but I have obligations which keep me in the vicinity of Paris. It is in my interests to remain here, where I will be able to take advantage of all opportunities to be of service.

I was permitted to attend a private Nativity Mass yesterday in the company of His Eminence Cardinal Mazarin, and was brought to his attention by the member of his embassy I have already mentioned. His Eminence received me politely and said he would re-

member my name in future, which is why I gave him our mother's, so that when you approve the change it will not require me to remind His Eminence of our meeting and his remark.

M. des Essarts has informed me that he will renew his recommendation for my advancement to the Musqueteers to M. de Troisvilles as soon as you have signified your approval of my use of our mother's family name. I pray you will not take too long to do this. I make full allowances for the roads, but this is December, and it would not be unreasonable to have your reply by February.

With my fidelity and devotion and my assurance to you that I will never dishonor the family, either our father's or our mother's, I will now sign myself to you for the first time,

Your loving brother
Charles d'Artagnan

On the Feast of Saint Stephen, 1642.

PART III
Atta Olivia Clemens

Text of a letter from Niklos Aulirios to Gaetano Fosso, acting major domo at Senza Pari.

To my able deputy, my thanks for your continued devotion to our mistress' interests. I have your letter from three weeks ago, and I am very pleased with the manner in which you have handled the delicate question of who is to be allowed to replace Uberto. You have been at pains to give no offence, and this is most praiseworthy. I believe that the new coachman, the Hungarian, will serve excellently.

Our mistress has asked that I send money to Uberto's family in appreciation for the long years of service he provided. He was dedicated and reliable, two excellent qualities that are often wanting in men. Death came far too early for him; he ought to have had another thirty years at least, and the pleasure of seeing his grandchildren. If it were not for the scratch of a rusty nail, he would be with us still and there would be no reason for grieving and finding a replacement for him. It is sad to learn how much he suffered before the end came. I have seen men bent like a bow before, and it is not a thing to be wished on anyone.

It is a year now since Louis XIII died; the French are still reeling from their double loss—Richelieu first, and six months later, his King—and the court is in turmoil, for to have a little boy on the throne is something none of them are prepared to accept. Of course Louis XIV is not a ruler; his mother is his regent, which has made for some trouble. She was so neglected and abused while her husband lived that now the courtiers who spurned her must do whatever they can to repair the damage they have done. She, in turn, has not been gracious about their past behavior: she continues guarded and suspicious, for she is convinced that the nobles are still against her.

Our mistress has become very popular because of this, for she is known to be part of Mazarin's suite and a woman of means. Since the Queen Regent trusts no one but Mazarin, those who are eager to gain her good opinion make an effort to cultivate Bondame Clemens as a first step to gaining the attention of Mazarin. It has its amusing moments.

All of which contrives to keep us here. The Cardinal has requested that we do not leave, and he is very persuasive. It is my hope that in another year we will be back in Italy once more, but I confess that it is not likely unless the court here becomes more regulated and the Cardinal's place as First Minister of France is undisputed. Once Mazarin has the reins firmly in his hands, we will be at liberty to depart. And considering the chore it is to transport our mistress' household from one place to another, a year might not be time enough to make all the necessary arrangements. Six carriages, with teams and relays, and the full complement of servants is hardly a minor venture. Even if a few of the servants prefer to remain here in France, the least we would have on the road is five carriages, and that requires arrangements and planning.

We have instigated changes and repairs at the stud farm near Tours. A few of our mistress' staff have been dispatched there for the purpose of seeing that her commands are carried out; it appears that there have been those who are willing to take the funds for upkeep and to do nothing more than pocket them. I need not tell you how ill this sits with Olivia Clemens. She abhors waste and mistreatment, of men, of animals, and of land, and all those things have occurred at Tours.

Your report on the yearling sale is encouraging. I would recommend continuing to use Napoliano, if his other colts show the same merits as Verga. Our mistress has expressed great satisfaction in how well the breeding has gone and she has requested that I thank you for your role in this success. She has remarked that she wishes her stud farm in this country could produce half the number of foals as Senza Pari and that they be of half the quality.

By the end of summer I will return to Senza Pari for a meeting with you and the tenants. Our mistress wishes me to evaluate the land and buildings so that improvements may be put in motion. I am eager to see Roma again, but I am also concerned that I will leave Bondama Clemens alone for at least six weeks. If only I knew the secret of being in two places at once! Then I might discharge my duties to her without leaving her side. Still, while I am gone I have the Cardinal's assurance that our mistress will be properly guarded, but this does not entirely end by apprehension. I have also the word of a young officer of the King's Guard who has vowed to care for Olivia no matter what may happen. I have more trust in Signor' d'Artagnan than I do in the Cardinal, because it is the Cardinal who places our mistress in danger in the first place.

When I have made my plans I will send you word, via the Cardinal's personal couriers, which will bring letters to you in the fewest number of days. In the meantime, I ask that you will send me monthly dispatches so that I will be prepared for our meeting, and you will have all your information ready. If any difficulties have arisen that you have not mentioned, I ask you to apprise me of them now, so that we may commence to resolve them as soon as I arrive.

You may depend on my gratitude; I pray for the well-being of all those who live at Senza Pari.

> Niklos Aulirios
> major domo of Eblouir at Chatillon

On the 30th of May, 1644.
Retain for household records.

· 1 ·

"It was poison!" Anne of Austria declared more emphatically, holding out the little flowered plate. "Why else did the King turn pale and cast up his meal?"

Mazarin shook his head, preparing for a long afternoon with the Queen Regent. "Majesty, there are a hundred reasons. The King is a child, and children are taken by strange humors all the time. Think of last week, when your younger boy had that terrible rash, and no one knew the cause. He was swollen and his skin was red and itching. And then, poof! it was over and the boy was smiling again. Children are like that. They fall ill, they have fevers—who can say from what cause?—and then they are as sunny as a May afternoon, and all in a matter of hours." He indicated a chair, and bowed her toward it. "Please, gentle lady, you are a little over-wrought. Quiet yourself and we will discuss this more carefully." He chose one of the plainest chairs in the room and brought it near to her, waiting for her nod of permission before he took his seat. "Please," he repeated.

Anne shook her head several times. "They want him dead, as they wanted me dead," she whispered. Her face, ordinarily pale, was chalky and her eyes seemed too bright. "They will find a way and then they will make one of their own King in my son's place, though he has the Right."

"For love of Our Lord, Majesty," said Mazarin, trying to still her passionate outburst. "Consider what you are saying."

"I have considered it," she said emphatically. "Why should I not?" Her face was set and there was a line about her mouth making her lips white. "I know this court of old. I have known it since I was little more than a child, and I know that it is filled with treason and a thousand terrible plots. The courtiers have banded against me before, and they will do so again. When it was my husband who ruled, there was nothing I could do, for he was the one who wanted most to be rid of me. Anything I did that might be construed as against his interests were used to isolate and degrade me." There were tears in her eyes, born of anger instead of grief. "I hated him for that, and I prayed to God to forgive me every night on my knees. But Louis hated me and he never asked for forgiveness, not from me and not from God." She looked away from Mazarin; her hand moving quickly to smear her tears away.

"It was a most unfortunate situation," said Mazarin at his most soothing. "The match was ill-advised and ill-considered."

"It was his mother's doing," said Anne, her anger unabated. "She was the one who thought I would be the one to change his tastes. She had it all planned."

"She was that sort of woman," said Mazarin, hoping that this outburst would not last long. "And she paid dearly for her folly."

"Exile!" scoffed Anne. "I was in exile for more than twelve years. I was ordered not to leave my apartments here for any reason." The little flowered dish she had been holding was suddenly flung across the room to break on the edge of the marble hearth. "I suppose if the Louvre had burned Louis would have ordered me to stay in the flames."

"Majesty—" Mazarin persisted.

"He made me the joke of the court, he encouraged them all to abuse and despise me, and it is no different now he is dead. They are too used to thinking of me as nothing, and they call me the same names they have always used, and they say my son has no Right, for Louis would never give me a child. He did not for so very long, that it could not be his. They say he is his brother's boy." She stopped, her voice dropping. "Or Richelieu's."

"Yes," Mazarin said in his most reasonable way. "I have heard that. I have heard even more ridiculous assertions. But you must remember that for so long the King made no attempt to hide his tastes, and he was so flagrant with those who were his favorites that it is not surprising that the courtiers now voice their suspicions." For the last year he had been saying much the same thing to her, trying to ease her fury whenever she was taken with sudden dreads, as she was now.

"It would not be allowed in Spain," Anne said, her hands locked in mortal combat in her lap. "It would not be tolerated."

"But this is France, Majesty, and both of us are suspect because we are foreigners." He was fully and formally dressed in red biretta, mozzetta, cassock, and lace-edge surplice. There was a diplomatic reception in two hours, and he knew that the Queen Regent could not appear in public in so distraught a state. He regarded her, one hand raised to invoke silence. "I will arrange for a friend to examine Louis," he said in his most even manner. "I will see that some effort is made to determine if what ailed him was natural to childhood or if it was the cause of something in his food. It may well be . . ." he said, tantalizing her with his speculation, "that some of the food was improperly prepared. It is worth considering, Majesty."

Anne was not prepared to relent. "I will want to hear everything this friend says. And I want to know who this friend is." She pulled her hands apart with effort.

"But if I told you that, we might inadvertently expose my friend to danger, and what then? In future, when other services are needed, my friend might not be there." He paused to let Anne consider what he had said. "I think it is wisest to protect those who protect us, Majesty: don't you agree?"

She fastened her hands on the arms of her chair. "Perhaps. If the friend is truly a friend. If not—"

"If not we will know it soon enough," said Mazarin.

"At the cost of my son!" Anne burst out, and once again began to weep.

"No, no, no, Majesty," Mazarin protested. "Never would I risk the King's welfare. I have sworn that to you and on the altar of God. The boy is my primary concern and I will do nothing that I believe might bring him into danger."

"He's just a child," she whispered. "To be so little and subjected to this!"

Mazarin sighed inwardly. He had been doing well, and then he had inadvertently triggered this new outburst. "Majesty, Majesty, calm yourself. You know that there are burdens that come with greatness, and your little boy will have to learn of them soon enough if he is to be a worthy King when he comes to rule. You are his mentor as well as his mother, and if he sees you so much alarmed, he may assume that he has many reasons to fear and will not strive as he must. It is not wise to make a King fearful, Majesty."

Her breath shuddered through her. "No."

"And so you must be more brave than he," he went on, warming to his subject and hoping that this time Anne would be able to control her outburst. If word got back to Austria that this Spanish Hapsburg was not as capable as her Austrian cousins, she would find herself with far more to contend with than restless courtiers. "He will take courage from you, Majesty, if you will offer it to him."

Anne pinched the bridge of her nose between her two forefingers. "How can I prevail?"

Mazarin gave her his most charming smile. "Ah, no, Majesty; how can *we* prevail. This is not a decade ago, when your husband flaunted his favorites to all the world, this is a new time for you. You are Regent, not any of those favorites. And Louis XIV is your son. It would be wise to remember that, for it gives you great strength, no matter how the fops whisper behind their hands, no matter how many lies are told: the Church and the Kingdom of France accept you."

"Outwardly," she agreed.

"It is all we may believe," said Mazarin, anxious to keep her from more dire speculations. "We know that there are those in the country who are displeased that your husband is dead, just as there are those who are displeased that I am First Minister. But until God raises up your husband, or you dismiss me from my position, then they must accept this or be called traitors and pay the price of their treason."

Anne had stopped crying, but her face was mottled and her eyes were rimmed in red. "Oh, God; how am I to manage?"

"As you have in the past, but with help and with the might of France to enforce your word," said Mazarin, apparently endlessly patient. "You have a son who is depending upon you to guide his steps and his Kingdom until he is capable of acting for himself. Consider what that will mean to the boy."

She made a vague gesture. "How am I to protect him?"

For a moment Mazarin had an urge to reach out, take the Queen Regent by the shoulders and shake her. None of this showed in his unruffled demeanor. "Let me act for you, Majesty. I have an oath to fulfill even as you do, and it would please me to know you have allowed me to pursue your interests. I will continue to keep you apprised of all I do, and I will notify you if anything untoward occurs. That will spare you this constant anguish which has brought you such great burdens."

"How can you act for me?" She was looking at him curiously and not quite as trustingly as before.

"In whatever way you choose. You have only to tell me how you would wish me to aid you, and you may be sure it will be done." He went down on his knee at her side. "Majesty, I am your servant as much as any lackey or scullion in the Louvre. You have only to command me and I will hasten to do your bidding."

Anne smiled a little, though her mouth was hard. "I will give it some thought. Speak to me of this again, in a fortnight, when I have had time to pray and contemplate." She held out her hand to be kissed, indicating that their private discussion was ended for the time being. "I must prepare for the reception," she said distantly, though she did not rise from her chair. "I have so many things to prepare for."

"Certainly," said Mazarin, getting to his feet and executing a proper bow.

"I thank you for your good counsel," Anne said formally, using the proper phrase for dismissal. She rose in order to curtsy and kiss his ring, then stood straight, her eyes bright but focused at some distant point as Mazarin withdrew from her presence.

Knowing that it was irresponsible to show anxiety of any kind when leaving an audience with the Queen Regent, Mazarin adjusted his features to reflect mild curiosity. He walked down the wide hall, one of his lackeys following three steps behind, taking care not to hurry. He acknowledged the greeting of courtiers with grave courtesy but with no gestures of distinction; he was not reckless enough to play visible favorites with the future of the little King so uncertain. Only once did he deliver a direct cut to a greeting, and that was from Monsieur du Peyrer de Troisvilles; Mazarin had clashed with the Commander of the King's Musqueteers from the first and was not willing to accept apologies from the fellow now. If he saw the answering scowl on de Troisvilles' face, he ignored it as he swept on to his private apartments in the Louvre.

Jacques Vidal Jumeau, the youngest of Mazarin's secretaries, was waiting for him, his new cassock looking out of place on this rugged youth from Provence. He ducked his head as he had been taught to do, then knelt to kiss the Cardinal's ring. "There are two messages brought this afternoon," he reported dutifully.

"And they are?" Mazarin displayed a brusqueness with his secretaries he would not have shown to the world at large. He held out his big, elegant hand. "Give them here."

"At once, Eminence," he said, and went to the locked desk where all such documents were kept. "One was brought by a page, the other by a lackey from a courier."

"Um," was all the response Mazarin ventured. "The first is an invitation for a fete to honor our Austrian guests. Pray inform le Duc that I shall be delighted to attend. You know the form; say that I will be accompanied by . . . three guests. That should be sufficient for the occasion." He dropped the first note. "You need not destroy that." Now his attention was on the other message, this one more lengthy than the first, and written in a hasty scrawl, the page crossed so that it was difficult to decipher as if it had been a code. He frowned as he read it. "Jumeau," he said suddenly. "Who was the messenger for this note?"

"The lackey did not tell me." Jumeau hesitated. "I . . . I did not think to ask."

"Yes," said Mazarin. The message was from Pere Chape and it was profoundly troubling, as much for the vagueness of the language which hinted more than explained, as for the implication that there was a great deal more at stake than he had first suspected. "I will need a courier, at once." He tapped the page against the base of his thumb, as if that might shake some more information out of the sheet. "Two couriers."

Jumeau bowed, but then stood in confusion. "Mounted or on foot?" he finally brought himself to ask.

"One on foot, one mounted." He started to pace, his elaborate surplice and cassock swinging with the vigor of his stride. "They are up to something, those plotters who desire to bring down Louis XIV before he ever mounts the throne. They are working against the Queen Regent, which is treason, and against the monarchy, which is contrary to God." He rounded on Jumeau. "I despise them all, these cravens who do not fight in the open, as men, but creep about in the dark, like rats." He flung down the paper. "Get that Guardsman, the one who's devoted to Bondame Clemens. Have him carry my message to her."

"D'Artagnan?" suggested Jumeau.

"That one." He took another turn around the room. "The Queen Regent is concerned about poison in the boy's food. Little does she realize how much more she has to fear. He is a child. It means little when he vomits if there is no blood and he does not take a fever. I will order new cooks be found for Louis—that is a minor thing. But there are measures we must take at once if we are to protect the monarchy." He stopped abruptly. "Where are the couriers? Why are you standing there? Stolto! E perche indugia—" With a visible effort he mastered himself and returned to his impeccable French. "Why do you linger?"

Jumeau had gone quite red in the face, though whether from embarrassment or contained anger even he could not tell. "I do not know which . . . to do first, and how."

Mazarin gave the young man a long, serious look. "Very well," he said, sounding more self-contained. "I wish you to summon one courier for delivery of a message in Paris. That young man, the one who was such help to Richelieu—what is the name?"

"Fontaine de Rochard?" suggested Jumeau, eager to get something right for a change. "He is a lackey."

"Yes; he was a page not so long ago: he. Find him and bring him to me. And then get that Guardsman. I want to see them before the reception for the Austrians." He stopped and rocked back on his heels. "I don't like the Austrians coming now. I don't like the way they are pressing the Queen Regent."

"Eminence?"

"Go do it. Send word to the barracks of the Guards and ask the major domo to find de Rochard." He folded his arms, his large brown eyes no longer warm. "I will have the conspirators if I must upset every noble household in France; that I swear before God."

"Yes, Eminence," said Jumeau before he bowed himself out of the door, leaving Mazarin alone to write and seal two messages. By the time Jumeau returned, Mazarin was his usual urbane self, watching his secretary with tolerance if not approval while the young man did his best to report.

"De Rochard will be here shortly," he said as he rose from kissing Mazarin's ring. "He is . . . pleased that you remember the service he performed for Richelieu. He asked that I render his thanks for this opportunity to serve you."

Mazarin nodded. "And the Guardsman—what of him?"

"I have sent word to the barracks, as you ask, informing Monsieur des Essarts that you wish to see d'Artagnan at once." He did not look directly at Mazarin as he spoke, but set his gaze at some unknown spot slightly above the Cardinal's left shoulder.

"Des Essarts," he mused. "I wonder how trustworthy he is? I know that du Peyrer de Troisvilles is my enemy, but des Essarts is another matter, I think." He examined his two sealed dispatches. "I pray they are in time."

Jumeau had not been Mazarin's secretary long enough to contain his curiosity. "How do you mean, Eminence? It is not my place to inquire," he added hastily as he saw the darkening expression in the Cardinal's eyes.

"It is better you do not ask such questions," said Mazarin with a faint smile. "If you do not know, you cannot tell."

The young prelate looked genuinely shocked. "I would never reveal anything you were gracious enough to impart to me."

"Then you are less human than any other man alive," said Mazarin with a little shake of his head. "To never breathe a word to a confessor or a comrade or a brother or a mother or a lover, you must have a will of steel." He put his hands over the sealed messages. "There are reasons why we destroy notes like these, Jumeau. Excellent reasons. Those reasons are more compelling than the first, for they insure your safety as well as my own and the safety of the throne."

Jumeau had been nodding repeatedly through this recitation. "I meant no intrusion," he said when the Cardinal was silent.

"Of course not," said Mazarin in a tone so smooth that it denied his words.

"I did not," Jumeau protested more forcefully.

"So you have told me," Mazarin said, rising from his writing table. "Attend to my answer to le Duc, Jumeau. You have writing materials in your quarters." It was as blunt a dismissal as Mazarin was likely to give.

Jumeau's face had turned pale now. "Eminence, you are mistaken in your thoughts." He knelt and kissed Mazarin's ring.

"It is possible," the Cardinal said at his most polite. "Pray attend to my instructions, Jumeau."

With a sensation of cold growing in his chest, Jumeau did as he had been ordered.

Fontaine de Rochard arrived not long after, his new livery making him look smaller and more gangly than he was. He knelt to the Cardinal, his voice cracking as he said, "What is it to be my honor to do for Your Eminence?"

Mazarin studied the youth; there was less than five years separating Jumeau and de Rochard, but their differences were marked: Jumeau was a man grown, set on the path determined by his family and his fortune; de Rochard, too, was a son doing his duty, but he had shouldered the burden long ago and without resentment— Jumeau felt limited and trapped by the cassock he had been compelled to don. "You served Richelieu well; he told me often of your service."

"God provided an opportunity for me," said de Rochard as modestly as he could.

"And you were sensible enough to seize it," agreed Mazarin. "And now, once more there is no reason to demur," he added. "If you are willing to act on my behalf in a certain matter, I will express my gratitude." He paused again. "As I recall, your family is not well-circumstanced."

"No, we are not," said de Rochard with unapologetic candor.

"Then you would be wise to accept my commission and to act on my behalf to the full extent of your capabilities." He lifted one of the sealed messages. "I require that this be delivered."

"You have only to tell me to whom and I will do it," said de Rochard with such feeling that Mazarin decided that the young lackey's dedication was fairly sincere.

"Excellent," he said. "You are to go with this message to the church of Saint-Etienne, near the fish market. There you will find a priest named Pere Chape, an Augustinian. Give it to no one but him, and watch him read it. I have already specified in this message that you are to do this, and if you fail me it will go ill for you."

"I will abide by your orders, Eminence, whatever they are." He was wise enough not to hold out his hand until the Cardinal actually gave him the message.

"When you have done this, you are to return here and wait for me. I may be some time, for I must attend the reception for the Austrians. Nevertheless, I wish to have your report this evening. You may inform my secretary that you are to have supper if the hour grows late. He will arrange it." Mazarin took the smaller of the two sealed packets. "Here. Serve me well and your family will have reason to thank you."

Fontaine de Rochard kissed both the seal on the message and the Cardinal's ring before he rose. "On my honor, Eminence."

Mazarin nodded thoughtfully. "Get a cloak," he advised after a moment. "One that covers your livery. I want no notice taken of your visit."

"As you wish, Eminence," said de Rochard. He rose but did not start toward the door yet. "Eminence . . . is there anything more?" He was aware how foolish it would be to depart before Mazarin had specifically ordered it.

"No. On your way, de Rochard." He kept his eyes on the papers on his writing table as the young lackey left, but once the door was closed, he rose and began to pace again, growing more and more aware of the impending reception, fearing that d'Artagnan would not arrive in time to carry his sealed message to Olivia. He could not keep the Austrians waiting, yet he dared not delay sending word to his associate. He was considering what alternatives he might have when there was a brisk knock on the door and before Mazarin could answer, the door opened and Charles d'Artagnan, his face a bit flushed, his amber-brown eyes bright, strode into the room, removing his plumed hat and dropping to his knee at the last moment.

"You sent for me, Eminence?" he asked when he had kissed Mazarin's ring.

Mazarin drew his hand back. "Are you drunk?"

"I've had two pots of country red, if that's what you're asking. That's hardly enough to fuddle a man." He rose, replaced his hat, and looked about the room. "Des Essarts' man said it was urgent." His irrepressible smile squeezed out the corners of his mouth.

"It is," Mazarin said, a bit testily. "Are you in any condition to ride?"

"Naturally," said Charles, his smile widening to a grin. "With what I have to celebrate, I could ride to London without a boat."

"All you must do is ride to Chatillon," said Mazarin, not quite disapproving.

"Olivia," said Charles with such unguarded emotion that Mazarin was taken aback.

"Yes; it is most important." He hesitated. "I want you to give her this message and bring her answer to me. That is all. My business is urgent and she is part of my embassy; do you understand that? There is no time for you to dawdle away an hour or two with her; I require the response before morning. Is that clear?"

Charles gave a brisk nod. "Yes, Eminence."

"I do not want to alarm you, d'Artagnan, but I depend on your absolute secrecy and your discretion." He said this last with a little doubt in his voice. "No one must know you have carried this message, or who has written, or who has received it." For emphasis he met Charles' eyes uncompromisingly with his own.

"Have no fear, Eminence. No one will pay any attention to me. I have made that ride so often that there will be no notice taken." He put his hand to the hilt of his sword. "If they do, well, no matter: I will silence them for you."

Mazarin clapped his hands together in exasperation. "Don't be more of a fool than God made you, Guardsman. I do not want your route littered with bodies—what better way to inform the world of where you have been than to kill a few men along the way?" He gave one, very Italian, gesture. "You are said to be a sensible man, d'Artagnan."

"All right," Charles said. "No bodies. I will go in disguise, if you like." This last impish suggestion was met with a hard, flat stare.

"I do not issue orders lightly." He put his hand out to the message. "If you are not willing to treat my commission in the correct manner, then I will find another to deliver the dispatch for me."

Charles sobered at once. He came to attention and lowered his head respectfully. "I crave Your Eminence's pardon. I intended no offence; the news I have been given today has made me joyous, and I fear that it has colored my behavior. Pray believe me to be willing to serve you in whatever capacity you require in the interests of France."

In spite of himself, Mazarin smiled. "All right—any man who can manage so careful an answer is not drunk, and not one to compromise his mission, either."

"Thank you, Eminence," said Charles, his expression so wooden that Mazarin relented.

"Oh, don't look so like an automaton." He waited while Charles relaxed his stance. "Before I give you this dispatch, what news is so welcome that it could do this to you?"

Charles was almost able to contain his smile. "I doubt you'll be as pleased as I am: I had it from Isaac de Portau. He's a Musqueteer, a Bearnais, as fine a fellow as any in the world. He told me this afternoon that he had it from de Troisvilles himself—"

"That fellow!" snapped Mazarin.

"I said you might not be pleased," Charles reminded him somberly. "Anyway, de Troisvilles told de Portau that the next time there is an opening in the Musqueteers, it is mine!"

Mazarin bit back the sharp response that rose to his tongue and said, after a brief silence, "It is what you have wanted, isn't it."

"Oh, yes, from the time I came to Paris." Charles did his best to contain his enthusiasm, his attention now more thoroughly on the Cardinal.

"And now it can be yours," he said slowly. "I congratulate you, then." He turned away and picked up the dispatch as if wholly unaware of Charles' astonishment. "In the meantime, see this is delivered to Bondame Clemens, watch her read it and bring her answer back to me. At once."

"Eminence," said Charles, doing his best to cover his confusion as he doffed his hat again and knelt to kiss Mazarin's ring.

∗   ∗   ∗

Text of a letter from Ragoczy Sanct' Germain Franciscus to Atta Olivia Clemens. Written in the Latin of Imperial Rome.

To my dearest, most treasured Olivia, my greeting from this strange and distant place.

Only recently have we been told that the French King is dead and his heir nothing more than a child. The news was a long time in coming, or you would have heard from me sooner, so close as you are to Paris, and that Italian Cardinal.

You said in the last letter I had from you that you were being *pursued by a dashing young man and that you were in doubt as to what to do. You, of all people, to doubt. I hope with all my heart that he is capable of knowing you and loving you, and that you have that joy and consolation to aid you through the danger of court life. I do not doubt your skills, your good sense, or your intelligence; I am worried about the intrigues that must surround the court with Louis dead. Have a care, Olivia, for my sake if not your own.*

You inquired about this place: I wish I could tell you of the things I have seen here, but there are so few words to describe the way in which these people live, or the ferocity the Spaniards have in their determination to extinguish that way of life, for sadly, these people are rich in gold, and the Crown and the Church covet it.

Not since Egypt, long before I knew you, have I seen so much gold, and so much of it squandered in burial tokens. They struggle to bring the gold from the earth so they can return it to the ground along with a corpse. The richness of the tombs in these mountains beggars the imagination. I have been told that there are priests and monarchs buried encased in gold, on catafalques of gold, with golden attendants to guard them through eternity. That does not mean that the people are rich; they are much the same as the rest of the world, most of the people peasants and farmers and artisans, ordinary humanity, in fact. But their dead are glorious.

Not since I crossed from China to India through the Land of Snows have I encountered mountains like these. They are more enormous than anything Europe can boast; only in Asia have they any rivals. To stand so high, on ancient roads, which until the Spaniards came never knew the wheel, and see the peaks rising high above is an experience few have been fortunate enough to have. Were it not for the ongoing war between the people here and the Spanish, I would recommend you come to see this for yourself, but not if you have to join the massacre, as I fear it is fast becoming.

I write this to Paris, certain that Mazarini has not yet released you. With all that has happened, he must have more need of you now than before, when he was detained in Roma. I have yet to meet this second cousin of his, though I have been told he is in the New World. But the New World is a vast place, Olivia, and who can tell if his path will ever cross mine?

It is late and the courier leaves at dawn. I will hand this to him before he retires so that it will come to you now; the next courier will not arrive for more than a month, and by the time the journey

is made over land and across the sea, whatever news I can send you
will be musty.

Perhaps that is why I have gone on so long: I wish there to be
something of merit in this letter beyond my concern and my love for
you. If there is not, then the concern and love must suffice.

Sanct' Germain
his seal, the eclipse

By my own hand, on the 11th of March, 1644.

· **2** ·

Olivia adjusted the girth a final time and set her foot in the
stirrup, ignoring the shocked looks around her. As she swung into
the saddle, she nodded to the groom holding the three-year-old's
head. "You can let him go," she said coolly.

"Madame, he is . . . fresh," the groom protested, his face becoming more wrinkled as his worry increased.

"Let him go," she repeated in a tone that ended all argument. "I
have been riding horses for longer than you know, Evraud. Let
him go."

With a miserable gesture of helplessness, Evraud released his
hold on the colt, stepping back hastily to avoid the sudden rush he
feared would come.

From his place by the fence, Perceval watched unhappily. By
now he knew better than to question Bondame Clemens about
anything she might do, including ride her half-broken horses while
dressed in breeches and cavalry boots. Bondame Clemens, as he
had reason to know, was not dissuaded by sensible argument or a
servant's threats. He could not wholly conceal his shudder as he
watched her ease up on the colt's head. In a secret part of his mind
he hoped that the colt would toss her off quickly, so that she would
come to her senses. At least the arena was covered so that she
would not be seen by anyone but those of the estate. His chagrin

as he thought of the gossip that would spread through the neighborhood made him look away from Olivia as she started the colt to a steady walk around the edge of the arena. "Thumaz," he called out in order to do something, to show a little authority, "see you man that door."

Thumaz paid no heed to Perceval, as was the privilege of his age; he was watching Olivia handle the colt, riding very carefully in her fine deerskin-covered saddle. He noted with satisfaction that she was alert but not nervous, and that her arms had sinew enough to hold the powerful mouse-colored colt. As Olivia started the colt into a gentle turn, he gave a toothless smile of approval.

Suddenly the colt balked, refusing to go forward, bouncing a little on his front legs.

"Stop," Olivia said firmly and calmly. She tightened her grip on the reins. "Hold."

The colt paid no heed. He began to toss his head in a steady, determined way, pawing with his off-side front hoof. He gave a low, defiant squeal as his pawing became more emphatic.

Perceval brayed out an order and started to climb reluctantly over the high wall into the arena, expecting to see his mistress trampled by the outraged colt before he could reach her side.

"Stay where you are; you're making it worse," Olivia called out in the same steady tone, her attention never leaving the colt, her hands firm as before. "Stop where you are until I have him moving again."

"Moving!" Perceval exclaimed. "He will bolt."

"Yes he will, if you keep irritating him." She shifted her position in the saddle, rising a little in the stirrups, her heels forced farther down. "He's trying to have a temper tantrum and I will not allow it."

Perceval wanted to order her out of the arena at once and call for the grooms who handled the stallions; let them bring their big whips and stout cudgels to control the animal. He knew what young stallions could be like, and how a reasonable man should handle them. But Olivia was mistress here, little as he approved of it, and he was at her mercy. He stood, his hands all but flapping at his sides in consternation.

The colt changed tactics and bounced on his back legs, his ears angled, his head too high up. The whites of his eyes showed now, and not in fear. He gave a loud whinny of challenge.

"Don't be silly," Olivia said loudly, as if correcting a wayward child. "Come to order." She let him have his head for an instant, but only so that she could better set the bit in his mouth. She was pressing with her lower legs, urging him forward.

Finally the colt bounded ahead three steps, then came to an abrupt halt, as if he had realized too late that he had followed her orders. He gave his head a shake and started to rear.

"Mere Marie!" Perceval whispered, closing his eyes so he would not have to watch Olivia fall.

Olivia sunk one hand in the colt's long mane and with the other she used the reins to turn his head to the side, holding it there as the young stallion rose in the air, neighing. "Back on the ground," she told him, keeping her seat with little effort. "If you want to get rid of me you have to do better than that."

The colt paid no heed to her. Once his front hooves were back on the plowed earth, he reared again, this time with so much energy that he very nearly overbalanced.

Perceval turned and ran for the fence.

"You are not helping, Perceval," Olivia called out to him. "Stop where you are until this fellow comes to his senses." She rocked back in the saddle, deliberately throwing the colt off-balance so that he had to bring his front feet down or fall. As she shifted her weight again, she thought back to that night, so very long ago, when she had scrambled onto the back of Sanct' Germain's big blue roan, and hung on for dear life as Sanct' Germain set the horse cantering away from her tomb on the Via Appia. It had been her first time on a horse, and she had resolved then that she would learn to ride properly. It had taken longer than she had anticipated, but almost three centuries later Niklos had made a real horsewoman of her. She pressed her lower legs tight to the colt's side and eased up on the rein. "Go on," she said, starting him moving again.

At last the colt walked naturally, almost as if he were at liberty instead of saddled, bridled, and mounted. He dropped his head into a more responsive position, his neck slightly arched. At Olivia's signal with rein and heel, he turned away from Perceval, who was all but frozen with terror.

Thumaz watched with an expression that bordered on approval, his big, gnarled hands moving in sympathy to what Olivia was doing. "She knows horses, I'll give her that," he said to Evraud in a measured way. "I don't hold with women on horses, mostly, but she isn't a ninny about it."

"No," said Evraud, fascinated at how skillfully Olivia rode. "But breeches—"

The only answer Thumaz ventured was a shrug. "She's mistress here."

As soon as Olivia had the colt moving away from him, Perceval scuttled for the wall, clambering over it with more alacrity than so portly a man might be expected to possess. He paused on the far side of it to wipe his brow with the hem of his smock. He was panting and his face was a plummy color. "It shouldn't be allowed," he said, just loud enough to be heard.

"Who is there to stop it?" said Evraud, striving to keep from smiling. He had found a place on the wall where he could sit in comfort without endangering Olivia as she rode. As he looked over his shoulder at Perceval he gave a discreet sign of contempt toward the acting major domo. Improper though she was, Evraud thought his mistress was fascinating.

The colt had gone around the arena twice in good form and was starting a third circuit when there was a sharp sound from inside the stable. Immediately he brought his head up and tensed before Olivia had a chance to shift her seat. The colt sprung sideways, all but dislodging his rider with the suddenness of his action; his calm deserted him.

"Magna Mater!" Olivia swore as the colt leaped into the air, landing heavily and badly, jolting the both of them as his hooves came down. She righted herself in the saddle as the colt skittered sideways, but in the next instant had to cling to his neck as he reared.

"Saint Antoine!" Thumaz spat, watching the colt dash toward the wall of the arena. He tugged the door open and stepped into the arena to try to help to bring the horse under control.

"No!" Olivia shouted. "No one move!" She had brought herself upright in the saddle again and was doing her best to get the colt's attention.

There was a second louder report from inside the stable, almost as if someone had fired a gun in one of the stalls.

This was too much for the colt, who neighed in distress and took the bit in his teeth. His eyes were wild as he started a bucking run toward the open door.

Thumaz stepped back and pulled the door closed an instant before the colt crashed into it.

The colt staggered, his body shuddering, and in the next instant, he toppled, landing heavily just as Olivia got out of the saddle.

"Madame!" cried Evraud as he came off the wall, rushing toward her.

Olivia's face was dark with anger as she knelt beside the dazed colt. "Who made that noise?" she demanded in a tone of voice that none of the men had heard before. "Who?"

Evraud stopped, afraid to come nearer. "I . . . I do not know, Madame," he said, frowning as he watched Olivia stroke the colt's neck.

"Someone get me a cold towel. Do it now," Olivia ordered sharply. "And find out who is responsible for this."

Thumaz made a clicking sound with his few teeth, and then hastened away into the stable, more willing to face the cause of that explosive sound than to remain and take the brunt of Olivia's temper.

The colt was breathing hard, thrashing his feet, but Olivia kept weight on his neck. "No, boy, not yet. You aren't getting up until I'm satisfied you're all right," she said to the colt, her voice as soft as it had been insistent. Her gaze lighted on Evraud. "Well, get the towel. Now."

Evraud ducked his head. "Madame," he whispered, and hurried away to do as she told him.

Perceval had come back to the wall and now he stared into the arena, his eyes darting nervously. "Is there anything you wish—"

"Make sure there are no more noises. And fetch Dione. I want this colt checked thoroughly," she said, keeping her voice low so that she would not startle the colt. "Now."

"But Dione is . . ." Perceval let the words trail off. If he said where the farrier was, he would also reveal some of the activities that were carried out here without Olivia's knowledge or permission.

"He is off with those thieves, I suppose," said Olivia, and if she noticed the shock in Perceval's expression, she did not comment on it. "But fetch him. This is more important than the booty of a few robbers."

Perceval bowed at the waist and started to leave.

Olivia's voice pursued him. "And Perceval, tell your brother that I will not tolerate him using my stud farm for a storage house for his theft. Is that understood?"

"Yes, Madame," he said, feeling as if the weight of ten sacks of grain had been placed on his shoulders. He wanted to turn to her, to ask her how she knew of Octave's enterprise, but his body remained stubbornly turned away from her and his tongue would not form the questions that were in his mind.

The colt gave a strong whinny and lashed out with his feet.

"Steady, fellow," Olivia said to the colt. "Not yet, not yet." She leaned forward so that she could see his head. There was a bloody patch on the side of his forehead, but he did not appear to be badly cut. She patted his neck and made herself stop shaking so that her distress would not communicate itself to the colt.

A face appeared over the edge of the arena wall. "Oh, Madama!" Avisa cried out as she saw the horse down and Olivia kneeling beside him.

"It is nothing, Avisa," said Olivia, knowing that her maid was not worried about the colt. "There was an accident."

"Are you hurt?" Avisa asked, her face creasing with anxiety. "What happened? Gran Dio!" She crossed herself and leaned a little closer.

"The horse is hurt, not I," said Olivia, adding, "As soon as the farrier arrives I will stand up. This is for the horse's protection." She patted the colt's neck, noting with alarm that he was sweating more. "Keep your voice low, Avisa; he is very easily frightened."

Her eyes round with apprehension, Avisa put one hand to her lips as if to hold in all words and sounds. She blessed herself and stood quite still.

Just then Thumaz came back to the arena. "Something happened in the feed locker," he said as he opened the door into the arena. There were bits of grain and straw all over his clothes, as if he had been caught in a high wind.

"How do you mean, something happened?" Olivia asked. She could hear the colt's labored breathing, which troubled her. In all her years with animals, she had never accustomed herself to their patient capacity for suffering.

"Not doing well, is he?" He shook his head sadly. "Poor lad, could be a cracked head."

"I hope not," said Olivia, fearing that it was.

Thumaz came closer, moving carefully and speaking softly. "I don't know what to say to you, Madame," he began. "It is like something out of a battle. Evraud says it is like an explosion."

"It certainly sounded like an explosion," said Olivia brusquely.

"Then it might have been, though what there was to explode in the locker, I don't know. We keep no musty grain, Madame, and Octave knows enough to keep his activities away from the stable." Thumaz nodded to Olivia. "Get up, if you like, and I'll handle him."

"In a moment," said Olivia, who was reluctant to give over the care of the young stallion to Thumaz or anyone else. She stripped off her gloves and stuffed them into the wide belt holding her breeches.

"As you wish," said Thumaz at his most philosophical. "If you want to inspect the locker, Evraud is guarding it. We're waiting for your instructions."

"You will have them." She stroked the colt's neck, making sure there was strength in her hands so that the horse would be reassured instead of frightened. "Where is Perceval?"

Avisa pointed away from the arena. "There," she said.

"Fetch him back," said Olivia. "I've changed my mind." She did not like admitting, even to herself, that the farrier could make no difference for the colt, but she knew it was so. "Avanti, Avisa," she said. "Or presto."

Obediently Avisa hurried away, not quite running—inconceivable in a lady's personal maid—but at a kind of trot. She called out to Perceval, first in Italian, then in French. "You must return!"

Perceval was relieved to be halted, and he quickly obeyed his new instructions, coming back to the arena at Avisa's side.

Olivia heard their approach; she waited until the two were near enough to hear her speak without raising her voice. "I have another task for you, Perceval."

At the sound of his name, Perceval stuck his head over the top of the arena wall. "Madame?"

"I want the gates to the entire estate closed and guarded. At once." Her words were crisp, stern.

"But the farrier—" he began, then stopped.

"I will attend to the colt," she said, wishing she would not have to. She was pragmatic enough to know she ought to have issued this order first, but she had been too worried about the colt. "Post the guards. Anyone coming or going is to account for his actions, and if there is any question whatsoever about his actions, then bring him to me at once. Or her," she added, knowing that Octave's band made use of sisters as well as wives to bring them what they desired. "No exceptions."

Perceval bowed. "As you wish, Madame."

"And see that I am notified at once if anyone leaves the estate unexpectedly. Do it now, Perceval." With that, she turned her attention away from him, not waiting to see how swiftly he carried out her orders. She glanced from the colt to Thumaz. "What do you think?" she asked the old groom, seeing the answer in his eyes before he spoke.

"He's not good, that's sure," Thumaz answered carefully.

"He's getting worse," said Olivia. "Listen to how he breathes. And he continues to sweat."

"I have a towel, if you want it," said Thumaz, recalling her first orders.

Olivia shook her head. "No, I guess not." She got up, releasing the horse, then watched with sinking hope as the colt struggled slowly and dazedly to his feet, wobbling as he stood. "It's the skull or his neck, one of the two," she said, as much to herself as to Thumaz.

"As you say, Madame," Thumaz agreed with a lack of emotion that was more telling than any outburst would have been.

"What a stupid, stupid waste!" Olivia said with sudden heat. She patted the colt. "Hold his head, Thumaz," she said, starting toward the young animal. "He's confused."

"Truly," said Thumaz. "What are you going to do?"

Olivia's expression was incredulous. "Unsaddle him, of course."

"Ah," Thumaz said with a wise nod. "It's bad luck to have tack on a dead horse." He secured the colt's head, making sure to stand to the side so that the horse could see him. "Go ahead. The way he's breathing, no telling when he might fall again."

"Yes," Olivia said sadly as she started to unbuckle the girths. "I'll need a primed pistol," she said as she loosened the breastplate. "One of the heavy ones; I don't want to misfire and I don't want to do more harm than good."

Thumaz had his mind more on the colt than on what Olivia was saying, but he knew what was expected of him. "As you wish."

"The wheel-lock from Brescia," Olivia said, knowing that pistol better than any of the others she had at this estate.

"As you wish," he repeated, then said, "I will tend to it, Madame. It isn't suitable that you—"

"He's my horse," said Olivia as she pulled the saddle from the colt's back, taking care not to move too suddenly for fear he would fall with the sudden shift in weight. "Poor boy," she said, seeing his labored breathing and his uneven stance as he strove to stay on his feet.

"It isn't . . . fitting work for you," said Thumaz with as much formality as he could muster.

"Who better?" Olivia asked. She carried the saddle to the wall and lifted it onto the rail. "You'd better keep the bridle on him. I'll hold him while you get the pistol for me."

Thumaz coughed. "The trouble is, Madame, I do not know how to load the wheel-lock."

Olivia pinched the bridge of her nose before replying. "Then bring me the materials and I will see to it." It had to be done, she said to herself. It had to be done and it was best to get it over with as soon as possible. The mouse-colored colt was in pain and his condition was growing worse as she watched him. Unwelcome memories flitted like shadows through her mind, conjuring up other times, other horses.

"Madame?" said Thumaz, watching her face.

"I'll need the pistol. Get it. In the case with the ducksfoot."

Thumaz made a gesture of approval. "A formidable weapon, the ducksfoot. Nine barrels." He handed the colt's reins to Olivia. "I will not be long, Madame."

"Good," Olivia said, her voice somewhat distracted as she looked into the unfocused eye of the young stallion. The white was tinged with red now, she noticed.

Avisa, who was standing near the door to the arena doing her best to be invisible, moved a little nearer. "Madama, you aren't going to . . . to . . ."

"To shoot him?" Olivia said, trying not to let her voice sound harsh. "What else can I do? Look at him."

"But you . . . Madama, your groom is right—it is not fitting." She put her hand to her bosom and touched the large silver crucifix that hung there. "Madama, you must not. Let the others tend to it. They are rough men, and they will not flinch from the task."

"Meaning you think I will?" Olivia countered. "My aim has always been good, and at this range"—she touched her hand to the colt's forehead—"I'm not likely to miss."

Avisa blanched. "Madama!" she protested.

"It is part of the work, Avisa. I breed horses, I must be prepared to deal with their ills." She blew gently into the colt's nostrils, trying to calm him. "It won't be much longer, boy, and then it won't hurt anymore."

"Arcangeli!" Avisa whispered. "Madama, there will be blood. On your clothes."

Olivia was not able to smile, but there was a trace of grim humor in her hazel eyes. "Then you'll have a good excuse to be rid of these reprehensible breeches," she said, not taking her eyes off the colt.

Avisa turned away, her face blank, her voice colorless. "I . . . I must go inside, Madama."

"All right," said Olivia, secretly pleased that she would have one fewer thing to worry about. She had seen Avisa faint before and was certain that if she remained, it would happen again. "I will want a bath drawn," she added as her maid started away.

"Certainly, Madama," said Avisa, going quickly toward the main house.

Left alone with the colt, Olivia gently eased him so that he could lean on the arena wall. He was less coordinated now and when he walked, his legs almost buckled. "Not much longer, boy," she said to the colt as she checked his eye and found more red. "Whoever's responsible is going to answer for this. I promise you." Not, she added to herself, that it would do anything for the horse. "I'm sorry, boy." She looked up as Thumaz once again approached, carrying an inlaid box.

"I have it, Madame," said the groom, holding the box out to her as if it were an offering.

"Did you load it?" Olivia asked.

Thumaz shook his head emphatically. "I have never handled that kind of a pistol. I am afraid of them." This confession was made with shame, but also with determination. Thumaz was wary of guns. "My brother had a wheel-lock pistol from Germany that blew his hand off when he fired it."

"It can happen," said Olivia, trying not to think of it now. What would happen to her, she wondered, if her hand were blown off? Would it regrow? She had sustained other injuries and had them leave no trace on her body. Would the loss of a hand or a foot be the same, and in a year or two or three she would have another? She had asked Sanct' Germain once, but he had no answer for her, though he had admitted he doubted so much damage could be undone. "It is one thing to have no scars, Olivia," he had said to her, more than a thousand years ago, "but an arm or a leg is . . . shall we say, more ambitious." Olivia sighed, knowing that her memories were as much to avoid what she had to do next as to give her courage. "Thumaz, take his head again, will you? And hold it up. He's trying to go down."

"As you wish, Madame," said Thumaz, coming to her assistance and leaving the inlaid box by the door of the arena.

The pistol was beautifully made, with an inlaid and filigreed handle and a straight, shiny barrel. Olivia took the tamping rod and attached a bit of oiled rag to it to be sure the barrel was clean. Then she set about preparing the wad and loading the ball. When she had charged it to her satisfaction, she gave it one last quick inspection, then said to Thumaz, "Take care. He'll go down hard."

"I will, Madame," said Thumaz, his eyes narrowing in respect and shock as he realized that Olivia was quite prepared to shoot the injured horse.

"Good," said Olivia, doing what she could to block the sudden rush of sympathy she had for the colt. He had such promise; she hated to act hastily where a good horse was involved; he might turn out to be a good sire for her mares here, and the colts he would throw would be as good or better than he. She made herself stop. There was more blood in the white of the colt's eye, which meant that there was bleeding in his skull. She could not alter that. The colt's breathing was more labored, his balance more precarious. The only thing she had left to do was give him the mercy of a swift death. She raised the pistol to the center of his forehead and fired.

The horse did not even stagger. His legs buckled and he collapsed, falling to his side, his neck flopping once as his head came down.

Thumaz bent to take off the bridle, his face stoney.

"Never mind that now," said Olivia distantly. "I want to see the feed locker."

"Yes, Madame," said Thumaz, stepping back from the colt. He hesitated, turning toward her. "What do you want done with him?"

Olivia blinked, as if the question were unanticipated. "The monks at Sacres Innocentes can make use of the meat, I suppose. Let them have it." She rubbed thoughtfully at her hands, getting the spatters of blood off them. "In which case, we'd better have someone from the kitchen tend to him at once. Fetch one of the cooks while I see about the feed locker." Her features were unreadable. "Go, Thumaz." She reached out for the inlaid box and put the wheel-lock pistol back into it, noting to herself that it would need cleaning later.

"Madame," he said, and hastened to carry out her order.

As Olivia left the arena she did not look back. Going down the long ranks of box stalls, she saw that the horses were nervous, a few of them pacing in their confines, others on the alert, ears pricked and heads up. At the sight of Evraud, she said, "Go and turn out the stalled horses. They need to be out."

"But there is no one to guard—"

"I intend to give this place a thorough going-over. You may return to help me as soon as you have the horses in their paddocks." She entered the narrow room and sneezed. "What an infernal mess it is."

"The dust is the worst," said Evraud as he bowed. "I will be back shortly." He walked away briskly, whistling the signal he always used with the horses; a few whickered in response.

"Yes," Olivia said. "See that you are." She fanned the air with her hand, looking around in the half-light. There was a window on the far side of the locker, and she made her way toward it, the gloom no hazard to her night-seeing eyes. The air felt thick as porridge.

As she pulled back the shutters, the locker brightened, and the extent of the damage was apparent at once: two barrels of crushed oats had been blown apart and their contents turned to grit and dust. A barrel of rough-ground maize had been damaged as well, and flecks of the yellow grain were mixed everywhere with the oats. Three other barrels had been knocked over by the blasts, and their contents were spread over the floor, the millet making walking especially risky.

Olivia stood surveying the damage, shaking her head in disbelief. "Well," she remarked to the chaos around her, "if there is a device of some kind, it will be here somewhere." She turned on her heel once, twice, assessing the severity of the damage. Finally she knelt down in the debris from one of the barrels of oats and began to feel her way through the pulverized grain. It took her some little while, but eventually she found something, a scrap of dark metal. She lifted it up and perused it. "A pomegranate," she said after a short silence. "Who knows how to make pomegranates?" The small, hand-held bombs were most often used against infantry, she recalled. The King's Musketeers were infantry, she reminded herself inconsequentially as Charles' face filled her thoughts, blotting out the little shard of a bomb in her hand. Then she made herself think more clearly. There had been two reports, one after the other. That meant there was a second bomb. And perhaps a third, or a fourth.

Olivia stood up very slowly. This would take more care than she had anticipated. Holding the bit of metal she had discovered, she retreated from the locker, going more carefully than she had before. Once she was in the wide corridor of her stable, she took care to close the stout door and put the brace into its brackets.

Shortly after that, Evraud returned, this time carrying a shovel. "The horses are out, Madame, and I thought this would be useful."

"Yes," Olivia agreed, her manner a little distracted. "Evraud, how many people in this area know about Octave's ventures?"

Evraud looked startled, and he answered hesitantly. "What do you mean, Madame? Perceval has sworn that . . ." He made a gesture to ward off the Evil Eye. "This is not his doing?"

"Who else would want to put a bomb on this estate?" Olivia asked. She held out the metal fragment for him to see. "There were two bombs. There may be more. That's why I've closed the locker for the time being."

"More?" Evraud asked, dazed. "I was guarding . . ." His words faded.

"Yes," Olivia agreed. "Had I been aware of the risks, you would not have been left here, exposed to such danger. What sort of madman puts explosives in a stable?"

"It would have to be a madman, or . . . you have enemies, Madame." He made the suggestion gingerly, as if he were afraid that his mistress might number him among those enemies for mentioning the possibility.

"I?" she asked, startled. "Who? There are those in Paris who would be glad to be rid of me, but here, who is there?" She answered her own question. "Other than Octave, of course."

"Octave would not . . . not here, Madame," said Evraud, then added, "I have no dealings with them, not directly. But those around here, they understand."

"Convenient," Olivia whispered. At that moment she wished fervently that Niklos was not in Roma at Senza Pari, that she could raise her voice and have him appear at her side to aid her and chide her for her perplexity. With determination she set such useless reflections aside. Niklos would be back in a month, and by then this trouble would be long past, a thing she could joke about when she told him of it. "And is Octave so considerate, or only those he deals with?" Her eyes were on the piece of a bomb. "Perhaps not everyone is familiar with his rules."

"Perhaps," said Evraud with a degree of wariness that had not been present before.

"And I may be jumping at shadows, mayn't I?" She said it lightly enough but there was nothing in her eyes that made Evraud suppose that she intended to amuse him. "Still, two bombs; it is something to think about." Or Charles, she thought. Charles knew about bombs, as all infantrymen did. He would be able to advise her. In the next instant she was deriding herself for thinking of so young and inexperienced a man as her lover was.

Evraud stared at his feet. "Two bombs."

"Possibly more," Olivia reminded him. "Which is why I want to know who has been across my land today. If Octave has had a hand in this, he will answer to me and to the King's Magistrate."

It was a vow that Evraud had heard before, but never had he believed it; hearing Olivia speak the words, he was convinced that she would do what she promised. "Octave does not carry his battles here."

"For which I must be grateful. But perhaps his battles have come to him," Olivia said, in that same light, brittle tone she had used before. "I will not allow it. I want you to be certain of that, Evraud; you and Perceval and all the rest of you who work here. I will not tolerate injury to my stock or risk to my workers, is that clear?"

"Why do you say this to me?" Evraud asked her, opening his hands to show his innocence. "Do you think I would defy your orders? Why do you doubt me?"

"Because you are Perceval's cousin, which means you are Octave's cousin as well, and unless the world is a very different place today than it was yesterday, blood has a bond." She gave him a quick, critical look. "I want word passed to Octave tonight. If there is any repetition of this, it will be on his head as well as any rival of his. Be sure he comprehends."

"I will try, Madame," said Evraud, not knowing what else to say. "Word will reach him. By nightfall."

"Excellent," said Olivia, lifting her head as she caught the sound of approaching steps. "That will be Thumaz and the cooks." Her tone changed, becoming more distant and impersonal. "Have a donkey cart hitched up, so that we can carry the meat to Sacres Innocentes when it is ready."

Evraud bowed twice, glad for the chance to get away from Bondame Clemens. "At once," he promised.

Her eyes clouded. "There's no need to hurry," she said in a soft voice. "It will take them a while." She looked down, as if for the first time noticing the blood that dappled her chamise and breeches. "I had better change." Avisa would have her bath waiting, and she could wash away the grime and the blood—everything but the memory. Her eyes fixed on a spot far away. "Put the saddle in the tack room, Evraud."

"Yes, Madame," he said, following her back toward the arena, and hoping he would not see anything of the work the cooks were doing. Never in his life had he become used to the sight of butchery.

As she reached the arena, she picked up the inlaid box containing her pistol. "Remember what I have told you, Evraud," she said. She did not wait for an answer, but walked quickly away toward the main house.

* * *

Text of a letter from Pere Pascal Chape to a man identified only as Le Fouet, written in code.

To my great and patriotic friend, my greetings. Once again I have the opportunity to aid you and your cause and to bring you news of the adulterous Queen and her bastard offspring.

As you have undoubtedly learned before now, the Queen is much taken with the notion that there are those plotting to kill her children and herself. We have known for a long time that she is prone to fancies and suspicions that were the product of her dreams and woman's weaknesses. Given the way she comported herself while her husband lived, it is not surprising to any of us that she would feel herself in such danger, for she continues to foist off her by-blows on the people of France as if they had the Right instead of being the living proofs of her lusts.

It is true that her Italian lover has been diligent, and in his Cardinal's robes he presents a very attractive picture of virtue, which masks all the more his great sins with the perfidious Queen. They are constantly in each other's company and she has made it apparent that she depends upon him for every kindness and aid, as if his position as First Minister gave him privilege with her. But no one is fooled. They rut like animals and their stench rises to God and fills all France.

You have said that you are with us, that you seek to aid our cause in bringing down this despicable pair and the two brats of her lascivious couplings with the loathed Richelieu. Your position and nobility are beyond any dispute and this shows to those who doubt that we are not malcontents seeking to rise in the world while France is in the hands of a weak and capricious woman, but that we have justice and righteousness in our cause, and we proceed from the most elevated of principles for the most worthy gains.

As I have said, the Queen dreads poison, and she has spent hours with the physician appointed to treat her sons, pestering him with her fancies about this mania of hers, requiring that the boy be purged often, in the hope that any poison that might have escaped detection before might be driven from his body before it can do its work.

While I seek no evil whatsoever to come to the Royal House, I am constrained to pray for the downfall of this Spanish whore and her two whelps so that France may once again be free of this intolerable taint. The Hapsburgs have no place in France, and the children of a Hapsburg woman must not be allowed to sully the Royal House of France for one day longer than is absolutely necessary for our purposes and the success of our cause.

You have said many times that you are sworn to the cause of the righteousness of the Throne. I and those who think like me applaud your stance and beg that you will consider joining them in their efforts to end the shame that has been brought on France by the terrible conduct of the woman who was chosen as wife and consort to our King Louis XIII of glorious memory. In remembrance of him, I ask you to weigh what I have said, and if you find in yourself *some sympathy for our goals, you will meet with us at Advent in the city of Lyon for the purposes of learning more of our actions and our purpose. There are many who are eager to welcome you to our number and to join their might to yours for the purpose of ending the rule of the Spanish trollop who calls herself our Queen Regent, and who flaunts her children and her lover in front of all the world as if there were no shame in anything she has done. Should you decide to attend, send me word and I will supply you with further instructions and such material as passwords and identifications. If you, upon reflection, find that you cannot aid us, then I end with the supplication that you will not betray those who act in honor and for the honor of France and the Royal House.*

With my prayers and the assurance that this brings you the good faith of those who, like you, have reason to abhor the disgrace of France which besmirches us all, I sign myself

Pere Pascal Chape

Canons Regular of St. Augustine

On the 2nd day of November, 1644.

Destroy this.

· 3 ·

De Portau ordered the third pot of wine for both of them, his ruddy cheeks glowing with the fire of the grape. "Keeps out the cold," he explained owlishly as he took a generous swig of the drink. He wiped his mouth with his lace-edged cuff and grinned his approval. "Keeps in the warm. Good wine stokes the fires, Charles, that's certain."

Charles reached over the rough-hewn table and patted de Portau on the shoulder. "You're a great fellow, Isaac. No man finer in all the Musqueteers." At that he chuckled. "And now that includes me."

Both de Portau and Charles laughed loudly, and de Portau raised his tankard in another toast. "To the newest Musqueteer," he declared roundly, his words slurring a bit now that the impact of the wine was reaching him. "Welcome to the ranks, boy, though you are a Gascon and not a Bearnais; see that you comport yourself well."

"Of course," said Charles, taking umbrage at the suggestion that he would do anything else. "On my honor."

"Of course, of course," de Portau soothed. "Didn't mean anything else." He leaned forward and lowered his voice to a dramatic whisper. "You are the sort of man we seek. You have courage, mon brave. You have mettle. Just see that you keep out of duels. Word to the wise: Peyrer de Troisvilles doesn't like duels. Says it's a waste of good men." He held up his hand to keep Charles from a new outburst. "You should have heard him this time last year. Arnaud d'Athos was found dead in la halle du Pre aux Clercs: dueling for sure. Killed with a sword in Clercs. There was no proof, but what else do you do there? De Troisvilles won't have it."

Charles nodded four times. "Yes. I understand," he said, but his eyes grew dark. "I will refrain except when honor is traduced."

De Portau slammed his fist onto the table, all but upsetting the winepots. "Damnation! what have I been saying to you. No dueling, honor or no honor." Suddenly he winked. "At least not where it will be found out. You're only just admitted to the Musqueteers; there's no reason for you to ruin all your chances over a misunderstanding, is there?" He leaned back, at pains now to be as calm as he had been excited. "Keep your head, Charles, that's what matters."

"I will try," said Charles, meaning it but having no notion how to go about it.

At the adjoining table a group of six Musqueteers had just sat down, and the oldest of them was bellowing for service.

"Don't be too eager with the others," de Portau added, seeing the enthusiasm in Charles' eyes. "Until they know your worth, they will treat you like a puppy. If you don't want that, then you must restrain yourself. Once they see you under fire, they will have the measure of you, and you will earn their respect." He lifted his hand to a long-faced newcomer. "Henri, over here. Never mind de Beusseret, have a drink with us."

The new arrival wore the blue mantle of the King's Musqueteers and carried himself well, with pride and a bit of a swagger but nothing too flamboyant. He came over to the small table where de Portau and Charles sat, casting about for a stool for himself. "God give you good evening," he said rather formally, nodding to Charles. "I have been looking for you, Isaac," he said to de Portau.

"To you as well," Charles responded automatically, doing his best to gather his wits in the presence of the stranger.

De Portau grinned again. "We're celebrating," he said unnecessarily.

"So I assumed," said the other Musqueteer. "What is the occasion? Why are you drinking with one of the King's Guards?" The jibe was delivered with a broad smile so that no insult would be construed.

"Because," said de Portau portentously, "he is no longer a King's Guard, he is one of us. He'll be given the mantle at the New Year, at the fete."

"Ah," said the other, his manner at once becoming more cordial. "Well, then I must drink your welcome, too." He hooked a stool with the toe of his boot and dragged it toward the little table. "We'll have a round on my purse, boy," he said to Charles.

"I do not like to be called boy," Charles said, his attitude growing defiant.

De Portau wagged a rebuking finger at him. "Until you stand in battle, you might as well get used to it. We all are called boy at first. I was. Henri was. Weren't you?" He addressed their new companion directly.

"Often," Henri assured them as he sat down.

"And he's some kind of cousin to de Troisvilles—if he is not spared, none of us can hope to be." De Portau finished up the wine in his tankard. "Five days until Christmas. I don't want to be sober until the Mass of the Nativity." He looked at Charles with an inquisitive air. "And you?"

"Ah," said Charles. "My purse won't stretch that far. And," he added more seriously, "I have obligations for tomorrow, and I had best be sober for them."

"How unfortunate," said Henri. "Is it for your family?"

"No, for my mistress," said Charles, unable to resist the urge to preen. "I am pledged to visit her then, for three days." He was delighted to see that he had made an impression on the other two Musqueteers.

A ragged cheer went up from the patrons of the tavern as two of the cooks, red-faced and panting, emerged from the kitchen with a roasted pig on a spit. As it was deposited with ceremony on the stand in front of the hearth, there was applause and whistles. The cooks took large knives from their belts and began to cut up the pig, accompanied by rhythmic stamping of the patrons nearest the hearth.

"A mistress," said Henri, not quite doubting him. "And who is she?"

"I cannot tell you her name. She is a widow, a woman of means." He leaned back and crossed his arms, waiting for the two to ask more questions, so he would have the luxury of refusing to answer.

"Some companion or maid, perhaps?" Henri suggested mildly.

"Hardly that," said Charles, stung at the suggestion. "She has a maid of her own, a woman who travels with her."

"Oh, so she travels?" de Portau asked with just enough suspicion that Charles was goaded into answering.

"Of course she travels—she's not French." He glowered at the other two. "And I won't tell you any more."

"A widow who is not French, who has a maid and who travels," said de Portau to Henri. "What do you make of it?"

Henri shrugged. "He says he can tell us nothing. Eh bien, let us have more wine and forget this widow for tonight."

"She is very beautiful!" Charles burst out.

"Certainly she is, since she is your mistress," de Portau said, soothing his younger companion. "We don't question that, boy." He raised his hand and waved it energetically in the air. "And Lisette is the prettiest woman in the world, if only she'll bring us another drink."

Since the three women who were employed at the tavern were plain and stout, Charles turned to de Portau, his face darkening, the ends of his brows tilting upward even more, giving his face a devilish look. "Are you saying that my mistress is like these creatures?"

"Of course not," de Portau said, but his small, merry eyes were bright with amusement. "Remember what I told you about dueling. It's a bad idea to begin with one."

To make matters worse, Henri started to laugh. "Isaac, you always were one to find how to tweak a man's temper. It's amazing you have lived so long. It will be a miracle if you reach thirty, the way you are going."

De Portau threw back his head and let his laughter rumble out of him. "It will be worth it, if I die for amusement." He reached out and once again patted Charles on the arm. "Take no offence from me, Charles. Ask d'Aramitz there: I mean nothing by these sallies, but to see how much you will endure from me."

Lisette, her face shiny with sweat, pushed her way through to the table. "More wine," she said, making an obvious guess.

"Queen of all bottles and spirits," de Portau enthused at her, "O estimable wench!" He reached out and gave her buttocks a squeeze through her heavy skirts and petticoats. "Firm. It's always best when they're firm."

Henri d'Aramitz guffawed and looked questioningly at Charles. "Well, boy? Do you agree? Is your mistress as amply endowed as Lisette here?"

Lisette gave Henri a cuff on the side of his head. "You be good to the boy. You see him reaching for me? He's got sense, this one." She showed Charles a smile with only three teeth missing.

"Bring each of us another tankard and a bottle," de Portau ordered, clapping his hand to his chest. "And some of that pig!" He made a gesture as if he had a sword in his hand and was about to skewer the thing. "Two slices each, and onions."

"And some of those little pickles," added Henri, touching the ends of his moustaches. "They're delicious."

Charles tossed a coin to Lisette, saying, "Bread and cheese as well."

"And money," said Lisette approvingly. "How useful." She tucked the coin away in a leather purse tied to her belt. "Wine, pork, onions, pickles, bread and cheese."

As Lisette pushed her way through the crowd de Portau turned to Charles. "Why give her the money before she brings our drink?"

"In the hope it would hurry her," said Charles. He patted the mantle he wore and grinned at de Portau. "Not many more days of this, Isaac."

"What company do you enter?" asked Henri out of courtesy.

Charles grinned. "The First. The Grand Musqueteers. Same as Isaac." He hooked a thumb toward the other group of Musqueteers. "They're second company, aren't they?"

"Yes," said Henri with a shrug. "There's little difference between the Grand and Petite, as you'll discover in battle soon enough. We'll be on campaign before spring is over." He glanced toward de Portau. "Are you ready for a new campaign, Isaac?"

"Always," said de Portau at once. "It's the reason I'm a Musqueteer, isn't it? What man joins a fighting regiment if he does not want to campaign?" He pulled out a large, plain handkerchief and wiped his brow. "They're always the same, these tavernkeepers— all we have to do is have a little sleet in the air and they cannot resist heating their taprooms as hot as their ovens."

"It's worse in the summer," Henri said philosophically.

"Flies," de Portau agreed. "And the air as thick as carded wool. But this is no better."

"Do you think the Queen will order us to fight?" Charles asked, trying to recall the few things Olivia had told him about Anne of Austria.

"If she won't, de Troisvilles will, or the Italian First Minister Cardinal," said Henri, sighing. "He covets the regiment, that fellow."

"You mean Mazarin?" Charles said, surprised that Henri would speak so slightingly of the Cardinal.

"Speak to my kinsman," said Henri, meaning de Troisvilles. "He did not get on well with Richelieu, and he has been opposed by Mazarin at every turn. Mark my word, Mazarin is ambitious for his own family. He is a Colonna with nephews to consider. He will not permit my cousin to continue to command the Musqueteers if he can persuade Her Majesty to permit him to displace de Troisvilles."

"Surely you're mistaken," said Charles, feeling awkward now that the conversation had changed.

"No, he's not," said de Portau suddenly. "Not about Richelieu, in any case. He was never one to help de Troisvilles, or to plead his case. This Italian is just another such prelate, and he is more obdurate than Richelieu ever could have been." He pounded his fist on the table twice. "Mark what I say—if there is no peace between de Troisvilles and Mazarin, our days are numbered. You may come to regret wearing our mantle, Charles." He picked up his handkerchief and stuffed it into his lace-edged cuff.

"Never," said Charles with feeling, his cheeks flushing as if he were a boy. "It is the greatest honor, the only honor I have ever sought, to be a King's Musqueteer."

"So I thought myself, not so long ago," said de Portau, his features growing briefly sad. Then he brightened deliberately. "Still, it is the best fighting group in all France, and with the grandest tradition, so I do not regret my choice, no matter what comes of this dispute between Mazarin and de Troisvilles."

"It would be unfortunate if there were more arguments," said Henri, then made a sudden lurch to his feet as Lisette waded toward them bearing an enormous tray heavily laden with food and drink. "A meal, and I am hungry enough to eat half an ox."

De Portau clapped his hands. "Food. Food." He swept his arm across the rough planking of the table, scattering bits of debris and old scraps. "There's room enough for all of it." Then he dug his fingers into the purse he carried and drew out two gold angels. "Here, Lisette. To keep the wine flowing."

As soon as she had put the tray down, she reached for the coins, testing them between her teeth before giving de Portau an appreciative smile. "There will be wine until dawn, if that is your wish, Musqueteer."

De Portau could not resist fondling her rump again. "A pity more women aren't like you, Lisette. More of us would be content to stay home if we could find another like you."

She boxed his ears playfully. "You are teasing me," she chided him with a giggle. "Eat your meal and drink your wine and be happy."

"I would be happier for your company tonight," de Portau told her, taking hold of her grease-spattered arm. "It would be a warmer night for both of us if you were to give me a little of your time."

She shoved him away. "Go on," she said, and moved away from him through the crowded taproom, pausing once to look back over her shoulder and give him a playful wave.

"Ah, what a loss," said de Portau before he took his dagger to the thick slices of fragrant pork on the plate before him. "To think that a woman like that is going to waste."

"She may not think that," Henri said, taking pleasure in goading de Portau. "It may be that she does not fancy a soldier."

"Nonsense," said de Portau through a mouthful of pork. "Any tavern wench fancies soldiers. Fact. Every one of them longs for the day when we will make them our field of conquest." He chewed thoughtfully, then took a generous swig of wine and went on, warming to his subject as he went, "You see, they know the worth of a soldier. They have seen us prove our mettle, at table and in battle, though we do it for amusement. And they know we will not fail them, that we will not falter, that we can give them as good as they give us."

Charles had torn one of the two loaves of bread in half and was ripping that into more manageable bits. "Why should Lisette want a soldier more than any other man?"

"Because she knows that whether we use a musquet or a lance, we accept no defeat in battle." He chuckled through his food. "What wench doesn't seek that in her bed partner?"

Henri had stuck his dagger into a generous pork collop and was nibbling at it. "But if she wants a soldier, why a Musqueteer? Why not one of the King's Guards, like your friend here still is for a few more days?"

"Because the Musqueteers are the bravest men in the army, that's why," said de Portau promptly.

"Ah," Henri said with a sage nod. "Naturally. And you are the bravest of the Musqueteers."

"Certainly," said de Portau at once. "Ask anyone; they'll tell you that no man is more courageous than Isaac de Portau." He chuckled again and reached for some bread to soak up the sauce from the pork.

"The cheese is good, too," recommended Charles, reluctant to be drawn into boasting before he had faced the enemy in battle. Should he falter under fire—not that it was possible—he did not want any remarks coming back to haunt and mock him.

"The tavernkeeper buys it from old Batiste," said Henri. "The same who supplies us in war."

"Familiar as a favorite boot," de Portau approved, cutting a portion of the round for himself. "It is a luxury, spending the evening like this."

"Yes," said Henri, then continued, "Since you're new to the regiment, you won't know this . . . ah . . ." He faltered.

"The boy's name's Charles d'Artagnan," said de Portau. "His brother's Paul de Batz-Castelmore."

"A worthy family," said Henri, unwilling to abandon his subject. "Since you're new to the Musqueteers, d'Artagnan, you will have much to learn. You will have to find out a few things for yourself, as we all do. It is an honor to be a Musqueteer, and every one of us takes pride in the mantle we wear. But you will discover before you are with us very long that we do not have the opportunity to spend such a pleasant evening as this one very often."

"All the more reason to enjoy the time we have," said de Portau, and tore off a section of pork from his dagger with his teeth. He chewed vigorously, grinning around the meat.

"We have our duty, and our vow to defend the King unto

death," said Henri, with a dissatisfied look. "And these days, that means we must try to save the kingdom for a little boy whose mother rules him and us, and is the sister of our enemy, the King of Spain." He reached down and helped himself to the pickles he had ordered. "And she herself is under the control of a handsome Roman courtier hiding in a Cardinal's robes."

Charles frowned. "We still must defend France. Perhaps now more than ever."

"Yes, we must, no matter what the rest demand of us," said Henri, reaching for his tankard. "They say it will be colder tomorrow. There could be snow."

"So early," said de Portau as he chewed. "Most of the time, it waits until the Nativity at least. Well, it may be a cold year in other ways as well." He helped himself swallow with a large tot of wine. "Not a bad vintage for a place like this."

"If it were vinegar, you would say that," Henri remarked as he drank again. "But you're right, it isn't bad."

"What do you think, Charles?" de Portau demanded, swinging around on his stool to face him.

"I think it is good wine for soldiers," said Charles, remembering the wine that Olivia had offered him the week before. It had come from the Rhone Valley, he recalled, was a deep, bluish shade of red with a taste that was like the feel of fine velvet. She had given him the whole bottle as he sat at dinner, watching him while he ate. She had played chess with him, though neither of them cared who won, and when they tired of the game, they had gone to her private apartments where tall wax candles burned for them until long after midnight. There had been another cup of wine then, after their lovemaking, yellow as butter and so sweet that it was better than honey. What was in his cup now was so rough and sour that he knew Olivia would not permit it to be poured for her servants. "It's frisky," he said candidly. "It's hearty."

"All those things," Henri agreed with a wicked amusement in his eyes. "And not quite as bad as sheep's piss."

De Portau started to laugh, but choked on his food and coughed instead, his face going suddenly dark red, his small bright eyes pushing out of his face. He hooked his fingers under his jabot and tugged in an effort to loosen it.

Charles reached over and pounded de Portau once, sharply, between his shoulder blades, thumping twice when de Portau gave a signal for more. He waited as de Portau finally got his jabot untied. "Again?"

"No," de Portau whispered, his coughing over. The dark suffusion that colored his face began to subside. "No, I'll do fine now. Just wait a moment."

"Have more wine," suggested Henri as he refilled de Portau's tankard. "What a sound you made, terrible, like bears in the spring."

"Bears in the spring," said de Portau as if the words were unfamiliar. He wiped his mouth with the ends of his jabot. "Agh. That was . . . that was worse than enemy cannonfire."

"Serves you right, bolting your meal the way you do," said Henri. "A man should take care eating when he is drunk."

De Portau folded his jabot and thrust it into the outer pocket of his coat. "I am not drunk now," he said, and his voice was cool and sober. "Put a noose around a man's neck, and it will bring him to himself at once, I promise you." He reached out and took another sip of wine. "If it were not required, I wouldn't wear anything around my neck. For just such reason as you can mark here." He touched his neck. "And do not tell me that a jabot will protect me from a sword or a musquetball, for that is ridiculous." His petulance was as out of place as it was unexpected, and he sensed it as well as his two companions. "I have, occasionally, dreamed that I was hanged."

Henri, seeing the abrupt change that had come over de Portau, looked at his fellow Musqueteer with a serious expression in his eyes. "It could have been enough to do for you, my friend. If your new recruit had not helped you, I might not have done it in time." He served himself more wine and then poured some into de Portau's tankard. "You can use a bit of this, Isaac."

"True enough." He sounded a little hoarse. "My throat will be sore in the morning."

"So will your head," Henri pointed out. He dipped a chunk of bread into de Portau's wine and held it out to him. "That will ease you a little."

Charles was still watching de Portau closely. "Did the meat stick in your throat?"

De Portau shrugged. "Something did. I wasn't paying much attention. Well." He picked up his tankard. "To my new companion-at-arms," he toasted sardonically. "If you are as quick in battle as you were to assist me here, I need never fear for my safety again."

"If battle is not more confusing than this crowd, I can see no difficulty," said Charles, reaching for his tankard, and only then realizing that his hands were trembling. He drank quickly, not only to conceal the tremor, but to banish it.

"Well, to the Musqueteers," said Henri, a bit more formally than before. "For as long as we continue."

"Shame, Henri. You'll ruin our festivities. There's no reason our future must be so dire," said de Portau. "You make it sound as if the Cardinal is going to exile us all by tomorrow."

"Not tomorrow," said Henri, and cocked his head toward the next table. "But soon. He cannot afford to have de Troisvilles against him, and a regiment of fighting men prepared to oppose him as well." He hitched his shoulder as if to reveal that it meant nothing to him. "I suppose one can always return to the King's Guard"—he indicated Charles' mantle—"or you might not want to give it up."

"All I have wanted to be," said Charles with feeling, "is a King's Musqueteer." He drank again, then clapped de Portau on the shoulder. "And how could I wish for any better comrade than Isaac? The Musqueteers have to continue, if for no other reason that this: the finest fighting men in France are Musqueteers, and France needs all of them."

"Fine sentiments," said de Portau, a little of the twinkle coming back into his eyes. "Let's see if you still have them after you have stood against cannon and cavalry."

"If I am alive, I will believe it, for it is the truth," said Charles, leaning forward so that he was no more than a handbreadth from de Portau's face. "And Isaac, you believe it." He emphasized the *you* enough to demand a response from de Portau.

"Yes," he admitted as he met Charles' gaze. "I believe it. I believe it."

Charles pursued his advantage. "Every Musqueteer believes it," he insisted.

Though Charles addressed de Portau, it was Henri who answered. "No, not every Musqueteer; most of us, I'll allow you that, but there are others who are here because it is demanded of them, and they, well, they believe nothing." He offered a pickle to de Portau. "Try this, Isaac. It's very good."

"Who does not believe it?" asked Charles, refusing to be turned away from his purpose.

Henri sighed. "Oh, Beusseret probably does not. The man is nothing more than a bully in a mantle. I doubt that de Montlezun de Besmaux believes it. He's an insinuating little rat."

"He's also the poorest man in the regiment," said de Portau, not as cynically as he would have liked.

"If he has less money than I do, he's hardly more than a pauper," said Charles, chuckling to let the other two know he did not mind being without money.

"You're both Gascons," said Henri. "You can determine which of you is poorer if it is important." He looked at de Portau with some concern. "Are you really all right, Isaac?"

"I am improving," said de Portau. "Who would have thought it?" he went on, determined to make light of his discomfort. "Here we have a Gascon debating with two Bearnais to determine who of us is . . . the least rich."

"I know de Montlezun de Besmaux a little," said Charles, doing his best to remember the fellow from the King's Guard. Both of them were sergeants, he knew that, but he had no strong impression of the man other than his obsequious behavior to des Essarts and his other superiors.

"The man's a self-serving little weasel," said de Portau. "Probably treacherous as well."

"You don't like him," said Henri, dismissing de Portau's comments. "And you're a suspicious fellow, Isaac. Have another pickle." He winked at Charles. "Don't take what Isaac says too seriously, at least about de Besmaux. It's not de Besmaux's fault that he has a long nose and the manners of a notary."

"Hah!" de Portau scoffed. "I am a reasonable man, a fair man, a man of excellent judgment. And," he added with the return of his one-sided smile, "you are right, I dislike him."

Charles took up his tankard. "Then we dismiss him." He drained his tankard and wished it was as simple a thing to put Olivia—who haunted his life like an honorable and tender, half-healed wound—out of his thoughts as it was to ignore the existence of Francois de Montlezun, Sieur de Besmaux.

*   *   *

Text of a letter from Perceval, acting major domo at Atta Olivia Clemens' stud farm in Tours to Niklos Aulirios, dictated to Frere Aubri of Sacres Innocentes.

Greetings to the most excellent major domo, Niklos Aulirios, who has honored me with the task of being his deputy in my lamentable brother's place, from the stud farm of the widow Atta Olivia Clemens, of Rome, whom we both are fortunate to serve.

I have been most diligent in following your instructions, and I have put men to investigate the various mishaps which have taken place here since summer. This will serve as my report on our activities. First, we have not been able to determine who set the two bombs in the feed locker that apparently began the most regrettable series of mishaps which have plagued this farm for many months. We were not able to find any more of the two bombs than the fragments which Bondame Clemens herself found. We have arranged for Thumaz' great nephew to guard the stables at night. He sleeps in the tack room, on a pallet provided for that purpose, and we are paying him as you recommended. Second, we have placed wardens at all the entrances to the stud farm and have kept careful records of all who have crossed the land or made other use of it. Aside from the Freres of Sacres Innocentes, the only men using the entrances often have been shepherds and two cowmen from the adjoining estates. We can produce these records upon your request or the request of Bondame Clemens. Third, we have not been able to discover the cause of the fire that destroyed part of the east wing of the central house of the villa. There were some sticks of wood found which it was thought might have provided kindling for the blaze, but nothing is certain. We have set builders to making the necessary repairs and will include the changes Bondame Clemens has requested. We have not yet begun work on the bath because the earth from Roma has not been delivered. We are told to expect it within the month, but with the winter so hard, it is not likely that we can do much more on the addition until spring. Fourth, the culprit who placed tripwires in the larger paddock has not been found. We have had to destroy eight of the yearlings turned out there, and the farrier has said that one, a filly, may be lamed for life. Since she may be used only for breeding, Bondame Clemens will have to decide if the filly is to be kept or not. Fifth, two more of the wardens have been wounded while on patrol. My brother Octave has sworn on the *soul and the grave of our mother that he is not responsible for this dreadful thing, and has offered to send his men to aid the patrols until those who are doing these terrible things are caught and condemned for their crimes. If it were not contrary to Bondame Clemens' orders, I would be glad to accept Octave's offer, but I am determined to abide by her instructions, and so I have refused. Sixth, I have requested that the good Freres of Sacres Innocentes keep us informed of suspicious strangers in the area, for many of them come to the monastery for food and shelter. I have been given the assurance of the Abbe that he will extend his cooperation as far as his office permits, and will request that other religious in this neighborhood do the same.*

The winter crops have been disappointing, due to the severity of the weather. Even the number of cheeses are not as high as last year because the cattle and goats have produced less milk. Our sheep have been producing more and thicker wool, which may be the only success we will have this winter. We have two three-year-old geldings, a four-year-old stallion, and five four-year-old mares Evraud recommends be placed on sale, and he has indicated reasonable prices for all. A complete accounting has been placed in the muniment room for your review.

The footbridge over our stream was badly damaged by rising water and debris three weeks ago, and I have assigned men to work on rebuilding it. In the meantime, a log-and-plank bridge has been set up for those who must cross the stream at that point. Those with carts, oxen, or horses we are instructing to use other routes, for the temporary bridge will not hold up more than simple foot traffic. If there is not more flooding, the bridge will be in good repair by April.

In the last four months, we have had the Cardinal's couriers come here six times, which is quite an increase over the previous year. Because of this, I request that Bondame Clemens authorize me to issue arms to the chief warden and a few of the household staff, for as things are, we are not able to protect these men, nor their messages. Should we encounter any serious attempts to intercept the messages carried by these couriers, we would not be able to stop them, which would disgrace us as well as Bondame Clemens. In that regard, we have taken to putting the couriers in the hidden room between the pantry and the smaller salon. The space may be small, but at least it can offer some protection as well as the advantage of concealment, if this is required.

While no one here seeks to become embroiled in the affairs of the

Cardinal, we do wish Bondame Clemens to know that we are good Frenchmen, loyal to the King and the Crown, and we will do all that is necessary to defend this kingdom against the enemies of King Louis and France. If we must aid these couriers and lend assistance to that Italian, we are willing to do it, so that France will not be left at the mercy of her enemies.

Four of the household servants have become ill this winter, and one has already died. They have all burned with fever, been subject to the flux, and eventually become severely weakened. The woman who has died suffered with a cough for the last two days, and could not find relief in spirits of wine mixed with honey and tincture of monkshood. We fear for the welfare and safety of the others, and have taken care to isolate those who have become ill so that the rest will not take the contagion. However, we have spoken with the monks, and they tell us that with the winter so hard, we must expect that God will call many to His side before spring comes again.

Let us recommend to Bondame Clemens that if she attempts to come here before spring that she take the road leading through Chartres rather than Orleans, for there has been so much flooding on the Loire between here and Orleans that the road, usually preferable to the road through Chartres, is worse than the muddiest cowpath. My mother's second cousin, a spinster living in Blois, has had to leave her house and take refuge with us because there is so much flooding.

We have heard rumors that there is to be war again. If at any time Bondame Clemens hears that we may be in danger, I ask that you arrange for us to hear of it at once. We are prepared to defend this estate, and to offer shelter to those made homeless by battle and soldiers, but we are not able to do these things without a little warning. We are relying on Bondame Clemens and her high position to keep us informed of the movements of troops as well as the risks of battle here. In accordance with Bondame Clemens' orders, there is food enough in the root cellar to last us for two to three months, provided that we do not need to extend hospitality to more than two dozen more persons. We also have rolls of bandages and the medicines left for us by Bondame Clemens, and which the monks assure us they know how to use properly. There is also feed enough for the stock for two months, providing that the horses must be kept in the stable. The dairy also has hay enough for two months, and a good supply of salt so that the cows will not go off giving milk.

This report is given with respect, and I swear that it is as complete and accurate as I am capable of making it. I pray that it is satisfactory. *May God show His Grace to you and to the most esteemed Bondame Clemens.*

> *Perceval de Rodat*
> *his mark*
> *by the hand of Frere Aubri*
> *at the monastery of Sacres Innocentes*

On the Feast of St. Hilary of Poitiers, 1645.

· **4** ·

"That tree branch ruined all the shutters on the ground floor of the east side," Niklos informed Olivia as they viewed the damage caused by the two-day storm.

She nodded, her manner calm now that the worst was over. "Do we have any in the lumber room we can put up for the time being? They don't have to be pretty, but they need to fit."

"I'll have Meres tend to it," said Miklos. "I still haven't got a complete report from the stables."

"Small wonder," said Olivia, who had been there earlier in the morning and tried to calm the horses with little success. "I hope that we don't have to go through another night like the last two—too many of the horses are almost insane from the storm already."

"We could turn them out," said Niklos without much conviction.

"If they had been out for most of the winter, I suppose we might. But they would be no calmer, they would just have more room to run and hurt themselves." She started to pace, going the length of her grand salon before coming back toward him. "I must send a message to Mazarin. His courier was supposed to be here three days ago, and even if the storm has delayed him, it has been too long." She stopped and rubbed her face. "Unless there has been an accident."

"Or worse," said Niklos, voicing her fears for her.

"Yes, or worse." She pulled her fichu more tightly around her shoulders and tightened the knot that held it. "I think I will change to my riding habit. It's warmer. And it doesn't have these infernal panniers," she went on, slapping the wide, flat hoop that supported her velvet skirt. She looked at where water had stained her lavish carpet. "It would probably make sense to rearrange the furniture. The maids will never get this out."

"Today?" Niklos ventured as he made some notes with the charcoal stick he carried.

"Of course not," Olivia said. "This is merely cosmetic. There is too much damage to be repaired first. I only mention it because—"

"Because you've made up your mind to ride to Paris and talk with Mazarin yourself," said Niklos, his ruddy-brown eyes revealing his amusement.

"How did you guess?" Olivia asked him.

"Long, long acquaintance," said Niklos, doing his best to give the impression of patient suffering. He indicated the tall windows. "They will need to be sealed again," he pointed out.

"Yes. Can we hire a chandler to help the staff? If there's one thing a ship's chandler can do, it's keep out water," said Olivia, striving to be amusing. "If you haven't one in the household records, then find someone who can recommend one."

"What about Charles? Couldn't he suggest someone?" asked Niklos with the assumption of great innocence.

"He's a Musqueteer," said Olivia, "not a naval officer." Her eyes narrowed as she looked over the windows. "Still, I may ask him."

"As good excuse as any," said Niklos, failing to keep the smile from his face.

"Do I require an excuse?" Olivia inquired.

"Not from me," said Niklos gallantly, then went on simply, "Is he what you longed for?"

"Charles?" Olivia asked, though she had no doubt what Niklos meant. "He is something I never thought to have." She fell silent, but when Niklos did not respond, she continued, speaking in the Latin of first century Rome. "Before you knew me, before I died"—her hazel eyes took on a distant shine—"there was Sanct' Germain. Without him I would have perished then. He was my truest ally and most cherished friend when I thought that I was completely abandoned. He was my lover and my deliverer. But he was not my suitor. He did not, he could not court me." She walked slowly toward the hearth as if drawn by the flames. "Charles wants me. He knows what I am and he wants me, not because of what I am, but because of me." She shook her head as if coming out of a doze. "I'm saying it badly."

"You aren't," Niklos told her quietly.

"I have thought often this last year of the many times Sanct' Germain has told me that he desires of all things to be known for what he is, all that he is, and accepted as what he is, for himself. I used to think it was the one truly nonsensical thing about him, because I couldn't imagine that such a thing was possible for those of our blood." She gave a short sigh and her brow creased with a little frown. "Only now, I find that it is possible, and now that I know it is, I know that I have yearned for it just as Sanct' Germain has, but unlike him, I have denied it, and pretended I had no need, because I had no hope."

Niklos came to Olivia's side and laid his hand on her shoulder. "And you? Now?"

She tilted her head so that her cheek rested on his fingers. "I think I am . . . blessed, though I do not believe in blessings." She looked away. "And I feel, occasionally, a little guilty, because I have stumbled upon the very thing that Sanct' Germain has sought for so long. I have it as a kind of gift, unasked-for. And Sanct' Germain has yet to find it."

"Perhaps that is the only way it is found: as a thing unasked-for." Niklos felt Olivia's sadness and understood it enough to sympathize with her.

"Perhaps," she said, then stepped away. "And if I continue this way," she said at her most bracing, "I will probably become melancholic and useless. There is too much to do." She started across the room, her step determined. "I will have Avisa help me dress. In the meantime, find me a horse that isn't entirely crazed by the storm and see that you use the heavy cavalry saddle on him. I'm going to put breeches on under my skirts, and let those who wish to stare."

Niklos gave her a laconic salute. "All right. Do you go with escort or alone?"

"Alone," said Olivia as she reached the door. "And do not trouble yourself to object. I know you do not like me to ride by myself, but I will go faster on my own."

"And will they let you enter Paris when you arrive, astraddle and unescorted?" He deliberately kept his tone light and teasing, for any other approach was apt to annoy her. "How do you intend to greet Mazarin? He puts a fair amount of importance on decorum."

"He also puts a fair amount of stock on information, and the delay of his courier outweighs a question of dress. At least I won't be going to the gate in armor." The corners of her mouth twitched. "Not that I haven't done so in the past."

"Perish the thought," said Niklos, remembering Olivia in armor. "I gather it is useless to try to dissuade you."

"It is," she said, opening the door. "I will spend the night in Paris."

"Not alone, I trust," said Niklos, then added with some concern, "Olivia, give me your word you will go to Charles. If there are more plots against Mazarin, I don't want you keeping near him. Charles will take care of you better than an army of the Cardinal's Guard could do."

"You have my word," said Olivia as she started out of the room. Before closing the door, she looked back at him. "I would have done it without giving you my word, as well." She did not stay to hear him laugh.

Avisa was outraged at Olivia's instructions about breeches under the skirt of her riding habit. "I suppose that means you will be using a man's saddle as well," she burst out indignantly as Olivia started to paw through her drawer of chamises. "What will you say if you are stopped, dressed that way?"

"I will say I am in a hurry, that it is winter and I want to keep warm. Where are my boots?" Olivia had pulled out one long-sleeved chamise of fine wool dyed a light sage-green. "I want the slate-colored habit, with the capes. And I will need a wide-brimmed hat; that partial tricorn should do, the one edged in black piping."

Avisa flung her hands into the air to let the world know that she was helpless against Olivia's determination. "You will disgrace us all if anything happens to you."

"Nothing will happen," said Olivia, doing her best to sound wholly confident.

"You are determined on this madness, aren't you?" said Avisa as she took a pair of heavy leggings out of one of the smaller drawers. "You'll need these, at least. And your boots are in the chest, where they always are. I had Urbain polish them yesterday. Not that it matters, given the weather." This last was so glum and foreboding that Olivia looked around at her personal maid.

"What's troubling you?" She had taken a seat on her chaise and was unfastening the bodice and corsage of her dress. "Let me have the chamise."

"Haven't you heard anything I have said?" Avisa demanded, her eyes rolled heavenward as if imploring reinforcements from the angels. "Are you wholly immune to sense?"

"Of course not," said Olivia as she tossed the velvet bodice across the room onto her bed. She started to work on the lacings holding her skirts and panniers. "You must recall that I have an obligation, a sworn duty to the Cardinal. The weather and the current mode does not excuse me from that duty."

"Then send Niklos," begged Avisa.

"It is not Niklos' responsibility," said Olivia as she started to fasten the front of her chamise. "I hate corsets," she remarked to the air.

"Then why wear them?" Avisa demanded sarcastically. "You care little enough for other conventions. You don breeches like a man, you ride in a soldier's saddle, Dio mio, why stop at corsets?" She gathered up the clothes Olivia had tossed aside and began to fold them. "There's a tear in the arm of this," she pointed out, holding up the bodice-and-corsage, indicating a little rip at the top of the sleeve.

"Repair it," said Olivia, paying very little attention.

"But it is velvet; it will show," warned Avisa.

"Well, embroider something on it. Put several bits of embroidery on both sleeves, so it won't look like you're hiding a tear. Have you seen my waistcoat?"

Without a single word, Avisa went to the smaller of two chests-of-drawers and all but threw the waistcoat at her. Then she folded her arms defiantly, waiting.

Olivia was adjusting the garters above her knees, flexing her toes to make sure the garters would not loosen while she was in the saddle. "While I'm gone, I'll want you to help Niklos determine how much damage was done by the storm. I need to know who in the household has livery or bedding that has to be replaced, and if there has been anything destroyed, such as crockery or napery or similar goods, I want you to make note of it, so that we can review it when I return."

"You think the Cardinal will permit you to return? Once he sees how you comport yourself, he will probably return you to Roma in a curtained coach." She crossed herself at the thought of such an event.

"Wouldn't that please you?" Olivia asked as she pulled her waistcoat over her head. "Get my habit, please."

As Avisa took the heavy woolen habit out of the armoire, she made one last attempt to dissuade Olivia. "Madama, please. I beg you to reconsider. This is very, very ill-advised, and it could lead to offending the First Minister. You cannot want to do that, Madama. You must not do this."

If Olivia had paid any heed to what Avisa said, she gave no indication of it. "My habit, if you will. And my boots." She did not ask Avisa to get her breeches, but went to the press at the foot of her bed and got them for herself. As she drew them on and fastened them to the rosettes of her waistcoat, she gave Avisa one more chance. "I'll need a heavy jabot, something in wool or silk. Something dark."

Avisa closed her eyes as if in silent prayer, then said in a flat tone, "What about the Hungarian silk? It is grey."

"Fine," said Olivia, "Bring it." She took the long jabot and began to wrap and knot it expertly around her neck. When she was satisfied, she reached out for the voluminous skirt of her riding habit, stepped into it, and dragged it over her leggings and breeches. As she adjusted its fastenings at her waist, she nodded toward the coat. "Open the lacings," she said as she bounced on her toes to be sure the skirt would not shift while she rode.

"Madama, how can you do this?" Her protest was feeble this time, and she spoke it while she was unfastening the lacings of the habit coat.

"How can I not, when it is so clearly my duty?" She reached out for the coat. "Thank you. Now bring the brushes; I have to do something about my hair."

Avisa gave a kind of whimper and hastened to do as she was told, her back stiff with disapproval and worry.

By the time Olivia walked into the stable a short while later, Niklos had carried out her orders and had a rangy bay mare waiting for her, the cavalry saddle already in place, the bridle being held by a groom while the farrier made a last check of the bay's shoes.

"She's twelve, so she's sensible," said Niklos, indicating the horse. "Just be a little careful of her mouth."

"Have you ridden her?" asked Olivia with some surprise.

"No, but I've asked those who have." He patted the horse's neck, scratching a little at her fuzzy winter coat. "She's got enough hair on her to keep her warm, I think."

"Good," said Olivia, not paying much attention as she watched the farrier. "Is there a problem?"

The farrier shook his head in doubt. "If the road is clear, I don't think so. If you have to cross rough ground, I can't be sure." He indicated the off-side front hoof he had resting against his knees. "The shoes are new enough, and she's a steady goer, but . . ."

"No one can anticipate everything," Olivia said, eager to be gone. "Niklos, give me a leg up, will you?"

Obediently, Niklos bent with his hands joined. "The girths ought to be checked frequently," he reminded her as she put her foot into his hands.

"I'm not completely a novice at this," she reminded him as he lifted her into the saddle. She spread her skirts as best she could to conceal the saddle and provide a little warmth and protection for herself and the mare. As she drew in the reins, she glanced down at Niklos. "Is that all?"

"They say it will rain again before nightfall," Niklos told her in his steadiest way. "If that happens, find shelter."

"If I can," she said, not permitting him to try to change her mind. "I will be back tomorrow, and if I am not, I will have a messenger come from the Cardinal."

"If it can be arranged," Niklos reminded her.

"I will arrange it," Olivia said with greater purpose than before. "If it must be arranged."

"Remember what you promised," Niklos said as he went to the mare's head.

"I gave you my word," said Olivia, adjusting her seat to the mare's long stride. "What is her name?"

"Mite," said the nearest groom. "She's a little shy about the ears."

"I'll keep it in mind," said Olivia as she checked her hat. "How is she in rain?"

"She'll do," said the groom, his approval of the horse apparent.

As she rode into the courtyard, Olivia glanced up at the sky, studying the clouds scudding overhead. "How does she go in the dark?" Olivia called back over her shoulder.

The oldest groom, standing in the open stable door, answered after he considered a moment. "Well enough, if you do not press her."

"All right," said Olivia, taking the crop that Niklos held out to her. "Don't worry, Niklos. I have managed far worse than this, and well you know it."

Niklos nodded once, his face grim in the muted light. "Yes, I know it. And *you* know that every time you have taken such risks, I have worried about you, so do not tell me I ought not to; by now it's a habit with me."

Olivia's hazel eyes softened. "I know. But take heart, old friend. All your worrying has been for naught." She used the crop to salute, then started Mite off at a walk, peering ahead toward the distant walls of Paris.

Most of the road was axle-deep in mud as several mired wagons at the edge of Chatillon revealed. Olivia skirted them, then decided to cut across the fields, using the country lanes. It might be a longer journey, she thought, but her chance of arriving without mishap was greater. Belatedly she also thought that if Eblouir was being watched, the watchers might not think it significant for her to ride away from her house if she did not take the main road to Paris.

It was windy, though no longer storming. Now there were playful gusts instead of great howling bludgeons, and while the branches of the cypress at the side of the lane bent and moaned, they no longer thrashed.

"It's not too bad, girl," she said to Mite, patting her neck with a gloved hand. "We'll make good time." She glanced toward a windmill with torn sails, shaking her head at the damage she saw around her. "Don't let the flapping cloth bother you," she advised the mare as the horse brought her head up, ears pricked at the sight of the tattered sails.

A farmer stood at the edge of a nearby field, hands on his hips, surveying the damage where the roof of a shed had fallen in. He glanced at Olivia as she rode by, giving her a truculent nod of his head and calling a greeting that could not be heard.

Olivia waved back and continued on, watching for the next turn that would take her to Vanves. She had decided that her best route from there would go to Issy-les-Molineaux. It was not as direct as Montrouge. "You are being overly cautious," she said to herself and the mare. "You have no reason to be so careful." But, she argued inwardly, what if the main road was as impassable at Montrouge as it was at Chatillon? What if there were guards out? What if she was being observed, her progress marked? "That's foolish," she said, all the while thinking that if the Cardinal's courier had come to grief, she might have reason to be afraid. "The poor fellow is probably at an inn, nursing a dislocated shoulder or some similar mishap." She heard the doubt in her voice and saw Mite's ears twitch as if the mare were as unconvinced as she was.

The road forked ahead, and Olivia chose the eastern branch, taking care to avoid the deep puddle in the center of the crossroad where deep ruts disappeared in slick-looking mud. She peered down the road and saw only an oxcart being led by two half-grown children. Relieved, she set Mite into a slow trot, liking the athletic way the mare moved.

One of the youngsters made a rude gesture as Olivia rode by him, and the other whistled through his teeth, laughing as Mite skittered sideways at the sound.

Olivia held the mare together and mentally cursed the two youngsters. She could feel the wind increasing; her thick woolen habit no longer seemed able to hold out the cold slice of the air; her hat flapped like a captive bird. With a quick, impatient swipe, Olivia pulled the two pins securing it free from her hair and watched as the tricorn sailed away, then she pulled the mare in and continued toward Paris.

Torches burned in the gateway when Olivia arrived at the Porte Notre Dame. The portcullis had been lowered more than an hour before, and the two guards on duty huddled together against the driving rain.

Olivia, bedraggled and exhausted, had to pull on the bellrope four times to get one of the guards to bestir himself. "It is too late," he said as he came to the edge of the gateway. "The gate will open tomorrow morning at first light."

"I have an urgent message for Cardinal Mazarin," Olivia announced in her most commanding manner.

"And I am the Duc de Lorraine," said the guard, turning away.

"I have authorization," Olivia called after him. She was glad now that she had insisted that Mazarin provide her with a safe conduct when she had first come to France. "Inspect it, if you like."

"You?" The guard gave a sweeping and condemning look at her, at her muddy horse and cavalry saddle. "How could the likes of you know the Cardinal?" He guffawed with listless malice. "In the morning we'll let you through."

Olivia swung out of the saddle and pulled Mite after her as she walked up to the gate. The rain which had been falling since day's end glistened and ran over her, shining where the light of the torches struck. "You will let me through at once, guardsman, or in the morning you can present your excuses to His Eminence and pray that he is feeling beneficent." She fumbled with the lacing holding her coat closed. Her hands were almost numb with cold and strain. "I have the Cardinal's letter here; you had better read it."

The guard looked at Olivia again, as if noticing her at last; this time there was a randy light in his eyes. "Favor for favor?" He leered at her, revealing discolored teeth.

The smile that Olivia offered him was ferocious. "You set one hand on me, you worm, and you will regret it." She was able to draw the letter from her inside pocket; she thrust it through the bars toward the guard. "You know Mazarin's seal?"

The guardsman took the parchment from her and gave it a cursory inspection. "Not bad," he said as he went to open the gate. "I'll have to have verification."

"This isn't sufficient?" Olivia asked in disbelief as she led Mite through the gate. Her skirts were sodden and their damp had long since penetrated Olivia's disgraceful breeches. She wanted nothing so much as a warm bath and an opportunity to dry off once the mud and grime of travel were washed away.

The guardsman signaled her to wait while he went into the one-room customshouse built into the wall of the gate. As he passed through the door, he wadded up the parchment and tossed it aside, making a tuneless, anticipatory whistle.

Olivia watched in disbelief. She wanted to accuse the guardsman of insubordination, but she could not frame the words, for she was suddenly sharply afraid. With tremendous effort, she said very calmly, "Who will go to the Cardinal's palace? you, or your fellow guardsman?"

The guardsman laughed, a sound like metal scraping brick. "In time one of us will, I'm sure. When it's proper."

It was difficult to pretend she did not understand him, but Olivia strove to appear only irritated; if the guardsman thought she was unaware of his intentions, she would have a slight advantage with him. She made her Italian accent stronger. "Listen, fellow," she said querulously, "I have not ridden through this infernal rain and, I think, damaged my mare's foot so that you can idle away the night waiting to send word to His Eminence. I require to be taken to his palace at once." Her back was straight and her head up.

"All in good time," said the guardsman with more insinuation in his tone.

Olivia tossed her head, feeling the wet strands of hair against her face and neck. "Well, while you prepare to go, or whatever it is you are doing, I will see to my mare's hoof." And before the guardsman could stop her, Olivia turned and was out the door.

"What?" The guardsman swung around just in time to see Olivia pull herself into the saddle. As he started toward her, she raised her riding crop and brought it down smartly across his cheek as she backed the mare out of the narrow passageway and into the street. The guardsman swore eloquently and shouted for his partner. "Stop her! *Stop her!*"

It was hard not to look back, to see whether the guardsmen were coming after her, and it was harder not to try to kick the exhausted horse into a canter, but neither of those things would be wise, Olivia told herself with all the force she could muster. She kept Mite to a trot, watching every doorway and alley for footpads and more sinister folk, knowing that there was more danger in being unescorted in the streets of Paris after dark than there was on the road from Chatillon. She wished now that she had taken the time to charge a pistol, or tuck a dagger into her boot. "A sword would be better," she whispered to the mare as she ducked to avoid a shop sign hanging over the way, hanging onto the reins to keep the mare from falling when she slipped on the muddy paving.

At last she saw the bulk of the Cardinal's palace ahead, and she all but shrieked with the consolation the building gave simply by its existence. She drew Mite down to a walk and went to the central gate, once again looking for the bellrope.

An officer of the Cardinal's Guard answered her summons, and listened to her tale in patent disbelief. "Where did you say your safe conduct is?" he asked her when she had finished telling him who she was and why she had come.

"If you had been paying attention to what I have been saying," she pointed out with exasperation, "you would know that the guard at the Porte Notre Dame has it."

"Convenient," said the officer in polite disbelief.

"Actually," Olivia said sharply, "it is exceedingly inconvenient. If I could produce it, this door would be open by now." She sighed. "Send for Fontaine de Rochard, the Cardinal's lackey, and ask him to identify me. If Pere Chape is here, he will vouch for me." She hoped that these names might influence the officer, for she was perilously close to being angry with him. "Magna Mater, I am part of His Eminence's suite!"

The officer hid a yawn behind his hand. "All right," he said, making up his mind. "I will send for de Rochard, but if he does not approve you, then you will be sent away from here with ten blows from a stout cudgel for your impertinence."

"Fine," said Olivia, meaning it. As she wiped the rain from her face, she hoped that her efforts would prove worthwhile. She patted Mite's side before she unbuckled the saddle girths. "Well, girl," she said to the mare, watching her drooping head, "you've earned your oats and a long rest for this ride." Then, as she tugged the wet saddle off the mare's back, she saw Fontaine de Rochard coming across the courtyard inside the gate, an anxious expression on his youthful face.

"Madame Clemens," he called out, signaling to the officer of the Cardinal's Guard to open the gate. "At once," he insisted. "God save you! what has happened?"

Olivia slung the saddle over her arm and waited while the gates were opened for her.

✵   ✵   ✵

Text of a letter from Jean-Arnaud du Peyrer de Troisvilles to Cardinal Jules Mazarin.

Eminence,

It is no secret that you and I have been at odds for some time, and in spite of the generous offers various of your henchmen have made to me over the last two years, I wish to make it clear to you once and for all that I have no interest in accepting a more favorable position at court than the one I now occupy. I have no ambition beyond continuing to serve the King and France as the commander of the King's Musqueteers. I have risen to my current position through my service to the Crown and I intend to do so until I die.

I understand that you wish to bestow my regiment on your very young nephew Philippe Mancini, le Duc de Nevers, who has no skill as a commander of armed men. You show great respect to your family, which is laudable in any man, but you have no regard for the Musqueteers, who will risk their lives in the defence of the King at the order from their leader. It is necessary, if their lives are not to be wasted, that men of experience and judgment give the orders, not untried and well-born youths with no idea of the reality of battle.

I have heard you remark that we Bearnais are cunning, and I agree insofar as it is true that we seek to employ sense and wisdom in our dealings. You have said that I, alone of everyone in Europe, doubt you, and for that you have claimed that all your work has been thwarted. I have long made it a practice to be direct and candid in everything I do and say, for to indulge in any other practice can only serve to provide my opponents at court with more fuel than I am willing to give them. If in so doing I have slighted you, I ask that you will pardon me, as I freely pardon you for the many unkindnesses you have shown me in the last year. If it is that Her Majesty has seen fit to elevate Troisvilles and bestow upon me the title of Comte, I can only remind you that such elevation was not of my seeking, nor was it the reason for my service to the Crown; and while I am honored far more than I can ever express, I am also nothing more than the servant of the Crown.

Undoubtedly we can agree on one or two essential matters: the King must be protected from the treachery often present in the court, for a little boy is too easily influenced by those who appear to show him favor. And it is apparent to both of us that the Queen Regent is in need of protection and guidance so that the Crown will not be in greater danger than it already is.

I pray you will consider this and then be willing to meet with me and discuss our difference in the light of the things we concur are of paramount value and importance. We do ourselves and the Crown no good by our continuing bickering, and we endanger what we intend most to defend. It is not my desire to continue to run counter to your wishes when it is apparent that our devotions are the same.

Believe me to be the King's true subject and the loyal commander of his Musqueteers.

   Jean-Arnaud du Peyrer, Comte de Troisvilles
On the 24th day of March, 1645.

A bona fide copy of this letter is included in the files of the King's Musqueteers.

· 5 ·

"Do you really prefer me clean-shaven?" Charles asked as he peered into the mirror at his bedside. "Beards and moustaches are more gallant."

"Not to me," said Olivia, propping herself on her elbow and watching as he stropped his razor. The morning sunlight angled in the window, making brilliant golden splotches on the flowered carpet; one small section of this was caught in Charles' mirror as well, and reflected some of the brightness onto his face. "I like to be able to see you."

"Why?" His smile was joyful. "You see so much of the rest of me, why do you want to see my face?"

"I like your face. I like all of you," said Olivia as she pulled the bedding up around her shoulders and was content to watch him lather his face before working his razor over the chiseled line of his jaw. She enjoyed the way he moved, the way his long, blunt fingers held the steel. "I wish you didn't have to leave."

"Do you?" He was finished with his cheeks and had tilted back his chin to work under his jaw. "It is my first real opportunity to demonstrate my skill as a soldier. If I do well, there is recognition and advancement for me. Doesn't that please you? Don't you wish me well?"

"I wish you safe," she said, her affection giving way to asperity. "You are not proof against musquetballs and cannon and the swing of a sabre." She said the last softly, not quite looking at him anymore.

"Well?" he challenged. "I am a Musqueteer. I am a soldier sworn to the King. Musquetballs and cannon and sabres are part of my life, Olivia." He completed shaving and wiped the excess lather from his face, suddenly impatient. "You know how much I have sought this, and you know that any success I am to have in this world will come through battle and war. Why do you question that now, when you have known it all along?" He rounded on her, not quite glaring.

"Because you are leaving to fight, and I fear for you," she admitted slowly. "I dread you will go into battle and all that will emerge will be your corpse." Her words were as harsh as her eyes were sad.

"Is that likely?" His manner lightened at once. "After what there is between us, why should I be in danger? Look how long you have lived. Why shouldn't I be as fortunate?" He was teasing her, the ends of his flying brows raised even more, making his face pleasantly devilish.

Olivia was not mollified. "I have been much more lucky than I have any right to be," she said brusquely. "And I have had the good sense not to face cannon."

"No, you train horses instead," he answered in the same sharp tone. As he turned toward her, his body, naked from the waist up, shone in the glow of morning light. "And from what you have told me, if you break your neck, you would be as dead as I would be with my chest blown to pieces by enemy fire." He slapped his towel down on the post at the foot of the bed. "Do not tell me that there is any difference between my danger and your danger. At least I do not pretend that battle is safe."

"In battle," Olivia said sternly, "you may be certain that someone will be trying to kill you. My horses do not want to kill me, they do not intend to kill me—or very few of them," she amended honestly.

"Your neck would still be broken, whether the horse wanted to kill you or not," said Charles, his voice very low. "I don't think I could bear that."

Olivia gave him a long, direct look. "Then you know how I feel when you tell me you are going to war." She sat up, drawing her knees up under the covers and resting her chin on them. "It has happened before, many times. I have been assured that there was no chance, none in the world, that my . . . companion could come to any harm. But it wasn't so. And I knew as soon as the breath was out of them. It is the way of those of my blood to know such things."

Charles leaned toward her, into the shadow of the damask hangings, his straight arms braced on the bed. "And what of me? I am of your blood already. I have tasted your blood, and you are as much a part of me as I am of you, aren't I?"

"In some ways," said Olivia carefully, wishing for the moment that he were not so dear to her. "But you have not yet died and wakened."

"What does that matter?" he demanded of the air. "What would that mean? I have taken you as part of me, and I am glad to have that privilege, I welcome it. But since it is mine, let me have it." Abruptly he reached out and took her head in his hands, leaning forward to kiss her with a passion that bordered on anger. He held her for some little while, his mouth on hers, until her lips opened to him; his defiance faded as her arms went around his neck. "Teton de Marie," he murmured as they drew apart, "why are we fighting?"

"Because we are afraid," said Olivia, remembering too many other times when she had not been willing to admit her fear.

"I am afraid of nothing but the loss of you." He had stretched out, angled across her, his face—now filled with love and concern—close to hers, his hand still at the back of her neck. "We are fools, Olivia."

"I grant you that," she said, brushing the strands of long chestnut hair back from his face. The scent of the soap he had used for shaving was sharp in her nostrils.

"I want to be angry with you," he confessed. "So that while I am gone I will not miss you, or so that I can lie to myself and say that I am too furious to miss you." His smile was tentative, chagrined. "I would rather face charging cavalry than have to miss you, Olivia."

"Don't face charging cavalry," she protested, pressing the tips of her fingers to his mouth. "Promise me."

"If I can avoid charging cavalry, I will," he said, dismissing her concern with a swift gesture that pulled her more closely to him. "Will that satisfy you?"

"It must," she said, her expression distant. She leaned into his shoulder, unwilling to meet his eyes. "I can't help being worried. If anything happens to you—"

He cut her short. "I worry for you, as well. And not because of the horses, not only because of your horses. That courier of Mazarin's died hard, Olivia. You did not see his body. I did, when they brought it back to Paris, all wrapped in a torn windmill sail. They showed it to us, to convince us that there are troubles. They explained what was done. If anyone did such things to you . . . I think I would go mad." This time his kiss was light, nothing more than the brush of his lips on hers.

Olivia took a deep, unsteady breath. "It will not happen; you have no reason to be concerned." She stared up at the canopy of her bed. "I have servants here who guard me well, and money to keep them attentive and faithful. If any of my staff is dissatisfied, I discharge them, so that none of the household can be easily bribed. And I have Niklos to protect me."

"They might not be enough," said Charles, then, as he tightened his hold on her, he went on roughly, "Listen to me: the courier was tied to the base of a tree, and his arms were tied to the bent limbs of another. When they let the limbs go, they pulled his shoulders from their sockets. One of his arms was almost off. They let him bleed to death from that torn arm; he was so white that his body was pale as cheese when we found him. That was why he never arrived here, Olivia. That's what Mazarin's enemies did to stop him."

"I cannot bleed to death," Olivia said softly. "None of us can, not after we change. Only the living can bleed to death."

"You can be tortured, and it might happen that you are. What then, if there is no death to spare you?" He kissed her again, urgently this time, breaking away before he could succumb to her nearness. "You are known as the Cardinal's Italian friend, you are part of his suite; everyone *knows* that. No one at court doubts that you act on his behalf, that you receive messages and documents for him, and that his couriers come here for private meetings. Don't you understand the hazards you run?"

Olivia shifted, moving the bedclothes so that she could lift them for Charles. "All right; I know I am at risk." She beckoned to him. "There is less danger for me than there would be for most others."

"That does not make it acceptable," Charles said, vexation in his voice now. "It is not acceptable to me."

"Yes; I have the same sense when you tell me you are going into battle." She indicated his breeches. "Take those off."

"I will not change my mind simply because you give me your love." There was more pain than resistance in what he said. "I can't forget."

"Neither can I," Olivia said, her fingers laid lightly on his chest. "But it will be a while before I see you again, and I want . . . oh, I want to sate myself with you before you go, so that I will not grieve too much while you are gone."

"Do you think you can?" he asked with an impulsive, mercurial smile. "Sate yourself, I mean?"

"No," she said.

"Does that mean you will try to drain me?" He asked it to tease her, but her reaction was genuine shock and dismay.

"No!" She started to move back from him, to seek refuge in the engulfing blankets and sheets. "How can you ask that of me, when you have tasted my blood?"

Charles was contrite, reaching out to her as he condemned himself for a fool. "Olivia, no. No, darling love, no, no." He hardly touched her, but he made her face him. "I didn't mean that. It was a jest—a poor one." He kissed her brow. "If I believed you would truly do such a thing, I would never say so to you."

"Wouldn't you?" She was terribly cold all at once, her skin feeling raw with it, though the sheets were warm to the touch. "And why not?"

"Because I love you," he said simply. "I would never mock you for anything you are, because I love you."

"Even though I am a vampire." As she said the word, other times in her life rose unbidden in her mind. That word, that one simple word that branded her a monster and worse was no longer hard to utter, but she had never learned to be able to acquiesce in the horror others felt: that word and what she was damned her as no court, no church, could.

"You could be a shrieking demon from the lowest pit in Hell and it would make no difference to me as long as you were also Olivia." He slid close to her. "And you are not a shrieking demon, are you?"

"Not just at present," she said stiffly. "How can you be certain I am not?"

His chuckle was low and filled with warmth. "I have been your lover for long enough to know what you are. I have tasted your blood, and though you are not willing to believe me, I know as much of you as you know of me through that bond." His kiss now was deliberate, as if he were trying to give up his soul to her. He ran his hand down her flank, over the rise of her hip and down the muscular curve of the thigh.

"Charles," she whispered when he at last permitted her to speak, "I did not mean to offend you."

"But you doubt me," he said, taking care that there was no trace of accusation in his response.

"I don't want to," she said, kissing his fresh-shaven chin. "But after so many, many years, I find it difficult to think that anyone could know what I am and not . . . despise me."

"I do not despise you; I never could." His hand moved up her body, around her breast, his thumb lightly pressing her nipple before his lips closed there. He felt her shiver as he drew her nearer, touching her as if he held fragile treasure in his hands.

There was no point in resisting him, Olivia told herself with that remote part of her mind that could still think. She did not want to, in case it was the last time. Over the centuries she had come to cherish the few and precious moments when souls and bodies joined; Charles sought the very core of her, searching for it in every part of her being. And she loved him, not only for that, but for the way the sun shone on his hair, on those loose chestnut waves that would not take a fashionable curl; for the way he walked, his heels leaving the ground almost as soon as they touched it; for the scent of him, and the way his sweat tasted when they lay together, their limbs tangled as vines; for the strength and clarity of his passion; for his blood that was forever part of her.

"Olivia," he said, quietly as a prayer. He bent and, in spite of the engulfing bedclothes, began to wrestle his way out of his breeches. "Wait."

Olivia, startled by this swift change, blinked as she looked at him, and then, realizing what he was doing, laughed.

"How can you do that?" he demanded with flagrantly false indignation. "Can you find the garter, for God's Nails?"

She could not stop her giggles, but she complied, ducking under the covers and reaching for the ornamented cuff of his breeches that was secured with rosette garters just below his knee. She worked the fastenings of the garters until they were loose enough to permit him to slide them over his feet, helping him to wiggle and kick his way free of his clothes. "Wouldn't it have been easier to get out of bed to do that?" she asked as she appeared at the mound of pillows at the head of the bed.

Charles grinned. "Possibly. But this is more fun." With one extravagant gesture he threw his breeches across the room, then rolled toward her, wrapping her in his arms once more. "How good it is to be with you," he said, nuzzling her neck. "I like this place, just here, under your ear." He kissed her several times there to make his point.

Olivia flung her head back, her eyes half-closed, her smile ecstatic as he resumed his ministrations. "What am I going to do for you?" she asked when he paused.

"Enjoy yourself," he answered, breathless in his delight. "I want you to be transported with pleasure, so that I can be part of it. I want you to fill yourself with the sweetness of love, so that when I fill you, there will be more than enough for both of us." His kisses went from quick and light to long and deep. His hands had an imagination and purpose of their own that served to make them both light-headed. As he moved over her, he looked down on her face, and could not believe that a saint in the sight of God was more beautiful than Olivia. Her flesh welcomed him as he entered her, and she moved with him as their rapture became delicious frenzy. He trembled, and felt her lips on his neck as his fulfillment overtook him.

They lay as they had been, the sheets rumpled around them, the blankets in disarray. He used his elbows to keep from crushing her, and to let him move enough to be able to look at her again. He grazed her upper lip with a kiss and the tip of his tongue.

She opened her eyes slowly, watching him grin at her. She hooked one foot inside his ankle. "I have you," she murmured.

"Not because of your foot," he whispered back at her.

It was too much trouble to say anything; she slipped her hands around his waist and locked them easily behind his back, giving him a lazy smile in answer to his grin. "I could stay here all day."

"If that's what you want," he said, easing off her but not breaking her hold on him. "I will explain to de Troisvilles that I was unavoidably detained." He stroked her fawn-brown hair. "He will understand."

"Why shouldn't he?" she asked, but there was a sadness in her flippancy.

Charles kissed her neck on the same place she had touched his. "Would it make sense to do it again?"

"Sense has nothing to do with it," she said, stretching with the lithe contentment of a cat. "Do you love me because it is sensible?"

"If I don't, I should," he said, smoothing the damp tendrils from her brow. "Answer my question."

"It always makes sense to make love," she said, slightly puzzled by his insistence.

"No," he said, his knuckles caressing her ribs in a parody of a blow. "Would it make sense for me to taste your blood again? You have had mine—"

"So often that it wouldn't matter if you hadn't tasted mine," she said, feeling strangely old as she answered. "If we had been lovers for a short while, it would be another matter, for there would not be the . . . bond; but . . . it has been years." In spite of her qualms, she smiled. "It . . . anything more would be . . . redundant."

"Would it be better?" He pulled one of the pillows under his side and used it to prop himself over her.

Her hold on him was broken, but she kept one hand on his lean hip. "Better? How?"

"Would it seal our love more?" His brown eyes were warm with tenderness. "Would anything serve to do that? Will you tell me?" He ran the tips of his fingers over her face, concentrating on every contour of skin and bone.

"With all there is between us, you can ask that?" Her eyes pricked, as they had done whenever she desired to weep—tears had been lost to her when she left her tomb, but the need for them remained.

He bent and kissed the arch of her brow. "I didn't think so, but I hoped there might be."

"Ah," she said, not quite sighing. "If such things are possible, I have never known of them." She unhooked her foot from his ankle. "What we have exceeds what most others know."

"But if there is more, I want it," Charles said, bringing his foot around to capture her ankle.

Olivia swung her free leg over Charles' back, holding him as if she were in the saddle on a newly broken horse. "And I have compounded it," she told him with a wistful laugh. "Oh, Charles, you must come back to me. I don't want to lose you. I'm not ready to lose you."

"And I am not ready to lose you, either," he said emphatically. "Not now, not a year from now, not a decade from now."

Her question came unbidden to her lips: "How can you be sure of it?" Once she asked, she wanted to hide from any answer he might offer her.

"I am sure because I know you," he said simply. "You are not one of those females who will try all life long to bend and mold herself to the will of her father or husband or son, and you are not one who will demand that her father or husband or son become what she demands they be. You are yourself, and as long as you are yourself, I will love you with all the passion in my soul, with the same passion I give to God and to the Kingdom of France. If I cannot offer myself to them, I have no right to offer myself to you." He leaned forward and kissed her eyelids. "You have no reason to fear."

"You are very young," Olivia reminded him, hoping that her oblique comment would not distress him.

"I am not so young as you might think," he objected. "I am not a pampered child of wealth and privilege who has never done a day's labor; I have worked the land and defended it since I was old enough to swing an axe or master a horse." He flopped back against the pillows, his luminous brown eyes on the gathered damask canopy. "It was required of us all; if I had been the oldest son instead of my brother Paul, they would have demanded that I spend more time in the schoolroom, to learn to write for magistrates and nobles, and to do sums. Paul is very good at such things, and he takes great care of Batz-Castelmore as well. While he was writing formal requests, I was learning how to use a sabre, how to throw a dagger, how to handle a lance, how to load and fire a musquet." He put his hand to his chest. "I don't mind about the figures, but I am sorry now I did not learn my letters better, so that I could send you notes and poetry while I am away on campaign." He was suddenly embarrassed. "I have a friend who has sworn he will write for me. But the things I would want to tell you, I am not certain I could speak aloud for him." He coughed once. "I will try, if that would please you."

Olivia took a deep breath. "It would please me very much. And if you would tell me where to find you, I would answer you with notes of my own."

Charles waved that suggestion away. "It isn't wise. You would have to use the Cardinal's couriers and that might increase danger to us both. Let me use the couriers of the Musqueteers—the notes will not be as swift in delivery, but they will not mark me as one of the Cardinal's creatures. Which," he added with a bit more vehemence, "I am not."

"No, you are not," Olivia agreed with him at once. "You are a King's Musqueteer, new to the service, and you have reason to prove yourself, or so you tell me." She freed herself from the confusion of their legs. "It shall be as you wish, Charles."

"It isn't what I would wish—I wish I had my own private couriers to carry letters to you every day, and I wish I knew how to write well enough to tell you every day how much I love you and how I miss you. But instead I will arrange for you to receive word from me as often as possible, and I will ask Isaac to write down what I tell him, and hope that I will not suddenly be struck dumb." He reached out to finger her hair. "Will you give me a lock of this, to wear in a locket around my neck? My sister Claude gave me a locket with a picture of Saint Michel on it, with room for a lock of hair. I haven't worn it—until now, I thought it was silly."

"I'll give you a lock of my hair," said Olivia, and was startled to realize that she had bestowed such a token only three times in the past. Not since that Sardinian troubador, three hundred years ago had she even considered such a gift.

"What are you thinking?" Charles asked, seeing some ghost of her memories on her face.

"I was hoping you would not regret your choice," she said, assuaging her misgivings by realizing it was close enough to the truth: so many times before those who had come to her life had discovered that it was not what they had anticipated; sooner or later, they had given it up. For most of them, their end had been at least partially welcome.

"Is that all?" Charles persisted.

"No," she admitted, "but the rest would mean little to you." She was staring toward the window, noticing how much higher the sun had risen while they had been wrapped in each other's arms.

Charles sighed. "I pray you will decide to tell me about your reservations, someday." Suddenly he gave her shoulder a gentle slap. "Come. I must eat and leave."

"How uncivil," said Olivia, managing to smile in spite of her renewed apprehension at his leaving.

"It is, isn't it?" he agreed cheerfully as he got out of bed. "But if you will hurry, you may watch me leap onto my horse and dash off to join my regiment." He had gathered up his breeches, but before pulling them on once more, he gave her a long, intense stare. "I don't want to go."

"I wish you didn't have to, as well," Olivia said as she rose more sedately. She took her night rail from the chair near the bed and draped it around her shoulders.

"You know that nothing is dearer to me than my honor," Charles said, in a deep, steady tone that Olivia had heard only once before. "But if you were to ask it, I would give it up, and gladly, to have your love."

It took a short while before Olivia trusted herself to answer. "Well, then you are fortunate, for I would never ask that of you, Charles. And if I did, my love would be worth less than the dust on the road."

His smile was faint but the glint was back in his eyes. "Touche, my beloved." With that, he went back to dressing, and the things they said were simple, inconsequent comments, less painful and dangerous than the turmoil each stirred in the other.

*　　*　　*

Text of a letter from Cardinal Jules Mazarin to his second cousin Gennaro Colonna, now with the Spanish forces in Mexico. Written in French.

To my errant kinsman now in the New World, your cousin in France sends greetings, and the hopes that his prayers will aid with those of others to bring you once again to honor and Grace, for the reputation of our family and the triumph of our religion.

You have informed me in your most recent letter that you have encountered nothing but the most heathen of savages, all of them decked out in gold and jewels and flaunting their false gods in the face of the Christian monks and priests who have come to teach them the ways of Christ. I have read other reports that show some of the same observations, but without the consequences of your own impressions. Your sense of frustration at the lack of faith on the part of these heathen, and their lack of Grace, is understandable enough, and if that were all your message, I would rejoice and inform our relatives that at last you have set your feet on the true path and have started the journey that must ultimately lead to the salvation of your soul and the restoration of your position within the family. But, sadly, you do not stop there. You are not content to observe those who are obdurate in their resistance to the teachings of Christ, and the tranquility of soul that comes with acquiescence in the Will of God, which is the reward on earth given to true Christians. You give it as your opinion that since these heathen are not won to the cause of Christ and are not willing to bow down to the Cross, that they are therefore unworthy of anything but the most unforgiving treatment, and any sort of degradation that you and your companions, as soldiers of the True Faith, can mete out to them for their obstinate refusal to accept Christ.

For the sake of all the Saints, why should they, those poor, ignorant savages, accept the promise of salvation and paradise when you, who carry His banner, treat them as you would hesitate to treat animals. Your letter describes—with hideous pride—the way in which you violated the women of a chieftain's family, and then killed them all by pulling out their intestines and nailing them to the floor. This is not the act of a good Christian soldier, and certainly not the act of one who professes to accept the laws of Christ as binding on his own fate. This is an overwhelming denial of the very nature of the Word of Christ, which is postulated on peace and love in His Name. To cause such terrible carnage shows a complete lack of respect for the oath you have taken as a soldier fighting in the name of the Christian King of Spain and the Church. You say that this was not the only incident, but the most recent, and therefore the one you have most knowledge of. You say that without such acts the heathen will not be subdued to the Christian faith. You claim that the fact that these are heathen excuses everything you do, but I cannot and I do not agree with you. You have taken the teachings of Christ and perverted them to your own nefarious purpose, making them worse than the most intolerable behavior of Nero and other debauched Emperors before the salvation of Christ found its heart in Rome.

I will offer you this homily in the fervent hope that it will create within you some understanding of the enormity of your trespasses against the Holy Spirit, and will stand you in good stead in future when you are tempted to indulge again in those excesses you have described and have not repented of, either in the act itself, nor in the sins that drove you to such atrocious errors.

There was a man who had lived all his life in disfavor, with his family and with his God. He was not a bad man, if badness is measured by the ferocity of his sins, but he was one who viewed the world and those around him with contempt; he respected no one and nothing in this world, and feared nothing in the next. He was thought to be a man without conscience by those who had cause to work with him, and as a hardened sinner by those who heard of him from others. He cared nothing for their thoughts of him, and when questioned on the matter, he said he was well-content to live alone and thus be freed from the company of rogues and fools. He was so unwilling to enter into the society of his city and his family that he chose to live away from them, and to regard them as nothing more than travelers, with no obligation or claim shared with them greater than their human necessities, which for him did not include love, honor, or religion. It was his contention that to have friends was to have liabilities, and to have family was to have constant unjustified demands made on him. When he learned that his father had dis-owned him and taken away his inheritance, the man was amused for it justified his vexation with the world. He declared that he had had nothing from his father while the man lived and it was nothing to him that he was disowned.

Think of this unfortunate being, my cousin, and apply his la-mentable actions to your own life. Before I continue with the tale, I wish you will take the time to review your own statements and letters which are not unlike the contentions of this most unhappy mortal. You may think that there is nothing to see, but I assure you that there is, and I am convinced that you have fallen into the same terrible trap as this fellow did. If you are able to discern the similarities, then hear the end of this unhappy story, and profit by it. You have said that you do not wish to be read lessons and that you have seen enough of the world to know what is what, but I, as your affectionate cousin, cannot agree with you.

Let me continue with this narrative, with renewed implorations that you read what is here as being for your benefit, a timely warn-ing—albeit an unwelcome and unsolicited one—given to one of my own blood who appears to be willing to damn himself forever as a gesture of pique.

The man, the fellow I have mentioned who cared so little for his fellow man, was rumored to have wealth hidden in his house. Be-cause he kept few servants and did not pay them well or treat them with respect, two of them were willing to speak of their master with strangers who accosted them in a local inn. They revealed, for the price of a small meal and two tankards of wine, that they had never seen the treasure their master was supposed to possess but had never been given any information by him that it did not. They were venal enough to accept a small bribe to inform these strangers of the best way into the man's house, and then, being full of food and wine, wended their way back to their master's house smug in the knowledge that they had at last some profit for their dealings with the man.

The strangers were, of course, thieves, and desperate men, who two nights later broke into the house and began to search for the treasure they wished to find. The man had only three servants who slept in the house itself, the others being required to stay in the farmers' houses of his estate, and these three were quickly overwhelmed by the robbers. Had their master shown them more regard and thereby sealed their loyalty, it might have gone otherwise, for it was apparent that his servants were not much moved to protect him. So it was that the robbers plundered through the house, searching for the treasure said to be hidden there. When none was found, the robbers determined to extract the location from the man who owned the estate, and they took up the task with skill and determination. First they bound him and hit his ankles with metal rods, demanding that the man tell them where he had hidden his gold. It was useless for the man to protest that he had none, that his father had left him none, and that he was of a solitary nature and not merely a miser. The robbers, as is often the case with such violent men, did not believe him, and so worked greater harm on his flesh, culminating in blinding him. Then they set fire to the house, so great was their disappointment and anger at not discovering the gold they were sure was hidden there.

So the man was now without any property, he was crippled from the blows to his ankles, and he was blind. In vain he called for his servants, who had fled upon the arrival of the robbers. No aid had been summoned on his behalf, no one had come to help him when he had cried out. He might have died in the fire that consumed the house but that the robbers had left one door open and the man was able to drag himself out of it. Once beyond the door, he collapsed, and it was there he woke in the morning, quite alone. None of his servants returned to aid or succor him. When he hauled his maimed body to the nearest church, he was turned away from there because of his apostasy, and the monks of the monastery had no place for him when he at last reached their portals. They promised to pray for him, as they had always done in the past, but they could offer him *no shelter and no food, for he had disavowed the company of those in the true faith of God.*

So this maimed and ruined man was left to be a beggar on the road, without shelter or aid. His relatives, after a few attempts to find him, abandoned the search and brought the man's nephews to work his land and rebuild his house. They revered his memory as one dead to them already and they strove not to speak ill of him; in consequence they spoke very little of him at all. The man knew suffering without end and distress beyond imagining because he turned from those who would have been his staunch support in his ordeal, and he mocked the very soul of charity, so that it was no longer available to him. When he died he was left to rot in a ditch, and wild dogs fed on the flesh of his carcass while his soul descended to Hell, to the ministrations of devils more cruel and cunning than the robbers had ever been. His prayers were useless then, for he had not repented and God no longer had jurisdiction over his soul.

I pray that you will come to your senses in time to keep from treading the same road this unfortunate man trod. I beg you to think of your soul and the souls of those as yet unconverted, for they are as much in your hands as are the souls of innocent children who entrust you to bring them protection from evil. You will find no profit in what you do, and you will not thrive if you continue in this way. I urge you to seek the advice of the priests who accompany you and to act upon their recommendations, for that way is the road to salvation and the preservation of your life.

This letter will be carried to you by Frey Andreas on the **Sagrada Familia** *which departs for the New World on the 22nd day of July, the Feast of Marie Madelaine; it would do well for you to remember her in your thoughts and your devotions, for she was guilty of far more serious sins than you have committed— or so I trust—and was absolved of all of them when she undertook to live a virtuous life. Consider how grievous her trespasses were, and how exalted she is now. You are not incorrigible unless you will make no effort to improve yourself. God will lend you His strength if you will but ask for it. That is the promise which His Son won for all of us with His precious Blood. Do not spurn it, cousin, and never despise it, as you have professed once to do. That Blood was shed for you, and your soul is as much a treasure in Heaven as that of the holiest monks and nuns. Repent your past sins and resolve to sin no more; God will welcome you with the blessed if you will truly*

*put your errors behind you. Mere Marie will intercede for you
if you will ask it in her Son's Name. How can I tell you what
joy it would bring to me to learn that you had put your past
behind you? It is always in my thoughts.*

*With all my prayers and all my hope that you will turn from
your disastrous course and establish yourself with the righteous
and the blessed, I send you my blessing.*

Your cousin,
Jules Mazarin
Cardinal and First Minister of France
On the 8th day of July, 1645.

· 6 ·

Pere Chape wished he could leave; he had never liked cemeteries, and this one, at night, was more distressing than he had
anticipated. He stood in the shadow of an enormous and ancient
tomb, staring at a new statue of a warrior Saint. He shivered,
though the autumn night was not chill. He sniffed, convinced that
he was in danger from the miasma of the place, but in fact feeling
sorry for himself.

There was the crunch of a boot on gravel and dry leaves, and
then the soft footfalls were muffled by moss growing beside the
path. There was the scent of brandy and perfume, and a shadow
next to that of the armored, angelic statue. "You wanted to speak
with me?"

"Yes," Pere Chape said, adding, "there is a white eagle in the
sky."

His unknown visitor sighed and answered with the rest of the
recognition code. "There is a red mouse on the ground." He
moved a little nearer so that the shadow of the tomb covered him
as well as Pere Chape. "What is the trouble? You know that it is
hazardous for us to meet."

"Certainly," said Pere Chape with the assumption of dignity. "But since that messenger was killed, the Cardinal has been so much on his guard that I am not certain it is any less hazardous sending you messages."

"Mazarin is in Amiens now, with the Queen Regent and that child we must call King instead of bastard." The tone was more condemning than the words. "I hope that Richelieu, wherever he is in Hell, knows that we will not tolerate his brat ruling the Kingdom of France."

"If God is just," said Pere Chape, a little apprehensive at the soft-voiced wrath he heard in his visitor's words, "He will favor our cause."

There was no response for a short while, then the other man said, "So."

"Monsieur . . ." Pere Chape began, then could think of nothing more to say.

"What was so urgent that you had to speak with me? And why now?" The voice was still low, courteous, almost seductive. Pere Chape was afraid of the man.

"It's the courier," he blurted out. "The one that was killed? You know—bound to tree limbs?" Even saying it made him writhe. He had never approved of killing the courier; he had said so when the plan was first considered. He had been absolutely against torturing the courier. He had kept to the position that if it had to be done, then let it be swift and painless. This soft-voiced fellow had given the order.

"I am aware," said the other man, his tone a degree less accommodating.

"Well," Pere Chape said, trying to remain calm, "it has been decided by the Cardinal that the couriers will now ride not to Eblouir but to the Roman widow's stud farm in Tours, and from there the letters will be carried by one of his Guards. He made up his mind just this afternoon."

"How can you know that? Mazarin is at Amiens with the Queen Regent and Richelieu's spawn."

"But he sent word, with one of the Queen's messengers. It was delivered to his secretary this afternoon. Had I not been at the Cardinal's palace, I would have known nothing of it. I thought that . . . that it was important to tell you. As soon as possible." He was finding it difficult to breathe and his tone had become rough with apprehension.

"And that was why you summoned me instead of sending a coded message?" The softness was now dangerous, a steel blade wrapped in fine satin. "What reason do you have?"

"I . . . I knew you wanted to keep track of the couriers, to be able to follow them. You know that Mazarin wants to use military men as couriers, and so far, des Essarts and de Troisvilles have opposed the request. But their days are limited—in another year, who knows who will head the Musqueteers and the King's Guard?"

There was a rustling in the hedge behind the tomb, and both men fell silent, Pere Chape prepared to bolt on the instant. Neither man moved until a large, dark, battle-scarred tomcat burst from the undergrowth, head up, a dying rat dangling out both sides of his mouth. He trotted away, giving the human intruders no notice.

The stranger did not speak at once. "Are there couriers on the road now?" he asked when the cat was gone from sight.

"I believe so. A courier from the Vatican is expected in the next three days. And someone has come from the young Duc de Nevers."

"Philippe Mancini!" said the other as if the name were the most vile obscenity. "Another Italian adventurer!" He took an impetuous step away, gravel rasping under his heel, then he turned back, his rage once again under control. "That boy will be his final error," the stranger declared in his low-voiced fury. "By le Bon Dieu and my right hand, I swear it."

"May God hear and aid you," Pere Chape said quickly, trying to keep from sounding as terrified as he felt. "An end to the Italian, I say."

"And to Richelieu's get." The man fell silent once more, needing time to regain his self-control. He tapped the hilt of his sword in a steady tattoo as he strove to keep himself from bellowing his ire. "They will fall," he said at last. "Mazarin, and all those with him. We will bring them down, and send that Spanish woman back to her brother, if he'll take her and those disgraced children of—" He stopped. "The watchman."

Pere Chape clasped his hands, and prayed that his bowels would not give way. "What if it's worse than the watchman?" he made himself whisper, his throat cracked with terror.

"You mean les Plumets or les Freres de la Samaritaine?" the other asked, so quietly that Pere Chape had to strain to hear him.

"Les Plumets do not enter cemeteries. And les Freres only prey on those near the Pont-Neuf." He paused. "Besides, this is les Grisons territory." He held up his gloved hand. "Step into the doorway of the next tomb on the shadow side. It's safe there."

"And you?" Pere Chape squeaked, torn between dread and relief.

"I will draw the fellow off a little and return," said the other man, his face obscured still, but a hard smile in his voice. "I'll whistle like an owl when I come back."

Pere Chape saw the swing of the other man's coat, worn cape-like over his shoulders—easily shrugged off in a fight—and heard the quiet fall of his feet on the gravel of the path, and then only the night breeze. He all but tumbled into the shadowed door of the next tomb, and he remained there as much from his overwhelming fear as from prudence.

It was not long before the watchman, using his tall staff for a cane, stumped by, his lanthorn giving off a a small, golden puddle of light at his feet. He was humming without actually making a tune, and his threadbare soldier's cloak from thirty years before was gathered around him to ward off the night chill. Near Pere Chape's hiding place he paused for two voluptuous sneezes, then continued on his way while he wiped his face with the cuff of his chamise.

Pere Chape recoiled from the sneezes as if he had been shot, and then crossed himself, letting the cold granite walls of the tomb hold him up.

Some little time later there was the brief sound of a scuffle, and a low cry of dismay. Then once again the only sound was from the wind.

When the stranger came back, Pere Chape saw that he was wiping the blade of his sword on the lining of his coat. He came near to the door where Pere Chape cowered, and said quietly, "He will tell nothing."

"You mean he is dead?" Pere Chape muttered, knowing that he ought to go to the watchman and give him his last rites; he could not bring himself to act. "Was it . . . necessary?"

The stranger paused in returning his sword to its scabbard. "Would I have done it otherwise?" He drove his sword down.

Pere Chape had no answer for that question, at least not one he cared to think about. He gave a gesture compounded of fatalism and dismissal. "God will summon him on the Last Day, when He will call every one of us to Judgment."

"Amen," said the other as he crossed himself. "All of that." He found himself a place in the shadows. "Very well, I begin to believe you were sensible in summoning me. I fear that our Italian has been more subtle than we thought. It is too easy to underestimate the man, with his constant tales and parables and chatter. He is clever." His hand closed on the hilt of his sword once more. "But he cannot out-talk cold steel."

"No," Pere Chape breathed, staring at the line of the sword beneath the man's gloved hand.

The stranger laughed, very, very softly. "Do not doubt I will use it, mon Pere. I have lived for the day I could end the reign of this foreign Cardinal since the damned Richelieu summoned him to France." He looked away, his face completely lost in the shadow of the tomb and his plumed hat. "I did all that I could to stop him coming, and now that he is here, I will do all that I can to send him away once more, to Italy or Hell, it makes no difference to me."

Pere Chape had the impression that the man had given a bleak smile, but he was not entirely certain. "You will succeed," he said, with more conviction than before, knowing that if his high-born sponsor did not achieve his goals, then they would share the same ignominious fate. "In the meantime, how would you want me to deal with these couriers?"

The stranger thought. "The Roman widow, that's the weak link. If we could introduce someone into her household, someone with an excellent reason to be there, someone that Mazarin trusts and who could be your tool, then it might be possible . . ." He sighed. "It would have to come from Mazarin, that's the trouble."

"Is it?" Pere Chape asked, suddenly feeling very bold. "I cannot be certain," he went on, keeping his voice low with an effort, for now his terror was replaced with a heady rush of confidence that gave him the impetus to continue. "One of Mazarin's secretaries—he's a prelate, not a bad man, but thwarted—has said that he needs more activity. He has mentioned as much to Mazarin himself. If I could promote his interests with Mazarin, he would be grateful; in future he might be very useful."

"Do you trust him?" asked the stranger, and Pere Chape had the impression of blue eyes like the heart of a swordsmith's flame. "Well?"

"No," said Pere Chape directly. "But I trust what I do not trust." He folded his arms, rejoicing in the attention he was being given. "If I could suggest to Mazarin that for the sake of all his couriers using the holdings of Bondame Clemens, the presence of one of his own staff might be useful, I am certain that he could be persuaded to appoint Jumeau to the position. Then it would not matter whether the courier comes through the gates of Paris; we will know who has come and gone."

"And the widow?" asked the stranger in a sharp tone, for once without the smooth grace that marked his speech.

"She is more interested in her horses than the state of the Kingdom of France. It is said that she despises politics." He recalled his two brief conversations with Olivia, when she had responded minimally to Pere Chape's questions.

"Well, and so do most women," allowed the other. "They are not made for such contests." He spat. "Which is another reason we cannot tolerate that Spanish woman. No woman is capable of leading a kingdom, of guiding the state through the tribulations of diplomacy and war."

"She depends on the Cardinal for that," said Pere Chape with the greatest condemnation.

"That's the only sensible thing I've heard about her," said the other man. "But her judgment is what you would expect of her— her dead lover said for her to trust Mazarin, and she does, with no consideration for his background or family." He folded his arms. "Very well. Approach this Jeau—"

"Jumeau," Pere Chape corrected. "Jean Vidal Jumeau. His family comes from Provence."

"How long has he served the Cardinal?" He turned away. "No, never mind. Years mean little." He gave Pere Chape a slight bow. "I am pleased you sent for me, after all. But do not do it again. Next time send a deputy, someone who has never done this before."

"But why?" Pere Chape demanded, growing afraid once more.

"Because if you or I or both of us are being followed, there will be no pattern for the watchers to report." He took a few steps away, then turned back. "Send me reports at the start of every month. Use the new code we gave you, the one on the farmers' poems." This time when he moved off again, he did not turn back.

Pere Chape stood very still, trying to penetrate the night to discover if there was anyone watching. If there had been, surely they must raise the cry soon, for the death of the watchman. That, more than any other apprehension, goaded him into action.

Slowly at first, and then more rapidly, he made his way down the gravel paths, through the avenues of tombs and graves, toward the side gate that was never closed. With every step he took, he stared and listened, hoping to detect the presence of someone else, someone sent to watch him. A grue, like a single shard of ice, went down his spine as he stepped through the gate and out onto the dark, cobbled street.

And now a new fear possessed him, that of dread for the street gangs who made the avenues of the city unsafe for any but themselves at night. The stranger had joked about les Plumets and les Freres de la Samaritaine, and les Grisons. But there were also les Manteaux rouges, and their most bitter rivals les Rougets, every one of them a dangerous criminal with no regard for the law, or God, or His priests. Pere Chape crossed himself and chose the side of the street with the fewest doorways, where one of these young monsters might be lurking.

During the day, it was a brisk walk of about half an hour—as timed by the clock on the tower of the Pont-Neuf—from the Cardinal's palace to the cemetery. On his return that night, Pere Chape took slightly less than two hours; he had hidden in alcoves and doorways, in the shadow of carts and bales; once he had all but tripped over a sleeping beggar he had mistaken for a pile of stinking rags. By the time he entered the servants' door of Mazarin's palace, the earliest lackeys and scullions were at work, and the first tasks of the day had been started.

"Mon Pere!" exclaimed one sleepy cook as he saw Pere Chape in the bright glow of the hearth. "Has there been an accident?"

Pere Chape, knowing that he was disheveled and filthy, conjured up an explanation as best he could. "I . . . I was summoned to an . . . acquaintance. Someone quite ill."

"How . . . unfortunate," said the cook, casting jaundiced eyes over Pere Chape's cassock. "What ails your friend?"

"Nothing, nothing," Pere Chape said hastily, his thoughts now racing ahead of his words. "But you know how it is when someone is gravely ill. You do not like to leave them. He wanted to hear Scriptures, to comfort him. I . . . stayed too late, and was waylaid in the street."

"Footpads! Attacking a priest!" The cook crossed himself, his massive chest heaving with emotion. "Where was the Guard?"

"Oh, the Guard." Pere Chape shrugged, thinking that the cook meant the Paris Guard.

"No, no. Did you not take an officer of the Cardinal's Guard for escort?" The cook stared at Pere Chape in astonishment. "Mon Pere!" This time the words were a shocked admonition.

"I had no . . . idea that I would need them. As I have said, I stayed later than I had thought I would. Now I think it might have been better to wait until morning, but—" He crossed himself. "Only with the aid of God did I escape the rascals."

"I should think so," said the cook. "Gracious!" He stared around the kitchen at the scullions, and pointed to one of them, a husky boy of about fifteen. "You there! Attile! Set water going for a bath for Pere Chape. Now. Use the big kettles. We don't want our priest to freeze before he's washed."

Pere Chape began to protest, thinking that he needed to find Jumeau as soon as possible. "Later in the day," he pleaded.

"Mon Pere," the cook rebuked him kindly, "God will forgive you if you do not attend first Mass this morning. And the congregation will thank you for it. You do not notice it, perhaps, but there is ordure on your clothes, and in your hair."

It was all Pere Chape could do not to reach up to find out. "Oh," he said, chastened. "I see. Perhaps you're right. I was not aware . . . I cannot visit the Cardinal in such a state, that's certain." No, he added to himself, that privilege was left to hoyden widows who rode with shameless breeches under her skirts. He allowed the cook to persuade him. "I thank you, Valerot." It was good he was able to recall the cook's name. "No doubt you are correct. I will attend Mass when I am in proper attire."

"Excellent. There will be hot water for you in the bath house shortly. Attile will see to it." This last was directed far more at the stocky young man than at Pere Chape. "It will not take too long to do the task."

Pere Chape put a hand to his face. "I will find my razor before I bathe, so that I will not have stubble on my chin, either." He gave Valerot a sketchy blessing, then started for the stairs leading to the less magnificent part of the palace, which was far from complete.

In his quarters—noticeably better than the upper-servants' quarters, but nowhere near as lavish as the apartments for the Cardinal's suite and guests—Pere Chape took off his cassock and examined it, shaking his head at the state of it. He would not be able to wear it again, that was certain, unless he was intending to plough a furrow with his own hands, or to load the dung carts back of the stable. He would have it cleaned, at least. He might have need for just such a ruin sometime.

The trouble was, he thought as he looked into the simple armoire that stood opposite his bed, he had only two other ordinary cassocks, and one of them was starting to show wear at the cuffs and the neck. He would have to ask the Cardinal for an allowance to replace it. He sighed. That would be the greatest humiliation, to accept such a favor from Mazarin when he wanted nothing more than to exile the impertinent fellow forever. Reluctantly he took the older cassock from its peg, and found a clean chamise in the bottom drawer of the armoire. His shoes were simple, with none of the extravagances of rosettes and raised heels that were being worn at court these days. It was frowned upon in the clergy to ape the fashion of the court; most of the time, Pere Chape was pleased to obey the strictures on dress. But once in a while, he would hunger for silks and satins, with lace collars as wide as a mozzetta, leggings that showed the curve of his calf below ornate garters, and a coat with dozens of brass buttons. He made himself promise himself that he would do penance for such sinful thoughts, and with that for company, he trudged down to the bath house.

By the time he was scrubbed to pinkness, the first Mass was over and the household was bustling. When he entered the kitchen again, Pere Chape found fourteen cooks already working on preparing the mid-day meal that would be served to the Cardinal's guests who remained at the palace while the Cardinal himself was in attendance on the Queen Regent. Pere Chape approached the cook Valerot and, after offering him profuse thanks, inquired casually about Jumeau.

"That one," scoffed the cook. "He is probably in the garden. He goes there during breakfast, so that he will not eat. He has said that he does not wish to add flesh. He prefers to be skinny as a rake."

"Perhaps it is a pious discipline," suggested Pere Chape gently.

"That one wouldn't know piety if it were a pigeon dropping on his shoulder," Valerot declared roundly. "He does it to be interesting. Pious men do not have that look of discontent and anger to their faces." He gestured with a ladle. "Try the garden. On the side away from the herbs. And when you have done, I will make you an omelette with mushrooms and little peas."

"After Mass, I am afraid," said Pere Chape, wishing he could afford the luxury of accepting the offer now, while he was so ravenous.

"Bien sur," said Valerot. "You have only to come to me." He went back to measuring out precise amounts of a thick, savory sauce into a huge tray of small pastry shells, muttering all the while about the poor quality of the minced lamb that would be added before the upper crust was placed on them.

The mist of the Seine was thick enough that the garden was wet from it; in the hazy light it was difficult to make out the young secretary among the sculptured shrubbery of the small garden. He was seated on a bench, a book in his hands, his eyes fixed in a hostile stare on something beyond the walls. As Pere Chape approached, he looked up, forcing a welcome expression onto his face. "God be with you, mon Pere."

"And with you, mon fils," said Pere Chape, offering a blessing. "I was told you were here."

"Oh?" There was more suspicion than greeting in his ambiguous response.

"Yes." He sat down on the bench opposite the one Jumeau occupied. "I have been thinking about what you said to me."

"And what is that?" It was not an encouraging reaction, but Pere Chape did what he could with it.

"About your station here," said Pere Chape, doing his best to appear conciliating. "You have said that you are capable of more than answering invitations for His Eminence, or keeping track of which letters are to be burned and which are to be saved. I can see that you are capable of greater service than that, and it distresses me that the Cardinal is not yet aware of the treasure he has in you." It was as much as Pere Chape dared say, and even then, he feared his effusion might arouse Jumeau's distrust as much as his vanity.

"And what have you decided?" Jumeau's tone was deliberately snide, and he started to rise.

"No, good secretary, hear me out," said Pere Chape. "What can it hurt you to listen? If you dislike what I tell you, you may always deny I have ever spoken to you at all." He indicated the bench Jumeau had just left. "Please, my friend. Listen."

Jumeau crossed his arms over his chest and remained standing. "Say what you have to say."

This was more daunting than Pere Chape had expected. "All right," he said heavily. "Perhaps I was mistaken, after all. Forgive me for imposing on your solitude." He got up and turned to leave.

His ploy worked: "Mon Pere," Jumeau called as Pere Chape took his first few steps away, "I was over-hasty, perhaps." He resumed his seat and waited while Pere Chape returned. "It is only that the hour is early and I slept badly," he offered as an excuse for his surliness.

"I have had such mornings myself," said Pere Chape. He sat down again and fussed with the simple ruffles at his wrists. "Still, we must persevere." When he was satisfied with the ruffles, he looked directly at Jumeau. "We are living in a dangerous time, and in a dangerous place."

"God knows it," said Jumeau, and crossed himself.

"Those with sufficient courage may discover advances for themselves, if they are willing to risk themselves." Pere Chape stared down at the plain toe of his simple shoes. "Our superior is a very great man, a man who has had a great burden placed on his shoulders; we, who are his supporters, must do all that we can to ease that burden."

"Of course," said Jumeau, his eyes narrowing with the intensity of his unasked questions.

"And yet," said Pere Chape, deliberately taking his time, "it is difficult to know whom to trust. With so much at risk, the Cardinal cannot assume that anyone near him is truly disinterested."

"We all have families," said Jumeau, with more hostility than he knew.

"And other concerns as well," said Pere Chape. "And it is fitting that we strive to do our duty as best we may to all concerned, as they merit it." He leaned back and peered into the luminous fog as if he could read the future there. "I am worried about one of the Cardinal's suite: an excellent woman, without doubt, but a woman, for all of that. She has taken on more hazard than she was prepared to deal with, I think. And it is fitting that someone aid her in her efforts on the Cardinal's behalf. If you, or one such as you, were posted to her estate, the dealings with couriers would not have to concern her any longer, and she would be free to continue with the entertainments the Cardinal has asked her to prepare for those he wishes to know better." He clasped his hands, not quite in prayer. "It would provide a splendid opportunity for someone as eager as you, and it would spare that good woman, Bondame Clemens, any more danger than she has already endured."

Jacques Vidal Jumeau crossed himself, this time with genuine feeling. "I would be honored if the Cardinal saw his way clear to permit me to serve him in this way. And I would be forever in your debt."

"Nonsense," said Pere Chape in his best bluff manner. "I am not a man who collects favors. It isn't tolerated in priests, and it is against my nature." He leaned back against the hedge behind him. "But here I see a capable young man languishing and bored, and I see a woman in the Cardinal's suite enmeshed in matters she can know nothing about. In the Cardinal's interests, I believe that all would benefit if this situation were to change so that you alleviated her burden." He waited a moment, like a capable fisherman sinking a hook; then he said, "When the Cardinal returns, I will mention this to him." He got up, ignoring the expression of rapt ambition that suffused Jumeau's lean face.

✳   ✳   ✳

Text of a letter from Charles d'Artagnan to Atta Olivia Clemens, dictated to Isaac de Portau.

Olivia, my dearest, dearest love;

We are preparing to return; the orders came down yesterday, and there was not a man among us who was not gladdened in his heart to hear the news. But I am certain I was the most glad of all, for none of the others will be returning to you. That delight is reserved to me.

As I told you in my last letter, there was some bloody fighting, but most of what this campaign has been is nothing more than long stretches of waiting. It is inconceivable to think of how long it takes to move an army. The commanders congratulate themselves if we make any distance in a day. It is not just because of all the supplies and arms we carry, but, in our return, there are many wounded, and what we have lost in supplies we have more than gained in injured men.

The wound I received is minor and nearly healed. I am a little stiff yet, but there was no real damage done to my shoulder and I can promise you that aside from an interesting scar there is no lasting damage from the musquetball. I was afraid that there might be, but the physician attending the monks at a nearby monastery has confirmed that my recovery should be complete by the time I come through the gates of Paris, or the doors of Eblouir.

I do not intend to alarm you, but we have been hearing rumors. I know that the army is always rife with rumors; worse than prison, they say. However, since these rumors touch on Mazarin, and, through him, you, I wish to warn you, so that you may make adequate preparations to deal with any problems that may arise. I am confident that any truth that may be present in these rumors is very small, and that what has happened is that a minor remark has been taken as a battle cry for those who did not comprehend the scope of the remark. Nevertheless, it is being said that there are certain nobles who are dissatisfied with the regency of the Queen and the rule of Cardinal Mazarin, and they do not mean des Essarts and de Troisvilles, whose opposition to Mazarin is well-known by everyone. I know that there have been rebellions before now, some of them recent. It could be nothing more than the same complaints repeated, and therefore of no immediate concern. But it is also possible that there may be some nobles who are doing more than grumbling. It is possible that a few are making plans, preparing to obtain more power for themselves, with whatever cost that may bring to the Queen Regent and the King, who is so young. I think that is what is most vexing to me, that they would think to plot against a little boy who has already lost a father and has had to listen to the gossip of court impugn the honor of his mother and the late Cardinal Richelieu. That is not the way noblemen should conduct themselves. It is more to be expected of the peasants and the tavernkeepers than men of rank who have sworn allegiance to the Throne.

You will do me the favor of preparing yourself against unfortunate developments. I want to see that you are ready to make any necessary changes, so that I will not be so worried for your well-being. It sickens me to think that this intrigue could harm you in any way. And do not protest that you cannot be harmed, for you have admitted otherwise to me. The Cardinal can protect you only so long as he himself is secure. In these times, you cannot depend upon that; the Cardinal is as much or more the target of noble displeasure as the Queen Regent is, and no one forgets that he is a *foreigner, no matter how he spells his name. So I ask you, Olivia, for my sake if not your own, to be on guard, and take care to protect yourself from the actions of venal and greedy men who may attempt to harm the King and those who have made it their cause to see that he arrives at the age of rule unscathed by these times.*

I will send word as soon as I am in Paris, and I will inform you then when I will be given a few days leave, or when I will be permitted to leave the city. I would ask you to come to Paris to meet me, but after what I have just said to you, it would be foolish of me to make such a suggestion, would it not? But, oh, it is tempting, very tempting. Do not offer to come to me, for I would not be able to resist you, and it is not wise that we meet in the city, for the risks are much greater there.

Now I must prepare to march. My friend de Portau tells me that his hand is exhausted and that he is ready to blush at all I have said. He is an excellent fellow, and good-hearted, and I gave him my word I would say so before I ended the letter, which I shall sign myself.

> *Charles d'Artagnan*
> *King's Musqueteer*

De Portau again, Bondame: on the 3rd day of September, 1645. After the siege of Bourbourg.
Destroy if necessary.

· **7** ·

His monk's habit was cumbersome and restricting, but Nino bore with that inconvenience for the sake of the advantages it gave him; in this habit, he could cross the estate of Bondama Clemens without question or other imposition. He took another swig from the bottle he carried and had to stop himself from singing a chorus of a rowdy song he had learned while he was still a soldier. He carried two sacks of round, smelly cheeses on his back, which served to disguise the other, more sinister things that were hidden under his monkish garb.

As he reached the widest of three streams that flowed through the estate, Nino stopped and sat down on the bank. The ground was damp from recent rains and the fallen leaves were beginning to turn musty. He inspected the bridge without appearing to be doing anything more than resting his feet. The stream was still low, the first rains having done little more than dampen the parched ground. Nino glanced up and down the stream, trying to estimate how high the water could be expected to rise. Nodding at what he saw, he leaned back, for all the world like a man who has nothing better to do than admire the end of the autumn, taking a last look at the golden sun before it hid itself in winter clouds.

When he was satisfied that he was not being watched, he reached under his habit and pulled out a short, brutal saw. He had taken it from the monks' carpentry shop earlier that day, in anticipation of this walk. Getting up slowly, and leaving his sacks of cheese behind him in the shade of an oak tree, he ambled over to the bank near the bridge, and then, as agilely as his lamed leg would permit, he scrambled down to the nearer supports that held the bridge. He patted the two uprights—both enormous rounds of oak, almost whole trunks—and looked up at the floor of the bridge. Then, smiling, he set to work, using the saw on the inside of the supports, straining as he labored, cutting both of the uprights almost in half before he was satisfied with his labors.

He was sweaty and covered in sawdust when he finally hauled himself back up the bank, standing to admire his work and catch his breath at the same time. He dragged his grimy palm across his brow, leaving a wide streak of woodchips and mud there. "Next time you ride this way, Bondama Clemens," he said through his teeth, "you had best pray that your angel rides with you." He stepped gingerly onto the bridge and was relieved that there was no immediate shifting or groaning of the timbers to give warning. He patted the handrail. "Last long enough to drown her, that's all I ask." He went back to the oak to retrieve the cheeses and to hide the saw once again under the folds of his habit. Then he hoisted the cheese sacks onto his shoulder again and started in the direction of the monastery. He went slowly, for not only was his leg hurting from the unaccustomed exertion, but he wanted to be certain he arrived after the monks had assembled for prayers so that he would be able to return the saw to the carpentry supplies without being noticed.

Frere Gautier met him later, as the monks and the tertiary Brothers like Nino took their places for their evening meal. "I hear you brought us a real treasure."

"If treasure can be chunks of hard milk, I suppose I have," said Nino, remembering to laugh so that Frere Gautier would share his amusement and not wonder at his state of mind.

"You're always such a dour fellow, Nino," Frere Gautier declared. "You'll have to learn to be more accepting if you are going to become a monk."

Nino lifted his hands to show his helplessness. "Until I am given a vocation, I can be nothing but a tertiary Brother. You and the Abbe and all the rest have said so." He crossed himself. "If God inspires me to more charity, to more goodness, then, well, we will see. I am in His hands."

"That is a first step," said Frere Gautier, clapping him on the shoulder. "Humility is a fine beginning."

The two men entered the refectory, Frere Gautier going to his place with the other tonsured monks, Nino to sit with those taking charity at Sacres Innocentes, which included the few tertiary Brothers at the monastery.

Today's fare was a bean soup, fortified with scraps of mutton; round loaves of bread with thyme and nutmeg served with fresh butter; and a large bowl of cooked vegetables, most of which appeared to be cabbage.

Frere Aubri was given the honor of reading the lesson for the day; he stood before the simple lectern, his face shadowed by his cowl so that only the words of Scripture might be heard and no thought given to the monk reading them. He raised his hand and blessed himself. "In the Name of the Father, Son, and Holy Spirit, Amen."

Everyone in the room copied the gesture and repeated the "Amen." All of them were anxious to eat, but most of them tried not to appear so, though the food was in front of them and turning cool as Frere Aubri spoke.

"From the book of Proverbs, the 24th chapter. 'Have no envy of wrongdoers, nor wish to be like them. Their hearts are destructive and their words are deceptive. It is wisdom that builds enduring houses, and comprehension that gives it form; knowledge is the treasure of the house, and learning makes it pleasant. The man who is wise has true strength; his strength is increased through gaining knowledge.'" Frere Aubri paused, his eyes moving down the page.

Nino listened, doing his best to keep his face attentive while he strove not to let his temper be reflected in his eyes. Who was Frere Aubri to read such a lesson, and what right did he have to judge Nino? Under other circumstances he might have challenged the monk to explain himself, but he checked his urge, trying to convince himself that it was merest chance that caused Frere Aubri to read that lesson on this day. He glowered at his wooden tankard which held a generous measure of raw wine. If he opposed the lesson, it might lead to difficulties, and that might upset his plans. He was too close to achieving his revenge to be distracted by monkish moralizing.

Frere Aubri went on. "'Take no satisfaction in the misfortunes of your enemies, and do not be happy when they falter. God knows your heart and it does not please Him to find evil therein. Do not be vexed by the wicked, and do not look on them jealously. There is no reward in doing evil, and all that is gained thereby is lost. Let all of you respect and fear God and the King; do not enter in with those who seek alteration; their sought-after change will come upon them tenfold, and none shall know the extent of their ruin.' Hear the words of God and ponder them as you give thanks for the food He has provided to nourish your bodies as His Scripture nourishes your soul."

Once again a ragged "Amen" was offered in response to this lesson, and everyone was secretly pleased that it was as brief as it had been. As soon as Frere Aubri stepped away from the lectern, there was a sudden increase in the level of noise in the cavernous room, the cacophony increasing as the rattle of wooden utensils on wooden plates grew louder.

It was a simple meal, soon finished; the monks made a point of rising as soon as they had completed their meal, so that they would not be thought gluttonous, or given to the pleasures of table. Frere Gautier, eating with a soldier's speed, was always one of the first to finish.

"I have to see to the cows in the dairy," he said to Nino as he came across the room. "Will you lend me a hand?"

"Certainly," said Nino. Frere Gautier, far more than the other monks, was friendly to Nino, and did not criticize him the way many of the others did. He wiped his bowl and spoon with a rag, then went to put them in their place on the shelf. "Is there something the matter?"

"Not really," said Frere Aubri. "But at this time of year, you know how it is; the ground is damp and you know how that is— some of them have troubles with their hooves. I have to wash their feet in turpentine. Bovine Apostles, I suppose," he added, grinning at the impertinence of his joke.

There were few things that Nino liked less than caring for cattle—great, smelly beasts with wet noses and enormous tongues— but he said at once, "You have only to ask and I will assist you."

"That's good," said Frere Gautier, already halfway to the side door. "A few of them get fretful when they have their feet touched." Just as he was about to close the door behind him, he hesitated, realizing that someone was gesturing to him. His greeting faded as he recognized the monk. "Frere Crepet," he said, his attitude guarded.

Nino stayed back—he disliked Frere Crepet more than any of the others—hoping he would not be noticed.

"I . . . I thought there were two of you," said Frere Crepet in his vague way, his head to the side as he spoke to Frere Gautier.

"My assistant and I have to tend to the cows," said Frere Gautier in his most patient manner. "If you will let us be about our tasks?" He started to pull the door closed, but once again was stopped by Frere Crepet.

"I saw where our tertiary Brother went today," he said, this time making a point of speaking directly to Frere Gautier.

Listening, Nino froze, his eyes suddenly expressionless as painted wood. No matter what Frere Crepet said now, he knew he would have to offer some explanation to Frere Gautier if he did not want to be regarded with suspicion.

"He brought cheeses," said Frere Gautier, dismissing the other monk. "Two bags of them."

"He crossed a bridge," declared Frere Crepet.

"He probably crossed several of them," corrected Frere Gautier, treating the comment as a reasonable one. "There are seven of them on Bondame Clemens' estate alone. More than ten on the des Achates estate. Four each on Etangrise and Raidebas. Everyone crossing those lands must cross bridges also, except in high summer."

"This was a different bridge; a special bridge," said Frere Crepet, then turned away, but not before he had looked Nino full in the face and nodded once.

As he pulled the door between them and the refectory closed, Frere Gautier said, "God has laid a burden on Frere Crepet, and it grows heavier with each passing season."

Nino decided to take a chance. "What do you think he meant about the bridges?" The answer he was given would determine what he would or would not do to the monk. "Why would he mention bridges that way?"

"Not bridges," Frere Gautier corrected. "A bridge." He stepped into the creamery joining the dairy. "Well, who can say?" he asked as he opened a tall, plank-fronted cupboard. "He may have a certain bridge he believes to be special and he thinks you may have crossed it today. That's one possibility. Do you see the turpentine anywhere?"

"No," said Nino, who had not been looking for it.

"It has to be in here somewhere." He moved a few stoneware jars aside. "I wish the others would be more careful about how they store supplies," he said over his shoulder.

"You miss the army," suggested Nino, half in jest.

"At times like these I do," Frere Gautier said seriously. "Most of the time I thank God for letting me find my salvation in His service, but every now and again, I would like to have a sergeant to keep order." He tried the next shelf down. "Ah. There it is. Find me a good-sized bucket and several rags. We'll need a lamp as well." As he straightened up, he put a hand to his back. "I am getting old, Nino."

"As is everyone," he said, thinking that he had seen but one person in all his life who seemed impervious to age, and that was Atta Olivia Clemens. He cursed her for that as well as for her role as the author of all his misfortunes. While he tossed half a dozen rags into a bucket, he said to Frere Gautier, "Do you think it would be useful for me to speak with Frere Crepet, in case he has something he—"

Frere Gautier shook his head. "It is useless, I fear," he told Nino. "We know that something addled his wits and that he continues to suffer. Why make his suffering worse, by reminding him of it?"

"But if there is something about one of the bridges, perhaps I had better find out what it is." He brought the bucket to Frere Gautier.

The sharp, oily scent of turpentine bit the air. As he poured generously, Frere Gautier shrugged. "If he mentions it again— which I doubt he will—you may want to talk with him, but not until then." He peered into the bucket, watching the level of turpentine rise. When he stopped pouring, he gave Nino a worried look. "Is there something you think we should know about those bridges?"

Nino was suddenly and unpleasantly on the alert. "What would I know?" he asked, his eyes narrowed.

Frere Gautier paused in the act of putting the jar of turpentine back in the cupboard. "I don't know," he said, his voice growing testy. "You seemed so . . . caught up."

"Caught up," Nino repeated. "No." His laughter sounded unconvincing to him, but he went on in any case. "I cannot help but wonder if there is something . . ." He suddenly had a notion, and seized it. "When I was a child, there was a man in the village, one who was afflicted in his wits, not quite as Frere Crepet is, but similarly. He sometimes saw the future, or had visions—it was a little difficult to tell which—and I thought perhaps Frere Crepet might be like him. There may be something about one of the bridges he has seen in a vision." And, he added to himself, when Bondama Clemens is injured, Frere Crepet will have the attention. He could not resist adding, "I thought that someone like Frere Crepet must have gifts from God, as well as curses and burdens. If he knew—"

"He's never had visions that I heard of," said Frere Gautier as he opened the door into the dairy, motioning to Nino to follow him. The night was cool, with a low-lying mist forming over the fields; the cows had already been milked and were no longer restless.

Nino looked into the darkness of the barn, knowing that a lanthorn hung by the door on a bracket. "I'll see to the light," he offered, glad to have the chance to change the subject.

Over the next several weeks, Nino made several crossings of Olivia's estate, and each time he used part of his time to do more mischief while he was there. He cut the supports of two other bridges, hollowed out the slope under the farriers shed, then later left materials to make a bomb. He built a tripwire that could be raised and lowered quickly, without leaving cover. And while he did this, he waited for Olivia's return to her stud farm, knowing that once she arrived, he could adapt his plans to hers. By spring, he promised himself, he would be revenged on this Roman widow.

It was three days before Christmas when Olivia came, her coach the lead of three, all of them under armed escort loaned to her by Mazarin from his Guard. The party arrived toward dusk on a dank, cold afternoon, causing alarm to the household staff, who had not expected the group for two more days.

"Perceval," Olivia said as she entered the house and peeled off her gloves, "why this continued disarray?"

"It is . . ." Perceval said, dithering at once, "simply your arrival. At this time of year no one arrives early, Madame, only late. We assumed—"

"Assume nothing," said Olivia sweetly, putting her hat beside the gloves. "I will require warm spiced wine for my guests and a meal to be served within—shall we say?—two hours." She nodded her approval to the fresh paint in the large salon. "Very nice. And beeswax on the furniture. A great improvement, Perceval."

"It would have been greater still had you arrived two days later," said Perceval, not quite pouting.

"Well, take consolation in approval, Perceval," said Olivia, gesturing to the first of her guests. "Come, Marquis, let my staff take your cases to the . . . the blue suite, I think, Perceval. The Marquis and Marquise are continuing from here to Poitiers after the Nativity, and their horses will need to be completely rested and well-fed when they depart. Tell Evraud to attend to that." She hoped she would not have to spend much time with the young nobleman and his newly pregnant wife. It was one thing to support Mazarin's work, but something else again to put up with bores. "Also," she added as if it were nothing more than an afterthought, "the Marquis' cousin will be joining us here tomorrow, God willing."

"A cousin?" said Perceval, keeping his voice even.

"So I believe. His duties demanded he spend tonight in Orleans. But tomorrow he will be permitted to enjoy the Christmas festivities with his relations." She could not entirely stop her own smile.

"How fortunate for the Marquis," said Perceval with no expression whatsoever.

"You are doing very well," Olivia approved, and left her guests alone with her staff.

It was icy the next morning; the ground glittered and the horses' breath was white smoke on the air as Olivia reluctantly agreed to take her guests on an inspection of her estate. "I do not wish to hunt at this time of year," she had said when they left Eblouir, and she reiterated now. "There is game to be had, but I am not of a temperament to enjoy stalking boar, which is the best sport we can offer."

The Marquis, who truly loved such hunting, had accepted the decision of his hostess. "An inspection is very generous," he said, trying not to be rude.

"Had there been more time to prepare," Olivia said as she mounted her favorite light-dun gelding, "my staff would certainly have been able to do more, but as this is a stud farm and not a hunting ground, we have not the facilities here—"

The Marquise, ungainly enough now to have difficulty getting into the saddle, added her own comment. "Surely you understand, dear husband, that it is not fitting for women to maintain a hunting lodge." She secured her left leg around the saddlehorn and gathered up the reins. "There. I am grateful for so tractable a mount."

In Olivia's opinion, the mare the Marquise rode was little better than a plug, but she said only, "I am pleased she suits you so well," and turned her dun toward the wide track leading away from the stables and arenas. Thank goodness Niklos would be arriving that evening, she thought, wondering what she was going to do to amuse her guests until her major domo got there.

Recent rains had swollen the streams crossing Olivia's estate; the sound of rushing water announced each bridge well before they reached it. Olivia made a point of leading the way, taking the duties of a host upon herself.

They were just passing over the widest bridge on the estate when Olivia's horse balked, throwing up his head and whinnying, big eyes rolling.

Olivia wished she were riding straddle, and did her best to hold him with her hands without the help of her legs. "Quiet, Sabbioso; quiet," she said as she tried to hold her mount steady.

The dun was not having any; he half-reared and started to spin just as the far side supports of the bridge gave an ominous crack, and then the bridge itself slid, canting to one side as Sabbioso scrabbled for traction on the planks.

"Madame!" cried the Marquis, starting to rush forward, reaching out to pull Olivia from the saddle.

With a vitrolic oath, Olivia set her spur to the dun's side and sent him into a disorganized bound at the far bank of the stream, protesting his ill-use in a loud squeal. As the horse clawed his way up the far bank, Olivia clinging to his mane to stay in the saddle, the bridge at last broke and part of it dropped into the muddy waters.

"Madame!" shouted the Marquis, staring across the stream at Olivia. "Are you well?"

"A little out of breath," Olivia called back, annoyed at herself for the fear she had felt. She brought Sabbioso to a halt, and when she was certain his attention was no longer scattered, she got out of the saddle and went to his head. "You did well, boy," she said quietly to him.

"By Saint Denis, that was as fine a display of riding as I have ever seen a woman show," the Marquis called to Olivia, grinning as he did. "You're good enough for the cavalry, Madame, if you will not be offended to hear it."

Olivia did not answer at once. "I was fortunate in my horse," she said candidly, not wanting to imagine what might have happened had she been on a less sensible animal.

"Horses are brutes," the Marquis said, dismissing the part Sabbioso had played. "It was your will that saved you both."

It would have been pleasant to give the man a sharp retort, but Olivia knew that it would be a foolish indulgence. She patted the flower mark between the gelding's eyes. "Don't pay him any mind, Sabbioso; we both know you saved the day." Then she waved to the Marquis. "Your Marquise is looking very pale, Monsieur. At such a time, you must look after her."

At once the Marquis turned to his wife, his large eyes filled with alarm. "Are you ill, Madame?"

The Marquise did not answer at once. "I am . . . a trifle faint, husband," she said. "The sight of that dreadful accident, so nearly a tragedy—" She broke off, one gloved hand held against her mouth.

"Get her back to the chateau," Olivia recommended, going on, "I will return shortly. I'll have to take another bridge, I'm afraid, and after what happened here, who knows if Sabbioso will be persuaded to cross it." She saw the indecision in the Marquis' face and added, "Send Thumaz and Evraud after me, with a remount, if you would be so kind."

It was enough; the Marquis saluted and wheeled his horse away from where the bridge had been toward his Marquise and the protection of Olivia's house.

As she watched her guests go, Olivia said to the dun, "Did you notice that support pillar, Sabbioso? I'll wager it's been cut." She flipped the ends of her reins against her hand. "Why would anyone want to do that? What's the point?" She cocked her head as if waiting for the dun to answer; when he did not, she asked the more difficult question. "Who do you think sabotaged the bridge, boy?"

*   *   *

Text of a letter from Gaetano Fosso to Niklos Aulirios at Eblouir.

To that most excellent and respected major domo who has it as his privilege to serve Bondama Clemens, a woman of enviable repute, my greetings to you, with my hope that you will be good enough to review the reports I am sending to you.

First, it is my unhappy duty to inform you that Susanna, the wife of the blacksmith, has died in childbed, and her twins with her. This was the third time she had tried to deliver without being able to bring living babies into the world. She has been buried, and they with her, at Santissimo Redentore. I have given Gabrielle five golden angels in her name, as Bondama Clemens has requested of me in the past at such times. I have also tried to find someone to care for Gabrielle's house, but so far I have not been able to discover someone willing to tend to the place for him. I have asked various of the tenants on the estate if they can recommend anyone for the work, but no name has yet been forthcoming. Gabrielle is in need of help, and he is not so ancient that it would not be wise for him to find another wife; many men are grandfathers at thirty-six, but it does not mean that life is over.

We have sold over forty lambs this autumn and the prices they have fetched are excellent. I have two pages to complete the accounting to you. It would please me to have you take time at once to read through these figures, so that we may better plan what is to be done in the spring. We have gained something of a reputation for the quality of the sheep we raise, and it would be best to make the most we can of such good odor.

The request you sent that the west side of the estate be given new and sturdier fencing has been carried out, and the price for this is part of the figures I have sent. I believe that you would do well to extend the fencing now, if it is your intention to continue to improve the fencing, for not only have we needed supplies, we have workers who are not occupied for the winter and who would be glad of a few more coins to put by for this year. Also, since the fencing has begun, there are those who expect the task to be completed.

Guido has recovered from the fever, but is not yet strong enough to return to his duties. I have continued his pay at the same rate as before, though it distresses me to do it. Bondama Clemens is much too lax in these matters, and her insistence that those who are suffering adversity not be turned off, while it is admirable in many ways, is also foolish because it encourages malingering and other discreditable behavior.

The family of Antonio Nuccio have asked to enlarge their market fields. I have refused, but I will grant permission if Bondama Clemens insists that I allow it, though it makes me quite troubled in my mind; I warn you that it will bring about discontent among the rest, and unless we grant all of them more land for their own market fields, there will be open unrest among those who work the land. I beg you will impress upon Bondama Clemens that this is no mere idle fear on my part, but the result of long experience and the knowledge of human nature such dealings impart.

We have had very good harvest from our hives this year—far better than in the last four years. I have instructed the staff to prepare more jars for the honey and to make appropriate storage. To attest to the fine quality of the honey, I will send to you a dozen jars so that you may determine for yourself the quality of the honey.

Our vineyards have been a trifle disappointing, for we had cool weather before it was expected and the grapes were not able to come to full ripeness before our harvest was necessary. It will be some time before we can determine how the wine will be. When we know how the vintage will age, I will inform you. Given the generally inferior quality of last year's vintage, I do not hold out much hope for a remarkable year.

On behalf of Bondama Clemens I have sent proper gifts and remembrances to Paolo Germoglio da Luccio, who in the last three months has endured the loss of his wife and three of his seven children, and one remains ill. The physicians have not been able to save any of them, and though there have been prayers said at Santissimo Redentore, these children, and many others in the district, continue to die. The cause of the disease is not known, but it has been established that all children have run a very high fever after two or three days of flux and all its discomforts. During this time no food or water would be accepted by the body, and no remedy yet attempted has been successful. While there have been only two deaths among the tenants of Senza Pari, and we pray that there will be no more, we also are aware that we are more fortunate than many another family where all the children have succumbed, as has happened to four different households on this side of Roma.

We have now three new coaches of the finest design and construction. Every one of us is eager to have the Bondama back here, so that she may enjoy these carriages for herself. No one in the area has even one coach of so excellent quality, let alone three. These, as you instructed, are maintained in readiness against the day that Bondama Clemens will return to Senza Pari. It will be a great venture, moving her from France back to her estate. She cannot anticipate how much planning and how much labor will be required in order to bring her and her goods and servants home. I am told it will take at least three days for us to prepare these coaches for nothing more rigorous than their journey north when they will be all but empty. It is difficult to imagine what they will be like when they are fully laden and Bondama Clemens herself has given the order to carry her goods. I am reminded of the great work in taking her to Paris, and I have been told that the return is likely to be more difficult, for not only are there goods, but as she is identified as part of the Cardinal's suite, there is every reason to suspect being the interest of robbers, who are likely to follow the coaches. It will be necessary for her to retain an armed guard to bring her home without mishap.

But those considerations are for the future, for that day that is still far-off, when Bondama Clemens will be released from her vow to Mazarini and his embassy. Before that time, you need only provide five weeks' warning and the coaches will stand at Eblouir, God willing and the Cardinal approving. Then, unless the weather is prohibitive, it will take seven weeks at most to bring her and her household back. As you see, we are ready to work in haste on behalf of our mistress.

I have appended the reports of all the areas of the estate so that you and Bondama Clemens can examine what we have done and what the costs and profits have been. I fear that the charges of the harness-maker may appear excessive, but these new coaches have required new harness for the horses, and because it is new, the first harness made proved to be incorrect. Also, the cooper has had to raise the price of his barrels because of the higher cost of the wood, especially the northern oak. He asked me to assure you that he had not intended to charge so much.

I have taken the liberty of increasing the amount donated to San Andrea and to Santissimo Redentore for the alleviation of suffering, not only for those with fever, but for those who were left without adequate food because of the early rain. There are more than ten families within a day's walk from here who will be in desperate straits because they lost their crops before they could be brought to market. I know this is in accordance with Bondama Clemens' orders; it is my desire to inform her that I continue to carry out her commands whether I agree with them or not. I agree that it is wise to end tribulation, but I fear that this concern of hers does more to coddle than to aid.

I pray for your safe return and for God's Grace upon you while you are far from us. All of us here say prayers for the protection of Bondama Clemens, and ask that she come back to us still in the bright favor that took her away. As far as it is my poor ability to do the task, I have striven to care for Senza Pari as it would satisfy Bondama Clemens to do were she here now herself. My greetings to both of you and my hope that all will be well in France.

Gaetano Fosso
acting major domo, Senza Pari

The 10th day of January, 1646.
Retain for estate records.

· 8 ·

Not long before sunrise, Fontaine de Rochard left the Louvre through the eastern river gate. He was wrapped in a long cloak and he carried a lacquered leather case close to his body as if to keep it warm. He made note of the King's Guards standing near the Pont Neuf, and of the sentries at the other end of the wall. In the slate-colored light, he could just see the reflection of Notre Dame in the river. He could hear the first clanging of church bells and the occasional distant sound of watchmen on the boats moored in the Seine. For a terrible moment he was afraid he would sneeze; then he stifled the urge and stepped into the street.

As he came to the end of the street, he held out the Cardinal's safe-passage, doing his best to appear bored as the sergeant pondered his way through the letter. "What are you carrying?" he demanded as he gave the pass back to de Rochard.

"I wish I knew," said de Rochard with the assumption of annoyance. "You know what the mighty ones are like—fetch me this, bring me that, carry the other thing—and this Cardinal is a mighty one." He patted the case under his cloak without revealing it. "So I am carrying what he has ordered brought to him."

The sergeant laughed. "And have you a long way to go?"

"Not far, no," said de Rochard. "I hand it to another servant and that is the end of my part in it. I probably won't be here in time for breakfast, but . . ." He shrugged eloquently, sharing a wink with the sergeant.

"Stop by the sign of the Red Cat," suggested the sergeant. "They have food every hour of the day from dawn until two hours after dark. They'll see you have something to eat, and you will not have to go through the morning with your innards growling." He gave de Rochard the gesture permitting him to pass, stepping back for him and waving him on.

"The Red Cat," called de Rochard. "Thanks. Perhaps I will." He started away from the river, toward the northeast quarter of the city, trudging along at a steady pace in the frosty morning.

There had been snow two days before and most of the streets were slushy, ice forming in the muddy ruts. De Rochard took care to be wary, for a single fall might imperil the documents he carried. He kept his cloak pulled tightly over his livery, for Mazarin had impressed upon him how urgent and important the papers were. The warning was so stringent that it was all he could do not to look at the documents, to discover what it was he carried. Jumeau had taunted him over his reticence, calling him a dupe to carry messages and not know what they were.

"Alms!" cried a feeble voice from a doorway. "For love of God and blessed charity, Monsieur."

De Rochard had a few coins with him, and he tossed the beggar the least valuable of them, saying, "Pray for the King and the First Minister, fellow."

The voice—no longer so feeble—laughed. "I'd rather pray for the hoards of the pagan Turks to overrun France; it would be a quicker, more honest death."

Although he knew it was unwise, de Rochard began to move faster, not quite running, being careful where he put his feet in his attempt to break away from that jeering beggar behind him. He tried to remind himself that his first duty, his only duty, was to see the case he carried into the messenger's hands, and to obey whatever additional instructions the messenger gave him.

He slipped, his foot going out from under him as he skidded in the deep, ice-rimmed groove in the road. He gave a single, wordless cry of distress, then steadied himself and got back onto his feet. His cloak was heavy with vile-smelling mud, his leggings and low boots were wet, and he had scraped his shin. He stood still to assess the extent of the damage, and decided that his vanity was the greatest casualty. He brushed at the mud and succeeded in smearing it over more of his cloak than before. It took him a short while to make his appearance as neat as was possible given the circumstances, and then he resumed his walk.

He had never been to Amiens; he often saw reports from there, and when the Cardinal was in Paris, he kept messengers moving between Paris and Amiens, maintaining his contact with the Queen Regent and the boy King. Three months ago the lackey had gone as far as Beauvais for the Cardinal, to deliver another case to a different messenger. In a year or so, de Rochard thought, it might be possible to ask for the privilege of carrying a message all the way to the Queen, since he had been halfway to Amiens already; as far as Beauvais, he knew the road. He smiled wryly at the idea, trying to imagine what he would have to do to attain that degree of confidence on the part of the Cardinal. Whatever it was, it could not include falling into mud, he decided as he looked down at the wreckage of his garments. His scowl went unnoticed except by a lean, brindled cat, who gave a low, musical growl before slinking away into the dull morning shadows.

As de Rochard reached a small place where the only sign of habitation was the fragrant smoke coming from the baker's shop, he looked around for the old round church of Saint-Etienne. He had been instructed to meet his courier there and to give him the case. The place was little more than the convergence of five streets where the buildings crowded together as if vying for the best place for trade. Some of the houses were tall and lean, sagging on their neighbors like old folk leaning on the strong shoulders of their children. De Rochard remembered being told that some time before, in the time of Abelard, this place was the center of a small village, not part of Paris. He could not recall who had told him that; possibly Bondame Clemens, who often spoke of the past.

Finally he located the ancient stone church tucked in behind a mercer's shop; he touched the rounded walls once, as if to convince himself that they were real. Then he looked for the door, trusting it would not be barred. He saw the enormous iron brackets that must once have held a bar to brace the doors closed, but the brackets were rusty now, and no stout length of wood was in sight.

There was a baptismal font carved inexpertly from a single granite stone, and over it a small faceted window let enough light in for de Rochard to be certain that he was alone in the place. He sighed, and saw his breath before his face, all white. He wished the new messenger would arrive, so that he would be able to pass the case to him and then have some rest. He yawned, feeling a little guilty although there was no one there to see.

A short time later a white-haired priest came tottering in, and began to recite the Mass in a low, emotionless voice. He was accompanied by a gangly youth who stared at the middle of the ceiling during the whole of the service, performing his parts of the ritual only when the aged priest motioned him to act. As the Mass continued, de Rochard had to force himself to keep from dozing.

Then the altar candles wavered, bowing, as the door to the little church opened and someone strode inside. There was the ring of spurs on the rough stone floor, and a pause as the messenger genuflected. Then the man was sitting beside de Rochard, his hat pulled down low over his brow. "The Cardinal greets you and says that the enemies of Caesar are the enemies of God as well." He coughed.

"The enemies of Caesar are the allies of Hell," said de Rochard, relieved to hear the new passwords. "I have the case for you."

"Everything the Cardinal wanted?" asked the messenger, his voice thickened as if he could not quite keep from coughing again. He busied himself brushing at his mud-spattered cloak. "The farmers in Beauvais said it would rain by tonight, and the roads are all but impassable as it is."

"There has not been much snow," de Rochard observed. "At this time of year, we have often had snow." He caught a glimpse of the messenger's reddened face. "But there is much wind."

The messenger nodded. "I thank God I am not a sailor." He leaned back against the unpadded plank behind him. "I think I might have taken a chill. My head aches enough for it." He cleared his throat and remembered to cross himself and give response to the Mass, nudging de Rochard with his elbow as he did. "I have told the Cardinal that he needs fighting men to be his messengers and couriers. Many and many a time I've told him. Now that he's succeeded in having de Troisvilles put out, he ought to find a few of those precious Musqueteers to carry his documents and letters to him." This time his cough was much worse; his face reddened, and when he was quiet once more, two bright spots remained in his ashen face.

From the sanctuary the Mass continued as if the church were completely empty.

"Are you well enough to ride?" asked de Rochard, hating himself for the hope that rose in his breast. "Do you think you can safely make the journey?"

The messenger shrugged. "I must," he said simply, but wiped his brow. "Dry," he said, examining his handkerchief. "That's . . . not good."

De Rochard knew as well as anyone that a hot, dry forehead meant fever. He looked at the messenger in some alarm. "How long have you felt . . . like this?" He did not know if it was safe to challenge the messenger more directly, for most of the men in private service to the First Minister of France were touchy about their honor, and that often included their fitness for their work.

"Yesterday I was not myself," the messenger admitted grudgingly. He made a sound in his chest as he tried again, unsuccessfully, to clear his lungs.

With an irritated gesture the old priest prepared to elevate the Host, glancing over his shoulder once but looking at neither of the men there. He continued the service, paying no attention to the two men.

"Do you need a physician?" de Rochard suggested tentatively. "One is available at the—"

"No one is to know I am in Paris—well, no one but you—and certainly no one is to discover that I am not well." He took a long, ragged breath. "I will have to take a draught of pansy. Yes. Pansy.

That will help me." He nodded several times, convincing himself that old nostrum was sufficient to restore him sufficiently to permit him to carry the sealed case back to Amiens. "Pansy and an hour or two of sleep and I will be ready to travel."

"Of course," said de Rochard, doing his best to agree, though he was keenly aware that the messenger needed more than a draught of pansy. "When Mass is over—"

The messenger waved this notion away. "Why remain? You know how it goes." His chuckle became another cough. "Is there a tavern nearby where I can get some hot wine? And an apothecary, so I may purchase the pansy?"

De Rochard was shocked: here was a messenger of Cardinal Mazarin who dismissed the Mass with nothing more than a gesture of his hand. "The Mass is—"

"I've heard it, and the Cardinal's business is more important than a few hosannahs." He genuflected, coughing again as he got to his feet. "I've been sitting through Masses since I was old enough to hold myself up. If I miss one from time to time, God will not mind, since I miss them on His business." He favored de Rochard—quite unnecessarily—with an inclination of his head and two fingers to the brim of his hat. He started for the door without waiting to see if de Rochard was accompanying him.

As he left the pew, de Rochard was keenly aware of what a very sorry figure he cut with the mud starting to dry on his cloak, and his legs crusty. He dropped to his knee and crossed himself, then rose and followed the messenger, the case still clutched tightly beneath his cloak. "I have not bothered to discover where the tavern or apothecary is."

The messenger was standing in the door now, peering out at the feeble sunshine that seeped through the clouds. "Not a promising morning," he remarked to himself. Then he looked at de Rochard. "You don't know where the tavern and apothecary are? Is that what you said?"

"I don't come to this part of the city very often," de Rochard admitted, feeling odd that he could not at once provide the information the messenger wanted. As the Cardinal's lackey, he was convinced that he should have all such knowledge at the ready. How could he convince Mazarin of his usefulness if he could not accommodate this messenger?

"We'll find them together," said the messenger with a greater show of purpose than de Rochard had seen from him. "There is usually a tavern near a place, especially an old one like this, to cater to the folk on marketday." He stepped out onto the cobbles, then stopped as another, more alarming, fit of coughing overcame him.

"I will find a physician," said de Rochard, now very seriously concerned.

"No you won't," the messenger countered, reaching out to grab de Rochard's arm. "You will tell no one I am here. You will not betray me."

"Betray you?" de Rochard repeated in disbelief. "I am sworn to the Cardinal; I could not betray you."

"Send for a physician and you will discover otherwise," said the messenger, indicating the bakery. "We will go in there; surely they know where the tavern is."

Unwillingly de Rochard tagged along behind the messenger, growing more convinced with every step that the man was very ill. He noticed that the man's shoulders drooped and that he trembled when he stood still. De Rochard could think of no way to address the matter again. "I have a few coins," he volunteered. "I will buy us some bread."

"Save your coins for hot wine," ordered the messenger. "Hot wine is more healing than bread." He had almost reached the door of the bakery when he almost bent double, swearing comprehensively. "And piss on God's toes, too," he ended, making himself stand straight once more.

De Rochard was appalled; the messenger had ordered him not to send for a physician, but he wanted to summon some kind of aid for the man. "You need—"

"—a drink!" said the messenger with ferocious good-humor. "A drink and a woman and three hours to call my own." He staggered through the bakery door, bawling out, "Where does a man go to get wine?"

The baker turned a suspicious eye on the messenger and de Rochard. "Good Christians do not take any but Communion wine at this hour," he informed them.

De Rochard saw the messenger stiffen belligerently, and he decided to intervene. "Of course, and we have just come from Mass. But as you see"—he gestured to his muddy cloak and to the travel-stained garments of the messenger—"we have been on the road, and for us, this is the end of the day, not the beginning. We would like a little wine in order to rest before we continue about our business." He ended with a little bow to the baker.

The baker folded his massive arms. "There is a tavern at the far end of the place. It is very old, with blackened ships' beams thrusting over the street. The Silver Ship." He indicated the racks by the oven where the first baking of the day was cooling. "Bread goes well with wine," he said, making his hint as broad as possible.

"Surely," said de Rochard, taking out a few more of his coins and offering them. "Two loaves."

The baker nodded and selected the largest. "Your friend looks ill," he said, fright coming into his deep-set eyes.

De Rochard knew that to admit the messenger was ill could bring more attention than they could permit. "Yes; he had the misfortune to be kicked by his horse, and it has left him short of breath and queasy." He took the change the baker gave him and signaled to the messenger.

"Better have a physician look at him. Kicks like that can be ruinous." The baker watched them leave, his face set in order to hide his feelings.

"Why did you say that about the horse?" asked the messenger. "It's shameful to say that about a messenger like me. We're expected to be, you know . . . those things . . . the ones that were men in front and horses behind?"

"I know what creatures you mean," said de Rochard. "And while we speak of horses, where is yours?"

The messenger gestured vaguely. "There is a stable for travelers. The Cardinal's messengers use it often. They'll remount me when we're through with our work." He rubbed at his forehead. "My head's about to split."

De Rochard spoke bluntly this time. "You are very ill. That's why your head is sore and that's why you cough. You need a physician and a bed to sleep in."

The messenger glared at him with reddened eyes. "I need some hot wine, some pansy, and a good horse." He all but choked on the words. "I don't need a child telling me how to care for myself." He spat bloody phlegm onto the worn cobbles. "No more from you, puppy, or I will complain of you to the Cardinal when I deliver the case you are still carrying."

"He would not approve of me permitting you to carry his documents if you were too ill to guard them and yourself properly." De Rochard clutched the case more tightly. "And now I am not sure you are able to carry them."

"Are you going to stop me?" the messenger challenged, attempting to laugh. He had to steady himself by putting one hand against the wall of the nearest house. "How old are you? Not more than fifteen or sixteen, I warrant. I am twenty-nine, boy, and you are no match for me." To demonstrate this, he made himself walk briskly, swaggering a little to conceal his shivers.

"You are ill," de Rochard protested, following after the messenger. "You need medicines, more than the apothecary has. You need rest."

"I shall have both when I return to Amiens," said the messenger, as if conceding a strategic point. "I'll give you my word on that." He grinned and pointed. "The Silver Ship. Hot wine. And we'll eat that bread, since you paid for it." As he spoke he shoved open the tavern door, calling out as he did, "Hot wine with spices, two tankards."

De Rochard blinked, his eyes adjusting to the darkness. There were lanthorns by the hearth, but the fire had not been laid and amid the ashes only a single log smoldered. He tugged at the messenger's sleeve and indicated a table near the bar. "We can sit there, friend." For the first time he felt awkward not knowing what name to call the messenger.

"Don't worry about it, boy," said the messenger, taking the chair de Rochard had pointed out. "It's just as well that we know very little about each other. That way, if anyone asks us, we can deny everything without lying outright."

"I would not answer," said de Rochard, his eyes brightening as his face flushed.

The messenger shook his head. "We all would answer, boy. Every one of us. It might take longer and be more painful, but if we were asked by experts, we would tell them everything, eventually." His expression grew distant. "I saw a messenger once, who had betrayed his comrades. They had put out his eyes with hot irons and yanked out every tooth in his head; they had mashed his legs to jelly with the boot and bound burning pitch in the palms of his hands. So he told them." He looked up as a small, thin man came into the taproom and bowed. "What is it? We ordered two tankards of spiced wine."

The small man bowed again. "Of course, of course, and it is being prepared. But, you see, it is so early in the morning, and there is only one cook in the kitchen . . . it will take a little time." This time he only inclined his head.

"Well, get to it as soon as you can," said the messenger, pointing to the two loaves of bread de Rochard carried. "We can start on this."

"Of course, of course," said the small man with yet another bow. "It will not take long, but I did not want you to think that you were forgotten or neglected."

The messenger flipped a large silver coin to the small man. "There. That promises we'll be here, to have our money's worth." He stifled another burst of coughing and then dismissed the man with a gesture. "Let me have my loaf."

"Of course," said de Rochard, imitating the little man as he handed over the bread and placed his own loaf on the table before him. "It smells good."

"All bread smells good," said the messenger as he broke his into three parts. "Always do this, for the Trinity."

De Rochard copied the messenger, inhaling the aroma of fresh bread as he did. "When I was little, I used to watch my sisters bake."

"Your sisters, not the cook?" said the messenger through a mouthful of bread.

"There wasn't much money for cooks," said de Rochard stiffly. "And my mother believed that all women should know how to make bread and omelettes."

The messenger nodded in vigorous agreement. "And so they should. All women should know some cooking, from the highest to the lowest, they should cook." He broke off more of the bread and popped it into his mouth.

The small man returned; this time he was not alone. Two tall fellows dressed in caped cloaks over bronze livery were with him, both of them conspicuously armed with pistols and swords.

"I am sorry to interrupt," said the small man, bowing, showing very little nervousness, "but it appears that these men wish to . . . discuss something with you."

The messenger was already rising, one hand on the hilt of his sword. "I am not one to discuss anything," he said, shrugging his cloak back and moving away from the table.

"It is in your interest," said one of the two men. His accent was that of Metz, flavored with German.

De Rochard had also risen, and wished that he had come prepared for this. A knife, a sword, even a stout cudgel would be welcome against these two. He held the case close against his chest as he moved clear of the table.

"Another one of the Cardinal's cherubs," said the second man, making the term obscene. "What use do you suppose he is, Martel, beyond the obvious?" He was deliberately goading de Rochard, enjoying the insults he offered. "They're so willing when they are young and pretty, aren't they?"

"You know that better than I," said de Rochard, keeping his temper in check with an effort. He gave a single, swift glance toward the messenger and saw that the man was quite pale, his eyes ringed by darkness.

Martel clicked his tongue in wonder. "Well, well, he has learned more than how to bend over." He turned his attention to the messenger again. "So, Sigloy, here you are at last."

The messenger glowered, smothering a cough with his hand. "It is nothing to you, Martel."

"You are right," said Martel, mockery in his demeanor. "Were it for me to decide, I would ignore you, for you are so unimportant in yourself." He cocked his head toward de Rochard. "You are less than he is, and he is nothing more than a pet."

It took all of de Rochard's self-discipline not to throw a chair at the man. It was infuriating to listen to him, all the more so because he knew that Martel was deliberately provoking him, trying to goad him into a rash attack. De Rochard held himself in check and covertly began to look for a weapon. He wanted to say something to the messenger, but was afraid that Sigloy—if that was truly his name—would be distracted, and off guard, prey to the sinister intruders.

"Look, Martel," said the other man. "Sigloy is sweating. His face is wet. I can smell him, like a dying rat."

"A pity," said Martel with patently false sympathy. "How does it happen that such a man is reduced to this, do you suppose; running errands for the Italian Cardinals instead of fighting him with true Frenchmen?" Casually he closed his hand around the hilt of his sword. "How can you have fallen from honor so far? Or did you never have it?"

With a roar, Sigloy hurtled at the two men, drawing his sword as he did.

"No!" yelled de Rochard, making a last, futile attempt to block the fight. Then he reached for one of the chairs and, hefting it with his right hand, half-pushed and half-threw it at Martel and his companion as Sigloy crashed into them.

There were howls and shouts and rich cursing as all three went down in a tangle of thrashing limbs. The messenger changed his grip on his swordhilt and slammed it into the jaw of Martel's companion, grimacing with pleasure at the ominous crack it made. He got onto his knees and dragged his sword all the way out of the scabbard as Martel scuttled backward into the protective cover of the next table.

"You!" the messenger bawled toward de Rochard. "Get out of here! *Get out of here!* Go. Go!" The order ended on a deep, braying cough as the man all but collapsed.

De Rochard hesitated, not wanting to leave a sick man in such danger. He looked about, as if expecting help to spring out of the walls, all the while clasping the case he carried close to his chest.

"For the King!" the messenger gasped. "Go."

This time de Rochard was spurred to action. He spun around, relieved to see that the messenger had only one man to battle; surely Martel would not harm so ill a man. He sprinted toward the door, his mind suddenly filled with thoughts of glory. He would find a horse and ride to Beauvais, then on to Amiens, the documents in the sealed case kept safe by his speed and his determination. He would arrive at Amiens and be received by the Cardinal, and then presented to the Queen Regent and the King, who would thank him for his diligence. His future would be assured.

He did not realize at first that the blow on his back was a pistol ball, or that the odd warmth spreading down his body was his own blood. He fell through the door into the street, to lie with his face pressed against the cobbles.

Martel walked up to him and nudged him over with his boot. "What's that foreigner thinking of, to use boys like him for this work?" he asked, addressing the messenger over his shoulder.

Fontaine de Rochard, looking up, thought that perhaps Martel was pointing at him, for there was something like a cold finger laid on his brow.

"Martel, don't!" came the choked cry that ended in a fit of coughing.

"Sorry, Sigloy, but I have my orders. We need the papers in that case. If there was another way—" said Martel in a tone that was very nearly genuine. "He's put paid, anyway."

The noise and the blackness came together.

*   *   *

Text of a letter from Jules, Cardinal Mazarin to Jean-Arnaud du Peyrer de Troisvilles.

To the most dedicated and constant of the King's military leaders, that most excellent man le Comte de Troisvilles, my greetings and the assurance that I take no satisfaction in the recent developments that have resulted in the—shall we hope?—temporary disbanding of the King's Musqueteers.

I have your recommendations in hand for the two men among the numbers of others in your command who best suit the needs I outlined to you in January. I appreciate your help in this, for it benefits not only these most worthy officers, but increases the likelihood of the Musqueteers being reinstated at some later time.

When I requested your aid in this matter, I particularly required that the men you selected should be those of the very least fortune in the Musqueteers, having nothing to call their own but their mantles and their swords, so that they would be wholly dependent on me and, through me, upon the King for their very well-being. The two names you have sent are not entirely unknown to me, and I must commend you for your thoughtful reply and your candid assessment of these two Musqueteers. I will keep your recommendations among my papers so that they may later have access to proof of your good opinion, should it be required.

I am aware that you are no supporter of mine, and I know that it was not easy for you to give me the information I asked for, since it would not serve your ends. A good commander such as you have been in the past must realize that there are times when those who command in battle must avoid entering into the court life or the affairs of state. Too often there are disputes that cannot be resolved between those who excel in battle and those who must treat and bargain on behalf of the Crown.

Let me offer you an example in the hope that it might ease the bitterness between us and unite us both more closely to the Crown: very many years ago, before Charlemagne came to rule, there was a monk, known for his piety and devotion, a man without guile who sought simply the presence of God and longed only to purge his soul *of sin.* Those who knew him regarded him with veneration because of his saintly acts and purity of heart. So it was that his reputation grew, and he discovered that there were many who sought him out for the benefit of his wisdom and his holiness.

At first he was delighted, for he saw that there were many who could be brought to Christian profession through his example and his teaching, and he thanked God for this opportunity to share his knowledge with those who had not yet confessed in Christ. He rejoiced at each new student, and in time declared he would establish a community for those who desired to live in Christian and sinless fellowship. He established his community under the Rule of Saint Benedict and prayed God would send him others to join with his community in the pursuit of Christian unity and the worship of God.

Now, all these attainments are virtuous things, and it is most honorable to pursue righteousness. This monk was doing as Our Lord enjoined all His apostles to do, and he was bringing many to the worship of God, Son, and Holy Spirit. He upheld the virtues of Christians and offered a true example for those in his community to emulate. The monk had in no way erred and he was faultless in the spiritual goals he pursued for himself and the members of his community.

But not all his followers were as honest and guiltless as he, and not all of them found the same peace in the worship of God as he did. Many of them were desperate men hoping to elude the consequences of their sins; some were willing to follow any who would give them protection. And some were the tools of Satan, intent on destroying the community this monk had created. It was not to the credit of the monk that he tolerated such men among the members of his community, for their contagion spread more quickly and more profoundly than anything that could be done by the monk to stop it. Where there had been piety before there was now spite, and the monk did nothing to stop it, for he believed that it was not his right to move the hearts of men once they sought God. He would not punish any for transgression in the community and he refused to confess to the world that corruption and dissipation had touched some of those who had come to the community. He allowed himself to be seduced by these men who wanted only his ruin and destruction. His greatness of soul could not endure the necessary excision and cauterization to save his community. And so, in time, all of them succumbed to the debauchery of those who were not truly seeking God and Christian worship. In time the community was shunned and the monk's name was cursed, though he himself had led a life that was blameless in every way but one.

I pray that in time the Queen Regent will allocate the necessary funds to restore the Musqueteers to their place of honor among French regiments. If it were not so precarious a time, I am certain that she would not have made this decision, but with the King so young and unrest in the country being what it is, the Queen Regent does not wish to impose another tax on her subjects and nobles, especially one that might appear to be in preparation for another war. All France is sick of war, I think, and of taxation for it. Given these circumstances, however, I cannot but support her decision, unpleasant though I find it. It is lamentable that the most acceptable sacrifice was your justly famed regiment.

I will, if you wish, report to you annually on the activities of Francois de Montlezun, Sieur de Besmaux, and Charles d'Artagnan. They are ideally suited to be my personal couriers, and without doubt they will serve me and the Queen Regent well. I have promised both men promotions and favor in the Musqueteers when that regiment is reinstated, as I am certain it must be. For such consideration, they, and I, have you to thank, which I do, with my prayers.

May Heaven look upon you and your endeavors with favor, and may you receive the recognition and favor you have earned with so many years of service to the Crown. I am confident that you will be able to rise again to favor when the time is more auspicious.

With my blessing and gratitude,
Jules Mazarin, Cardinal and
First Minister of France

On the 4th day of March, 1646.
A bona fide copy of this letter is retained in my records.

PART IV
Charles d'Artagnan

Text of a letter from Charles d'Artagnan to Cardinal Mazarin, dictated to Isaac de Portau.

To the First Minister of France, Cardinal Mazarin, my respectful greetings, and my assurance that I have followed your instructions regarding the disappearance of your lackey Fontaine de Rochard, as is the duty you have assigned to me.

I have been able to determine that he did meet with a man who was possibly your messenger. Both the priest in the church where they met and the baker in a shop nearby saw them together. They agree that the man he met was ill with a cough. The baker told me that they asked the way to the nearest tavern in order to have hot wine. He told them how to find the Silver Ship. They bought some bread and left his shop. It would appear that the baker was the last person to see the two men. No one at the Silver Ship saw, or admits to having seen, these two men. I spoke to the cooks and the tapster, and all of them say that no one came to the tavern that morning. I was not able to learn anything more from anyone at the tavern, and was told that I was not wise to make such inquiries. It was apparent to me that if anyone in the tavern knew anything, it would take more than a few questions to discover it. Once I revealed that I was your courier, I was regarded with veiled anger, which I am convinced was not entirely because I am an officer, but because I am employed by you. No one in the tavern vouchsafed anything of importance, except through what they did not say.

However, I have also been told by a sensible woman who lives in the house across the street from the tavern that she saw a large man shoot another man with a pistol on that same morning when your lackey met with the courier. She swears that there were three or four men in the tavern, and furthermore, she says that one of the men had a bad cough. *This woman is the wife of an upholsterer and known as a good housewife and virtuous spouse. She is honest and industrious and clearly not one to make up stories, or to turn the banging of a shutter to the marching of an army. If she says that there were three or four men in the tavern, I am inclined to believe it is so.*

Going on the information this woman provided, I asked others in that part of the street if they had been aware of any commotion on that morning. Most refused to speak with me, and a few made threats that were not welcome or courteous, but a mercer who keeps a shop in the place said that he heard a dispute or fight in the tavern, and recalls that there may have been three shots fired, though he is not so certain that he would swear to it. Also, a cowman bringing butter and cream to the bakery that morning says he saw a quantity of blood on the street in front of the Silver Ship. This cowman is a simple fellow, but I have no reason to doubt what he has told me, and I am sure he knows what a puddle of blood looks like.

From this, I must assume that your lackey has met with ultimate misfortune. If the coughing man with him was truly your messenger Jean-Baptiste Sigloy, then I fear that he, too, must be numbered with the fallen.

I have ordered the Watch to report on any bodies they may discover improperly buried in the district, and to make note of any rumors of harm done to messengers. After so long a time—nearly three months—I fear that anything we discover will be of little use to us, but I wish to have a record of those unexplained deaths and improper burials. If those who attacked your lackey and messenger were wise, then messenger and lackey were buried in holy ground. If that is the case there must be a record of it somewhere, but I have not been able to find such a record. Therefore all reports on bodies discovered may eventually offer some indication of what happened to those men.

This is to be carried to you by Montlezun de Besmaux; I am returning to Eblouir to await the arrival of the courier from the Vatican. When he arrives, I will bring his messages to you at Amiens with all haste, and without entering the walls of Paris. I will ride in ordinary garments and without my mantle, as you have insisted.

May God protect you and the King, and may He lend you His wisdom in this troublesome time.

> Your courier
> Charles d'Artagnan

On the 19th day of May, 1646.

· 1 ·

As the lackeys finished loading his carriage, Mazarin took Niklos Aulirios aside, his features more serious than usual. Gone was his charm and diplomacy; he was worried. "I have to know," he began after he had satisfied himself that they were out of earshot, "what arrangements Olivia has been making in regard to her return to Rome."

Niklos shrugged. "Nothing much. Her retainers at Senza Pari are prepared to send her coaches north upon her order, and the staff here have taken certain measures that—"

"Yes," Mazarin cut in impatiently. "That is what I wish to speak to you about." He was nervous, fidgiting with the lace-edge of his mozzetta. "There are rumors now, very dangerous rumors, that . . . my embassy is . . ." He turned quickly as a lackey approached. "We are not to be interrupted!"

The lackey blanched, bowed, and retreated, his eyes blank.

"Eminence," said Niklos when the lackey had gone, "what is the matter? You are not yourself."

"No," Mazarin agreed with a twitch of a smile. "And being myself has become quite an effort." He made a visible attempt to master himself. "You know that three of my messengers have been killed since the first of the year? Yes." He nodded with Niklos. "Yes. None of my Italian couriers yet, but the messengers are another matter. They are more . . . obvious, working between the Queen Regent and myself. At least the Papal couriers move beyond such limits." He stared away across the fields, his expression softening. "I still like the windmills," he said softly and inconsequentially.

Niklos returned to the matter at hand. "What has this to do with Bondame Clemens?" He waited for his answer, and when none was coming, he asked, "Or what has it to do with Charles d'Arta-gnan?"

"They are both at risk," said Mazarin quietly. "All those close to me and the Crown are at risk, in these times." He glanced away, then met Niklos' eyes directly. "There are rumors that I am plan-ning to flee, to leave the Queen Regent exposed to the nobles. It is part of the continuing attempts to discredit her and me. The rumor suggests that my flight would be proof that the Queen Re-gent was the mother of bastards."

"Married women cannot have bastards," said Niklos, his brows drawing together for emphasis.

"You know that means nothing for a Queen, especially for this Queen." Mazarin placed his large, long hands together. "And who is to say the rumors are not right, and Richelieu was the father of those children. It is easier to believe that Richelieu was than that Louis XIII was their father, and I say that with no disrespect to the Cardinal." He hesitated before going on. "If Louis XIV is to reign, it will be because I am stalwart, no matter what the nobles try to do. I gave my word to Richelieu and to God that I would defend and uphold the Queen and her children."

"Yes," said Niklos, unsure what Mazarin was implying. "Why does this concern Olivia?"

"It . . ." He dropped his hands. "If it is known, or even sus-pected, that Bondame Clemens is planning to leave France, it may be interpreted as an indication that I, too, am preparing to leave. If that is believed, then the nobles will do more than plot, they will act. At this time, it would not be easy to defend the King, and it is necessary that he be defended. At this time, my presence gives some force to the Queen's regency; if that appears to lessen, then she will be far more vulnerable than she is already."

"Or to put it another way, Olivia is not to leave, or to prepare to leave yet," said Niklos with asperity.

"I'm sorry," said Mazarin. "Truly, I am sorry. I know I prom-ised her that she could return to Rome by the end of this year, but it is much too hazardous. She will need to remain here for a while longer."

"Why tell me, Eminence?" Niklos challenged. "Why not tell her yourself, or does that trouble you? She may be a woman, but she is not a fool, and she deserves an explanation."

Mazarin did not protest. "I accept your rebuke. You are right, of course. It would be better if I were to speak with her directly. But I am abashed. I promised her it would be arranged for her to leave before winter, and now, I must withdraw that promise." His expression became more somber. "I know it was an intrusion to place Jumeau in this household. I know it is more than our arrangement called for. But circumstances here are more difficult, more . . . complex than I had anticipated. I truly hoped that she could depart before now, with my thanks and favor. I never thought it would be wise to have a member of my staff as part of her household, but with messengers being killed, I can only defend what I have done by the loss of their lives."

"You should be saying this to Atta Olivia Clemens," Niklos told him.

"It is not appropriate," Mazarin declared, and from the tone of his voice, he would not change his mind. "When this is over, when she has returned to Rome, then, perhaps, I will be at liberty to discuss these circumstances with her." He stood a little straighter. "I respect her for her wisdom—few women have her understanding—and I am grateful for all she has done to aid me and the work I do. But be aware that she is a woman, for all her good sense, and that to burden her with cares such as these would be no benefit to her."

Niklos' smile was sardonic. "I would like to hear her answer when you tell her that." He folded his arms. "Very well; what do you expect me to do, other than endure that prig Jumeau?"

Mazarin paced a few steps, then came back to Niklos' side. "I hope you will stop these preparations for departing. It would be most useful if it seemed that Bondame Clemens would live here forever. If it is not possible to do this, then all that you can do to end the rumors that Bondame Clemens is planning to aid my . . . escape would be welcome. It is important that there be no doubt about this."

"I will have to speak with Olivia," said Niklos. "I take my orders from her."

"Certainly. But strive to make it clear to her why I have requested this assistance from her. Tell her of the risk she runs if she continues. The more the rumors appear to be correct, the greater the chance of the nobles acting on them." He gestured toward the carriage and his waiting escort. "I must return to Paris. I have to speak with the Spanish Ambassador tomorrow. Again," he added drily.

"With a Spanish Queen, is it more difficult dealing with the

Ambassador?" Niklos asked, partly in genuine curiosity, partly to keep from arguing with the Cardinal.

"Some days it is one way, some days another." He gave Niklos another direct look. "I rely on you to protect your mistress, Aulirios."

"That you may do with complete confidence," said Niklos with a bow.

"Good." He was about to turn away when one last thing occurred to him. "There is also Monsieur d'Artagnan; he is in danger, as well. If there is a rebellion, he will be caught up in it."

"She is aware of that," Niklos said with gentle severity.

Mazarin gave a small bow. "As you say," he agreed, and at last started toward his carriage. His manner changed as he did: he stood straighter, his face lost its exhaustion, and except for the darkness under his eyes, he might have been refreshed by his sojourn in the country. "Thank your mistress for the use of her house, and tell her that I am deeply appreciative that she was willing to go to Tours while I was here."

This time Niklos gave him a proper bow. "Certainly, Eminence." He signaled to the footmen and lackeys to prepare the carriage for the Cardinal. "It is our honor to entertain you here at Eblouir at any time."

As the steps were pulled down, Mazarin blessed Niklos and the other servants of Eblouir who were allowed to watch his departure. "Please extend my greetings to her and relay my messages, if you would be so kind."

"It will be my privilege," said Niklos, not quite as gently as he intended. He knelt to kiss Mazarin's ring just before the steps were taken up and the carriage door closed.

The Cardinal signed to his escort to move; the coachman raised his whip and the party moved off toward the distant walls of Paris, raising dust and drawing the attention of sheep grazing in the next field.

Niklos stood watching for some little time, and then made his way through the house to his own apartments, his frown deepening to a glower as he went. By the time he left his quarters, it was almost sunset. The plans he had made did not please him, and he was pondering how to discuss them with Olivia when Meres found him.

"Aulirios," he said, offering a half-bow for form's sake.

"What is it, Meres?" He was preoccupied and disinclined to talk. "Is it urgent?"

"I don't know what you would call it," said Meres with a slight smile. "Word has just been brought from the stable that Bondame Clemens has just ridden in. She is accompanied by one of the trainers from Tours, a fellow named Evraud. What is required now? I was told to get your orders."

Niklos stood straighter at the mention of Olivia's name. "You have done properly," he said, and issued orders for Olivia's bath to be filled, for a room to be made ready for Evraud, and for a meal to be prepared. "Inform Bondame Clemens that I will need to speak with her at her first convenience."

"Gladly," said Meres, adding, "I'm pleased she's back."

"So am I," said Niklos. He sent Meres off, then went to find Avisa.

Olivia was already soaking in her bath when Niklos entered the room by a side door. "If the staff ever learned you do this," she said after she had blown him a welcoming kiss, "they would be shocked."

"There are many things about you and me that would shock them," said Niklos as he sat down on a low bench beside the large, sunken tub.

Her response was no longer playful. "You're right, I fear." She leaned back, half-floating in the steaming water. "What is so urgent and so private that you must speak to me secretly?"

It was a moment before Niklos gathered his thoughts enough to answer her. "Before Mazarin left, he had a request to make of you. He . . . he was very . . ."

"Very what?" Olivia asked when Niklos did not go on.

"Anxious, I suppose," said Niklos as he considered his conversation with the Cardinal. "Not without reason, sad to say." He bent down so that their heads were no more than two handbreadths apart. "Olivia, remember the problems you anticipated last year?"

"What of them?" Olivia asked, her attention sharp and fixed. "What has happened?"

Quickly Niklos outlined what Mazarin had asked of him, adding, "You sensed it when it began, but you thought it would fade. Now it seems that it has not, it has only changed shape a little. There are nobles determined to discredit the young King and to be rid of him, his mother, and Mazarin."

"And Giulio thinks that they are watching me, that I will cover his escape, or provide the means." She began to rub her face with a cloth. "You're annoyed as much as you're worried; what is it? Are you afraid that Mazarin is right? Or is it something else? Is it about the nobles? Do you think there is going to be a rebellion after all?" She saw the answer in his face before he spoke. "In Greek," she warned in that tongue.

"Mazarin certainly fears it." He stared at the wall. "He does not want it to appear you are going to leave France. That's the one thing he's set on. He is convinced your leaving will trigger the rebellion, by making the nobles believe that Mazarin will leave with you." His gesture indicated he did not know what to think. "I don't think the nobles pay that much attention to you, but it would not take more than one or two to spark things, I suppose. Still, I hope that it is nothing more than Mazarin's fear for the Queen and her sons speaking, but . . ."

"But," Olivia concurred. "We must never forget the but. Well, then we must cooperate, at least for a while." She indicated a glass jar filled with bath salts. "Hand me that, will you?"

"You don't seem upset," Niklos remarked as he complied.

"It's because I'm not surprised. Had this been unexpected, I would probably have been furious." She leaned back as she poured more of the bath salts into the warm water. "Every house should have a caladarium like this. How do they manage without hot baths, I want to know."

"You're being a Roman again," said Niklos with affection. "But I warn you, Olivia, I will not be turned from the subject. We have matters we must discuss."

"The ploy has worked before," said Olivia as she put the lid back on the jar. "You were more easily distracted, eight hundred years ago. Now you are a task master: very well, let us consider what is to be done, since it seems we are condemned to remain here for another several months."

"Or years," said Niklos heavily. "And before you tell me, the answer is no, I will not leave you here and go back to Senza Pari to administer it for you. Do not ask me, do not order me. I stay where you are." His handsome features were no longer as pleasant as they usually were; his implacability would have amazed most of those who knew him.

"I wasn't going to suggest that," said Olivia as innocently as she could. "I wasn't."

"Such charming mendacity," said Niklos, his eyes narrowing in amusement. "I know you; it's been on your mind for months."

"True," she admitted, "but I have said nothing. That is signifi-cant, isn't it?" As she slid deeper into the water, so that just her head rose above the surface, she said, "I think we had better make sure we can get to Tours on short notice, however. It is one thing to abandon all plans to leave France, but another thing to be ready to leave Eblouir, if we must."

"So you *have* been thinking of it," said Niklos with a trace of relief. "You are not adverse to a little strategy."

"No, I'm not," said Olivia, suddenly very tired. "I am growing weary of it, but not adverse to it." She moved languidly, almost floating in the hot water. "But I wish that it were not necessary, this constant shifting and adjustment that we must do to survive. The Cardinal does not understand what he is asking of us, not really. And Heaven forbid he should learn! Have you ever considered what might happen to us if Mazarin discovered all there is to know of me? Or you?"

Niklos shook his head. "I don't want to think about it."

"Neither do I," said Olivia. "But I must. Especially now that Charles has . . . has learned so much. He is endangered by what he knows and what he will be." The vertical line between her brows deepened. "What would Mazarin do if he found out that I am a vampire, and that Charles will be one as well when he dies. A member of his embassy and his personal courier—he would not take it very well, I suspect." She gave a single, sad laugh. "We would receive more than a scolding."

"More than a scolding, yes, but not so much as you might have had once. It is 1646, and this is Mazarin we speak of, not the Bishop of Bilbao, or some of the others. He is not like the churchmen of even two centuries ago," said Niklos, but with less conviction than he liked.

"Are you hoping to convince me or yourself?" Olivia asked, and went on briskly. "No. You're right. They probably would not pile the faggots in the Place Royale and reduce us all to ashes and cinders. But they would not welcome us, either." She wiped her damp tendrils of hair off her face. "And it would be awkward returning to Rome if it were known that I am a vampire and you are a ghoul. We might have to go find Sanct' Germain in the New World. Which means traveling by ship." This last was said with real detestation.

"None of it need happen," said Niklos, suddenly eager to dispel her sense of foreboding. "We will make preparations and continue our usual precautions. If we are fortunate, we will not have to deal with any of these problems."

"If we are fortunate," she said, tweaking the water to splash him a little.

"Best not," he warned her. "If the servants notice I am wet and they know you are bathing, they will become suspicious as well." He took care to move out of range.

"They suspect something of the sort already," said Olivia.

"Actually," Niklos said, not quite able to be amused, "I have said that we are brother and sister, but that I was born on the wrong side of the blanket. The only way our father could give me a share of his wealth was to appoint me your major domo."

Olivia regarded him with bemused humor. "How inventive of you. How many times have you trotted out this farrago in the last few hundred years?" There was a little indignation in her hazel eyes but no anger. "You might have mentioned it to me."

"I might have," said Niklos, glad that they had a language that the servants did not know: it not only provided the privacy that he and Olivia sought, it also added strength to their supposed kinship. "But the staff puts more stock by it since you do not acknowledge the tie, though you receive me as if I were one of your family."

"And now that you have revealed your ruse to me, what am I expected to do?" She shrugged, then indicated the large drying sheet beside him on the bench. "Give that to me. I want to get out." She rose as she said it, the water streaming off here, the level in the tub half-way up her thighs.

"Avisa will be horrified if she finds me here," said Niklos as he gave her the drying sheet. "She is horrified by what she has learned of me already."

"If she is horrified, it also means she is curious. I had best think of something to say that will put an end to it for a while. With the Cardinal so apprehensive, I do not know who might try to suborn the servants." She wrapped herself in the sheet and gave Niklos a careful stare. "I want to know anything that occurs that way—any attempts or rumors of attempts to get information from the servants. Don't be obvious."

Niklos chuckled. "I will do as I have done before: I will say that someone offered me a bribe and I refused; I will be very outraged but also greedy, as if I might have said something else if I had been offered enough. If there have been inquiries made, I will learn of it soon enough." He got to his feet and went toward the side door. "You had best pay no attention to these changes of plans, as if one way or another makes no difference to you."

"That's sensible," said Olivia a bit distractedly as she let her hair down from the pins that had held it in a knot on her head. "I will go to my study when I'm dressed. If there are any papers that I need to inspect, bring them to me there."

"Of course," said Niklos, giving her a sudden grin of wicked amusement. "Sister mine," he said in French.

"Wretch," she responded in the same language as she blew him a kiss. She waited until Niklos was gone, and then rang for Avisa to come.

The maid arrived so promptly that Olivia was almost certain that she had been listening at the door. Avisa bobbed a curtsy and said, "What clothes am I to set out, Madama?"

"Oh, I think the green brocade with the umber velvet will do," said Olivia as she dragged her comb through her fawn-brown hair. "It is a bit more formal than I would like to be, but with so many messengers and couriers coming and going, I must be at my best to receive them."

"Certainly," said Avisa in a toneless way. She was about to leave the room when she added, "Madama, I have had a letter from my sister. You recall I have mentioned her to you before."

"The one with six daughters and five sons, who married a lesser nobleman from Bologna or some such place. Is she the one you mean?" Olivia had heard sporadic tales of this sister many times, and considered Leatrice as unhappy as Avisa occasionally felt herself to be; Olivia knew far too well what it was to be sold into marriage, as Leatrice had been. She hoped that Leatrice's husband Onorio was kinder than her own. "What has she said to you, your sister?"

Avisa did not answer directly, but said, "I mentioned several months ago that we would probably be returning to Italy before the end of this year." She glanced nervously at Olivia. "You told me it was all right. At the time, it was thought to be so. And you have said to me often that if I wished, I could have several months for myself, to compensate for living so far from my home and family."

"Yes," said Olivia, who extended the same offer to all the Italians who had come with her, as would have been proper in her father's household, sixteen hundred years before. "I assure you that the offer is genuine."

"But," Avisa went on in agitation, "you see, I assumed we would be in Roma by now, that we would be at Senza Pari and it would be possible for me to claim that time to myself that you offered me. And now, instead, the rumor is that we are to remain here for at least a year more."

"It seems likely," said Olivia, doing her best to sound indifferent to her predicament. "I have been told that the Cardinal expects us to discontinue our arrangements for traveling south, at least for the time being. We are here to assist him, not to cause him embarrassment."

"That means we will be here through the winter," said Avisa. "It is impossible to move your household in winter. There are too many things, too many people to move while the roads are mired. You would be a fool to attempt it, Madama." She had taken the dress Olivia specified out of the armoire, but now she held it as if she had no idea what to do with it or what it was for.

"Avisa, prego, don't dither," said Olivia as pleasantly as she could. "Tell me what it is you want and I will do what I can to assist you."

"But you will be displeased," she said miserably, "and if you are displeased, you might turn me off here, without taking me back to Roma or giving me a recommendation so that I could find employment elsewhere. I would be destitute in a foreign land." She threw the dress onto the bed and gave way to weeping.

Olivia stopped fussing with her hair. "Magna Mater! what is the matter with you?" she demanded, too puzzled to be angry. "Avisa, what nonsense are you talking?"

"It . . . it is not . . . nonsense." She went on crying in a steady, hopeless way that baffled Olivia.

"I give you my word, no matter what you have done, I will not turn you off without a character in France." She wondered if someone had approached Avisa, but doubted that her maid would be so undone by mere bribery. "What is it?"

Slowly Avisa regained her self-control; between hiccoughs and sniffs, she explained. "I told my sister—she is my half-sister, actually, as you know; we have the same father but not the same mother, my mother having died in childbed not long after I was born—I was their second child and the only one to live beyond the age of three—and my half-sister is years younger than I am—when she informed me that her oldest daughter was about to marry that when my niece—for I regard her as much my niece as any relative I might have that was not a half-sister or step-niece—was brought to bed with her firstborn, I would come and care for her, since my sister cannot do this, having children of her own to care for. When I told her, I was sure that we would be back in Roma by the time she gave birth. Fiorella—my niece—has been brought to bed with twin boys, and . . . I am still here and I cannot help her."

"Do you wish to go to her, Avisa? Do you want to go back to Italy?" Olivia asked as her maid gave way to another bout of tears. Over the years, Olivia thought, she had heard several variations on the tales of Avisa's family; which, if any of them, were true? she wondered. "Shall we arrange it for you?"

Avisa nodded, and finally said, "Yes, Madama; I very much want to go home."

Olivia sighed. "Then, of course, you shall," she said with as much heartiness as she could assume. "I want you to send word to your sister and your niece that you will leave here in two weeks. You will go directly to your sister and you will remain as long as you believe it is necessary. You will continue to draw your pay for a year, as I have promised you before, and at the end of that time, we can arrange how we are to continue. If you decide you prefer to remain with your niece and her family, then terms can be worked out." She motioned to Avisa. "Bring me my clothes. This drying sheet is now wetter than I am."

Avisa obeyed, averting her face. "My face is very red; you need not deny it, I know how it is. And my nose is the reddest of all." She assisted Olivia into her corsets and then opened the rear lacing of the bodice so that she could lift the garment over Olivia's head.

While Avisa busied herself tightening the bodice laces, Olivia said to her, "I will need to find a proper replacement for you, but that will not delay your departure. Tonight I will speak to Niklos about it and tomorrow I will tell you how we will proceed." She plucked at her skirts and watched the way the fabric fell. It was warm enough to make the garment uncomfortable, but Olivia was almost inured to it. "You will be able to write to your family tomorrow," she said as she took her seat and let Avisa put up her hair.

She was almost finished with arranging the crimped locks around Olivia's face when Avisa said, "Madama, there is something I meant to tell you earlier."

Olivia steeled herself for whatever this might be. "Yes? What is it?" She was pleased that her voice did not betray her apprehension.

"It's . . . probably nothing. It is . . . well, I went to your study this morning, while the Cardinal and his party were still here?" Though she still held the comb, she had given up attending to Olivia's hair.

"What about them?" asked Olivia more sharply.

"It was that secretary, the one sent by the Cardinal. The young one with the scowl." Avisa was rubbing her reddened eyes; Olivia did not have the heart to tell her she was making them worse, not better.

"Yes, that would be Jumeau," she said with an expression of mild distaste. "An officious man, but what does it matter?" She had told Mazarin once that the young prelate was arrogant and autocratic; the Cardinal had spoken to him and since then Jumeau had made an effort to be pleasant.

Avisa began to pleat the edge of her long apron as she went on. "I went to your study. I wanted to put fresh flowers in there, for your return."

"I saw the flowers; they are very nice," said Olivia, not certain where all this led.

"He was in the study. Jumeau. He was at your writing table, Madama." She gave Olivia a sudden stare, with the shock not quite faded from her eyes. "I thought he might be . . . reading something of yours."

"He might have been getting something for the Cardinal," Olivia said, though she was not entirely pleased with that notion. "Mazarin was conducting a meeting—"

"A private meeting," corrected Avisa. "And that Jumeau was upset when I found him. He told me that he was looking for a knife to trim his pen and could not find one. He said that he had looked elsewhere and would not have touched anything if he had found the penknife." She let go of her apron and tried to smooth the pleats out of it.

Olivia found this revelation troubling, but she knew better than to reveal her concern. She shrugged for Avisa's benefit and said, "He probably felt as awkward about the encounter as you did. Certainly it would have been more correct had he found Niklos and asked him for a penknife, but after living here for several months, Jumeau probably did not want to be bothered. I will have Niklos speak to him about my things."

"As you say, Madama," said Avisa uncertainly as she tried to put her attention on the work she had to do. "I am not one to carry tales, but when I found him at your writing table, I was afraid that he was up to no good."

"I'll mention it to the Cardinal," said Olivia, and let Avisa get on with tending her hair, all the while pondering: what was Jumeau looking for on her writing table?

* * *

Text of a letter from Le Fouet to Pere Chape, written in code and delivered by unknown messenger.

To that most worthy Augustinian, Le Fouet sends thanks and greetings for the labor done on his behalf and on behalf of the Kingdom of France; when order is restored you will be given praise and recognition for all you have done on our behalf.

I have your report of August, and I note that Mazarin has ordered more guards for the Queen Regent and her bastards as well as increased protection for those in his employ. He has heard something, that is certain, but I doubt it is enough to make it possible for him to interfere with the work we have in hand. Your observations on his actions, on his concern for Anne of Austria, even while she keeps her misbegotten sons in Amiens, has given me and those who share my sentiments much to assess. Without your reports, we should have to make dangerous guesses.

I wish to know more about the activities of these couriers of Mazarin's. Where do they go? Who passes messages to them? We will need to have all such information before we make our final plans. I am especially eager to know where Mazarin will be sending his couriers in the next several months, and where his messengers are to go. The couriers, bearing the documents they do and having the license to cross borders, are of greater significance, but the lowliest messenger can be revealing if the material carried is properly used. Do what you can to learn more of this, I ask you, and send me word at the first opportunity. I am awaiting your communication. Use the new code I have provided you, and do not *trouble yourself with apprehension for discovery. You are among friends, Pere Chape, and your friends will come to your aid if ever you need them. You need have no fear for yourself, now that you have made our cause your own.*

I require to know more about those among the nobility who have been at pains to ally themselves with Mazarin. Those nobles are the enemies of France, and they are to be treated accordingly. I have no sympathy, no emotion but contempt for these despicable men; they are the most reprehensible traitors. With your guidance, I will bring down those who have defamed the Throne by elevating a child not of the Blood Royal. They are more loathsome than maggots in a corpse. Only let me know who they are and I will see them broken on the wheel.

Also I will require to know how much time Mazarin will be spending in Paris and how much in Amiens. This is very crucial information and I will need it to be accurate to the day, if you can obtain such specific plans. If we are to strike, it must be at a time when Mazarin will be the least prepared for such an attack, and will therefore be unable to marshall his troops to defend himself. We require the element of surprise but can only attain it if we have full knowledge of those who are opposed to us. If you cannot get such determinations, then send the plans as you find them, but indicate which plans are set and which are not. Your preparation can tip the balance for us; I want you to appreciate that. Your actions can spell victory or defeat for our cause.

Recent events in England have shown how precarious a thing a crown can be, and although we abhor Cromwell as the outraged peasant he is, we applaud the actions which have placed King Charles in the hands of the Scots, who will know how best to deal both with King and commoner. It will prove a fine example for us to emulate when the time comes: doubtless there will be redress of wrongs and Charles will return to the Throne with a chastened heart and a greater number of his nobility to aid and guide him in future. We can take this as our model, for there are those of the Blood Royal who are content to listen to their nobles and be guided by them, and who can understand the lesson taught by England, and hope that France is wiser than they. In sum, while we must decry the usurpation in England, we also praise the warning it gives us all, for France cannot and will not tolerate the Throne being held by despotic foreigners and base-born false heirs. Let France never forget that Spain is our enemy, and that Queen Anne is Spanish, that the children she has born are not of Louis XIII's loins and they corrupt all they touch.

We need an issue to arouse the people of Paris as well as the nobles against Mazarin. We need some incident that will reveal to all the extent of the perfidy of Anne of Austria and her Italian lapdog. There will have to be a single event or actions that will clearly delineate the disgrace we have suffered at the hands of the Queen Regent and her children. It is necessary to have a demonstration that all will grasp. It is of the utmost importance that this person and event catch the full emotions of all Parisians, or there will be no uprising great enough to overwhelm the King's Guard. Therefore I ask that you take note of the plans Mazarin is making for changes in the administration of France, Paris in particular, so that when the time comes, we will be able to rouse the people at once, and have the nobles prepared to act.

I admonish you, Pere Chape, to enlist more in our cause. Among the nobles our numbers continue to increase, and as they increase we take courage that our just cause will prevail, and we will bring down Mazarin and Queen Anne and rid France of the shame of her bastards. The existence of Louis XIV is a stigma on the face of France. To have to endure Richelieu's by-blow, to show that disgusting little boy respect is more humiliation than any well-born Frenchman should tolerate! How can we not act when the cause is so clear, and when France herself is in great danger from traitors and foreigners within the court and on the Throne?

Take heart, and be bold in all you do. We who seek to restore honor and glory to France uphold your actions and encourage you to persevere. Use my words to fire others, if it will be useful for you. It is not yet safe to reveal my identity to the world, but the day is not far off when all will know me and those who follow me, and they will flock to our lily banner in triumph as France is once again truly French and not a vassal of Spain and Italy.

With my commendation and blessing,

Le Fouet

On the 29th day of August, 1646.
Destroy this.

· 2 ·

By the end of the first week in October the leaves were changing, turning the woods near Chatillon to all the colors of good wine—dark red, bright red, gold, and straw yellow. The scent of earth was on the wind, and the evenings were chilly with the first hint of winter.

"An early autumn," said Charles as they strolled through the small vineyard attached to Eblouir.

"Yes," said Olivia distantly. She looked over her shoulder, then turned to him again and smiled. "Forgive me. I am nervous and . . ." Her gesture finished the thought.

"Why would anyone follow you?" Charles asked, putting a protective arm around her waist. "Aside from the fact that you are the most beautiful woman in the world, of course."

She rested her head on his shoulder, but her smile faded. "That's not it," she told him seriously. "I wanted to believe it was the result of all the troubles Mazarin is having, that I am catching it from him, like a cough."

"You never cough," said Charles.

"Sometimes," she corrected him. "But not often. I am never ill." Her eyes once again grew distant. "There is something here, something wrong. I sense it."

"Women sense things," said Charles, stopping and taking her in his arms. "I'd rather you sense me." He tweaked a tendril of her crimped hair. "I don't have much time. Mazarin is sending me on another mission in a day or two. He allowed me as much time as he could to be with you, but there isn't much to spare."

"I know," she said, for they had discussed this when he arrived a few hours earlier. "I wish there were more time. I wish we had all your lifetime to be together. Then it wouldn't be so hard to know the time will come when we will no longer be lovers." She was surprised to hear herself say this, and more surprised to realize it was true.

"We will always be lovers," said Charles. "Don't joke about that, Olivia."

"I'm not joking. I've told you that once you come to my life, we will no longer be able to be lovers. Those of our blood require life; it is the one thing we do not have to give." She touched his chin, remembering that he had shaved off his beard for her. "You are so dear to me."

His arms tightened. "You are life to me." His lips were more persuasive than his words. Their tongues met, tantalizing, making promises for more to follow. As they moved apart, Charles whispered to her, "I will have you for eternity, Olivia."

"Eternity?" She laughed gently. "Aren't you afraid I would bore you, after a few centuries?"

"Never," he said, without a trace of cajolery. "Listen to me, Olivia," he said, stopping in front of her and facing her with determination. "You tell me that you have lived for more than fifteen hundred years. Very well. I cannot imagine that, but I believe you because you tell me it is true. As difficult as it is for me to imagine all that time, it is more difficult still to think of a time, now, or thousands of years from now, when you would bore me. You are everything I have dreamed of, and all the things I have longed for in a woman and despaired of finding. Nothing about you bores me. You never could. You never will."

What was it about this young—very young—man that compelled her so? Olivia asked herself as she had every night since they had first become lovers. Why should he, of all the men she had known down the years, have the power to captivate her, to hold her? It was not his youth: she had rid herself of the folly of mistaking youth for character more than a millennium ago. It was not simply his ardor or his desire, or his damned flying eyebrows. It was *him*; it was that Charles de Batz-Castelmore d'Artagnan was Charles de Batz-Castelmore d'Artagnan. "I love you, Charles," she said, her hazel eyes intent on his bright brown ones.

He grinned, and there was passion in his eyes. "Why not go in now? Why not fill that shocking bath of yours and loll about like the Romans of old?" His brows lifted at the corners. "Is that what you Romans really did? loll about in hot water and eat grapes?"

"Occasionally. Most of the time I tried to think of ways to avoid my husband and the men he . . . he brought to me." She felt his arm harden against her back.

"I would wish that husband of yours were alive today so that I could have the honor of killing him." He pointed toward the terrace of the chateau. "There's your major domo." As he waved back to Niklos, he said to Olivia, "Was he ever your lover?"

"That was a long, long time ago. And he did not change because of me; he is not of my blood, if that is what you're asking." She broke away from him, walking a little faster through the rows of vines. "We have finished the harvest," she remarked to Charles. "You should have smelled these fields a week ago. The air was enough to make everyone tipsy."

"And you?" Charles asked as he followed her. "Did it make you tipsy?"

She started up the steps to the terrace. "I don't know. I am not sure it is possible for me to be tipsy, now. Or not from smelling wine." She glanced toward Niklos and saw that he was frowning. "What is it?"

Niklos motioned her to come nearer, and to speak softly. "This was brought this afternoon," he said, handing a packet of papers to her. "From Tours."

"Tours?" Olivia repeated, motioning to Charles to approach. She broke the seal on the packet and spread out the contents to read. "There have been more accidents," she said in a still, clear voice. "Five horses have been killed and one of the cottages has collapsed." She continued to read. "Perceval has been hurt: this is from Abbe Gottard. They have taken Perceval to Sacres Innocentes. His leg was broken."

"Octave?" asked Niklos. "Would he harm his own brother?"

"I don't think so," said Olivia, shaking her head in concern. "That is what troubles me. If it is not Octave, then who is it?"

"Mazarin has enemies in France and you are part of his embassy," said Niklos in a colorless tone.

Charles bristled. "Mazarin would not knowingly expose Bondame Clemens to any risk."

"Certainly he would," said Olivia. "He warned me of the risks when he sent me here, and he has never said that we were safe here." She put her hand on Charles' arm to stop another outburst. "I will have to send him word. Oh, not by you, Charles. You have tasks in other places. I will send Meres." Her face became set. "And I want you, Niklos, to go to Tours and find out how Perceval fares. Discover, if you can, what happened and who was the cause."

"When?" asked Niklos sharply.

"Tonight. Ride as long as you can. Meres can leave in the morning." She refolded the letters. "Put these in my study. I want to go over them before I notify the Cardinal of these events."

"And you?" Niklos demanded of Olivia. "What are you planning to do?"

"Remain here," she said, looking a trifle startled that Niklos would ask. "Charles has a little time, and so I will not be completely without protection while you are away."

"And once you leave?" Niklos asked Charles. "What then?"

Charles bristled. "I will request the Cardinal give me permission to remain with Bondame Clemens until you return, so that she will not be unguarded."

Olivia interrupted them before they could fall into useless arguing. "Will the both of you stop this?" She waited until the men visibly relaxed. "I am capable of handling arms, I know how to shoot, and I am not afraid to use a pistol if I must. I am reasonably competent with a sword. And I have been on my own before—as well you know, Niklos."

Niklos folded his arms. "And I have never been at ease when you were," he reminded her pointedly. "I am never more worried than when you must fend for yourself."

"Thank you for your confidence," said Olivia, her sarcasm softened by a chuckle. "But if it is my safety that distresses you, all the more reason to go to Tours and find out what threatens me there. Or would you rather I went?"

"Gia. Sta bene," said Niklos, lifting his hands in mock surrender. "I will leave tonight." He directed his next remarks to Charles. "Do your best to gain permission to remain here while I am gone. Surely Mazarin can be made to see the necessity of a guard here."

"I will dictate a request for the lackey to carry," said Charles to Niklos, his jaw square with determination.

"How thoughtful of you both to make these arrangements," said Olivia. "I know how to defend myself. I am not about to impose on Mazarin when he is already vulnerable. We can make appropriate arrangements here and inform the Cardinal of what we have done. Jumeau can prepare a full report for him; that ought to be sufficient until we learn more." She put her hand on Niklos' arm.

"I treasure you, old friend, and I am touched to know how much you are prepared to do for me, but, Niklos, I don't require it. I would rather not use more preparations than we need, if only because that would alert the Cardinal's enemies."

Charles rubbed at his chin. "You have a point, Olivia." He nodded to Niklos. "How quickly can you get word back from Tours with news if you travel at speed? Chartres the first day and Cloyes-sur-Loire the second? That puts you at Tours on the third day. You can be back in a week." He laid his hand on the hilt of his sword. "Can you do that?"

"If Perceval sees me and there is a reliable remount for me at the usual places, then yes. You have made the journey in that time, haven't you?" Niklos challenged. "Then I will be able to also."

Olivia regarded the two men. "Very well; leave as soon as you can, Niklos, and try to get to Tours in three days. I will give you authorization on the Cardinal's mandate to get remounts along the way; you know the places and you can pace your horses to them. I doubt Mazarin will think I have abused privilege if I do this."

"You will be gone before I come back," Niklos said to Charles. He touched Olivia's arm affectionately as he went on. "You are not the only one who values her. Make sure you leave her safe."

"I will not leave otherwise," Charles promised, and went on to Olivia. "No. Don't object. I won't dispute with you, love. I will not abandon you if you are in danger—do not ask it of me." He gave Niklos a little bow. "I am grateful to you."

"Do either of you wish to hear my opinion?" Olivia asked them, then held up her hand to keep them from answering. "I want Charles to depart as he has been ordered to do by Mazarin. If he does not, we will once again give warning to these enemies—whoever they are." She slipped her arm through Charles'. "I will welcome your protection, Charles, for as long as it is right for you to provide it. And I will do all that I can to ensure our safety. To begin, get Meres on his way, Niklos. Do it without display or remark, for it is not unusual for me to send a message to the Cardinal. Make this just another such errand. If there are any questions, dismiss them. You can add that if the message were urgent, surely Monsieur d'Artagnan would carry it. As it is, Meres, a lackey, is taking a simple report to Mazarin." She nodded her dismissal to Niklos, calling after him, "Ask them to fill my bath for me, will you?"

Niklos offered her an old-fashioned Roman salute, then continued on his way, humming as he went.

"He is more than your servant. He is devoted to you," said Charles when Niklos was gone.

"Does that upset you?" Olivia asked, unable to read his expression.

"No; I am . . . grateful to him." He put his hand on her shoulder, pressing with his fingers. "I am entrusted with your protection, and I have given my word. I don't want to leave you alone. Don't ask it of me."

"I don't," she said reasonably, giving him a steady look. "The Cardinal does, however, and you are his courier. There is no reason to fret: we have a few days, and we will use them to good advantage"—she felt his fingers tighten—"not just as lovers, but as comrades in the same battle."

Charles pulled her close to him. "If we must, we must," he said through a sigh. "I would prefer to spend it making love, but . . . but you are right."

She slipped away from him, keeping hold of his hand. "Come. I have some notes to write and then the bath will be ready for us. Meres will be on his way shortly, and so will Niklos. They need my messages. Then there will be nothing else to bother us."

Jacques Vidal Jumeau was arranging books in Olivia's study when she and Charles came through the door. He looked up quickly, dropping the volume he held. "Madame Clemens . . . I had no idea—"

Olivia indicated her writing table. "I am sorry to inconvenience you, Jumeau, but I have a few letters to attend to. Perhaps you might have one of the cooks give you an early supper while I write them?" She waited for his response, and noticed that his neck reddened at her suggestion.

"As you wish, Madame," he said with a bow of great and insulting civility. "I will avail myself of this opportunity. How pleasant to eat in the kitchen with the servants." This last was said through clenched teeth as Jumeau swept out of the room.

"What—?" Olivia looked after him in consternation. "What have I said to offend him so?" she asked Charles.

"Oh, you know clerics; they take on airs. He does not want to associate with servants. Most of them don't," said Charles offhandedly. "How do you bear that officious fellow, Olivia?"

She sat down at her writing table and took four sheets of fine paper from their box. As she opened the standish and selected her pen, she said, "I have little choice; he was sent here at the Cardinal's suggestion. Apparently Chape—you know the Augustinian that is part of Mazarin's embassy?—he thought it was a wise idea to have Jumeau here, though I am not certain why. Mazarin agreed, and I have no reason to protest." She dipped the pen in the ink and began to write. "I hope he is not too annoyed with me; I may need to enlist his aid once you are gone."

"Fine aid!" Charles scoffed. "To think of you depending on a cassocked freak like that one—" He broke off and took a turn about the room, as if his pacing would convey his feelings more than words.

"How do you mean a freak?" Olivia asked a little later when she had signed the first letter and sanded it. As she listened she drew out a stick of wax and lit a candle to melt it.

Charles stopped moving and looked at her. "He is not cut out for Holy Orders. He reminds me of a cat deprived of a mouse. It's in his mouth, the line of it. He is consumed with anger, not with zeal." He snapped his fingers. "I am no judge of clerics, Olivia. Pay no attention."

"That is precisely why I do pay attention," she said as she set the seal on the first and started the second letter.

"That makes no sense," he said fondly, stopping across the table from her and watching as she wrote. "Perhaps I should learn my letters better," he said as she completed the second note and sanded it.

"Is it necessary?" Olivia asked, curious to hear what he would answer.

"I don't know," he admitted, staring in fascination as she began the third letter, watching in silence while she wrote.

Meres had taken his message and left, Niklos was in the stable saddling Souris for the first leg of his ride to Chartres, Jumeau had returned from the kitchen somewhat mollified with word that Olivia's bath was full.

"Not that it is my place to deliver such notice," he added as he watched Olivia rise from her writing table.

"Then I thank you twice for your service," she said, motioning to Charles. "I want to wish Niklos a safe journey. I will join you directly. Wait for me in private." She left the room quickly, hoping that Charles would not decide to engage Jumeau in conversation.

Souris was restive but not nervous as Niklos led her out of the stable into the yard. Around them the vermilion sunset turned the world red.

"I will be as fast as I can," Niklos promised Olivia as he swung into the saddle.

"You mean you will be as fast as is safe," she corrected. "I will look for you in a week. If you have not returned in ten days, I will notify the Cardinal to send his Guard to find you." She took his extended hand in hers.

"You are troubled," said Niklos. "You will not say so, but I feel it in your hands."

She shook her head. "I do not know what I am. I feel I am walking on a board over a chasm, a board that shifts under my feet." Her voice became ironic. "I should be used to that sensation by now, wouldn't you think?"

"I think you do not want to admit you are in danger." He stared down at her. "Do you think you are in danger?"

"I think we are all in danger," she said somberly. "Take no risks, Niklos."

"Certainly no unnecessary ones," he promised with a wink. "And you, you take care. I am far less a target than you are, and they know where to find you."

"Whoever they are," she said darkly.

"Yes; whoever they are," said Niklos, echoing her tone. Then he let go of her hand and picked up the reins. "In a week. Keep safe, Olivia."

"And you," she said, stepping back so that he could clap his heels to Souris' sides, starting her into her strong, enduring trot. She watched him pass through the gates of Eblouir, then brought her hands to her eyes as if, after all these centuries, there might be tears there. Stop it, she ordered herself, and lowered her hands as she returned to the chateau, trying to shake off the desolation that swept over her.

Charles was waiting for her in the bath as she had expected, his chestnut hair wet and shining. "I have started already," he said, watching her slip out of her robe de chambre. "I wanted a chance to wash before you—" He did not go on as she sank into the large tub across from him.

"Yes?" she said to his silence.

He stared at her, his eyes enormous. It was as if he had never seen her before. "It would be my death to lose you, Olivia. Without you there is no life for me." His voice was husky with the emotion that seized him.

She looked at him through the steam. "What a strange thing, to think I am life. You know what I am, Charles."

"Life," he insisted, and moved toward her.

"Life," she repeated, wishing once more that she had the ability to weep. As their hands touched she gave a tiny cry.

Immediately he took her in his arms, his face against her hair. "What is it? What is this sorrow you feel, Olivia? Have I caused it?"

She shook her head. "Not you. Never you. Possibly it is my fear for you." Her lips were against his shoulder; she could taste his skin. "Charles, Charles."

He bent his head and kissed the lids of her eyes. "You are my love and my life, Olivia."

Her need for him was acute within her. Her hands quivered with the force of her need. She touched his nipples, and felt his flesh awaken under her fingers. As his hand moved to cup her breast, she shivered, shaken to her core. She tried to speak, but words failed her.

Charles felt her tremble, and drew her close to him. "Have I hurt you? Olivia? Have I done something to—"

"No," she whispered as she found her voice at last. "No. You have done nothing to hurt me." She answered his kisses with her own, her esurience growing as she opened her soul to him. "Your life is my life, Charles."

"As your blood is my blood," he answered, the urgency of his arousal suddenly unbearable. "It is too soon, but I must," he murmured, lifting her in the water so that she could fasten her legs around him. He clamped his jaw shut so that he would not shout for the joy of it as he went smoothly and deeply into her, ecstasy making him weak and powerful at once.

Olivia could not stop trembling. She was like one suffering a fevered delirium, the frenzy of rapture that seemed too great for mere flesh to contain. Her thoughts scattered before a passion more encompassing than reason; she gave herself up to it, a reverent visionary at worship. She clung to him, hardly aware of how they moved together so great was their union. When she felt him shudder and clasp her more closely she strove to sustain their gratification as she bent her head to his neck, her ardor turning to glorious serenity with his fulfillment.

The water was cooler when they finally left the bath. Both moved with easy languor, finding excuses to touch each other, to kiss, to laugh softly.

"Here," said Charles, tossing a drying sheet to Olivia. "Your hair—"

"No worse than yours," she replied as she started to rub the wetness from her hair.

"I'll have to find a comb," he said in mock complaint as he shook his head vigorously, sending spray over Olivia and the walls. "No wonder dogs do this when it rains."

"You're being foolish," she said, but it was not a criticism of him. She took two steps toward him and put her arms around his neck. "I hope with all my soul you will never regret loving me."

"If I regret loving you, then put me in a madhouse, where I belong. I would be a lunatic to regret loving you, Olivia." He held her near, but without the hectic desire he had felt earlier.

"It would kill me, I think, having you repudiate me." She let their kiss linger this time, and as they drew apart, she added quick, feathery kisses to the corner of his mouth and the edge of his jaw.

"You have nothing to fear," he promised her, his words so deep and still that at last she believed him. "I will love you until the day I die and all the days after that I am un-dead with you." He placed his right hand over his heart. "Before God and His Angels and the Hosts of Hell."

"Ah," she said, as if seconding him, unable to make light of his vow. In that moment she wondered how she had ever been able to doubt him, how she could have thought his youth was a barrier to their intimacy.

He looked down at her face and slowly, marveling, he smiled. "At last," he said, reading her thoughts in her eyes.

"There is a bond with the blood," she said very quietly.

"Yes, there is," he answered. He took the ends of her drying sheet in his hands and tied them behind his back. "There is a bond in the flesh, as well."

She laughed, too happy to cavil. "Come. Minette will be bringing me hot wine and a biscuit—"

"But you never eat," he objected.

"Then you can have the hot wine and biscuit," she said as she loosened the drying sheet. "But since she is new to my service, I do not want her thinking I am too strange. If she brings me hot wine and biscuits, she pays less attention to the meals I do not eat." Olivia started toward the door that led to her private apartments.

"Will this new maid be shocked if she finds me in your bed?" Charles asked, hesitating.

"She would probably be more shocked if she did not. She has been listening to the tales the other servants tell about us, and I believe she has been looking forward to your visit." She bent to pick up her robe de chambre from the bench, then opened the door. "Do not tease her, Charles. She has a squint and cannot help it; her eyes are weak."

"And she's a lady's maid?" Charles said skeptically as he followed her, making sure that his drying sheet was securely wrapped around him.

"There is nothing wrong with her close work, it is only a question of seeing things at a distance. Her sewing is remarkable and she tends clothes to perfection. And she does not ask too many questions about what I do for the Cardinal." She closed the door as Charles came up beside her. "She may have retired already."

"Or she may be in your bedroom, waiting to catch us," he said, giving her a quick kiss on the cheek. "Shall we give her something to see?"

Olivia returned his kiss but shook her head. "You are incorrigible," she said with pleasure. "Let me go in first, just in case you're right."

He shrugged but allowed Olivia to open the door. As she gasped, he came hastily to her side, his easy delight gone at the sound. "God and the Martyrs, what is it?" he asked.

She pointed; a biscuit lay on the floor at the foot of her bed, and beside it an empty wineglass had fallen. Next to them there was a hand, the nails a dusky blue. "Minette," Olivia said quietly, and went slowly toward the body.

"Jesu et Marie," muttered Charles as he crossed himself.

The maid was lying as if she had fallen off the bed, a rumpled heap of petticoats and linen fichu, her cap askew, her eyes open and staring, her lips the same blue as her nails.

"She was poisoned," said Olivia with quiet certainty.

"How do you know?" Charles asked, his mind reeling: while he and Olivia had been locked together in their exultation, this poor creature had been dying.

"Look at her hands. Nails that color mean poison. Her mouth, too." She reached out and took Charles' hand again. "We had best summon help and prepare another note for Mazarin," she said, resignation coming over her. The world was intruding again, leeching the bliss from her life, separating her and Charles. It was strange how much his nearness had come to mean to her, and how alone she felt when he was not with her.

"Tonight?" Charles pleaded, feeling his jubilation slip away from him as he stared at the corpse.

Olivia nodded, knowing that they both had duties to fulfill. "But you need not leave until morning. I will have the servants tend to her, and we can sleep in your chamber. That will give us a little more time. There is nothing we can do before morning, except move her body. The magistrate will not come until then." She bent and picked up the wineglass. "Poor Minette."

Charles spoke sharply, saying the thing he dreaded. "That was your wine she drank."

"Yes," Olivia said as she turned the glass in her fingers. "I know."

*　　*　　*

Text of a letter from Gennaro Colonna to his second cousin Jules Mazarin, written in Italian.

To my esteemed relative, the First Minister of France, Jules, Cardinal Mazarin, my greetings and much-belated thanks for the interest you have taken in my welfare. I have only now come to appreciate your efforts on my behalf, and I wish to inform you of my gratitude for all you have done.

Let me tell you how this comes about: the company of fighting men in which I was enrolled was ordered into the coastal mountains on the west side of the southern Americas, to the place where the Incas live. During our journey here—partly by sea, partly over-

land—I took a fever. It was severe, and it did not improve. The physician of the company feared for my life and my companions were ready to dig my grave by the time we reached our destination. I remember little of the travel, for the illness had me in its grip and I was often not wholly in my right mind. Oftentimes I was taken with chills that left me palsied and weak as a sick puppy; other times I burned with fever and raged. It is not remarkable that my comrades despaired of my life and were more willing to send for a priest than another physician.

Yet, to my everlasting thankfulness, a physician came. He was with another party of soldiers and priests, and he had been in these mountains for almost ten years. He was identified as a tertiary Brother of the Carmelite Order, serving religious and soldiers with equal deliberation. Being a tertiary, he is not bound by monkish vows, but lives with the Carmelites and follows their Rule as far as he is able, as he was not born Catholic. He travels with the monks and treats those whose wounds or illness require his skills. He recognized my malady and at once set about to procure cinchona bark. He told me that Pedro Barba had used this bark to cure la Condessa de Chinchon, and as it returned her to health so it would return me. It mattered little to me, for I was certain that I would die and that God had numbered me with the goats bound for Hell. I tried to resign myself to death and damnation, but took the elixir given me by this tertiary Brother. Either from his skill as a physician or the Grace of God, or both, I began to recover.

It is now two months since I made my first improvement. I am not yet strong enough to fight with my company, but I am able to aid my physician in his treating others, and I have found great solace in this. San Germanno—for that is the name of the physician who has cured me—tells me I have some ability as a physician and has suggested that I take up the study. I have given him my word to consider this. Before I was taken with fever, I might have dismissed the notion—to be candid, it would have seemed ridiculous to me—but now, having come so near death, I find I cannot ignore what I have survived, or the suffering it gave me. In six months I have sworn to give San Germanno my answer, and while I am weighing my decision, I have promised to continue to assist him, to learn from him, although I know I will never attain his degree of ability. Daily I am amazed at the capabilities of this man, whose genius exceeds all physicians I have known of before now. I have asked him where he came by this extraordinary skill and he has said that he learned it in Egypt.

I mention this man not only because he has saved my life and shown me another way to live, but because he claims to know one of your embassy, the Roman widow Bondama Clemens. He has informed me he knew her when she was much younger and that he has maintained an occasional correspondence with her over the years. From what he tells me, they are relatives of one sort or another, for he has said that he and she share the bond of blood. I ask that you commend me to Bondama Clemens and convey my admiration for her relative to her. Surely one such as San Germanno is a credit to any family, and she must know that she is blessed to be of the same blood as he.

That brings me to my last observation of this letter: in the past I have regarded your instruction as unwelcome and ludicrous, and I have been inclined to dismiss everything you were kind enough to impart to me. Now I am aware that I have been worse than lax in my behavior and my thinking. You have not been a bothersome intruder, but a pardoning sage, willing to try to pull me back from the brink I was so determined to cast myself over. I wish you to know that I truly value all that you have striven to do for me, and in future you will find me an attentive and grateful student, eager for instruction.

This letter will be carried by Frey Estanislao on the ship Los Sacramentos, bound for Spain in ten days. I pray passage will be swift and the seas quiet, so that you may receive this before the start of Lent next spring.

It is presently my intention, should I be able to progress as a physician, to take my mentor as my example and become a tertiary Brother of the Carmelites. I will not be beyond the reach of my family that way, and will have no monkish vows to uphold if the family makes other plans for me. In time, that may change, but for now, I believe that I was saved for more reason than whim, and I know I have turned away from all that was worthy in my life and endangered my body and the salvation of my soul. No more need you or any others of our family fear for me. I have seen the danger at last, and I have drawn back from it as I would from the fires of Hell itself. Your prayers have been heard, cousin, and I hope with all my heart that my previous abuse had not made me odious to you so that my awakening has come too late for friendship between us.

Every night and every morning I number your name in my prayers. I beg you not to shut me out of your heart, but to accept *me, penitent, as one who seeks your guidance. If you continue to pray for me, then petition Madre Maria and San Lucca to aid my learning so that I may, in time, be a capable physician.*

Your cousin, in contrition,
Gennaro Colonna
On the first day of November, 1646.

· 3 ·

There was a pelting rain slanting in on the north wind that turned the whole world dark grey; Paris looked like a charcoal sketch by the time Montlezun de Besmaux and d'Artagnan answered the summons to meet with Mazarin in his palace.

"Do you know why we have been sent for?" Montlezun de Besmaux demanded of Charles as they presented themselves to the chief lackey.

"His Eminence does not confide in me," said the chief lackey in tones intended to stop all speculation. He indicated a small antechamber where two branches of candles burned and a bottle of wine stood open. "If you will wait here until I come for you?"

Charles nodded his acknowledgement and led the way into the little room. "At least it's warm," he said, going to stand by the hearth. "I was thinking of asking for my cloak back."

"But it's wet," said Montlezun de Besmaux, sounding offended.

"True. But it is also dry," said Charles as he went to pour the wine. "You'll have some?"

Montlezun de Besmaux gave a nervous gesture of acceptance. "How long will he keep us waiting, do you think? Very long?"

"As long as he wishes," said Charles, holding out one of the glasses to Montlezun de Besmaux.

After two quick sips of wine, Montlezun de Besmaux began to pace, his free hand moving restlessly over his mantle, the hilt of his sword, the lace at his wrists. "I wish I knew why we are here. I don't like this. Why should he send for both of us like this, and then keep us waiting? Are you sure you do not know what the Cardinal wants?"

"I have told you before," Charles said with no attempt to disguise his irritation, "I have no more idea than you do."

"But it is so unusual," objected Montlezun de Besmaux. "He has not called both of us with so little notice before." He tugged at his mantle again, then twitched the lace at his neck. "I did not have time to dress properly."

"Saint Etienne give me patience," said Charles. "You are presentable. You are wearing your mantle. Your hat is wet, but it is raining. You need nothing more than this for a correct appearance. The Cardinal does not employ us because of our clothes." As he spoke, he hoped that Mazarin would finally pay the bonus he had promised his couriers at Christmas; a month had gone by and still he had seen no gold.

"I do not like this," Montlezun de Besmaux said in an undervoice. "Why both of us?"

Charles rounded on him. "I know no more now that I did when the message arrived. We are the Cardinal's couriers. We are at his disposal. We serve him at his pleasure. If His Eminence wishes us to sit here for the next two days, it is what we will do." He looked up as the chief lackey returned to the antechamber.

After a grave bow of just the right mixture of superiority and servility, the chief lackey said, "Cardinal Mazarin begs you will excuse the delay, but he is currently entertaining the suite of the Dutch Ambassador and cannot absent himself quite yet. I will return when he is ready to speak with you." He glanced at the bottle of wine. "I am to see you have refreshments and drink. I will have another bottle sent, and a plate of meat pastries." He lowered his head without any loss of dignity, and left them alone again.

"You see?" Charles said when the chief lackey had departed. "We are here at the Cardinal's convenience, not our own. We might as well enjoy the fire and the wine."

"And the meat pastries, if they send any," said Montlezun de Besmaux. "I hope that Mazarin is not all night with the Dutch Ambassador and his suite. What need has he to speak with them, in any case?"

"He is First Minister of France," Charles said as if addressing a wayward child. "Would you rather leave the task to one of the Ducs? You know what would happen then—there would be war tomorrow." He took a long drink. "And perhaps then we could be Musqueteers again."

"Musqueteers!" Montlezun de Besmaux exclaimed derisively. "Oh, yes. No doubt you long for another campaign, with treks that last for days in dust and mud, and bad food and water, with guns and wounds and death waiting for us."

"And glory," said Charles simply. "I do miss battle. I am a soldier and that is what I wish most to do, serve France and the King on the field of honor."

Montlezun de Besmaux finished off his wine and poured more. "You are a fool. There is no reason to fight but to gain power and influence. War is fought for power and influence, and those of us who fight should keep those objectives in mind, or we are nothing more than burnt offerings, nor do we deserve to be anything more. If power and influence cannot be had, then battle is useless." He glowered at Charles, daring him to contradict him. "You know I speak the truth."

Charles was about to give Montlezun de Besmaux a cutting retort when the door opened and a priest stepped into the room.

"Forgive me this interruption," said Pere Chape. "I have been sent by His Eminence to escort one of you to his presence." He looked from Charles to Montlezun de Besmaux. "Which one of you wishes to be first? The Cardinal expressed no preference."

Montlezun de Besmaux waved to Charles. "I leave the first assault to you, since you are so fond of battle," he said as he lifted his glass in an ironic toast. "When you are finished, you may tell me what I have to contend with."

Charles was about to refuse, then hitched his shoulder. "Why not?" he said, and favored Pere Chape with an extravagant bow. "I place myself in your hands, mon Pere." He cast a quick, scornful look at Montlezun de Besmaux. "When I return I will do what I can to put your fears to rest."

"Many thanks," said Montlezun de Besmaux imperviously.

Pere Chape held the door open. "Then come with me, Monsieur . . . I fear I do not know which of you is—"

"I am d'Artagnan," said Charles. "He is Montlezun de Besmaux." He gave a slight bow to his fellow courier, then stepped into the hallway behind Pere Chape. "It is unusual for His Eminence to call both of us to him at the same time," he observed in the hope that Pere Chape might help to prepare him for whatever was to come.

"It has been a strange day, and this evening is no different," said Pere Chape. He was not walking quickly or with any apparent purpose. "We have a short time to ourselves. The Cardinal will not be in his private study quite yet."

"Then why escort me now?" Charles wondered aloud.

"He wishes not to have to wait for you," said Pere Chape, his face showing mock dismay. "It is the fate of those of us who serve the great ones to be always at their beck and call."

"Of course," said Charles, curious enough to add, "Do you know what he wants of me?"

"No," said Pere Chape. He led the way up a narrow staircase. "But there are many great ones who are not so capricious in their demands, aren't there?"

Charles stopped at once, halfway up the flight of stairs. "What do you mean?"

"I mean," said Pere Chape with care, "that the Cardinal is inclined to be unreasonable in his demands, and those who are in his employ often find—"

In three quick steps Charles was beside Pere Chape, one hand on his sword, the other at the priest's throat. "Forgive my impertinence, mon Pere," he said as he shoved the priest back against the wall. "You must not say such things to me, even in jest. I am the sworn courier of the First Minister of France and I find no humor in such remarks."

Pere Chape was immobile with fear. "Monsieur," he panted as Charles loosened his hold just enough to permit him to speak. "You . . . you mistook my meaning."

"Then you must pardon me," said Charles relentlessly. "It is my vow, you see. I have given my word to God and the King that I am the true servant of His Majesty and His Eminence. So you fail to amuse me with your wit, mon Pere." His hand tightened again. "It was your wit, was it not? that made you speak as you did."

Pere Chape managed to nod decisively twice, his face going pale as he saw the determination in Charles' eyes. He wriggled under the pressure of Charles' hand. "It . . . it is a bad . . . a bad joke. I never . . . never intended—" He stopped as Charles released him.

"Certainly you never intended any disrespect or disloyalty to the Cardinal, did you?" Charles held him now with the force of his eyes. "I misunderstood your purpose. Didn't I?"

Pere Chape smoothed the front of his habit and tried to restore his dignity. "Most certainly," he said huffily. "You cannot believe that I, a priest and a servant of His Eminence, would compromise the Cardinal?"

"Because," said Charles in the same light, firm tone, "if I thought you had done so, I would be obliged to mention it to His Eminence. But," he went on less harshly, "if I have your word that you—as priest and servant—intended nothing more than amusement, I will not have to speak of this to His Eminence." He gave Pere Chape a speculative look. "Well? What am I to do, mon Pere?"

Pere Chape turned away from him. "It was a . . . jest. A poor one, I admit. But . . ." He put his hand to his throat as if to protect himself from further assault.

"But?" Charles prompted.

"I . . . suppose I had to make it. Your pardon, Monsieur." He had almost regained his composure. With sudden decision he moved away up the stairs, leaving Charles to follow after, his brow creased with thought.

"Certainly," Charles said distantly, distracted by the turmoil in his mind. Why had Mazarin tried to test him in this way? Did he suspect he was being betrayed? How could he believe that he, Charles de Batz-Castelmore d'Artagnan, would be party to such dishonor? A little of these reflections showed in his eyes. Mazarin had chosen Charles as his courier and had accepted his oath to himself and the King. What had caused him to question that oath now?

"It is the second door," said Pere Chape, indicating the narrow passage off the corridor. "There is a guard at the far end; no one may enter or leave unobserved." He sketched a blessing in Charles' direction. "May God guide you."

"And you, mon Pere," said Charles, going toward the indicated door with little more than a flick of his hand that could be taken as a salute. He stepped through the door to find Mazarin standing by the hearth, his face made ruddy by the fire. Charles dropped to his knee to kiss the Cardinal's ring.

"Good evening, my courier," Mazarin said as he motioned to Charles to rise. He selected one of three simple chairs and sat down, indicating that Charles was to sit as well. "I must speak to you. It is distressing."

So I guessed right, Charles told himself. The exchange with Pere Chape had been a test. "What is it I am to have the honor of doing for you and France?"

Mazarin shook his head, his dark hair showing a few wisps of grey now. "No courtesy, d'Artagnan. Courtesy means nothing when there are so many dangers at hand." He touched his long, large fingers to his forehead. "I understand from Bondame Clemens' major domo that no one has yet discovered how her maid came to be poisoned?"

"No," Charles said, all suggestion of levity or belligerence gone from him at once. "No."

"It bodes ill," Mazarin said, fingers still pressed to his head, his eyes closed. "I had hoped it was—" He stopped and looked at Charles as he lowered his hand. "It does not matter what I hoped."

Charles was puzzled, but he said only, "Eminence," to indicate that he was alert and listening closely.

Outside the door, Pere Chape lingered only a moment longer; he had no desire to have the guard report he had been listening to the private interview taking place within. He folded his hands piously and went quickly away from the room, back to the antechamber where Montlezun de Besmaux waited. As he entered the room, he saw that the servants had brought a plate of pastries and a loaf of bread.

"Back again?" Montlezun de Besmaux asked as he looked up from his wine. Without waiting for an answer he waved a hand toward the food. "This is very good. Have some."

"Thank you," said Pere Chape, "but no. I have had my evening meal, and now I fast until morning. But you," he went on as if the pastries were his own generosity and not the courtesy of Mazarin, "enjoy yourself. If you want more, you have only to tell me and I will send for some."

"Excellent," said Montlezun de Besmaux as he took a second meat pastry and bit it in half, sprinkling his collar and moustache with flakes from it. "The cooks here are very good," he said through his chewing.

"Yes, the Cardinal insists on it, as did Richelieu before him." He went and sat on the upholstered bench near the fire. "A miserable night to be out," he observed as Montlezun de Besmaux refilled his glass.

He paused in his pouring, giving a one-sided shrug. "Well, it is the fate of servants to wait upon their masters, isn't it? If His Eminence wished for us in the dead of night in a snowstorm d'Artagnan and I would be obliged to present ourselves." He set down the bottle and lifted his glass. "Still, servants can find ways to spare themselves the worst of those demands."

Pere Chape made himself appear uninterested. "I suppose it is possible," he was able to say after a moment to collect his thoughts.

"Of course it is. You know it as well as I do. It's only fools like d'Artagnan who cannot make their way in the world. If d'Artagnan wishes to stay a poor Gascon soldier, it's all one to me, but I have my sights on higher prizes than he." He took a long drink, finished off the pastry, and went on, warming to his subject. "Only an idiot seeks glory. A fighting man needs his reputation, certainly, but glory is for those who are blind martyrs. I do not intend to wear my mantle to the end of my days, and add nothing to the worth of my family. I will leave this world better-placed than I came into it; glory does not provide that, but good sense does."

Now Pere Chape was hopeful. "How do you mean?" he asked, masking his satisfaction with curiosity. "I understood that a mantle, a commission, and a sword was the greatest attainment a Gascon desired."

Montlezun de Besmaux's laughter was jeering. "There are those who believe in the honor of Kings, as well, and the sanctity of the Church—your pardon, mon Pere," he added as he remembered Chape was a priest.

"Oh, I do not disagree with you," Pere Chape said, wanting to encourage Montlezun de Besmaux to continue. "I am forced to agree that the Church is often called upon to act in matters which have little to do with her sacred offices here on earth." He crossed himself, taking care that Montlezun de Besmaux saw him do it. "And I have prayed many times for guidance when my position here demands . . ." He let his words die away.

"My point exactly." Montlezun de Besmaux pounced on the silence. "Every man must make his way as best he can. All the rest is sham." He bit another pastry in half.

Pere Chape sighed. "I am troubled, too, by what I have heard about the court, about the Queen Regent, and her sons." He lowered his head. "I pray and I pray, but I cannot find the answer."

"To what?" asked Montlezun de Besmaux.

"There are rumors," said Pere Chape darkly. "They will not be stilled. They say that Louis XIII of revered memory was so taken with his own . . . lusts, that he never made a wife of his Queen.

Never. And that the children she has are base-born." He coughed delicately. "If that is so, then the disgrace to France must be expunged."

Montlezun de Besmaux chuckled cynically. "Do you think this is the first time a bastard has worn a crown? Louis XIV is nothing more than a child. He is a pawn. His mother is a pawn. When the game is over, we'll see which side of the board has won. It will make little difference except to those who chose the wrong King." He tore off a section of bread and spread it with butter from the little crock provided.

"Do you truly believe that?" Pere Chape asked, uncertain about his next move: if Montlezun de Besmaux proved to be as adamant in his way as Charles d'Artagnan, he ran a great risk of being exposed.

Montlezun de Besmaux considered as he drank. "Some of what I think is the wine talking, but . . . yes, I am an ambitious man, and I am a realistic fellow. If the tide should turn, I will turn with it, as will any sensible man." He set down his glass and finished buttering his bread. "It's too soon to tell which way the tide is going."

"Is it?" asked Pere Chape, adding quickly, "I have not yet learned to measure these things; being here at court, I am often caught off guard." He thought the room was growing uncomfortably warm, but he said nothing, not wanting to break Montlezun de Besmaux's train of thought.

"Who wouldn't be?" said Montlezun de Besmaux. "Rather face cavalry than a courtier, that's what I think." His laughter was immoderate. "Not that I seek to face either. I'd prefer to serve the Cardinal as long as it is advisable."

"And how long is that?" Pere Chape inquired as if asking after Montlezun de Besmaux's health.

"As long as he is in a position to grant advancement and favor," was the prompt answer. "All else is lunacy." He began to chew his way through his slab of bread.

"I see," said Pere Chape. He could not make up his mind about this man. "Suppose the tide does turn, what then?"

"The only priest I will tell that to is my confessor, who cannot repeat it," said Montlezun de Besmaux. "I may be nothing more than a poor Gascon, but you will not trap me with so obvious a ploy." He reached for the wine bottle and saw that it was empty. "Is there more to be had?"

"Of course," said Pere Chape, rising and starting for the door. "Will the same do for you?"

"Anything will do for me, so long as it is not vinegar." He gestured extravagantly with his bread. "But hurry. Eating is thirsty work."

Pere Chape was annoyed at this change of interest. He was pleased at how well he had been able to draw Montlezun de Besmaux out, and was almost certain that he would be able to enlist him in his cause. But that had to wait on another bottle of wine. He hoped that Charles d'Artagnan would remain with Mazarin a little longer, so that he might learn more about Montlezun de Besmaux.

While Pere Chape went in search of the serving lackey, Mazarin was listening to Charles' impassioned plea for permission to remain with Olivia. "It is for her protection. If I am there, you will always be kept fully informed of what has occurred." He paced the length of the small room, slapping his gloves into the palm of his hand as he went. "I do not say that Niklos cannot be trusted—clearly he can, and he has proved that many times before—but he cannot be everywhere. Neither can I, but between us, it would be difficult for anyone to harm her, or any of your couriers and messengers who use her estates as meeting places."

Mazarin watched him with reserved interest. "This has nothing to do with your being her lover, of course."

Charles stopped pacing and faced the Cardinal directly. "It has almost everything to do with it, Eminence," he said softly, then continued, "Oh, as your courier I am sworn to protect you and your embassy as well as the documents I carry for you. If any of those in your suite were in as great danger as I fear Olivia is, I would recommend the same thing, for that is my duty to you as your courier."

"Very commendable," said Mazarin without inflection.

"But it is Olivia," Charles went on. "And she and I are lovers. I have my duty to you, as I have said; I have a duty to her as well." He went back to pacing. "She does not seek my protection—in fact, she is convinced it would make matters worse if she were obviously guarded—but I cannot leave her so vulnerable."

"And if I say you must," suggested Mazarin, his voice gone cold. "What then, d'Artagnan?"

Charles stood very still, facing the closed door. "Then I must do as you order me, or be dishonored."

"I am relieved to hear you say that," said Mazarin. He shifted a little in his chair. "I hope it may not come to that, but I am not sanguine."

"And if there are other attempts on her life, what then?" Charles demanded urgently. "Do not ask me to stand by and watch her be killed, Eminence."

"I will endeavor not to," said Mazarin, feeling exhausted. "The King is a little boy, more vulnerable than Olivia Clemens will ever be. He is the hope of France, and you are sworn to defend him with your life. Do no forget that oath." His stare was thoughtful.

"I will not," Charles promised him.

Mazarin accepted this. "Do not think too harshly of me; I will do what I can to guard Bondame Clemens; my word on it." He held out his hand, indicating that the interview was at an end. "There are documents that must be carried into the Low Countries. You will receive my mandate tomorrow, and leave the day after. You will be gone a fortnight. During that time I will send one of my own Guard to Eblouir. Does that satisfy you?"

Charles bowed in acquiescence. "Eminence."

"Send that other Gascon to me, d'Artagnan. I have tasks for him as well as for you." He watched as Charles knelt and kissed his ring, and very briefly he felt a pang of grief for his courier for no reason he could fathom. "You are a brave man, d'Artagnan. Do not let that be your downfall."

"Thank you, Eminence," Charles said as he bowed his way out of Mazarin's presence.

"So, are we in disgrace or is His Eminence seeking to impress us with his power over us?" Montlezun de Besmaux demanded with angry laughter as Charles returned to the antechamber.

"Neither," said Charles, taking in the other courier's state with a single sweeping glance. "But given your condition he might be persuaded to condemn us." He folded his arms and shook his head. "He is waiting. Where's the priest?"

"Gone to get more wine," said Montlezun de Besmaux. "He told me that he would bring more. Have the pastries," he offered grandly, indicating the last two on the plate. "They're very good."

"Not yet," said Charles, regarding Montlezun de Besmaux. "You had better put some water on your face. You've got crumbs everywhere." He did not want to show his disgust, but though he maintained his conduct, the tone of his voice gave him away.

"You are a fine one to hold yourself above me," said Montlezun de Besmaux haughtily. "The clothes on your back were bought by a woman, a rich widow, they tell me." He was never able to sneer for Charles launched himself across the room, striking Montlezun de Besmaux in the face with his gloves.

"If my oath allowed it, I would meet you, Gascon or no." His voice was low and tension made it rough. "And should you ever say such a thing again where anyone but I can hear you, I will ask you to name your friends. My oath does not require me to be dishonored, not for you or any man."

Montlezun de Besmaux stepped back so hastily that he almost tripped over the leg of the upholstered bench. His eyes were shiny with fright and wrath, and for an instant his hand hovered near the hilt of his sword. "No; no," he protested, raising his hand to where the gloves had struck him. "You misunderstood me, d'Artagnan. You insult me as well." He busied himself brushing crumbs from his collar. Where was that priest now that he had need of him? He watched Charles covertly and improvised. "I am . . . a bit drunk, I admit it. And like other men, my jests are not always made well when I drink." He tittered. "Why should I wish to insult you? We are both couriers. We have been Musqueteers. We are Gascons. Mere Marie and the Saints, I am as poor as you are. I only intended to say that I . . . that I wish I had a patron, one who would provide what His Eminence does not." He smoothed his moustache. "I have not yet received the gold we were promised at the Nativity, and my purse is as empty as Herod's treasure house."

Charles' voice remained low. "What I told you stands. I will not have my name, or the name of my mistress, defamed."

"What man would?" asked Montlezun de Besmaux, as if appealing to an audience. "You are very right. I did not realize my wit would fail me." He moved as far away from Charles as the room would permit, the imprint of the gloves becoming a bright swath above his beard. "It's the drink."

"If that is certain," said Charles with icy politeness, "then I excuse your remarks. And I will never hear them again, will I?" This last, so gently spoken, was heavy with threat.

"Naturally not," said Montlezun de Besmaux, becoming more sober with every breath. "It is a bad night; I must be tired, and the wine went to my head before I knew what was what." He glared at Charles. "Will that suffice, or must I grovel?"

Charles gave him a formal bow and a terrifying smile. "I am satisfied with your apology now. If it ever happens again, I will demand your life."

Montlezun de Besmaux swore in an undervoice, then looked directly at Charles. "You are a madman, d'Artagnan. Madmen should be humored." He licked the butter off his fingers as he watched Charles narrowly. "I must attend His Eminence."

"He is waiting," said Charles in oblique agreement.

"I wonder what he would think if I told him what has transpired here?" The gleem in his eyes was speculative and irate. "Considering your oath and all."

"The woman whose honor you impugned is part of his embassy," Charles pointed out coolly. "You might discover that His Eminence shares my opinion." He glanced at the door as it opened and Pere Chape, an open bottle of wine in his hands, came back into the antechamber.

"Oh!" exclaimed Pere Chape, startled to see the Cardinal's two couriers poised to do battle. "I did not know—"

Charles moved back, his attitude changing quickly. "Do not keep the Cardinal waiting, Montlezun de Besmaux. If there is anything more to say, we will discuss it later."

Montlezun de Besmaux's bow was so slight it was barely civil. "I have no doubt," he said as he swept from the room.

Pere Chape stared after him, sensing some of the violence developing between the two men. He put the bottle of wine down and regarded Charles. At last he said, "If you wish some—"

"No; but thank you," Charles said absently. He had come near the fire and stood staring down into the smoldering logs. After a short while, he asked, "Will His Eminence require my presence any further tonight?"

"I don't believe so," said Pere Chape, bemused by the question.

Charles reached for his plumed hat. "Then convey my compliments to Montlezun de Besmaux; I am going to return to my quarters." He started toward the door.

Pere Chape moved to detain him. "You ought to wait. It is advisable for you to wait." He had almost touched Charles' sleeve, but drew his hand back quickly, as if the fabric were hot. He made himself stop. "I will ask the lackey to bring your cloak," he offered, but made no move to do so. Then he added in a kind of panic, "And if there is any remark on your departure, be it on your head. I will not answer for you."

The smile Charles gave him was wide and fierce. "How kind you are," he said with all the false sincerity of a practiced courtier.

Watching him depart, Pere Chape did his best to appear self-effacing and apologetic; he had the nagging sense that he had not

convinced d'Artagnan of his disinterest. He started to give a blessing, but the words and the gestures would not come, and he remained still as Charles closed the door.

❊   ❊   ❊

Text of a letter from Isaac de Portau to Charles d'Artagnan.

To my good comrade-in-arms, my greetings.

*We have been chasing that infernal Elector Maximillian all over
his damned Bavaria. What the man expects to gain now I cannot
guess, for he is outnumbered and outmaneuvered, but continues to
fight on. Both we French and the Swedes have had our fill of this
place. The campaign is becoming boring: each time we meet his
forces, we win, he retreats, we give chase, and then we fight again.
It would be better if you were here instead of careering off in any
direction Mazarin sends you, but that would end the favor he
shows you. I would then have someone to laugh with.*

*I took a ball in the shoulder a week ago, and have come through
the fever with only laudable puss to show for it. The farrier attended
to my wound, which is why I have survived, I think. Left to the
physicians I would probably be laid in my grave by now: you know
what physicians are.*

*The result is, as you have probably guessed, that I am to be sent
back to Paris for three or four months while I recover my strength.
At least the season will be pleasant, not too hot as it is in high
summer, and not insufferably cold as it has been in winter. If Maximillian is brought to heel in that time, I will remain in Paris. That
will be a mixed blessing until the Musqueteers are reactivated, for
unless the Guard takes me on campaign, I will be on half pay, like
the rest of the Musqueteers not fighting with other companies. It is
my hope that you will have a few hours to share with me. A bottle*

of wine, a dish of soup, a joint of meat, what more could we ask? I will leave the women to you for the time being, until my arm does not hurt quite so much. Then we will see which of us has the greater success. If I must be inactive in our duty, I will put my attention to more pleasant tasks.

There are rumors again that the Cardinal will reinstate the Musqueteers. True, there have been such rumors before and I have not heard it from anyone I trust enough to believe, but the rumor is a persistent one, and so it may be that we will be back in the First Company again before this year is out. I confess that war is not the same without the Musqueteers. It is all well and good to fight with the Guard, but there is no glory in it. Glory comes with the musquet and the first position in battle. I need not tell you this, I know; we are of like thought in this matter.

I will be at the barracks of the Guards until I can find better lodging. I'd like a room at a tavern, somewhere near the Guards barracks if they are not already full of soldiers. If you hear of one such, tell me. Or better yet, tell the landlord and secure the place for me. I have money coming yet and will repay you for your trouble. Choose somewhere with good food and not too much noise, if that is possible. Yes, now that I read over it all, it seems to be a dream, but if you will do what you can you may be sure there will always be a place for you to go to ground if you must.

You told me before I left on this absurd campaign that you might be able to find me a good horse for a reasonable sum. I would greatly appreciate that now. My grey was shot out from under me last September and the dun was taken over by one of the Swedes and I have not seen her since. If I am to be of any use at all, I will need a horse—a good horse, mind you, strengthy and sensible—not one to balk at every shadow or a worn-down creature that trots no faster than an old dog.

I see I have asked quite a lot of you. No doubt I am imposing on our friendship. Well, I will not expect you to do all of the things I mention, but sitting here with my arm bound up, I am given to daydreaming, and you are reading the results. Do as you wish, and I will look forward to many evenings of wine and food and boasting. The rest is not so important as the camaraderie. We will drink to being Musqueteers again, and to the First Company, the best of the lot of them.

Isaac de Portau

On the 9th day of March, 1647.

· 4 ·

To celebrate the Resurrection, Anne of Austria allowed Mazarin to persuade her to come to Paris to give a grand fete. She brought her children with her and kept them constantly surrounded by nursemaids and King's Guards for the two weeks she required to prepare for the event.

After the glorious celebration of Easter Mass, she went at once to the Louvre, for she needed three hours to dress for the banquet and gala of the evening. She paid little attention to the whispers that followed her, or the occasional snubs she was given by the most arrogant of the nobles, though she promised herself that each of them would pay dearly for what they did.

The galleries and halls of the Louvre were ablaze with the light of thousands of candles. Lackeys given the task of making certain that none of the candles were extinguished went about with long poles in their hands, with lengths of fuse on the end. As the guests arrived in their finery, many were spattered with hot wax dripping from the chandeliers, but no one noticed this minor inconvenience, for the occasion was too splendid for such trivial complaint. Four little orchestras played in the largest room, each group of musicians playing music selected to represent the Four Humors. Two banquets were to be served, one at sunset and one at midnight. Five hundred guests were invited, and almost all of them attended.

Olivia arrived shortly after the first banquet was served. Her carriage, being one of the last to arrive, had to be taken to an inn on the other side of the Seine once she was delivered to the fete. Bueve warned her from his box that it would take at least an hour from the time she sent for her carriage until they could be certain to appear. "Take one of our own lackeys, Madame," he suggested for the fifth time.

"I will," she said as she stood beside the carriage looking up at him. "The Cardinal has already made arrangements." She handed him a gold coin in thanks for his service. "Do not drink too much while I am here," she warned him with a smile.

"Cider only, Madame," he promised, and glared at the two footmen clinging to the back of the coach. "And they will have no more than one brandy apiece, or I'll have the hide off them."

"Make sure the horses are fed and watered," she ordered, adding, "and clean their hooves before harnessing them tonight."

"Yes, Madame," said Bueve, touching the brim of his coachman's tricorn hat. Then he took the reins and started the carriage moving once more.

Four lackeys had watched this interchange expressionlessly. As soon as her carriage was gone, the senior lackey approached Olivia and bowed to her. "What name, Madame?" he asked with the most elegant bow.

"Bondame Atta Olivia Clemens, of Jules, Cardinal Mazarin's suite," she said formally as she followed the lackey indoors where she surrendered her dark velvet cloak to a very superior lady's maid.

In the light her gown was magnificent, more in the Roman style than the French; the bodice, outer sleeve, and overskirt were of the same bronze-colored damask silk, the corsage was embroidered with topazes and tourmalines. Her petticoat, stomacher, and undersleeves were of golden satin embellished with seedpearls. The high waist of the gown and the sleeve bands at the elbow were of dark brown velvet. Instead of lace cuffs, she had two wristbands of pearls and topazes in a rosette pattern. Her fawn-brown hair was simply dressed, the crimped locks falling in precise curls, the back of her hair done up in a complex knot contained by a golden net.

The lackey, who had been looking at finery all through the fading afternoon, stared at her. He recovered himself enough to repeat her name and pass this information to the herald who announced her.

Since more than half the guests were at dinner, Olivia's arrival did not attract much attention beyond the awe of the lackey. She found herself a place to sit near the orchestra playing music that was thought to be bellicose, and gave herself a little time to gather her wits while the rambunctious melodies surged around her.

"Madame Clemens," said a fair young man she did not recognize in accented French as he bowed to her. He was gorgeous in a cerulean blue satin coat lavishly laced in silver.

"You have the advantage of me, Monsieur," she answered, rising and favoring him with a moderate curtsy. "I fear you are not known to me."

He kissed her hand, hardly touching her fingers with his lips. "I am commanded by Cardinal Mazarin to bring you to him." He offered her his arm. "I am Jan Maarten Procopius," he told her. "My title these days is in dispute."

"The Low Countries are very uncertain," said Olivia, knowing that whatever side of the question the young man favored, he would agree with her.

"Yes." He drew her into a receiving room, saying as he brought a chair for her, "If things continue as they have gone thus far, I think I might be tempted to join Peter Stuyvesant's company in Nieuw Amsterdam." The look in his candid blue eyes was unhappy. "War or the New World," he said, sighing.

"How sad," she said, thinking of the number of times in her long life she had faced such decisions.

"If the war ends soon, it would be one thing. If it does not, then I must reconsider." He bowed to her and indicated the door. "I will fetch His Eminence."

Left alone, Olivia permitted herself a bemused smile. How like Mazarin to be so cautious, she thought. She looked around the room and was delighted to discover two alcoves on either side of the massive hearth that contained tall shelves full of books. Impulsively she rose and went into the nearer one, peering at the spines, for the alcove was in shadow and reading, even for her night-loving eyes, required concentration.

She had taken down a handsome volume of Gomez de Quevedo y Villegas' *La Historia de la vida del Buscon,* and was thumbing through it when she heard the door open. She was about to put the book down and greet Mazarin when she realized she did not recognize the voices.

"It is not wise for you to be seen with me," said the deeper of the two.

"No one knows of this. Look; we are alone. They are all eating. We are safer here than we will be again until midnight." This second man had a cultured voice, the voice of someone used to command. "By then, half these rooms will be filled with those having assignations. I don't want to try to talk while others are coupling."

Olivia retreated to the darkest part of the alcove, wondering if she could offer a plausible excuse for her presence if she needed one.

The man with the deeper voice was speaking. "But, Francois, it is not safe to mention Le Fouet here. There are too many spies. Have you seen how many Guards are in attendance? And there are more lackeys than are necessary."

"And who knows who Le Fouet is, but those who have reason to share our cause?" said Francois with an arrogant snort of laughter. "If a lackey hears Le Fouet, what does it mean to him?" He walked toward the fire.

In her hiding place, Olivia sank down to her knees, hoping that the light from the fire would not reflect on her shiny gown.

"It may mean something to his master when he reports it," said the first man. "Francois, I do not want to vex you, but I think it is ill-considered to do this. If you must gather more nobles to our cause, do not attempt to do it here."

"What better place?" Francois asked grandly. "Everyone is here, and there is no reason to remark upon it. The Spanish whore has given us our opportunity. If we had a few more to stand beside us, we could end this disgrace tonight." Fury had come into his voice, cold and implacable. "I have sworn to see honor restored to France, and I will do it or I will die."

"But not here," said the other man. "For the love of God, Francois, think a little." He pulled up a chair and sat down, his back to the fireplace. "You are not prepared yet."

"That is why I must speak to those who are here tonight. Do not be concerned, mon Duc. I will be at pains to mention no name but my own. Your role, and the role of the others, will not pass beyond this room." He paused. "Mon Duc, are you going to countenance this continued insult from our . . . hostess? Are you willing to bow down to her boys, knowing what you do?"

There was a brief pause, then the Duc answered. "I am not pleased with the situation; not many of us are. All the more reason for care. If we are exposed here—" His voice became even deeper. "You know my thoughts."

"If we do not take this opportunity, it will take us months to bring all our allies together; we are too scattered for direct action. On our estates we are powerful, it is true, but you and I know that the Italian Cardinal watches where we go and whom we see. Here there is no danger, not tonight. Tonight we could be able to do so much if you will give me permission to speak to those who wish to hear." Francois was now quite emphatic, his words coming quickly, like hammerblows.

Olivia held very still, listening intently. All her attention was fixed on what the two men were saying. She was hearing treason, treason that was especially dangerous to Mazarin, and therefore to her as well. She would not let herself think what would happen to her if the two men found her now.

"But that is the problem," said the Duc. "We do not know, not for a certainty, which among our numbers truly agrees with us and which may not. Not yet. We must be certain before we proceed. If we are not, then the Queen and her bastards live, the Italian lives, and we will be lucky to have a quick death. Do you wish to risk all that on convenience? for you are proposing just that."

Francois brought his foot down. "Yes!" he burst out. "Yes, yes, yes. We must be bold. Now is the time for us to act, to be rid of the Italian and the Spanish woman once and for all. You are too timid, mon Duc. I tell you: it can be accomplished tonight. This night."

"Or all might be destroyed," said le Duc gravely. "That is what I fear. I cannot say so more directly than this: we are not ready. If we forge ahead now, before we have strong commitments from those who say they might stand with us, then we are apt to fail. And if we fail here, Francois, that will be the end of us, of Le Fouet, of all we wish to do. We will not make ourselves martyrs to France, we will become the forgotten ones."

"They will rally to us," Francois insisted with zeal. "They will see that we are right and they will come to us with glad hearts." He stopped. "Is someone at the door?"

Olivia listened to him cross the room and open the door; all the while she did not want to admit that they might somehow be aware of her presence. She deliberately looked down at the floor instead of in the direction of either man; Sanct' Germain had told her fourteen hundred years ago that it was dangerous to stare at persons from hiding, especially their hands or heads. He had shown her how often such staring brought about discovery. She stared at the floor and listened.

"Well?" the Duc asked as Francois closed the door.

"I saw no one," he said, but with doubt. "Possibly someone—a servant—went by."

The Duc chuckled twice. "Are you still so certain you want to bring our cause to a head tonight? You are apprehensive when you think just one man might—I say might—be listening to our conversation. Yet you want to reveal your intentions to all the nobles here. You are inconsistent, my friend." The chair scraped as he again moved nearer the fire. "Take my advice. Wait. Listen to everyone you see tonight, and guide their talk to our advantage rather than rush blindly ahead. Be circumspect, Francois. Use this gala to examine more of those who have expressed their discontent with the present state of affairs. If they are like-minded or have similar complaints, tell them what you believe must be done to change this, and then take the steps that will be necessary to lay careful plans. Once the time comes to act, there will be no occasion to draw back. We will have a single opportunity. Then we will triumph or we will fall."

"We cannot fall," insisted Francois. "We have right with us." He strode around the room, expounding. "France has become nothing more than a vassal of her enemies, all because we have a Queen who is sister to our enemy in Spain, and she is guided by an Italian Eminence to raise up the children of Richelieu."

It was tempting, so tempting, to want to look, to discover who these two men were. She chided herself for her folly and hoped she would be able to remember their voices.

"Just the one son," said the Duc. "I am told she is determined to make sure the younger one shares the same vices as her husband did; she wants him to be a catamite. She clothes him in dresses and surrounds him with young men who crave unnaturally for boys." He spat. "Vile woman. After her marriage, she does this. It is unthinkable to do that to a second son. What if her Louis does not live to reign? France will be as it was before, with a King who cannot insure the succession. She was a married Queen without a husband, and she wishes another woman to live as she did." His chair scraped. "You asked me to give you my thoughts, and you have heard them." He walked away toward the door, his step weightier than Le Fouet's. Then he stopped. "You know, Francois, the son of Richelieu is not the worst King we might have. This is not the child of a groom or a lackey, but the First Minister of France. He was a true Frenchman, Richelieu; noble, and no man has guided the kingdom with a truer hand, little though you or I liked him."

"He was not of the Blood Royal," said Francois, shocked.

"No," agreed the Duc. "This is the sticking point for me. But there are many who may be willing to forget that, especially if this

Italian really can bring about peace at last. The Queen will not stop him making truces, because of her little boys. She does not want them faced with battle because they are so young. We have been at war for more than fifteen years; put a man on the Throne and we might war for another fifteen. The cost for such a venture will be thought too high by those who have smaller holdings or have lost more than you and I have. A boy may be a more acceptable King to many than any man grown." He opened the door. "Bon chance, Francois."

"But you are with me," Francois said desperately, his voice rising again. "Mon Duc, you have—"

"I have pledged you my life," said the Duc. "I will stand by that as binding for as long as there is breath in my body. I have sworn my honor, Francois. Are you so lost in our cause that you no longer know the worth of that vow? What I want to impress upon you is danger of acting as precipitously as you propose. Too many nobles remember de Soissons and the others. They know what happens to those who conspire against the Throne, and they will not hurry to the same fate. I tell you these things so that you will be ready to answer the arguments you may encounter, not because I believe them. But if you insist on questioning the Queen and her children, you will encounter objections, no matter how much Mazarin is distrusted or the Queen is despised."

"For love of Mere Marie, close that door!" ordered Francois in an undervoice. "Mon Dieu, why not announce to the world that I am Le Fouet? Close the door."

The door remained open. "We have been closeted too long; someone will notice," said the Duc in a polite but critical way. "For every spy you have in the Cardinal's household—and I recall you have at least three close to His Eminence—there are a dozen watching this gala tonight. Whatever you have learned, they will learn tenfold more." The Duc left the room, calling from the hall. "Will you join me? The orchestra is about to resume playing sanguine music in the next hall."

"A ridiculous conceit," snapped Francois, but he followed after the Duc, slamming the door behind him.

Olivia remained in her hiding place until she heard the distant sound of music. She rose to her feet, telling herself it was cowardly and foolish to think that one of the two men had remained to apprehend her, and was waiting for her to make herself known so that he could silence her. At last, holding the book she had been reading—she could throw it or use it as a shield—she stepped tentatively out of the dark alcove into the light from the hearth.

The room was empty: the only sign that anyone had been in it was a small gold button on the floor by the chair. Olivia had just knelt to pick it up when the door opened once more.

"Magna Mater!" she exclaimed, turning, the book at the ready to throw.

"Olivia," said Cardinal Mazarin, between amusement and consternation. He extended his ring to her, then offered her his hand to help her to her feet. "This is an unusual reception even for you."

Olivia stood, and turned to the mantel in order to set the book aside, then smoothing her clothes with unsteady hands, she directed her attention to Mazarin. "I apologize, Eminence," she said, then switched from French to Italian. "I have just passed several minutes listening to two men discuss the overthrow of you, amico Giulio, the Queen, and the Throne." As he looked at her in dismay, she went on to repeat as much as she could remember.

"But who were these men?" Mazarin asked when she had finished. He sank down into one of the chairs, crossing himself as he did. "They are so ready?" he asked distantly.

"You knew about them?" Olivia watched him closely, not entirely willing to trust him to answer truthfully.

"Yes," he said with a bitter smile. "There is no reason to deny it, not to you." He touched his hands together. "Le Fouet. Are you certain of that name?"

"Yes, and Francois," she said. "The other man was a Duc, but no name and no title were revealed." She held out the gold button on the palm of her hand. "One or the other of them was wearing this."

Mazarin took it out of her hand and laughed mirthlessly. "A single gold button. At a royal gala. We might as well look for a scrap of lace, or a pearl." He looked closely at the button. "Nothing remarkable."

"You were hoping for arms on the button?" Olivia suggested, her hazel eyes dancing more with danger than humor.

"It would have been useful," said Mazarin as he tucked the button away. "A Duc, possibly a Royal Duc," he mused. "Many of them are ambitious and a few are discontented. But which one? If I accuse the wrong man, I succeed only in turning another noble against me." He glanced toward the alcove. "Are you sure they did not know you heard them?"

"I am certain that I would not be speaking with you now if they had discovered me," said Olivia in a hard voice.

"And, of course, they know you are part of my embassy," he went on, more to himself than to her. "They would be suspicious if you were to show any undue attention to them."

"I don't know which 'them' they are," Olivia said bluntly.

"And it would be dangerous for you to attempt to find out," Mazarin finished for her, and continued in French, "I think it would be best if you were to have many conversations tonight. Nothing serious, nothing very long. That way, if you can recognize the voices, you may have a better chance of hearing them." He rose. "Why Francois? Why not something unusual, like Baltesard or Paulot or Ulisse? There are so man Francoises!"

A discreet knock on the door was followed at once by the chief lackey stepping inside, leaving the door open. "Eminence, the Queen urgently desires your attention."

Olivia gave Mazarin a sharp look, and finished his observation for him. "Why not have a single Duc here, as well," she recommended. "Then there would be no difficulty determining who he is." She gave a full curtsy as she kissed his ring, knowing that her position in his suite demanded such formality.

Mazarin blessed her. "We will speak later, Bondame Clemens," he said, then went to the lackey. "Take me to the Queen, and then place yourself at Bondame Clemens' disposal. She has much to do on my behalf."

The lackey bowed, first to Cardinal Mazarin, then to Olivia.

"I will be in the next hall," said Olivia as the lackey started to leave the room. She did not want to be in this little room any longer, for it suddenly seemed to her to be worse than a baited trap. "Find me there."

"Madame," said the lackey as he left with Mazarin.

For the next three hours, Olivia followed the Cardinal's instructions. She had rarely spoken to so many people in so little time as she did at the gala. Her conversation ranged over every topic she could think of, from the collapse in the price of tulip bulbs in the Low Countries some ten years ago, to the rumors of an outbreak of Black Plague in Spain, to the Dutch and English importing fur from Nieuw Amsterdam and Hartfort, to the preference for Belgian lace, to the Portuguese trading with Japan, to the comparative superiority of French and Italian velvets, to the Turkish efforts to wrest Crete from Venice, to Evangelista Torricelli's invention to measure the pressure of the air, to the difficulty of obtaining fine emeralds from India, to speculation on the possible fate of King Charles of England, to the victories of the French forces in the Rhineland.

Shortly before the midnight banquet was to be served, the chief lackey took Olivia once again for a private audience with Cardinal Mazarin, this time in the withdrawing room where the musicians kept the cases for their instruments and their part scores.

"Well?" Mazarin asked without preamble.

He was looking exhausted, Olivia thought, and decided that he must need sleep badly. "I cannot say," she answered. "I have been listening all evening, and I have heard a few conversations that were not flattering to you or the Queen, and one or two of the guests have said disparaging things about the King, but . . . I did not recognize the voices." She looked down at one of the sheets, a page of music for alto basanello, and wished that voices were as easily identified as music.

Mazarin accepted this with a resigned gesture. "I did not truly expect you to discover the men. I hoped, nothing more." He put his hand to his forehead. "My wits are out tonight." He laughed unhappily. "You know how it is with me—I love the chance to tell a story or a parable or a homily. Tonight, nothing stays in my mind. I cannot follow the thread of my own tales. I keep wondering if I am speaking to someone who is plotting to kill me, or someone who expects to replace the King on the Throne of France, or who has vowed to see the Queen Regent killed. It is worse than hearing a lying confession, or a perjured oath." His large, deep brown eyes were filled with tears. "What can I do that will not put every one of us in greater danger? I have prayed for guidance, but . . . nothing comes. And then I fear that I have erred, and that I am truly bringing disgrace to France, that my oath to Richelieu was false and I am filled with shame." He stopped himself, bringing himself back under full control. "I . . . I did not intend to speak of such things."

Olivia gave a faint smile of sympathy. "No. We never do." She folded her hands. "But I am relieved to know that I am not the only one with such doubts, Giulio," she said in Italian.

"E vero," he agreed. He watched her a little longer, evaluating her state of mind. "Do you wish to remain the rest of the evening?"

"No," she said bluntly. "I am . . . tired. I also fear that if I remain, those with Le Fouet might—"

He silenced her with a gesture. "No more risks, not tonight." He waved her toward the door. "I will send for you in the morning, and we will talk then, when everyone else is half asleep, and the servants are too busy gossiping about the gala to notice what you and I say."

"As you wish," she said, adding, "Where do we meet?"

"I will send you word," Mazarin told her. "After morning Mass. Be ready."

"I will," she said, curtsying formally once more. When she had kissed his ring she added, "If I knew who these people are, I would not be so frightened. It is not knowing that makes it so hard to endure."

There was a wistful, angry light in Mazarin's eyes. "I thought the Papal Court prepared me for this. I assumed I had seen all of the sins political life could bring. But it was not the same in Roma, where you could identify your enemies, if not their henchmen. I have come to wish for a vendetta, for all its blood, because there would not be this maddening courtesy to penetrate. In Roma, if a man is your enemy, he will acknowledge it in private, if not in public. But here in Paris, who is enemy and who is ally when all behave like . . . like puppets. 'God give you good day, Eminence,' 'A vastly fine entertainment, Eminence,' 'Most admirably done, Eminence,'" he mimicked, with bows. "How do you know which man is your friend?"

"Well, the Paris Parlement seems to be against you," Olivia offered ironically.

"They are," said Mazarin emphatically. "And I am grateful for that. I know their complaints. I know what they wish me to change. I know that they blame me and are suspicious of the Queen because we are foreigners. But the court, the nobles—that is where the power lies, and where the real traitors are. And I cannot find them."

Olivia met Mazarin's eyes with her own. "Will there be a rebellion? Will they try to bring down the King?"

"Like England?" Mazarin asked. "No. I don't think that is possible. They have no Oliver Cromwell and the Protestants in France are contained. Richelieu saw to that." He coughed once. "Protestants are only an inconvenience. The ones to fear are all gathered for this gala."

"'Kill them all; God will know His own'?" Olivia quoted the ferocious twelfth century bishop who had destroyed the city of Albi to be rid of the Catharists there.

Mazarin could not bring himself to laugh, though his mouth twitched at the corners. "Yes. It would be the simple answer, and I would no longer need to worry about the court. As it is, I see a lackey I don't recognize and I think he may have been sent to kill me. That is because I am Italian, and I have been taught to be wary of servants. The French are not like that. The courtiers—how am I to separate those who are trustworthy from those who are deadly?—are most troublesome. How do I conduct myself? What do I advise Queen Anne to do?" He favored Olivia with a bow as she rose. "I can no longer conceive of this court without treachery."

"No," said Olivia, recalling that treachery was not limited to this court, or this country, or this time, nor despair to Jules, Cardinal Mazarin. "No more can I."

❊   ❊   ❊

Text of a letter from Gaetano Fosso to Niklos Aulirios.

To the most respected major domo of the esteemed Bondama Clemens, who honors us both with her employ, Niklos Aulirios, I, Gaetano Fosso, serving in your stead at Senza Pari, send my greetings and the assurance steps have already been taken to comply with the requests you have sent.

As per your orders, we have dispatched riders with horses to the remount places you have indicated, with money to support them and a single groom apiece to care for them. The funds will pay for a full year at the remount places, and are to be renewed on your order, as I understand it. I do not mean to press or to question these instructions, but I am concerned, for it seems to me that since Bondama Clemens has her own stud farm at Tours, it would be more sensible for her to supply these remount stations from there rather than have her horses come all the way from Roma. I mention this not as refusal, but to satisfy those employed at Senza Pari who are as baffled as I am. There is also the matter of the lack of coaches required. With the horses sent, why was it that Bondama Clemens did not ask for her coaches as well? Or do these horses have nothing to do with her return to Roma and are instead to be put at the disposal of Cardinal Mazarini and his couriers and the couriers of the Vatican? I pray that some answer be provided in order to silence the gossip that had been thriving since the grooms and horses left here more than a week ago.

In answer to your inquiry, the current yearlings are to be culled before the end of May. Nine are very promising and will remain here, but there are thirteen others, five stallions and eight mares, that will be offered for sale, all but one of the stallions as geldings. One of the mares died with her foal at birthing. Both were underweight and the farrier guesses that the mare had succumbed to worms, and because of the worms her foal could not thrive. We have continued to use the preparation that Bondama Clemens has provided to reduce the incident of worms, but they cannot be stopped completely. This would appear to be one of those cases.

Yes, I concur. It would be most welcome to all of those of us who live at Senza Pari to have Bondama Clemens return to us. I have realized in the last month that fully half of those who are employed on the estate have never seen Bondama Clemens, and know of her only through what those of us who have been here more than ten years can tell them. This is a difficulty for us, since it is irregular enough to be employed by a woman, widow or not, let alone one serving in an embassy in a foreign country. There has been much speculation about her that I have done what I might to depress, for it is not wholly to Bondama Clemens' credit, and we must not permit those who work for her to speak of her disparagingly, though they have never met her.

Our hives have produced very well and the honey is of good color and sweetness. We will be able to get top price for it, and for the wine bottled last autumn, for the cellar-keeper informs me that all but two of the small barrels have produced an excellent wine, the two whites being a trifle sweeter than usual, which will require very delicate handling. The Loire Valley vines have at last produced vines and the cellar-master has said that the wine is of fine quality.

We will not have much of it for the next several years, but unless there is another blight, each vintage should be a bit larger than the last. I have ordered all but a few bottles cellared so that they might be served by Bondama Clemens when she returns.

To that end, we have taken over the wine cellar at her other estate, the Villa Vecchia that she has had restored. The cellars there are superior to the ones we have here, and are much larger as well. I have sent eight men to the Villa Vecchia to tend to the cellar and care for the wines.

The building itself is in much better repair than it was five years ago, and improvements will continue for some time. There are a total of twenty-six people permanently employed there, mostly carpenters and those with similar skills. I have even found an artisan skilled with mosaics, for as Bondama Clemens advised me long ago, the floors there are ancient, going back to the time of the Caesars. Restoring them is a long and difficult task, but if that is what Bondama Clemens truly desires, I will see it done. I have also instructed the staff here and those in residence there that they are to put themselves at the disposal of a Conte da San Germanno, who has been in the New World. Since we have no information on the time of his possible arrival, we will attempt to be prepared for him at any time. It is my understanding that he has a single servant traveling with him, and that will provide some indication of the man. I would appreciate other ways to identify this Conte properly, so that I will not make the error of entertaining and caring for the wrong man. I would feel the disgrace of that act most keenly.

I have had word from Avisa's sister, and the news she has sent is sad: that Avisa took a serious fever during the festivities of the Nativity. She was abed for ten days, during which time the physicians bled her thrice. According to what her sister writes through the good offices of her confessor, Avisa then rallied, but a short time later was again filled with fever and palsy, and quickly passed beyond the skill of the physicians attending her. She was given Extreme Unction while in a fevered trance and three days after died. She was buried before the beginning of Lent in the church Santa Croce where her sister and her family worship. I have sent the sum Bondama Clemens provides for the dead who have been in her employ. Avisa, being Bondama Clemens' maid for so long, deserves the highest sum, and I have taken the liberty of providing the marble for her marker as well, all in Bondama Clemens' name.

There have been other deaths as well. Our senior groom suffered an apoplexy and after a week was called to Grace. He was tended at Santissimo Redentore and I am certain no one could have had better care. Benedetto, the nephew of the farrier who was learning the trade, has suffered a wasting malady; one side of his body has become shrunken. The monks were ready to take him in, but he committed the ultimate sin and took his own life when he was told that his arm would never be strong. The wife of our Hungarian coachmaker has died in childbirth leaving him with four young children. We do not fear that he will find another woman to marry, and have been casting about for someone suitable, but I am aware of the warnings Bondama Clemens has issued on the place of stepchildren. They are to enjoy the same position and protection within a family as the children of second and third marriages. I will take care to see that her admonitions are heeded, both in finding an appropriate woman for him and in making arrangements for sums paid to the family. It is lamentable that this fine craftsman has had so great a loss; his life has been hard and his children must suffer with him, for which we all pray that God shows him mercy.

In regard to children, nine have died on the estate since the Nativity festival. Two of them drowned, one was killed by a fall of brick, the other six died of illnesses, two of them from children's pox. Also, the oldest son of the second dairyman has been struck blind by a fever, and whether or not he will regain his sight is in the hands of God. I have provided the payments Bondama Clemens has always given in these instances, and have made provision for the blind boy, so that he will not be a beggar. It is rare in a landlord to be as generous as Bondama Clemens, and it is my most fervent hope that she will never have cause to condemn her generosity. But the heart of women is soft, and it is not in their nature to deprive those in need, for they were made to serve men, and to care for the young.

I will be deeply pleased to welcome home Bondama Clemens. It has been too long since I have been able to pay my respects to her myself, and have the advantage of her instruction. She is a very worthy matron, and I am wholly at a loss to comprehend why she has gone unwed these long years, for she is young enough to be a prize any man might pride himself on winning. I am aware that her husband was a nobleman, but surely there are other noblemen of sufficient rank that a marriage could be arranged. It troubles me to see her alone, for it is too great a burden for women to be without the support and sense of a man to guide them. God has made them weak creatures, in need of the protection and care of men, as He has made men to be strong and capable that they may care for women. *It is not natural for Bondama Clemens to be so long without a mate if she is not called to Holy Orders.*

Forgive me for my blunt opinions, but I say nothing that is not intended for Bondama Clemens' good and for her protection. If she holds her husband's memory in such esteem, it would be more fitting for her to enter a religious community than to remain active in the world where she is at the mercy of nearly all the assaults and plagues that are the burdens of men. If her estate is somehow left that she cannot retain it if she marries again, let her approach Mazarini or one of the Cardinals she knows in Roma, for they are powerful enough to exert their influence with the magistrates on her behalf. There can be no disapproval of such an inquiry, given the time she has been widowed. She is not hoping to have a Will altered with her husband's pulse hardly stopped. I am certain that she would not have to sacrifice her entire inheritance if she married again. I have no doubt that the Cardinals are of a like mind with me and will urge her to find a new spouse if she is willing to ask them for their support. She has done much for them, and it is fitting that since they have employed her they give her the advantage of their protection for her service.

I await your next instructions and will provide my usual report in another two months. In the meantime, my prayers for the favor of God for Bondama Clemens and for you continue as they have for all the time you have lived in that foreign land, so far away from us. May you prosper and live in virtue and the gracious favor of the Saints and Martyrs.

> Gaetano Fosso
> acting major domo of Senza Pari

On the 24th day of May, 1647.

· 5 ·

Heat lay like a heavy, invisible hand on Tours, bringing all but the most necessary work to a halt. Spring had been warm, and now that June was almost over, summer was already making mid-day a furnace. Few travelers moved on the road, nor would they until the first shadows of evening made their comings and goings less torturous. At Olivia's stud farm, most of the horses kept to the shade of buildings and trees, their heads carried low, only their tails active against the constant torment of flies.

Olivia was occupied in the cellar, inventorying the materials stored there. "Why on earth did they keep these dried apples?" she asked Niklos as she held one of the desiccated little fruits out to him. "Look at it. It's more like a walnut than an apple. I don't think you could persuade the horses to eat it. There are dozens of them on that shelf. See?" She raised the lanthorn she carried, revealing at least thirty of the ancient apples. "Have them cleaned out, and any other dried fruit that is more than a year old. This is ridiculous!"

"They will be removed," said Niklos, tossing the apple once, then bringing it closer to his eyes. "How old is this, do you think?"

"Who knows?" she asked. "I would like to find a date or two on these various jars and bags. I cannot rid myself of the worry that most of them have lain here since before Richelieu was born. They certainly smell that old." Her nose wrinkled as she spoke, and in the next moment she suppressed a sneeze.

"If this is such a chore—" Niklos began.

"It is better than walking in the sunlight. And that has nothing to do with my native earth in my shoes, my friend; it has to do with the heat of the day."

"Then a nap, perhaps?" Niklos said, gesturing around the cellar. "Tell Perceval you want this cleaned and ordered down here. You have set a fine example: you've been down here all morning, and there are five sacks of things to be discarded." He indicated the sacks where they lay at the foot of the stairs. "They have to be disposed of, as well. You've made your point. Now let Perceval get around to his job."

"He's been very careful since he was hurt," she said, sighing a little. "I was afraid he was dead at first. Imagine being worried about Perceval." She shook her head in surprise.

"You have always been careful of those you employ," Niklos observed. "Remember that page in England? It would have been an easy thing to let him be caught with the silver he had stolen."

"And see him hanged?" Olivia asked, her hazel eyes growing serious. "No, thank you. Life is short and hard enough for those who have not changed." She looked at the list she had made.

"You're right," she allowed, then smiled. "In any case, I want an excuse to stop and yours is perfect. I will leave word for Perceval to tend to this, and I will spend an hour or two on my bed or in my bath."

"Not in the bath," Niklos said as he followed her toward the stairs. "For one thing, it would be no cooler than tepid, and for another, it is not fitting to ask servants to carry water in heat like this."

She nodded as he spoke. "Of course. I'll bathe tonight, when it is cooler and no one will faint for bringing those enormous tubs to the bath." Her eyes shone with memories. "A pity we cannot have spouts, as we did so long ago."

"That was another time," said Niklos as he added one more sack to the pile. "Possibly one day we will have them again."

Her face grew closed. "I have told myself that for more than a thousand years, but I have yet to see it. There are times when I wonder if I dreamed it all, and Roma were nothing more than a wish I had."

"It was real. It was real even when I was there, and by then the best was over." Niklos put his hand on her shoulder. "No despair, Olivia. We will be able to go home soon. Mazarin will not keep you here forever." He shone his lanthorn around the cellar once more. "They say there are tunnels down here, as well. I haven't been able to find them."

"Besides, where would they go? Who would use them?" She shivered. "Sometimes, in places like this, I remember my tomb." With a quick breath that was not quite a sob, she started up the stairs, motioning to Niklos to come after her. "And find Perceval for me, so that I can tell him what needs to be done."

"Very well," said Niklos, coming up the stairs behind her. "At least Perceval took your instructions to heart—you do have food enough for two months, if you are not too selective in your fare."

"Oh, yes, that was done well. But it might have been better if the cellar had been inventoried and cleaned before putting in what I ordered." She smiled as they reached the door, opening it herself instead of waiting for Niklos to do it for her. "The hinges need oil, too," she added at the low, metallic shriek.

"It would keep anyone from sneaking in through the cellar," Niklos said as philosophically as possible. "Consider what a difficult time a robber would have. No wonder Octave has stayed away from here."

"His brother has nothing to do with it?" Olivia asked as Niklos turned the large key in the lock and added it to the ones on the massive keyring hanging from his belt.

Niklos did not answer at once. "I don't know. I would have to see them together before giving an answer. I have no reason to think that Octave wishes Perceval harm, but Perceval will limp for the rest of his life, and it could be that Octave was the one who injured him, though not purposefully." He shoved his way through a stack of empty barrels. "This estate has cost you a lot of money these last two years, Olivia."

"Are you saying that the money has been lost foolishly?" she asked as they stepped into the pantry. The air was noticeably hotter and there was a faint, pervasive scent of rancid oil.

"No; I am saying that the estate should be making money, as it has in the past. The losses you have suffered here are not simply the misfortunes of agriculture, they are the result of deliberate attempts to compromise this estate." He looked around the kitchen. "You're right—the ovens need replacing, and that open hearth is much too old-fashioned. I will arrange for something new to be built here."

Olivia gestured her agreement, but was not yet willing to change the subject. "Do you think that it is the estate or the Cardinal or myself that brings this about?" she asked. "You have kept very silent on that question: it isn't like you, Niklos." She had crossed the kitchen and now stood at the entry to the antechamber to the dining room. "And don't tell me you haven't formed an opinion."

"I've formed several," said Niklos, guarded but affable. "That's the trouble. Every time I think I have sorted out the trouble, something else happens, and then I am at a loss once more." He went through the antechamber and into the dining room. It was not nearly as grand as the dining room at Eblouir or Senza Pari, but it was a pleasant place, with tall windows on the north side that fronted on a garden, now almost brought back under control. The table was small, seating only twelve, and the two sideboards were little more than trestle tables.

"How is that? Will you tell me?" Olivia pulled out one of the chairs and gestured Niklos to take the other. "I've been at a loss to understand it, myself."

Niklos sat down, and looked out into the garden for a short while before he replied. "If the estate is the target, then why has the estate been damaged? What neighbor, no matter how greedy, would damage the thing he wished to acquire? If it is Octave attempting to hide his activities here, then why bring attention to the place by causing so much misfortune? The magistrates have searched the estate four times, and that cannot be in Octave's interest if he is hiding his men here. If the intent of whoever is causing these mishaps and accidents is to compromise the Cardinal, how does killing half a dozen horses accomplish that? The couriers can demand remounts from any landholder in the area, so killing your horses would not stop them. The estate is not used much for meetings of officials and couriers; most of the time it is for rest and remount. So there is no advantage in rendering it suspicious, because such suspicion can only bring about a minor disaccommodation, which means next to nothing to the Cardinal. Then there is you, but who have you offended that this would be the response? You are not here often enough to be known, and it is not easy to have dedicated enemies if there is not direct confrontation at some point." He slapped his palm down on the surface of the table. "So. That leaves me with no answers at all."

"Then what have you decided?" Olivia asked him, leaning back in her chair and waiting.

"I think, perhaps, that one of the nobles who distrusts the Queen and Mazarin because they see them as foreigners has decided to act against all the foreigners who are allied with Mazarin and the Queen. I think that possibly it is the wish of this noble to isolate Mazarin and Queen Anne, so that they have no place to turn. Then the nobles might decide to have a proper rebellion, and bring about the downfall of the little King along with Mazarin and Queen Anne. There are others of the Blood Royal to take the Throne, and if the man I postulate exists, then he may have a preference among those of the Blood Royal, and wishes by these acts to secure influence with him."

"Quite a gamble," said Olivia when he had finished.

"If that is the reason, and if I have guessed correctly," he reminded her. "There is no indication that I am right. Just as there is no indication that I have stumbled upon the actual reason for what has taken place here." He hit the table again, but with less force than before. "Go lie down. Perceval will wait upon you in an hour or so. And I will have a little time to dine in private." He gave her a quick wink. "There is a plump kid, not one that would be saved. I have chosen it for myself." He got up, glancing toward the door. "There will be another patrol of the main buildings in two hours, when most of the staff will want to move again."

"Fine," said Olivia, leaving her chair. "Tell me when the patrol starts, will you, Niklos?" She looked apprehensive. "I don't know what to expect here. I used to think I did."

"Do you still want us to go armed?" Niklos asked.

"You, most certainly. I am not certain about the others." She put her hands to her hair and swept the limp tendril back from her face. "A pity one cannot rest in the cellar on a day like this. But that is too much like the tomb," she added. "And I would not want to make the servants here suspicious about me. They are frightened already."

"And that worries you, doesn't it?" Niklos regarded her with sympathy. "You are afraid that they might, somehow, stumble upon the truth, and then you would be a fugitive again." He saw her nod. "Rather be worried about what this destructive unknown is going to do next than what the staff might discover about you. Another bomb is more terrifying than a vampire, Olivia, even to these people."

She went to the door, her face revealing nothing of her fears. "No doubt you are right, Niklos, and I am letting myself be ruled by dread, not by reason." She pointed to the draperies secured at the corners of the windows. "Close those for me, will you? I hope it will help keep the room cooler. The view isn't as nice, but . . ."

"It also keeps out prying eyes," said Niklos as he went to do as she ordered. "A wise notion."

Olivia was able to laugh once as she left the dining room.

Niklos made certain the draperies were completely closed, and so he did not see the shadow in the garden that did not move with the other shadows, but slid away from the flowering shrubs and spindly new trees toward the rear of the chateau and the storage sheds away from the stable.

Under his habit—which was worse than a suit of armor on such a day—he carried three small bombs, each with a long fuse. He ignored the sweat that poured off him except when it ran into his eyes and made it hard to see. In his various searches on the grounds of the stud farm, he had discovered an old abandoned root cellar that was connected to one of the tunnels leading out of the cellar of the chateau. He had dug his way into the root cellar over the last two months, and now he was ready to have his revenge. Three bombs, he told himself. Three of them, set at intervals along the tunnel, each with fuses that would go off at the same time: the chateau might easily be destroyed. At the least it would be damaged, for the foundation would be wrecked. Bondama Atta Olivia Clemens would not be able to keep her stud farm. With luck, he would see the house fall in on her. He hurried toward the hole he had dug and then concealed with brush.

In spite of the heat he worked quickly, his body feeling strong but for the ache in his hip. He pulled the brush aside and set it up to screen his activities, and then he plunged through the small opening into the darkness of the old root cellar. He sat for a short while, letting the earth cool him, smelling the soft pungency of turnips and onions and cabbages long since turned to earth. When he no longer felt scalded by the sun, he made his way to the tunnel door, tugging it open in a hurried, angry way. The ladder leading downward was old and rickety, but Nino set himself on it without hesitation, going down into the darkness swiftly, his wrath greater than his caution. Once a rung broke under him, but he held on, and then eased himself the rest of the way.

He could not quite stand upright in the tunnel, and he knew that the air was bad. It would not take long, with the fuses cut so that all three bombs would go off at once. He panted as he worked, feeling chilly for the first time in days as the cool of the earth replaced the swelter above him.

The first bomb, the one nearest the door into the chateau cellars, was the hardest to place, for it had to be in a location that would make the fuse burn evenly. Nino cut a groove in the earthen floor to make sure that the fuse would remain lit, and he built up a little nest of pebbles to contain the bomb. The second one was set in the wall of the tunnel, the better to bring down more of the structure. The third, only three strides from the ladder out, was placed high up the wall, so that the explosion would be more jarring when it occurred. He reached the foot of the ladder, then took flint and steel from under his habit. He faltered at the first strike, but not the second, and the fuses glowed as they set about their deadly purpose.

This time Nino did not climb as well, his fright making him clumsy, his very need for haste causing him to fumble his way into the root cellar. He was panting, the sweat on him now stinking of fear, not heat. He lugged the door back into position, then hurried to the hole he had made and scrambled through it. He could not linger there safely, though he was sobbing for breath and his flesh was raw where he had scraped himself coming up the ladder. He left the brush where it was and staggered away from the root cellar.

"Frere Nino!" called Frere Servie from some little distance away. "My poor Brother, what has happened to you?" He came puffing across the open field, his face ruddy with heat and effort.

"Away!" Nino shouted, waving his arms to keep the monk from coming any nearer. "Trouble!"

It was the wrong thing to say. Frere Servie only moved more quickly. "Then we must help. God and the Saints, look at you!" he burst out as he got nearer. "Have you been captured by outlaws? Frere Nino, what has happened to you."

Nino shoved him, cursing as he did so. "Get away!" he insisted, trying to get out of range.

"But if there is trouble, we must give assistance," said Frere Servie in confusion, standing uncertainly much too close to the old root cellar.

"No!" he shouted, grabbing Frere Servie by the elbow and hauling him away. "You buggering old turd, it's going to explode!"

"Explode?" demanded Frere Servie, wrenching himself away from Nino. "What nonsense—"

The ground heaved up, then thudded back on itself. The noise, muffled at first, at once became an eruption. It was accompanied by shattering glass and then the groan and cracking of stone as the kitchen of the chateau shifted, then crumbled. Part of the west side of the chateau began to disintegrate, breaking away from the rest of the building like a section of cliff at last surrendering to the sea.

Frere Servie threw himself to the ground, his mouth open and distorted by a scream that no one heard, not even himself.

The roof of the chateau shed slates as if an enormous cat had clawed them loose. The kitchen was already lost under rubble, and partly sunk into the ground where a portion of the cellar had given way. The sound of hysterical whinnying and the thud of hooves was the first sound beyond the destruction of the house that Nino could hear. Only then did he realize he had crouched low as the building shattered. He got to his feet, paying no attention to Frere Servie, and started across the fields, toward the bridge that had been rebuilt just two months before. As he looked back, he saw a small herd of horses galloping away from the chateau in panic, a few of them headed for the place where Frere Servie lay in a helpless stupor.

How long would it be before he learned what happened to

Bondama Clemens? Nino avoided the gates, though monks were permitted to use them, for he did not want to have to answer any questions. He had found a break in the fence over a year ago and from time to time he used it, assuming poachers had put it there. He did not want to have to answer any questions about his disheveled appearance until he arrived at Sacres Innocentes, where he would be able to tell of the terrible explosion he and Frere Servie had witnessed. It was an effort not to whistle, and he swung his lame leg with gusto as he made his way toward the road that led back to the monastery.

When he saw a figure on the road ahead of him, Nino slowed down, and changed his stance to one who was suffering from great shock. He almost staggered on the narrow path, and he stopped, apparently to steady himself against a tree, but in fact to try to discern who was blocking the way.

"Bon Frere," said the man, taking off his enormous hat with the long plumes and bowing a little. "You seem to have come upon trouble."

Nino pressed one hand over his heart. "There was an explosion," he said faintly, pointing back toward the break in the fence.

"We heard it," said the man, and at a signal five more men stood behind him. "What occurred?"

"The chateau. There has been a bomb. Or"—belatedly he realized he had said too much—"some such thing," he added carefully. "I was a soldier once. It sounded like a bomb."

"Did it?" The man was not only tall, he was massive, a slab of a fellow with shoulders as wide as a horse. "Is that why you ran rather than give help?" He motioned to one of his companions. "Help the Brother to come closer, will you, Herve?"

One of the companions detached himself from the group. As he neared Nino, the long red scar on his cheek was revealed. "Come, Brother," said Herve, taking Nino firmly by the arm. "Come. Lean on me."

"I . . . I can walk for myself," said Nino, trying to keep from shaking. "It was . . . very terrible. Part of the house fell in."

The big man stood more straight, his eyes suddenly keen. "The chateau? Do you say it was damaged?"

Part of Nino was filled with pride of his accomplishment; it was all he could do not to boast of his bombs and what they had done. But something in the big man's eyes silenced him, and he shook his head numbly. "Part of the house . . . fell in."

"Blaise, Ignazet, Frasier, go see what has happened. Give what help you can. Go now. Hurry." He made a blunt gesture with his arm, and three men rushed away to do his bidding. "You," he went on, his baleful gaze now directed to Nino once again, "how does it happen that you are covered in dirt? How can it be, that you would run instead of giving aid?"

"I . . . I was filled with fear," said Nino, and it was for once the truth, for this large man was more threatening to him than the officers who had ordered him out of the army. "I am a weak man, and I ran." He hesitated. "I wanted to find help, to bring some-one . . ."

"Bring someone?" asked the big man sarcastically when Nino fell silent. "Who would you find on this trail?"

"I wanted . . . to get back to the monastery," he said, his voice rising in spite of his attempts to keep it under control. "I thought that the monks would come." He looked around, as if expecting to see the Brothers emerge from the trees as he spoke.

"Truly," said the other. "A gesture of . . . what? . . . compensation to those you left behind. A way to salvage a little virtue from this unmanly display?"

Nino longed to avenge the insults this man had given him. He wanted to set his clothes on fire, to fill his mouth with a bomb and watch it explode. He thought of the two bottles of wine he had hidden under the straw mattress in his cell at the monastery, and wished now he had brought one of them along. At last he was sure of himself. "I know I have been a coward, and I pray that God will forgive me. I entered His service to gain courage, and I have failed my God."

"You have," said the large man, one thick hand hooked under the bandolier slung across his chest. "You will have to answer to God for what you have done, but you will also have to answer to me." He rocked back on his heels. "If I learn that anyone was killed because of you—" He smiled instead of going on, and the smile made Nino shrink.

"Please, I must get some assistance." He looked at the scar-faced Herve who held him. "There are people hurt. I shouldn't have run away. I've sinned, running like this. I should minister to those who need me. If you come with me, we might do more—"

"Come with you?" the big man challenged. "I will go with you to the chateau. I want to know what has happened there. But I am not a fool, me. I will not go to the monastery with you, on the road for all the world to stare at me. I do not go where I can be seen." He came two rolling steps closer to Nino. "If I learn that anyone at the chateau was harmed, you will have to answer to me for it, and you will not enjoy it, I promise you."

"But what have I to do with that?" Nino asked, dreading the answer he would get.

"That is what I am going to find out," said the big man as he gestured to Herve. "Bring him along."

Nino wanted to shriek his protest, to insist that this large barbarian had no right to detain him. But he could feel the way Herve held his arm, and knew that the scarred man liked giving pain. He permitted himself to be led along quietly, while he cursed and blasphemed in his thoughts.

As they approached the break in the fence, one of the three men dispatched to bring information came running up. "Octave," he said to his leader, "we cannot find your brother, and a fire has broken out where the kitchen was."

"A fire," said Octave. "Continue the search, Ignazet; let me know who you find and what they tell you of this. The mistress is here—discover if she is well. If she is not, we must leave at once. They will blame us if they can." He looked over his shoulder at Nino. "God must like His little coward. I will spare you until I learn of Perceval's fate."

Nino blessed himself, more for the benefit of those watching him than in any belief it was required. He lowered his head and sought for a word or a phrase that might save him from Octave's wrath. "I have sinned, it is true, and I have sinned as a monk, which must enhance the offence to God." He stared down at the ground and went on, "I deserve punishment for my sin, and I will try to accept it with a charitable heart, because I am the one who sinned, and the pains of the body on earth are minor compared to the pains of the soul in Hell. It is right that I answer for my sins, as we all must. But I ask you, because I am a monk, let me be punished by monks, my Brothers who will view my transgressions through their own vows."

"Judged by monks, is it?" Octave turned and looked at Nino, a canny appreciation in his eyes. "All right, little poltroon, you can have your monks sit in judgment on you, providing they will permit me to testify—if my brother is alive. If Perceval is dead, I will roast you over a slow fire." He was moving faster now, taking long, impatient strides toward the ruin of the chateau.

Nino, still held by Herve, trailed behind him, and for once in his life he offered up genuine prayers: he prayed fervently for the life of Octave's brother Perceval.

* * *

Text of a letter from Le Fouet to Jacques Vidal Jumeau, written in code.

To that most worthy and farseeing cleric, Jacques Jumeau, Le Fouet sends his greeting and his admonitions to be more persevering in his work on the great work at hand.

It is not only the Parisian Parlement that suffers the diminishing of their time-honored rights, it is all the other Parlements as well. With the country staggering under the weight of the costs of a long war—necessary for the survival of the country, but burdensome nonetheless—additional taxes demanded at this time are not as easy a thing to come by as the Italian seems to think they are. Appointing intendants to oversee and overrule the decisions and policies of the Parlementaires is the most egregious error Mazarin has made yet, and it is one which will not go unredressed. This tyranny of intendants who are nothing more than lick-spittle servants to the Cardinal is loathsome to every Parlementaire in the land. For the sake of the kingdom and our established traditions, it must be abolished. Let the Parlements meet with a free hand once more; they will not refuse honorable and just taxes if they must be levied. But to continue to demand monies from those who have already given too much is absurd and cruel. You must be aware of this. You must understand the strength of my feelings on this matter. You must be willing to be more diligent so that we need not continue under the heel of these abominable intendants.

I will not insult you by asking you to listen at keyholes—that degrades our cause more than it aids it. I will not demand that you forget your vows of your station in life: those who ally themselves with Mazarin might require such things of you, having no respect or honor. We who wish to return to the traditional ways and values need to have more men of your character, of moral rectitude who are not content to be blown about by the wind of expediency. However, it is necessary that we learn more from you than we have. It is important that you take the time to note everyone who comes to Eblouir and everyone who leaves, even to coachmen and lackeys, for it is apparent that there have been changes made for which we were unprepared and we have had to act before we were ready. Had you been more attentive and relayed more information to us, we would have not had to undertake our countermeasures before they were fully developed.

Therefore, I beseech you to be vigilant, I order you to be staunch in your purpose. We must have copies or summaries of all documents that come through Bondame Clemens' estate. We must know who carries messages, where they come from and where they go, even if it is only to another messenger at another relay point. From such information, we can learn much, including what it is that the Italian wishes us to believe. His couriers are especially interesting, for they cross the frontiers of other countries, and that can tell us with whom the Cardinal is treating. It will not do at this crucial time to give Mazarin and the Spanish whore the slightest advantage. We must take care to be ahead of them at all times, and better informed than they think we are. So long as we can gather knowledge in secret, we will not be caught napping when it becomes necessary to act.

How horrible to think that we might have lost all because we have not received needed intelligence. It could come to that. It has been perilously close to that before. If we surrender now, we will be forever in the clutches of that Italian Cardinal and the Spaniard. Consider, Jumeau: Spain is our enemy. Spain is allied with Rome. And we have an Italian First Minister and a Spanish Regent. It is clear to anyone with eyes to see that these two are not prepared to defend France with their lives, nor are they willing to forget their birth in order to serve France, just as we cannot forget ours. We are Frenchmen, and this is France. While there are some in the nobility who find it acceptable that France is no longer ruled by Frenchmen, we who are true to the kingdom cannot agree. Those of us who are of noble birth have an obligation to defend France, and to preserve it. It is necessary to be rid of the foreigners and their unacceptable ways so that we may once again restore the glory of the kingdom.

Events in England should be warning enough to Mazarin and Anne, but they do not seem capable of learning from the misfortunes of others. They are determined to continue as they have been, trampling our time-honored customs and institutions underfoot and undermining the fabric of society with intendants in place of Parlements. Be sure that no King may count himself secure if his nobles are discontented, for as the nobles raised him up, so they will bring him down. I do not mean to harm a little boy who has no father, I mean to be rid of two foreigners who are poisoning his mind, making him unfit to rule.

If we are to have a Louis XIV, let it be Louis de Bourbon, Duc de Conde. He is a Prince of the Blood, he is a great hero, he has experience leading men in battle, he has shown himself courageous, a man to be reckoned with. He is more entitled to the Throne than is a child who has yet to master a pony and Latin verbs.

France has been at war for more than thirty years. That must indicate to any sensible man that we cannot have the kingdom drift, rudderless, at this time. De Conde will serve France better than the little boy can. He will strive to give the kingdom her rightful place in the nations of the world, as the great kingdom she is. We must not tolerate indecision and weakness while there are so many treaties and similar negotiations to enact. What child understands the smallest part of such negotiations? What child is capable of maintaining the honor of France? For we can have no less that such a one as our King. Now France is like one of the husbands in Moliere's plays—led about by the nose by a cunning woman and her sly lover.

I wish to hear from you shortly. I wish to have news and information of everything that transpires at Eblouir, no matter how insignificant it may appear. Be cautious, for it would not do for you to be caught. But do not use caution as an excuse not to act. Nothing is trivial at this juncture. Nothing is minor. Never has Mazarin been more suspicious or more treacherous. We must equal him, or we will go down to defeat, and France will be the greatest victim of all.

Le Fouet

On the 9th day of September, 1647.
Destroy upon reading.

· 6 ·

As Meres trimmed the stems on the last of the cut roses, he heard the door into the library open behind him. He continued at his task, using the small sewing scissors he had been given for the task; he looked over his shoulder for an instant, and saw the sweep of a black habit. "Jumeau," he said, giving the man a slight bow, though it was hardly a required courtesy where he was concerned. "Has Bondame Clemens returned from her ride yet?"

"Not that I am aware," said Jumeau curtly. He busied himself putting more sheets of fine paper in the pigeonholes of the desk, and adding a little water to the standish so that the ink would not dry or clot. It was so tempting, having three sealed messages all but under his fingers, yet not daring to touch them because a lackey was in the room.

"Soon, perhaps," he said, indicating the window with a gesture of his elbow. "The clouds have blown in."

"It may rain, or so the cook says," Jumeau reported, wanting to throw Meres bodily out of the door.

"Well, at this time of year, we might have rain at any time. It's not as bad as England, of course, but—" He made a philosophical gesture with his scissors and went back to the flowers. "These are the last until next spring, I'm afraid."

"Weren't there roses at Christmas last year?" asked Jumeau, trying to sound natural. He looked in the drawer for Olivia's sealing wax. "Ah, she has sufficient."

"The roses were from Tours," said Meres softly. "We won't have any this year." He took the stem ends and rolled them up in a rag, then stood back to look at the faded bouquet. "It's not going to last more than a day or so. Such a pity." He put the scissors into the flat leather wallet hanging from his belt. "I'll leave you to your work, Jumeau. But I think you might have to let Bondame Clemens relax in here."

"Oh?" said Jumeau, trying to sound irked rather than eager.

"She has another report on Tours to review. If I know her, she will be at it until late in the evening. The last three nights, I have retired late, and yet she was still here, poring over the information from Tours." He gave a single chuckle. "She is a most enterprising woman, not at all like most women. I never thought it would be rewarding to be in a woman's employ."

Jumeau smiled hostilely. "There are women in the world who would interest any man who was weak enough for them."

Meres started toward the door, but turned at that. "No, I don't mean that. I don't suppose a courtesan is any more interesting than a housewife, if you are not partaking of her pleasures. Bondame Clemens isn't like that, though. She's so much herself, and so much a . . . a woman"—he pursed his lips as if trying to taste the right word—"a woman to be appreciated. Almost as if she were a man." He took the latch in his hand and opened the door. "I will tell her you want to speak to her."

Jumeau looked startled. "Why do—"

"Why else would you be here, if you did not want to speak to her?" Meres laughed a little. "I know it's nothing either of you can discuss. It's the Cardinal's business, isn't it? something you have to tell her in confidence for His Eminence. I know that she has many such secrets." He did not wait for any response Jumeau might give, but went out of the room and closed the door behind him.

Meres was in the pantry selecting crockery for the servants' supper when he heard the clatter of hooves in the courtyard. He put the large soup plates aside and stepped out into the lowering dusk. "Madame Clemens," he said, bowing as one of the grooms hurried over to take the reins of her mare.

"Good evening, Meres," said Olivia as she got out of the saddle. She said to the groom, "Aulirios is a little way behind me. His horse picked up a stone and went lame on him. They're walking." Though she was as steadily polite with her staff as she had always been, Meres noticed that there was a certain inattention in her courteous manner, as if her mind were on more important things. He thought about the disaster at Tours and knew the reason why. "I have done as you asked," he said quietly as Olivia walked up to him.

"Good," she said quietly. "Is the seal correct?"

"From the one you gave me," said Meres. "There are two letters, actually; the one you prepared yesterday and the one we did not use last week."

"Very good," said Olivia with a single tight nod. "It would suit me to the ground to see this scoundrel exposed for the culprit I suspect he is. It would also satisfy me to know that there is false information going to Le Fouet—whoever that Francois is—instead of the real work we have done. Le Fouet is not a foolish man, but perhaps he is gullible; I am gambling that he is."

Meres opened his hands. "What do we know of plots?" he asked rhetorically. "You are a Roman widow, and as such know nothing of statecraft."

"Naturally," Olivia said drily, then turned and looked at Meres with respect. "You show great promise, my friend. I anticipate the need to find you a proper patron before I return to Rome." She let him open the pantry door for her. "Would you like to be a major domo?"

"I would like to be a Comte, but I doubt that will be possible. We're connected to a noble house somewhere on the family tree, but we are not so well connected that it would gain us any real advantage." He led her through the kitchen as quickly as possible, leaving the rest of the staff to continue with their work. "I think I can also duplicate the handwriting of Cardinal Bagni, if that is necessary. It might be wise to have a new note from the Vatican as these plotters grow more bold. If Le Fouet thought that the Pope might intervene, it could force his hand." He opened yet another door, and emerged into the main hall of Eblouir, the grand dining room on the left, the study on the right. "Do you want to inspect what I have done?" He favored her with a bow.

"Is Jumeau in the room?" Olivia asked in a whisper.

"Yes; or he was when I left. He will have had time to be busy, and we will know of it. I prepared well: I have put a single hair under each seal, so if he has broken them, we will know it." He put his hand on the door latch, then hesitated. He was smiling like a boy bent on havoc. "Are you ready, Madame?"

Olivia returned his smile fleetingly, but without the bravado he showed. "I will be sorry to lose you, Meres. And the day will come when I shall lose you. You are truly a prince among lackeys. Let's venture it."

"A thousand thanks, Madame," he said as he bowed her through the door.

Jumeau was sitting by the fire, a copy of *Exercitatio de Motu Cordis et Sanguinis*—which he had evidentally mistaken for a religious text—in his hands. He was frowning over Harvey's diagrams of arteries as Olivia came into the study; hastily he set the book aside. "Madame Clemens." He bowed with more formality than grace, looking at her with what he thought was veiled contempt. "Was your ride pleasant?"

"In fact, it was not," said Olivia directly. "Aulirios had to walk when his horse went lame, and the weather was so blustery that there was little enjoyment to be had, for the horses were very nervous. You know what they can be like on stormy days." She removed her jaunty-but-windblown hat and tossed it onto the chair beside her writing table. "Have you had a worthwhile afternoon, Jumeau?"

"I've had time to myself," said Jumeau, a bit puzzled that Meres had not gone to bring refreshments. "I have used it to study, as you see. I knew nothing of this theory of . . . circulation, and so I read what I could, but find I do not have the . . . stomach for this anatomy." He indicated Harvey's book with a flip of his fingers. "Surely an erudite man, but to waste his intelligence on the circulation of the blood!"

"There are few things more important than that, Monsieur Jumeau," said Olivia. She took her place on the settee and patted the wild strands of hair back into approximately the right place. Then she looked at Jumeau again. "I have been told to expect a messenger sometime in the next two days," she said conversationally, as if she were mentioning something he already knew. "If the weather continues, it could be three days."

"The next two days?" Jumeau was not able to appear as uninterested as he wished. "Two days. Or three days. There have been . . . a goodly number of messengers as late."

"That is because the Cardinal has need of them, I suppose," said Olivia, picking up the Harvey book and thumbing through it. "A most excellent work. So many things are explained once you understand that the blood is a single system that circulates throughout the body. In my youth . . . quite some time ago . . . they still subscribed to the old notion that there were two different systems for blood, one hot and one cold. Health and temperament were determined by which system was the stronger, and in what way." She returned the book to its place on the shelf. "I am pleased that this book has been written."

Jumeau shook his head ponderously. "This is hardly an appropriate subject for you to discuss, Madame. Women are not moved to learn these things, for it is not their purpose in life to learn and study, but to care for the young and be protected by a husband." He gave her a short, triumphant glance. "No wonder you remain a widow, when you pursue such works as Harvey's."

Olivia's smile was distinctly sardonic. "I remain a widow, Monsieur Jumeau, because I wish to remain a widow." She dropped a sealed packet on her writing table. "I will attend to that later, after I have bathed." She started toward the door. "Is there any word yet out of Germany?"

"What sort of word?" asked Jumeau, who knew what she was asking but would not admit it. He found Olivia's affair with Charles repugnant, for to his mind no French soldier with a sense of honor should become ensnared by an experienced foreign widow like Atta Olivia Clemens. He was also offended that she was so beautiful a woman, youthful and active, not bent, crabbed, and surrounded by lapdogs, as a proper foreign widow would be.

"Why, about d'Artagnan," said Olivia, as if there were no shame in taking a young and portionless lover. "Have we been told when he will be back?" She picked up her hat and brushed the brim. "It was bad enough while he was in England; while he is in Germany, I worry that he will be shot by some zealous soldier of Maximillian's." She went to the door, adding as she left the room, "I will want to have this room to myself in an hour or so."

Jumeau glowered at the closed door and said three words under his breath that demanded his immediate repentance, but he knew he would never confess. He looked at the packet Olivia had left, and it seemed to him that the oiled cotton pouch glowed as hot as the heart of a fire. If it were filled with diamonds it could hold no more desired treasure for him than the dispatches it contained. He leaned forward, his elbows braced on his knees, his hands laced in front of his chin. It was so tempting and so easy to reach forward and pull the entire pouch apart, but that was not possible, not if he wished his perusal of the contents to go undetected. There had to be some other way, he told himself in that vehement manner he used when he was determined to do a thing. He studied the pouch without moving, then rose and paced around it, as if he suspected it might be alive. Finally he sat down and lifted it up, once, weighing it. The cords holding it shut, he saw, were cleverly tied, and the knots would not easily yield to his fingers. That was vexing. He grew more committed to his desire to see the contents of the pouch; for him, secrecy gave a spice to his endeavors that nothing else had provided him. He set himself to the pleasure of working out this intricate puzzle, regretting only that there was so little time to do it.

There was a discreet rap on the door and Meres entered the study. "I ask your pardon, Monsieur Jumeau, but it is now time for supper in the servants' dinner room. We've rung the bell twice. We do not wish to start without you, and there are some who would like you to pronounce the blessing on the meal."

Jumeau ran his hand down the front of his habit. "Of course," he said; he rose quickly, as if he had nothing better to do in all the world. "The bell rung twice, you say?" He shook his head in self-condemnation. "I forgot the time." He motioned to the weight-driven clock near the hearth. "And that is not a very reliable instrument." He stretched his joined hands out in front of him, trying to make it appear that he had been dozing. He did not want it noticed that the pouch was lying on the table.

"Yes," Meres agreed. "Not even the water or saw clocks do much better, though," he pointed out. "I hope I have caused no intrusion." He was able to keep from laughing only by remembering that the game was a deadly one.

"Oh, no," said Jumeau, looking innocent and eager to please. "I still count myself something of a stranger in this household, and it . . . touches me when I discover that there are those who seek to include me in their activities." At the door he nodded toward the fire. "Do you need to bank it?"

Meres shook his head. "I shouldn't think so. It won't go out for two or three hours, and you will be back at work here before then; you can build up the fire to suit yourself. I will see that it is banked for the night."

Jumeau bowed, keeping strictly to the required social form in the belief that it was the most appropriate shield he could use. He fell in behind Meres and allowed the lackey to lead him to the servants' dinner room.

While the staff were eating their soup course, Niklos arrived back at Eblouir, his temper as frayed as the cuffs of his shirt. The long walk had made him as grumpy as his horse; his feet hurt, his head hurt, he was hungry. He sought out Olivia as soon as the gelding had been placed in the farrier's hands.

"I'm sorry, I'm sorry," he said as he came into her sitting room and before she could speak. "I should never have let this happen. Today of all days, there had to be this!"

Olivia, who was magnificently en deshabille, said, "Oh, certainly; I hold you accountable for every stone in the road, and each step your horse takes." She flipped the enormous lace ruff of her robe de chambre. "Be realistic, old friend. Neither one of us could have anticipated this happening. You have no reason to apologize." She ran her ivory comb through her hair, bringing the long, sleek strands over her shoulder. "What do you think of this friz by the face? I can't make up my mind if it is very attractive or a bit silly."

"It's probably both," said Niklos. "And don't think you're fooling me by changing the subject, Olivia. I should have been here, no matter what you tell me. Jumeau isn't the kind of man you can trick easily."

"Oh, I agree, Niklos," said Olivia, giving her head a toss.

"I mean it, Olivia," he said, a bit more belligerently.

"Yes, I know," said Olivia, so sweetly that she was almost intolerable. She indicated the chairs in the room. "Sit down before you collapse, and I'll tell you what Meres has done. Between us we have covered most of the possibilities. I think you will agree that our lackey has a knack for this service. It might be wise to mention this to Mazarin."

Niklos did not appear much mollified, but he allowed Olivia to persuade him to sit down and take off his caped coat. "All right," he capitulated. "How many pieces of false information have we supplied to Jumeau so far?"

"I think it's seven, that's assuming he has accepted everything as genuine—I'm not sure he has, but—and passed it on in that complicated code of his. Honestly," she went on in mock exasperation, "to base a code on books and chapters of the Bible, so that the number of the specified chapter tells which letter to start from, and even numbers say every other number, odd say every number. It's too unwieldy for me." She frowned suddenly. "I wish I knew which of his cohorts destroyed my house at Tours."

"I don't think he would want to tell us," said Niklos. "How long do we give Jumeau with the pouch?" He sat down on the satin-covered settee by the window. "You realize, Olivia, we could be mistaken, that our assumptions are wrong and the spy in this household is not Jacques Vidal Jumeau?"

"I realize it is possible for the sun to rise in the north, too, but I don't expect it." Olivia picked up a small bell and rang it. "Meres is waiting for my signal."

Niklos nodded but his eyes remained troubled. "I am serious about this, Olivia. What if it is not Jumeau? What then?"

"Well, who else can it be?" Olivia countered. "Who else has regular access to the dispatches and letters, knows the messengers Mazarin uses, is familiar with the negotiations in progress? Surely you don't think that one of the lackeys here has been suborned, do you? How likely is that? Recall, if you will, that the problem began a month after Jumeau arrived. We were through this already. He is the only person who has had access to the records and—"

"So has d'Artagnan," said Niklos, his voice low and the room suddenly very quiet.

Olivia stared at him. "You don't really suspect that Charles is a traitor to France, do you? Do you believe he could do that? Charles? Charles de Batz-Castelmore d'Artagnan, work against France?"

"But you know that the rebels appeal to the love of France in those they recruit. Why not d'Artagnan?" He held up his hands. "I am merely being Devil's Advocate; I do not believe my own questions, but I must ask them."

"Yes, I know." Olivia's sigh was short and hard. "Charles swore an oath before God to be loyal to Mazarin and to King Louis XIV. He will honor that oath for as long as he lives. Or longer. And he is not literate enough to substitute forgeries for the real documents. You know that as well as I. We know that Jumeau is the spy." She put her comb down and stood up. "Do I look like a widow wakened from sleep by some disturbance?"

"No," said Niklos bluntly. "You're much too well-ordered for that. You need to have your hair in a braid down the back and a cap on your head to protect you from draughts, and that robe de chambre is far too alluring for a chaste widow to wear."

"How nicely you compliment me," said Olivia, a little of her usual mischief back in her manner. "Come. I want to see what is going on in the study. I've asked Meres to help us out. He ought to be there soon."

"Does he realize that Jumeau might have armed himself?" Niklos asked as he hauled himself to his feet.

"I have warned him, but I think he is convinced it is all some kind of delightful game. I don't know how to convince him other-wise." She had lowered her voice so that it was little more than a whisper as they went down the hallway toward the stairs to the main floor.

"The game costs lives," said Niklos, his eyes on Olivia again. "How can you be certain it was sensible to bring that youth into this?"

"I'm not," she snapped. "I am only saying that he is enjoying himself." She was going faster now, without appearing to hurry. Niklos lengthened his stride to keep pace with her. "By the Saints, Olivia, what is the matter? You—"

"I'm nervous. I want to find that man with his fingers on the letters." She was almost at the door when she gave a gasp, then followed it with shaky laughter as Meres stepped out of the shadows. "Don't do that," she admonished.

"It's exciting," he said, making his bow sketchily. "Ever since you told me what you are going to do, I've been wanting to tell the world—"

Niklos took him by the shoulders at once, his attitude uncompromising and serious. "You cannot mention this, Meres. Not now, not later, not to your confessor, even when you are dying. What we do here has never happened."

Meres nodded several times, his face flushed with excitement. "I know, I know. Bondame Clemens told me all about it, and how wrong it is to reveal these things. I would not ever say anything that she would not like." He put his right hand over his heart. "By the Cross and Mere Marie, I swear I will never speak of this to anyone but God in my prayers."

Niklos released him, shrugging. "If he breaks that oath, he will not be the Meres we know now," he said to Olivia.

"I will accept that as guarded approval," she said, pausing by one of the hall sconces and taking the candle from it. She shielded the candle, then gave a shrill laugh and flung open the study door, as if she fully expected to find the room empty.

Jumeau was seated at Olivia's writing table, and under his hand was a letter with a broken seal dangling from one of the two ribbons that crossed it. He brought up his arm, as if to protect either his face or the document from a downward blow, though his countenance was more disbelieving than fearful. Because of the light, he did not see the two men in the hall beyond.

Olivia stood in the doorway, the candle held aloft, her hair rioting about her face. Tiers of ruched lace cascaded over her robe de chambre, and it was closed provocatively with satin rosettes. She took two slow steps into the room. "Jumeau," she said after a short hesitation.

"Madame Clemens" was his guarded acknowledgment.

"What are you doing at my writing table?" she asked, trying her best to sound affronted rather than angry. "It is not fitting for you to be there, Monsieur."

Jumeau was already halfway to his feet, his left hand swiping at the letter he had been reading. "I . . . I thought it was best . . . for the Cardinal . . . yes. I thought it was best," he said with a bit more confidence, "that I read through all the material you have received. After all, I am here to tend to various of the Cardinal's messages and—"

"Jumeau," Olivia interrupted, her voice so soft and sweet it slid over him like warm honey, "you are sweating. Your face is shiny. Have you taken ill? Should I send for the physician to bleed you? And your hands!" She pointed. "Look at them: they are trembling, Jumeau."

He joined his hands behind his back like a recalcitrant child. "It is nothing, Madame. Your concern is most generous." He spoke as if the words were steeped in poison. "I assure you I am perfectly well. It is . . . a little late."

"But you *are* shaking," Olivia protested, coming nearer to him. "I can tell. It may be you are reading something dangerous, and that has caused a grippe. And what letter is this?" She reached out artlessly with her free hand and lifted the letter. Her gaze fell on the seals, still intact. "Why, Jumeau, you have not broken the seals," she remarked. "Dangerous indeed. How very curious."

Jumeau audibly ground his teeth. "If you will leave me to the tasks the Cardinal has set me," he said hastily, snatching for the letter.

But Olivia had moved deftly away, and was holding her candle so that she could read the dispatch. "Oh, dear," she said, turning to look at Jumeau. "This is not something you ought to have read," she informed him. There was a subtle change in her voice and the way she stood. "And I suspect that you know it."

"Madame!" he blustered. "Madame, I would never—"

Olivia dropped her pose. She turned and faced Jumeau with her direct hazel eyes fixed on him. "Would never what? Would never betray Mazarin's trust? Well, we know that is a lie, don't we? Would never intercept messages? Oh, of course not. That would be unthinkable. Though the evidence suggests otherwise. Would never oppose the King? Well, you cannot expect a little boy to command the allegiance of grown men, can you? It's not reasonable. And you are such a reasonable man." In the silence that followed her denunciation, Olivia walked toward Jumeau, the letter held in her hand. "Or would you like to offer another explanation for this? One that might be accepted."

He moved back as if from a deadly insect. "No," he said in a strangled tone. "Not when we are so close."

"So close to what?" Olivia asked with exaggerated care. "The culmination of your treason?" She moved so quickly that her candle almost burned out. "Tell me! You will not leave here until you do, Jumeau. Tell me what you have done," she demanded as she blocked his way out of the study.

"You have to let me go!" he shouted at her. "You won't dare let Mazarin hear of this—he'll make you leave the country, you whore!"

In the hallway, both Niklos and Meres bristled at the word, though only Meres started to move. Niklos touched his arm and shook his head.

Meres made a rude gesture with his hand, but kept still.

"Stay where you are," Olivia warned Jumeau. Now her voice was steady and her eyes were calm. "I think you have confused a few things, my friend. I think you do not believe I have an estate in Rome and funds of my own. It serves your purpose to believe that I am Mazarin's tool, his pawn. You assume I am an impoverished relative dependent on Mazarin for my place in the world, and therefore willing to be of service to him." She shook her head, the beginning of a smile at the corners of her mouth. "But you see, you are wrong."

"You are a courtesan, a harlot!" He lunged at her, but she stepped out of his way, though not enough to give him sufficient room to reach the door.

"Don't be more foolish than God made you," she said. "Your beliefs about me are a lie. Your assumptions that I would not be able to discover who in the household was purloining reports and substituting forgeries was false as well. What made you think that it would not be noticed? Do you think that Mazarin's friends are stupid? Do you think that there is only one set of dispatches carried at any time? Did it never occur to you that there would be questions and comparisons, and that eventually the road would lead to you? There were so few candidates, you see. Mazarin has only six secretaries, and all but two of you work at his side. It was just a matter of time until we unearthed you, exposed you. Used you." She saw the shock in his eyes. "Oh, yes, we used you. And, incidentally, we have been guilty of a little forgery ourselves." She watched his face turn ashen. "Oh, yes. Those reports you have taken such pride in, those documents you have copied with different information, they were made from deceptions." She shrugged. "If this is the game you wish to play, Jumeau, you need to be more deft."

"Deft!" he bellowed, and rushed at her, his head low.

This time Niklos could not restrain him: Meres charged into the room, ready to do battle with the world. He threw himself directly at Jumeau, catching the cleric on the shoulder, both men staggering under the impact.

Niklos barreled through the door, reaching out to pull the combatants apart. He yelled a long curse in Greek and strove to find a hold on the struggling bodies.

Olivia tossed her candle into the fire. "You handle Jumeau. I will take Meres," she ordered, and did not wait to see if Niklos complied, but came as close as she dared to the grunting, rolling men locked in battle. She was almost in position when she heard a muffled report; her eyes flew to Niklos'. "A shot?"

Dumbfounded, he nodded, then he moved in with more determination. Meres started to shove himself off Jumeau, his young eyes filled with amazement. Then a bubble of blood formed on his lips, expanding, breaking, and he fell back on top of the man who had killed him.

Olivia, holding a poker in her hand, prodded Jumeau in the side. "Move," she said, her mouth tight and white-lipped.

Slowly, with dawning terror in his soul, Jumeau did as she commanded. He hunkered back in the shadow of the settee and felt a sense of protection when Niklos came and seized him by the back of the collar.

Olivia knelt down beside her lackey. She pushed his hair back from his forehead, and eased him onto his back. With the gentlest touch she crossed his hands on his breast, then made the sign of the cross on his forehead.

"You believe?" Jumeau barked, and cringed at the look she gave him.

"No. But he did." Resolutely she turned her face away from the body on the floor. There were no tears in her eyes, for she had none to shed, but there was an abiding anguish in her soul that was worse than tears would have been. She looked up at Niklos. "It's such a waste."

✿   ✿   ✿

Text of the confession of Frere Gautier presented to Luc-Simeon Gottard, Abbe of the monastery Sacres Innocentes.

In the Name of the Father, Son, and Holy Spirit, Amen. I offer this confession to purge my soul of error and to submit to the judgment of my Brothers and God for the Glory of God. I know that I am stained deep with sin and that what I say here is not for my forgiveness, but to set down the extent of my straying.

I accuse myself of bringing unrest and sin to Sacres Innocentes by nominating Nino Colonnello of Rome to join our numbers as a tertiary Brother. I did not adhere to the Rule of our Order, praying for guidance and searching my soul for the truth, but thought instead of my days in the world, when I was a soldier and spent my hours at war. This Nino Colonnello was another such as I, or so I deceived myself, and permitted his sinful ways to cloud my prayers and my duties. Had I not persevered in attempting to bring this man among our numbers, we would not now be so shamed and disgraced through his wickedness; for this I ask forgiveness of all my Brothers, and of Mere Marie.

I accuse myself of obstinacy where Nino Colonnello is concerned. I was remiss in my tasks the better to plead his case, and when he was allowed to begin his training as a tertiary Brother, I would make provision for him, so that he would not have to undertake the full rigors of monastery life until he was more accustomed to the burden. I offered myself the excuse that I was concerned because of his injured leg, and I thought, mistakenly, that my actions were

*charitable. I could not see how steeped in malice and envy this man
is, nor how willing he was to bend me to his purpose. I know that I
led him into error and encouraged him to persist in error.*

*I accuse myself of bearing false witness, through the lies this Nino
Colonnello told me in regard to the widow who keeps the stud farm
that marches with the monastery land. He claimed she had used her
influence to have him unjustly blamed for laxity and other crimes,
and that because of her he could no longer live with his wife. He
swore that this widow had forced them to separate and would not
permit him any access to his wife at all. He said that she corrupted
all she touched, and that he sought only to save his wife from her
predations. There were similar allegations, but it disgusts me to
catalogue them, for I know now that they were the very heart of his
lies, of his sin. I listened to every poisoned word and I did nothing
to warn a blameless woman of the danger near her, nor did I believe
there would be any event so devastating as the destruction of half of
the chateau and a portion of the out-buildings of her estate. Had I
not harkened to Nino Colonnello, that house would still stand, and
those who labor there would continue to do so in peace and without
harm. It is more shameful that Nino Colonnello was apprehended
by a highwayman and his troop, instead of you, my Brothers, and
for that I am deeply repentant, for that is a fault that must be laid
at my door with the rest.*

*I accuse myself of lack of vigilance, for even when I began to have
doubts, I made no attempt to learn what the truth of this man's
assertions might be, and I continued to assume that his threats of
violent revenge were more the signs of wrathful fancy, such as soldiers often express, rather than true intent. I always assumed that
Nino Colonnello would not actually do the things he threatened to
do. I did not anticipate he would actually construct grenada bombs
and use them to turn her house to a ruin. I accuse myself of cowardice, for when I discovered the extent of his perfidy, I still did not
speak out as my Vow demands. I was too much in the world, concerned about reputation and the honor of men who fight in battle. I
did not say to any of my Brothers or to our Abbe that I had known
of Nino Colonnello's plans, I could not admit that I had heard him
plot and that I did nothing.*

*I accuse myself of my fall, of my loss of any claim to the habit I
wear and the Rule I have sworn to follow. Each sin is more grievous
than the last. Had I been willing to make a larger escort to take
Nino Colonnello from his cell here to whatever punishment the*

magistrates would mete out to him, I am certain he would not have escaped and Frere Herriot would still be alive. I did not suppose he would have hidden bottles of wine in his mattress, or that he would use them as clubs. What honorable man would do that? I was too arrogant to see that Nino Colonnello is not an honorable man. I must answer for the life of my Brother in this life and before the Throne of God. I sinned through pride, which is the greatest sin of all, and I have been cast out of the company of those seeking Grace.

I beg you, Abbe, my Brothers, let me determine my penance, and pray that I will fulfill it. I will not look for the facile way now, I will not be taken in by the appearance of goodness. I wish to remove myself entirely from the world, and to devote myself completely to prayer. I ask you to immure me, sealing the door of my cell so that nothing less than the fall of the walls of the monastery will open it again. I will want nothing more than bread and water, and the wine of Communion. Otherwise, I implore you to leave me there until I am dead. I ask no word from anyone, no comfort or wisdom; I will accept complete silence with gladness, and embrace my state as I would embrace the Feet of God. I request only that if Nino Colonnello is ever found and brought to justice, that one of you tell me of that great blessing, for that will be my sign that I may be redeemed at last. I do not hope for that joy in the world, but perhaps, if God is good, He will show me Nino Colonnello in Hell when I am come there.

I will pray every day for the repose of the soul of Frere Herriot, I will pray for the wronged Bondame Clemens. I will pray for all those who have suffered injustice, and all those who are blameless but bear the burden of another's crime. I will pray that God, in His Mercy, will bring each of you to joy and peace, and that those who enter our walls never again be instruments of sin. May Saint Michel, who was my patron once, pity me for my weakness and give me courage to endure my penance with a thankful heart. May Saint Dismas, who died with Our Lord, expunge my crimes from the minds of men. May you, my Brothers, forgive me, so that your prayers may guide me. Benedictus qui venit in Nomine Domini.

Frere Gautier

At les Sacres Innocentes on the Feast of Saint Odo of Cluny the 18th day of November, 1647.

Retain with monastery records.

· 7 ·

"Have you noticed the broken windows?" de Portau asked as he strolled past the Louvre toward the river. "A bad sign, very bad." He raised his gloved hand. "Three right in a row."

"Windows are forever getting broken," said Charles with a dismissing motion toward the Hotel de Ville. "The trouble is, it's so much work to replace them, and then someone comes along and breaks them once more."

De Portau thrust out his jaw and shook his head. "No; no that's not it." They had reached the river and had turned to walk along it. "This is more than an occasional misfortune, this is what happens when the windows are broken deliberately. You mark what I say to you, Charles: it's this Parlement question, that's what's behind it."

"And the nobility is behind the Parlement question," said Charles, touching the brim of his hat to two veiled women going by. "It's as bad as those Turkish puzzles, with boxes inside boxes inside boxes." He raised his gloved hand to shade his eyes as he looked up into the afternoon sky. "When must you return to the barracks?"

"Before changing the Guard," said de Portau, slapping his mantle with the back of his hand. "I wish we were Musqueteers together again, my friend. It does not suit me to continue with the King's Guard until I am posted underground."

Charles gave him a speculative glance. "Would you like to be one of the Cardinal's couriers? With four of his messengers killed in the last year, he needs good fighting men to work for him. I could mention your name."

De Portau shook his head, his little eyes bright as glazed raisins. "I'm not poor enough for that," he said, went on quickly, "meaning no offence to you. I have seen Mazarin at work and I must ask myself: why would the Cardinal employ two unlike men as Montlezun de Besmaux and de Batz-Castelmore d'Artagnan? The first answer is obvious—both are Gascons. But they are such unalike Gascons. Montlezun de Besmaux is such a fawning, servile worm to Mazarin, and you are all bluntness and bravery. So it is not that you are Gascons. You have not married, Montlezun de Besmaux has. That's not it. You have not fought in the same campaigns. Your battle records are markedly different. What then is your commonality? I ask myself. The answer appears! You are both poor. Neither of you has more than two sous." He flung up his hands at the announcement. "While I am not a rich man, I am far from poor, Charles. Mazarin would not take me because he could not—" He stopped abruptly.

"Could not own you?" Charles asked without rancor. "You may say it; it's true enough. My brother Paul cannot afford to maintain me as a soldier, and so I must depend on the Cardinal to do it." He gave an eloquent shrug. "These days, that is not a certain thing."

"The broken windows?" de Portau guessed shrewdly. "The Italian knows what they mean, then?"

"Oh, yes," said Charles. "But Queen Anne does not, and does not want to learn."

"Foolish woman," grumbled de Portau.

"A frightened one," Charles corrected.

"Comes to the same thing. They're obstinate as mules, frightened women. I'd rather face a line of Swiss pikemen backed by Dutch cannoneers than one woman stubborn with fear." He opened his arms. "I'd comfort her, naturally, give her a little bravery. But that might not be enough to change her mind." He sighed and added slyly, "Do you think that's what the Italian does? gives her a little bravery the soldier's way?"

To de Portau's surprise, Charles gave his question serious consideration. "I've wondered," said Charles as they made their way around a puppet show attracting its last crowd of the day. "And I have come to think not. I can't say quite why."

"They say Richelieu was her lover. She might have a taste for Princes of the Church." He thumped Charles on the arm and pointed upward. "More broken windows. There's going to be worse until this argument with Parlement is settled."

Charles was momentarily taken by the grotesque little actors on the puppet stage: a figure in Cardinal's robes with an enormously long head and huge black eyes was using a bishop's crozier to bash an ermine-caped noble over the head; the noble was defending himself with a jeweled mace. The third figure, who was a gross parody of the King of Spain, capered with glee as he watched the fray. Most of the crowd watched closely and cheered. "That is what bothers me," he said to de Portau. "This is not an isolated incident. There is evidence everywhere that the people are tired of plots and battles. This dispute between Mazarin and the nobles will not vanish, and I cannot see that either side will compromise."

"Why not? It's the way of statecraft to compromise." De Portau removed his glove, reached into his wallet and drew out a small silver coin which he dropped into the hat of the puppeteer making his way through the crowd.

"But how can they? The Parlement will not pay for the supplies the army must have. Mazarin cannot compromise on that, not with victory within our grasp."

"I've heard that before," said de Portau.

"It is. The Parlement will not levy new taxes. And all the Parlements are angry about the intendants, who they claim are usurping their functions, and all in the name of Mazarin." Charles turned so abruptly that he nearly collided with a hatter carrying his wares. He sketched a bow in the fellow's direction, ignoring the curse that was flung at him.

"Well, aren't they?" de Portau asked reasonably. "The intendants are acting for the Cardinal and the work they do supercedes the Parlements. What else are the Parlementaires to think?" He saw a seller of broiled chicken on a skewer standing by his small, portable stove nearby and signaled him to come closer. "Have one with me, d'Artagnan. On my purse." He grinned impulsively, and had the coins out before Charles could object. "When you are wealthy, I expect a handsome reward for this service."

"You shall have it—when I'm rich," Charles promised lightly, but went on seriously at once. "What is the worst in all this," said Charles as he pulled off his glove with his teeth and took the proffered skewer, "is that I am concerned for Olivia, because she is in danger. She is part of this whether she wishes to be or not, and she has encountered trouble because of Mazarin. It is easier to harass a widow living in the country than a Cardinal in the heart of Paris." He blew on the fragrant meat and tested it with his tongue. "Hot."

"It will cool," said de Portau. "You told me about that secretary they apprehended—what? two months ago?—a bad business. You said that the fellow was one of Mazarin's secretaries, gone over to the nobles, who knows how long ago. Good thing your widow winkled him." He sniffed at the fragrant steam from their food. "Rosemary and garlic. Perfect."

"It's very good," said Charles absently. "You are right, it was a bad business. She managed it cleverly, but she did not know that the man carried a pistol. Well, he was in Orders: who expects a cleric to be armed? It is incidents like that that give me nightmares. What if there is another spy in her household? What if the nobles send one? How is she to be defended? The worst of it is I cannot be much help. The Cardinal has been keeping me moving this last year: Germany, England, Rome. Now he wants the border garrisons reinforced so that none of our enemies will think to catch us napping while the peace negotiations are continuing. I will have dispatches to carry, and I will not be able to do my duty and guard Olivia the way I would want."

"Ah," said de Portau.

Charles took a first, tentative bite of the chicken. "It's good," he pronounced.

"Yes," said de Portau, waiting.

It took two more bites for Charles to gather his resolve. "I wish to ask you to guard her in my stead," he said in a rush, as though he would stop entirely if he slowed down at all.

"And how am I to do this?" de Portau asked, wholly unsurprised by the question. "I am in barracks here, she lives to the southwest of the city. She would take ill to having a stranger skulking about the place, and if she is as attentive as you tell me she is, she is not one to accept excuses." He bit into his chicken. "Would you want another?"

Charles took a moment to realize that de Portau was asking about chicken. "No," he answered distractedly. "What if I can persuade the Cardinal to post you to Chatillon to watch Eblouir? We know about Jumeau now, so there is reason to suspect that there may be others in that area working against the Cardinal. That is where the danger comes to Olivia, don't you see?"

"Yes, I do," said de Portau. "You don't want your Roman widow in the middle of a crossfire."

"That's right," Charles said, adding, "Isaac, would you do it? If Mazarin approved, would you do it?"

"That would depend," said de Portau after a short silence. "It would, I think, require the consent of the lady. And it would be necessary for the Cardinal to arrange matters properly with des Essarts. I will have to be given formal leave to do this, Charles." He bit off more of the chicken, and as he chewed he added, "I don't want to jeopardize my place in the Musqueteers when they are reinstated."

"Are you certain they will be?" Charles asked doubtfully.

"Yes; oh, yes, I'm certain they will be." He wiped the grease from his mouth with the back of his hand. "Now we are trying to end wars, and so we do not need our Musqueteers. But soon enough the wars will start up again, and then—poof!—they will want us to reappear like a magician's poppet. They need Musqueteers to use against cavalry. Put us at the front of the lines and let us shoot the horses out from under the enemy. We can take the brunt of horse and foot soldiers, and there's precious few troops that can do that and live to boast of it."

Charles nodded, his mouth full of chicken. He swallowed twice, then was finally able to speak. "It's a sin to pray for war, but I am a soldier and I want a soldier's glory."

"Well, encourage Mazarin to bring back the Musqueteers. And find a way to make the Parlements pay for it." He tossed away a bit of bone to emphasize it, then watched as a stave-ribbed cat darted out of the shadows to claim it as prize. "I will say this to you, young Gascon—"

"Not so young anymore," said Charles.

"You are six years my junior, and among soldiers, that is a lifetime," said de Portau, unwilling to be put off. "I will say this," he resumed. "I will watch over your widow, and I will respect that she *is* your widow if des Essarts will allow it. If he will not, then I will do what I can to help you make other arrangements with one you can trust."

Charles grinned. "You are the best friend a man ever knew, I swear it on my mother's grave." He looked across the river toward the dark flank of Notre Dame. "No windows broken there yet. They're intact."

"For the time being," said de Portau, suddenly very dark in his mood. "You don't know how much I yearn for an honest fight, man against man, matched for strength and weapons, and the right prevail. I hate this game of subterfuge and deceit that we are made to play at."

Charles nodded slowly, losing his taste for the chicken. "Yes. It is as bad as tainted meat." He let his skewer drop. The cat appeared again, bristling defiance as it dragged its feast away.

De Portau shied his skewer toward the riverbank and did not watch where it fell, saying, "Let the rats have the rest." He continued along in silence, and then confided, "There was a man from one of the Ducs who came to the tavern, two, three weeks ago. He was careful not to say which Duc. But he offered many advantages—in veiled terms—to the men in the tavern if, when the time came, they would give their support to the nobles rather than the foreign Cardinal and Queen." He drew out a large handkerchief and wiped his hand, staring down at his fingers in the fading light. "All he said was vague, but everyone knew what he wanted: if the nobles rise, or Parlement resists again, and the magistrates will not bow to Mazarin, we would be expected to look the other way, not to fight, or to fight with the nobles. He implied there were rewards for those who promised their aid now, before the day arrives. It disturbed me, Charles, to see how many of the men were listening to him."

"Did any of them take his offer? Did they swear to give their allegiance to the nobles or the Parlement?" Charles asked, and held his breath for the answer.

"None that I saw," de Portau said carefully. "But I listened to how they talked—including Montlezun de Besmaux."

"He was there?" Charles asked, startled.

"He is everywhere," said de Portau vehemently. "He is like a weasel, stealing chickens." His tone lightened. "He looks like a weasel, too. Doesn't he?"

Charles smiled. "Yes." It was a relief to be able to say these things to de Portau, for there was no other soldier he knew who was trustworthy enough to keep such damning words to himself. "Why was he there?"

"He said it was for the Cardinal, but I suspect it was for the betterment of the Sieur de Besmaux. He is the sort who would gather information and sell it or his silence to the highest bidder." He spat to show his contempt. "Poverty is not reason enough to employ that one, and so I would like to tell Mazarin. He has gold in you, and dross in Montlezun de Besmaux."

"He is ambitious," said Charles, "but so am I."

"Yes—he for wealth and influence, and you for a Marshall's baton." De Portau pounded Charles on the back, signaling the end of his complaint. "If you arrange it, I will watch over this Roman widow of yours, and doubtless curse myself that I was born a man of honor."

Charles cuffed him lightly in return. "I will warn Olivia that you are a dangerous rogue." He laughed outright. "I would give a month's pay to see what she would do to any man fool enough to try to seduce her."

"A fire-eater, is she?" de Portau asked wickedly. "Now, that's tempting."

"No," Charles answered, no longer joking. "She is not like that. She can handle a pistol and a sword and she rides better than half the men in mantles do." He looked past the bulk of the cathedral toward the west. "You'll understand once you meet her," he said with certainty.

"You think I will get permission to do this?" de Portau inquired, having less faith in that eventuality than Charles did.

"I believe we must," said Charles simply. He lapsed into silence, and de Portau accepted it, strolling through the darkening afternoon with his friend. They were almost to the old ferry where livestock were taken across when Charles spoke again. "The nobles will rebel. I am as sure of it as I am of life beyond death. The intendants are an excuse; they want to bring the Throne under their control while Louis is a child, so that he will be in their thrall. It is not only that Mazarin and the Queen are foreign, it is that they will not accept the old authority. They must fight if they are to regain their suzerainty. They must fight or accept the Cardinal as the leader of France, and they will not do that."

"So more broken windows," said de Portau philosophically.

"And broken heads, I expect," said Charles. "Broken windows can be repaired, but broken heads—"

"Such as your widow's head," interjected de Portau.

"Among others. There is also the King." He added the last drily. "There is reason to fear for him, as well."

De Portau bowed his acknowledgment. "Very well, so it will be arranged and I will keep watch on the widow while you storm the countryside with alarms and warnings." He snickered. "You didn't think that you would spend so many hours on horseback when you became a Musqueteer, did you?"

"No," said Charles, and could not resist adding, "but luckily Olivia provides me with excellent horses." He ducked as de Portau took a playful punch at him, returning it in the same spirit, and grinning as their hands slapped together. "Be good to her, and she may give you one as well."

"For your sake, no doubt," said de Portau.

"No doubt," Charles seconded, then turned as he heard the sound of breaking glass some way behind them. "Nom du Nom du Nom," he muttered.

De Portau put his hands on his hips. "It will get worse, boy; I warn you. It will take a while, but the boldest are carrying slings now, and others will join them, some because it is the fashion, and some because they want advantage." He rocked back on the thick heels of his boots. "I hate these skirmishes in the streets. I hate barricades."

"It will be settled before then," said Charles confidently.

"No it won't," de Portau contradicted him emphatically.

"When the peace is made, all this will be forgotten," said Charles, pointing at the newly broken window. "This is the last of the war, being fought here." He thought over what he had said and decided he had done it neatly. "When we have peace again, the nobles will stop this constant wrangling."

"You're wrong," said de Portau, holding up a single finger to punctuate his pronouncement. "It is when peace comes that the nobles will be more fractious than ever. There will be nothing for them to do but brood on the powers they have lost to the First Minister, and that will ferment like bad wine. You wait. Two weeks after the victory Te Deum every window on this quai will be broken." He stopped as he once again heard the sound of breakage. "Now it is a single window here and there. Later it will be every window, everywhere."

"You've turned into a cynic," said Charles.

"I was born one," de Portau corrected him. "But that is nothing. Soldiers are cynics by profession." He winked at Charles and said softly, "Are you aware we are being followed?"

"I thought we were earlier," said Charles in some alarm, forcing himself not to look back over his shoulder or draw attention to them in any other way, "but I did not think that they were still with us. Three men, do you think?"

"Two men, in long cloaks, look like deckhands, both of them. They're by that knife sharpener. Not the place I want them to be," he added. "It might give them ideas I don't want them to have. Knives are what that lot favor."

"I have my sword," Charles said indignantly. "And I don't fear a fight."

"Oh, Devil take your sword. You're the Cardinal's courier, and you do not honor your duty to Mazarin by brawling in the street.

And des Essarts would have me flogged for it. This is not the place to stop them, in any case."

"How do you mean?" Charles asked, feeling encouraged by this last. "You have a plan to catch them?"

De Portau did not answer at first, but signaled Charles to remain where he was while he ambled over to a young woman selling sachets of violets. He exchanged a few compliments with her, flattered her outrageously, and paid her twice what the sachet he bought was worth, then strolled back to where Charles was waiting. "There's too much traffic here. We would not be able to accost them without a fight."

"Then where?" Charles asked, eager for the chase.

"A little farther on there is an old fountain with a tiny place around it, little more than a widening of the roadway," de Portau said. "Very old houses there, and an apothecary's—"

"I know it," Charles interrupted.

De Portau went on as if Charles had not spoken. "There have been workmen repairing the quai in front of it. The roadbed was washed down, sometime last winter; it's being fixed. This morning all the workmen's material was still there. You and I and a handful of bricks ought to discourage them."

"What if they raise the alarm? If the Watch comes, we will have to answer to Mazarin and des Essarts." Despite his warning, Charles could not suppress the grin that spread, wolflike, over his features. "But it is necessary, isn't it; since they're following us."

"Of course it's necessary," said de Portau with a grin of his own.

"So," said Charles, setting off in the direction of the fountain. "Let us hurry."

"Let us not," said de Portau seriously as he grabbed Charles by the sleeve once more. "If you rush, those behind us will take up the chase in earnest. We don't want that to happen," he said, then laughed loudly and put his arm through Charles'. "Walk as if you had nothing on your mind but a little boasting, and do not give your attention to any part of the street. You and I are having a chat. We're old comrades-in-arms and we're catching up on each other's escapades."

Chagrined, Charles lowered his head. "I am sometimes too hasty." He pointed to where an apple-seller was dining on his unsold stock. "That fellow, he has the right idea."

De Portau approved vigorously. "That's the way of it. Now, a little faster. We don't want them to get too close, either." He slipped past a group of students in their university robes, and cocked his head at them. "Filling their heads with Greek, I'll wager, and the forms of different leaves. I have a cousin who's a scholar, did I tell you that?"

"I don't remember," said Charles. "You tell me so many things." He bowed as he passed the students, for two of them were looking offended.

"And at least half of them are true," crowed de Portau. He sidestepped a heap of dung and pointed to the fountain not far ahead of them. "A pity it doesn't produce wine and ale as well as water." He went up to the ancient stone fountain but did not drink. "Half the beggars in Paris come here. They probably bathe and piss in it as well as drink it." He laughed, and pulled Charles closer. "Go find a brick."

Charles touched the brim of his hat. "There's a hoe, as well, and a trowel."

"Good devices, all of them," said de Portau, winking at Charles before he reached out to seize his brick. "Not like facing the Dutch or the Germans, but it keeps me in practice," he observed to the air as he turned around, arm at the ready.

One of the two men who had been following them was only a few steps behind; he skidded to a stop, poised to run as Charles lunged at him, throwing himself full-length against the man, his arms wrapping around his knees, bringing him down.

The other was far enough behind that he had time enough to see what was happening to his companion; he had already turned to run when de Portau's brick thudded into his back. He gave a guttural cry, stumbled and fell.

"In one shot!" de Portau shouted, rushing forward, shoving some of the passersby aside in his hurry to get to the fallen man. He dropped to his knees, one of them on the man's back, reaching to secure his hands. "I have you now, villain," he announced to the man as he secured his hands with his jabot.

The man de Portau had caught swore in the lowest of gutter Parisian as he rolled onto his back, then struck out with his knee, attempting to slam into de Portau's groin.

"That's enough of that," said de Portau, and hammered his locked hands into the man's stomach, stepping back as he collapsed.

Charles was still struggling to hold the man he had caught; he had been bruised in his face and shoulders but had not released the ruffian's legs. He was determined that no matter how the man fought, until he lost consciousness he would not let go. With that, he was able to endure the blows being rained on his head, face, and shoulders. He dreaded what would happen to him if his captive found a weapon of any kind and started battering at him. He needed time; he knew that time was his only protection, and he sought for a little to aid him. He forced both of them to roll over, closer to the low barrier between the quai and the Seine, and as he rolled he saw the other man reach out to grab a trowel.

Then a boot kicked the trowel away and de Portau stood over them both with his sword drawn. "The Watch will be along shortly, and we had all better be gone by then," he said, breathing hard but perfectly amiable. "Get up, and you"—he pointed his sword at the captive man's throat—"just get to your feet, your hands behind you."

Slowly, truculently, the man obeyed. He hawked and spat but did not attempt to flee. The curious people who had gathered to watch the fight only seconds before now vanished. The four stood alone at the edge of the river.

Charles retrieved his hat and ran his fingers through his hair before putting it on. His head still rang from the drubbing it had taken, and he could feel cuts on his lip and his cheek. He forced himself to pay no attention to the discomfort as he pulled off his jabot and used it to tie his captive's hands. "We will tend to you, never fear," he said when he felt the man's arms tighten in resistance.

"Gracious, yes," said de Portau heartily. "My companion and I want to know why you were following us. There are a few others who might be curious as well. A silly request, I know, but one you might comply with, don't you think?" He prodded his prisoner with the hilt of his sword. Neither of the men spoke, but this did not appear to distress de Portau, who marched his prisoner in front of him, and whistled as they went.

Charles followed after, too sore to join in the merry whistling, and too worried to feign lightheartedness. He kept his captive moving at a steady pace; his sword was sheathed but ready. As the last of the afternoon faded into evening, Charles felt that the light was being taken from his life as well.

✿   ✿   ✿

Text of a letter from Le Fouet smuggled into Jacques Vidal Jumeau in prison. Taken by prison guards and not delivered.

To my aide Jumeau, my greetings.

You are to say nothing, no matter what they may offer you as incentive. I have it in my power to give you more than anything, anything they might hold out to you. I have it in my power to give you all that you desire or to have your life snuffed out like a candleflame at bedtime. I want you to believe that I will reward your service to me in whatever way is appropriate.

It is said that the Italian widow has brought complaint against you. She has proof that you were spying in her household, and I must reluctantly agree that what she has presented to the magistrates and to the intendant will be supported in trial. You will stand accused of espionage at least, and of treason at most. We are fortunate that the widow is not French, or there is every chance that you would automatically be sentenced to death. As it is, there is a slim chance that I will be able to plead for you with the Parlementaires who will then decide your fate.

In order to do this, I must have your help, for if you falter now there is nothing I can do to save you. You must remain staunch in your denial; say that it was never your intention to work against the interests of the Cardinal and the King, and that you have always been loyal to the oath you gave to the Spanish whore. Say all that, and do not budge from it. If they accuse you of reading dispatches, insist that it was because you wanted to know what had transpired so that you might better expedite the information that arrived and more swiftly direct it to those with need of it. If you are accused of substituting forgeries for true dispatches, tell them that you thought there were spies intercepting the messengers and couriers, and that you had a plan to foil them, through substituting false material, so that you could evaluate the results of your actions and thereby discover the true criminal. If you are accused of endangering Bondame Clemens, say that you were told that she was not truly working for the Cardinal, but for the Pope and was charged with reporting on the progress of wars and negotiations in France so that the Pope might better regain greater control of Europe. This woman comes from an old Roman family, and it would take little to have such an assertion believed, or at least accepted as grounds for action.

I have been told that you are supposed to be tortured once, but I have sent word to prohibit that. You are to say that your health is fragile and that excesses of pain would be mortal to you. I will arrange for a physician to support you, and swear that you cannot tolerate torture, or other physically damaging methods. I expect you to be willing to appear to faint or to have a fit if there is any attempt to do more than ask you simple questions. You are dealing with rapacious, subtle men who will not let your vows stop them from wresting all they desire from you. You are as mortal as the rest of us, and do not be so proud as to think that you could resist what they do: that is done by dying and nothing else. So we must have them believe that you will not respond well to torture. At such times we must be as ruthless as they are, and you must be firm in your purpose or we will not prevail.

If you fear that you may not be able to resist what they would do to you, then get word to the night jailer and inform him of it. He will get word to me and I will provide you with sufficient poison to end your life before they can injure you too badly. Do not tell me you flinch from this if it becomes necessary. You don't suppose God really cares if you do this when the Cardinal's men are about to do the same thing, only more painfully and slower. Say your prayer and take the potion if it is needed, and be glad you were spared the torments that would destroy you and our cause at once.

There are more nobles with us at all times. They are growing certain that it is Mazarin's intention to break their power and seize it for himself. They know this would be the greatest disaster to befall France since the Black Plague. They see the example of England, and they know that they must act, or none of them will have the mandate of their position. You must buy us the time we need, for half a year should do it; then every nobleman in France will be carrying a sling and breaking windows until that perfidious Italian turns tail and runs for Rome, taking that Spanish whore and her bastards with her.

Have courage and be true to France, Jumeau.

Le Fouet

On the 23rd day of March, 1648.
Destroy this.

· 8 ·

Mazarin shifted against the squabs as his coach bowled down the road. Behind him Paris seemed to be a toy city, made of painted wood for a fortunate child. He held in his lap a leather dispatch case, and as he looked at his other passenger, he shook his head despondently. "I have no idea how best to advise you, cara mia," he said to Olivia in Italian as he reread the letter he had received the day before. "Abbe Gottard is a trustworthy man, and if he says that one of his tertiary Brothers was spreading such lies about you, then—" He lifted his hands.

"What lies are these?" Olivia asked. She was dressed in court finery, having come from the semi-annual Parisian reception for Queen Anne of Austria. She found the elaborate clothes binding and uncomfortable and not particularly flattering, but all she did was remove the large emerald-and-pearl earrings and tuck them away in her brocade purse. "They were about to stretch my ears to Greece."

"Very beautiful, though," Mazarin said with a touch of his old gallantry.

Olivia relented. "Go on, Giulio," she said quietly. "Tell me what the Abbe says. What are these lies that were spread about me, and who spread them?"

Mazarin glanced at the letter again, shaking his head with disapproval. "Abbe Gottard had a tertiary Brother at les Sacres Innocentes—an Italian, worse luck, who'd been a soldier—who was taken in hand for being the man who was responsible for the destruction of your house. While he was held by the monks, he said he did it to protect Tours from you. He said you were a demon, that he knew you were much older than you looked, that you had not changed at all in ten years, that you were preying on young men in order to keep your youth. He said you would corrupt all the monks, and because he could not bear to have that happen, he destroyed your house. The Abbe tells me he believes none of this, but he is afraid that there are many who have heard the rumors, and those rumors have grown, so that he is now advising me that it would not be wise for you to venture to Tours again. There are too many people who have heard the whispers and believed them just enough to want to prevent your return. I do not want to send you into such a place now, for I cannot guarantee your safety. I can hardly guarantee that in Paris, let alone Tours." He said this last with bitterness.

"Eminence," Olivia said, "there was bound to be trouble. The nobles were bound to resent your coming. You said as much yourself."

He did not have the French way with a shrug, but he was able to convey resignation, skepticism, unconcern, and lack of confidence with his. "I thought I was prepared for it, but it is as if everything I try is . . . blocked, anticipated. I fear I have spies around me—I know I must have—and it makes me slow to act when I need most to be decisive."

"You will prevail, Eminence," said Olivia with more sureness than she felt. "You will not fail now."

"I think I may have already." He looked at the letter from the Abbe again. "This is the sort of thing that has been plaguing me at every turn. You have been my truest support, you have not faltered when times were difficult. By being away from the court, you have performed all sorts of inestimably important tasks for me, and all without attention. But this makes it impossible for you to do that, and not because of the ridiculous lies about you. You are no longer isolated or remote, you are someone who is known. This makes you noticeable, visible, and a person attracting speculation. Which ends the wonderful luxury of the privacy you have afforded me and my messengers." He put his hand to the page. "Tours is already dangerous for you, we both understand that. And I believe that Chatillon may be as well. Once rumors of this sort begin, they spread and grow more vicious."

"I have been the subject of rumors before," Olivia remarked; she stared at the page as if she wanted it to burst into flame. "I do not know what to do, Eminence; what do you advise? Do you want me to make plans to leave?"

"No," he said at once. "We have discussed why before, and that has not changed. You must remain here. I want you close at hand.

Your departure would be assumed to herald my own. I will have to make other arrangements. I think that perhaps I will find another place in France for you, away from the court, until it is safe to bring you back. Or better yet," he said, brightening visibly, "if you were to come to Paris, to wait attendance on Queen Anne when she is there, it would be even better. Niklos can remain at Eblouir, if you insist, but I think it might be wise—"

"Eminence, you know my aversion to court life," Olivia reminded him with a sinking feeling.

"Yes, and that is what makes this difficult." He folded the letter carefully. "I am grateful to Abbe Gottard; that is certain and I have no lack of respect for him and all he has done for me and for the Queen Regent. But he could not have chosen a worse time to have this happen."

"The time does not seem to have been of his choosing," Olivia reminded Mazarin. "From all you have said, this was thrust on him by that tertiary Brother."

Mazarin lifted his dark brows in patient agreement. "It is a poor time no matter who has chosen it."

"What was the name of the tertiary Brother who defamed me?" Olivia asked, not wanting to catalogue other disappointments. "Did he mention that? It might be someone I know, or have heard of." She did not expect to recognize the name, but sensed that her question would be welcome for them both.

"I did not know you had such enemies," Mazarin said stiffly. "A man who would blow up a building, for no other purpose than ruining your house, is a formidable foe."

"Neither did I know," Olivia responded. "But it would appear that both of us have been wrong. I suppose it may be one of the men from Italy who thought he could have a place with my estate because I come from Roma, and was refused one. I have been told some came to the estate and were turned away. I had no part in that decision, but it could be I was considered responsible. That has happened to me before. If he approached Perceval, then he would have been refused out of hand. Perceval has employed local men only." She studied her fingers in her lap. "I can't conceive of any other reason for this to happen to me, not that is not connected to what I do for you."

"That could be what has happened," said Mazarin, pursing his lips as he thought. "Soldiers in a foreign land sometimes trade on their fate with others from the same country. This fellow might be that sort. The name is Colonnello, the Abbe says. Do you know someone named Colonnello?"

Olivia shook her head. "No. I only know Colonnas," she said, making an obvious joke on Mazarin's family name.

He dutifully chuckled, but it meant little. "I don't suppose," he said remotely, "that he is lying about being Italian."

"Probably not," said Olivia. "It's in the speech, isn't it?" She knew a sad amusement as she mentioned that, for her own Italian had an archaic flavor to it, an old-fashionedness that occasionally provoked comment.

"He might be a Spaniard," said Mazarin darkly. "Corpo di Dio, he could be anything. And the name Colonnello could be just another ruse, to anger me. He may have another name entirely, and we might never discover it." His frown deepened as he spoke, making his handsome face look older and less attractive. He put the letter back in the dispatch case. "I have talked to d'Artagnan, and on his recommendation, I will have his friend given temporary assignment to my Guards, and then posted to guard you."

"His friend," Olivia repeated. "De Portau?"

"Yes. They were Musqueteers together. De Portau is with the King's Guard. His record is very good, and I doubt you need worry once he is present."

"I already have Niklos," Olivia pointed out. The idea of entrusting her safety to a stranger did not appeal to her at all.

"He has other things to do than guard you," Mazarin said, dismissing Niklos. "I think you require someone who will have it as his duty to accompany you and be certain you are not harmed no matter where you go."

"Is that truly needed?" Olivia asked, hating the plan already. She despised being watched and guarded and hampered and confined. "Can't there be another way? It's as bad as being in prison, Eminence, to be guarded in that way."

Mazarin smiled. "You love to overstate your case," he observed. "I am aware of your dislike of constraint, but in this instance, your good sense will prevail. You need a guard until the nobles and the Parlements have accepted the intendants and once more taken steps to supply the army in the field. All those in my service will be at hazard. Take this de Portau in as your guard, for d'Artagnan's sake if not mine. He will be no earthly use to me if he is forever caught in worries about you." He glanced out the window. "I used to love the windmills. Now they remind me of . . . enemy ships, I suppose." He touched his hands together. "You're a sensible woman, Olivia. I shouldn't have to remind you what is wanted at this time. You have been through enough to know that you must protect yourself until this dispute I have with the nobles is resolved."

"But you cannot send me back to Roma?" she persisted. "It isn't something I could do overnight, Eminence. I will require two or three months to be fully prepared, and you know that a household moves slowly in travel. How could such preparations appear like the beginning of flight when they are so complex and slow?" She watched his face, trying to fathom his thoughts by his expression and the angle of his head.

The coach lurched, the two men on the box swore loudly, and for a moment the carriage canted alarmingly. Then it rocked back onto the road, the horses whinnying in distress, one of the lackeys riding behind yelling out that he had almost broken his arm and the next time he'd like a warning.

In the carriage both Mazarin and Olivia reached for the hand-loops by the door, but neither was quick enough. They were tossed onto the seats and the papers in the leather case went slithering across the seats and onto the floor. As soon as the coach was back on the road, Olivia knelt and began to gather up the papers, handing them silently to Mazarin.

"Take care you get them all," he warned her, a little breathless from being flung around.

She made a careful check when she was through and found one small notecard lodged between the upholstered squabs. As she handed this to Mazarin, she said, "You might always tell the world that you disapprove of my affair with Charles, or that my uncles want me to marry again."

"What uncles?" His challenge received no answer, nor did he expect one. Mazarin did not press the matter. "When your house was destroyed in Tours, I supposed that it was done by the brigands in the area, and that the tertiary Brother they captured was only a scapegoat to permit the brigands to escape unscathed from their own nefarious act. But when you told me that the chief of the brigands is the brother of your major domo there, and had once been major domo himself, I was less certain about the brigands. That is one of the reasons Abbe Gottard has kept me informed on this tertiary Brother, and why we are all distressed that he escaped and has not been recaptured." He gave Olivia a short time to respond; when she did not, he continued, "You do not believe that this man was anything more than a misled or angry peasant, do you?"

"Peasants have enrolled in the army," said Olivia, curious though she did not want to be. "From what you have learned, I can think of no reason to assume that this man was anything more than a cashiered peasant soldier who was angry that he could not find work at the stud farm. You are flinching at shadows, Eminence, and there are too many real dangers around you for you to waste time with this." She adjusted the fall of her skirts. "Eminence, listen to me," she went on persuasively, "who can you think of who would bother to come all the way to Tours—Tours, Saints save us!—establish himself at a monastery just for the pleasure of blowing up my house?"

Mazarin took a long breath. "I do not want to find out you are mistaken, Olivia," he warned her affectionately. "I have reason enough to know that there are the most adamant foes who will lie in wait for you for years. I do not want you plagued by one such because of me."

"But I am neither Cardinal nor First Minister of France," she said reasonably. "I am a widow in your embassy, and it makes sense to me that it is your embassy that is being threatened, not Atta Olivia Clemens of Roma." Her hazel eyes grew brighter. "And if it turns out that someone is attempting to disgrace you through me, then we will have to deal with that trouble as it arises." She reached across the narrow space between the seats and patted the dispatch case. "There are more pressing concerns in these sheets, Eminence, and you would do well to review them. It is not fitting that your position should be compromised because of gossip about me. That priest who takes your messages to the Vatican from time to time—Pere Chape—he might be called upon to help us if we have more trouble."

Mazarin listened to her attentively, and was almost convinced she was correct. "I have to review our agreements with Sweden. Now that this endless war is almost concluded, we have certain concessions each of us must make for the benefit of the other. They are valiant fighters, the Swedes, but I do not comprehend their temperament."

"They were not always as they are now," said Olivia, remembering the iron-helmeted Norsemen who had come a-viking up the rivers of France and England, drunk with mead and the thrill of battle.

"War has taken a toll of us all," said Mazarin, not understanding her. They were approaching Chatillon now, and Mazarin began to relax. "Away from Paris, I am less troubled than when I can see broken windows. In Paris I fully expect a Parlementaire to challenge me to defend my honor."

"Challenge a Cardinal?" Olivia asked, knowing that to do so was to be excommunicated, which not even the boldest of Parlementaires would risk. "Who is foolish enough to do that?"

"I don't know," Mazarin admitted with a shame-faced smile. "But that does not rid me of the sense that it will happen. And in a way," he went on thoughtfully, "I would not mind, for it would end this uncertainty and suspicion that has been my daily fare for so long."

"If you wish it ended, why not demand it, rather than waiting for one of the others to act? Insist that the nobles or the Parlementaires state their case at once or cease their protests." She knew it was not as simply done as she proposed, but she did not like to see Mazarin so harried.

"How?" asked Mazarin, his dark brown eyes on hers. "And how can I do it without exposing the Queen and the King to the machinations of the nobles? You know how that would be—the King would end up in the hands of a different regent and the Queen would be returned to Spain in disgrace. I have an oath to defend, Olivia." He glanced out the window again. "The turn to Eblouir," he said as the coach rounded a curve a bit too sharply.

Olivia righted herself on the seat. "You will have a change of horses from my stable, and I will arrange for your escort to be fed," she said, repeating the offer she had made earlier. "If you decide that you would rather, there is room to house you for the night, and it would honor me to—" She had been looking out the window toward her chateau, and as it came into view, she fell silent, her face frozen.

"What is it?" asked Mazarin when she did not go on. "Olivia? Is something the matter?"

Her voice did not sound like her own. "All the windows are broken," she said.

Mazarin looked stricken as she spoke. "What?"

"All the windows are broken," she repeated, lifting the shutter on the window to get a better look at the chateau as the coach came up the drive and through the arch of the gate.

"God and the Angels," whispered Mazarin as he raised his window's shutter.

"Niklos," said Olivia, unable to keep from staring at the ruined windows, blind as empty eye sockets. "Where are the servants?" Impulsively she reached out as if to open the door of the carriage, but Mazarin restrained her.

"In a short while, cara mia," he told her gently. "Let the driver bring the coach to the stable and stop before you try to get out." He crossed himself, then reached out to take her hand. "I never intended any of this to touch you."

"But it has. First at Tours and now here," she said, wanting to scream at him for the satisfaction of screaming.

"If I could apologize, Madama, I would do it, on my knees." He folded his hands and murmured a prayer before looking at her directly and saying, "You will have to come back to Paris with me. We will arrange it now. Your staff will send along the things you need—clothes, horses, whatever you designate—but you will come back with me. Tonight." Now that he was aware of the danger near her, he was without the doubts that had so tormented him earlier.

"You said yourself that Paris is not safe," Olivia reminded him, a bit nonplused at his change of demeanor.

"No, but safer than this," he said, indicating Eblouir as the coach drew up in the stable courtyard. "Let my men—" he warned, but before he could finish, Olivia had opened the door and got out.

"Niklos!" she shouted as she started toward the pantry door. "Niklos Aulirios!" It was hard not to call for Meres as well, though Meres was dead. "Niklos!"

With the aid of his lackey, Mazarin descended from the carriage and came to her side. "My men will search the house."

"I'll do it," said Olivia as she gathered up her skirts, cursing their cumbersome abundance, and began to run toward the pantry door.

"Madama!" Mazarin called after her, but she would not stop.

As she reached the door, she discovered it was bolted from the inside. She cried out in frustration, then started around toward the rear entrance to the house, between the creamery and her bath. She did not bother to check her speed, but let her enormous vampire strength take her. Behind her she heard one of Mazarin's escort exclaim in astonishment, but she ran on.

Around the back of the house, the heavy walls that framed the open hearth of the kitchen and the backing of the huge ovens.

Then past the shed containing cut wood, and at last to the little door that led to the dressing room adjoining her bath. As her hands closed on the ring latch, she felt the door open to her.

"Olivia," said Niklos, hugging her as she rushed into his arms. "I was afraid you would come back while they were still here."

She lifted her head from his shoulder and looked at his face. "You're not hurt?"

"Not I. There are a few in the household who are bruised, and two are cut a little. As soon as that group that said they were a hunting party came through the garden, I ordered all the doors bolted and windows barred. We didn't have time to put up the shutters. Well, you know that, don't you?" He patted her back and looked away, slightly embarrassed. "I didn't want you to see the house like this."

"Did you think you could repair it in an hour or two?" Olivia asked, her voice shaking just a little. "Magna Mater! is there any window that isn't broken?"

"Less than a dozen." Niklos released her. "But I could have had one of the grooms meet you on the road, to tell you that the place was . . . under siege." He took her hand and led her down the narrow hall back toward the kitchen. "Most of the servants are in their dining room. The windows there are high, and protected. The lackeys did a good job, Olivia. And the grooms helped, after they secured the stables. There was only one horse injured, and he was out in his paddock. We didn't have long enough to bring him in." They had almost reached the kitchen; he stopped her and said in a low voice, "Most of the staff are upset. Some of them are angry."

"I am not surprised. I am upset and angry, myself," said Olivia with asperity, then softened her tone. "You mean that they may blame me."

"Yes," said Niklos bluntly. "The men in the hunting party shouted your name."

"That probably wasn't all they shouted," she said sardonically, then remarked, "You'd better let in Mazarin and his escort. They're waiting outside, trampling the broken glass into the court-yard, no doubt." She looked at Niklos with a direct, intent stare. "We have dealt with worse, you and I."

"That we have," said Niklos, his attitude at its most stalwart, with doubt showing only in his ruddy-brown eyes. "I will tend to the Cardinal and his men." He looked toward the alcove of the pantry door. "Will they deign to come in through the kitchen?"

"They'd better; they're not coming in any other way," Olivia said, and started toward the servants' dining room. She looked back at Niklos once. "We will manage, old friend."

He answered with a gesture of affirmation.

In the servants' dining room, discussion was carried on in irate, hushed voices. The two cooks bickered about the ruined garden, the scullions listening with distress in their young faces. Four of the lackeys were trying to explain to the others and one another why the hunting party had dared to attack the house. The other three lackeys were too disgusted to join them, but kept to haughty silence. The grooms were restless, just like the horses in the stable, though only one of them actually made any complaint. Of the five maids, one was sitting with a wet cloth on her forehead, another was applying ointment to a bruise on the senior lackey's arm, and the other three were sitting apart from the rest, their heads together.

Olivia opened the door and stepped inside, waiting for her servants to give their attention before she closed the door. "I am pleased that there were no serious injuries to any of you," she said, schooling herself to speak calmly. "I am also chagrined that you should have to endure this while in my employ." She looked from one servant to the next, making an effort to meet the eyes of each in turn. "What has happened here is inexcusable, for you as well as for me, and it is intolerable for you to remain here as long as risks such as this remain."

One of the maids put a shaking hand to her mouth too late to stop the sob of worry. A lackey looked away in disgust.

Olivia ignored these things. "I cannot require any servant in my employ to face danger in my name. It is not honorable for me to do this; I will not demand it of you." She moved a few steps into the room. "I will arrange for each of you to be given a full year's pay, as well as the salary for all of May. If you have family depending on your earnings, inform Aulirios and I will make provision for you and for them so that no one need suffer privation because of what these arrogant noblemen have done." She looked at one of her grooms. "Is the stable all right?"

"They wanted to break windows; most of the horses didn't interest them. They took after Jeudi because he was loose, and he liked to jump." He looked away from Olivia to some place on the floor near the table leg. "One of them shot him. It was the only time they fired a pistol. For the windows it was slings and stones. They rode around the house, shouting and breaking windows. Jeudi was so excited . . ." His voice trailed off, and guiltily he wiped his eyes with the back of his hand.

"They wanted to shame you, Madame," said one of the new lackeys. "They called you many names that nobles should not use to well-born women." His stare was insolent. "But you are a foreigner and in the suite of Mazarin. There may be some truth in their accusations."

Three of the others were nodding in agreement when the door opened behind Olivia and Mazarin swept into the room, his hand with his episcopal ring extended.

Though most of Olivia's staff had seen Mazarin from time to time when he visited Eblouir, they had never been subjected to one of his full state entrances. All but two of them dropped to their knees at once; the maid with the cloth on her forehead slid from her chair to the floor in a swoon.

"Someone attend to her," said Mazarin, indicating the unfortunate woman. "You," he went on, selecting the youngest lackey. "See that she is decorously seated at once." He gave the gathering his blessing, then, as they arranged themselves once more, he said, "Your mistress has been ill-used by those whose birth should render such abuse impossible. If you think otherwise, you do her and me a disservice." He walked past Olivia to the modest hearth and used that as his pulpit. "For her good service and loyal aid, I am taking Bondame Clemens to Paris, where she will not be subjected to insults of this sort again. I will dispatch workers to repair this chateau. And when it is repaired and ready, it will be hers to use again, if she will be gracious and forgiving enough to accept it." He made an eloquent and courteous gesture to Olivia, then continued to her servants, "You can offer thanks for such a mistress in your prayers, as you will pray for the redemption of those who have done this disgraceful act. Not many households in France can boast of a more just mistress than Bondame Clemens, and none has one more kind." Again he offered his blessing in his grandest manner, then moved impressively to the door. "If I hear that any of you were party to what happened here, it will go hard for you." He nodded gravely once, and left the room.

Olivia stood still, aware that her servants were staring at her with stronger and more mixed emotions than before. She gathered her thoughts with an effort. "For the time that the Cardinal has been magnanimous enough to order Eblouir repaired, your salaries will continue unless you would rather seek employment elsewhere, in which case Aulirios will provide you with a recommendation. Those who wish to remain will be paid as I have stated already." She looked around, feeling as if she stood on shifting sands. "I must inspect the damage," she added, and left the room, knowing that nothing would be said among the servants until she was gone.

Niklos was waiting for her outside the door. "Is it true what the Cardinal says?" he demanded as soon as the door was closed. "Olivia?"

"I don't know," she said, a trifle light-headed. "He has been saying so many things." She started toward the hall leading to the rest of the house.

"Are we going to Paris?" The words came out sharply, matching the frown making a deep line between his brows.

Olivia stopped walking and considered the question. "I think you are staying here. If Charles were not dispatched to the Marquis d'Hocquincourt, I would ask to have him here as a guard so that His Eminence would be willing to let me remain. But I suspect that I am indeed going to Paris."

"Because Mazarin thinks you'll be safer there?" Niklos said incredulously. "He's mad if he believes that. Paris is the center of this . . . this noble discontent. It is the Parlement of Paris that resists Mazarin most consistently." He swung his arm impatiently. "What about the Queen Regent? He isn't bringing her to Paris, I wager."

"I don't know," said Olivia thoughtfully. "I suspect he might, if only to show that he is not frightened by threats." She fiddled with the sash at her raised waist. "If he would simply allow me to return to Roma. Half of my house in Tours is a ruin and the other half is little better than a byre. And now this. It was called Eblouir because of all its windows. The glazers will need a long time to restore it." She opened the door to an alcove, a room most often used to hold cloaks and wraps, but empty now. "Come in, Niklos," she said.

"What is it?" he growled.

"Mazarin cannot object now. You will have to pack most of the goods here in any case, to protect them against vandals. Let me try to convince him that they can be shipped south, in small amounts, without attracting attention." She sagged against the wall, saying as much to herself as to Niklos, who closed the door so that they could not be overheard, "Why does Giulio tempt them this way? He is the master of the great gesture, of skillful negotiations, but he does not know how to wait, and waiting is making him skittish."

"Then leave." He said it harshly out of worry, but he touched her arm at the same time. "This is not your risk, not your fight."

"No, but I gave my word to His Eminence, and to the Cardinals Bagni and Barberini and Bichi. They would not look kindly on my leaving at such a time." She shook off her lost look. "I want my ducksfoot pistol and two swords. And I want the four best horses in the stable. If I must remain here, I intend to be prepared." This time she was able to smile with a little of the roguish charm she displayed occasionally. "Since I am to be in the storm—"

"Is this because of Charles?" Niklos interrupted, his tone low and sharp. "Because if it is—"

"I think it is, in part," she said. "If he were not Mazarin's courier, then I would have gone when Tours was wrecked. As it is, I know that if I displease Mazarin now, I will be putting Charles at risk, and perhaps I would not see him again. After all this, I don't know if I could endure losing him as well. So I will do as Mazarin wishes, and hope we win through."

Niklos paced the length of the small alcove. "Doesn't Mazarin know what he is asking of you?"

She went to Niklos' side and leaned her head on his shoulder for a moment. She spoke softly, her eyes all but closed. "He hasn't said; it would make no difference if he did."

"Be damned to him," hissed Niklos, a quick jerk of his head indicating the way Mazarin had gone.

"Very likely," said Olivia with a faltering smile.

* * *

Text of a letter from Charles d'Artagnan in his own hand to Atta Olivia Clemens

My love Olivia,
You are not safe now. The victories and the Te Deum were too late. The Parlementaires Broussel, Charton, and Blancmesnil are the cause of the trouble since Eminence and Queen ordered them arrested. Now the nobles and the Parlementaires are together and will not be stopped.
I want you to leave. Trust the man who brings this. Go with him to Avignon, and then to Rome. Wear men's clothes and take arms. I want to come, but I must be with Eminence and King. My soul hurts to do this, but you will not be safe here, and I cannot make you safe. Go with de Portau. He is my good friend. Wait for me in Rome and I will come, dead or living.
I pray for you. Your love is with me that makes me strong.
                                                      Charles d'Artagnan
Burn this.

· 9 ·

His bow was perfunctory, and he spoke just above a whisper. "Will you do it?"

Olivia held the scrap of paper to the flame of her candle and watched as it started to burn. "So you are de Portau," she said, still looking at the paper.

"And you are d'Artagnan's famous widow." From another, such words might have been insults; from de Portau, they were almost affectionate. "He did not over-praise you, Madame."

"I am Olivia, not Madame, if we are to flee like felons in the night," she said. "I will not summon the maid," she went on, "so I will need some help with my boots."

"Of course," said de Portau, trying hard to conceal the astonishment she wakened in him. "How long will it take? We must be gone before the night Watch is relieved, or we might not leave the city."

Olivia smiled as she looked at de Portau. "I am not dressing for a ball, Monsieur. I am dressing to escape. I have some experience of escapes and I know the rules." As she said this, she went to the armoire at the far end of the chamber and opened the two lower drawers, pulling out dark men's clothes, a hat and riding boots, leaving them in a puddle of dark on the rose-patterned carpet. "I don't want to offend your modesty, de Portau. But I warn you I am about to dress. You may bring a screen if you think you'll need it."

De Portau shrugged with more sangfroid than he felt. "As you prefer, Madame."

"Olivia," she corrected him. "And you are—?"

"Isaac," he said, staring as she pulled off her night rail and stood naked amid her pile of clothes. "Your mirror—"

"I won't require it," she said with a quick twitch of a smile as she reached down and pulled out her underwear, a serviceable unboned corset and brief drawers. She dressed without any trace of coquetry, as efficient and meticulous as any soldier readying for battle. Her heavy grey chamise was on and she was tugging into her breeches when she said, "There is a case under the bed. Will you get it for me, please?"

"We can't carry much," de Portau warned.

"You'll want what's in that case," said Olivia as she fastened the rosettes of her breeches at the top of the peplums of her dark wool doublet.

De Portau pulled out the case and opened it suspiciously, then stared in renewed astonishment at what he saw. "Madame!"

This time Olivia did not bother to correct him. "Take one of the purses for yourself, Isaac. Be careful with it, because we may need much gold before we are out of France. Give me the other." She held out her hand and took the purse he gave to her. It was satisfyingly heavy. "Do you want the duck'sfoot or shall I carry it?"

"Can you use it?" he asked, amazed to find the multibarreled pistol in the case.

"Yes. Why would I keep a weapon I can't use?" she asked, straightening up. She took her dark jabot and tied it around her neck, adjusting the fall so that it gave extra protection to her throat. She went to her dressing table and picked up a small pair of scissors. "I can't do this for myself," she said, holding them out. "Here."

De Portau took them. "What do you want me to do?"

"Cut my hair," she said as if the answer were obvious. "I won't pass as a man if I have all this trailing down to my waist. Cut it shorter than yours, so that the friz by my face will not be as noticeable."

Reluctantly he took the long, light brown strands in his fingers. "It is beautiful hair, Madame. It is a shame to cut it." He flinched at the thought of what Charles might say if he were given this task.

"It is a greater shame to be caught because of it," said Olivia pragmatically. "Cut it."

De Portau could not argue with what she said; he took the scissors and started snipping, saddened by each lock of shining fawn-brown that fell amid the carpet roses. He tried to comply, as if cutting hair for a page, but he had to admit that he did not do a very good job. Finally he stood back. "I've done," he said sadly.

Olivia ran her hands through her short hair, shaking her head to loosen any unfallen bits. "I hope your cuts are surer with a sword," she said with a chuckle as she realized how ragged her hair was.

"I have some experience of swords," said de Portau. He put the scissors aside and went back to the case. "I will take the ducksfoot, I think," he said.

"Make sure it's charged, then," said Olivia, not willing to argue. "I don't want to have to stop for that if we are pursued."

"Of course," said de Portau, a bit huffy at having his good sense questioned.

Olivia relented at once. "I do not mean to impugn you, Isaac. When I am in . . . difficult circumstances, I think aloud; that way I am less likely to forget important things." She took the other two pistols from the case and put them on the foot of her bed. "And I need a sword," she said, indicating the empty scabbard that hung from her belt. "And that dagger, for my boot." She reached out for it, then went to put on her high, soft-topped boots. "I have horses in the stable, and tack. It will not take long to be ready. Will you give me a hand with these boots?"

De Portau obliged at once, coming and taking her foot in his hand so she could push against it as she tugged her boot on. As she was drawing on the second one, he lifted a finger, indicating the need for silence.

Olivia was instantly still. Her hand closed around her dagger. There was a discreet knock at the door. "Madame Clemens?"

"Who?" de Portau mouthed, making no sound.

"A priest," she responded in the same way. "Yes, Pere Chape?" she asked as if just wakened from sleep.

"Are you all right?" He was just outside the door. "We have had warnings of more prowlers in the palace."

"I am fine," said Olivia. "Is there any danger?"

"Of course not," said Pere Chape with false assurance. "It was only my duty to be certain you were well."

"Very well," said Olivia, frowning now.

"Then I will not disturb you further. God be with you."

"And you," answered Olivia, her frowning deepening. She motioned de Portau to utter silence as she got up and moved to the door, her footstep muffled by the carpet. She stood listening, then came back to the bed. "Listen to me," she whispered, so low that he had to bend near to hear her. "He is still at the door. He is still listening. He is waiting to catch me, or us."

"But why?" de Portau asked, puzzled. "He is one of the Cardinal's men, isn't he?"

"Who knows?" said Olivia, her eyes hardening. "With Mazarin leaving so hurriedly, Pere Chape might want to go over to the Parlementaires." She checked her pistols. "I'll charge them in the stable," she said in an undervoice. "Gather up the hair and put it in here. Then put the whole thing back under the bed." She was opening another small case, and drew out pistolballs. "Hurry," she hissed to de Portau, who was trying to pick up all her hair.

He had just closed the case and was sliding it back under the bed when Olivia slid back toward the door, listening intently. She gave a sign that indicated Pere Chape had not left. Cautiously she came back to de Portau and again whispered. "We go out through the maid's room and by the servants' stairs. It means someone may see us, but with Pere Chape in the hall, I can think of nothing else to do. I have a copy of the Cardinal's seal, which might or might not help us to leave the city." She went to her dressing table and reached under the bottom drawer, then pulled out a sheet of vellum with Mazarin's seal impressed in red wax at its center. "It might get us out of the palace, at least," she said.

"Possibly," said de Portau as softly as he could, "or it may mark us as spies."

"We run that risk no matter what we do," she reminded him, then looked around the room one more time. "If we can only gain a little time. Most of them will be looking for the Cardinal and the Queen. They will not bother with us, not at first. If we are lucky, that will be enough."

At her signal, de Portau followed her to the small door leading to the empty room which would ordinarily be occupied by her maid. As he closed the door carefully, so as to make no sound, he said, "What of remounts? We might get away from Paris, but it is a long way to Rome."

"I have horses stabled along the route," said Olivia, her voice a little louder now that there was more distance between them and the waiting Pere Chape. "That is the least of our worries, Isaac. Pursuit is more crucial than remounts."

"Is it?" He allowed her to lead the way through the maze of little hallways and down precariously steep stairs toward the back of the palace. The whole building moaned and sighed due to the broken windows and the wind. "I don't like it," he said as they neared the servants' common room adjoining their dining room. "It's too risky."

"Would you rather walk out the grand entrance?" she asked. "There are still nobles watching, in case Mazarin has decoyed them with a third coach." They were almost through the common room when the kitchen door opened and a thin page wandered in, clearly still half asleep.

Olivia and de Portau stopped, waiting to see what the boy would do, and listening for the approach of others.

The page looked at them, his eyes growing wide. Then he yelped and ran from the room.

"Quickly," whispered Olivia, and all but dragged de Portau through the door leading to the pantry. She kept him moving through the next two rooms, one of which was filled with pots and pans, the other of which had sacks of wheat and unground grains for use in the palace kitchens. The door beyond that opened onto a little courtyard in front of the creamery.

"There may be guards," de Portau warned her as she began to make her way through the shadows toward the stable.

"We have this," she reminded him, patting where Mazarin's seal lay under her doublet. "If there are any questions, the guard will honor it."

"Are you certain?" de Portau asked as he moved after her.

"No."

The stable was unguarded. Half the stalls were empty, and the main tack room was not locked. The grooms were not in their quarters and there was no sign of any of the stablehands and farriers who might usually be found there at night. As Olivia and de Portau passed the stalls, the horses whickered.

"They're hungry," said Olivia, wondering if the animals had been fed at all that day, or given water.

"There's no time to feed them," warned de Portau as Olivia pointed him in the direction of the little room where his own tack was kept. "Perhaps we should let them loose. They might find some food, and it would slow pursuit."

"If we have time," she agreed reluctantly. "But better get grain for our mounts, then. They will do better with a bit of food in them. Take one of the small sacks, as well, in case we need to stop on the way; they can eat then." She was already taking her saddle, breastplate, and bridle off their racks, then chose a leather-backed pad for the saddle. Her brushes and picks were in a farrier's apron which she donned. "Hurry. Nothing more than a quick brush, and check the hooves," she warned him. "There isn't time for more."

The mouse-colored mare was nervous, but the quick grooming Olivia gave before saddling her served to calm her a little. She took the grain she was offered eagerly, and when it was gone nudged Olivia's arm requesting more. By that time Olivia had the saddle on and was buckling the breastplate to the saddle. The mare lifted her head as de Portau swore in the next stall.

"What's wrong?" Olivia called in an undervoice.

"Damned horse stepped on my foot." He did not sound injured. "Is this a Spanish horse?"

"Partly," said Olivia, readying the bridle. The mare took the bit and brought her head into a neat tuck as Olivia buckled the reins and led her out of her stall. "Isaac?" she called as she pulled off the apron and tossed it back into the stall.

"Just a little more time," he answered. "The fellow's trying to eat through the grain sack." His slap on the horse's rump was the loudest sound they had made yet. "Almost ready," he assured her, and then opened the stall door. "There. Do you have a crop I can use?"

Olivia had taken two from the tack room. She gave him one and slipped the thong of the other over her wrist. "We'd better mount in here. There's no telling what we'll find outside."

"True enough," said de Portau. He checked the stirrup, then swung up into the saddle, holding the bay in as the horse started to move. "Stand, you barbarian."

As Olivia mounted, she noticed a movement near the open tack room door. She peered through the dark, her eyes not as hampered by night as others were. The only thing she could make out was a black sleeve, but it might be nothing more than a piece of canvas caught by the wind. She cocked her head, listening, but heard nothing louder than the soft clatter of the horses' hooves. She let the mare take a few steps nearer the tack room, then held her, not wanting to court discovery. Slowly she brought the mare back around and nodded in the direction of the stable door. "Isaac? Are you ready?"

"For anything, Madame," he answered with a flourish of his hat. "Let us proceed."

The streets around the palace were slick with broken glass. A few drunken Watchmen staggered their rounds, paying no attention to the destruction they saw, questioning no one. They threw stones at the shuttered windows, imitating the earlier window-smashing attack, laughing when their small rocks struck. As Olivia and de Portau rode past them, they made an extravagant point of looking the other direction, and then laughing immoderately when the two were far enough away that they would not return to thrash them for their impertinence.

"We got away," said de Portau as they crossed the Seine and started toward the southern gates. "I never thought it would really happen. The risk was enormous," he said as if revealing a tremendous secret. "We got away."

"I hope we have," said Olivia, unable to shake the sense that they were observed. She rose in the stirrups and looked behind them again, then pulled her cloak more tightly around her. "It's cold for this time of year."

"Just as well. The horses will last longer," said de Portau, his hands gathering in the reins. "How do we get through the gate? Are they alerted, do you think? Do they know yet that the Cardinal and the Queen have fled Paris? Have the nobles suborned them yet? Will that seal work?"

"If I make them think that I am a Vatican page, it will. Not even the Parlementaires and nobles want to anger the Pope." She took her gloves from one of her pockets and pulled them on, then cast another backward glance. "There is someone there; I would swear it on my mother's grave."

"You're fanciful, Olivia," said de Portau, daring to use her name for the first time. "If we had been followed, we would know it. Who would bother now that we are almost out of the city?"

"We are not almost out of the city, we are approaching a gate, and we may not be permitted to leave. Then it will not matter how far we came, if they do not allow us to pass." She settled herself in the saddle again, and set the mare into a slow trot, thinking that if they could increase the distance between them and their pursuers, they would stand a better chance of being allowed to leave.

The Seine was leaden in the wan moonlight; shadows of buildings fell like immense voids along the bank; as Olivia and de Portau left the quai and turned toward the ancient church of Saint Medard, the long shadows engulfed them, so that they were darker places within the dark.

At the Orleans Gate a single Watchman looked at the Cardinal's seal, gave a laconic glance to the two dark-clad travelers and waved them on, holding up his bottle of wine in an ironic toast. "You tell the Pope that his puppy has had his tail bobbed," he called after them, chortling at his own drunken wit.

"That was lucky," admitted de Portau as they continued along the river.

"The news must not have meant much to him. Give the Watch another day and they will be dragons," said Olivia, her mind casting back to many bitter experiences. When she had wanted to leave Cordova, it was not permitted; when she had wanted to leave Tyre, it was not permitted; when she had wanted to leave Krakow, it was not permitted. This time she had got out before the doors closed too tightly. "And we are still in France," she said aloud, looking apprehensively over her shoulder again.

"What matter? We are ahead of most of them. If we make good time and have fresh horses, we will be out of the kingdom before the Ducs realize they have the upper hand." He patted the bay on the neck. "Not a bad horse."

"Thank you," said Olivia, her attention on the road, not on the compliment. "I try to raise good horses."

"So Charles has told me," said de Portau, relaxing visibly now that the walls of Paris were behind them. "Where do we remount? Is it far?"

"I have horses stabled both in Savigny-sur-Orge and Saint-Genevieve-des-Bois. We can choose which is best when we are nearer." She pulled the mare into a walk once more. "It won't do to push them too hard now. We may need their speed later." She looked toward the east. "Four hours to sunrise, wouldn't you say?" Her face showed almost no emotion, but the feeling of urgency was pressing her more insistently.

"Yes; four hours. We got away in good time." De Portau rubbed the stubble on his cheeks above his beard. "I can ride until two hours after sunset, and by that time we will be a goodly way on our journey. I'm a soldier, but I'm not a stripling anymore—I am all of thirty-five, getting on for a soldier. I need sleep two nights out of three. So, after sunset, if there is a place we can be safe, I will have to have rest then or be no use to you." He coughed delicately. "You will be tired then, too, Olivia."

"Very likely," she responded, not wanting to tell him that she had had little need for sleep for almost sixteen hundred years. "By then we may be beyond Fontainebleau."

"That might be a problem, Fontainebleau," said de Portau carefully. "It has been one of the nobles' strongholds. They might be there still. It is hard to know." He sighed. "I wish, while we were remembering the grain for the horses, we had also remembered a leg of chicken for us as well."

Olivia hesitated before she answered. "There will be food if you want it when we change horses. I thought it was more important for the horses to be fed than for us." She hitched her thumb in the direction of the sack of grain tied to his saddle. "We'd better continue to carry that with us. For the horses."

"As you wish," said de Portau, sounding cast down, but with a glint in his small eyes. "I'd hate to see you on campaign, Madame, and that's the truth. I wouldn't wonder if you couldn't put all our generals to shame."

"Why do you say that?" Olivia asked, and then motioned him to silence. Her eyes were intent, inward directed. "There are horsemen behind us."

"There are always horsemen on this road," said de Portau, attempting to disguise the sudden cold fear that gripped him.

"They are moving quickly," said Olivia. "A goodly number; seven, perhaps eight." She looked back in alarm, as if she expected to see them. "They're a way distant yet."

"They might have nothing to do with us," said de Portau without conviction. "They might be carrying word to Fontainebleau or . . . somewhere else."

"Would you care to make a wager?" said Olivia as she touched the mare's sides with her heels. Obediently the mouse-colored horse began again to trot, the sound of her hooves on the road lending a steady beat to their progress.

De Portau put his mount to the trot as well. "Is this fast enough?" he asked, permitting his apprehension to show for the first time. "A trot is well enough, and they can keep it up longer than a canter, but if we are being chased—"

"No, it isn't fast enough," she admitted, and nudged the mare into a canter. "But you're right; I don't know how long she can keep this up." She moved in the saddle for better balance. "And I don't know what the road is like ahead." Her words came in spurts as the force of the canter rocked her.

"Neither do I," said de Portau, urging his horse to keep pace with hers. "Who is it behind us?"

"I don't know, but I would wager that they're from the nobles or the Parlementaires—I don't think the Cardinal sent them. He has no reason to come after us, and the others have every reason in the world." She put all her attention to the road, watching for anything that might injure or slow her mare. Most of the roads in France were in poor repair, for most of the taxes levied had gone to pay for wars, not building roads. Ordinarily Olivia would not plunge along this road in the dark, but with those unknown riders at her back, she dared not do otherwise, no matter how imprudent.

A little farther along the road, Olivia and de Portau passed through a sleeping hamlet. Dogs woke, barking, at their passage, then fell silent, only to bark again a short while later.

"There, you see?" Olivia said to de Portau. "We are not the only ones abroad tonight." She could feel her horse begin to flag, the pace getting to her. "Pull in to a trot," she called to de Portau.

"Is it safe?" he shouted to her.

"It's not safe to keep going as we have." She was as breathless as her horse. "We need to get them a little water, too. Not the river. At the next village, find a well."

"What about the men behind us?" de Portau demanded as he brought his bay up beside Olivia's mare. "They are still chasing us? Can you tell?" It was as far as he would go to believing that she had the ability to sense the presence of their hunters.

"On horses just like ours. If they push their mounts too hard they will kill them; they can't catch us on dead horses," said Olivia curtly. "We might find a place to hide, as well."

"Won't they be expecting us to do that?" de Portau asked. "And won't they look for places we might hide?"

"Not at that pace," said Olivia. "They do not have time to search at the canter. But if they slow down, then they will be searching for us, you may be sure of it." She could feel her mare's deep breaths and pounding heart through the flaps of her saddle. The horse needed time to recover her wind and to gather her strength once more. Olivia touched the handle of one of the two pistols she carried. "If they get too close, we will have to discourage them."

"I have the duck'sfoot," de Portau reminded her. Now that they were not rushing as fast, he was aware of how cold he was, and of the steady ache in his shoulders. He straightened his spine against the hurt, blanking it out of his mind as if he were in battle and ready for the foe. That pain was a sign of being tired, he reminded himself, nothing more than that. Simple fatigue, and unexceptional in a man who had been up since sunrise. He reminded himself that he had given his word he would ride until the two hours after sundown, and that was a long time away. He blinked his eyes hard twice, and settled in to the steady trot of the bay. "If we must, we can see if we can get behind them, become the hunters." The last was garbled by a yawn he could not stifle.

"You're tired," said Olivia in a tone that invited no contradiction.

"A little," he admitted. "I will come about after dawn; it is the dark, it makes me sleepy." His quick smile was abashed, as if he had been caught doing something very naughty. "When we stop, I will splash some cold water on my face; that will wake me, and I will be fine."

Olivia kept her thought to herself, but she began to worry about how long he would be able to last. There was no reason, she thought, for him to be embarrassed by his exhaustion, but it was clear to her that he was embarrassed. She held her mare to the trot and scanned the distance, searching for the signs of another hamlet: fenced fields, windmills, a cluster of small buildings, that would be enough for her to be sure.

"What are you looking at?" said de Portau, having cast a glance backward. "I still do not see anyone, or hear them."

"That's to the good. They might have slowed for the sake of their horses." At last she caught sight of a group of small houses flanking the road some distance ahead. "Another little town. We will look for water there," she said, knowing it would be more than a quarter of an hour before they reached the place. The mare would trot that far, she knew, but she might not want to trot farther. "Water, and a couple handfuls of grain for them both. That should help revive them." She patted the mare's neck and pretended she did not feel the uneven rhythm of her stride that warned of some harm to the horse.

"How much farther to Savigny-sur-Orge?" de Portau asked.

"Another hour, perhaps," said Olivia, not quite sure of where they were. "Not much more than that."

"The bay should hold up that far." He cracked out a single laugh. "What if they reach us before then, could they do that?"

"We will have to fight, if they are after us and reach us," said Olivia, certain now that the mare was starting to favor her on-side front foot. It was the one thing she had gambled on, that the horses would last all the way to the remount place. And now it appeared that this mare was going lame. Another time when she was not being pursued, she would have dismounted and led the mare, taking all the time that was needed to reach the remount location. It distressed her to have to use this mare so, but she realized that most of those she knew would not hesitate to ride a horse to death if that were necessary.

"You are troubled, Madame," said de Portau, his manner solicitous. "Are you tired, too?"

"Of many things," she said, and made herself listen again. "They are distant yet, but it will not continue so, not with this mare no longer truly sound."

"What do you mean?" de Portau asked sharply, turning her way so abruptly that his horse almost swung in front of Olivia's.

"She is going lame. I won't be able to push her much farther." Now that she had admitted it, she was not as worried as she had been.

"But she will go far enough," said de Portau, the tone of his voice urging her to give him the reassuring answer he demanded. "She can reach Savigny-sur-Orge, can't she?"

"I doubt it," said Olivia, hating herself for speaking the words aloud. "She cannot last much longer. She's beginning to breathe hard, and see how she nods," she added, pointing out that telltale drop of the mare's head when she stepped on her painful leg. "There. It is getting worse."

"Hell and damnation and perdition!" de Portau burst out, then immediately hushed his voice. "Sorry, Madame. I did not mean to do that. But it is more than flesh can bear to see this happen when we have got away so handily."

"Yes," she agreed, once again looking ahead. She squinted at the dark as if that would bring the things she wanted to see into sharp relief. Then she stared again. "I think I may see something," she said cautiously.

"What?" de Portau asked, unable to pierce the darkness. "What do you see?"

"It is an old building of some sort, an inn or a chapel or hostel for the sick," she said, realizing it was a six-sided stone building so ancient that most of the roof was gone. "It isn't the protection I would want, but it is better than what we have now, and the mare can rest awhile."

"And we can eliminate those who follow us," said de Portau at his most decisive.

"There are seven or eight of them," Olivia reminded him.

He did his best to snap his gloved fingers. "Nothing to it. Seven or eight against one Musqueteer, it's hardly fair to those seven or eight. I was in the First Company with Charles, the Grand Musqueteers," said de Portau with pride. "They're the best of the lot."

"But there are seven or eight men behind us, and for all I know, they have been Musqueteers, too," said Olivia, taking care as they neared the strange old building, in case it turned out to be inhabited. "The ducksfoot has nine barrels, and I have two pistols, that means we may only have one shot misfire."

"I'll aim for the horses," said de Portau.

Olivia winced as she heard that, but knew it was the most sensible thing he could do. "But that does not stop the men."

"It does if the horse falls on him," said de Portau, beginning to enjoy himself. "We'll conceal the horses and give them grain, so that they will be less tempted to whinny, and that way we can pay attention to the road instead of these beasts. A pity we haven't time enough to make a better ambush," he went on, warming to the prospect. "Still, they won't be expecting us to waylay them, will they?"

"We could simply let them pass and ride on after them," said Olivia in forlorn hope, wanting no more of fighting; but she was not convinced herself that this was a good notion.

"And when they find we have not reached the remount place, they can wait in ambush for us? No thank you, Madame. I would rather be the one setting the trap instead of them."

They had almost reached the six-sided building, and Olivia saw that it was one of the old Plague hostels, for travelers who were victims of the Black Plague, almost three hundred years before. She looked at the age-darkened stones and felt a touch of pity for the miserable people who had died there.

"It isn't as good as many places," said de Portau as they rode up to it. "But it is much better than most." He dismounted, his groan as he lowered himself to the ground revealing how demanding the ride was for him.

Olivia kicked her feet out of the stirrups and slipped down from the saddle lightly so that she would not injure the mare. "I will take them behind the building and give them nosebags," she said, pleased that the grain sacks de Portau carried would serve that purpose.

"And I will see what I can." He started off toward the road, drawing his sword as he went. It would have been better, he thought, if they were a bit nearer dawn, so that he could see what he was doing. But then, the men pursuing them would see as well, so he decided it might be best dark after all. He noticed that the road curved beyond the six-sided building and he considered that as he walked back to where Olivia was hobbling the horses now that their nosebags were tied on.

"What do you think?" Olivia asked.

"We hide behind here and challenge them. If they attack, we kill the horses and fight them as best we can. If they are our friends, and can prove with more than words that they are our friends, then we ride with them as far as we can."

"All right," said Olivia, taking her pistols from her belt and setting about charging them.

"You're adept at that, Olivia," said de Portau as he checked the duck'sfoot. "It's not often a man meets a lady who can charge a pistol and ride a horse as you do."

Olivia's response was wry. "I trust that is a compliment."

"Oh, certainly." He held his sword with his left hand, hefting it to be sure he could handle it and the wide, unwieldy pistol at the same time. Only then did he hear the distant sound of hoofbeats.

"They're coming," said Olivia, raising her head as the sound grew louder.

"At the trot. You are right. They are hunting." De Portau swept her a short bow. "Be ready, Madame. We will only have one chance, I think, to hit them. After that, they will have the advantage." He set his pistol aside in order to bless himself and whisper a brief prayer. "Well, God will defend His true servants, won't He?" he asked, and before Olivia could answer, he strolled around the six-sided building.

The riders approached fast, and halted in disorder as de Portau stepped onto the road and bellowed at them to stop. "Who are you, and why do you follow us!"

One of the men swore, but another silenced him, and a third brought his horse closer to de Portau. "Who are you, fellow, that you stop honest men on the King's road?"

"Another honest man," said de Portau, "who asks you to get back." He made a quick gesture with his sword.

The man laughed and the sound raised hackles. "We were informed by Pere Chape that a Roman whore who is a spy for the Italian Cardinal has attempted to escape, carrying lies to the Pope," he called out, the harshness of his voice making his horse sidle under him.

"How good of Pere Chape," said de Portau. "Yet there is no Roman whore here, soldier, only a King's Guard." He held up the duck'sfoot. "With lead enough for all of you, if you are not the men of King Louis and the Queen Regent."

"Spanish whore," muttered one of the other men.

"Dear me," marveled de Portau. "A Spanish and a Roman whore. The Cardinal has had his hands full, it would appear." His smile glinted. "What do you intend to do to this unlucky woman?"

"That's a matter for the Parlementaires. And us," said the leader, urging his horse closer to de Portau.

"Move him back, Monsieur," said de Portau cordially, "or I will be forced to cut his legs. It offends me to hurt innocent horses when the rider is the sinner."

This time the leader was more deliberately aggressive. "You will tell us where you are bound, and why, and if we are not satisfied, then we will take you with us and you will aid us in the capture of this spy."

Olivia had moved to the other side of the Plague hostel, thinking that though she was almost behind the mounted men, she was not much of a deterrent to their retreat. She held one of her pistols at the ready as she watched the men on the road.

"I am for Fontainebleau," said de Portau, "not that it is any of your concern." He would not move from the center of the road. "Who did you say dispatched you after this Roman woman?"

"Pere Chape," said the leader. "He is a true Frenchman, working to restore France to her nobles, free from foreigners. He has devoted himself to learning all that he might of the Italian Cardinal; he has given years to our cause."

"It seems to me," said de Portau, deliberately insulting, "that you are looking in the wrong place for a spy."

The leader swore and in the next moment had a pistol in his hand. As he fired, his horse reared, and the shot went wild, though the others were now drawing their weapons, their restless horses adding to the confusion.

Olivia moved closer, aimed, and shot the last man in the group out of the saddle. She was grateful to her night-seeing eyes, for it gave her an advantage in shooting. Her second shot was not as effective, catching the second man from the rear high in the shoulder. His scream bubbled, and she realized with horrible satisfaction that the ball had found his lung.

Two of the others were struggling to bring their mounts around so that they could get a shot at her, and one of them was able to aim at where her pistol had flashed, though she had moved away from the place.

De Portau had fired twice, once directly into the chest of the leader's horse—the animal was now on his side, his rider pinned under him as he coughed and kicked out his life—and the second time at the man behind him, aiming for the lower brim of his hat. The fellow screamed and slipped out of the saddle. He landed heavily, tried to rise and crawl, then fell.

More shots were discharged, and de Portau staggered as a pistolball ripped into his side. He rocked on his feet, then fired at the man who had shot him, knowing that the ball went wild. He fired his next into the man's thigh as he rode forward, then hacked upward with his sword, catching the man at the waist and pulling him screaming from the saddle.

The second man Olivia had shot was barely staying in the saddle. He had fallen forward against his horse's neck and the gelding was whickering in distress, milling unguided against the others.

The fourth man in the group, taller than the rest, started toward de Portau, his sword raised to strike. Olivia broke from cover, reaching for her dagger and throwing it with skill and all her tremendous strength. It lodged in his back, just below his shoulder blade. He threw his hands high as if surrendering to God, then fell backward onto his horse's rump before dropping to the ground.

One of the pursuers had already pulled his horse back; he was about to wheel about and run when Olivia reached his side, grabbed his arm, and thrust her sword upward into his chest. She stepped aside from the man as he fell and grabbed the reins of his horse, pulling the raw-boned blue roan aside for her own use.

De Portau was faltering under the attack of the last of the men. The bullet in his side was hot as a brand; his vision was wobbly and he had to fight against nausea as he beat the other man's sword aside. He felt his arm weaken, and he knew the next blow would hurt him badly.

But it never came. Olivia attacked from the other side with an upward cleft so ferocious that she almost severed his arm from his body. The man howled, kicked his horse into a choppy trot, then tumbled to the ground.

"Ah," said de Portau, wondering how he came to be sitting in the road. The last he was aware, he had been standing, sword in hand, and two shots left in the duck'sfoot. He looked up and saw Olivia kneeling beside him. "I think I'm done," he said, and was startled to hear the thread of his voice.

She could not bring herself to deny it. "They're all dead," she told him.

"You got the leader?" he asked, and ended with a single cough that tore through him with fangs and claws. He shook as he tried to make the pain stop, but all he was able to do was hold it in abeyance.

"Yes." She had made sure all the men were dead before tending to him.

He heard this with satisfaction. The coppery scent of blood filled his head, like the air of a slaughterhouse. He gathered his strength so that he could speak again. "It was a good fight."

"Yes," she said.

He lifted his hand to bless himself, but it was now much too bothersome and he let his hand drop, thinking remotely that he had not yet put down his sword.

Olivia finished the cross for him, her emotions and thoughts carefully banked like a night fire. She shifted her saddle from her mouse-colored mare to the blue roan—she had had a weakness for the color since Sanct' Germain had taken her away from her tomb and Roma all those centuries ago—untied the hobbles, then brought the bay de Portau had been riding. With no one to see, she could use her preternatural strength to lift the dead man across the saddle. She tied him there, then cut the reins on the horses that remained in the road so that they would not stumble over them and injure themselves. She slapped each in turn and set them trotting away nervously into the night, away from the carnage on the road.

As she mounted the blue roan and took the reins to lead the bay, the first pale line of approaching dawn lit the edge of the eastern horizon. Olivia felt the first diminishing of her formidable stamina and was morosely glad that she had done the necessary tasks before the sun made her dependent on the native earth that lined the soles of her boots. She looked for a church or a monastery now, somewhere she could leave de Portau's body with honor before she made her way south, ever south, for Fontainebleau, Avignon, and Rome.

*　　*　　*

Text of a letter from Niklos Aulirios to Atta Olivia Clemens.

To my most esteemed bondholder and all-but-eternal friend, greetings from Eblouir. This comes with yet another two carriages of your possessions, released with the permission of the First Minister, and duly exempt from customs.

You will be pleased to know that the windows have finally been completely replaced and no one has come to break any of them for well over a month. Thus it would appear that Mazarin has the upper hand again at last. He has most of his windows repaired, as well, but he is not as sanguine about his state as he was a year ago. The Parlement has been made to accept most of the royal edicts, and Mazarin has consolidated his position very well. In spite of Mazarin's successes, the Queen Regent has been slow to return to public life. She is afraid for the lives and welfare of her children— not without cause—and she has become less willing to concede to the nobles' requests for access to the King. It is her decision to live a more retired life and to be ready to flee if such is necessary. The events in England prey on her mind, or so Mazarin thinks, and she has visions of someone executing her son.

She may have some cause for alarm. The Great Conde, Louis de Bourbon himself, who commanded the troops that ended the Fronde last year, has been taking on airs of late, demanding that he be given a higher place in the world. He is a Prince of the Blood, of course, but he has said that he does not think that Mazarin is grateful enough for his deliverance. It is possible that he may change his position in regard to the rebellious nobles if he cannot maneuver Mazarin into the position he wants.

Comminges, the lieutenant of the Queen's Guard, is very much opposed to these assertions of de Conde; it was Comminges who was able to escort the Queen and her children to safety during the Fronde. Charles will tell you all you wish to know of that, and more, if you will let him, since he was with Mazarin on the same expedition. Once again, the nobles are waiting to see what de Conde will do before they act, but I expect another round of broken windows before too long. I am growing nervous whenever I see a sling, in case that means another smashed window.

Octave has once again returned to the Tours estate as the major domo, as a tribute to his brother. He has his men searching the region for the monk who set the bombs that ruined the chateau; if the man is alive and anywhere between Orleans, Chartres, Alencon, Angers, and Poitiers, they will find him. I begin to agree with Octave that the fellow fled as soon as he escaped, and if mischance has not killed him, he is probably in Spain or the Low Countries or Germany by now. It would please me to bring the man before the magistrates—either local Parlements or intendants, it makes no difference—and see justice done for his act. Seven people died because of him, and it galls me that he has been able to run free. I know that if Octave's men catch him, there will be no need for magistrates, but I have Octave's word of honor that he will inform me if the miscreant is found, and I believe him.

I have asked Mazarin to give permission for a dozen of the Tours horses to be taken to you in Roma. He has been using the estate for some remounts, but not enough to require the number of horses we keep there. With so much rebuilding to do, it would be sensible to reduce the number of horses. I can get permission to place them on sale, and no doubt Mazarin would be happy to receive them as contributions to his own stable, but I have authorized such donations already, and I believe it is time that a few of the horses be sent to you. If you would rather I do not press this question now, you have only to tell me and I will wait until a more opportune moment, say, perhaps, when I am bound for Roma myself, which I am assured will be before autumn rains make the roads too dangerous.

Three weeks ago I was able to present Charles with the gift you sent to him; he was overwhelmed at what he called your gallantry, for he said that two matched musquets is a princely present and that he is not worthy to have it. He also offered to behead me if I attempted to take them back. He misses you, Olivia, in a way that I find so touching that there are no words for it. He has asked Mazarin several times to give him permission to carry dispatches to Roma for no reason other than it would give him a few hours in your company. I think that in his own way he is faithful to you in his heart.

So far there has been no official report on de Portau. As far as the official records are concerned, he has simply disappeared. There are a few who think that he might have aided the rebels of the Fronde, and others who have said that he took the opportunity given by the Fronde to leave France for the New World, where he might do more to gain his own fortune. I have said nothing, and will not unless you instruct me to; I have taken the liberty of informing Charles because it was he who sent de Portau to aid you. As almost a year has gone by since that night, I assume that there will be no more inquiries into his whereabouts and he will be among the many who have vanished.

I have arranged for Masses for his soul, as you requested, and have told Charles of that, as well.

Pere Chape has been put into prison, though he is not to be officially tried. Like de Portau, he will vanish, but into a dark cell for the rest of his life, with no recourse to the Church or the law. He was finally convinced to give a full confession, so that he might have an occasional book to read rather than nothing at all. I suppose it is not a bad trade, the truth in exchange for books. He has implicated a Padre Fabriano Riccono, a secretary at the Vatican, but if the Pope will act upon this depends a little on how His Holiness and Mazarin negotiate the problem.

This talk of the Pope and the Vatican makes me homesick. I have almost forgot what it is to contend with the Church. With reasonable fortune, I will see you before the New Year. If there are more delays, I will tell you of them as quickly as a messenger can bring you word. Whenever we meet again, I will be overjoyed for it.

Niklos Aulirios
major domo Eblouir
Chatillon, near Paris

The Feast of the Blessed Virgin, 1649.

· 10 ·

This was the third time since Olivia had left France that Charles had been sent to Roma. He had arrived at Senza Pari early on a misty October morning, dressed as a Jesuit and carrying two cases of property and documents to Olivia.

She met him in the small salon that faced on the old garden, decked out in a very fashionable day-gown of sea-green silk over two exposed petticoats, one of fine embroidered muslin and the other of striped taffeta. The corsage had a narrow ruff of standing pleated lace and she had her hair caught up in ribbons. Her smile made her face luminous.

"It's been too long," Charles said when he stopped kissing her. "I would have come sooner, but—"

"But Mazarin has suffered too many changes of fortune to permit you to come here unless there is business to do," she said, trying to keep the wistfulness from her voice. "I think he would not let me come to Paris again for similar reasons."

"It is five years, Olivia," said Charles, his smile lopsided as he went on. "You no longer seem an older woman to me; now we are the same age." He touched her face. "Is that how it will be with me, too? That I will look no older than the day I . . . die?"

"Yes," said Olivia seriously, then put her arms around his waist once more.

"Don't think of it now, my love. If we had days and days to do nothing more than ask each other silly questions, it would be different, but—"

"But," she concurred. "Come; Niklos will see that you have breakfast and a little time to yourself, if that's what you want, and—"

"If I wanted time to myself, I would remain in Roma at the Lateran," he said bluntly. "I am here to be with you. Let me have an hour or two to sleep with you beside me, and then we can forget the rest of the day together, and the night as well."

Olivia could not keep from smiling into his eyes, her face radiant. "How wonderful," she said.

"It is, isn't it?" He bent and kissed her once, lightly. "The hall to your room is at the top of the stairs, isn't it? I remember correctly, don't I?" He touched her hair. "It's still short, isn't it?"

"Not as short as it was," said Olivia. "It will take another six or seven years before it is as long as it was in Paris." She reached up and flipped off his priestly hat. "No grey, that's pleasant," she said. "It has been more than two years, Charles. I was . . ." It became hard for her to speak. "I was afraid you had decided I was not worth the—"

He put his fingers to her lips. "If you say anything more I will be angry with you, and I do not want to be angry with you, I want to be drunk with love of you." He slid his hands to her neck, so that he could turn her face up to his. "I could never believe you were not worth whatever price was placed on you."

She laughed with feigned indignation. "Now you make me sound like one of my prize mares," she said, and as she saw the stricken look in his eyes, she went on, "I am teasing you, Charles. Think nothing of what I saw. I am so filled with happiness that you are here that I don't know what to do with myself. And I am a little frightened of how ecstatic I become when you are here because I am so devastated when you go; it is hard to lose you when you are so much to me."

"Then I will not return," he said, pulling her tightly against him. "What will your servants think, if they find you embracing a priest?"

She kissed the corner of his mouth. "If they mistake you for a priest, they are too simpleminded to be a servant of mine." The last words were all but lost as she gave herself over to his kisses again. "Come," she said, a catch in her throat. "There will be time later."

He obediently followed her, ignoring the occasional curious glances from servants who saw them. He went quickly up the stairs, unfastening the front of his coat as he went, pulling at his linen neckcloth before they reached the door of her private apartments, unbuttoning his chamise before the door was quite closed.

"Unfair," she protested when she saw how much he had undressed already. "And I have all these petticoats and laces to unfasten."

He was now in nothing but his boots and breeches. "I will be your ladies' maid; you needn't worry about all those petticoats and laces," he said, pulling her close against his chest, pressing lace and taffeta against his skin. "Send your maid away and let me tend to you."

"My maid is with her cousin's family today," said Olivia, glad now that she had given Nicola a few days to spend away from Senza Pari. "And tomorrow. And the day after."

"I will try to be here that long," said Charles, turning her around so that he could unlace the bodice of her dress. "Where are the ties?"

"Tucked under at the waist," said Olivia, and grinned as he fumbled with them. "You are a man of experience, Charles; how is it that you've never learned how to unfasten laces?"

He rested his chin lightly on her shoulder so that he could whisper to her, "That's because I've never had to wait for them to be loosened.

She reached back and pinched him lightly. "I might have known you'd have an answer." Her attitude grew more somber. "I have heard that Mazarin has urged you to marry, to find a suitable woman and have sons."

"He has mentioned it," said Charles in a tone of voice that suggested he did not want to discuss it.

"And you have refused," Olivia said, not abandoning the matter. "Why is that?"

"Not that it is any of your concern," said Charles, "but I know no one I want to marry. But you, Olivia. You have said already that you will not marry; so, then, neither will I." He finally got her laces undone; he removed her bodice and went to work on the skirt and petticoats. "You still will not wear boned corsets, will you?"

"Not unless I must," she answered. "It is worse than wearing armor." She hesitated, then added, "It is part of my heritage. We did not wear stays when I was young." She closed her eyes as he nibbled kisses on her shoulder.

"I have the skirt unfastened. Two petticoats"—he turned her face so that he could kiss her again, this time with more passion and less playfulness than before—"to go."

"And the corset," she reminded him, feeling the long months of separation vanish. "Magna Mater! how I have longed for you. I have spent nights in my library with no mind for the books because all I could think of was you. When I have waited through the dark for a foal to be born, I have to clap my hands over my eyes to keep from envisioning you with me." She sighed as her petticoats dropped around her feet.

"I am curious about your corset," said Charles as he plucked at the lacing down the back. "I am curious about how you wear it, how it holds you. Like this?" His arms went around her from behind, his hands cupping her breasts. "Such sweetness, Olivia. How can you live with so much sweetness?"

She leaned back against him. "You give the sweetness. For me this is just flesh. But I am happy that you find sweetness." Now she put her palm against his thigh. "Were you going to rest before—"

"Yes; I'm too tired to be much good to you, or to me, if it comes to that. I'm not the boy you met." He was rueful and just apprehensive enough that Olivia knew he was worried that he might disappoint her.

Olivia pressed her hand. "Every age has its strength, Charles. If you were still climbing onto coach roofs to help women caught in the middle of riots, I would be nervous for you. I think now it would be wisest for you to command the troops that end the riot completely." She could feel his posture change and took strange satisfaction in realizing she had said nothing more than the truth.

He placed his hand over hers. "By noon I will be yours until long after nightfall." With that, he pulled the laces from her corset and let it fall atop the petticoats. "You do not know how much I have wanted you, Olivia. No woman alive can move me as you do." He turned her around, his hands as adoring as acolytes. "I cannot tell you how much I cherish my time with you. I value this more than the triumphs I have had in war. We have had just three times together in five years, none of them longer than a week, but those few days have sustained me in everything I do. It is not easy to remember that our time together is so short when it is the savor of all my life." He got out of his breeches and tugged off his boots. "A little sleep, Olivia, a few hours only, with you close to me, that's all I will need. Your presence will refresh me most of all."

She grinned at him. "I may hold you to those few hours."

"I expect no less," said Charles, leading her to her own bedchamber where he flung back the covers for her. "Will it be warm this afternoon?"

"Only in the sun. At this time of year the shadows are cold." She went to close the shutters over the windows. "That will keep out prying eyes, love."

"Excellent." He had thrown himself on the bed exuberantly and lay there naked, watching her set the latches on the shutters. "You are more beautiful every time I look at you."

She decided to make light of his words, so that he would not feel he had to recant them later. "That is either a faulty memory or—"

"Or it is that I love you more with the passage of time," he finished, seriously but with amusement in his brown eyes. His flying brows were slanted even more sharply up in his face, giving him an impish look.

"Then I am more blessed than most of the women in the world," said Olivia seriously as she turned away from the windows, satisfied that the shutters were securely latched.

"That is because I love you," said Charles with satisfaction. "If it were otherwise, I could understand why you would have doubts." He picked up a pillow and held it as a shield as she threw herself at him. In the low light, it appeared that he was wearing a heavy tunic.

"You're impossible," she accused him, laughing and joyous because she was certain now that he was not merely seeking to reinforce a memory of passion. They wrestled gently, then lay back, breathless and grinning.

"A little rest," repeated Charles sternly, and destroyed his command by giggling once. "Oh, God, what would the Musqueteers think of this?"

She did not know how to ask if a decision had been reached regarding the reinstatement of the regiment, and so she said, "Are you so sure you are the only fighting man who plays at battle in bed?"

"No, but no one does it as well as I do," he answered, stretching out and drawing the blanket up to his chest. "I will not require you to waken me; I am used to waking on order, from habit."

"Your own order, you mean?" she asked, settling down beside him, liking the way their bodies fit together, enjoying the smell and the heat of him.

"Naturally. Being the Cardinal's courier means that I cannot rely on anyone but myself to sound trumpets." He yawned, and the beginning grooves in his cheeks deepened, another sign of the years. "You don't have to sleep—I know you don't sleep much, but stay with me, Olivia, so that I will have you even in my dreams."

"I will," said Olivia, and slid her leg over his, one hand across his chest, her head pillowed against his shoulder. "If this will not disturb you."

"Cannonfire disturbs me; this is my greatest pleasure." He turned his head to kiss her forehead, then stretched and, catlike, was quickly asleep.

Olivia felt the breath move in him with the same steadiness of waves on a beach. She let herself be rocked by it, feeling how much his breath was himself. Though she did not sleep, she dozed, and welcomed the waking dreams of the other times they had spent the days and nights in a world that consisted of little more than their arms and bodies and kisses and union. It would be hard, she thought, to have to leave that behind when he came to her life, but once they both were vampires, they would not be able to give each other that inescapable need—life. In all her hundreds of years, Olivia had never been jealous of those sought by the men of her blood, but she suspected that this time it might be different, that this time she would begrudge every partner he had the life they could give him when she could not. She was both smug and shamed by this realization, and wondered how Charles would feel in a century's time? Would he still yearn for her, or would she be his most treasured memory and most enduring friend?

There was always the chance, she reminded herself, that he would not change when he died, that the predations of war would destroy his body so that he would not wake into her life. The idea was so distressing, so distasteful, that she thrust it away as she had for so long held off all memories of her years of torturous marriage to Cornelius Justus Silius. Rather that Charles have dozens of lovers, each more doting than the last, and that he adore every one of them, than that he fall, shattered, on the field of battle.

"What's wrong," asked Charles, his arm pulling her on top of him.

"No . . . nothing," said Olivia, taken by surprise. The light in the room had shifted, and she realized that it was now past midday.

"What nothing?" Charles insisted, looking directly up into her face. "What nothing, Olivia?"

She gave a small, jerky shrug. "Unhappy thoughts, that's all. I suppose any woman who loves a soldier has them from time to time."

"You mean you fear for my life when I fight?" he asked as directly as he could. "That's a foolish thing to do. I will not die as long as you love me. You are my talisman against all harm. I swear it, Olivia," he insisted as he saw her dubious expression. "As long as you love me, I am invincible." He drew her down to a long, searching kiss, one that left them both with widened eyes and deeper breath.

"I will try not to worry, then," she said, her skin warmed and acutely sensitive where he touched her. It was a special magic that Charles alone possessed, she thought, this subtle awakening that reached to places within her that had remained hidden before to everyone, even herself. For all her love for Sanct' Germain, there had been no chance to make such discoveries before she changed and came into his life. After that, it had taken her from the time of the Emperor Vespasianus to now for her to know such utter happiness with any lover.

"Not too quickly," Charles murmured as she found her way over him, hands and lips seeking, exploring. He caught her arm and drew her back to him, opening his mouth to hers, and then expanding his own quest, his brown eyes bright with exultation as he felt her excitement and delectation. "Your skin is better than satin," he whispered. "Especially here."

She could not answer him, not with words. The wonderful delirium he caused in her continued, a rapturous frenzy that was so all-encompassing that she wanted nothing more in the world than the glorification of their bodies, the innovation of their desires, the fulfillment of their shared passion, and the communion of blood.

It was near day's end when they finally rested from their exchanges of delight. The bedroom was darker, the light warmed to a pale russet glow where fine lines of it penetrated the shutters and colored the walls.

"I always think I can remember how you make me feel, and I never can," said Charles as he kissed her ear. They were lying together like spoons now, his arms around her. Tendrils of his chestnut hair still clung around his face; the clean, sharp smell of his sweat was caught in the damp sheets.

"I can't remember, either," said Olivia, giddy with contentment. She wished she knew how to purr. She turned in his arms and kissed his shoulder, low, soft laughter shaking her when she saw how matted his hair was. "I will have Niklos warm the bath for us," she offered. "And I will arrange for you to have supper. You must be hungry."

"And wanting more of what I have fed on," he said outrageously, adding, "If you were ticklish—"

"I would never have any peace," she declared, sitting up and reaching for the bell that would summon her major domo. "And wine? Some food, wine, and then we will go play like dolphins in hot water?"

"As you wish," he said, grinning lazily at her. "I wish I could remain here for the rest of my life, Olivia." His eyes clouded. "I mean that, or almost."

"You mean it as a wish," said Olivia gently. "You mean it as you pray for peace in the world and hope for men to bear themselves with dignity and goodwill," she said, looking down at him. "And I share your feeling. I would keep you here forever if that would not cause you to hate me, in time."

"I could never hate you," said Charles, shocked at the suggestion. "Olivia, don't make light of what I say: I could never hate you, no matter what you did."

"Possibly," she allowed. "But you would not respect me if I compromised you, would you?" She motioned him to silence. "No, don't argue. I would not want you to be otherwise, because then you would be a stranger to me, not my Charles who—" She broke off and looked up at the discreet knock on the door. "Come in, Niklos."

"Olivia!" Charles protested in a whisper.

"He knows you are here," said Olivia, "and he has few illusions about me." She sat cross-legged in the bed, her covers pulled up as high as her waist; as Niklos came through the door, she took one of the pillows and held it out to hide Charles.

Niklos rarely bothered to bow to Olivia when he spoke with her privately, but on this occasion he did. "You and your guest are giving yourselves some time to recover?" His tone was more affectionate than sarcastic.

"Yes, and Charles is hungry. Small wonder," she added as she lifted the corner of the pillow and winked down at him. "He will require supper, wine, and honied warm milk."

"And you want the bath heated and filled, unless I miss my guess," said Niklos. "I have only to give the order and it will be done." He gave a slight bow to the pillow that concealed Charles. "Is there anything else you need, d'Artagnan?"

"No," came the muffled answer, and a burst of laughter. He emerged from behind the pillow. "Yes. Two branches of candles for this room. I do not want to lose sight of Olivia for one instant I am here."

"As you wish," Niklos said, with a quick, wicked wink to Olivia. "Your bath, the meal, the wine, honied milk, two branches of candles. And robes as well, I assume. I have Monsieur d'Artagnan's waiting for him."

"From so long ago?" Charles asked with the semblance of surprise.

"You are the only man who has been here as Olivia's guest since she returned from France, and that was more than five years ago, now," said Niklos. "There is a suit of clothes for you, a robe, two cloaks and a coat, a pair of boots, two pistols and a sword, as I recall, in the armoire she has set aside for you." He retreated toward the door. "There is a minor piece of business, Olivia, but it can wait, if that is your preference."

"What is it?" Olivia asked out of long habit.

"There is a report from the Villa Vecchia," he said, using the name by which Villa Ragoczy had been known for several centuries.

"And?" she inquired and waited.

"They have finished the ground floor and want permission to begin work on the second floor. It will mean hiring more men, as well as requiring more supplies. Shall I authorize the expenses and the time?" He looked at Charles and added apologetically, "We might as well settle this. It won't take long, and then neither of you need think about it."

"By all means," said Charles, trying to match Niklos' casual manner without entirely succeeding.

Olivia had frowned as she listened and now she said, "All right, how long do they expect this to take and how many men do they anticipate needing?"

"If they hire another twenty, it will take three or possibly four years. If they hire double that, it will be two or three years. In either case, the supplies will be about the same. If we have bad weather, of course, that will delay the work a little, but the longest it will take is seven years." He folded his arms. "What do you think?"

"I think that Sanct' Germain says he plans to stay in the New World for another fifteen years at least. He has found more of the native priests and physicians, and you know how such things fascinate him." She bent and kissed Charles on the forehead. "Tell them to hire the twenty men, and they can take up to ten years for all of me." She rubbed her hands together. "Just tell them I would rather take longer and do it right than hurry the work and have to do it over because it is not correct." She grinned at Niklos. "Is that answer enough for you?"

"It will be for Enrico," said Niklos, referring to the overseer at Villa Vecchia. Once again he bowed, this time with so much respect that Olivia hooted with laughter. Then he was gone and they were alone together once more.

"I don't know if I could wait so long to see a thing accomplished," said Charles when Niklos was gone.

"That is because you haven't lived as long as I," she said, leaning back against him. "Come. If we stay here you will have no food until midnight." She gave his shoulder a gentle slap. "Niklos will bring robes for us shortly, and we can go down to the smaller reception room."

"Why should we bother?" he asked as he reached for her. "We can have them bring supper here, to your sitting room."

"That would mean we are clandestine lovers, and we are not," she said, her head up. "If it were up to me, we would go to the old baths in the center of Roma and sport there naked, so that everyone from the Pope to the urchins would know that you are the man I love. But Mazarin would not like his courier the object of attention, and so, we will do what we may." She tossed the covers aside and stepped out of the bed. The room was growing chilly but there was no sign that she was cold.

Charles sat up, watching her as she looked for a pair of silken slippers. "I don't know what to say," he confessed as he watched her retrieve her slippers from under the bed. "You tell me this, and yet there is no marriage for you."

She stood up, slippers in hand. "Charles, think: how can there be? You know what I am. How do I swear to be a wife until death, when I have been dead for so long?"

"You're not dead," he protested with some heat.

"Not in the usual way," she said, sitting down to don her slippers. "But there are too many questions that would be hard to answer. I have aged very little since I died. If I were to live with one man, how long do you think it would be before someone noticed? And when it was noticed, how long do you think it would be before there were rumors, rumors I could not always refute. And how long do you think it would be before my husband became disenchanted with his unchanging wife? Now, you say it is nothing, but in twenty years, what then? In twenty years, you would be—what? fifty-three? fifty-five?—and I would be . . . as I am. It will not be a trivial matter then." She reached out and took his hand; amusement and something much more enduring and profound glowed in her hazel eyes. "But if any man ever could change my mind, Charles, it is you. You."

He brought her hand to his lips, kissing her fingers one at a time. "Then I am encouraged," he said, as he met her eyes. "And I will persevere, every time I am allowed to come to Roma, I will pester you until you forbid me to mention marriage."

Her expression grew remote and lonely, "Do you think you will?" When he started to protest, she raised her hand to silence him. "Perverse creature that I am, nothing would please me more than for you to prove me wrong. Who can say—I might forget every jot of good sense I possess and permit you to convince me next year or the year after."

"Do it come morning," Charles urged her. "It isn't as flamboyant as bathing in the center of Roma together, but it would attract some attention."

She pulled away from him. "Mazarin would not be pleased. He does not want me to return to France and it is not likely that he will post you to Roma," she said, forcing herself to be rigorously pragmatic as she had striven to be in the past. "If, when you return, Mazarin agrees, then let us talk of this again, assuming it is still your desire."

Charles glared at her baffled. "What do you mean to tell me? I will not alter, Olivia, not now and not at the end of my life." He got out of bed as he heard Niklos give a discreet rap on the door. "What will it take to convince you?"

She was spared having to answer by Niklos' return, heavy cotton chamber robes in his hands. As she took the one held out to her, she said to Charles, "If my loving you is not enough, then nothing else will be enough, either."

If Niklos was aware of the tension between Olivia and Charles, he carefully avoided showing it. He bowed to the air in the center of the room. "Supper is being laid in the small reception room; the bath will be ready in an hour."

Charles paid no attention to Niklos. His whole being was fixed on Olivia. "Because the blood is the bond?" he said as he drew on the robe. "And that it is enough to bind us from year to year when we cannot be together? Is that what you want me to believe?"

She shook her head as she held out her hand to him. "No, dearest, my most treasured Charles, not because blood is the bond; because life is."

* * *

Text of a letter from King Louis XIV of France to Paul de Batz-Castelmore.

Louis by the Grace of God King of France and Navarre, to Our dear Gascon noble, Paul de Batz-Castelmore, in regard to your most gallant and well-beloved brother, Captain-Lieutenant Charles de Batz-Castelmore Seigneur d'Artagnan of the First Company of Our Musqueteers, the Grand Musqueteers.

It is with the most profound regret and inestimable sadness that We take pen to inform you of the heroic demise of Our said Captain-Lieutenant Charles de Batz-Castelmore d'Artagnan on the 25th day of June in this year of 1673, during the battle for Maestricht in the Low Countries. As Captain-Lieutenant of the Grand Musqueteers, Our well-beloved d'Artagnan distinguished himself by rallying Our forces in the very heat of battle, and, taking his men, fighting mounted and upon grey horses, led them into the very heart of the fray.

We mourn with many others to learn that the First Company took heavy casualties while turning the tide of the battle: of the Grand Musqueteers, fifty were wounded and eighty were killed, truly calamitous losses. In fact, so great was the chaos that reigned, it was not until the roll of the First was called that any realized that Our esteemed Captain-Lieutenant had not returned with his men. Under the leadership of the senior First Company sergeant, Monsieur de Saint-Leger, a search for Our Captain-Lieutenant was mounted at once.

We are distressed to tell you that your beloved brother, Our es-

teemed Captain-Lieutenant, was found at the head of his men, his throat shot away so that they feared his head was severed from his body. In returning his body to the lines of Our troops, four men perished.

For the records of the family de Batz-Castelmore, We have decided to impart to you a few impressions We have gathered over the years, from the time Our most admirable Captain-Lieutenant was a courier in the service of Mazarin until his advancement to the well-earned and illustrious post he held on Our behalf. We are minded to add here that We have written separately to Carlotte-Anne de Chanlency on behalf of Our beloved d'Artagnan's sons, so that in future years, they, too, will know of the exploits of their father. We are saddened that the boys have not known their father well because of the ill-match of their parents. It is lamentable that they should have become estranged after only six years together, but when a man is over forty when he marries, such results are not unknown. It is Our thought that Our much-trusted Captain-Lieutenant never wholly recovered from the death of his adored Roman widow, which occurred late in the year 1658; after such a love affair, and so tragic an end to it, he was not inclined to care for any other woman; the vision of his cherished Madame Clemens was ever before him. We have no strong memories of the Roman widow, for We met her but few times, and in Our youth, but We know how greatly he loved her.

We are aware that Our well-loved d'Artagnan had little or no fortune, and to that end, We assure you, as We have assured his estranged wife, that there will forever be a place in Our Guard and Our Musqueteers for the sons of so gallant a father. Very truly We believe that We should not now reign if Our well-loved Captain-Lieutenant had not been tenacious in his purpose and defended Us and Our Mother when there were few so brave as to demonstrate support for Us and the honor of France.

It was truly the skill of Our Captain-Lieutenant that he was able to inspire almost all he met with the desire to oblige him, and would thus perform his requests without loss of the good opinion of others, though what they did on his behalf was not always in their interests except as regards Our esteemed d'Artagnan. Such a gift is one that many another might envy. The loss of so excellent an officer is one that cannot be estimated. Monsieur de Saint-Blaise has said it very aptly, and We can do naught but repeat his words: "Honor and d'Artagnan are wrapped in the same shroud."

Given at Paris, by Our own hand in respect to the memory of Our most beloved Captain-Lieutenant, Charles de Batz-Castelmore, Sieur d'Artagnan, for such is Our pleasure, and affixed with Our name and Seal.

Louis of France

On the 12th day of July in the Year of Grace 1673.
To be kept with the honor of Batz-Castelmore.
The seal of Louis XIV.

· Epilogue ·

Text of a letter from Ragoczy Sanct' Germain Franciscus to Niklos Aulirios.

My good friend Niklos;
I knew when it happened. I was in a forest not unlike those in the heart of Africa, and the instant she died the true death, I felt her death was my own. I am grateful that Mazarin's cousin, Padre Gennaro Colonna, was able to carry word to you as swiftly as he did. Had I been then at liberty to come, I would have been with him. No doubt he informed you of those political circumstances that put me in prison.

That she should die because she restored my old villa: how much turmoil that thought has given me. Today, when I visited the place, and saw where the heating system had collapsed, I could not entirely believe that it was wholly an accident. I have read the report requested by the Pope that declares the builders did not know the proper way of installing the passages under the flooring in order to warm the house through a single holocaust. It may be that it is no more complicated than the use of the wrong mortar that caused the whole foundation to give way. Yet I cannot accept it. Perhaps my doubts are nothing more than my own wish to have no part, no matter how remote, in Olivia's death, but it may be that the mortar was not to blame, nor the holocaust, though it is said that it seemed to explode.

Senza Pari is yours, without question, as are the other holdings she left you. There is no reason you should share any of them with me. I have more than enough throughout the world to provide my needs, and your long bond to Olivia is deserving of every bequest.

Truly, I do not know what I will do about Villa Ragoczy yet. It may be twenty years since her death, but for me the place continues to be full of Olivia. She haunts the ruins, and I am not yet prepared to disturb her, though I know it is my memories I would disturb, and not Olivia, who is gone from me forever now. In time I will decide what is to be done, but not yet.

The single consolation I can have for comfort is knowing that she found what I still seek—love that knows wholly and still loves. At least she had that before the true death came. If I am as fortunate, I will think my nearly four thousand years well spent.

One last thing: did they ever learn who the elderly man with the crippled leg was? According to the accounts, his body was discovered near the place where the holocaust ruptured, and no one could identify him.

No more. I will welcome your visits before I depart for Hungary. Know I am grateful to you for your tireless loyalty to Olivia, if my gratitude does not intrude on your grief. You may always count me your friend.

Ragoczy Sanct' Germain Franciscus
(conte da San Germanno)
his seal, the eclipse